BY JACKIE COLLINS

LADY BOSS
ROCK STAR
HOLLYWOOD HUSBANDS
LUCKY
HOLLYWOOD WIVES
CHANCES
LOVERS AND GAMBLERS
THE WORLD IS FULL OF DIVORCED WOMEN
THE LOVE KILLERS
SINNERS
THE BITCH
THE STUD
THE WORLD IS FULL OF MARRIED MEN

JACKIE
COLLINS

SIMON & SCHUSTER

AMERICAN

STAR

A LOVE STORY

NEW YORK LONDON TORONTO SYDNEY TOKYO SINGAPORE

SIMON & SCHUSTER
SIMON & SCHUSTER BUILDING
ROCKEFELLER CENTER
1230 AVENUE OF THE AMERICAS
NEW YORK, NEW YORK 10020

SIMON & SCHUSTER AND COLOPHON ARE REGISTERED TRADEMARKS OF
SIMON & SCHUSTER INC.
DESIGNED BY EVE METZ
MANUFACTURED IN THE UNITED STATES OF AMERICA

1   3   5   7   9   10   8   6   4   2

LIBRARY OF CONGRESS CATALOGING-IN-PUBLICATION DATA IS AVAILABLE.

ISBN: 0-671-66625-8

While *American Star* contains descriptions of unprotected sex appropriate to the period in which the story is set, the author wishes to emphasize the importance of practicing safe sex and the use of condoms in real life.

*IN MEMORY OF MY
HUSBAND OSCAR*

THE SHINING LIGHT OF MY LIFE.

PROLOGUE

DECEMBER 1992

Today millions of fans across the world celebrate the thirty-fifth birthday of cult superstar Nick Angel, and the opening of his latest movie, Killer Blue.

A statement issued by Panther Studios disclosed that Nick will not be present at the Los Angeles premiere of Killer Blue *as expected.*

A spokesperson for Angel reported that the actor will spend his birthday in New York.

U.S.A. *Today*
December 1992

AMERICAN STAR

NEW YORK, DECEMBER 15, 1992

Mornings were always a bad time for Nick Angel. He lay in bed, eyes closed, unwilling to surrender the peaceful darkness, fighting the fact that he had to get up and face another day. Especially this day. His birthday.

Thirty-five.

Nick Angel was thirty-five.

Jesus! The newspapers would have an orgasmic overdose on this one. He was no longer the boy wonder. Age was creeping up on him.

He lay very still. It was probably past noon, but the longer he delayed getting up the better, for he knew that once he stirred they'd be all over him. Honey—his live-in girlfriend. Harlan—his so-called valet. And Teresa—his faithful karate-champion assistant.

He heard a sudden movement in the room. A subtle rustle of silk and the faint aroma of White Diamonds—Honey was a big Liz Taylor fan. In fact Honey was a fan, period.

So . . . why was he with her?

Good question. The problem was there were too many questions in his life and not enough answers.

Honey was on the prowl. Pretty blond Honey with the lethal body and vacant mind. He sensed her standing by the bed staring down at him, willing him to wake up.

Too bad, sweetheart. Get lost. Not in the mood.

As soon as he was sure she'd left, he quickly rolled out of bed and made it to the safety of his steel and glass high-tech bathroom, locking the door behind him.

Ah . . . Nick Angel in the morning. Not the man he once was, although still handsome in spite of ten pounds of excess flesh, bloodshot eyes and an altogether dissipated demeanor.

He hated the way he looked. The extra weight he'd put on disgusted him. He had to stop drinking. Had to get his life together.

Nick Angel. Longish black hair. Indian green eyes. Pale skin, stubbled chin. At five feet ten inches he was tall without being overpowering. His handsomeness was not perfect. More brooding . . . mesmerizing. And in spite of being bloodshot his green eyes were hypnotic and watchful. His nose, once broken, gave him the dangerous edge he needed.

And now he was thirty-five.

Old.

Older than he'd ever thought he'd be.

But the world still loved him. His fans would continue to worship because he was Nick Angel and he belonged to them. They'd elevated him to a rare and crazy place where nobody could expect to remain sane.

It's too much, he thought bitterly, splashing cold water on his face. *The adulation, the never-ending attention. Crushing . . . stifling . . . suffocating . . . Too fucking much.*

He smiled grimly.

Welcome to the insane asylum.

Welcome to my life.

Reaching for the phone he buzzed the underground garage, connecting with one of his team of driver/bodyguards.

"I'm on my way down," he said, keeping his gravelly voice low. "Get out the Ferrari. No driver. And call the airport, tell them to have my plane ready. I'm taking it up."

"Right, Nick. Oh, an' happy birthday, man."

Screw this birthday crap. He knew he'd hear nothing else all day.

Finishing in the bathroom he dressed quickly in the trademark black he always wore. Pants, shirt, leather jacket and black tennis shoes. All he had to do now was make it out of the apartment before he was forced to endure more congratulations.

As soon as he hit the hall they came at him. Honey, all pearly teeth and rounded breasts encased in a pink angora sweater, her short skirt swishing sexily around her thighs.

Harlan, a crazed black man with wild hair extensions and subdued makeup.

And Teresa, six feet tall with a face like a man.

What a mismatched trio! But they were his. He owned them. He paid for every move they made.

"Gotta go," he said edgily.

"Where?" Honey asked, thrusting angora-clad tits in his direction.

"Where?" echoed Teresa, staring at him accusingly. "I should come with you."

"Yeah, where ya goin', man?" added Harlan, joining the chorus.

"I'll be back soon."

Maybe.

Maybe not.

Cleverly he timed his words to coincide with the arrival of the elevator, and before they could nail him further he was out of there, downstairs, in his Ferrari, driving out of Manhattan as fast as he could.

It took him forty-five minutes to reach the private airstrip where he kept his two-engine Cessna. Several mechanics greeted him with birthday wishes.

Surprise, surprise. He'd known today was going to be a bummer.

He climbed aboard his plane, settled in the cockpit and guided the small aircraft down the runway until he was given clearance to take off into the unseasonably blue sky.

He sighed, a long heavy sigh. When did it all begin to get out of control?

Nick Angel.

Free at last.

But he had a solution. A plan he was about to put into action.

Color me dead.

BOOK
ONE

1

LOUISVILLE, KENTUCKY, 1969

"Do it!" the young girl cried out, her breath coming in short frantic gasps. "Do it, *do it!*"

"I'm tryin'," Nick Angelo replied heatedly. And indeed he was, but to his dismay the girl was so wet he kept slipping out.

Her voice was shrill and commanding. "Do it!" she insisted, wriggling back into position. "C'mon, Nicky. C'mon, c'mon, *c' monnnn!*"

Beginning to panic, he jammed the point of entry yet again, and thank goodness managed to stay in place.

"*Ummm . . .*" The desperate shrillness faded from her voice and she began to sound pleased. "*Ooooooh . . .*" She continued to sigh sweetly as he pumped away.

Nick hung on, even though he was sweating and uncomfortable. But he hung on anyway because jamming himself inside this girl was the most important act in the entire world.

Vaguely he remembered one of his friends telling him sex was like riding a horse—mount up, get in the saddle and take the trip.

Nobody had warned him it would be such a dangerous hot sticky journey.

And then it hit him. The most exciting, throbbing, out-of-control

21

feeling he'd ever experienced. Holy cow! He was coming! And he was inside a real female—his hand and some dirty magazine had nothing to do with it.

The girl screamed out her satisfaction.

He felt like doing the same thing. But he was cool, a guy had to stay cool—even if it *was* his first time.

Nick Angelo was finally making out—and he couldn't think of a more mind-blowing way of celebrating his thirteenth birthday.

EVANSTON, ILLINOIS, 1973

"Please, Nick, *pleeease* . . . I can't take any more."

Maybe. Maybe not. But he'd been giving it to her for twenty minutes and she'd only now started to complain—although it was hardly a complaint, more an agonized cry of ecstasy.

"Ooh, Nicky, you're the best!"

Yeah? So he'd been told. Now if he could only teach them not to call him Nicky . . .

Making out was his specialty. It sure beat homework or any of that learning crap. And it certainly beat spending time at home watching his old man drink himself unconscious while his mother was out busting her ass working two jobs to keep the lazy slob in beer.

Family life. Shove it. Just like he was shoving it up Susie or Jenny or whatever her name was.

One of these days he planned on taking off, getting out of this dump, and bringing his mother with him. But first he needed a job so he could score some bucks, then there'd be no holding him back.

Right now he was stuck in school because his mother thought education was important. Mary Angelo had this crazy fantasy that one day he'd get a scholarship to college.

Yeah, sure—a make-out college was the only place *he'd* get in.

Mary wasn't into reality—she was into dreams. At thirty-seven she looked ten years older. A birdlike woman—slight and nervous, with faded prettiness and wispy hair. She'd met Nick's father, Primo, on a blind date when she was sixteen and he was thirty. They'd gotten married exactly one week before Nick was born, and Primo had hardly worked a day since. A carpenter by trade, he'd soon realized that picking up unemployment while sending his wife out to work was a far better deal than actually doing anything himself.

The Angelo family moved often, trudging from state to state, living in rented houses, always ready to be on the move whenever Primo felt that restless urge. And he felt it often.

Growing up, Nick couldn't remember being in the same town for longer than a few months at a time. As soon as he began to settle in, they were on their way again. Eventually he gave up on any permanent relationships. New town. New girls to conquer. And on to the next. Now he'd gotten used to it.

"Can we go see a movie tomorrow?" Susie or Jenny or whatever-her-name-was asked. "It'll be my treat."

"Nah." He shook his head as he got up, pulling on his pants. They were in the back office of a small automobile showroom—a venue he used often on account of the fact he sometimes ran errands for one of the salesmen, and in return he got to borrow the keys.

"Why not?" the girl asked. At eighteen she was two years older than him. She had short hair, freckles and a well-developed chest. He'd picked her up the day before behind the counter of a Kentucky Fried Chicken outlet.

He tried to come up with a quick excuse. He excelled at sex. Hated to stick around. Past experience told him she wouldn't appreciate the truth. A screw is a screw—who needs it to be anything else?

"Gotta work," he said, brushing a hand through his unruly black hair.

"What do you do?" she asked curiously.

"I'm an undertaker's assistant," he lied, straight-faced.

That shut her up.

He waited for her to adjust her clothing, even helped her up. Then he took her to the bus stop, left her there and walked the mile home.

Currently they were living in a rundown house with Mary's sister—his aunt Franny—a big woman with dyed yellow hair and a bleached moustache. It was only a small house, but as long as Primo had a television to watch and a plentiful supply of beer, he was satisfied.

Nick hoped Mary was home from work. If she was, there'd be a chance of something to eat. Franny never bothered to cook. She was on a diet of Reese's peanut butter cups and diet soda—screw fixing meals.

Sure. Franny got fatter and everyone else starved to death.

Sex always made him hungry. Right now he'd kill for a hamburger, but he was broke as usual, so the only chance he had was working on Mary with his charm. Not that he'd have to do much work, his mother adored him. She put him before everyone, including Primo when she could get away with it—which wasn't often, for Primo demanded most of her attention when she wasn't working.

Nick's goal in life was to have as little to do with his father as possible. He hated the way Primo treated Mary. He couldn't stand listening to him bitch and complain about everything. And most of all he despised the way Primo sat on his big fat can doing nothing.

The truth was that Primo scared him. He was a huge, overpowering man, and whenever he was in a bad mood Nick felt the back of his hand or the sting of his rough leather belt across his backside. Mary always tried to stop the beatings—protecting him as best she could— even if it meant getting beat herself. Primo didn't care who got in his way—he lashed out good.

Sometimes Nick wanted to kill him. Other times he accepted the beatings as a fact of life. The rage he felt was muted, buried. There was nothing he could do—not until he was older, then he'd get him and his mother out.

Halfway home it started to rain. Pulling up the collar of his old denim jacket he bent his head down and began jogging along the curb, thinking about how great it would be to have wheels, imagining that one of these days he'd get himself a car—a gleaming red Cadillac with chrome wheels and a real fine radio.

Yeah . . . one of these days.

Primo was sitting on the steps outside Franny's house. Nick could see him as he approached. He tensed up; something was wrong. Why else would his old man have deserted his precious television and be sitting outside in the rain?

He approached warily. "What's up?" he asked, stopping and jogging in place.

Primo wiped the back of his hand across his nose and glared up at him, bloodshot eyes bulging. "Where've ya been?" he demanded, slurring his words.

Nick felt the cold rain trickling down the back of his collar and he shivered—anticipating bad news. "Out with friends," he mumbled.

Primo heaved a mournful, beer-soaked sigh and hauled himself to his feet. His shirt was stuck to his body. His thick graying hair fell in greasy clumps on his prominent forehead. Raindrops continued to drip from the end of his nose.

"She's gone," he said glumly. "Your goddamn mother went an' died on us."

2

BOSEWELL, KANSAS, 1973

Lauren Roberts was sixteen when a man stopped her in the street and asked if she'd ever considered a modeling career. Lauren had laughed in his face. Who was this stranger? And why was he picking on her?

It turned out there was a film crew passing through town, an odd bunch of people. Lauren had been warned—along with everyone else in school—to have nothing to do with them.

When she got home she told her father.

Phil Roberts nodded sagely and said, "A pretty girl will always be bothered, but a wise girl soon learns to take no notice."

Lauren agreed. Pretty was one thing, but wise was better. Her father was smart. He'd always taught her that relying on her exceptional good looks to get by was a mistake. Being an A student was better. Getting good grades. Excelling at sports. Helping out with community service. And even though Bosewell was only a small town—population no more than six thousand people—there was always plenty of community service.

Lauren was certainly pretty. At five foot seven she was taller than most of the other girls in her class. She had long legs, a slender body, and thick chestnut hair falling below her shoulders, framing an oval-

26

shaped face with expressive long-lashed tortoiseshell eyes, a straight nose and a wide mouth concealing a dazzling heart-warming smile.

Lauren Roberts was one of the most popular girls in school. Everyone liked her, even the teachers.

She was standing in the school yard with her best friend, Meg, when Meg nudged her conspiratorially and whispered, "Here he comes. You'd better watch out!"

"He" was Stock Browning—Bosewell High's very own football star. Lately he'd been noticing Lauren in a big way.

Lauren frowned. "Shut up," she muttered. "He'll hear you."

"So what?" replied Meg, tossing her blond curls. "I bet he's going to ask you out."

"No, he's *not*."

"Bet he is."

Stock walked like a cowboy, with a wide-legged rolling gait. His hair was white blond and crew cut, and his eyes a Teutonic blue. Big and tanned, he was well aware he could get anything or anyone he wanted. It helped that his father owned Brownings, the only department store in town.

"Hiya, Lauren," he drawled, stifling a strong desire to pat his crotch —snug in track suit pants.

It was the first time he'd called her by her name, even though they'd attended the same school for years.

I guess sixteen must be the magic number, she thought skittishly.

"Hello, Stock," she responded, wondering, as she had many times before, where his parents had come up with his name.

"How 'bout you an' me taking in a movie?" he suggested, getting straight to the point.

Lauren considered his invitation. In a way she was flattered; after all, Stock Browning was looked on as the catch of the year. But then again she didn't—like most of the other girls in school—feel "that way" about him. He wasn't her type.

"Hmm . . ." she said, caught off guard and stalling.

He couldn't believe she was actually hesitating. "Is that a yes?" he asked.

"It's a when," she replied carefully.

His eyes narrowed. "When what?"

"When did you have in mind?" she asked, trying to keep it light.

Goddamn it! Was she being difficult? Any other girl would be singing at the chance of a date with him. "Tonight. Tomorrow night. Whenever you like."

I'd like you to leave me alone, she decided. Even though she didn't have a boyfriend she was not interested in dating him. Absolutely not. He was too full of himself by far.

"Well?" He towered over her, and she couldn't help thinking of his big sweaty body pressing down on hers if they ever did it. Not that she had any intention of doing it. Not until she was married to the man she loved—whoever he might be.

She continued to stall, as she hated hurting anyone's feelings—even his. "I don't know, I've got a busy week," she demurred.

Now it was his turn to frown. A busy week! Was little Lauren Roberts actually turning down a date with him? Surely it wasn't possible?

"Call me when you make up your mind," he said brusquely, and stalked off.

Meg, hovering on the sidelines, giggled nervously. "You didn't say no, did you?"

Lauren nodded. "I said no."

"You *didn't!*" Meg clapped a hand over her mouth.

"I did."

They both burst out laughing and hugged each other.

"Holy cow!" exclaimed Meg. "I bet that's the first no *he's* ever had."

"Serves him right for ignoring us all these years," Lauren said.

"You're right," Meg agreed, although if Stock Browning had invited *her* out she would be boogeying down Main Street handing out flyers. "What are you going to do if he asks you again?" she asked curiously.

Lauren shrugged. "I'll worry about it when it happens, and quite honestly, I don't think it will."

"It will," Meg said wisely.

"So I'll deal with it." Lauren felt that Stock Browning had occupied enough of their time. "Let's go get a malt."

That night she told her parents about the encounter, expecting them to agree that Stock was rich and spoiled and even though he was the son of the most affluent man in town she'd done the right thing in turning him down.

Jane and Phil Roberts had been married twenty-five years—the first ten childless. Just when they'd given up hope, along came Lauren. She had received nothing but their love and devotion—it would be hard to find a more united family. So it came as a shock to discover that no, her parents did not agree with her. They considered Stock a very nice boy with a bright future, and certainly a suitable candidate for their only daughter to go out with.

Lauren was crushed at hearing they felt that way. "I'm *not* dating him," she said stubbornly, before rushing up to her room.

Twenty minutes later her father knocked on her bedroom door. Phil Roberts was a pleasant-looking man with sandy hair parted in the middle, a small moustache and a weak chin. "Lauren, dear," he said soothingly. "We want the best for you, surely you know that?"

The best? Don't you mean the richest?

"Yes, Daddy, I know."

Phil paced around her room, uncomfortable and ill at ease. "Spend an evening with the boy, give him a chance."

A chance at what? Her virginity?

"Okay, Daddy. Maybe," she mumbled, noticing that tonight her father looked tired, and she didn't want to upset him.

"Good girl," Phil said, looking relieved.

Meg was right, it didn't take Stock long to ask again. A few days later he invited her to his cousin's twenty-first birthday party. "Black tie," he announced grandly.

"I don't have a black tie," she dead-panned.

He didn't laugh. Bad sign.

"I'll pick you up at six-thirty," he said, patting his crotch—obviously a favorite habit.

Her parents were suitably pleased.

"We'll go to Brownings and buy you a new dress," her mother said.

Lauren nodded. *Do we get a discount if I let him jump me?*

On the appointed evening Stock turned up washed and brushed—bristly blond crew cut, reddish tan, well-fitting white dinner jacket. Her parents were impressed. In fact she'd never seen her mother so giggly and girlish as she lined them up for a series of quick snapshots.

Lauren's new dress was sludge green. She hated it. "Made in New York," the saleslady had pronounced in hushed tones. After that her mother had refused to look at anything else.

Stock put his arm around her for the photographs. She felt the heat of his hand through the thin material of her dress and held her breath. The rumor was that Ellen-Sue Mathison had been forced to leave town because he'd gotten her pregnant. And Melissa Thomlinson swore he'd tried to rape her.

She shuddered.

"Are you cold?" Stock asked solicitously.

"Oh, no, I'm just fine, thank you, Stock," replied her mother, twinkling gaily.

"Try this." Phil Roberts thrust a glass of champagne drowned in orange juice into his beefy hand. "One for the road. No harm, eh?"

Lauren was seeing her parents in a new light and she wasn't sure she liked it.

Stock drove a sleek Ford Thunderbird. He opened the door for her and helped her in, trying for a surreptitious peek up her skirt.

"Nice parents," he said, settling behind the wheel.

"Nice car," she responded dully.

"It gets me there."

Not with me it doesn't.

Now that he had her he didn't know what to say, and she wasn't about to make it easy. She was here under protest, and if he made one wrong move he'd find himself very very sorry indeed.

3

EVANSTON, ILLINOIS, 1973

Friday morning dawned bleak and icy. The rain beat down relentlessly, forming a muddy sludge on the ground.

Crammed into the back of a cab between Aunt Franny and his father, Nick felt the bile rise in his throat. They both smelled strongly of mothballs—due to the fact that they'd borrowed black clothes from the neighbors, one of whom, Mrs. Rifkin, had magnanimously decided to accompany them to the funeral.

Mrs. Rifkin sat in the front of the cab, chewing Chiclets and attempting to make conversation with the black driver, who was more interested in breaking the speed limit and dumping them fast. He sensed a small tip, and nothing pissed him off more.

Franny extracted a half-melted Reese's peanut butter cup from her worn purse, popped it into her mouth and said to Primo, "Well, now . . . when do you think you'll be moving on?"

Great, Nick thought sourly, his mother wasn't even cold and this old bag was trying to get rid of them. So much for family attachments.

Primo opened his mouth to reply, and the foul aroma of bad teeth and stale beer wafted in the air, jockeying with the mothballs for attention.

"What's your hurry, Fran?" Primo asked, letting out a not so discreet burp.

"Without Mary's paycheck I can't be lettin' you stay. Can't afford it," Franny stated, munching away.

"So you're throwin' us out? Is that it?" Primo said nastily.

Franny smoothed down the folds of her skirt, rubbing a newly discovered stain on the cheap material. She was damned if she was going to let her sister's lazy slob husband live off her. She hated the sight of his ugly face. "I plan on renting out your rooms," she announced. "The sooner the better. I—"

"Not to darkies, I hope," interrupted a panicked Mrs. Rifkin, forgetting who she was sitting next to.

The cab careened around a corner, throwing Nick up against his aunt's ample bosom. He wished he could throw up all over her, the old cow deserved it.

"An' how about Nick?" Primo asked, as if he wasn't sitting right there beside them.

"You'll take him with you," Franny replied, not even considering the idea of inviting him to stay on.

"He'd be better off with you," Primo insisted.

Franny rummaged for another chocolate. "What am I expected to do with a sixteen-year-old boy?" she said in an exasperated voice.

Primo wasn't about to drop it. "At least he'd have a home."

Was his father actually thinking of him, or was it the thought of being free that urged him on?

"Yes. An' extra food to buy. An' clothes, and all that other stuff young boys need," Franny said indignantly. "No thank you. He's *your* son. He goes with *you*."

Case settled.

Nick leaned forward, trying to stop the despair that was rising up within him, a despair so great he could barely manage to breathe. One day his mother was there. The next, gone—just like that. Heart failure, they said.

Heart failure at thirty-seven years of age? Desertion, more like. She'd left him alone with Primo because she simply couldn't take any more.

When they got out of the taxi at the cemetery Primo stood there fidgeting, until Franny realized he expected her to pay the driver. She threw him a filthy look.

"Must've left my wallet home," Primo mumbled sheepishly.

"Cheap monkey," she said sourly, counting out the exact fare. "You always were and you always will be."

The cabdriver snatched the money and zoomed off, the wheels of his vehicle splashing them all with mud.

Mrs. Rifkin was not pleased. She sprung open a faded umbrella, all the while muttering under her breath, "They shouldn't let 'em drive, that's what *I* say."

Nick shivered. How could his mother leave him alone with Primo?

Despair was replaced with anger. He wanted to shout and scream. If he could have gotten hold of her he would have shaken the life out of her.

Only it was too late, wasn't it? She was already dead.

A thin man in a shiny gray slicker with a sinister hood announced he would be escorting them to the grave site. "Is this all of you?" he sniffed, sounding disappointed.

"Yeah," said Primo belligerently. "Wanna make somethin' of it?"

The man ignored him.

"We haven't lived here long," Nick felt compelled to explain as they trudged past endless rows of neatly lined up graves. "My mother didn't have time to make friends."

"Oh, dear," said the man, with about as much interest as a fish. He just wanted to get rid of this motley group as fast as possible.

"She was a wonderful woman, though, really wonderful," Nick added, speaking too quickly, his words tripping over each other.

"I'm sure she was," said the man in the slicker.

Finally they arrived at a freshly dug plot where a cheap wooden coffin waited to be lowered into the ground.

My mother's in that box, Nick thought, suddenly losing it. *Oh, jeez! My mother's in that box.*

And so the short ceremony began. And the rain pounded down. And Nick didn't know whether he was crying or not because his face was wet, so very very wet . . .

Three days later they left. Franny was relieved to see them go. Just to make sure, she packed them stale cheese sandwiches and a flask of lukewarm instant coffee. She stood outside her house waving them on their way, even though it was still raining and bitterly cold.

"Fat bitch!" mumbled Primo, as they drove away in the shabby old van he'd had for ten years.

"Where we goin', Dad?" Nick ventured.

"Don't ask no questions an' you won't hear no lies," Primo said grimly.

"I just thought—"

"*Don't* think," Primo interrupted harshly. "Sit there an' keep your big ugly mouth shut. Ain't it enough I gotta be responsible for you?"

There was a thickness in Nick's throat. Oh sure, he was used to leaving town, abandoning his friends and starting afresh every few months. But he was not used to being without his mother's protection. She'd always been the buffer between him and Primo, and now there was no one who cared.

"Soon as we get where we're goin' I'll look for a job," he said, staring at the windshield wipers as they worked on the relentless rain, scratching against the glass with a dull scraping sound.

"Nah. Ya gotta stay in school," Primo said.

"I don't," he objected.

"That's where you're wrong. I made your mother a promise."

"*What* promise?"

"Mind your business."

Shit! It was *his* life they were discussing, surely he was entitled to know? And since when did Primo care about keeping promises?

Primo slumped into silence, his bloodshot eyes fixed on the road ahead, his big hands clutching the steering wheel.

Nick's mind kept drifting back to his mother being lowered into the ground, the rain soaking through the cheap wooden coffin. He was overcome with an unbearable sense of suffocation and loneliness.

Was she cold?

Was her body slowly beginning to rot?

Some kind of horrible wail began to beat and pound inside his head.

Why couldn't it have been Primo?

Why couldn't it have been his goddamn father?

. . .

They stopped for gas a couple of hours later. Nick got out and stretched his legs while Primo vanished into the men's room and didn't come out for twenty minutes. When he finally emerged he ignored his son and headed straight for the convenience store, where he purchased a pack of Camels and a six-pack of beer. Then he stationed himself by the pay phone and began making calls.

Nick knew better than to ask who he was phoning. He didn't care. It didn't matter what his father said, as soon as possible he would find a job, save his money and get the hell out.

He got back in the van. It stunk of gas. Idly he rolled down the window and watched a blonde in a miniskirt and boots make a dash from her car to the ladies' room, somewhat futilely holding a soggy magazine over her black roots.

Girls. They were all the same. He'd made out with enough of them to know exactly what they were like. In all his travels there hadn't been one girl he'd wanted that he hadn't had. It was hard to understand how some poor jerks agonized over getting laid, because it was so easy—kind of like fishing. Put out the bait. Reel 'em in easy. Go for the kill. And then take off. Fast.

Nick Angelo could score with anyone. And he did—as frequently as possible. It gave him his only real sense of identity.

Primo lumbered out to the van, threw the six-pack—depleted by one can—onto the seat and started the engine.

"Uh . . . it's illegal to drive with alcohol in the vehicle," Nick muttered.

Primo wiped his nose with the back of his hand. "What're you, a cop?"

"Just pointing it out."

"Well, don't."

Yeah. Shut up. Sit still. Butt out. The story of his life.

Leaning back he closed his eyes, drifting into a sort of half sleep—until he was jolted awake when they almost skidded into the back of a massive truck parked on the side of the highway.

"Fuckin' drivers!" screamed Primo. "They don't give a crap where they dump it."

"Why don't I drive?" Nick suggested. It was beginning to get dark and Primo was already gulping down his third beer.

"Since when do *you* drive?" Primo sneered.

"I took driver's ed in school. I got my license."

"Don't remember that."

No, he wouldn't, would he? And even if he did, he'd never have allowed him to use the van, but he'd taken it out on more than one occasion when Primo was slumped in a drunken stupor and he'd had no fear of getting caught.

The van skidded again. Primo grunted, finally deciding he'd had enough. Pulling over, he slid across to the passenger side, shoving Nick out into the icy rain.

Nick ran around the back and quickly jumped in the driver's seat. "Where we headin'?" he asked, gripping the steering wheel, anxious to get wherever they were going. Primo finished his beer, crushing the can in his big hand and flinging it out the window. "Kansas," he said, burping loudly. "Some piss-assed town called Bosewell."

"Why there?"

" 'Cause I got a wife there, that's why."

This was big news to Nick.

4

BOSEWELL, KANSAS, 1973

What started out as a simple date seemed to be turning into a relationship, and everyone was pleased except Lauren. She'd fallen into some kind of dumb routine with Stock. Dinner and a movie on Friday night. Dancing and a party every Saturday. And two family brunches. This had been going on for six weeks.

"What's happening?" she wailed to Meg. "I used to be a free person, how did I get myself into this?"

"Has he tried anything yet?" Meg asked, lighting up a forbidden cigarette.

She shook her head. "No. And stop pumping me all the time, you're like a district attorney!"

"No, I'm not. I'm dying to find out the dirty details."

"Why?"

"*C'mon*, Laurie," Meg pleaded. "You *know* we share everything. He must've kissed you at least."

"Maybe," she said mysteriously.

"Has he?" Meg pressed.

"Maybe," she repeated.

They were in Lauren's bedroom, and Meg began to bounce up and down on the bed, her face red with the frustration of not being able to get any good scoop out of her best friend. "Tell me, you rotten little cow!"

She didn't particularly wish to confide in Meg—after all, it wasn't that exciting—but now there seemed to be no choice. "Okay, so he's kissed me. Big deal. End of subject."

Meg's eyes gleamed. "Is he a good kisser?"

"He's got big teeth."

"What does *that* mean?"

"They get in the way. And besides," she sighed, "I *told* you, I don't feel anything for him."

Meg jumped off the bed. "Perhaps *I* should take him over. How's that for an idea?"

"Yes!"

"You don't mean it."

"I do! I do!"

Meg was exasperated. "You've got the hottest hunk in town panting all over you, and you're acting like it's no biggie."

"It's not."

"Then why don't you stop seeing him?"

She sighed again. "Because I can't. My parents like him. They like *his* parents. In fact, if you want to know the truth—my father's selling his dad some kind of big insurance thing."

Meg dragged on her cigarette like a veteran. "Oh, that's not so good."

"Don't I know it," she said glumly, trying to figure out exactly how it had happened. Their first date had been uneventful, Stock had behaved himself perfectly—he didn't even get drunk, while all around them his football buddies were staggering zombies.

She'd had no reason to turn down his second invitation, especially with her parents urging her on. And then suddenly *her* father was selling *his* father insurance, and there was no way she could mess that up.

Before she knew it, everyone considered her and Stock a couple.

Now she was stuck. And she wasn't happy.

Mr. Lucas, Bosewell High's history teacher, droned on. Lauren attempted to concentrate but it was difficult—the man was dull—and getting anything out of his class was almost impossible, he had no idea how to fire his students' imaginations. They sat in front of him— twenty-four bored teenagers engaged in a variety of activities. Joey Pearson, the class clown, was busy writing dirty limericks and passing them around. Dawn Kovak, the school tramp, negotiated with one of the boys about what she might do to him during lunch hour. Meg sketched fashion designs behind the cover of *World History*. And Lauren daydreamed.

Her biggest daydream was always about New York. When she was little her parents had taken her to see Audrey Hepburn in *Breakfast at Tiffany's* and she'd never forgotten the thrill of seeing the big city on the movie screen.

New York . . . she'd definitely decided that one of these days she was going there just like Audrey Hepburn. And she'd have her own apartment, a fulfilling job and a cat. Oh, yes, she'd *definitely* have a cat. And of course a boyfriend. A *real* boyfriend. Not Stock Browning with his white crew cut and macho walk. A man more along the lines of Robert Redford or Paul Newman—she was quite partial to the dirty-blond look.

"Lauren!" Mr. Lucas's waspish voice interrupted her reverie. "Kindly answer the question."

Question? What question? She quickly glanced at the blackboard and figured out what he'd been teaching, coming up with the correct answer just in time.

"You're amazing!" Meg whispered, stifling a giggle. "Even *I* could see you were somewhere in China!"

"New York," Lauren whispered back. "Although I wouldn't mind visiting China one day."

"Fat chance!"

She and Meg viewed their futures differently. Meg saw herself married with kids and living happily in Bosewell. Lauren knew there was a whole other world out there and she planned to explore it before settling down.

The bell sounded, signifying the end of class.

Stock was leaning on the lunch counter waiting for her. "I'll pick you up at six-thirty tonight," he said.

"You will?"

"Don't tell me you've forgotten."

39

"Forgotten what?"

"Dinner with my parents."

"Oh, yes," she said listlessly.

"Don't go crazy with excitement."

What did he want from her? She was going, wasn't she? Surely that was enough?

Bending down he pecked her on the cheek. He smelled of sweat and camphor liniment. The sweat she could take, but the camphor almost made her gag. It was definitely time she had a chat with her father about the insurance he was selling Mr. Browning. Was it a done deal? And if she stopped seeing Stock, would it upset everything? She was sure that any moment he was going to make the big move, and she had no desire to star as the struggling victim trapped beneath his bulk in the cramped interior of his Ford Thunderbird.

On the way home she stopped at her father's office—located on Main Street above the Blakely Brothers hardware store. The door was locked, the shade pulled down covering the glass. PHILIP M. ROBERTS, INSURANCE was printed on the door. He'd hinted it would one day read "Philip M. Roberts and Daughter." Lauren hadn't summoned up the courage to inform him she had no intention of going into the insurance business.

Disappointed he wasn't there, she continued on home.

Her mother was in the kitchen making a cake.

"Where's Dad?" she asked, sticking her finger in the mixing bowl and scooping out a taste of the creamy mixture.

"Stop that!" Jane Roberts scolded. She was a dark-haired woman with fine features and high cheekbones. It was easy to see where Lauren had inherited her good looks.

"Umm, delicious." Lauren stuck her finger in again.

"I said stop it," Jane repeated sternly. "There'll be nothing left. This cake is for you to take to the Brownings' tonight."

"No way!" she said, horrified. "I'm *not* taking them a cake, Mother."

"Then I'll have to ask Stock."

"No, Mother, *no!* You can't embarrass me this way."

Jane stopped what she was doing and wiped her hands on her apron. "What's embarrassing about baking the Brownings a cake?"

Lauren hesitated. "Well, you know, it's sort of like . . . uh . . . sucking up."

Jane narrowed her eyes. "Sucking up?"

"You *know* what I mean."

"No. I'm afraid I don't." Jane glared at her only child with a *How dare you talk to me like that—wait until your father gets home* expression.

Uh-oh. Mother was p.o.'d. Maybe she'd gone too far. "Okay, okay, I'll take the dumb cake," she mumbled, and rushed upstairs to her room.

It was quite obvious suck up was the name of the game, and right now there was nothing she could do about it.

Daphne Browning was a big woman with multiple chins and bright scarlet lips. She greeted Lauren graciously. "Your mother's *so* thoughtful. What a perfectly *lovely* gesture," she gushed. "Of course my doctor forbids that *I* eat chocolate, but Benjamin simply adores it, don't you, darling?"

Benjamin Browning barely glanced up from his newspaper. He was a tall man, thick around the middle—with dour features, iron-gray hair and matching bushy eyebrows. "Trying to diet," he grunted.

Stock prowled around the room, while Lauren settled herself stiffly on a damask chair in the very formal living room. A hovering maid whisked the cake away, never to be seen again.

"When are we eating?" demanded Stock.

Daphne ignored him. "Tell me, dear," she said, scarlet lips quivering as she turned toward Lauren. "Is Stock your first boyfriend?"

Lauren could not believe she was being asked such a personal question. If she wasn't so polite she would have replied, "None of your business." Instead she began furiously petting Mrs. Browning's Pekinese—a ferocious little dog who bared its teeth and growled viciously.

"What a cute puppy!" she exclaimed, trying to sound sincere. "How old is he?"

"She," corrected Mrs. Browning.

"What's her name?"

"Princess Pink Pontoon."

"How unusual." She patted the dog again and the little rat snapped at her with its lethal teeth.

Stock guffawed. "It'll take your hand off if it can."

"Stock!" admonished Daphne. "Princess would *never* do that."

"Dinner is served," announced a black maid, appearing at the door.

Mr. Browning put down his paper. "About goddamn time," he said irritably.

Dinner was a drag. This was one evening Lauren had no wish to repeat. Mrs. Browning was a snob. Mr. Browning was plain rude. And Stock was . . . well, he was Stock.

On the drive home he got straight to the point. "They like you," he said.

"That's nice."

"Even though you're young."

What was *he*—all of eighteen? "I'm thrilled," she said dryly.

He missed her sarcasm. "They gave us permission."

"For what?" she asked, stifling a yawn.

"To get engaged."

5

Aretha Mae Angelo opened the door of her trailer home and glared at Primo as if she were sick of looking at him. Actually it was seventeen years since he'd walked out on her, but she certainly wasn't about to let seventeen years stand in the way of a vigorous tongue-lashing.

Hunched in the van, Nick could hear every word as she tore into his father.

"What *you* want? Cheatin' slime. How come you sniffin' round here again? Y'ain't nothin' but a bum, so get outta here. Y'hear me? *Out.*"

She might be telling him to get lost, but Primo whined some kind of weak excuse, and before Nick could make out exactly what was happening the woman yelled more insults, dragged Primo inside the trailer and slammed the door shut.

Nick sat in the van and contemplated the last week. He was sixteen years old—nearly seventeen—and his life was over. Who cared about anything? He certainly didn't. His whole existence had been a lie.

Mary and Primo. His loving parents. Now Primo had informed him they weren't even legally married, because he'd still been married to this woman when he and Mary exchanged their wedding vows.

Primo Angelo was a bigamist.

And if that was so, what did it make him?

He didn't care to think about it.

The rain had slowed to a drizzle but it was still icy cold. Nick huddled in the van, hungry and tired—empty of any emotion.

Some time later Primo emerged from the trailer followed by the woman. Yanking open the door of the van he thrust a dirty blanket at Nick. "You'll sleep out here," he said gruffly. "No room inside."

The woman pressed forward, trying to get a look at him.

Nick noticed she was dark-skinned, very dark-skinned. With a sudden jolt he realized she was black.

In the morning the rain had stopped. Asleep across the two front seats Nick was awakened by a faint scratching sound. For a moment he couldn't figure out where he was. He sat up, banging his head on the dash. His gut ached with hunger, and he felt an urgent need to pee.

Staring at him through the side window were two small black boys. One of them was scraping his fingernails against the window. As soon as they saw he was awake they ran away.

In the light of day he took in his surroundings. The van was parked in the middle of a sparsely populated trailer park. A few skinny dogs loped around a cluster of dilapidated-looking trailers, while all around was mud, weeds, and, over to one side, a massive garbage dump.

This place made Aunt Franny's rundown house in Evanston seem like a palace.

He got out of the van. Crouching on the ground a few feet away lurked the two black kids, still staring at him.

"Hey," he said. "What's up?"

They didn't respond.

"Gotta take a piss."

One of the boys pointed to a ramshackle hut next to the garbage pile.

He made it to the hut and wished he hadn't—the stench was unbearable.

After doing what he had to do he hurried back to the van, his stomach rumbling uncontrollably. In his pocket he had exactly thirty-five cents. Not enough to do anything.

Leaning against the van, he thought about his future and decided that things certainly couldn't get any worse. He was stuck in a strange town, waiting around in some crummy trailer park while his father reacquainted himself with the woman he'd been married to for seventeen years and never told anyone.

One of the boys edged toward him, a handsome kid with bright eyes and dark chocolate skin. "What's your name, mister?" the boy asked curiously.

"Nick. What's yours?"

"Harlan. I'se ten. How old's you?"

"Sixteen."

"What you doin' here?"

He shrugged. "Beats me."

After a while Primo emerged from the trailer clad only in his grubby underwear, scratching his bulging belly, a rare smile lighting up his unshaven face. Nick knew the look. It was his father's *I just got laid, aren't I a fine stud* look.

"Howdja sleep?" Primo asked, as if they'd spent the night in a fancy hotel.

"I didn't. I was too hungry," he muttered, angry with his father, and yet not sure how to express himself. What he'd really like to do was beat his stupid lying brains out.

"Don'tcha worry 'bout that," Primo said jovially, as if nothing was amiss. "Aretha Mae's one fine little cook." He clapped his hand on his son's shoulder. "C'mon, I wantcha t'meet her."

Reluctantly he followed Primo into the trailer, while the two boys hovered close behind.

Inside it was a crowded mess, with clutter everywhere—clothes, magazines, old newspapers and junk piled high on every surface. In one corner was an unmade bed and, on the floor, two moldy sleeping bags.

Aretha Mae busied herself at a kerosene stove, frying ham and potatoes in greasy bacon fat. She was a sinewy black woman with frizzy dyed red hair and a wary look in her eyes.

"Sit yourself down, boy," she said to Nick over her shoulder. "You must be real hungry."

He squeezed onto a torn plastic-covered bench next to a rickety table stacked with dirty dishes.

Aretha Mae dumped a plate of food in front of him, sweeping the used dishes to one side. "Eat," she commanded.

Primo chuckled; he saw a home in his future. "I knew you two would get along."

"Shut your mouth," Aretha Mae said. "We be talkin' 'bout who gets along later. Don't go thinkin' you're movin' in."

Nick was impressed by her nerve, although he half expected his father to smack her across the mouth.

Primo didn't. Primo laughed, a big-bellied laugh. "Still a feisty bitch," he said. "I like that in a woman. You haven't changed."

Aretha Mae threw him a stern look. "Don't use no bad language in front of my kids," she said, indicating the two silent boys by the door.

"Listen who's talkin'," Primo said, scratching his stomach. "I can remember when that's *all* you used."

"Things was different then," Aretha Mae said primly. "Those was different times."

Primo continued to laugh and grabbed her ass. "They sure was."

She slapped his hand away and turned to Nick, busy wolfing down the greasy but delicious meal. "What your old man tell you 'bout me?" she demanded. "He tell you we was married? He tell you he ran out on me when I got pregnant? He tell you 'bout your half sister he ain't never seen—let alone supported?"

Nick stopped eating. Sister? What kind of crap was coming his way now?

"I didn't know . . ." Primo whined. "You threw me out. I didn't know you was pregnant."

"Liar!" she snapped. "The baby in my belly was *why* you ran." She glared at him balefully. "An' then whaddaya do? Fix another woman so you's trapped anyhow. Dumb chickenshit!"

Primo wrapped his arms around her from behind, caressing her bony body. "C'mon, hon, I'm back," he crooned. "You always *knew* I'd be back, didn't ya?"

Aretha Mae made an angry sound in the back of her throat. Not that angry. In fact it was becoming quite obvious she didn't mind having Primo's clumsy arms around her one little bit.

Nick thought of his hardworking mother lying in her grave and the greasy food turned in his stomach. He hated his father. He hated the whole stinking set-up.

Abruptly he stood up. "What sister?"

"She be away right now," Aretha Mae said quickly. "She be visiting relatives in Kansas City."

"I got me a daughter," Primo marveled. "I always wanted a girl."

"You got one, all right," Aretha Mae said. "Oh, yessir me, you *really* got one."

Several days later they moved in, after spending a few nights in Bosewell's only motel. Since there wasn't room for all of them in Aretha Mae's trailer, Primo made a deal with the couple next door to take over their rat-infested storage dump—a trailer with no wheels and cardboard covering the window spaces. "It'll do for the kids to sleep in," he told Aretha Mae. "Should clean up nice."

Nick spent three days hauling out junk, dodging rats, cockroaches and spiders. Harlan and his younger brother, Luke, helped out. They were jumpy little kids, petrified of their mother, who ruled them with an acid tongue.

The two boys attended school every day, leaving the trailer park at six in the morning. Aretha Mae left shortly after that to go to her job as a maid to a rich family in Bosewell. This gave Primo plenty of time to himself, and although he promised Aretha Mae he'd start looking for a job he had no intention of doing so. The moment she left he settled in front of her small black-and-white portable television, with a six-pack nearby. Nothing had changed for Primo. He knew his priorities and he stuck to them.

Nick hung around, he had nowhere to go.

After a couple of days Primo said, "Gotta get you back in school."

"I'd sooner get a job," he said, feeling restless and trapped. "Maybe—"

"I promised your ma," Primo interrupted, staring at the television. "Thought I told ya that."

"So what?"

Whack! Right across the mouth. It caught him by surprise, cutting his lip. He tasted blood and was filled with fury. There was no Mary to protect him now. School was in his future and there was nothing he could do about it, at least for now. As soon as he could he'd find a job, save his money and get out.

Nick Angelo planned to run, and nobody was going to stop him.

"How exciting!" screamed Meg.

"Darling, I couldn't be more pleased for you," said her mother.

"This is great news," announced her father, as proudly as though she'd just concluded a complicated insurance deal.

Idiot! She should have kept her mouth shut. All she'd done was tell them Stock had mentioned they should get engaged, and the next thing it was the town gossip. Now she was more trapped than ever in a relationship that totally confused her.

She was sixteen. She was too young. Oh, sure, her mother had gotten married at seventeen—but that was a love match between two people who were crazy about each other; they'd told her the story enough times.

Her situation was different—she hardly even *knew* Stock, and what she did know she didn't much like.

"I'm not getting engaged," she informed her parents, panic-stricken at the thought.

Jane Roberts smiled and patted her daughter like she was an excitable puppy that needed calming. "Nerves, darling," she said. "Marriage is a big step. You'll have a long engagement, get to know each other. Stock's a nice boy from a fine family. Your father and I are very happy."

Oh, good, *they* were happy. What about her? Wasn't *she* the one supposed to be grinning uncontrollably and walking ten feet above the ground?

Love. From everything she'd seen and read it was a magical feeling, and all *she* felt was sick.

In third grade she'd had a crush on Sammy Pilsner. She'd been eight years old and ecstatic. He'd made her shiver and shake whenever she saw him.

At twelve she'd fallen in love with her cousin Brad, a bony-looking boy three years older than her. He and his family only visited at Christmas, so she'd soon grown out of that.

At thirteen she'd had her first date. Disaster.

At fourteen her first kiss. Even worse.

And at fifteen she went steady for a satisfying six months with Sammy Pilsner.

Sammy didn't make her shiver and shake as much as he had when she was eight, but he was a good kisser and they got into many long lustful nights of heavy petting, although she never let him go all the way—she was too frightened of getting pregnant—even though he drove over fifty miles to a neighboring town to buy rubbers, and tried to convince her they should do it.

Eventually Sammy's father got promoted at his job and they moved to Chicago. She was a little bit heartbroken. She and Sammy corresponded for a few months, then his letters tapered off, and she realized she was free to see whoever she wanted. She dated several boys. They all wanted one thing. If she hadn't given it to Sammy, why would she surrender it to a casual date?

One thing about Stock, he hadn't jumped her. Yet.

"I don't want to get engaged," she confided to Meg.

"Everyone's *soooo* jealous!" Meg squealed. "Has he given you a ring? When are you going to *do* it? You'll *have* to do it now that you're engaged."

"But I'm not," Lauren protested.

Meg squinted at her. "Not what? Not engaged? Or not going to do it?"

"Not engaged, asshole."

"Nice talk from a virgin!"

"Asshole," Lauren repeated.

If her father ever heard her say that he'd kill her. Neither of her parents swore, at least not in front of her, although she'd once heard her father loudly groaning, "Christ! Christ!" when she was eleven and listening outside their bedroom door.

At least she knew what men said when they had sex. Although Sammy didn't. In the throes of passion, when she was doing something to him nice girls weren't supposed to do, Sammy Pilsner used to yell out, "Cowboys and Indians! This is an attack! Go for it! Go for it!"

Thinking of Sammy made her grin. His was the first and only penis she'd ever seen—she didn't count the time she'd walked in on her father getting out of the shower. He'd gone red in the face and screamed at her to get out. She was ten at the time. Shortly after, her mother had taken her to one side and told her to please knock before entering their bathroom.

Knock knock.

Who's there?

Daddy's penis.

I promise I won't look.

Sammy Pilsner was very proud of his penis, he wanted her to look all the time. In fact he wanted her to do a lot more than look.

She'd obliged, because at the time she thought she loved him, and at least you couldn't get pregnant that way.

She knew all about oral sex, having read about it in *Playboy*. Her father kept copies of the magazine locked in a storage closet in the basement. She'd discovered his stash one day and over the course of the next few weeks had read them all. Each magazine was full of naked women, sexist cartoons and articles about all kinds of sexual activities. She didn't enjoy looking at it, but it certainly taught her a lot. Sammy Pilsner couldn't believe his luck!

But that was the past—now she had Stock to deal with.

A few days later he sidled up to her during lunch break and informed her that his parents had decided to throw a big engagement party for them.

She wanted to say, "But I never said we'd get engaged." Instead she found herself nodding and listlessly agreeing.

Maybe that's what Stock liked about her—her total lack of enthusiasm. As the football hero and son of the town's richest man, he'd had girls fawning all over him since sixth grade. Perhaps he found her cool attitude a refreshing change.

"Saturday night," he said, sliding his arm around her shoulders. "My mother's talking to yours."

Oh, great! She should put a stop to this now. But somehow it just seemed easier to go along with it. Like that girl in *The Graduate*, she could take it all the way to the church, and then some handsome hero would rush in to save her and she'd run off with him, leaving Stock with his mouth open—probably patting his crotch to make sure she hadn't taken it with her!

One question. Who would the rescuing hero be? Sammy Pilsner? She didn't think so. Sammy was probably getting his penis licked by a cute little Chicago girl with long legs and a big mouth.

Idly she wondered if her mother ever did *that* to her father. The very thought made her shudder. No way. He probably didn't even let her *look* at it.

"I've got a big surprise for you," Stock said, surreptitiously checking out her bra strap through her sweater.

"What?" she asked impatiently.

"Never you mind, you'll see."

Asshole.

On the way home from school she stopped by her father's office. Once more he'd closed up early. She rattled the handle just to make sure. Nobody home.

Downstairs she popped into the Blakely Brothers hardware store. The Blakely brothers were identical twins, both fat and fifty with jovial smiles and drooping bushy eyebrows. She had no idea how to tell them apart.

"Hiya, Mr. Blakely," she said cheerily. "How's your wife?"

He beamed. "If I had one she'd be fine."

Foiled again! One was married, one single. The rumor around town was that the single one was a homosexual.

She grinned. "Just testing. I knew it was you!"

"No, you didn't." He winked. "I hear you're engaged. That's very nice, Lauren."

Her father the blabbermouth. This was obviously no secret.

"Have you seen my dad? He seems to have left early again."

"Didn't notice him go."

She had a ton of homework. Perhaps it was just as well her father wasn't around, they would have started talking, she'd get home late, and then she'd have to work all through dinner.

She'd never told her father she knew about his secret stash of *Playboys*. She'd never told her mother either.

"Your mom ordered light bulbs," Mr. Blakely said. "Since your dad has left . . ."

"I'll take them," she volunteered.

He handed her a large brown supermarket bag piled high. When her mother ordered she did it in bulk, imagining it saved her money.

The package wasn't heavy—merely cumbersome. She slung her schoolbag over her shoulder and grasped the paper bag with both hands. "Bye, Mr. Blakely."

"Goodbye, Lauren. You're marrying into a fine family. One of the best."

I'm not marrying into anything, Mr. Blakely. I am merely getting engaged. Temporarily. Because I can't stand the fuss of wriggling out of it. Because I'm always trying to please people. Because I hate to hurt anyone's feelings.

Because I'm an idiot!

Crash! Some jerk ran right into her at the swing door and her package fell to the ground, followed by the sound of breaking glass.

"Shit!" the jerk said. No "Sorry." No "Excuse me." Just a short, terse "Shit!"

She waited.

"You should look where you're goin'," he said rudely.

She was outraged. "*I* should?"

"Yeah. *You* walked into *me*."

"I did no such thing."

"Sure you did."

"No, I didn't."

They stared at each other, two furious strangers.

He was skinny and not very tall, with jet black curly hair, a pale complexion, a slight indentation in the center of his chin and intense green eyes. He wore a grubby white T-shirt under a frayed denim jacket, indescribably filthy torn jeans and battered sneakers.

She felt a shiver of excitement. "Aren't you going to help me pick everything up?" she asked, wondering who he was.

Nick returned her stare. Not bad. A bit square-looking. Hardly his usual type. But he was horny. God, he was horny!

"Okay," he mumbled, bending to help her.

"What about the broken bulbs?" she asked, finding two smashed ones.

"Get the store to replace 'em, you're on their property," he said, trying to decide how long it would take to screw her. Small-town girl. Possibly a virgin. Definitely more than one date.

He leaned closer, catching a whiff of her scent. She smelled like lemon soap, no cheap dime-store perfume. And her hair—long and shiny—was some sort of reddish brown color. He checked out her body. Slim but definitely acceptable.

"I can't do that," she said primly. "You'll have to pay for them."

He laughed. Not a very nice laugh. A sarcastic *Who do you think you're talking to* laugh.

"Sweetheart, I got enough to buy one pack of smokes an' that's *it*."

"Am *I* supposed to pay for them?" she countered.

"No." He nodded over to the counter where Mr. Blakely was busy with a customer. "I told you—go talk to old fatso. He'll give you back your money."

"Don't call Mr. Blakely that," she whispered furiously.

"He can't hear me."

"Maybe he can."

"What's he got—X-ray ears?"

Just as she was about to reply her father appeared, hurrying down the stairs that led from his office.

"Daddy!" she exclaimed, forgetting about the green-eyed stranger for a moment.

As soon as Nick heard the word "daddy" he was out of there. He'd learned at an early age to stay as far away from fathers as possible.

"Where have you been?" she asked, grabbing her father's arm.

"Upstairs, working."

"But I went upstairs. The shade was down, the door locked."

"Nonsense. What's all this?" He indicated the mess on the floor.

Flustered, she looked around. The boy who'd so rudely crashed into her was gone. "Oh, I dropped Mom's light bulbs."

Phil chuckled. "What's the woman doing—stocking up for the next three years?"

Lauren giggled, they were conspirators in her mother's excesses. "You know Mom," she said.

"Indeed I do," he replied. "By the way, Lauren, I haven't had a private moment to tell you how happy I am about your engagement. Stock is an upstanding boy with traditional values, his family is first class." A pause. "Your mother and I are very proud of you."

Shit! If a stranger could say it she could certainly think it.

I guess I'm engaged, she thought gloomily. No way out. For now.

7

Aretha Mae had arranged to get him into Bosewell High in mid-term. "Cyndra goes there," she informed him.

"Who's Cyndra?"

"She be your sister, boy, an' don't go forgettin' it. Good-lookin' girl, that's her problem. An' I don't want it bein' yours, seein' as you all be sleepin' in together."

Wasn't it bad enough he had to squeeze in with Harlan and Luke?

He cadged a couple of bucks off his father and made his way into town. They'd stayed in some one-gas-station towns in their time, but Bosewell took the prize. He explored Main Street, wandering into the hardware store, where he bumped—literally—into a girl he considered making out with for a moment, but then her father appeared and he was out of there fast. She wasn't his type anyway, too clean-cut.

The waitress in the drugstore was more like it. Mid-twenties, big knockers and a slight squint.

He slid up to the counter and ordered coffee.

"Black?" she asked, hardly taking any notice of him.

He winked to get her attention. "With cream, sweetheart. Lots of it."

"You new in town?"

"Howdja guess?"

" 'Cause if you wasn't you wouldn't be tryin' to hit on me. You'd know Dave was my husband." She jerked her thumb at the short-order cook, a burly man about ten years older than her with muscles to spare.

Nick refused to give up. "He keep you happy?"

She raised a sarcastic eyebrow. "Does Mommy know you're out?"

They both burst out laughing at the same time.

"Louise," she said. "Welcome to Bosewell."

"Dave's a lucky guy."

"And you're a fresh kid. What you doin' here anyway? Passin' through on your way to reform school?"

"My old man moved us here."

She poured him a cup of coffee, adding a generous amount of cream. "An' what does *he* do?"

"Fucks up a lot."

Louise sighed. "Don't we all, dear. Don't we all."

"I gotta go to school," he said, gulping his coffee. "But I wanna work nights an' weekends, score some bucks. Got any ideas?"

"What do you think I am? An employment agency?" she said, smoothing down her gingham apron.

"Just askin'."

She softened. "Maybe Dave'll know of somethin'."

Her attention was taken by a group of high school kids who came crowding in making a lot of noise. She moved over to take their orders.

Nick checked them out. He was used to joining new schools half-way through the semester, it was always the same deal. The other kids regarded him with suspicion and there usually was some jerk who tried to start a fight, while most of the girls pretended they didn't notice him—although they did.

Every time he had to prove himself, every fuckin' time. It meant pounding the shit out of the school bully and screwing the prettiest girl. Somehow he always managed to do both.

He had one golden rule. Don't play fair. It worked good.

One of these days he'd be out of school once and for all, the routine

57

was getting him down. Exactly how many times did he have to prove himself?

The group was asking Louise about him and staring over. A couple of the girls nudged each other. A big guy with a blond crew cut made a smart remark and they all laughed.

Instinctively he knew that this was the guy he'd have to deal with.

Tough shit, big guy. I'll give you a shot in the balls that'll take you all the way to Miami and back.

Louise returned and filled his cup.

He nodded toward Mr. Crew Cut.

"Don't mess with him, honey," Louise warned. "His daddy owns most of this town."

"Yeah?"

"You better believe it." She brushed a strand of lank brown hair out of her squinty eyes. "Lemme go talk to Dave, his brother George runs the gas station. You know anythin' 'bout cars?"

"If it stops I can fix it. That good enough?"

"We'll see, hon. We'll see."

Back at the trailer it was the same old scene. Primo sat glued to the television, burping, swigging beer and picking at a bag of pretzels.

Aretha Mae stood in front of the kerosene stove, her shoulders slumped as she heated up two-day-old meatloaf—a gift from her employer, who allowed her the choice of throwing old food away or taking it home.

Harlan and Luke played outside, kicking around tin cans and jumping in and out of the skeleton of what was once a car.

Nick strolled outside and joined them. "One of these days I'm gonna get me a Cadillac," he said. "A goddamn red Cadillac with leather seats an' lots of chrome."

"Can we ride in it?" Harlan asked, believing every word.

"Sure. Every day if you like."

The next morning he rode the bus to school with Aretha Mae. She told him where to get off and handed him a dollar.

"What's this for?" he asked, not wanting her charity.

"In case you need it," she replied stoically, staring straight ahead.

He wondered what the going rate was for maids in Bosewell. Or maybe her employer piled her up with old food and clothes and considered that payment enough.

Bosewell High was a pale gray concrete building with green lawns on one side and an enormous parking lot on the other.

Clusters of students headed toward the imposing front entrance, most of them coming from the parking lot.

Nick felt the usual hollow feeling in the pit of his stomach. He tried to ignore it. Stay cool. No nerves. Don't let the fuckers get you down.

Without having to ask, he found registration and made himself official. The school secretary ran a disapproving eye over his grubby uniform of jeans, T-shirt and jacket. "While we have no dress code here at Bosewell High, we do expect our students to look clean and well groomed," she said. "That means washed and pressed clothes at all times. And no torn jeans."

"Yes, ma'am." Hopefully he'd never have to see her again.

"Classroom number three, Mr. Angelo. Your teacher will tell you what books you need."

"Thank you, ma'am."

Old cow. He could charm her if he wanted to.

Who wanted to?

"Ohh . . . feast your eyes on *him!*" Meg nudged Lauren excitedly. "Now he's what I call *gorgeous!*"

Lauren glanced up from her desk, her mind elsewhere. "Who?" she asked vaguely.

"*Him.* Standing by the door. He must be the new student. Dawn spotted him yesterday at the drugstore and she's in *love.*"

"Dawn's in love every day."

"I know. But this one is—oh, I dunno—so sort of moody-looking." Meg jumped up. "I'm going over to welcome him."

Lauren looked over at the door. And then she looked again. Meg was talking about the boy she'd run into at Blakely's hardware store. The one with the green eyes and smart mouth.

"Who is he?" she asked.

Too late. Meg was halfway across the room, while Dawn was fast approaching from the other direction. Lauren sat tight. Let them make fools of themselves if they wanted to. He wasn't *that* great. Just different . . .

Meg was speaking to him now, eyes sparkling, cheeks flushed. Lauren watched her go for it. They were best friends, had been since elementary school, but sometimes Meg was too impulsive. She should have waited, let him come after her. Well-known fact. Boys liked to chase after girls, not the other way around.

Meg was pretty, with fluffy yellow hair and gray eyes. She was ten pounds overweight and on a permanent diet. Her two front teeth were crooked, which sometimes gave her a rabbity look.

Dawn Kovak on the other hand was a tramp. She had dyed black hair, prominent breasts, and wore too much makeup. She didn't look sixteen, she looked thirty.

Lauren observed them both in action, her best friend and the school dump—as Dawn was nicknamed.

He'd probably go for Dawn with her black hair and big breasts—they always did. Meg had "virgin" written all over her.

Surprisingly he chose Meg, allowing her to lead him to the only vacant desk, listening as she chattered on, giving her all his attention.

Lauren felt the smallest shiver of jealousy. Which was ridiculous really, because she certainly wanted nothing to do with him. She was engaged to Stock Browning. She was *very very* busy, thank you very much.

Hmm . . . maybe she should go over and greet him?

No need. Meg seemed to be doing a perfectly wonderful job of making him feel more than welcome.

She stopped watching and opened up her English Lit book. Concentrating was not easy. She couldn't help glancing up to see what Meg was doing. Meg was heading back to her desk with a triumphant expression.

Just as she got back, their teacher entered the classroom.

"He's *fantastic!*" Meg whispered, sitting down, a silly smile lighting up her face. "*And* he's asked me out."

"He has?"

"Yep. Tonight."

"Where?"

"Who knows? I'm meeting him in front of the drugstore at eight."

"Your parents'll never let you out on a school night."

"I'll say I'm over at your place studying."

"Meg, you don't know anything about him, how can you go out with him?"

"Holy cow, Lauren, you sound like my mother."

"I do not!"

"Yes, you do."

"Girls!" The high-pitched tones of Miss Potter, their English Lit teacher, interrupted them. "Will you be joining us today?" she continued sarcastically. "Or shall we set up a table for two outside so that you may carry on your conversation uninterrupted?"

"Sorry, Miss Potter," they chorused, sounding like a couple of second-graders.

Lauren couldn't resist one more quick glance over at the new boy. He caught her look and returned it.

Meg hid her face in her book, trying to choke down a giggle. "I'm so excited!" she whispered. "He's really gorgeous!"

"You're crazy," Lauren muttered, and for one brief moment wished that *she* was the crazy one.

The chubby little blonde came on to him like gangbusters. He chose her over the dark one because he had a strong suspicion the dark one had nailed every guy in school, and while he was interested in getting laid, he was not interested in catching a dose of the clap or, even worse, crabs.

It was easy. As usual. It had something to do with his green eyes. He could fix them on a girl—just for a moment—and they had this sort of crazy hypnotic effect.

Jeez! He was allowed to have *something*, wasn't he? And God had given him the eyes.

He caught the girl he'd bumped into yesterday watching him from across the room. She didn't mean to, but he could see she couldn't help herself. Maybe after he was finished with the blonde he'd go for her, give her a cheap thrill. Maybe . . .

Bosewell High was going to be easy compared with some of the inner-city dumps he'd been forced to attend. This school was strictly small-town, he could take his pick.

So far he hadn't spotted the beefy guy with the crew cut. The schlump was probably in a different grade, and that was good. If he played it smart perhaps he could avoid him altogether.

Deep down he knew this wasn't possible. Deep down he knew there was always one dumb asshole who'd go for his throat.

When school got out for the day he planned to return to the drugstore, find out if Louise had come up with a job for him, and then, if he was lucky, cadge a meal and hang around until it was time to meet Blondie.

The teacher noticed him and made him stand up and introduce himself to the class. *Jeez! What a drag!* He hated the way they all looked him over. Why didn't they ask for his rank and serial number while they were at it?

At lunch break he fell in behind the crowd and drifted down to the school cafeteria. He bought a cheese sandwich and a Coke, found a corner table and sat down.

Before long, Crew Cut made his entrance—trailed by an admiring group busy hanging onto his every word.

Nick ate his sandwich and surveyed the scene. Blondie waved at him from across the room. She was probably dying to talk to him again, but had decided to play it cool. Ha! He could even figure out how they thought.

And then the girl from the hardware store made her entrance, pausing in the doorway.

He knew she noticed him and half hoped she'd come over, but she didn't.

And what was this? Crew Cut was on his feet, racing across the room, putting his arm around her and leading her over to a table. Shit! She was his girlfriend!

Immediately Nick wondered if she was gettable.

Yeah. Why not? He was always up for a challenge.

"The party's all set," Stock said.

"I know," Lauren replied. "My mother and your mother are like this." She held up two fingers to show exactly what they were like.

Stock smirked. "My mother likes bossing your mother around."

Lauren took offense. "What do you mean?"

He shrugged. "My mother likes bossing everyone, including me."

Just for a second Lauren felt sorry for him. It must be awful having a mother like Daphne, a huge commanding woman with scarlet lips telling everyone what to do.

"Meg's got a date tonight," she found herself saying, anything to make conversation.

"Really?" He couldn't care less.

"With that new guy," she added.

"What new guy?"

"You know, the one that started school today."

"Yeah?" His lack of interest was all too apparent.

She gave up, there was only so much she could do.

Meg arrived at her house an hour before her date, barely able to conceal her excitement. She rushed up to Lauren's room and made a mad dash for the mirror. "How do I look?" she demanded, fluffing out her newly washed hair.

"Horrible," Lauren teased.

"*Whaaat?*"

"Only kidding."

"Don't do that," Meg wailed. "This is the first decent date I've had in months."

Lauren sat cross-legged on her bed. "How do you know he's decent?"

Meg was exasperated. "What's the *matter* with you?"

"What's the matter with *me?*" she retorted sharply. "Take another look in the mirror. You're all excited over a guy you don't even know. He could be a sex maniac, a rapist, anything . . ."

"You're really weird," Meg said, shaking her head. "I mean really."

"Thanks. All compliments gratefully accepted."

"Anybody would think *you* liked him."

She flushed, and jumped off the bed. "Don't be ridiculous."

"Forget it. *I* saw him first and he's mine. Anyway, you're engaged, or had you conveniently forgotten?"

Lauren pulled a face. "Would that I could."

"Nice talk," Meg said, adjusting the waistband of her new black skirt to make it shorter. "How do my legs look?"

"Like legs. What'll I tell your mother if she calls?"

"Tell her I'm in the bathroom. Anyway, she's not likely to."

"It could happen."

"You're a big help."

"Call me as soon as you get home. I want a full report."

Meg gave a jaunty wink. "You bet!"

"Hi." Meg felt suddenly shy as she approached Nick. He was leaning against the wall outside the drugstore, smoking a cigarette.

When he saw her coming he flicked the butt toward the curb with an elaborate flourish. "Hi," he replied, taking her arm as if they'd been dating for months. "You look nice."

She giggled nervously. "Thanks."

"I mean it," he replied. "Very nice." He'd scored a free hamburger off Louise, and a promise from Dave he could work at his brother's gas station Saturday nights. Things were looking up. Now all he had to do was get laid and perhaps he could get a good night's sleep, although it wasn't easy with Harlan and Luke coughing and farting the night away.

"Where are we going?" Meg asked, as he guided her along Main Street.

"Thought we'd catch a movie."

She'd already seen *The Poseidon Adventure* playing at the Bosewell, but so what? "Super," she said, eager to please.

Super. Hmm . . . Maybe he should have picked the sure thing with the black hair, this one was a baby.

When they reached the theater he steered her away from the box office. "Buy your ticket, go inside, an' then let me in through the fire escape door. Like I'm busted, y'know?" He gave her arm an encouraging squeeze. "Okay?"

Buy her own ticket? Usually on a date the boy paid. Lauren would *love* hearing this. Still . . . it made life exciting. "Okay," she agreed.

He gave her a little shove. "It's easy, you'll see."

She purchased her ticket and entered the almost empty theater. Then, when she was sure she wasn't being observed, she raced down the side aisle to the fire exit, opened the heavy door and let Nick in.

"Yeah!" he said, guiding her to the back row, which was conveniently empty.

The movie had already started. Putting his arm around her he settled back to watch. After a few minutes he moved closer. "I knew you and me would get along soon as I saw you," he said in a low voice. "It was like . . . y'know . . . uh . . . special."

"I know," she whispered back, thrilled they were thinking along the same lines.

"Sometimes these things happen," he said, massaging her back through her sweater.

"Right," she agreed, beginning to feel rather warm.

"Like it's meant to be or somethin'," he added, his hand creeping around to the front, dangerously close to her left breast.

She opened her mouth to agree again and without warning his lips were on hers, kissing insistently, his tongue probing.

She gasped for breath. This was all happening so fast. The last boy she'd dated had waited three whole weeks before trying anything. Now Nick's hand was definitely on her breast and she knew she should push him away, but at least she could enjoy it for a minute, couldn't she?

Nick stroked her nipple through her sweater, his thumb and forefinger moving in circles.

She let out an involuntary groan as he slowly began to push her sweater up, fumbling in the dark for her bra hook.

"Don't," she managed, realizing she'd better put a stop to this now.

He didn't listen. He was too busy unhooking her bra.

Cupping her left breast he bent his head, licking her nipple with practiced ease.

She tried to push his head away. "No!" she whispered urgently.

"Yes!" he whispered back.

"Someone will see."

"It's empty in here."

"I don't want you to do this."

"Yes, you do."

And it was true. She did. For a moment she relaxed, giving herself up to this glorious feeling sweeping over her. Was it so bad to feel so good?

He began to suck her nipple, at the same time reaching for her hand and jamming it on his penis—which somehow or other he'd managed to release.

Oh, God! She'd never touched one before. Oh, dear! There was no way she should be doing this. Nice girls didn't do this—unless, of course, they wanted to be labeled easy or a tramp, like Dawn Kovak.

With a sudden burst of resolve she attempted to pull her hand away.

"Hold it," he commanded. "It ain't gonna bite!"

"I can't," she said desperately.

"Yes, you can." He groaned, helping her hand move up and down —faster . . . faster . . .

And then it happened. He spurted all over her. Hot, sticky, wet.

"Jeez!" he groaned again. "Ohhh . . . jeez!"

"My skirt!" Meg wailed, horrified. "You've done it all over my new skirt!"

He leaned his head back, closed his eyes and took a deep satisfied breath.

Welcome to Bosewell. It had been one helluva day.

ick made the long trudge home thinking about Blondie. Nice tits.
Too shy. Not for him. Jerk-off action was for boys Harlan's age.

Who was he kidding? Once in a while a jerk-off was better than
nothing, and he knew if he'd tried to screw her she'd have bolted. As
it was, she was hysterical about her stupid skirt. What was it with girls
and clothes?

Best not to see *that* one again, he thought. Better to invest in a box
of rubbers and give the dark-haired one a chance.

Girls, they were all the same. Easy. And he never cared if he saw
any of them again. Once the sex was over he felt an emptiness, a
void.

When he got back to the trailer the two boys were sitting on their
pile of blankets flicking through well-thumbed comic books.

"What's up?" he asked cheerfully, taking off his jacket.

"What's up with you?" Harlan retorted.

"Nothin' much." He nodded over at Luke. "How come he never
speaks?"

"He jest don't," Harlan replied, suddenly sullen.

"Somethin' happen to him?" Nick asked, stripping off the rest of his
clothes.

"Not your business."

"I'm only askin' 'cause I thought I might help."

"Not your business," Harlan repeated fiercely.

Nick shrugged and settled himself down on his lumpy mattress, trying to find a comfortable spot. "No farting tonight," he said sternly, staring menacingly at the two boys.

Harlan stood up, pulled down his shorts, bent his rear end in Nick's direction and let one rip.

"Aw, god*damnit!*" Nick wrinkled his nose in disgust. "If I wasn't so beat I'd slap your skinny butt halfway across this trailer park."

Harlan burped. Luke laughed. At least he could do that.

Nick closed his eyes, and for some unknown reason began thinking about the other girl, old Crew Cut's girlfriend. No, he told himself sternly, mustn't look for trouble. The truth is they're all the same in the dark, and he'd never met a girl who could give him anything more than a hard-on.

In the morning he followed the two boys into the main trailer hoping to cadge breakfast. Aretha Mae handed out stale slices of bread smeared with congealed bacon fat. He grabbed one.

Primo snored loudly, sprawled across the rumpled bed.

Aretha Mae looked tired, her eyes sunken, her mouth pinched into a thin line. She clapped her hands together. "Out," she told the two younger boys. "Get movin' or you be late." She turned to Nick. "How 'bout I pay your bus fare the rest o' the week. After that you be on your own."

"Don't worry, I got a part-time job," he said quickly. "I'm workin' down at the gas station Saturday nights."

She was impressed that he didn't take after his idle father. "That's good," she said, wiping her hands on an old cloth. "That's real good."

He nodded. "Yeah."

Meg was late for class. She slipped into her seat and shuffled a few books around, attempting to look industrious.

"You didn't call," Lauren hissed. "I don't appreciate that kind of behavior when I'm supposed to be your alibi."

"I had more important things to worry about," Meg hissed back.

"Like what?"

"Like a ruined skirt."

Mr. Lucas coughed meaningfully and glared across the room at them.

Lauren returned her attention to her books. She'd had a miserable morning listening to her parents carry on about her engagement party. They were turning into a couple of social-climbing phonies right before her eyes—discussing what to wear, who would be there, how they should act.

"Today I'm going shopping for a new outfit," Jane had declared enthusiastically. "And Lauren, dear, we'll buy you a pretty new dress too."

Lauren hated the word "pretty," it conjured up visions of pale pink ruffles. "I don't need a new dress," she'd said.

"What nonsense! We'll go shopping after school today. Bring Meg."

She'd been unable to wriggle out of it. This engagement thing was getting out of hand.

As soon as Mr. Lucas signaled freedom she grabbed Meg. "Well?" she asked breathlessly.

Meg shook her curls. "You were right. He's a sex maniac."

"He is?"

"Oh, yes."

"Really?"

"I'm not lying."

"What *happened?*"

"He's crazy about me."

"I'm sure. But what did you *do?*"

Meg sighed, ready to tell her story. Before she could, Nick put in his first appearance of the day, strolling by on his way to math. Clinging to his arm as if she owned him was Dawn Kovak.

He winked at Meg, greeting her with a cavalier, "Hey, how're ya doin'?"

"Fine," she managed, her cheeks burning with rage and humiliation.

• • •

70

"They're putting up a tent in the garden," Stock said, flexing his muscles.

"Isn't it too cold?" Lauren asked.

He smirked. "They've got those heater things."

"Why the garden? Your house is so large, they could have everyone inside."

He proceeded to do a series of knee bends. "Beats me."

"Stock . . ." she began tentatively.

"Yes?"

"Maybe we don't need a big party."

He continued doing knee bends. "Sure we do. Once we get rid of the old farts it'll be a blast."

"But everyone's making such a fuss. I'm not certain it's what I want. I—"

"Listen, hon," he interrupted, standing up straight. "We're talkin' a good time here. Relax, you'll love it."

"I will?" she said unsurely.

" 'Course you will."

"Okay," she said, still not convinced, watching her mother pull into the driveway in the family station wagon. "I have to go. We're going shopping."

"Buy something sexy," he leered, unexpectedly pinching her on the ass.

She swatted his hand away. "Don't *do* that!"

He chuckled. "Why not? We're engaged. I'll soon be doin' a lot more than pinchin' your butt!"

Oh, no, you won't, she thought angrily. *I'm putting a stop to this as soon as I summon up the courage to tell my parents.*

"Okay, babe, see ya. I got football practice anyway." He swiped a kiss on her cheek and loped off.

"Lucky thing!" sighed Suzi Harden, coming up behind her.

Lucky thing indeed! Lauren didn't feel lucky. She felt like a cornered rat waiting for the trap to snap shut.

Sex with Stock was unthinkable. His big sweaty hands all over her. Crushed beneath his enormous bulk. No way!

"Where's Meg?" Suzi asked. "You two are always together."

"She didn't feel well—went home early."

71

And who could blame her? She was broken up over Nick's appearance with Dawn Kovak. One moment he was all over her, and the next he was consorting with "Anything Goes Kovak." Boys! Who could understand them? Who wanted to?

Her mother swerved the station wagon over to the curb and she got in.

"Where's Meg?" Jane asked, adjusting her rearview mirror. "I thought she was coming with us."

Maybe she should have a little card printed:

Meg is not coming.

Meg is humiliated and heartbroken.

All humans of the male species are sex-crazed animals.

Lauren shrugged. "She didn't feel up to it."

Jane looked concerned. "Is she sick? I hope not. We don't want *you* catching anything."

"She's sick of boys."

Jane laughed. "You girls!"

"Ha-ha!" Lauren thought sourly, catching a glimpse of Nick Angelo —she knew his name—sauntering out of school with Dawn Kovak clinging to his arm. Obviously Dawn was now a permanent fixture.

He was real moody-looking, a regular bad boy. She'd warned Meg, told her not to get involved. Meg should have listened.

Nick Angelo. Hmm . . . Meg had said he was a great kisser . . .

So what?

One thing he'd learned in life—if you're going to dump a girl do it quickly. No excuses. No hanging around. One sharp cut and it's over.

Blondie was a mistake. Dawn was definitely more his speed.

"How come it took you so long to get here?" she'd asked, approaching him on the way into school.

"What's *that* supposed to mean?" he'd replied, checking her out.

She'd touched his cheek with a long red fingernail. "I've been waiting for a guy like you all my life."

Soul mates. She was even using his lines!

"So," he'd said. "Here I am."

"So," she'd said, with a provocative wink. "I'm ready."

Dawn Kovak lived with her alcoholic mother on the wrong side of town. Not quite as bad as the trailer park, but getting there. She didn't have much going for her except her curvaceous figure and sultry looks, so she used them to full advantage. She might be the school screw, but at least her assets made her popular. During the day she filled him in about Bosewell. Small town. Small thinkers. No fun. No action. The nearest place where anything happened was fifty miles away—a town called Ripley—where there were bars and places to dance and a cool bikers' hangout.

"You got a car?" was one of the first questions she asked.

"I can get hold of one," he'd replied, thinking of taking the van one night when Primo was out cold.

"You an' me—we'll make our own good times," she'd promised seductively.

For now, Nick had thought. While it suits me.

But don't get too close, I'm only passing through.

When the Brownings did something they did it big. The garden was tented. A three-piece group played what was supposed to be dance music. The food was catered. And the tables set with fancy pink linen and fine silverware. After all, the Brownings were the richest family in town and once in a while they liked to show it.

Stock collected Lauren early and drove her straight to his house, proudly showing off the party preparations.

"When the old folks hit the sack we've got a disco all set up," he boasted. "And plenty of beer. I mean we're talking *plenty.*"

He was telling her like she was a big beer drinker or something. "Great," she managed, tugging at the bodice of the pale yellow dress her mother had talked her into buying. She hated the dress, it made her look like a flower girl at somebody's wedding.

"Right now I have something just for you," he said, grabbing her hand and pulling her over to the corner of the garden.

Oh, no! Was this the big moment? Was this the great attack?

"What?" she mumbled, praying he wasn't going to jump her—although it was highly unlikely in his parents' garden with sixty guests due any minute.

"This," he said, proudly pushing a small leather box into her reluctant hand.

She held it gingerly.

"Go on, open it," he said.

Easy for *him* to say. But when she opened it the net would tighten, for any fool knew it was an engagement ring.

"I always dreamt of going to New York," she blurted out, postponing the inevitable.

"We will," he assured her. "On our honeymoon if you like."

When was *that* going to be? Next week? Things were moving so fast she could hardly breathe.

"I figure we'll get married after I finish college," he said, as if reading her thoughts. "I know that sounds a long time—but when we're officially engaged it'll almost be like being married, won't it?"

Reprieve! Reprieve!

" 'Course, if you get pregnant we can do it earlier," he added.

Pregnant! Was he kidding? You had to have *sex* to get pregnant, and there was no way she was doing anything with him. *No way.*

With a feeling of relief she realized this was the answer to all her problems. No sex, no engagement. When she refused to put out, he'd break the engagement. *He'd* break it off. *She'd* be the injured party, and her parents couldn't be mad at her. Whew! What an escape.

With renewed vigor she sprung the box open and stared at a heart-shaped sapphire surrounded by more than a dozen diamond baguettes. "Wow!" she exclaimed. "This is beautiful."

"I knew you'd like it," he said, smirking proudly. "My mother picked it out."

"How romantic," she said dryly. As usual her sarcasm was lost on him.

"Put it on," he urged. "See if it fits."

She did so—imagining the day she would give it back.

He took her hand, pressing it on his tuxedo-clad crotch. "Feel this," he said with another proud smirk. "This is what you do to me."

She jerked her hand away. Their engagement was going to be shorter than anyone could possibly imagine.

Dawn Kovak was the girl of his wet dreams—ready, willing and always able. He knew her reputation—not that it came as any surprise, be-

cause Joey Pearson had already filled him in. Joey was a good guy—
funny, clever, a touch offbeat. They'd become instant pals when it
turned out they were both doing Saturday night shifts at the gas
station.

"Look," he'd explained to Joey, "I won't be stayin' long. What do I
care if she's screwed every guy in town? She's just the way I like 'em
—experienced."

Joey had laughed. "Yeah, there's nothin' like a girl who knows what
she's doin'."

Both of them had been recruited to park cars at the Brownings'
party—anything to earn a few extra bucks.

A maroon Cadillac made its way up the circular driveway. Nick ran
around to the driver's side and opened the door. A man got out. His
wife was in the passenger seat. Meg emerged from the back and made
a quick dash into the house.

"What happened with you an' her?" Joey asked. "Didn't you take
her to the movies or somethin'?"

"Nothin' happened," Nick lied easily. He wasn't about to tell tales.
"My mistake. Picked the wrong girl. It was my first week in town,
y'know how it is."

Yes, Joey knew how it was. His mother and he had arrived in
Bosewell from Chicago a year ago. His father, a cop, had been killed
in a bank holdup, and his mother immediately decided they should
move to the safety of a small town.

"When we first came here my ma said it was for my protection,"
Joey said, grimacing. "Like the minute I'm eighteen I'm outta here.
It's back to Chicago for me. I'm gonna do stand-up."

Nick looked vague. "Stand-up?"

"Y'know, like tell jokes an' stuff. Make people laugh."

"Sounds good to me."

Joey searched through his pockets and produced a battered cigarette. He snapped it in two and handed Nick half. They shared a
match.

"So . . ." Joey said, taking a deep drag. "I know what *I'm* doin' here.
What brings *you* to this pisshole?"

Nick sucked on his half of the cigarette. "My old man," he said.

"What does *he* do?"

Nick laughed bitterly. "Fuck-all."

"That's nice."

"Very nice. Like he was married to this woman . . . this black woman . . ." He paused. Joey didn't need to know this, nobody did. "Aw, shit. It's a bummer, it doesn't matter."

"Tell me about it," Joey urged.

Nick wasn't in the mood to reveal himself. "Some other time," he said, dropping the subject.

Joey shrugged. "I'm not goin' anywhere."

More cars arrived and they got busy.

"Y'know, Stock Browning is the asshole of the world," Joey said, running back from parking a Buick. "The schmuck tried to beat me up once—I kicked him in the nuts an' got myself a knife."

Nick laughed. "I knew we'd get along."

"The funny thing is," Joey continued, "when I was goin' to school in Chicago I never got beat up once."

"Maybe 'cause your dad was a cop."

"Bullshit. There weren't any jerks like Stock Browning around."

"You really love the guy, don'tcha?"

"He's a prick. I'd sure like to know why Lauren's gettin' engaged to him. Dumb move."

"You ever take her out?"

"No way, man. She and Meg—it's virgin city."

"Maybe she's changed."

"Yeah," Joey said disgustedly. "That can happen. Girls! Show 'em a wad of money an' it's legs in the air an' let's party!"

Another car entered the driveway and pulled up in front of the house.

"I'll toss ya for it," Nick said.

"What's the difference?" Joey replied. "We're splittin' all the tips anyway."

Nick nodded. "Right."

Meg was furious. "He's outside!" she complained to Lauren.

"Who?"

"Don't ask me who!" Meg snapped. "You *know* who. It's him. Nick.

77

Isn't it enough that I have to see him at school? Now he's here, parking cars. I'm so humiliated. I arrived with my *parents!* How could you do this to me?"

"Calm down, Meg. I had no idea he'd be here."

"Oh, no, *sure.* You're too busy getting engaged to notice *anything* or anybody. How do you think I *feel?*"

"Meg," Lauren said patiently. "Your date with him was three weeks ago. Forget it."

"Easy for you to say. Try putting yourself in my place." Her voice rose hysterically. "He practically *raped* me!"

Lauren looked concerned. "You didn't tell me that. You said he got your bra off and ruined your skirt. You certainly didn't tell me he tried to rape you. If he did, you should report him to the police."

"It's too late."

"If that's what happened, it's never too late."

Meg's face crumpled. "I hate him!" she cried out.

"So do I," agreed Lauren, ever the supportive friend. Although truthfully she couldn't say that she hated him, because she didn't even know him.

Of course, she knew he had green eyes. And black curly hair. And a great chin. And a James Dean slouch.

She also knew he was working part-time at the gas station, and that he and Joey Pearson were friends, and that most nights he saw Dawn Kovak.

She certainly found him intriguing, although she couldn't tell Meg, had to keep a tightly buttoned lip on *that* little piece of info.

"Are you enjoying the party?" she asked, moving the conversation along.

Meg narrowed her eyes and reached for a glass of watered-down punch. "Will you have to call your firstborn Stock junior?" she asked in a mean voice.

"Not if it's a girl." Lauren smiled sweetly and moved over to join her parents, who seemed to be having a perfectly fine time sucking up to the entire Browning clan.

Dawn was the uninvited guest; at least her name wasn't on the official list.

"Surprise!" she greeted Nick, arriving just before midnight in a car full of leather-clad friends who looked like they'd strayed out of *West Side Story*. "Stock told me to get here late."

This was not the rich kids' group. These were the tougher, older kids who smoked pot, drank alcohol and blasted Joplin and Hendrix day and night.

Nick hadn't exactly fallen in with them—but thanks to Dawn he knew most of them, and they'd accepted him as a cool guy.

Behind the car were six or seven motorcycles. Dawn had recruited more friends from Ripley.

"Hiya, Nicky." She licked his ear, suggestively sticking her tongue deep. "Now the party can *really* get goin'. Dump this gig an' let's go inside."

"Yeah, go on, man," Joey encouraged. "There's only a few more cars. I'll take care of 'em."

"I don't wanna stick you—" Nick began.

"Go. We'll split the tips tomorrow."

Why not? If Dawn was invited, he was entitled to tag along. He was certainly as good as any of these other creeps.

They blasted in noisy and out for a good time.

Stock greeted them surrounded by several of his football buddies all well on the road to oblivion.

"Hiya, sexy," Dawn said, provocative in an off-the-shoulder sweater and short tight skirt. She nuzzled in for a deep French kiss. "Takin' *you* outta circulation is a crime!"

Stock guffawed, winked and burped. "Let's get the disco goin'. You take care of it, Dawn."

"Sure thing, handsome—anything you want. An' I *mean* anything."

He stuck his tongue out, flipping it obscenely from side to side. "I've had *that*."

His friends roared. Dawn did too.

Nick headed for the bar. So Stock had screwed her. Big surprise.

He helped himself to a cold beer, swigging from the bottle and checking everything out. This was some set-up, it must have cost big bucks—what with the tent, a full bar, dozens of tables and chairs, flowers and all that crap. There was even a dance floor, which Dawn was now dragging Stock onto as the disc jockey took over from the sedate three-piece group, blasting everybody out of their seats with the Stones' raunchy rendition of "Satisfaction."

The last of the adults scurried toward the exit. Daphne and Benjamin Browning were long gone.

Nick helped himself to another beer.

"Oh, no!" Meg yelped. "He's here. What's he *doing* in here?"

Lauren was truly fed up with her friend, she'd done nothing but complain all night.

"I've got to go," Meg said frantically.

Lauren was in no mood to stop her. "I'll see you tomorrow," she said coolly.

"Are you staying?" Meg asked, surprised.

"It's my engagement party. Or had it slipped your mind?"

"I suppose *you* have to stay until the end. You don't mind if I go, do you?"

As a matter of fact she did mind, but there was no way she was begging Meg to stay. "No, that's okay."

"Thanks." Meg took off without a second thought.

Lauren sighed. So much for best friends. She wished she could say to Meg, "Stay. I need you." And she wished she could say to Stock, "Goodbye. I don't need you."

Her parents had enjoyed the evening. Phil Roberts had turned on the charm and talked up insurance to more prospective clients than he could remember. Jane Roberts had declared herself belle of Bosewell, dancing with every old man in town.

Lauren had danced with Stock and all his buddies. She'd even had to dance with Benjamin Browning, who'd held her too close and breathed whiskey breath in her face. Now she was ready to call it quits, but Stock had other ideas. He was all set to let the good times begin.

He reeled off the dance floor fresh from Dawn, and grabbed Lauren. "C'mon, sugar, let's rock 'n roll," he said, leering drunkenly.

"I'm really tired," she said. "It's been a long night."

"Are you kidding?" He rolled his eyes. "The evening's just beginning."

"Do your parents know you've invited all these other people?" she asked, gesturing at the crowd.

"What do *you* think? I told them I was havin' a few more friends come by. They don't care. This is my party, I can do whatever I want."

"*Our* party," she corrected. "And *I* want to go home."

He shook his head, perplexed. "Sometimes you're a real pain. Have a glass of punch. Relax. Get with it."

"I had a glass of punch, thank you."

"So have another one. One of the guys spiked it. Now the party'll *really* swing." He attempted a kiss. She pulled away.

He laughed bitterly. "You're a helluva fiancée."

The Stones gave way to a raucous Rod Stewart. Lauren gave him a little shove toward the dance floor, where all his cronies seemed to be having a great time. "Go dance with Dawn again. She loves it, I don't."

"If you're with me you'd better learn to love it," he said, slurring his words. Then he staggered back to Dawn.

What did he think this was, school? She'd learn to do exactly what she pleased and that was it.

Over by the door Nick caught the action. He didn't care about Dawn taking off—it didn't matter. Lauren was the girl that interested him, might as well admit it. And now was as good a time as any to do something about it.

Just as he was about to head toward her, a familiar voice said, "What in hell *you* doin' here, boy?"

It was Aretha Mae, a different-looking Aretha Mae with her frizzy red hair pinned back and a starched white maid's uniform covering her skinny body.

"I could ask you the same," he said smartly.

She glared at him. "*I* work here," she said. "An' you better be gettin' your ass outta here." She balanced a tray of dirty glasses and marched back into the house.

Screw her. She wasn't his mother. He didn't have to listen to anything she said.

Lauren was still by herself. Seizing the opportunity he sauntered over, sitting down beside her. "How ya doin'?" he asked casually.

She turned to look at him. They'd never been formally introduced, but what did that matter?

Oh, God! Meg would be furious if she talked to him.

"Uh, hi," she replied, trying to sound equally casual.

He nodded at Dawn and Stock on the dance floor. "They make quite a couple, huh?"

"Hmm," she said noncommittally.

"Isn't it supposed to be you up there with him?" he asked, helping himself to a cigarette from a box on the table.

He had his nerve. He knew perfectly well it was supposed to be her.

"How come *you're* not dancing with him?" he persisted. "Don't you like to dance?"

"Don't you?" she countered.

He gave her the benefit of his green-eyed stare. "Only if it's with somebody special."

She met his eyes for a moment, found them too dangerous and quickly broke the look. "I . . . I have to go," she said, getting up.

"Mr. Football Hero's in no state to take you home," he said, also standing.

She wondered why her heart was beating so fast. "That's not your concern, is it?"

He kept on staring at her. "Maybe it could be."

"I beg your pardon?"

This girl wasn't reacting the way they usually reacted. A little warmth would be nice. "How come you're so uptight?" he asked, trying to throw her off balance.

"I'm not uptight," she answered defensively. "You're rude."

"Yeah? What've I done?"

"Nothing—to me."

"What's that mean?"

"You know."

"No, I don't. What?"

She wished she hadn't brought the subject up, but there was no stopping now. The words tumbled out. "The way you treated Meg. You took her out, jumped all over her and then dropped her. How do you think she feels?"

Shit! That was the trouble with girls, they always confided in each other. "She told you about it, huh?"

"Meg's my best friend."

The truth, he decided, was the way to play it with this one. "And she's nice," he explained. "But not for me, so I . . . uh . . . didn't see her again. I thought I did her a favor."

Lauren faced up to him, fighting Meg's battle. "*That's* a favor?" she asked incredulously. "You don't lead someone on, then dump them."

Time to change the subject. "Why are you getting engaged to this jerk anyway?"

Two bright red spots stung her cheeks. "You're the jerk. You don't even know him."

"*C'mon*, you know he's a jerk." He paused for a moment. "I suppose you're gonna tell me you're the happiest girl in the world."

"Just exactly who do you think you are?" she asked angrily.

"Me? I'm just passing through, honey."

"And *don't* call me honey."

"Why?" he teased. "Does it turn you on?"

Their eyes met for a moment. He held the stare. Once more she broke it by walking away.

For some unknown reason her heart was still pounding as she hurried outside. Nick Angelo was dangerous and she knew it.

Cyndra Angelo had been traveling on the bus for hours. She was tired and dirty. Her clothes were rumpled and uncomfortable. Her feet hurt and she was hungry. She peered out the window. It was raining. It was always raining.

She'd had to change seats three times. Every time the bus stopped and new passengers got on there was always some guy who chose to sit next to her. After a few minutes he moved too close, started to talk, and she was forced to shift seats again.

It wasn't as if she did anything to encourage them, they came on to her whether she wanted them to or not. Pigs!

Kansas City had been a nightmare. Staying with distant relatives of her mother's, she'd found the men in the family only too eager to put their hands all over her. It seemed that every male she met wanted to lure her into bed. What was it about her? What did she do to encourage them? Nothing that she knew about.

She opened up her old tote bag, took out a compact with a broken mirror and studied her face. She wasn't white. She wasn't black. She was nothing.

It never occurred to her that she had the best of both worlds. That her skin was the most glorious olive—smooth and blemish-free. Her jet black hair was long and thick. Her eyes a deep rich brown. Her jawline strong and her cheekbones etched. She looked different from everybody else. The truth was that she was a very beautiful young girl indeed.

The bus stopped and two men got on. It didn't take long before one of them came sidling up the aisle and sat beside her. "Hiya, sweetie," he drawled. "Where you headin'?"

"None of your business," she replied, turning to face the window.

"No need to be unfriendly," he complained.

She ignored him until he finally got the hint and moved away.

Maybe she was crazy for going home when she could've stayed in Kansas City and gotten herself a job.

Oh, yeah, sure . . . some sensational job. Hooker, call girl, stripper, go-go dancer . . . there were a million and one opportunities for a girl like her. But Cyndra had bigger ideas. Somehow she was going to make something of her life, and nobody was going to stop her.

She'd gone to Kansas City for an abortion. Paid for, she suspected, by the man who'd raped her. Of course, nobody would admit he'd raped her. Her mother had said it was her own fault, that she'd encouraged him.

She'd never done any such thing. She hated him, always had.

Mr. Benjamin Browning. Big businessman. Happily married family man. Phony son of a bitch.

The Brownings. Her mother's employers. The fine, upstanding Brownings.

Oh, yeah, she could tell the town a thing or two about the fine, upstanding Browning family. She'd had the unfortunate distinction of knowing them all her life.

When she was a little girl her mother used to take her to the house all the time and leave her in a back room while she worked. Sometimes Benjamin Browning would come to that back room and touch her. She was too young to understand what he was doing, but as she got older she began to dread going there.

When she was five she'd tried to tell her mother. Aretha Mae had slapped her sharply and said, "Don't you dare talk 'bout Mr. Browning like that. I work for these people. Don't you *never* make up no bad things again."

So Cyndra had learned to shut up. At least her mother stopped taking her there—she put her into kindergarten instead, dropping her off on the way to work.

School was another bad experience. She was jeered at because of her dark skin, and ostracized because her mother worked as a maid. Several times she was beaten up by the older kids. Eventually she'd learned to look after herself. But not quite well enough, it seemed.

Damn Benjamin Browning! Mr. Fine Upstanding Pillar of the Community! Damn him and his money and everything about him!

She'd been away for a month. The abortion had turned out to be a frightening experience. It had taken place in the rundown house of a hatchet-faced woman and a gray-haired man with bony white hands, who'd called her "girlie" and treated her as though she was a prostitute. For hours she'd bled uncontrollably—until they'd had to rush her to the nearest hospital, dumping her on the front steps and abandoning her like a delivery of prime beef.

"What happened to you?" the doctor at the hospital had demanded. "We need names. You have to tell us who did this to you."

But she couldn't do that, so she kept quiet, just as she'd kept quiet her whole life.

Now she was on a bus coming home, and she didn't know if she was happy or sad.

"How old are you?" the doctor in Kansas City had asked.

"Twenty-one," she'd lied.

"I don't think so," he'd replied.

And he was right. She was sixteen. Sweet sixteen!

With a deep sigh she began daydreaming. One of these days she was going to get out of Bosewell. One of these days the name Cyndra Angelo was going to mean something.

By the time the bus dropped her off, the rain had almost stopped. The driver waved goodbye and she grabbed her bag and began the long trek to the trailer park. In a way she was pleased to be coming home. At least she had Harlan and Luke to look forward to, they were good kids and she genuinely loved them. She did not love Aretha Mae, although she grudgingly respected her for managing to survive on her own with three children to raise.

When Cyndra was six she'd asked who her father was. "Never you mind," Aretha Mae had replied. "That be my business, not yours."

She knew he was white and that's all she knew. Harlan and Luke were the offspring of a black man called Jed who'd lived in the trailer for two years, then moved out one day when Aretha Mae was at work. Jed had never been seen or heard from again—which was just as well, for his interest in little Cyndra had been more than stepfatherly.

As she walked along the deserted path she started thinking about Benjamin Browning and what she would like to do to him. Kill him, for starters. Maim him if that didn't work. String him up by his grungy old balls.

The truth was that she knew in her heart there was nothing she *could* do. It was her dirty secret and she was stuck with it.

She thought about how it had happened, and if there was anything she could have done to stop it.

No. Impossible. The man was an animal. Besides, he was over six feet tall and weighed at least two hundred pounds. Whereas she was only five feet five inches and one hundred and fifteen pounds. No contest.

It had happened on a Tuesday. Aretha Mae was sick with flu, so at her request Cyndra had taken time off from school to help out. The Brownings had another maid, but she was out sick too—so Cyndra found herself alone in the house. Mrs. Browning was shopping, Stock was at school and Mr. Browning was at his office.

He came home early coughing and spluttering. "I feel lousy. There's this damn flu going around," he complained, loosening his tie. "Be a good girl and fix me a hot tea with lemon. I'll be upstairs."

She didn't like him, but she had no reason to be frightened of him. She was a big girl now, and he hadn't touched her since she was five.

She made the tea in the spacious kitchen, putting the china cup on a tray with a matching saucer next to it containing several slices of lemon. Then she carried the tray upstairs to the master bedroom.

He was in his bathroom. "Leave it on the bedside table and turn the bed down," he called out.

She did as he asked, touching the fine-quality linen sheets, wondering what it must feel like to sleep in such luxury.

Mr. Browning emerged from the bathroom clad in a terry-cloth robe. It was a warm day and the window was open. Outside, the gardener worked on the lawn.

"Close the window," Mr. Browning said, clearing his throat.

She went over to the window and pulled it closed. Before she could turn around he grabbed her from behind and wrestled her onto the bed, pushing up her skirt and ripping off her cotton panties.

She was so startled she hardly had time to put up a struggle. "Stop!" she managed, trying to get away.

"Cunt, gimme that black cunt," he murmured excitedly, thrusting himself roughly inside her.

She was too shocked to scream, it all seemed to happen so fast.

Mr. Browning was enjoying himself. "C'mon, black bitch. Give it to me. Give it to me *good*," he grunted.

Frantically she struggled, still trying to push him off.

"That's what I like!" he crowed. "Keep on moving—I like it! I like it when you fight me."

He ripped into her, tearing at her insides, hurting her terribly. She thought she screamed but she wasn't sure. Whatever she did, he had no intention of stopping, he was beyond control—until with a long-drawn-out cry he was finally finished.

He collapsed on top of her for a few moments, almost suffocating her. Then he got off, and she heard him go into the bathroom.

Drawing her legs up to her stomach she began to sob.

After a few minutes he came out of the bathroom fully clothed as if nothing had happened. "I'm not going to shower," he said in a conversational tone. "I want your smell on me all day." He walked to the door and stopped. "Oh, and by the way, Mrs. Browning will be home soon, so you'd better stop that sniveling and get those sheets changed—they're covered in blood."

Six weeks later she realized she was pregnant. She had nowhere to turn except to her mother, so she'd told her everything.

Aretha Mae had listened silently, her face clouding over with anger.

When she was finished her mother said harshly, "You're never done makin' up stories 'bout these people, are you?"

"It's the truth—"

Aretha Mae slapped her across the face. "Shut up! You hear me, girl? I'll take care of it—but you must *never* talk 'bout this again. *Never.*"

Somehow Aretha Mae had come up with the money to send her to Kansas City for the abortion.

Now she was back, and she hoped Aretha Mae wasn't going to force her to continue school. It would be far better if she dropped out and got a job, they could certainly do with the extra money.

The rain had stopped, but the ground was still muddy. She wasn't frightened walking through the dark. There were no streetlights, but she knew every inch of the trailer park, it was the only home she'd ever known.

When she arrived outside their trailer she was surprised to see lights on and hear the television blaring. It wasn't like her mother to stay up so late.

She opened the door and walked in.

A man was sprawled on the bed watching television. He had a can of beer in one hand and a stupid smile on his face. He was laughing at something Johnny Carson had just said.

Cyndra stopped abruptly. "Who're you?" she asked, alarmed.

Groggily he sat up. "Who am *I*? Who in hell are *you*?"

"Where's my mother?" she demanded. "Where's Aretha Mae?"

Primo's eyes focused on this beautiful slip of a girl. "*Shee-it!*" he exclaimed. "You must be my daughter. Come on over here an' say a big hello to your daddy."

12

*S*ince their engagement party Stock had been suitably deflated. He'd caught hell from his parents for inviting too many people, and allowing the party to get totally out of control. When Lauren left he'd been drunkenly reeling around the place with his so-called friends—who'd proceeded to wreck the place, smashing glasses and bottles, pulling down half the tent, generally causing chaos. Mr. Browning was not amused.

"It wasn't my fault," Stock whined to Lauren. "You were there, why didn't you stop me from letting them all in?"

"Because I'm not your keeper," she said crossly. "It's your own fault." And it *was* his fault. Who did he think she was—his mother?

They bickered on and off. Lauren was miserable and yet she didn't know what to do. Should she give him back his ring? She knew that's what she *should* do, but she didn't want to do it while he was having trouble with his parents. His father had cut his allowance. His mother was barely speaking to him. How could she turn against him too?

Stock did nothing but complain. She decided that as soon as his complaints stopped she would make her move. Meanwhile, she threw herself into a student production of *Cat on a Hot Tin Roof*. She'd landed the plum role of Maggie the Cat, which was exciting, and her

husband, Brick, was played by one of the older boys, Dennis Rivers. Apart from being very good-looking, Dennis was a terrific actor. The rumor was that he liked boys instead of girls. Lauren couldn't care less who or what he liked, she felt privileged to be working with him.

Betty Harris was in charge of the drama group. They met after school at the old church hall once a week.

Betty was unlike the other teachers. A large, billowy woman in her fifties, she had flushed cheeks and straw-colored hair that never looked combed. She favored loose gypsy clothes and spoke in a breathy, excited voice encouraging her students to excel.

As far as Lauren was concerned, drama group was the high point of her week.

"I hear you got engaged, Lauren dear," Betty Harris greeted her. She nodded.

"Too young," Betty said, shaking her head knowledgeably. "Much too young."

Lauren nodded again. At least *someone* understood.

When all of her students were assembled, Betty made an announcement. "I have a big surprise for everyone," she said, fluttering her hands. "You've often heard me mention my brother, Harrington Harris, the famous New York stage actor. Well, next week he's coming to visit us here in Bosewell."

An appreciative hum went around the room.

"So you will see that I am not actually making him up," Betty continued, her rosy cheeks glowing. "He will be with us very soon." She paused, her protruding eyes darting around until they settled on someone in back. "And on another note, before we start rehearsals today, I'd like to welcome a new student into our group. Will all of you please say hello to Nick Angelo."

Lauren turned around, startled. Lounging at the back of the room in his familiar outfit of jeans and dirty denim jacket was Nick.

Meg nudged her. "I just died!" she whispered. "If I can only keep him away from Dawn, maybe I've got another chance."

"Do you still want one? I thought you hated him."

"I know," Meg agreed. "But who else *is* there? I mean, you've got to admit, he *is* gorgeous."

Yes, reluctantly Lauren had to admit it—in his own intense way, he certainly was.

Cyndra was shocked and angry to discover that while she'd been away her mother had allowed her longtime missing husband and his scummy son to move in. A husband Cyndra hadn't even known existed. And what's more, the man claimed he was her father. Her father, for God's sake! A white-trash piece of shit who made her sick just looking at him.

"I'm getting out of here," she threatened.

"Where you goin', girl?" Aretha Mae asked, her lip curling.

Cyndra was close to tears. "I'll get a job, find something. But I'm *not* stayin' here."

They argued back and forth until finally Cyndra realized it was useless. She had no money and nowhere to go. Once again she was trapped.

"You be sharin' the other trailer with your brothers," Aretha Mae said, glad to see her daughter, but sorry about the trouble she was bound to cause.

Cyndra moved into the battered old trailer next door. She put up a sheet dividing the already crowded trailer in two, and refused to speak to Nick. "Stay on your side," she warned him, "an' we won't have no trouble. Got it?"

He'd just looked at her, still trying to reconcile himself to the fact that he actually had a half sister, and a black one at that.

"What've I done to you?" he asked one day. "It ain't my fault we're stuck here."

"You and your goddamn daddy," she replied, her brown eyes flashing. "He's nothing to me."

"Oh, yeah—nothin' 'cept your dad."

"My dad your dumb ass," she fired back. "I hate both of you."

She was pretty but a real pain. He made no further attempt to speak to her.

Meanwhile he was doing okay at the gas station. Apart from Saturday nights he now came in on Saturday mornings too. He stashed away most of the money he made, after handing a few bucks to

Aretha Mae each week. When Primo found out he had a part-time job he soon made demands.

"Nothin' left," Nick said.

"What in hell am *I* supposed t'do?" Primo complained.

"Whyn't you try getting a job?" Nick replied, standing up to his father for once.

Whack! Primo lashed out, his heavy hand swinging through the air. Nick was old enough and wise enough to know when it was coming and duck out of range.

Cyndra refused to walk with him in the mornings or even sit next to him on the bus. At school he noticed she was even more of a loner than he was, although on Saturday nights she hung out with the biker crowd from Ripley.

Primo seemed to think they were living the great American dream. Now that Cyndra had returned he tried to play the concerned father. "Don't want that girl runnin' around all times of night," he informed Aretha Mae.

"You've left it too late to be givin' her orders," she said. "She ain't gonna take nothin' from you."

"She's my daughter," Primo roared. "An' *I* make the rules around here."

Aretha Mae shook her head wearily. She had Primo back after seventeen years, but the question was—did she really want him?

The scene from *Cat on a Hot Tin Roof* went extremely well. Lauren was glowing, she loved playing Maggie the Cat, especially with Dennis as Brick.

After class Betty Harris praised her. "Excellent, Lauren dear. You really have talent."

She was delighted. "I do? You know, one day I'd like to go to New York. Would I have a chance?"

"Acting is a tough business," Betty replied. She was wearing a voluminous caftan with multiple hanging gold necklaces, and every time she spoke the chains rattled against each other. "Too many actors chasing too few parts."

"But I'd love to give it a try," Lauren said earnestly.

"A try would be good, dear, but don't depend on acting to make a living, it's far too treacherous a profession."

Stock met her after class, took her arm possessively, noticed Nick and said, "What's that creep doing here?"

Lauren jumped to his defense. "He's not a creep."

"Says who? Take a look at him—always in that stupid get-up. Who does he think he is—James Dean?"

"Not everyone has to look like you," Lauren said coolly.

"Not everyone *can* look like me," he boasted.

They went to the drugstore for a soda. *The Way We Were* was playing at the local theater. Lauren wanted to see it, but Stock wasn't interested.

"I hate that sentimental crap," he jeered. "Give me Clint Eastwood any day."

She sighed. "You *promised* we could see it tonight."

"I got other ideas."

"Like what?"

"Going for a drive, talking about our future. It's about time."

"I guess so," she said hesitantly, taking a long deep breath. A drive was good, it would give her an opportunity to tell him she didn't think they had a future.

Stock drove like a rich kid showing off. His father had weakened and promised him a new car for Christmas, so he really let the Thunderbird rip, zooming down Main Street as though he was competing in a drag race.

"Not so fast," she said, clutching the dashboard.

"Calm down."

She hated being told to "calm down"—like she was hysterical or something. "Where are we going?" she asked.

"Over to the old athletic field," he replied, taking one arm from the steering wheel and placing it around her shoulders.

The deserted field just outside town was a notorious necking spot. "No," she said quickly.

"Why not?"

"You know why."

"We're engaged. We can go anywhere."

"That's what I want to talk to you about."

"I thought *I* was the one who wanted to talk."

"We should both talk," she said seriously.

Against her better judgment she allowed him to drive to the old field, where he parked the car, dimmed the headlights and immediately swooped.

"What are you doing?" she said, pushing him off.

"What I should've done a couple of months ago," he replied, his big hands roaming all over her.

She slapped his hands away. "C'mon, Stock, don't start this."

"What are you, Lauren? Some kind of ice queen?" He said, managing to clamp his lips down on hers.

She struggled free. "Will you stop it!"

He drew away from her, clenching his fists. "Christ! When do I get to first base with you?"

"Never," she replied heatedly. "This engagement is a big mistake. We weren't meant to be together."

He sat up straight. "What the hell do you mean by *that?*"

"I never should have said yes. I don't know why I did. My parents encouraged me. They like you, they like your family. They think we make a great match." She knew she was speaking too fast, but now she was on a roll and couldn't stop. "I'm not ready to get involved."

"You were involved with Sammy Pilsner," he said slyly.

"What do you know about me and Sammy?" she snapped, her cheeks reddening.

"Nothing much. Just that he used to tell all the guys he was getting a blow job from you."

She couldn't believe Sammy would have betrayed her. "I don't believe you," she said fiercely.

"It's true, isn't it? And if you did it to him, I want the same." And with that he launched himself upon her again.

She wasn't Meg, about to let some oaf have his way with her. "If you don't stop I'm getting out of the car," she threatened, once more slapping his hands away.

"Go ahead," he replied confidently. "It's a long walk home."

"You think that's going to stop me?"

"Aw, shit, you're behaving just like a dumb girl," he whined. "Anybody else would love being here with me."

He was nothing but a braggart and a bully. She glared at him furiously. "I'm *not* anybody else, it's about time you realized that."

Sensing her anger he rapidly changed tactics. "C'mon, Lauren," he wheedled. "I only wanna love you up a little." And it was hands all over her again.

Every time he launched an attack she felt incredibly vulnerable. He was so big and strong, it would be easy for him to overpower her. She knew she had to make a move, and make it fast. She groped for the door handle, sprung it open and bolted. "I'm out of here," she yelled. "You're nothing but a sex maniac!"

"And you're nothin' but a prick tease!" he yelled back.

"Get lost, Stock Browning!" Burning with fury she set off down the road.

Stock suddenly realized she was serious. He started the engine, turned the car around and drove after her. Winding down the window he leaned out. "Get back in. Stop being stupid."

"I don't need this," she replied, marching along the bumpy country road.

He was contrite. "I won't touch you again. I swear I won't."

She stopped walking and whirled around to face him. "What do you swear on?" she demanded, not relishing the thought of a five-mile walk home.

"My father's life."

"Big deal."

"Okay, okay, I'll swear on my *own* life. Does that make you happy? Now get back in the car." He threw open the passenger door and she climbed in. "I'll behave myself," he said, backing down all the way. "I'll wait until we're married. That's a promise."

You'll have a long wait, she thought. *A real long wait.*

13

The school play was due to take place a few days before Christmas break. Lauren was so immersed in her role that she decided to put the incident with Stock behind her and deal with him after Christmas. Her New Year's resolution was to get rid of him once and for all.

Her parents were driving her crazy—all they wanted to talk about was wedding dates.

"I was married to your father when I was barely eighteen," her mother said.

"I'm only sixteen," she pointed out. "And I'm *not* getting married."

"Why not?" Jane and Phil chorused.

What was it with them? Were they trying to get rid of her? Or couldn't they wait to share in all the perks that being related to the Brownings would bring them?

Rehearsals became the most important thing in her life. The only interruption was the arrival of Betty's brother. Harrington Harris looked like a famous actor. Tall, in his early forties, he had a receding hairline, long sideburns to compensate, lecherous eyes and a disarming manner. Every girl in the class immediately fell in love, including Meg. "Harrington's the most exciting man I've ever met," she confided to Lauren.

"Too old for me."

Meg winked. "Certainly not too old for me. *And* he's asked me out."

Here we go again, thought Lauren. "Maybe he's married," she said.

Meg was silent.

"Well, *is* he?"

"How do I know?"

"*Are* you going out with him?"

"Of *course* I am. It's an adventure."

"And I suppose I'm your excuse?"

"Of *course* you're my excuse."

At least Meg finally seemed to have gotten over Nick, which meant that maybe she could talk to him now. It wasn't easy pretending she didn't notice him—even though they kept on exchanging long looks, and she was painfully aware of everything he did.

Meg set off for her date with Harrington Harris full of her usual enthusiasm. The following day her enthusiasm had turned to outrage. "He jumped me," she complained.

Lauren shook her head in wonderment. "What did you expect? A cup of coffee and an intellectual chat? Naturally he jumped you. Sex. That's all men want. Didn't your mother teach you that?"

Meg giggled. "As a matter of fact she did."

"So what did you do this time?"

"I told him I was a virgin. That frightened him off."

"At least you're learning."

A few days later Meg came down with the mumps. Twenty-four hours later so did Harrington Harris. Unfortunately, several other members of the cast caught the dread disease, including Dennis, much to Lauren's disappointment.

"What will we do about the play?" she asked Betty Harris.

Betty was as upset as she was. She surveyed her class of high school students, searching their eager young faces for someone to replace Dennis, her eyes finally falling on Nick. He was such a handsome boy in an intense kind of way, and he certainly looked as if he might be able to handle it. Not that she had any idea if he could act or not, but she waved the script at him, and told him to get on stage and read with Lauren.

Sitting at the back of the class, he jumped to attention. "I . . . I can't do this," he mumbled.

"Come along, dear," Betty said crisply. "You joined this group, I'm sure you're perfectly capable of giving it a try."

Reluctantly he got up and made his way to the stage, where Lauren sat at a makeshift dressing table brushing her hair.

"This is the scene at the beginning of the play where Maggie and Brick have a confrontation," Betty explained. "You've watched the scene, Nick. You can do it."

He clutched the script tightly. Christ! He'd joined the group to get closer to Lauren, but he hadn't expected to get this close. What if he made a fool of himself?

He opened the script and stared blankly at the words. It wasn't like he hadn't watched Dennis say them enough times, and if Dennis could do it, so could he. Angry at himself for getting trapped, he began to read.

Lauren turned around and responded to his lines, her eyes flashing.

Soon he relaxed and started to get into it. Hey, it wasn't as bad as he'd imagined. Suddenly he wasn't Nick anymore, he was just an actor playing a role, and jeez, it was a kick!

When the scene was finished he dropped the script to the floor and reality came flooding back.

Lauren was staring at him. She had the most beautiful eyes he'd ever seen. He turned to Betty Harris, anxious for her reaction.

"That was very good, dear," Betty said, beaming happily. "I'm impressed. Now all you have to do is learn the words."

Learn the words. Was she kidding? "Ah . . . yeah, yeah, sure," he assured her, sounding a lot more confident than he felt.

"Then there's no panic," Betty said, relieved. "Class, you can relax —we have our Brick."

Outside the church hall it was cold and dark. Tiny snowflakes were beginning to fall. Nick leaned against the old bike Dave's brother had lent him. It certainly beat taking the bus. He waited patiently for Lauren. According to Aretha Mae, Stock and his parents were in Kansas City attending a family funeral, so there'd be no boyfriend lurking about.

She came out a few minutes later.

He stepped forward. "Hey . . . uh . . . I just wanted to say thanks," he said, kicking a pebble on the ground.

She stopped. "For what?"

"Y'know, for not letting me look like a jerk."

She held out her hand to catch a snowflake. "You handled it really well. You must have acted before."

He laughed. "Who, me? No way."

"Then you're a natural."

Now he was embarrassed. "Well, like I've seen a lotta movies, stuff like that."

"It's not easy the first time you have to get up in front of people. But honestly—you knew what you were doing."

He stamped his feet on the ground, warming up. "Thanks. That's a nice present."

"Present?"

"Yeah. It's my birthday today."

"Really?"

"Yep."

"How come you didn't tell anyone?"

"Hey . . . Seventeen . . . it's no big deal."

"My parents always make sure *my* birthday's a big deal. I have a huge cake and friends over to the house and lots of presents. What did you get?"

"My family don't give presents."

She wondered about his family, there'd certainly been enough gossip about them in school. "Aren't you going to celebrate at all?" she asked, half expecting Dawn to put in an appearance and drag him off.

He pulled up the collar of his denim jacket and stamped his feet again. "Nah, guess not."

"You have to do *something*," she said, prolonging the moment. "At least let me buy you a cup of coffee and a piece of cake."

He wasn't about to turn *this* invitation down. "Great," he said quickly. "Let's go."

"I've got a car," she said. "Leave your bike here and we'll pick it up later."

"Do I get to drive?"

"It's the family station wagon," she said apologetically. "Only I am allowed to drive it."

He grinned. "What're they gonna do, shoot you?"

"I guess they'll let me live," she said, smiling back.

Oh, God! Why was she doing this? She tried to tell herself she felt sorry for him, that nobody should be alone on their birthday. But it was more than that and she knew it. Nick Angelo was exciting, and she wanted some of that excitement.

They walked over to the car.

"Like one of these days I'm getting me a bright red Cadillac," he said. "Yeah, a Cadillac—that's the car for me."

"Why a Cadillac?"

"I dunno. It's just kinda . . . a cool car. An' it's made pretty good. It's American."

She smiled again. "You're very patriotic."

"You gotta be something, right?"

Their eyes met. "Right," she said.

The snow kept everyone home, and by the time they reached the drugstore it was almost empty. Nick guided her into a booth and slid across the other side. "What'll you have?"

"*I'm* buying," she reminded him.

"I'm driving, so *I'm* buying," he countered.

She laughed. "No way. It's your birthday."

Louise came over, tapped her order pad and threw Nick a disapproving look. "What'll it be?" she asked, pen poised.

"I'm starving," Lauren said. "How about two cheeseburgers?"

"Yeah, an' let's go for a couple of chocolate malts along with that," Nick added, winking at Louise.

"And fries," Lauren said.

"With ketchup—" he interrupted.

"And fried onions."

"Yeah! Right!"

They both burst out laughing as Louise walked briskly to the kitchen.

"I like a girl who eats," he said, grinning.

"From what I hear you like all girls," she replied, immediately thinking, *Oh, no! Why did I say that? It makes me sound like a jealous idiot!*

JACKIE COLLINS

"That's 'cause *I'm* not engaged," he said, staring pointedly at her ring.

She hurriedly slid her hands under the table. "Stock's very nice," she said defensively.

"Very nice, my ass."

"I don't know . . . maybe it's not going to work out the way everybody thinks." Why was she revealing herself to him?

He leaned across the table. "Are you telling me you're *not* engaged?"

She hesitated for a moment, then plunged right in. "I'm just saying certain people have expectations. My parents think we make a great couple. But what I really want is to go to New York and give acting a try. When I'm older, of course."

"Sounds cool to me. You told him?"

"No, and I don't have to tell him. My future doesn't necessarily lie with Stock Browning."

He nailed her with an intense stare. "So take his ring off."

"I didn't *say* I was getting disengaged. I just said my future might not lie with him."

Louise marched over, slammed their order on the table and threw Nick another sharp look as if to say *What the hell you doing with her?*

Lauren took a bite of her cheeseburger. "Where's Dawn tonight?" Damn! She'd said it again. Why couldn't she keep quiet about Dawn?

He shrugged. "Who knows? I only see her when I feel like it."

She wanted to know more about him, but she didn't dare ask.

He wanted to know more about her, but he figured he shouldn't push it.

They ate in silence.

"I guess this turned out to be a pretty good birthday after all," he said at last.

She wondered why she felt so light-headed. "It did?"

"Yeah. Like, y'know, bein' with you, getting the part in the play, it kinda makes today special."

"That's if Dennis doesn't recover and come back," she reminded him.

"Right," he said casually, pretending it didn't matter, although by this time he was hooked and it did matter a great deal. "Y'know, this

102

is my first birthday since my mother died. She never made me a cake or any of that birthday stuff—she was always too busy working. But sometimes she would like, y'know, slide me ten bucks."

"When did she die?" Lauren asked softly.

"A few months ago. That's why we came here. Turns out my father married Aretha Mae seventeen years ago, then skipped town. He never got a divorce—so he an' my mother weren't legally married. She didn't know—nobody did. When she died, my aunt threw us out. So we came here. We live over in the trailer park."

"What's it like?"

"Believe me, you never wanna know. I got this half sister who refuses to speak to me, an' a couple of half brothers, Harlan and Luke —they're okay. I share a trailer with them. My old man sits on his ass all day while Aretha Mae goes out to work. I'm stuck here until I get enough money to split."

"Where will you go?" she asked, her eyes widening.

"I dunno. New York, maybe." He paused and grinned. "Wanna come?"

"My parents would *love* that."

He was suddenly serious. "They wouldn't have to know. We'd just take off . . . Ever thought of doing something like that?"

Why was she feeling so dizzy? "You're crazy, Nick. I don't even know you."

He looked at her very gravely. "One of these days you will. That's a promise."

"Uh . . . the Christmas play is coming up," Nick mumbled, not quite sure whether to mention it or not.

Primo was lounging on the unmade bed, scratching his beer belly. "What?" he said, dragging his eyes away from "All in the Family" for a brief moment.

"I said the school play's coming up," Nick repeated. "And . . . uh . . . one of the actors got the mumps, so I'm playing the lead." He hesitated for a moment. "I dunno . . . thought you might wanna come."

"*I* wanna come," piped up Harlan. "Me and Luke."

"No, you don't," said Aretha Mae, busy at the stove.

"Sure they do," Nick said. "I'll get 'em seats."

"Wanna go. Wanna take Luke," Harlan chanted.

"No," Aretha Mae said sharply.

"Why not?" Nick asked.

"Because we don't belong with those people. We ain't gonna sit in no fancy theater watchin' you make a damn fool of yourself."

"I don't make a fool of myself," he objected. "I'm good."

"Good?" Aretha Mae arched her eyebrows and curled her lip. "You be good for nothin', boy."

What was *she* bitching about? He gave her money every week, which was more than anybody else in the family did. How come she didn't pick on Primo? The lazy slob hadn't even attempted to get a job.

"I'm going into town," he said, as though anybody cared.

He left the trailer, got on his bike and started the long ride. God, it was freezing. He didn't know why he was going into town anyway, considering it was Sunday and there was never anything to do. Everyone went to church in the morning and then retired into their houses all day. The drugstore was closed. The gas station was closed. The movie house was closed. What was he planning? A fast ride up and down Main Street? Very exciting.

He decided that maybe he'd pay Dawn a visit, seeing as they hadn't been together lately and he was feeling decidedly horny. Since he'd been rehearsing for the play he hadn't seen much of anybody except Lauren. And there was no way he could make a move on her.

Ah, Lauren . . . He couldn't figure her out. One moment she was his best friend, the next cool and businesslike—as if the play was the only important thing. They met at rehearsal and went through their scenes. The moment they finished she hurried off to meet Stock, who was always outside waiting to take her home.

He'd imagined things would be different after their one night together sharing cheeseburgers and a few home truths. But no. Everything was back to the way it was before.

He was mad that he'd opened up and told her about Aretha Mae and his father. It wasn't her business. She was just some rich girl, stuck-up like all the rest.

When he reached Dawn's house, her mother told him she was away for the weekend. Great, now he didn't even have Dawn to take his mind off things.

"When's she comin' back?" he asked.

"Tomorrow," Mrs. Novak replied, clutching a scarlet cardigan across her scraggy breasts. She was one of those rail-thin women with bulging eyes and a nervous tongue that kept darting in and out, licking her thin dry lips. She smelled of whiskey and stale cigarette smoke.

"Why don't you come in anyway and have a lemonade," she suggested.

Jeez, Nick thought, if she and Primo ever met they'd make a perfect couple. Fat and thin and both zonked out of their minds.

He declined Mrs. Novak's invitation and got out of there fast.

"How are you feeling, Dennis?" Lauren asked over the phone.

Dennis told her he was depressed about not being able to appear in the play with her.

"Don't worry," she said comfortingly. "We'll manage without you, but it won't be the same."

Liar, she thought as soon as she hung up. *It'll be even better because Nick Angelo is playing your part.*

She felt disloyal and confused, and yet she was savvy enough to know that Nick meant trouble. She also knew she couldn't stop watching him at every opportunity, and she loved acting with him. But there was such a thing as self-preservation, and she was aware that it was essential to stay away from him, which wasn't easy, because every time they did the opening scene between Maggie and Brick she sensed a great surge of electricity between them.

Now it was almost time to perform the play on the stage with half the town watching. She shivered. Would everyone be able to spot the chemistry between them?

Stock was back in her life with a vengeance. Big and bossy and full of himself because he'd taken delivery on his new car—a super-fast Corvette. She stuck by his side whenever she could. It was safer than allowing Nick to get close.

"You don't have to come to the play if you don't want to," she told Stock.

"I'll be there," he said. "You're my girl—wouldn't miss it. I'm sittin' with my parents in the front row."

Oh, great. That's all I need.

"I'm just saying you shouldn't feel obligated. I'm perfectly okay with the fact that you . . . you might be bored." She was almost stammering.

He didn't get it. "Is Dennis back yet?"

"Uh . . . no. That new guy's playing the role."

"That jerk, you mean," he said sourly.

It seemed that both Stock and Nick were programmed to insult each other whenever they could.

Sometimes she felt as if she was going to explode. There was nobody she could confide in. Not her parents, and certainly not Meg, who'd kill her if she knew she had these feelings for Nick.

Bury them, she told herself. *And Nick Angelo will go away. He's the kind of boy who comes to town, causes trouble and then takes off.*

There was plenty of activity in Bosewell at Christmas. First there was the play, followed by the school dance on New Year's Eve. Naturally, Stock had plans. "After the dance," he informed her, "some of the guys have booked rooms over at the motel. We'll have a party."

"What kind of party?"

"Oh, you know, music, good times an' a few strong blasts . . . Relax, Lauren. You're such a square sometimes."

She hated being told to relax—it was so patronizing. "Remember what happened last time," she said, to her horror sounding just like her mother. "Your allowance was cut off and you told me I should've warned you about inviting all those extra people."

"This'll be different," he promised. "Oh, and ask your girlfriend Meg if she wants to go with Mack Ryan."

Mack was Stock's best friend. Bigger than Stock. Blonder than Stock. But not as rich.

"Why doesn't he ask her himself?"

"Maybe he doesn't want to. Guys don't dig the idea of getting rejected."

Meg was delighted, she said yes immediately. At least we'll be a foursome, Lauren thought. Anything was better than being alone with Stock.

As the play drew nearer Betty insisted on more rehearsals. Lauren didn't mind, in fact she loved it.

Nick grabbed her arm one day on her way out. "Hey," he said. "Do I have to wait until my next birthday for you to talk to me like a human being?"

"I'm talking to you now," she said, trying to remain calm.

"Ha!" His laugh had a bitter ring. "You're back in the same old groove. You've got your rich boyfriend, your nice organized life, an' no time for me."

"We're working together," she said. "What gave you the impression it was more than that?"

He stared at her so intently she thought she might dissolve.

"You *know* it's more than that," he said.

"I . . . I have no idea what you're talking about."

"Yes, you do," he said. "Only you won't admit it."

She pulled free and rushed outside. To her relief Stock was waiting. Stock was always waiting.

The night of the play there was a blizzard. Betty Harris was in a bad mood because Harrington, whom she'd planned to show off, was still sequestered away with a bad case of the mumps.

Lauren was shaking. Why had she agreed to play the lead? Did she really want to stand up in front of the whole town in a skimpy silk slip and play Maggie the Cat, a sexy older woman? God, everybody would laugh her off the stage.

Nick was nervous too—he couldn't figure out how he'd got conned into this.

Before going on they wished each other luck. "Break a leg," Lauren said.

He looked at her incredulously. "Break a leg?"

"That's what they say in the theater for good luck."

"I always figured actors were a crazy bunch," he said, shaking his head.

She grinned. "I guess they are."

His throat was dry and he had a strong desire to run. "Well, anyway —we're gonna kill 'em. Right?"

"Right!"

Lauren made her entrance first. Nick waited in the wings, his heart thumping. But once he made it onto the stage he lost all fear and became the character. *Shit!* he thought. *I can do this—I can really do this.* And he was right, because the play was a smash. *Cat* was shocking and risqué for a small town like Bosewell; Betty had taken a risk putting it on. And the audience loved it.

As they were taking their bows, Lauren spotted a scowling Stock sitting in the front row with his parents. She couldn't care less, she was too busy enjoying the applause.

After five curtain calls the elated cast mingled backstage. She looked around for Nick and hurried over. "You were great," she said warmly.

"So were you." He broke into a grin. "Hey, we both were."

Betty Harris approached them, beads and gold chains jangling. "We're a hit!" she gushed. "You were *all* wonderful. If only my brother were here to enjoy our triumph."

"I'm sorry he's still sick," Lauren said.

"His balls probably look like an elephant's on a bad day," Nick whispered in her ear.

"What?" She couldn't believe what he'd just said.

"It's the mumps," he replied straight-faced. "Gets 'em every time!"

She choked back a giggle as a vivid picture of Harrington Harris with swollen elephant balls flashed before her eyes. Fortunately her parents appeared before she burst out laughing. She turned to introduce Nick, but he'd taken off.

A glowering Stock hovered behind them. "You never told me you were going to be up on stage half naked for everyone to get an eyeful," he complained.

Wasn't he supposed to be congratulating her?

"You never asked," she replied.

"We'll see you later, dear," her mother said, wandering off with Phil in tow.

"How does it make *me* look?" Stock demanded. "You up there with that creep playing opposite you. You made a fool of me tonight, Lauren."

"I did not," she said heatedly.

"Yes, you did."

She sighed. "Don't spoil it, Stock. This is a special night for me."

"It isn't for me."

"Then maybe you should go home."

"And what will *you* do?"

"I'll stay here and celebrate with the rest of the cast."

"Without me?"

"Yes, without you."

"You do that," he said, storming off.

Too bad. She wasn't exactly heartbroken.

Betty Harris had arranged dinner in one of the adjoining rooms for

the cast. They were high with excitement, milling around congratulating each other. When they sat down Lauren found herself next to
Nick.

"So . . . I guess that's it," he said, picking at a roll. "I won't get to
see you until school starts next year."

She sipped a glass of water. "Next year sounds like forever, and
we'll see each other at the New Year's dance. You are going, aren't
you?"

"Nah . . . don't think so."

"Why not?"

"I can't get into all that organized crap where everybody's supposed
to have a good time."

She bit her lip and tried not to say it, but out it came anyway.
"Surely Dawn will want you to take her?"

He gave her a quizzical look. "I thought I told you, me and Dawn,
we're not a couple."

"That's not what she says." *Oh God, Roberts. Shut up!*

"How come you're so concerned anyway? You've hardly talked to
me lately."

"I'm talking to you now."

He stared at her. "Maybe I'd like to do more than talk."

She looked away. She should have known he'd want to jump her,
just like he'd done to Meg. Why were boys so interested in sex? Didn't
feelings or getting to know someone ever come into it?

"Excuse me," she said, pushing her chair away from the table and
getting up.

"Where are you going?"

"I've got a present for Betty in my car."

Leave me alone, Nick Angelo. I am not interested.

Oh, yes, you are, Roberts. Oh, yes, you are.

She hurried outside to the station wagon and reached inside for the
brightly wrapped gift.

"Hey—" He was right behind her.

She turned around, feeling weak and vulnerable.

Without saying a word he moved very close and kissed her.

It was not like any kiss she'd ever felt before. His lips were insistent
and yet soft. His tongue was exploring, and yet not in a conquering
way. Without thinking she began kissing him back.

"I've wanted to do this ever since I first saw you," he murmured, pulling her closer.

She took a deep breath. "Blakely's hardware store. I was scrambling around on the floor—"

"Yeah, an' you looked pretty good that day."

She was about to say "So did you," but before she could he kissed her again, and the second time was so incredible that she succumbed, losing herself in it. She'd kissed boys before—Sammy Pilsner, Stock, several boys she'd dated—but it had never been like this. Never.

He pushed his hands through her long hair. "You're so beautiful."

Nobody had ever called her beautiful before. Pretty—yes. Nice—naturally. Beautiful was something else. But even so . . . she mustn't get carried away. "We can't do this," she protested softly.

"I'm not forcin' you," he replied, pressing close.

She took another deep breath, willing herself to make a move. "I have to go." Without waiting for a reply she turned around and rushed back inside.

For the rest of the evening she tried not to look in his direction or even think about him.

Betty Harris made a speech praising all her students, and when it was time to leave Nick was right behind her. "Can I drive you home?" he asked.

"No. I'm the one with the car, remember?" Lauren replied.

He grinned. "You're right."

"Good night, Nick," she said politely.

"Good night, beautiful."

All the way back to the trailer park he thought about her. Then his mind started racing in different directions. The play had been such a triumph. He'd really got off on the feel of an audience watching him, studying his every move. On stage he wasn't some nothing kid, he was Brick, he was someone they responded to in a positive way.

And then his thoughts returned to Lauren. When he kissed her it had been like nothing he'd ever known. Oh, sure, he'd had enough girls, but none of them had been like her—he'd never had that feeling of wanting to look after a girl, protect her, be with her all the time. This had nothing to do with scoring. This was different.

Was he in love?

Don't even think about it.

111

Maybe he could be an actor. The thought sneaked into his head unexpectedly.

Nah. He didn't stand a chance.

Or did he?

15

Once Nick decided what he wanted to do, he went all out. His first move was to visit Betty Harris and ask if she'd consider giving him private coaching.

"I can't pay you," he explained. "But one of these days I'll make it, an' then I'll pay you big."

Betty laughed. "If only I had a dime for every boy that thought he could be the next Marlon Brando or Montgomery Clift. You're no different, Nick. You're good, but you're no different."

"You don't understand," he said. "I'm not gonna be a nuclear scientist. I ain't got a chance of runnin' for President. I gotta go for *something*, an' I've decided this is it."

"Ah, yes, but I *do* understand," Betty said, pacing around her small living room. "When I was young I had the same ambition. In fact, I even went to New York."

He was surprised. "You did?"

"Yes. I made the rounds of auditions only to be told I was too tall, too short, too fat, too thin, too ugly, too pretty. Believe me, Nick, nobody knows what they want. They only know they want a carbon copy of somebody who's made it."

"So what did you do?"

"I got married," she said. "I married a man who liked to dress up in my clothes. He left me for another woman." She laughed dryly. "Thank God it wasn't for another man!"

"Go on," he encouraged.

"I suppose I got older and certainly wiser. Every so often I landed a bit part here and there, until eventually I came back to Bosewell." She sighed. "And here I am, teaching the high school acting class. Teaching you all to do something you're never going to have a chance at."

"Everybody's got a chance, Betty."

She smiled wryly. "Full of optimism. How old are you? Sixteen?"

"Seventeen."

"Well, Nick, I went to New York when I was twenty, came back when I was thirty. I'm now fifty. The last twenty years . . ." She trailed off, shaking her head, wondering where the time had gone.

"But your brother made it," he pointed out.

"It depends what you call making it," she said matter-of-factly. "In a town like Bosewell he's a star. But the truth is he's played three butlers on Broadway in the last six years, and that's the extent of his stardom. The last time he worked was advertising a cure for hemorrhoids on television."

"Harrington Harris?"

"Yes, the great Harrington Harris. But it makes everybody feel good when he comes back here. They *think* he's a star, and that's all that matters."

"Betty," he said earnestly, fixing her with his green eyes. "You gotta help me. I need to study, an' I have to do it with somebody who'll teach me things."

There was something about him that was so intensely sincere. Betty knew she shouldn't encourage the boy, but what did she have to lose? The winter was cold and lonely, and what else was she going to do with her time?

"Very well," she said. "You'll come over here three times a week at noon and we'll work from twelve until four. Be prepared to work hard and *never* call to tell me you have something else to do."

"I swear it," he said excitedly. "I'll be here."

She smiled. "Good. It's a start."

· · ·

Life at the trailer park was hard during the winter. The roofs of both trailers leaked, causing a rancid damp smell and numerous little puddles. It was almost like living outside.

Primo refused to do anything about it. "My arm hurts," he whined. "I ain't fixin' nothin'."

"You musta hurt it lifting a can of beer," Nick muttered disgustedly.

"You're gettin' a real smart mouth," Primo slurred. "I could throw you out any time."

"I thought you promised my mother I would finish high school?"

"Don't be so sure," Primo grumbled.

Out of school, Luke and Harlan were bored. They ran into town every day and Aretha Mae couldn't stop them. One day Harlan came home beaten up.

"What happened to you?" Nick demanded.

"Nothin'," Harlan said sulkily.

Nick turned to Luke. "What happened to him?"

Luke stared blankly.

"Jeez!" Nick exclaimed. "Open your mouth and talk, goddamnit!"

Luke ran out of the trailer crying.

Aretha Mae stood in front of the sink stoically washing dishes. Primo snored in his usual position.

"Don't you give a shit?" Nick demanded.

"He better learn to defend hisself. This won't be the last time," Aretha Mae said.

Cyndra had gotten herself a job down at the canning plant. She left early in the morning and arrived home late at night, barely acknowledging Nick's existence.

Finally he exploded. "You're a freakin' pain!" he shouted. "When you gonna lighten up?"

"When you leave," she replied brusquely.

"Don't hold your breath. I'm outta here on *my* time—not yours."

"Good," she said. "Make sure it's soon."

He kept himself busy. What with the work at the garage and visiting Betty Harris's three times a week and trying to do a few repairs around the trailers, he never had a moment to himself.

Working with Betty was a kick. She chose plays she knew would interest him. He particularly loved A *Streetcar Named Desire*. Reading Stanley to her Blanche was a real blast. The good thing was that he'd finally found something he could absorb himself in and it was pretty exciting.

The honeymoon was over for Aretha Mae and Primo. They'd taken to having long vicious yelling matches. Primo beat up on her pretty good. Smack! That's all the bastard seemed to know.

Nick wished he could apologize for his father. He wanted to say, *Look, it's not my fault. Throw us out. We'll go somewhere. Anywhere. We don't have to screw your life up, too.*

But now that she had him back, Aretha Mae had no intention of letting Primo go.

Christmas came and went. It was a dismal holiday. Aretha Mae brought home the remains of the Brownings' turkey and made a thick soup—that was the extent of their festivities. No tree. No presents. No nothing.

Nick didn't mind, he was more or less used to it. But he felt sorry for the kids, especially Harlan—it was useless trying to get through to Luke.

Occasionally he hung out with Joey, who wanted to know if he was going to the New Year's dance.

"Haven't thought about it," he said.

"There's nothin' else to do," Joey said. "We gotta make plans."

"How do we get in?" Nick asked. "Don't we have to buy tickets?"

"Nah, it's a high school thing. Why don't you take Dawn?"

He hadn't really thought about Dawn lately. He'd been so busy that the need to get laid hadn't arisen. "Yeah, I'll give her a call. Who'll you bring?"

Joey dragged on his cigarette and attempted to sound casual. "Maybe I'll ask your sister."

Nick looked surprised. "My sister?"

"Cyndra," Joey said. "I mean, it's not like I think she'd say yes or anything, but she always seems so . . . kinda, y'know, all by herself."

Nick made a face. "Hey, if you wanna get your balls crushed—go ahead."

He had no feelings for Cyndra. Maybe as a brother he was supposed to feel protective, but what the hell—she was a bitch, he didn't care who she went out with.

"What do we wear to this thing?" he asked.

"Tux," Joey replied. "We'll take a ride to Ripley an' hire a couple of monkey suits."

They set off for Ripley the next afternoon. Joey had a secondhand motorcycle and they made it in a couple of hours. The rental place was crowded with manic people struggling to get themselves an outfit for New Year's Eve. Joey pushed his way to the front, grabbed a salesman and picked out two tuxedos.

"I feel like a jerk," Nick said, trying his on.

"You look like one," Joey guffawed. "But that's okay, so does everyone on New Year's."

He paraded in front of the mirror. The pants were too long, the jacket too big. "Have I really gotta wear it?"

Joey slapped him on the back. "Only for a night. You'll live."

They paid their money and left.

"I know a bar where they got naked girls," Joey said with a wink. "Bare tits an' ass."

They'd both acquired fake ID's, so they swaggered into the bar full of confidence. Nobody stopped them. Nobody cared.

The place was jammed with construction workers busy watching the parade of half-naked waitresses—girls who wore nothing but black stockings, garter belts, frilly aprons and phony smiles.

Nick couldn't believe what he was seeing. He nudged Joey. "Ain't there some law against this?"

Joey sniggered. "Don't tell me you've never been in a topless bar before. They're the coming thing."

"Hey, hey, talkin' of comin'," Nick joked.

Joey laughed. "Let's have a little control here. You can look, not touch."

"Do they put out?"

"If you've got the bread."

Nick patted the top pocket of his denim jacket. "I got it," he said. "Yesterday was payday." He already had his eye on one girl—a pretty brunette with a sweet face who reminded him of Lauren. He hadn't seen her since the play, and sometimes he thought about her. But he tried not to—she wasn't exactly available. When the girl took their order he came on to her. "What're you doing later?" he asked.

She peeked at her watch. "I get off at three."

"I'm about ready to get off now," he joked. "How much?"

She tried to look insulted. "You think I'm a hooker?"

" 'Course not," he said. "How much?"

"Twenty."

"Twenty," he repeated. "What is it, mink-lined?"

"Ten for you because you're cute."

"You got a room?"

"If you wanna go to my place it'll be an extra five."

He weighed up the possibilities. He'd never had to pay for it before, but somehow it seemed fitting, a New Year's present to himself, a girl he didn't have to sweet-talk. "Okay," he agreed.

Her name was Candy and she lived in one room with two smelly cats roaming around, and a hamster in a cage.

"I don't usually bring people back here," Candy announced, shrugging off her coat. "But you seem like a nice guy. How old are you anyway?"

"Twenty-one," he lied. "How about you?"

"Twenty."

More like thirty, he thought. "You been doin' this long?"

"Doing what?" she said, scrambling in her purse for a joint.

"A little action on the side."

"Oh. I don't really do this," she said vaguely, lighting up. "I needed extra money this week . . . and like I said, you're kinda cute."

Sure, he thought.

She offered him a drag and began to undo the buttons on her blouse.

He drew deeply on the joint—it wasn't the first time he'd had marijuana—and watched her as she took her time removing her blouse. He'd already seen the goods on display in the bar, but it was more of a kick watching them revealed slowly just for him.

Underneath the blouse her small breasts were covered by a skimpy black bra. With a theatrical flourish she threw the blouse on the floor and unzipped her skirt, daintily stepping out of it. Quite obviously she hadn't bothered to wear panties. He felt that good old familiar stirring.

"What shall I leave on?" she asked.

He noticed she was chewing gum. "Your earrings," he replied.

She laughed, casually fingering her nipples. "Never heard *that* one before."

He stripped off his clothes. This girl was a challenge. She was a professional, and he wanted to see if he could make her feel as good as all his other conquests.

Candy plumped herself down on the bed and beckoned him over.

He made the trip across the room in record time and climbed aboard.

She took another drag of her joint and placed it in a chipped glass ashtray next to the bed.

"You're not really twenty-one," she said slyly. "Tell me the truth?"

No way was he admitting to seventeen. "Nah. Twenty-two," he said, pumping away.

Candy had obviously expended all her energy down at the bar. She lay there like a corpse, chewing gum and looking blank as he gave her a little of the Angelo magic.

As soon as he was finished he couldn't wait to get away. Forget about pleasing her—this was the first and last time he'd ever pay for it. He left the money on the table and beat a hasty retreat.

Later Joey met him at the bar and they got on the bike and headed for home.

"What happened, man?" Joey wanted to know. "Gimme all the filthy details."

"You want details, pay for it yourself."

"What's the matter? You fall in love?" Joey teased.

He groaned. "Don't even mention the word."

Love. Was *that* the feeling he had for Lauren? He missed her and yet he was nervous about seeing her when school started because he didn't know what would happen. He was so used to being in control with girls. He got beat up enough at home, at least there was one part of his life where he had the upper hand.

Now he had this dumb feeling and it wouldn't go away.

Lauren Roberts. She was the only special girl he'd ever met, and she belonged to somebody else.

The truth was it was about time he did something about it.

Lauren spent a miserable Christmas. Over the holidays her mother's brother Will and his wife Margo came to visit from Philadelphia. This time they did not bring Brad, their nineteen-year-old son. Lauren's crush on him had been a long time ago and she didn't miss his presence.

The day after Christmas they spent at the Brownings' house. Stock gave her a cashmere sweater and two cookbooks—obviously chosen by his mother. She gave him a simple pewter money clip and a photo frame. And all day long she wondered what Nick Angelo was doing.

At night she lay in bed and thought about her future. Only another two years and she'd be out of school. She was already campaigning for enrollment in an Eastern college. Her parents said Kansas City was as far as they'd let her go, but she had her mind set on New York.

Meg came by the house to find out about the New Year's dance. "What are you wearing?" As usual she was obsessed with clothes.

"I haven't thought about it," Lauren replied vaguely. "Maybe that dress I wore to my engagement party."

Meg frowned. "You *can't* wear the same thing again."

"Yes, I can," she said stubbornly.

"What's the *matter* with you? You're so . . . sort of . . . different lately."

Lauren wondered if she was different. All she ever thought about was Nick. On his birthday he'd seemed so sensitive and understanding, and the night of the play, when he'd kissed her, it was definitely something special. She couldn't believe he'd practically attacked Meg. The truth was that Meg had probably encouraged him and then backed off at the last moment, always a dangerous practice.

"*I'm* wearing black," Meg announced dramatically.

"That's exciting," Lauren murmured. Frankly she couldn't care less.

The night of the New Year's dance there was thick snow on the ground. Lauren stared out her window watching the snowflakes falling. She wondered if she could get out of going altogether.

No such luck. Stock called to announce he would be picking her up at seven. "Be ready," he said.

God, he was so overbearing. When had she ever kept him waiting? New Year's resolution: Get out of this engagement once and for all. Stop thinking about it and do it.

For a Christmas present the Brownings had insisted she visit their store and pick out an outfit. She'd done so reluctantly, and only at her mother's insistence. She'd chosen a short black off-the-shoulder dress. When her mother saw it she had a fit. "You can't possibly wear that, it's quite unsuitable."

"Why?"

"It's too sophisticated. Besides, young girls don't wear black."

"This young girl kind of likes the idea."

Jane sighed. "I don't know what's the matter with you lately, you're so argumentative."

Hmmm. Had she and Meg been talking?

Stock arrived with a corsage of white orchids and an appreciative "Wow! You look—" He was about to say "sexy," but since Mr. and Mrs. Roberts were hovering in the front hall he changed it to "sensational."

She smiled; for once he'd said the right thing.

Jane produced her camera. "Photo time!" she exclaimed gaily.

Dutifully she posed for a picture with Stock, then kissed her parents, said "See you later" and left the house. Usually there was a discussion about what time her curfew was, but since it was New Year's Eve and she was with Stock, it didn't seem to matter. All they were interested in was cementing the deal.

Mack Ryan was waiting in the car, and they set off to pick up Meg. When they arrived at her house she gave Lauren a filthy look. "You didn't tell me you bought a black dress. How *could* you? *I'm* wearing black," she muttered furiously. "And you *knew* I was."

Lauren shrugged; quite truthfully she'd forgotten. "It doesn't make any difference. We don't look alike."

"I wanted to stand out," Meg said, shaking her head petulantly. "Now we look like twins!"

"You do stand out," Lauren replied, thinking that her friend had put on a pound or two.

"No. *You* do," Meg said. "It's *always* you."

They got to the dance late, having stopped to drink some champagne in the car. Lauren wasn't used to drinking—she hated the taste, but she'd decided this New Year's was going to be different from any other. It was time she grew up.

When they arrived the dance was in full progress. Stock grabbed her by the arm, cutting a swath through his cronies as he led her onto the dance floor. "You're looking hot tonight," he said. "I didn't want to say it in front of your parents but, boy, have you got a body!"

Was this the first time he'd noticed? She decided to respond in kind. "Boy, have you got a body, too!"

He wasn't quite sure how to take this, so he pretended he hadn't heard, and began to gyrate his hips to the strains of "Honky Tonk Woman" played by the local band. Not quite Mick Jagger—as a matter of fact not even close.

Lauren felt a little dizzy as she started to dance, her eyes continually searching the room.

What are you looking for, Roberts?

I'm looking for Nick Angelo. Want to make something out of it?

To Nick's surprise, Cyndra said yes when Joey asked her to the dance. "I hear you're going with Joey," he said.

She glared at him.

"One of these days you're gonna realize you're taking it out on the wrong person," he said, trying to fix his stupid bow tie.

"When that day comes I'll let you know," she replied, brushing back her long dark hair.

"Gee, I'm holding my breath," he said, irritated by her pissy attitude.

They were interrupted by the sound of banging and screaming coming from the trailer next door. It was nothing new—ever since Christmas, Primo and Aretha Mae had been at each other's throat.

Cyndra glared at him with a spiteful expression as if it was his fault. "Maybe you won't be around here much longer."

"How many times I gotta tell you? This wasn't my choice."

"You belong to him, an' he ain't nothin' but dirt," she said vengefully.

"Yeah . . . well, let me tell you this—*you* belong to him too."

Her eyes were full of fury. "I don't believe it."

"Are you telling me your ma lied to you, is that it?"

Her dark eyes continued to blaze brightly. "I don't believe that dumb ox is my father."

"He is. Get used to it."

Joey arrived to pick her up on his motorcycle.

Cyndra stood at the door of the trailer peering out with an angry expression. "It's snowing," she said. "How we gonna get anywhere on that?"

Joey produced a rolled-up plastic raincoat, unrolled it with a flourish and threw it over her. "There you go. How's that for service?"

"Oh, this is classy," she grumbled. "A real classy date."

"What did you expect? A Kennedy?"

"Nothing," she said, her lip curling sourly. "Absolutely nothing."

Nick had been planning to ask Primo if he could borrow the van, but what with all that screaming coming from the trailer he decided to ride his bike over to Dawn's and see if they could borrow her mother's car.

He hated the rented tux, it was too big for him, and what the hell was he supposed to wear on his feet?

Fuck 'em. He'd wear his sneakers, and if anybody had anything to say about it he'd punch 'em in the mouth.

Harlan told him he looked nice. Luke stared at him like a zombie. It occurred to Nick that the kid should be getting some kind of professional help. Fat chance.

"What are you two doin' tonight?" he asked.

Silly question. What *could* they do? They had no way of getting into town unless they walked, and the snow was pretty deep on the ground. They couldn't even slip into the other trailer and watch television on account of the fact that Aretha Mae and Primo were busy killing each other.

"Tell you what," he said, trying to cheer them up. "Tomorrow I'll treat you both to the movies."

Harlan nodded, his face lighting up.

He set off for Dawn's on the bike. It was a long ride and by the time he got there he was soaked through.

Dawn greeted him wearing the tightest dress he'd ever seen. She did not believe in leaving anything to the imagination.

"Great date you are!" she said, shaking her head. "We've gotta get you dry before we can go anywhere."

"Can we borrow your mom's car?"

"It's all ours, handsome. She *was* gonna use it, but then she passed out. C'mon, get your clothes off, I'll try to dry 'em."

He followed her upstairs to her room and stripped. Two large posters of Elvis Presley sneered down at him.

She ran an appreciative eye up and down his body. "Hmm . . . sure you wanna go to the dance? My mom won't surface until tomorrow."

"Hey, I didn't ride all the way into Ripley to hire a freakin' tux to sit at home."

She winked suggestively. "Sitting wasn't what I had in mind."

"We can do that later, okay?"

"Whatever you want, big boy."

That was the thing about Dawn, she was much too obliging.

Lauren spotted him the moment he came in. In a way she hadn't expected him to turn up. In another way she'd hoped he would. And now here he was with Dawn hanging onto his arm like a leech.

She tried not to stare—she certainly didn't want him catching her. He looked great in his tuxedo, even if it was a little big. He'd obviously made an effort. Was it because of Dawn? *Bitch!*

Lauren immediately felt guilty. The trouble was that Dawn wasn't a bitch at all, she was a perfectly pleasant girl who just happened to be the school tramp. Lauren suspected Stock had slept with her. Not that he admitted it. Not that she cared.

Stock was having a fine time twirling her around the dance floor, full of himself as usual.

"Let's get a drink," she said breathlessly, breaking away.

He beamed. "That's more like it. How about going for the rest of the champagne out in my car?"

"I meant a soft drink."

"Excuse *me.*"

She hated it when he tried to be sarcastic.

Over by the bar Nick handed Dawn a glass of watered-down punch. "Try this poison."

Her eyes scanned the room and she shook her head. "I dunno what *we're* doing here. We shoulda gone to Ripley." She threw him a sly look. "Or stayed home."

He had to agree with her, they didn't belong.

Dawn swallowed a fake yawn, "We came, we saw, we got bored. Let's get the hell outta here, we can have more fun at my house. I'll show you mine if you show me yours!"

He wasn't prepared to leave until he'd seen Lauren. After all, she was the reason he'd hired a tuxedo and shown up.

"Hey, you told me you were such a hotshot dancer. How about showing 'em what a *real* dancer can do?"

Dawn was always up for a challenge. "Honey, I can beat any of 'em. Anytime. Any way."

"What are we waitin' for?" He pulled her onto the crowded floor. Not that he was into dancing, but he could make the moves if he had to.

Dawn enjoyed showing off. She had her assets and she knew how to shake them—especially in her favorite tight dress.

A small crowd gathered as they put on a show.

And then he spotted Lauren. She was sitting at a table with Stock and a group of his friends, and naturally she looked sensational.

He knew he had to make a move. He didn't know what he was going to do or when he was going to do it, but he wasn't leaving until he did.

17

"So?" Joey asked, leaning across the small table. "Do you like to dance?"

"No," Cyndra said, checking out the room with her dark moody eyes, wondering why Joey had invited her.

"How come?"

"How come what?" she snapped. "Just because I'm half black I'm supposed to have rhythm?"

"I didn't say that."

"No, but you sure thought it. Is *that* why you asked me tonight? Black chick ain't got no morals—she'll be easy."

"Huh?"

"You heard me."

"I heard someone with a big hang-up."

"What?"

"A hang-up—like in chip-on-the-shoulder shit."

She smoothed down the skirt of her green velvet dress—purchased at a secondhand shop—and tried to compose herself. She certainly hadn't dressed up and come out to get involved in a slanging match. "I don't have no chip," she said, controlling her temper.

"Maybe you should," he remarked. "It's a lousy deal—black mother, white dad—you can't figure out *what* color you are."

Unexpectedly tears stung her eyes. He was right on, she wasn't one thing or the other and it hurt.

"*My* dad was Jewish," Joey continued. "A Jewish cop in Chicago married to a nice Irish Catholic girl. I never tell anyone I'm half Jewish, it's not worth the aggravation."

"What aggravation?"

"Y'know—the name calling, the dirty words. You know."

Yes. She knew, all right. Mr. Browning crying out "Black cunt!" in the throes of his lust. Every man she ever met looking her over like she was there for the taking.

"You gotta learn to live with it," Joey said wisely. "*I* did."

She sneaked a quick glance at him. He was kind of funny-looking, tall and lanky with a shock of brown hair, a lopsided grin and crooked teeth. She didn't know why she'd accepted his invitation. Maybe because it was the first time anyone had asked her anywhere formal.

"Wanna dance?" He jerked his thumb toward the crowded floor.

She saw Nick out there breaking his butt with Dawn Kovak to the strains of "Sugar Sugar." "I . . . I don't think so."

He noticed her watching. "What've you got against him?" he asked.

She shifted uncomfortably. "Who?"

"Nick. What's he done to you?"

"He came here, that's what," she said fiercely.

"It wasn't his choice," Joey said, taking a pack of Camels from his pocket and offering her one. "He's a cool guy. You should give him a chance."

She waved the pack of cigarettes away. "You don't understand."

"Maybe one day you'll explain it to me. Sometimes it's good to talk —get it out in the open." He paused, realizing he was dealing with a touchy subject. "Whenever you like—I'm here. Okay?"

She narrowed her eyes and regarded him suspiciously. "What do you want from me?"

He shrugged. "Nothin', if that's all right with you."

"What time is it?" Meg asked, clinging to Mack Ryan as if *they* were the engaged couple.

Stock consulted his expensive waterproof watch—a present from his parents. "Twenty-five minutes before midnight. Come five past an' we're on our way."

"You got it," said Mack, placing his hand on the back of Meg's neck and giving her a rub and a tickle. "This little lady an' I—we want some privacy."

Meg giggled. "We do?" she said coquettishly.

Sure, Lauren thought. *And tomorrow this little lady is going to be complaining about how you nearly raped her.*

"Are we gonna *party* tonight!" Stock proclaimed.

Lauren took a hearty gulp of punch and immediately regretted it—the stuff tasted disgusting.

"C'mon," Stock urged, pulling her out of her chair. "They're playing my favorite."

His favorite turned out to be a soapy rendition of "Rocket Man." She hated it, especially when he began to get romantic, pulling her close, rubbing his crotch up against her leg and singing off-key in her ear.

Tonight's the night, she thought gloomily. *He's going to make a move and when he does I'm giving him back his ring.*

About time, too.

Across the dance floor Nick edged his way nearer to Lauren, guiding Dawn until she finally realized something was up and said, quite testily, "Where are we *going*? You're pushin' me around like I'm a vacuum cleaner!"

"We're gonna play excuse me."

"Huh?"

"Like I'll ask Lauren to dance—an' you'll take care of Stock."

"I will?"

"Yeah. We gotta liven things up."

"That'll liven things up, all right," she said, getting the picture and not particularly liking it. If Nick thought he was about to score with Miss Thighs Together Roberts he had another think coming. Sweet little Lauren wouldn't give him a second glance. And Stock would punch his brains out if he made a move on his precious fiancée.

As soon as he'd maneuvered them next to Lauren and Stock he gave Dawn a shove and an encouraging "Go for it!"

Dawn smiled provocatively at Stock. After all, she knew him well enough—they'd been secretly sleeping together on and off since eighth grade, and his engagement had certainly made no difference in his sex life. "My turn," she said gaily, pulling him away from Lauren, throwing a perfunctory "You don't mind, do you?" over her shoulder.

"Go ahead," Lauren said, one eye on Nick—who winked as if to say *How did you like the way I arranged this?*

Stock was easily led. Could he help it if girls found him irresistible? Dawn played her part, dragging him off to the middle of the dance floor, clinging to him tightly.

"Hey," Nick said, staring intently into Lauren's eyes. "Looks like you need someone to dance with."

She felt her heart begin to beat erratically. All of a sudden she could hardly breathe. "I guess so."

He took her in his arms, pulling her in real close. "Tonight you're breakin' your engagement," he said, very quietly.

"I know," she found herself replying.

He held her even closer. "Just so long as you know."

"There's gonna be trouble," Joey said.

"What kind of trouble?" Cyndra asked.

"Big trouble," Joey replied, nodding toward the dance floor.

Cyndra had no idea what he was talking about. As far as she could see, everybody seemed to be having a good time.

"You don't get it, do you?" he said.

She wondered what she was supposed to get.

"Stock Browning."

Browning. The very sound of that name made her shudder. Damn the whole disgusting Browning family, they were the worst kind of people.

"What about Stock?" she asked, trying to stay cool.

"Your brother's makin' a move on his girl."

She frowned. "How many times do I have to tell you? Nick's *not* my brother."

"Don't make no difference, he's gonna get his ass kicked."

"Good."

"You want him gettin' beat up?"

"I don't care."

"Yeah, well . . . I'll havta get into it."

"Why?"

" 'Cause he's my friend."

She studied the dance floor. Stock was gyrating with Dawn. Nick was way over the other side, slow dancing with Lauren. "Nothing's going to happen," she said.

"I hope you're right."

"I usually am."

"What's Lauren doing with *him?*" Meg said, staring furiously across the dance floor.

Mack was not listening to a word she said. "Y'know, I always had eyes for you—even when I was going steady," he said.

Meg was distracted. She was enjoying all the attention, but at the same time she didn't appreciate her best friend cozying up to Nick Angelo. "Where's Stock?" she demanded. "He should put a stop to this."

"You got the cutest little butt I've ever seen."

A compliment was a compliment. She forgot about Lauren for a minute. "I do?"

"Yeah. Cute butt. Cute face. I really dig you, Meg. Always did."

"Yes?"

"Let's go outside an' sit in the car."

"It's cold out there."

"We'll put on the heater, play the radio, finish up the champagne. C'mon, say yes . . . I wanna tell you about when I first noticed you."

How could she resist? "You won't . . . try anything?"

He looked suitably hurt. Girls were the most stupid creatures on earth—did she really imagine it was conversation he was after?

"Who, *me?* I have too much respect for you, Meg. I really do."

She allowed herself to be persuaded. After all, he was pretty damn cute himself.

"Well . . . all right."

Ten minutes to touchdown! With a great deal of effort he tried to keep his eyes off her plump, ripe breasts as he steered her outside.

As midnight approached a sense of anticipation hung over everyone. Excitement was definitely in the air.

The band was blasting out a Beatles medley. Nick's arms tightened around Lauren. "This is a very special night," he said, his voice low and warm. "The start of somethin' new."

"I know," she said softly.

"This time in ten years we'll be old."

"Sort of."

"Very."

"I guess."

"But we'll be together."

He sounded so sure, and yet she knew this wasn't going to be easy. Stock she could deal with—but her parents would go crazy if she ever started dating Nick Angelo.

Don't be negative, Roberts.

Okay, okay. Take it easy. I'll try to be as positive as I can.

The Beatles medley ended, and the band blasted into their own noisy version of "Born to Be Wild."

Dawn grabbed Stock's hand as soon as he began backing off. "Where *you* goin', big boy? We were just getting into it." She licked her lips suggestively and wriggled her hips. "Don't flake on me now."

Stock felt altogether foggy. "Gotta find Lauren, it's almost midnight."

"Oh, yeah, midnight," Dawn sneered. "Big deal. I can show you a better time than little Miss Goody—and you know it."

"Gotta find her," Stock repeated, slurring his words, his face red from too much Scotch surreptitiously sipped from his father's silver flask hidden deep in his pocket.

Dawn felt she'd done her part, she wasn't going to beg. Screw Nick Angelo—this wasn't how she'd planned on spending her New Year's.

Over by the edge of the dance floor Nick and Lauren were locked in each other's arms, oblivious to everyone around them. Stock spotted them and started over.

Joey stood up. "Here we go," he groaned, stubbing out his cigarette.

Cyndra toyed with her glass of watered-down punch. "Nothing's gonna happen."

The bandleader grabbed his microphone. "Five minutes to midnight!" he roared excitedly. "Five minutes to blast off! Are we ready?"

"Yeah!" the crowd roared back. "We're ready!"

The band switched to "Crocodile Rock"—they were in an Elton John mood.

"Lauren." Stock placed his hand on her shoulder and whined a plaintive "I didn't mean to dance with Dawn for so long. C'mon . . . it's time to go."

Lauren was startled, for a moment she'd forgotten about everyone and everything except Nick, Stock had ceased to exist. She turned to face him. "I . . . I don't want to go," she said quietly, her heart pounding.

"Why not?" he demanded belligerently.

"Because I don't."

Stock began to get angry. Was she giving him a hard time on account of his dancing with Dawn? For a moment he stood there swaying, suddenly realizing that while he'd been busy, Lauren had been cozying up to Nick Angelo.

"What the hell you dancin' with *this* dumb prick for?" he demanded. "Take a look at him—he's wearing sneakers, for crissake. Can't even afford shoes."

She felt Nick stiffen, ready for battle. Quickly she touched his arm, hoping to restrain him.

"Three minutes to midnight!" yelled the bandleader.

"You come with me where you belong," Stock said.

"No," she replied.

"You're my fiancée. Cut the shit an' do like I tell you."

Without saying a word she removed her engagement ring and handed it to him.

He was stunned. "What's this?" he said blankly, staring at the sparkling diamonds.

"It's over, Stock," she said, finally feeling in control.

"Over?" he said incredulously. "It can't be over."

"It is," she replied calmly, experiencing an overwhelming sense of relief.

He raised his voice, his face becoming even redder. "Nothin's over until *I* say it is."

She stifled a hysterical giggle. Was it her imagination or did he look like a boiled lobster? "Don't yell at me," she managed, without breaking up.

"Two minutes!" from the bandstand.

"Shit!" from Stock.

Now people were beginning to notice something was going on and couldn't help watching.

Nick decided the time had come to join in. He put his arm around her waist. "Let's go," he said.

"*You*—fuckin' butt out," Stock shouted, enraged. "This has *nothing* t'do with you."

"You've got it wrong there," Nick replied evenly. "It has *everything* to do with me."

"Fuck you!" Stock screamed.

"We're rollin' into countdown," the bandleader yelled, his microphone drowning out everyone. "So let's all do it together. Countin' back from sixty. Fifty-nine . . . fifty-eight . . . fifty-seven . . ."

"Jesus!" Stock smacked his forehead with the palm of his hand and glared at Lauren. "Now I know why I couldn't get into your friggin' pants. This cheap, nigger-lovin' prick got there first!"

"How *dare* you talk to me like that," she said.

"I'll talk to you any way I want. You're nothing but a tramp bitch —I should've listened to my mother."

Nick stepped forward. "This asshole is askin' for it."

"No!" She tried to block him from getting to Stock.

"Nineteen . . . eighteen . . . seventeen . . ."

"Get out the goddamn way," Stock warned her. "I'm teachin' this white-trash punk a lesson."

"Don't!" She tried to stop them; she hadn't wanted it to come to this.

". . . Eleven . . . ten . . . Okay, now everybody together. Let's hear you all!"

The crowd launched into a raucous chant.

Joey fought his way through, hoping to stop the inevitable. Cyndra trailed behind him.

". . . Five . . . four . . . three . . ."

Stock shoved Lauren roughly aside. Nick went to protect her, and before he realized it was coming, Stock hauled back and let one rip, sending him sprawling.

". . . Two . . . one. HAPPY NEW YEARRR!!"

Nick didn't have a chance. He fell like a slab of concrete. Just before he lost consciousness he saw balloons. Hundreds and hundreds of pretty pink balloons floating through the air.

18

He came to gradually, gasping for breath, his head aching like it was going to bust right open. Groaning, he raised his hand to his face and touched sticky blood. Slowly he opened his eyes.

Lauren was sitting on the floor, his head cradled in her lap. They were in the corridor outside the gym. A few people stood around watching—waiting to see if he was dead, no doubt.

Mr. Lucas, one of the school chaperons for the night, glared down at him. "That was disgusting behavior, Angelo," he said sharply. "We don't condone fighting in this school."

"*He* didn't do anything, Mr. Lucas," Lauren protested. "Stock hit *him*."

Mr. Lucas ignored her. "Somebody better get him home," he said impatiently, puffed up with his own importance. "I have to go back inside."

Now that the excitement was over, the few onlookers drifted away. Only Joey remained, Cyndra hovering close behind him.

"Jesus, man, you all right?" Joey asked. "I was on my way over when that moron laid one on you."

Nick tried to think straight. He felt like shit. Gingerly he touched his throbbing nose. "I . . . I think it's broken."

"Then we'd better get you over to the emergency room," Joey said, taking charge.

"What emergency room?" Cyndra asked. "This isn't Chicago, you know. We've got two doctors in town and they're probably both out celebrating."

"Are you sure it's broken?" Lauren asked, filled with guilt.

He touched his nose again. "Yeah, I'm sure."

His face was covered in blood, and some of it had dripped onto Lauren's dress, leaving big wet stains.

"I didn't mean this to happen," she whispered softly. "I'm really sorry."

He tried to make light of it. "Hey, a broken nose is worth it if it gets that asshole out of your life."

She considered his words. Yes. Stock was certainly gone, there was no doubt about *that*. "He *is* out of my life," she said quietly. "Forever."

"Well," Joey said, "this is all very cozy, but what're we gonna do?"

"We could take him over to the hospital in Ripley," Cyndra suggested. "They've got an emergency room."

"How'll we get him there?" Joey said, scratching his chin. "It's snowing, freezing cold, an' it's New Year's Eve. How'll we do it? On the back of my bike?"

"I guess not," Cyndra said.

"He can't go to the trailer park," Lauren said firmly. "It's too far. I'll call my father and ask him to pick us up. He can stay at my house tonight."

"Are you nuts?" Joey exclaimed. "Your parents will freak when you tell 'em you've finished with Stock."

"You're right," she said glumly. "But it's my fault he's hurt and I'll take responsibility."

Nick groaned. "I'd like to kick that asshole in the balls."

"What makes you think he's got any?" Cyndra said coolly.

He attempted a weak laugh. "So, it takes something like this for you to talk to me, huh?"

She shrugged. "Don't get carried away."

Lauren hurried off to call her parents. She stood at the pay phone, impatiently waiting for someone to answer. Then she remembered they'd gone to a party and probably weren't back, which was all the better to smuggle Nick into the house before they could object. She called the local taxi service and was lucky enough to get a cab.

By the time she got back, Nick was on his feet.

"Listen—I can walk. Let's not make a big deal out of this," he said, feeling embarrassed.

"Are you sure?"

"Yeah, I'm sure." He looked at Cyndra. "Tell 'em I won't be back tonight. Not that they give a shit."

"Like I'll be talking to them when I get home," she said sarcastically.

Back at her house Lauren led Nick straight up to her room. "How are you feeling?" she asked anxiously.

"Like a jerk. Your boyfriend took me by surprise. We should've taken it outside and I could've given as good as I got."

"Ex-boyfriend," she said matter-of-factly, pulling down the cover on her bed. "You'll sleep here."

He managed a weak grin. "With you?"

She smiled back. "Let's get serious."

He sat down on the bed. "Okay, okay. Just asking."

She soaked a washcloth and gently cleaned the blood off his face.

"Ouch!"

"Don't be a baby."

When she was finished he said, "Now what? Am I gonna roll between the sheets with all my clothes on?"

"I'll take care of everything," she assured him.

He grinned again. "Including undressing me?"

She shook her head, smiling. "One of these days . . . maybe. But right now you can do it yourself. You should get some sleep, we'll talk in the morning."

"Your dress is messed up. Hadn't you better change before your parents see it?"

He was right, her new black dress was stained with dark patches of blood. "I hated this dress anyway," she said wryly. "Let's call it my farewell present from the Brownings."

"Hey, Lauren," he said, reaching for her hand. "It was worth it."

"Say that in the morning when you look in the mirror."

By the time her parents arrived home she'd made up a bed for herself on the couch, changed into her robe and was waiting to greet them.

As they came through the front door she heard her father's angry voice. "Don't threaten me, Jane. Don't ever threaten me."

"I'm not threatening you," Jane replied in a strained voice. "But I can tell you this—" She spotted her daughter and abruptly stopped. "Lauren, what are you doing home so early?"

This was a new one. Home so early? It was one o'clock in the morning. "Uh . . . somebody got hurt at the dance."

"Not you?" Phil said quickly.

"No, I'm fine," she replied.

"Who then?" Jane asked.

"It . . . it's, uh, Nick Angelo. Remember? He was in the school play with me."

"What happened to him?" Jane asked, totally uninterested.

"He was in a fight. He didn't start the fight, but he got a broken nose and there was no way he could get home tonight what with the snow and everything, so I brought him here." She knew she was speaking too fast, but she couldn't stop. "Actually, he's asleep in my bed. It's all perfectly respectable, Mother. I'm sleeping on the couch."

Her father looked furious. "That boy is here—in your bed?"

"Yes, Daddy," she said patiently. "But I'm not. I'm downstairs with you. Right?"

Phil and Jane exchanged horrified glances.

"I do wish you hadn't done this without asking us," Jane fretted. "I don't like strangers sleeping over. Who is he anyway?"

"I told you, Mother. Nick Angelo. He was Brick in the play."

"Oh, him. Strange-looking boy," Jane said. "Somebody told me he lives over in the trailer park. Is that true?"

"Does it make any difference?" Lauren challenged.

Jane frowned; her daughter could be very stubborn, and she could see that this was one of those times. "Well, if you wish to sleep on the couch, I suppose there's nothing we can do about it. We'll see you in the morning."

Lauren gave them half an hour. She waited until they'd both used the bathroom and she heard their bedroom door close. After that there was the faint murmur of conversation, and eventually silence.

When the house was absolutely quiet she crept upstairs and looked in at Nick. He lay on his back, arms outstretched, eyes closed.

She stared down at him for a long moment.

Nick Angelo, you've changed my life. And I am so very very grateful!

In the morning Lauren was up at six. She'd decided it was better to get Nick out of the house before he had to face her parents. If she moved quickly and quietly she could borrow the family station wagon and drive him over to the hospital in Ripley before they were awake.

She'd hardly slept at all. Everything was changing and so was she. She knew she had to be strong, ready to stand up to all the opposition she was bound to face. For so many years she'd been good little Lauren, hardworking little Lauren. Now she'd be labeled naughty little Lauren because she didn't wish to remain engaged to the richest boy in town.

Too bad. She could deal with it. The problem was, could they?

Upstairs in her room Nick sat on the side of her bed clad in his ruined tux. She entered the room, put a finger to her lips and whispered, "Shhh . . . We're leaving."

He nodded, relieved to be getting out of there.

She hurried into her closet and pulled on jeans, sweatshirt and a heavy duffle coat. "Follow me," she whispered, and they crept downstairs.

In the kitchen she scribbled a note explaining why she'd taken the car and taped it to the refrigerator door.

Within minutes they were outside. "Whew!" she sighed, unlocking the car. "It's not easy acting like a criminal."

"I'll drive," he said.

"No," she replied firmly. "Not this time."

"Did you get any sleep?" he asked, getting into the passenger side without a fight.

"No. Did you?"

Ruefully he touched his swollen nose. "What do *you* think?"

She eased the car away from the curb. It had stopped snowing, but the roads were wet and slushy.

"I think we're both insane!" she exclaimed, perfectly happy.

"And you like it."

"I love it!" she replied recklessly. "I feel free for the first time in ages."

He looked at her intently. "Yeah?"

"Oh, yes. Stock was like a big dark cloud hovering over me."

"So why did you stay with him?"

"It seemed the easiest thing to do."

"Easy ain't always easy," he remarked sagely.

She sneaked a quick glance at him. "You look awful."

"Thanks!"

"How do you feel?"

"Like a tractor ran over my face. Apart from that—great."

"The doctor'll fix your nose."

"What doctor?"

"We're driving to Ripley."

"We are?"

"I owe you a new nose. It was my fault you got hit."

"Hey, any time—if it means sleeping in your bed." He grinned. "Loved the Snoopy sheets!"

"Don't make fun of me. My mother never throws anything out."

His nose continued to throb and he was in serious pain. So why did he feel like singing? After all, Lauren was only another girl. Yeah— only the most beautiful girl in the world!

He studied her perfect profile. "What're your parents gonna say about everything?"

She grimaced. "I'll let you know."

He reached for the radio, tuning it to a rock station. If only they could stay in the car and keep on going. Was it too much to ask her to give up everything and run away with him?

They made it to Ripley in an hour and a half and drove straight to the emergency room. New Year's Eve had taken its toll—the place was crowded with survivors of various battles. There were bloody knife wounds, a shooting or two, a couple of beaten women and a large black man screaming obscenities. Lauren clung to his arm as they took a seat.

"Hey, take it easy," he said, feeling somewhat queasy himself.

They waited nearly five hours before getting any attention, and then a harassed young doctor rushed Nick into an examining room and confirmed that yes, his nose was indeed broken. He set it and covered it with bandages.

"I feel like I was in a war," Nick joked as they left the hospital. Deep down he was wondering what he'd look like when the bandages came off. Hell, he'd always been happy with his appearance. Now what? Another stroke against him?

"Don't worry," Lauren said, reading his mind. "You'll look fine."

Outside the snow had started up again with a vengeance. "Big cities," she said, shivering. "They frighten me."

He laughed. "This ain't no big city. This is Disneyland compared with New York or Chicago." He slapped his hands together. "Jeez! I'm freezing!"

"So am I. And starving!"

"Me too."

She glanced at her watch. "It's nearly three. My parents will murder me! We'd better start back."

"Not until we get something to eat."

Her parents were going to kill her anyway, what difference did another half hour make? "Okay," she said, wondering if she should phone them. No, she decided; save the big confrontation for later.

They left the station wagon in the hospital parking lot and ran, slipping and sliding on the wet sidewalk, to a nearby hamburger joint.

A waitress approached their table. She had a cigarette hanging from the corner of her mouth and a jaded expression. "Yeah? What'll it be?"

"Double burger with everything on, a Coke and fries," Lauren ordered breathlessly. "Twice." She smiled at Nick. "Okay?"

He had twenty dollars in his pocket. "I'm buyin'," he said.

"No. *I* am," she insisted. "It's my fault we're here."

"Can't let you do that."

"Yes, you can."

"Two burgers or *what?*" The waitress was bored, she couldn't care less who was paying as long as the check got settled. Lauren nodded, and the waitress left.

Nick leaned across the table and kissed her.

"What's that for?" she asked, wide-eyed.

"Uh . . . I guess for bein' you."

She smiled. He decided she had the most beautiful smile in the world. "Hey," he blurted, unable to stop himself. "I think I . . ."

"Yes?" she asked eagerly.

"Aw—forget it."

Her eyes shone brightly, urging him to continue. "What?"

"Uh, like, I think . . . uh . . . y'know—like, I think I love you."

"Me too," she whispered softly, feeling as if she was going to melt with happiness. "Me too."

19

At first Jane Roberts was pleased when she awoke and found that Lauren had left with Nick Angelo; she hadn't relished dealing with a stranger in the morning. Besides, she had other things on her mind, there was no time to worry about her stubborn daughter right now.

She frowned when she reached the kitchen and discovered Lauren's note. Phil was not going to be pleased to find that Lauren had taken the car without his permission, it was so unlike her.

She reread her daughter's note.

BORROWED CAR.

BACK SOON.

LOVE,

LAUREN

When Phil came downstairs he was furious. "We give that girl too much freedom," he grumbled. "How dare she presume she can drive out of here in my car."

"What'll Stock say?" Jane fretted. "I hope she's back in time for the New Year's lunch with the Brownings, we're expected there at one."

"She'll be back," Phil said gruffly. "She's probably taken that boy home."

"I wonder who he was in a fight with."

"Who knows? Who cares?" replied Phil, opening the kitchen cabinet and reaching for a box of cornflakes. "Whoever it was, he was probably bigger. Lauren always protects the underdog."

"Yes," Jane said. "But it wasn't very nice of Stock to leave her alone."

Phil tipped the cornflakes into a dish and added milk. "We have to talk about us, Jane," he said.

Her face reddened. "We talked last night."

"Not enough."

"It was enough for me," she replied, her lips tightening into a thin line.

The phone interrupted what was about to be another fight. Phil picked up. "Yes?"

"Sorry, Mr. Roberts, did I wake you?"

"No," he said tersely.

"It's Meg. Can I speak to Lauren?"

"She went out early."

"Where did she go?"

He ignored her question. "She'll call you when she gets back."

"Uh . . . thank you, Mr. Roberts."

Shortly before noon Jane Roberts sat at her dressing table, adding a touch of powder here, a dab of rouge there. She had a new cinnamon outfit with matching pumps. She'd decided to wear her fur coat. It was five years old, but perhaps when Lauren married into the Browning family and Phil's business started improving he would be able to buy her a new one.

Phil walked into the room and stood behind her, tapping impatiently on his watch. "She's not back."

"Oh, dear," Jane said. "How can she do this to us?"

"It's snowing again." Phil moved over to the window and stared out. "I hope she hasn't had an accident."

"Lauren's an excellent driver."

"I know," Phil said, pacing up and down. "I don't understand where she can be."

"Nor do I," said Jane, more than slightly irritated that her daughter would choose today to mess things up.

The phone rang. "That'll be her," Phil said, grabbing the receiver.

It was not Lauren, it was Daphne Browning. "Phil," she said in her imperious voice, "let me speak to Jane."

"Certainly, Daphne." He covered the mouthpiece with his hand. "She wants to talk to you. Don't mention Lauren."

Jane rushed to pick up. "Happy New Year, Daphne," she gushed. "You left the Lawsons' party awfully early last night, but it was fun, wasn't it?"

Daphne was not into pleasantries. "I simply cannot believe your daughter's behavior," she said flatly.

Jane was startled. "I beg your pardon?"

"Lauren's behavior," Daphne repeated, as if she was talking to an extremely backward child.

"What happened?"

"Surely you know?"

Jane took a stab in the dark. "About the fight?"

"Disgusting!" Daphne exclaimed. "You might think Lauren would have the decency to stay with her fiancé rather than go running off with that no-account boy from the wrong side of town."

Jane took a deep breath, she had known Lauren's engagement to Stock was too good to be true. "Are you still expecting us for lunch?" she said tentatively, knowing the answer before she asked.

"I don't believe there's any point, do you?" Daphne replied. A long cold pause. "I'm extremely disappointed in Lauren. You should be too."

"Lauren's always done the right thing," Jane said, finally coming to her daughter's defense.

"Certainly not this time."

"Well . . ." Jane hesitated. "I'm sure whatever happened between them, Stock and Lauren will work it out."

"You're making very light of this," Daphne said disapprovingly. "You *do* know she gave him back his ring."

"Oh," said Jane blankly.

"He doesn't care," said Daphne, her tone snappy and spiteful. "Not after the way she treated him."

"I have to go," Jane said, not wishing to prolong the conversation.

"Fine," sniffed Daphne, hanging up.

Phil walked back into the room, adjusting his tie. "We should leave," he said. "You'd better write Lauren a note telling her we've gone ahead."

"Too late," Jane said. "The engagement is off. We are no longer invited to lunch."

By noon the news was all over town that Lauren Roberts had broken off her engagement to Stock Browning. It was also common knowledge that Stock had smashed Nick Angelo in the face, and nobody seemed to know where Nick and Lauren were.

Joey was alarmed, he'd seen the electricity between the two of them and knew it meant trouble. Shortly before noon he rode over to pick up Cyndra.

"Did you hear anything from Nick?" she asked.

"No. Did you?"

"We don't have a phone, in case you hadn't noticed."

Harlan was hanging around outside. "Nick was gonna take us to a movie," he said, sounding mournful.

"He got hurt," Cyndra explained. "He was in a fight."

"When's he coming back?"

"Later."

"He promised," Harlan said sadly. "Luke was lookin' forward to it."

"He'll take you another day," Cyndra said.

"Whyn't *you* take us?" Harlan asked, his eyes big.

"Some other time," she answered quickly. "Come on, Joey. Let's go."

Cyndra didn't care to admit it, but she was pleased to see Joey. When he'd taken her home the night before he hadn't even tried for a kiss good night. She felt safe with him. It was a welcome change to feel safe with a member of the opposite sex.

They rode into town on his bike and stopped by the drugstore. Joey settled her in a corner booth and went off to talk to some of his friends. When he came back he said, "Okay, so this is the story goin' around. Nick took a slug at Stock an' the big guy creamed him."

"But that's not true," Cyndra said heatedly. "Nick didn't have a chance. Stock hit him when he wasn't looking."

"Yeah, *we* know it," Joey agreed. "But since he's on the missing list it's difficult to defend him. Oh, an' Meg says Lauren's not around either. She's been tryin' to call her all day."

They both thought about it for a minute.

"Hey," Joey said at last, as if he'd had some kind of big revelation. "You don't think they ran off and did it, do you?"

Cyndra smiled, a sly smile. "Did *what*, Joey?"

He grinned back. "*You* know. What *we're* gonna do one of these days."

Oh, yeah? That's what *he* thought. "Don't bet on it," she said, sipping her Coke.

He threw up his hands. "Okay, okay. Only jokin'."

By late afternoon the light smattering of snowflakes had turned into a fierce storm. "I'm calling the police," Phil Roberts said. "I'll give them the license number and they'll track her down."

Jane looked dismayed. "How can she do this to us?" she asked, her voice quavering. "Doesn't she know we're worried out of our minds?"

Phil shook his head as he marched across the room to the phone. "I'm calling the police," he repeated.

Jane nodded. There seemed to be no other answer.

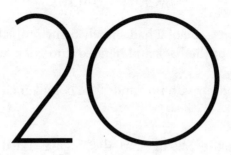

They sat in the hamburger place for two hours. They talked. They got to know each other. They gazed into each other's eyes. They held hands. They giggled. Neither of them had any idea of the time.

The two of them made a strange couple—Lauren all bundled up in her winter clothes, and Nick in his battered tuxedo, his nose bandaged, his dark hair falling on his forehead, his green eyes as intense as ever.

Eventually the waitress approached their table. "You can't sit here nursing a Coke forever," she said sharply. "Either order somethin' else or leave."

Nick stood up. "We're outta here."

"Old bitch!" Lauren whispered.

"No bad language," he said, laughing.

"I'm not the little goody-goody everybody thinks I am."

"Yeah—like I've noticed."

He grabbed her hand and they ran outside. Now the snow was really coming down in icy blasts.

"I'd better phone home," Lauren said, feeling guilty.

"They'll only yell at you," he said. "Let's hit the road an' get back."

When they reached the station wagon it was piled high with snow.

It was so cold that some of it had already turned to slabs of ice. Lauren got a shovel out of the back and handed it to Nick, who began trying to crack the ice.

"I'm gonna end up with no hands," he complained. "My fingers are frozen!"

"Can I help?"

"Yeah, get in the car an' start the engine. We'd better get goin' before it's dark."

The car wouldn't start. Lauren tried to no avail. She moved across the seat while Nick got behind the wheel. He gave it a couple of shots until the engine finally turned over and they set off.

The car began to skid and slide on the slippery roads. He tuned the radio to a news station. A weather warning announced heavy snow and impassable roads.

"What now?" Lauren asked helplessly.

"We can try an' make it."

"And if we get stuck?"

"I dunno."

"Maybe we should stay here," she said tentatively.

"Then you're *really* gonna have to call home. You can't let 'em think you're never comin' back."

"Okay."

"There's a motel over by the gas station at the edge of town," he said. "Let's see if we can make it."

"Fine," she replied, thinking about how she would explain this to her parents.

By the time they reached the motel she was shivering with nerves. While Nick booked them in she hurried to a pay phone.

Her father answered with a sharp "Yes?"

"Daddy?"

"Lauren," he replied, his voice harsh. "Where are you? Your mother and I are worried sick."

"I know. I'm sorry."

"You're *sorry*? We imagined you dead and buried under a snowdrift, and you're calling to say you're sorry. Get home *right* now! Do you understand me? Right now!"

"Daddy, I can't. I'm in Ripley. The roads are closed."

There was an ominous silence. "Who are you with?"

"I . . . I'm with Nick. I took him to the hospital. You see, it's my fault his nose is broken. I know I shouldn't have borrowed the car without asking you, but I didn't want to wake you. The emergency room was filled with people, we had to wait . . . I . . . I didn't realize it would take so long."

"Are you telling me you can't get home?"

"We thought we'd stay in a motel and drive back tomorrow."

"My daughter—in a motel? With that scum?"

"Nick's not scum," she said defiantly. "He's a very nice person. It wasn't his fault Stock smashed him in the face, it was mine."

"You'd better speak to your mother."

Jane grabbed the phone. "Your behavior is absolutely disgraceful," she said in a low tight voice.

"I'm sorry . . ."

"I don't wish to hear your excuses. If the roads are closed it's quite obvious you can't get home tonight. Since you are forced to stay in Ripley, promise me you'll stay in separate rooms and have nothing to do with that boy whatsoever. Can you promise me that, Lauren?"

There was no point in arguing. She crossed the fingers of her left hand and, just to make sure, her right hand too. "I promise, Mother."

"We'll deal with this tomorrow, young lady," Jane said. "And don't expect us to be lenient."

The motel room had fringed orange lampshades with scorch marks. The faded yellow bedspread had seen better days. The blue rug was threadbare. But there was a television, and the manager's office had soft drink and snack machines.

"It cost too much to get two rooms," Nick explained when she came back from the phone. "You don't mind sharin', do you?"

She didn't mind. She knew that when she got home it would all be over anyway—so why not make this a night to remember?

Once they were settled they both decided they were having a wonderful time. They'd stocked up on candy and potato chips, Cokes and 7-Ups, and now they sat cross-legged on the bed munching and watching an "I Love Lucy" rerun.

"This is great," Nick said, swigging Coke from the can.

Lauren smiled happily. "I can't believe we're here together."

"You know," he said, "I always had you figured as a timid little small-town girl—frightened to make a move."

"Then why did you come after me?"

" 'Cause I figured you were worth savin'."

"Thanks a *lot!*"

"You're welcome."

She began to laugh. "You look so silly with your nose all bandaged."

"Maybe I should rip it off. That doctor didn't seem to know what he was doin'."

"You were too handsome before."

"You thought I was handsome, huh?"

"Very."

"Not your type, though?"

"Yes."

"Nope. You like 'em big an' beefy."

She reached for a pillow and threw it at him. "Will you *stop.*"

"Only if you make me."

"I'll make you, all right," she giggled, rolling on top of him, attempting to pin his arms to the bed.

With one swift move he reversed the situation and had her trapped beneath him. "Now you're my prisoner," he joked. "I can do anything I like."

"Go ahead," she whispered, suddenly serious. In her heart she knew that when they returned to the real world she would be forbidden to see him, and while she could she wanted to be as close to him as possible.

He was filled with mixed emotions. His body was urging him to go for it—but his head kept insisting he'd better hold back. Lauren Roberts wasn't just another one-night conquest. She was pretty and sweet and talented and, most of all, special.

And yet he had a hard-on that could crack ice.

She gazed up at him, her eyes dreamy and inviting.

"Uh, y'know, maybe we shouldn't . . . ." he said.

"Yes—we should," she said earnestly, reaching up to touch his face. "I'm ready, Nick. It's what I want. It's what we both want, isn't it?"

"Only if you're sure . . ." he said uncertainly.

"I'm *very* sure."

He started to kiss her, slowly at first, but as things began to heat up it was all he could do to control himself. For a girl who hadn't been around, she certainly could kiss.

He reached under her sweatshirt, touching her breasts, groping to unhook her bra.

She helped him pull the sweatshirt over her head and went for the buttons on his shirt, tearing the material in her haste to get it off him.

He traced her breasts with the tips of his fingers—touching her softly, stroking her nipples until she began to make small gasping sounds.

Jeez! Her skin was like satin, her hair long and silky fanning out over the sheets. And she smelled so clean and fresh. Most girls he'd slept with favored heavy perfume and had cigarette breath. Dawn Kovak wore musk; he had to scrub to get her scent off him.

"Come on, Nick." Now she was leading *him*, reaching for his zipper, wriggling out of her jeans.

She had the longest legs he'd ever seen.

He peeled down her panties and tossed them on the floor, dipping his fingers, feeling her urgent need, and finally getting on top of her and carefully easing into the trip of a lifetime.

She opened up to him with no inhibitions. It was her first time but it didn't matter.

He broke through as gently as he could and took her all the way.

When they were finished he held her in his arms—cradling her until she fell asleep, a smile on her face.

He'd made love a hundred times since the first time when he was thirteen, but never like this—never had feelings been part of it.

Lauren Roberts.

Lauren Angelo.

It sounded good.

He'd finally found a soul mate, and as far as he was concerned their lives were forever entwined.

21

"You will *never* see him again," Phil Roberts thundered. "Do you understand me, Lauren? *Do* you?"

She understood him all right, and his harsh words came as no surprise—so why was her heart breaking into a thousand tiny pieces? Why was there a feeling of dread in the pit of her stomach? Why did she want to die?

She glanced over at her mother. Jane's mouth was set in a tightly compressed line. Lauren knew the expression; it meant *I'm not getting involved—don't ask me.*

"Daddy—" she began.

He held up his hand. "No! I do not wish to hear your excuses. What you did was unforgivable. Taking the car. Staying out all night."

"I called," she said defiantly. "I explained the roads were closed. I *couldn't* get home."

"And as for the way you've treated Stock, it's beyond my comprehension."

"He's a jerk, Daddy. He called me a prick tease."

"Lauren!" gasped Jane.

"How dare you speak like that in front of your mother," Phil roared.

Lauren imagined herself as a stranger watching this dramatic family

154

scene. Phil Roberts—red in the face, puffed up with self-righteous anger.

Jane Roberts—a faded beauty in a small town, her shoulders tense, standing by while her husband took charge.

And then there was Lauren. Sixteen years old and no longer a virgin. Sixteen years old and desperately, wildly, incredibly in love.

They couldn't stop her from seeing Nick. What were they going to do—lock her in the house?

The moment she'd walked through the door they'd started on her.

Why did you break your engagement?

Nick Angelo is nothing but trash.

How can you do this to us?

What will people think?

Who cared what people thought? *She* certainly didn't. For once in her life she felt absolutely, totally alive.

"Go to your room," her father said harshly. "And stay there until we give you permission to come out."

Good. All she wanted was to be alone so she could think about Nick, relive every wonderful magical moment. The touch of him, the taste of him, the sheer thrill of being in his arms. She turned to go upstairs.

"We're very disappointed in you, Lauren." This from her mother.

Oh, go bake a cake! You have no idea who I am anymore.

Her room was a mess, just the way she'd left it—her bed unmade, the sheets rumpled from Nick's overnight stay. She bent to sniff them, maybe catch his odor. Oh, God! She had to see him again soon, she missed him already.

Her rock heroes—John Lennon and Emerson Burn—gazed down at her from above her bed. Once her idols, it now seemed silly to worship from afar. She unpinned the posters, rolled them up and put them in her closet. Then she stared at herself in the mirror, deciding that she looked exactly the same—no real change, except maybe the expression in her eyes. There was something new there—something intangible.

After making love she and Nick had slept in each other's arms all night as close as two people could be. And in the morning they'd made love again, and this time she'd enjoyed it even more. She'd cried out for him to enter her, and then she'd cried out from sheer pleasure as her body jerked in response to his loving and she'd experienced a feeling so sensational, so amazing that she'd wanted to burst into happy tears.

"What was *that?*" she'd gasped.

"What?"

"That feeling I just had."

"You came," he'd told her.

"Came where?"

And he'd explained that making love wasn't only for the man's satisfaction.

"How do you know so much?" she'd asked, feeling a strong twinge of jealousy.

" 'Cause I got taught by a whole bunch of older women. Now I can teach you."

She'd reached for him. "How about teaching me more."

They didn't leave the motel until eleven in the morning. He drove slowly along the treacherous icy roads, while she snuggled next to him. By the time they reached Bosewell it was almost two-thirty.

"I'll get out at the gas station," he'd said. "Unless you'd like me to come in an' face your parents with you. I don't mind."

"*I* do. It's better I handle them alone."

He'd pulled the car up across the street and jumped out. "I'll call you later."

She'd laughed and slid behind the wheel.

He'd come around and kissed her through the open window. "I . . . uh . . ."

She had a right to be demanding. "What? *Say* it."

He'd attempted to make light of it. "I love ya."

"You too."

And she'd watched him run across the street—her hero in a blood-stained tux with a battered nose.

Now she was back to reality.

As soon as she reached the safety of her room she picked up the phone to call Meg and find out what had been going on in her absence. Before she'd finished dialing her father appeared at the door. "No phone privileges," he said, his face long and dour.

"But, Daddy—" she started to object.

"I said you will *not* use the phone," he repeated sternly, entering her room, pulling the phone from its jack and carrying it off under his arm.

They were angrier than she'd thought, probably because she'd broken up with Stock. It wasn't that they resented Nick, she rationalized; they didn't even know him. Maybe after a few weeks she could introduce him into their lives and they'd soon realize what a terrific guy he was.

The real truth was there was no way they could stop her from seeing him. School resumed shortly and then she'd be with him every day whether her parents liked it or not.

Right now it was quite obvious they weren't going to let her out of the house. No car. No phone. No contact with friends. She was a prisoner. A prisoner with her thoughts.

Ah . . . but her thoughts were going to keep her very happy until she saw Nick again. Very happy indeed.

"You dumped on us," Harlan said accusingly, sitting on the steps outside the trailer, zinging pebbles at an empty can.

"Hey, that's not true. I couldn't make it. I had an accident. Take a look at my face," Nick said.

"You promised us a movie," Harlan said glumly.

"I wasn't here," he explained, edging past him into the trailer. "I told you why."

Luke lay listlessly on top of the mattress he shared with Harlan.

"What's the matter with him?" Nick asked.

"I dunno." Harlan followed him in, shrugging. "He got sick."

"What's your ma say?"

"She ain't here."

He went over to Luke and placed his hand on his forehead. The kid was burning up.

"When did he get like this?"

"Dunno," Harlan said, sighing.

Nick stripped off his clothes, realizing there was no way he could ever return the tuxedo. It was good that when Joey had checked out the clothes from the rental place he'd given a phony address. "Where's Cyndra?" he asked, pulling on his jeans.

"Out with Joey." Harlan leaned against the door looking miserable.

"Tell you what," Nick said cheerfully. "Soon as Luke's better we'll go to that movie."

"You said that before."

"Yeah, but this time I ain't gonna be stuck in Ripley with a broken nose."

"You look funny," Harlan said, staring at him, his head to one side.

"Yeah, yeah, I know."

He wondered what Lauren was doing. After she dropped him at the gas station he'd worked for a couple of hours, but it was so quiet he'd finally made the trek home, picking up his bike from outside Dawn's without ringing her doorbell. Joey hadn't been at work, so he had no idea what the buzz around town was. He'd been planning on going back to the drugstore to see Louise and Dave, but now he didn't feel he should leave Luke.

"Anybody got a thermometer around here?" he asked.

Harlan gazed at him solemnly. "What that?"

"Forget it," he said. "Hang on, I'll ask Primo."

His father was in his usual position—stretched out like a sleeping rhino, snoring heavily. The television was blaring, and there were three cans of beer stacked in a row on the floor next to the bed. He wore a torn undershirt and dirty underpants. A half-eaten bag of potato chips spilled out on his chest.

Roughly Nick shook him until he came to, bleary-eyed and puce-faced. "Whassamatter? Wass goin' on?" he griped, burping loudly as he hoisted himself into a sitting position. His rheumy eyes focused on his son. "Wadda *you* wan'?"

"It's Luke," Nick said, trying to get through to him. "He's burnin' hot an' just lyin' there."

"Ain't my problem." Primo yawned, automatically reaching for a beer.

"It could be if anythin' happens to him," Nick said, hating his father even more, if that was possible.

"Whyn't ya tell Aretha." Primo's attention was now taken by a bikini-clad blonde with jiggling tits cavorting across the television screen.

"She's at work," he said shortly.

"Quit botherin' me. Throw a bucket a water over him—that'll cool him down till she gets back." Primo reached into his underpants to scratch his crotch. "An' don't tell her 'bout Luke till she done fixin' my supper."

For a moment Nick stood there trying to figure out what to do. Then he spotted the keys to the van on the table and swiped them on his way out. Fuck Primo. Fuck the fat pig.

By the time he got back to the other trailer Luke was breathing funnily.

He made a fast decision. "We're takin' him into town," he told Harlan. "Wrap him in a couple of blankets an' let's get movin'."

"Sit down, Aretha Mae," Benjamin Browning said.

Aretha Mae hovered in the doorway of his study, her expression wary and suspicious. "Why?"

Benjamin picked up a silver pen from his desktop and twirled it between his thick fingers. He did not relish the job Daphne had landed him with, the sooner it was done the better. "Because I say so," he said irritably. "Come in. Close the door behind you and *sit down, goddamnit*."

She did as he requested, albeit reluctantly. Once she was seated he swiveled his leather chair at an angle so that he didn't have to look her in the eye.

"Yes?" Her voice betrayed her impatience.

"I am terminating your employment," he said coldly.

She was startled. "What you sayin'?"

"I'm firing you. Your services are no longer required."

A nerve twitched beneath her left eye. "Oh, they ain't, huh?"

"Mrs. Browning and I have decided you deserve six weeks severance pay on account of your years of service with us." He passed a signed check across the desk. "Mrs. Browning has requested that you do not return to work after today. Is that clear?"

"Clear . . ." she muttered.

He thought she was accepting her termination without argument. Thank God for that.

"Well . . ." he said, willing her to go quietly. "That's all."

"That's all," she repeated his words, not moving.

"You may go," he said, dismissing her with a cursory wave.

Aretha Mae stood up, placed both hands on his desk and glared at him. "I ain't goin' nowhere, you son of a bitch," she said, forcing him to make eye contact.

He'd known she would try to cause trouble. It was too much to expect that she would go quietly. Once . . . many years ago when she'd first come to work for them, she'd been lovely. Young and vibrant with long legs, big breasts and a sassy smile—just like Cyndra —a juicy little piece, hot and sexy. Now, seventeen years later, she was a dried-up, bitter old woman. Skinny and wild-eyed with sunken cheeks and dyed red hair. Even Daphne had aged better than her, and Daphne was ten years older. Not that he fucked his wife any- more, but once a year on their anniversary he made her get down on her knees and give him a suck. He knew how much she hated it, and it gave him immense pleasure to watch his penis vanish into that scarlet slash of a mouth. Daphne didn't dare refuse him. Daphne would never give up the grand title of Mrs. Browning.

"I'm firing you," he repeated. "Don't you understand English? You *have* to go."

"No such thing as Aretha Mae havin' t'do nothin'," she snapped, sitting back down. "No such thing, an' you know it."

He threw his silver pen down on the desk, full of exasperation. "I'll double your severance pay if that's what you're after. Three months' wages and out of here today."

"Ain't goin'," she said stubbornly.

Now he was getting really angry. "Why not?"

" 'Cause three months down the line I ain't got no job, no money, no nothin'."

"You can find another job."

"In Bosewell? No shit? What other family got themselves a full-time maid?"

"There's always work in the paper factory or the canning plant."

She jumped up again. "No!" she said forcefully. "I work here—an' this is where I stay."

He was silent for a moment before saying, "What do you want?"

"Same money I'se gettin' now for the rest o' my natural life. An' five thousand dollars in the bank for my Cyndra. Oh, yeah, an' a lawyer's letter t'say I gets it regular."

"That's blackmail."

"*Your* word—ain't mine."

"And if I refuse?"

"Then the whole town gets t'know who Cyndra's daddy is, an' the filthy things you done t'her."

"What are you saying?"

"You *know* what I'se sayin'. Cyndra's *your* child."

Benjamin paled. "It's . . . it's not possible."

"That it is."

"How?"

"Remember when I first came t'work here?"

His throat constricted. "Yes."

"You was chasin' me day an' night—soon as your wife left the house you was after me—an' I was sleepin' in that room down in the basement. Well, one night you came there, held your hand over my mouth, an' shoved your thing inside me even though I didn't want it."

"You wanted it," he said angrily. "After the first time you were begging for it."

"You got me pregnant an' I didn't know what t'do. So I ended up marryin' the first man who'd have me—an' we moved t' the trailer park. Thing is, when I told him I was pregnant he ran out on me— an' all these years I been alone. But I kept on workin' for you—an' you kept on pokin' me till I wasn't young 'nuff for you no more."

"My wife and I supported you, and this is how you pay us back— by lying?"

She gave a hollow laugh. "Supported me—*shee-it!* I worked my black ass off for you an' your family, an' don' you forget it. Washin' your dirty underdrawers, cleanin' the shit in your johns, wipin' up all the mess."

"And now you're going to blackmail me with this far-fetched story?"

"I'm gonna get what's right for me an' that child o' yours."

"She's not my child," he said vehemently.

"Want me t'tell the town 'bout how you was screwin' me all those years? Want me to tell them how you raped your own daughter?"

"You wouldn't do that."

"Honey," she said bitterly. "*I* ain't got nuttin' t'lose. How 'bout you?"

22

Nick drove the van to the drugstore, parked in back and entered through the kitchen, grabbing Louise as she passed by carrying an order of ham and eggs.

She stopped and let out a whistle. "Lookit you! Your damn face is one big mess."

"I need a doctor," he said urgently.

"Seems like you shoulda thought of that before."

"Not for me. Luke's sick—my kid brother. I got him in the van. Who can I take him to?"

"Gee . . ." She hesitated. "Doc Marshall's away, an' Doc Sheppard don't like bein' bothered at home."

"Where does he live?"

She placed her order on the counter and gave him her full attention. "What's wrong with the kid?"

"I dunno. He's hot, can't breathe good."

"Maybe I should take a look before you go waking up Doc Sheppard—he's an ornery old bastard." She untied her apron. "Hey, Dave," she yelled, "I'm takin' a break, have Cheryl fill in."

Out in the van Luke was shivering uncontrollably. Harlan sat beside him looking miserable.

"Thought you said he was hot," Louise said accusingly, placing a hand on the child's forehead. "Oh, shit, yeah—he's hot, all right."

"What do you think it is?" Nick asked.

"Dunno. But it ain't good." She climbed into the van. "Let's go. We'll wake up old Doc Sheppard. Hang a left, then take the second street on the right. An', Nick—put your foot down."

The bus ride took longer than ever. Aretha Mae sat by the window gazing out. Usually she let her mind go blank—ridding herself of the cares of the day. But today she was filled with pent-up emotions—feelings she hadn't allowed to surface for seventeen years.

Benjamin Browning was Cyndra's father and she was glad she'd finally told him. Yes—glad to see the expression on his pompous white face when the full impact struck and he'd realized what he'd done.

Filthy pig. He was no good—only his money saved him from wallowing in the gutter.

With a deep sigh she recalled the day she'd started work at the Brownings'. Her mother had answered an ad in the newspaper, and Mr. Browning had agreed to pay her bus fare from Kansas City if she could start immediately. "My girl be there," her mother had assured him, delighted to be rid of one of seven daughters. Her mother had lied and said she was eighteen. The truth was she was barely fifteen and just out of school. "Work hard. Stay quiet. Don't get in no trouble." Those had been her mother's parting words.

Six months after she left home her mother was killed by a drunken driver. She had no father.

At first Aretha Mae liked working in a house with running water, indoor toilets and unheard-of luxuries like a refrigerator and TV. But Daphne Browning was not pleasant to work for. She'd recently given birth to Stock, and she had no intention of caring for the child unless he was clean and fresh at all times and never crying. Although she had all the housework to do, Aretha Mae soon found herself caring for the baby as well as attending to her other duties.

Benjamin Browning watched her like a tiger stalking its prey. She was aware of his lecherous eyes and roaming hands, but she managed to stay clear. He was in his early thirties then and quite good-looking. A self-made man with an abundance of energy and a canny mind. Daphne had pale skin, yellow hair and large breasts. They made love every night. Aretha Mae knew because she got to change the messy sheets.

The first night Benjamin came to her room he was drunk—he'd been out at a bachelor party. It was late, and she was asleep. He ripped the covers off her bed, placed a firm hand over her mouth, lifted her nightgown and thrust himself inside. She hadn't dared to complain. What good would it do? She had nowhere to run to.

When he was sure of her silence it became a weekly habit—sometimes twice or three times a week, depending on his mood.

After a while he stopped putting his hand over her mouth.

After a while—to her shame—she began looking forward to his nocturnal visits.

And then she got pregnant.

Aretha Mae was no fool—she knew if she mentioned it they'd throw her out, so she said nothing, merely bided her time, desperately taking hot baths, swigging gin when they were out, in hopes the baby growing in her belly would quietly go away.

Primo Angelo arrived in town at exactly the right time. He was a big handsome man with a cocksure swagger and a glint in his green eyes. A carpenter by trade, he was doing work on the new school building. Aretha Mae did everything in her power to seduce him. She flattered him, babied him, told him he was the most handsome man she'd ever seen, and refused to sleep with him.

What was a man to do? He married her and they moved to the trailer park—although she did not give up her job at the Brownings'.

Primo stopped working immediately. "I need my strength to make love to you," he told her. The man with the silver tongue and the lazy ass.

When she informed him she was pregnant he took off without so much as a fast goodbye. She was miserable for five minutes. Men— what could you expect? They were never faithful, never true.

When she had her baby, everyone believed her vanished husband was the father. But she knew the truth, and she hugged it to herself like precious gold. One day the information would pay off.

Now—finally—that day had come.

The bus reached her stop and she climbed off, weary but triumphant. Benjamin Browning had agreed to her terms. He'd promised to arrange the papers with his lawyer, and soon—for the first time in her life—she'd be secure.

Dr. Sheppard lived in a large comfortable house with a big garden and a sign hanging over the front door that read: COME ALL YE LITTLE SHEPHERDS AND GATHER HERE FOR SUSTENANCE AND COMFORT. Nick pounded on the door while Louise and Harlan stayed in the van with a steadily worsening Luke.

Nobody answered, so he pounded some more.

An upstairs window shot open and a white-haired old man in bright red pajamas leaned out. "What's all that din?" he shouted in a crotchety voice.

"Somebody's sick. Can we come in?" Nick shouted back.

"Now?" replied Dr. Sheppard, his surprise evident.

"No, tomorrow morning, jerk," Nick muttered under his breath.

By this time Louise was beside him. "Dr. Sheppard," she yelled. "It's me. Louise. From the drugstore. Remember? You gave me that internal examination a couple of months ago. Said I had a lovely pelvis."

She'd succeeded in getting his attention. "I'll be right down," he croaked.

"Dirty old geezer," Louise said disgustedly. "Stuck his finger up me like he was flippin' a pearl! Never again."

"You get the door open, I'll carry Luke inside," Nick said.

By the time he got back to the van Harlan was crying. "What's the matter, kid?" he asked.

"Is Luke gonna die?" Harlan whimpered, seeking assurance, tears rolling down his cheeks.

"No, he ain't gonna die," Nick assured him, gathering Luke up into his arms. "Don't think nothin' like that. You stay out here—he'll be fine."

He carried the small boy up to the house, not sure what was going to happen—he only knew it didn't look good.

Louise had the door open and was proceeding to charm Dr. Sheppard—a short man with hairy hands, a halo of white hair and big pop eyes. He was old and crusty and took a lot of charming.

"What's this?" he said, when Nick appeared with Luke in his arms.

"This child is sick," Louise said quickly. "Can you take a look at him, doc? *Please*."

"I'm off duty," the miserable old man said.

"I know." Louise kept her voice soft and persuasive. "But I figured you'd do us this one favor—what with Doc Marshall bein' away an' all, an' you bein' the only doctor left in town." She paused, giving him a seductive look. "I'm coming in to see you next week. I had those stomach cramps again, thought you could look me over."

Dr. Sheppard cheered up.

Louise continued to pour it on. "I guess I need another of those . . . uh . . . exams you're so good at giving. I felt so much better after the last time."

"Yes, yes," the old man said. "Bring the boy into the examining room."

She winked at Nick. He carried Luke into the examining room and laid him on the cold table.

The doctor bent down and peered at Luke. "This boy is black," he said indignantly.

So? Nick wanted to say. *What the fuck does that matter?*

"We thought he was too sick to drive to Ripley," Louise said quickly.

"That's where *black* people are supposed to go," Dr. Sheppard muttered bad-temperedly, rubbing his bulbous nose with the tip of his thumb. "I'm not supposed to look after coloreds."

"Hey—" Nick couldn't help himself. "It's the seventies, for God's sake, an' we ain't even in the South."

Dr. Sheppard turned to glare at him. "Who are you, young man? I've never seen you before."

"Thank God for that," Nick muttered, and then loud enough for the doctor to hear, "I'm his brother."

Dr. Sheppard's bushy eyebrows shot up. "His brother?"

"Just take a look at the kid, will you?"

Ten minutes later they were out of there. "Nothing wrong with the boy," Dr. Sheppard had said. "All he needs is a good night's sleep and an aspirin."

Nick didn't believe him, but what could he do? "How about that other doctor he was talking about—the one in Ripley?" he asked Louise.

She shrugged. "I dunno. Never heard of him. I'm sorry, I gotta get back to work. Dave's gonna be pissed, you know what he's like."

He dropped Louise off and began the drive to the trailer park. Maybe the old doctor was right—maybe all Luke needed was rest and an aspirin.

On the way home he spotted Aretha Mae trudging along the road. He swerved over to the side.

"What you doin' with your father's van, boy?" Aretha Mae asked sharply.

Quickly he explained about Luke. She jumped in the back, took one look at Luke and was as panicked as he was. "I told him not to play out in the snow," she fretted. "I told him he was gonna catch cold. He's got somethin' bad, I know it."

"Yeah," Nick agreed. "That's why I took him to see Dr. Sheppard."

"That dumb old fool—he's no good," she said, shaking her head in disgust. "He won't treat us—whatever the law says. We gotta take him to Ripley."

"The roads ain't clear yet. It took hours to get back earlier."

"We have t'go," Aretha Mae said obstinately.

"What about Primo? He don't know I've taken the van."

"Too bad," she said.

He shrugged. "Okay. Ripley it is."

He drove as fast as he could, considering the condition of the roads. Even so, it was midnight by the time they reached Ripley.

Aretha Mae directed him to a house in a rundown neighborhood, and when he got there she jumped out of the van and rang the bell.

An Indian woman in a sari answered the door. She didn't seem at all surprised to have patients arriving in the middle of the night.

"It's my child," Aretha Mae said. "He be real bad."

"Bring him in," the woman said graciously. "I'll get my husband."

Dr. Singh Amroc was a slightly built Indian man, totally bald with a thin black moustache. After a cursory examination of Luke he said,

"This boy has pneumonia. It's essential he be admitted to a hospital at once."

They all set off, crowding into the van, the doctor too.

On the way to the hospital Nick began thinking about Lauren. He hadn't called her, would she be mad? Girls were funny about things like phoning when you said you would—but he was sure that when he explained everything she'd understand.

He wondered if her parents had given her a hard time. He missed her already and couldn't wait to see her again.

At the hospital he sat in the waiting room with Harlan while the doctor and Aretha Mae filled out the forms to get Luke admitted.

Harlan stared at his half brother. "Thanks, Nick," he said solemnly. "You're my best friend."

"Hey—" He shrugged, embarrassed, "It was nothing."

Primo's rumbling stomach awoke him. Bleary-eyed, he groped for the large clock ticking away on the floor. It was late, very late, and where the hell was Aretha Mae?

He staggered to his feet, brushed a scurrying cockroach off the side of the bed and went outside, taking a piss in the nearby brush.

Then he lurched back inside, grabbed a can of beer and sat and brooded. After ten minutes he went outside again and kicked open the door of the kids' trailer. Nobody was around.

"Where the fuck *is* everybody?" he yelled. "Where the fuck is my dinner?"

He noticed his van was missing. "Goddamnit!" he muttered, making his way back to the main trailer. The bitch had taken his van and the kids. The bitch would pay for being home late. *Nobody* treated him this way. *Nobody* kept Primo Angelo waiting and got away with it.

Luke had to stay in the hospital.

"There ain't no way I'm leavin'," Aretha Mae said, her mouth set in a stubborn line. "No way at all."

"If you're stayin', we're stayin'," Nick said.

"No—you'd best get back. When Primo finds his van's missin' he'll be mad."

"I'm not goin' back without you and Luke."

"Yeah, me too, Ma," Harlan joined in.

"Suit yourself." She was too tired to argue.

"I know a cheap motel," Nick said. "We can all spend the night there."

"What'll we do about Primo?" Aretha Mae worried.

"I'll call Joey in the morning. He'll stop by the trailer an' tell him what's goin' on."

She nodded. "Good. Now you take Harlan to this motel while I stay here."

"Why don't we stay with you?"

She shook her head. "No. Don't want Harlan comin' down sick, too. You go rest up."

Reluctantly he got up. "We'll be back first thing tomorrow."

"You got money, boy?"

"Well . . . don't know if I've got enough."

"Here." She rummaged in her purse and counted out fifteen dollars in worn bills.

"Thanks," he said, pocketing the money. "We'll get back here early."

They left the hospital and drove straight to the motel. The man in the manager's office recognized him. "You here again?" he said, winking lewdly. "Must've been a good one."

Nick ignored the comment. "We'll be stayin' one night," he said, paying in advance.

He took Harlan into the room, settled him in front of the television and hurried to the pay phone. For a moment he stood in the ice-cold booth wondering if he should phone Lauren at this late hour. No way. It was even too late to contact Joey—his mother would be seriously pissed. Shit! There was nothing left to do except go to bed, he'd call everyone in the morning.

Harlan awoke at six a.m. "I got a bad feeling, my gut hurts," he whined.

Nick got out of bed and stretched. "Don't worry about it. Everything's gonna be fine."

Harlan shook his head. "No, it ain't, Nick. It ain't."

"Quit worryin' an' get dressed. We'll get to the hospital early."

Outside the wind was howling. Shivering, Nick pulled up the collar of his jacket, stuffed his hands in his pockets and ran over to the van. Harlan followed him and jumped in the passenger seat.

Five minutes later they were standing at the hospital reception desk. "Luke Angelo," Nick said.

The nurse consulted her admission book. "Ward five, fifth floor."

They took the elevator. At the nurses' station on the fifth floor Nick asked again, "We're here to see Luke Angelo."

The nurse glanced up. "Relative?" she inquired.

"Yeah. I'm, like . . . uh . . . his brother."

"The doctor is with Mrs. Angelo right now," the nurse said, all business. "Please take a seat."

"Uh, Luke . . . he's okay, right?"

"Take a seat."

They waited over ten minutes before Aretha Mae appeared, clutching her thin winter coat—a Brownings cast-off—around her.

Harlan ran down the corridor and threw himself at his mother.

Nick knew it before she said a word. He got up and walked slowly toward her. His throat was dry and his stomach churning.

Aretha Mae shook her head hopelessly. "He's gone," she said, her voice no more than a hoarse whisper. "My baby is dead."

Harlan let out a wail that could be heard from one end of the hospital to the other. It was a sound Nick would never forget.

23

"Did Nick call?" Every morning Lauren asked the same question, and every morning her parents gave her the same stupid answer. "It doesn't matter whether he did or not. You are *never* seeing him again."

"I don't care," she replied, her heart beating fast. "I just need to know."

"It makes no difference," her father said harshly.

"It makes a difference to me," she replied, wondering how she had ever imagined her father to be a kind and sensitive man.

"Then in that case he has *not* called you."

She didn't know whether they were telling the truth or not. She sat in her room and brooded. Did Nick consider her easy? Is sex all he'd wanted? *Oh, God, no! Please, God, no!*

They'd been so close and now they seemed so far apart. She knew he didn't have a phone, so she couldn't call him. Not that her parents would let her get within ten feet of a telephone. They had her trapped in the house, guarding her as if she was a maximum-security prisoner.

"What have I done that's so terrible?" she asked one day.

"You were engaged to one of the finest boys in town," her father replied, his face stony. "You should have taken into consideration that I was doing business with Stock's father before recklessly breaking off your engagement."

"I didn't realize it was a business arrangement," she muttered.

"You owed it to us to tell your family, not the whole town," her father said.

She couldn't believe they were being so mean. "I've never done anything to upset you in my life," she said. "No alcohol, drugs or any of the things some of the kids at school get into. All I did was borrow the family car, and you're punishing me like I'm a criminal."

Together—the perfect team—they said in unison, "You have to learn the hard way, Lauren, or you won't learn at all."

"What will happen when school starts?" she asked. "You can't watch over me every day then."

"When the new semester commences we hope you'll have learned your lesson," Phil said.

And what if I haven't? What if the first time I see Nick we run off together?

As if reading her mind her mother chimed in with, "If you see Nick Angelo at school, I want your solemn promise you'll have nothing to do with him."

She crossed her fingers behind her back. "Okay, Mother, if that makes you happy."

Yeah. Good little Lauren was learning to play the game their way —and it was their fault.

On her first day back she bumped into Meg on the way to history class.

"OhmyGod! OhmyGod!" Meg exclaimed excitedly. "I've been *desperate* to see you. I've called you *dozens* of times. I even came by your house and begged your mom. She wouldn't let me in. What is going *on?*"

"*You* tell *me*," Lauren said. "I've been held prisoner, cut off from everything."

Meg lowered her voice. "There's been rumors you were *pregnant* and had to have an abortion."

"Are you serious? Surely *you* know what happened?"

"You mean at the New Year's dance?"

"Right—when Stock hit Nick, broke his nose, and I drove him to the hospital in Ripley. I'm sure you heard we got stuck there over-night, the roads were closed and we couldn't get back. My parents were furious."

"Oh," Meg said, sounding disappointed. "Is that all?"

"Isn't that enough?"

Meg wanted to know more. "What happened with you and Nick?"

"Nothing," Lauren lied. "I was punished for absolutely nothing."

"Nick Angelo is the worst. How come you drove him to the hospi-tal? Stock's been so upset. Mack and I have tried to look after him but he's, like, heartbroken." Meg shook her head. "You treated him badly."

Lauren was incensed. "*I* treated *him* badly? How about the way *he* carried on?"

Meg continued as if she hadn't heard a word. "Throwing his ring at him and everything. *I* heard it was Nick who tried to attack *him* and *that's* why Stock broke his nose—he was only defending himself."

"That's not true."

"Yes, it is. Nick Angelo is an animal. Look what he did to me."

Lauren attempted to remain calm. "What *did* he do to you, Meg?"

"Practically raped me."

She had a strong desire to smack her friend's smug face. "Oh, and I suppose you didn't provoke it?"

"What do you mean?"

"It seems to me that every time you go out with a boy the same thing happens."

Meg flushed. "It certainly doesn't."

"I thought you were my friend," Lauren said sadly.

"And I thought you were a friend worth having," Meg replied, with a spiteful glare.

Miserably Lauren sat in class, her eyes searching the room for Nick. He failed to appear.

Shortly before lunch break she spotted Joey in the corridor and hurried over. "Hi. Can we talk?"

He gave her a dirty look. "Oh, *you* resurfaced, huh?"

"What does *that* mean?"

"It would've been nice if you'd called Nick after all that happened."

"After *what* happened?"

"His little brother dying and all."

She was genuinely shocked. *"What?"*

He could see she wasn't acting. "You didn't hear?"

"I've been grounded since New Year's."

Joey felt uncomfortable. "I'm sorry. Nick told me you wouldn't talk to him."

She wondered how much Joey knew. "Why would I avoid him?" she asked carefully.

"He called your house enough times. Your parents said you didn't want to speak to him."

"That was them talking—not me. Please, Joey, tell me what happened."

"His half brother got sick with pneumonia. Doc Sheppard refused to treat him, so they had to take him to another doctor in Ripley. The kid died in the hospital there."

"Oh, God! That's so awful."

"Yeah."

"Where *is* Nick? I have to see him."

"He won't be back in school."

"Why not?"

"He was thrown out on account of your boyfriend."

"You mean expelled?"

"Yeah. The Browning family didn't want him around—they put on the pressure. 'Course it didn't help that he smashed up the sign in front of Doc Sheppard's house, and threatened to beat the shit outta the old fart."

"He did?"

"Yeah, Cyndra went with him. The old fuck called the sheriff. Nick spent the night in the can. Cyndra wanted to join him—but I managed to persuade her it wasn't the coolest move in the world."

"Where is he now?" she asked, thinking about what he must have gone through.

"Workin' down at the garage full time. Old man Browning tried to stop that too—but George wouldn't listen. If the Brownings had their way they'd run him out of town."

"Can you take me there?"

"Sure, but if we get caught there'll be big trouble."

"Don't tell *me* about trouble."

"Okay. Meet me in the parking lot in five minutes."

"I'll be there."

"An' don't mention it to your big-mouthed girlfriend either. She's real tight with Stock an' all his buddies."

"I understand."

She hurried to her locker and grabbed her purse and jacket. On her way downstairs she ran straight into Stock and a group of his ever-present cronies. Their eyes met. The group went silent.

"Uh . . . hi," she said, trying to make the most of an awkward situation.

Stock's jaw tightened, his right eye twitched, his hand strayed toward his crotch. Then he totally ignored her—pushing by as if she didn't exist.

Okay with me. If that's the way you want it, Stock Browning, I can handle it.

Joey was waiting out in the parking lot, revving up his motorcycle. "Climb aboard," he said. "We'd better split before we get ourselves busted."

She jumped on the back of his bike and they took off. Whatever the consequences, she didn't care. She was on her way to see Nick, and that's all that mattered.

24

"Thanks, sweetie." The woman in the maroon Cadillac had enormous breasts stretching the confines of a tight pink sweater. She'd been in twice this week to gas up her car—not that she needed to, the second time he'd almost had an overflow at three gallons.

Nick strolled casually around the car. "Want me to check your oil an' water?" he asked.

"Why not, sweetie?"

While he was checking under the hood he noticed she was checking out her face in a flashy silver compact. The woman scrutinized first the eyes—heavily mascara'd and outlined in black. Next the nose—powder, powder. And lastly the lips—full, sexy lips glossed and ready for action. She had long reddish hair and wore a fur coat which did not succeed in covering her outstanding sweater-clad breasts. She was old, at least thirty. Nick was an expert at figuring women's ages.

"Who is she?" he'd asked George, the first time she came in.

"Never seen her before," George had said, chewing tobacco. "Illinois plates—must be visiting."

"You got a johnnie here?" the woman asked, snapping shut her compact.

"A what?"

"Little girls' room."

He pointed.

She got out of the car.

She was tall—which was fortunate, Nick thought, because with the pair she was carrying, falling flat on her face would otherwise be a distinct possibility. Her fur coat ended at the hip. Under it she wore a short skirt and thigh-high black patent leather boots.

"You from around here?" he asked, knowing she wasn't.

She ran her tongue across her front teeth. "Passing through on my way to civilization. Staying a week with my sister."

"Having fun?" He could have kicked himself. What kind of a dumb question was that? How could anyone have fun in Bosewell?

She looked him over slowly—seductive eyes raking him from top to bottom. "Nope," she said, sauntering off to the restroom.

George winked conspiratorially. "She's got the hots for you, boy. Better watch it! Didja get an eyeful of those gazumbas? Wouldn't mind a mouthful myself." George began to chuckle and wheeze.

A few weeks ago, Nick thought, this woman might have been a challenge. But now . . . who cared? All he was interested in was making money—plenty of money—and as soon as he'd saved five hundred bucks he was on his way out of this pisshole.

The woman had left her open purse on the front seat. He noticed her wallet poking out—crammed with bills. When she came back he pointed it out to her. "You shouldn't leave your purse open like that —it's askin' for trouble."

"Story of my life," she said, smiling laconically. "How was my oil?"

"Fine."

"I don't need anything?"

"You're perfect."

She handed him a credit card and he put it through the machine. Genevieve Rose. He'd already noticed the wedding ring—a fat band of diamonds.

"Where you from?" he asked, as she signed with a flourish.

"Chicago. Ever been there?"

"My friend has. His dad was a cop."

Another dumb remark. Jeez! What was the matter with him today?

"A cop, huh? The worst kind." She slipped him a five-buck tip and drove off without another word.

"Hey, she gave me a five," he told George.

"Frame it," George said. "It's the first an' last time you'll see a tip like that."

"Yeah." He went into the restroom and sniffed—her perfume lingered. He rinsed his face with cold water and noticed the mirror above the sink was still cracked, George said it wasn't worth having fixed. Peering at himself he gingerly touched his nose. It wasn't the same—it would never be the same—but it didn't look too bad. Not straight like before, slightly bent and rough-looking. But somehow it gave his face more character and certainly made him appear older than seventeen. Betty Harris said his broken nose gave his face a strength it hadn't had before.

He wasn't sure.

"When you're famous you can always have it fixed," she'd said.

Famous! Holy shit! For her to say a thing like that was a compliment indeed.

Betty Harris had turned out to be the one constant presence he could trust. Now that he no longer had school to contend with, he divided his time between work for money and work for pleasure. The long sessions with Betty were pure pain mixed with intense pleasure. Acting satisfied him in a way nothing else had. Since he was thirteen he'd always had sex to get lost in, but after Lauren, mindless sex did not hold the same appeal, so now he took all of his pent-up energy and channeled it into the roles Betty allowed him to play. Hamlet was a particular favorite, and Stanley in *Streetcar*. Oh, yeah, he could really let rip—pouring every emotion into the highly charged complex characters.

Betty was impressed. She praised him constantly, and her encouragement really helped. When he'd got himself thrown into jail for messing up the outside of Dr. Sheppard's house, Betty had put up his bail. He'd been charged with defacing property. If he'd had his way he'd have defaced the old white-haired gnome of a doctor from here to eternity. But for that old man, Luke might still be alive.

After the initial shock Aretha Mae had reverted to her usual stoic self. Primo was unaffected—Luke hadn't meant anything to him. Cyndra was sad. And Harlan inconsolable. Night after night Nick listened to the kid sob himself to sleep. A few times Cyndra took

Harlan into her bed and comforted him with stories and songs. Sometimes Nick joined in. The three of them formed a bond. For the first time since his mother died he really felt he had a family.

Primo had tried to cause trouble over him borrowing the van. For once Aretha Mae shut him up with an acid tongue-lashing he wouldn't forget in a hurry. Primo had slunk off like a beaten dog.

When they'd thrown him out of school he hadn't bothered telling his father. What was the point? George gave him a permanent job at the garage, and every buck he made he put away—stashing it under his mattress—watching the pile of bills grow larger every week.

As for Lauren—he'd shut her out of his mind. When he didn't hear from her . . . when there was never any message, he'd felt a deep sense of betrayal. He'd opened himself up to another human being and look where it had gotten him—exactly nowhere. Never again. Love—you could shove it.

Emerging from the restroom he bumped into George, who said, "You got a visitor. Use the office."

"Who?" he asked, but George was off doing something else.

He entered the small, cramped office and there she was—Lauren—perched on the edge of the old warped desk, looking as beautiful as ever.

"Hi." Her soft voice was almost a whisper.

Jeez! Who needed this? "What're *you* doin' here?" he asked roughly.

She got off the desk and came toward him. "I made Joey bring me."

"Good for him."

"I came as soon as I could."

"A few weeks late," he said coldly, "but I s'pose you were busy."

"My parents wouldn't let me out. I had no idea what happened." She moved closer. "Nick, I'm so sorry to hear about your brother. I didn't know. I thought I'd see you in school today and when I didn't . . ." She trailed off, shrugging helplessly. "You've got to forgive me—it wasn't my fault."

It sounded logical. Only why had both her parents sounded so sincere when they'd informed him she had no wish to speak to him and would he kindly stop bothering her? Still . . . parents . . . those fuckers could lie better than anyone.

He made one last effort to back away. "Hey, I'm cool. You don't have to feel sorry for me."

Her eyes filled with tears. "Sorry for you? Is that what you think?"

"Listen, it's—"

"I *love* you," she interrupted, her voice breaking. "I honestly love you."

Her words melted the ice, and suddenly she was in his arms, soft and sweet-smelling. There was no way he could resist her. There was no way he wanted to.

They talked for over an hour, clearing everything up, and by the time she left, they'd worked things out. Joey would be their liaison— he'd deliver notes and set up meetings.

"One of these days I'll talk my parents into meeting you," Lauren promised, "and then we can be together as much as we want."

Yeah, he thought. Don't bet on it. Parents and him—not a good mix.

She kissed him before leaving. She wasn't even gone and he couldn't wait to see her again.

"Soon," she promised.

He wasn't so sure it would be as easy as she thought.

25

And that's how they handled it—as carefully and secretly as possible. Of course, there's no such thing as a secret once more than two people know. Joey knew, and Cyndra and Harlan. And George—who confided in Louise and Dave.

As the months passed and they grabbed furtive meetings here and there, Lauren began to show the strain of lying to her parents. She'd become an expert at inventing elaborate excuses that wouldn't rouse their suspicions, but still it was tough.

Nick felt it too. He didn't want to pressure her, but being with her in short sharp bursts was doing him no good. He wasn't a kid, and he was beginning to think he couldn't take one more evening of groping and fumbling—he needed more. He needed to be as close to her as two people can get.

As the weather improved and spring took root he came up with the idea of bringing her to the trailer. Harlan was at school, Cyndra at work, and Primo never stirred.

The trailer was hardly the ideal place—but it was a lot better than the old abandoned car in the back of the gas station where they'd been forced to spend most of their time together.

He set it up, arranging for Joey to bring her to meet him at the gas station.

She was excited about the plan, and on the appointed day she told her parents she was doing community service after school and would be home later than usual.

The day of their meeting dawned crisp and sunny. Lauren had settled into a stilted polite relationship with her parents. They thought she'd forgotten all about Nick Angelo—the bad boy who'd come to town and disrupted her life. Little did they know.

She left for school at the usual time, entered through the front, avoided roll call and exited through the back. She knew she was living dangerously, skipping school was full of risks—the wrong word in the wrong place and she could be busted, then what?

The risk was worth it.

Fortunately she didn't run into anyone likely to question her. The close friendship she'd had with Meg was long over. Meg was part of Stock's group now, and Stock refused to speak to her.

How her life had changed over the last few months—and yet she was happier than she'd ever been.

Joey was revving up his bike in the parking lot, ready to go. "Come on," he said. "Jump aboard an' let's get the fuck outta here."

At first it was awkward—the trailer being such a dump and all. Nick had tried to clean it up—shoving all the clothes into a corner, smoothing out the worn blanket on his mattress, but there wasn't much he could do to improve twelve square feet of space shared by three untidy people.

He could see Lauren was shocked by the shabby conditions, but she covered it well.

"Okay, so it's a pisshole," he said with a cocky grin. "But who promised you the White House?"

She pretended to look solemn. "I'll have to leave then."

"Yeah?"

"Maybe."

"Oh, really?"

"I think so."

"Come here."

"Why?"

"You know why."

He fell on the mattress, pulling her down beside him. They started to kiss, slowly at first—savoring each other's lips—and then faster until they both wanted more.

He moved his hands under her sweater, feeling her breasts. "I've missed you so much," he murmured, working his way under her bra, trying to concentrate on something other than the feeling he was experiencing.

"You too," she managed.

He pulled her sweater over her head and unhooked her bra, bending to kiss her breasts—his tongue moving slowly from nipple to nipple.

She sighed—a long-drawn-out sound.

It was too much. The moment of no return was upon them before either of them had time to stop and think, and even though she'd planned to ask him to wear a rubber . . . who cared? It didn't matter. Nothing mattered except the fusing of their two bodies.

He was more aggressive than the time before—entering her with a burst of energy, riding her like his life depended on it. And now that she knew what to expect, she responded with a wildness and abandon she had not known she possessed.

Together they rocked the world—riding the roller coaster until it peaked on the highest point of all, pausing for several mind-blowing seconds before cruising smoothly all the way to stop.

"Oh . . . jeez!" he exclaimed. "That was the best ever."

"It was?"

"It was."

"Me too."

"C'mere, me too."

And she curled into his arms wet and sticky and fell into a blissful sleep.

When she awoke it was afternoon and he was lying on his back beside her, hands behind his neck. Slowly she traced the contours of his chest with her tongue—tentatively at first because she wasn't sure if he'd like it. He obviously loved it—so she really got into it, licking and sucking, teasing him with little love bites.

"Where'd you learn t'do this?" he asked, groaning.

"Hmm . . . wouldn't *you* like to know?"

"Yeah." He reached for her breasts but she brushed his hand away. "I think I would."

"Lie back and enjoy it," she said, leisurely traveling down his body until she reached his hard penis.

"Lauren, you don't have to—"

"Yes, I do," she whispered, teasing him with her tongue. "Because I want to."

By late afternoon they both knew they had to make a move. "You'd better get dressed," he said, wishing they could stay in bed forever.

"Uh . . . where's the bathroom?"

"I don't know how t'break this to you, but we ain't got one."

She thought he was joking and laughed.

"No, seriously—we don't."

"No bathroom?"

"Sorry."

"Where do you shower?"

"Down at the gas station. It's not exactly a shower—but I don't think you want the details."

She felt bad that she'd asked, she didn't want to embarrass him.

"Maybe we can come here every week," he said, getting up and pulling on his jeans. "Just you an' me—shut out the world."

"I can't take too many days off school."

"Yeah. An' I suppose George wouldn't be too happy if I ducked work on a regular basis."

"Nick . . ." She stared at him, her face composed and serious. "What if I got—"

"Whoa—*no way!* I pulled out in time."

She was relieved. "You did?"

" 'Course I did. Wouldn't risk it."

"Thank goodness."

"Hey, you gotta learn to trust me. You know that I . . . uh . . . ."

"Say it!"

He grinned. "Love ya."

She smiled and softly touched his face. "Yes, I know."

. . .

"How was school today?"

"Huh?" Lauren tried to squeeze past her mother, who was standing in the front hall blocking the stairs.

"School," Jane Roberts repeated.

If Lauren wasn't so intent on getting upstairs she would have noticed a tenseness in her mother's voice.

"Oh, the usual—boring math, dull history. And P.E. *I hate* P.E. In fact the showers were out of order—I feel all sweaty. Maybe I'll take a shower now."

Jane did not budge. "Anything unusual happen?"

Warning bells rang in Lauren's head. Something had gone on at school that she didn't know about.

Gotta play it smart, Roberts. Wouldn't do to get busted.

"The thing is, Mother," she said quickly, "I wasn't going to worry you—but after P.E. I didn't feel so good. The nurse suggested I lie down for a while."

"Really?" Jane's tone did not warm up. Usually she would have been full of concern.

There was a short uncomfortable silence. Since her mother didn't seem inclined to move, she decided to head for the kitchen. But Jane followed her in—there was no escape.

Opening the refrigerator she grabbed a carton of milk and turned around to find her mother staring at her with cold accusing eyes.

She couldn't take it anymore. "Is something wrong?"

"Why do you ask?"

She shrugged, reaching for a glass. "I don't know. You seem kind of . . . funny."

She wondered if she could make a dash past Jane and get upstairs without further questioning.

"Lauren," her mother said in slow, measured tones. "We've always brought you up to be a good girl. Truthful at all times."

Oh, God, something was definitely up.

She tried to look innocent. "Yes, Mother?"

"You weren't at school today, were you?"

Now she had a choice. Did she continue to lie and take a chance? Or did she tell the truth?

Dear Mother, I spent the day in bed having sex with Nick Angelo.

Did you, dear? How nice.

Gee, thanks, Mom, you're so understanding.

She bit her bottom lip—there was only one way to go. "I told you, I *was* at school, but I didn't feel good."

"The school secretary phoned to inform me you have probably been playing truant on and off for the last few months."

She managed to look amazed. "What?"

"Apparently you've been absent on several occasions with various excuses. A sore throat, a cold, a visit to the dentist. And all your excuse notes were supposedly signed by me. Miss Adams is no fool. Eventually she became suspicious—especially as this morning you were seen leaving on the back of a motorcycle."

Oh, God, here it comes. She was in deep trouble.

"We've always trusted you, Lauren, and now this. Your father is on his way home."

Naturally.

"It's *your* fault," she blurted out, her cheeks reddening. "You can't stop me from seeing Nick. We're in love."

"In love?" Jane laughed derisively. "You're sixteen years old, what do *you* know about love?"

More than you think, she wanted to yell out. *More than you'll ever know.*

Words came tumbling out. "Don't you understand? Nick doesn't have anybody except me. I can't turn my back on him like everyone else. I can't do it."

"You'll do exactly what your father and I say you will."

Dread swept over her. This was no idle threat. Somehow she was going to have to deal with it.

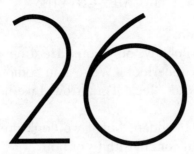

"We're outta here," Joey said.

"Huh?" Nick slid from under the Lincoln he was servicing. "Whatcha talkin' about?"

"I mean we're leavin' town, me and Cyndra."

"You don't have enough money," Nick said, wiping oil off his hands.

"Sure we do," Joey replied. "I been workin' two jobs, remember? And Cyndra's been doin' time at the factory. We've had it with this town."

Joey and Cyndra—the two people he was closest to were taking off. Wasn't it bad enough that he couldn't see Lauren anymore?

"Anyway," Joey said, lighting up a butt. "We did some talkin', an' we figured if you wanted to come with us it's okay."

"Where you plannin' on goin'?"

Joey shrugged. "Chicago. I got relatives there, friends, people who'd put us up until we find a place."

"You told your mother?"

Joey dragged on the butt, inhaling every last bit of smoke into his lungs. "Are you shittin' me? I'll leave her a note. She'll freak whatever I say."

"How about Cyndra?"

"She ain't tellin' nobody, only you." He dropped the butt on the ground, crushing it underfoot. "We're goin' tomorrow."

Nick shook his head. "Jeez! Tomorrow! Like how about givin' me notice?"

"I know it's kinda sudden, but if we don't do it now we'll never make the move. You comin' with us or not?"

He was torn. Sure he wanted to go, but how could he leave Lauren? Even though he hadn't seen her for six weeks he still loved her. It wasn't her fault she'd been grounded, it was his—he should have made certain they were more careful.

Things were a mess. They'd really blown it. Her parents had gone crazy. Phil Roberts had even turned up at the trailer. He'd listened as Phil attempted to confront Primo—like the fat slob gave a shit. Some fucking joke.

"I want your assurance your son will have nothing more to do with my daughter," Phil Roberts had said, standing stiffly at the door.

"What in hell ya talkin' about? Get the fuck outta here," Primo had replied, a true gentleman.

Phil Roberts had retreated fast.

Nick unbuttoned his greasy overalls. "I dunno what t'say, Joey. I'm real tempted."

"Look . . . I understand it ain't easy."

"I can't run out on Lauren without seein' her."

"Whyn't you write her a letter? Tell her you'll be back for her when you got the bucks."

"Like when?"

"What am I, a fortune-teller? Who knows? But you're sure not securin' any future for the two of you hangin' around here."

Joey was right. If he took off he could do anything he wanted, start a new life—anything—and when Lauren was eighteen she could tell her parents to screw off and they'd be together.

"Let me think about it," he said, peeling off his overalls.

"Don't think—do," Joey encouraged. " 'Cause I ain't plannin' on endin' up here—an' neither is Cyndra. We're on our way, Nick—an' if you're smart you'll come with us."

He thought about it all day, and the more he thought, the more appealing the prospect became. Take off. Say goodbye to Primo, Bosewell, all the shit that plagued his life. Jeez, it was tempting.

Then he began thinking about Harlan. How could he dump the kid? Especially with Cyndra leaving too.

Hey, man, what are you, a baby-sitter? Think about yourself for a change.

He needed to see Lauren, but that wasn't possible. Writing her a letter seemed like a good idea. He could explain everything so she'd understand. That way she wouldn't think he'd run off without her.

After work he stopped by the drugstore. Louise greeted him, her usual cheery self, "What's up, Nick?"

"I need a big favor."

"What else is new?"

"Can you see Lauren gets a letter if I leave it with you?"

"You mean hand it to her when she comes in?"

"Yeah. Only not if she's with her mother."

"No problem."

"Lend me a pen an' paper, I gotta write it."

As obliging as ever, Louise set him up with paper and pen and he hunched in a corner booth trying to figure out what to write.

Dear Lauren, I'm going, but I'll be back for you. It's dumb for me to hang around since we can't see each other anyway, so I'll keep in touch and you'll always know where I am.

That didn't exactly cut it. He tried again.

Dearest Lauren.

Too flowery. And once more . . .

Lauren—I miss you so much that every night when I go to sleep all I can think about is you. I see your face. I feel your body. I smell you.

Nah, that sounded rude. He started again, and finally got the words right. Then he sealed the note in an envelope and wrote her name on it, adding a large PRIVATE! and URGENT! on the front. Now all he had to do was tell Joey he was going with them.

As he left the drugstore, Stock Browning drove up and got out of his car with a couple of his cronies. He swaggered past Nick, seeing this as a perfect opportunity to show off—his favorite sport. "Smell something, guys?" Stock said with a rude snigger. "Like an open garbage can?"

His friends guffawed.

Nick had been waiting for this ever since his broken nose. "Hey, man," he countered. "How come y'always travel with bodyguards? Scared shitless you might run into me, huh?"

"Into *you*?" Stock smirked, showing off for his pals. "I squash white trash like you under my feet."

"Yeah . . . well, they're sure big enough."

"What did you say, *jerk*?"

"You heard me, *asshole*."

Stock thought he'd be a big man in front of his friends. Since he'd creamed Nick once, he figured it was easy. He turned toward him, his hefty right arm raised, ready to throw a punch.

This time Nick was ready. "Fuck you," he spat out, kneeing Stock in the balls, following up with a sharp kick in the shin.

Stock let out a roar of pain.

Nick chopped him across the neck, and before anyone knew what was happening Stock was sprawled on the ground.

"Hey," Nick said, prodding him with the tip of his sneaker, "I guess I owed you that." Turning his back he walked away.

Cyndra was in the trailer when he got home, busy cramming everything she owned into a small backpack.

"Joey told you, huh?" she said, rolling up her favorite sweater and squeezing it in.

"Yeah."

"What have you decided?"

"I'm gonna come."

She jumped up, threw her arms around his neck and kissed him. "I'm real happy, Nick."

"So am I."

They grinned at each other. It had taken time, but they'd finally formed an alliance.

When Harlan came home he immediately knew something was up. "Where're you goin'?" he asked Cyndra, his big eyes accusing.

"Nowhere," she said, unable to look at him.

"We gotta tell him," Nick warned her in a low voice.

"Look, I love him as much as you do, but there's no way we can drag a kid along. I know my mom—she'll get used to me splittin'— but if we take Harlan, she'll send the cops after us."

"We can't just walk out on him."

She stared at Nick, sour-faced. "If we tell him, he'll run straight to Aretha Mae."

"Not if he makes us a promise."

"What's goin' on?" Harlan asked, edging nearer.

"C'mere, kid," Nick said, patting his mattress. "Howdja like to have this trailer all to yourself? You're gettin' older now, you can bring girls here, throw wild parties, huh?"

Harlan's eyes filled with tears. He'd known it was bad news. "You an' Cyndra goin' away, ain'tcha?"

"Yeah—we gotta go," Nick said. "But it ain't that bad."

Cyndra joined in. "One of these days I'll come back for you. That's a promise."

Harlan shook his head. "No, you won't."

"Yes, I *will*," she insisted. "Wanna bet?"

"I'll take the bet," Nick said. "An' if she don't, *I* will. How's that?"

Harlan was unconvinced. He wiped away his tears with the back of his hand and tried to pretend it didn't matter.

Nick felt bad—but what could he do? He'd made a decision and he intended to stick to it.

The next morning dawned exceptionally bright and clear. Since it was payday the plan was for everybody to go to work, pick up their checks and meet around six. Joey told his mother he would be away for the weekend. Cyndra told Aretha Mae the same thing. Unfortunately Primo overheard and launched himself into a sitting position. "Where you goin'?" he demanded, as if he had a right to know.

"None of your business," Cyndra replied sharply, hating the sight of him.

Aretha Mae sensed something going on. She pulled her daughter to one side and said in a hoarse whisper, "You got money comin'. Real money."

Cyndra was surprised. "I have?"

"Mr. Browning—he came through."

"Why?" Cyndra asked suspiciously.

" 'Cause I told him he hadda do what's right."

"I thought you didn't believe me."

"Maybe I did, maybe I didn't. It don't matter—he owes you."

"How much money?" Cyndra asked quickly.

"We'll talk about it next week," Aretha Mae said.

"Why not now?"

"Now's not the time."

On their way to work Cyndra told Nick about the conversation. "She knows," she said, nervously biting her thumbnail. "That's why she's telling me 'bout this money now. Whyn't she tell me before?"

He shrugged. "Dunno. Why is old man Browning givin' you money anyway?"

"It's a long story," she said, clamming up.

He didn't push it; she'd tell him when she was ready.

Now that he'd made the decision to leave he was impatient, although he did want to take the time to say goodbye to Betty Harris. She'd been good to him, and he owed her that.

Since leaving the Brownings, Aretha Mae had been working over at the canning plant. It was a tougher job than maid's work, but at least it was a job. She hadn't told Primo she'd quit the Brownings, it was none of his damn business. Taking Primo back had been a mistake. She'd thought she might enjoy having a man around again, but what did he give her? Pure nothing.

Benjamin Browning had kept his word. He'd had no choice really —he couldn't risk Aretha Mae revealing him for the pervert he was. She'd banked the five thousand dollars he'd handed over in cash. What a fine day that had been!

At first she hadn't planned on telling Cyndra about the money—it was there for an emergency. But that morning she'd had a funny feeling when Cyndra said goodbye. The girl was up to something— and that's why she'd mentioned the money. She didn't want her daughter doing anything foolish—like running off with Joey Pearson. A girl with Cyndra's looks could do far better than him.

On Fridays Aretha Mae worked a half day. Lately she'd been meeting Harlan after school, taking him down Main Street and treating him to ice cream. They were both lonesome since Luke's death.

She thought of Luke often, and her heart was filled with sadness. Poor Luke . . . poor baby . . . he'd never had a chance.

Harlan was standing outside school when she arrived. She tried to take his hand but he pulled away from her.

"How ya doin', baby?" she asked, thinking what a fine-looking boy he was.

"Don' call me that, Mama." Harlan glanced around, making sure none of his schoolmates had heard.

"Gonna buy you ice cream," Aretha Mae promised.

Harlan's heart was heavy. He didn't want ice cream—he wanted God to bring Luke back. And maybe at the same time God could persuade Cyndra and Nick to stay.

Betty Harris wasn't surprised. "I knew you'd be on your way one of these days," she said, inviting Nick into her living room. "I didn't realize it would be so soon."

"There's nothing for me to hang around here for," he explained, flopping down on her overstuffed couch. "I gotta get away from my old man before I end up like him."

"What makes you think that would happen?" Betty asked.

" 'Cause if I stay anywhere near him I ain't got no chance."

"And you imagine you'll have a chance in Chicago?"

"Why not? It's a big city."

"Big cities can be cruel places," she said quietly. "You're young and good-looking. I'm sure you'll get plenty of offers—perhaps not always the ones you expect."

"I can take care of myself," he said edgily.

"I know that." She sighed, thinking how vulnerable he was—in spite of his tough exterior. "I'll miss you, Nick. Teaching you has been a wonderful experience, you're really a talented boy. You have a natural ability to become whatever character you're portraying." She hesitated before giving him what she considered the ultimate compliment. "Sometimes you remind me of a young James Dean."

He laughed, slightly embarrassed. "Hey, let's not get carried away or maybe I won't go."

Betty Harris watched him, her expression serious. "If people see you, if you get the right opportunities . . . I shouldn't encourage you, because acting is the most difficult profession in the world." She sighed again. "You *do* know that most actors are out of work most of their lives, don't you?"

"I gotta take the chance," he said, wishing she'd cut out the negative shit.

She nodded wisely. "Yes, that's the right attitude. Positive thinking. Wait here a minute."

She left the room and he got up and paced around. He loved being in Betty's living room, it was so warm and comfortable, a real home. There were photographs in silver frames and stacks of interesting books. God, how he wished he'd been encouraged to read as a child. He hadn't even known what a book was until his first day of school.

He picked up a picture of Betty in a white lace gown, her hair tumbling in soft curls around her youthful face.

"I was pretty, wasn't I?" she said, coming back into the room and startling him.

"You still are," he replied gallantly.

"So young and so smart. There'll always be a woman to look after you."

"That's not what I want."

"I know." She smiled and handed him a padded envelope.

"What's in it?" he asked, weighing it from hand to hand.

"Something I want you to have," she said earnestly.

"If it's money I can't take it."

"It's not."

"Can I open it?"

"Go ahead."

He tore the envelope open. It was Betty's precious signed copy of *A Streetcar Named Desire*.

"Betty . . . Jeez, this is great."

"Good. I want you to have it."

He tucked the book under his arm. "Betty, I gotta tell you . . . you've been so good t'me, I'll always remember you."

"I'll remember you too, Nick. Take care of yourself." Impulsively she stepped forward and hugged him. He hugged her back, tightly. Betty represented his last vestige of security and he was going to miss her and their intense sessions.

When he left her house he did so without a backward glance. It was time to move on. His new life was just beginning.

They met at six o'clock on Friday night—excited, maybe a little bit frightened, but none of them showed it.

Joey had the trip all planned. The last bus to Ripley, and then they'd hop a freight train all the way to Kansas City, and from there —Chicago.

The three of them stared at one another.

"This is it!" Joey said.

"Goodbye, Bosewell," Cyndra said.

"I ain't comin' back till I've made it," Nick said confidently. "And I *will* make it. Then I'll come back for Lauren. Bet on it."

27

Every morning Lauren awoke with the same blank feeling. As soon as she opened her eyes she felt a dull ache of despair, and there was nothing she could do about it.

She'd begun to hate her parents. Walking into the kitchen and having breakfast with them was an effort. Sitting at the table and listening to their inane conversation. Didn't they realize they were killing her inside? Didn't they realize they were mean-spirited and unrelenting and, above all, wrong?

She thought about Nick all the time and in her heart she knew she had to see him. But how? That was the big question: *How?*

Every day her father took her to school and her mother met her afterward, driving up in the family station wagon, giving her no chance to escape. This had been going on for six weeks—ever since she'd been caught.

"When are you going to trust me?" she asked one day.

"When your father and I feel that we can," her mother replied with a pious expression.

There was no point in pursuing it. Trying to change their opinion of Nick was useless.

Today it was Monday, and Nick was on her mind more than ever. She walked over to her bedroom window and gazed out. The sun blazed hot and steady—unseasonably so. Downstairs she could hear her mother calling out, "Lauren! Breakfast is ready."

Soon she would have to sit in the car next to her father as he dropped her off at school. Delivered and collected. And she knew they checked with the school secretary every day to make sure she hadn't taken off.

Listlessly she wandered downstairs, ate the breakfast her mother had prepared—picking at the food with absolutely no appetite at all —and collected her books.

Phil Roberts appeared five minutes later. Was it her imagination, or did the atmosphere between her parents seem tense? They hardly seemed to talk anymore. She was sure she was responsible. It had to do with the fact that her father had not concluded the insurance deal with Benjamin Browning, therefore her mother had not received the social and financial boost she'd expected, and this had obviously put a strain on their relationship.

Too bad. It was nothing compared to what she was going through.

"It's hot today," Phil grumbled, struggling into his jacket and grabbing a slice of toast on his way through the kitchen.

"The weather report says it will be hotter than yesterday," Jane remarked.

Phil did not look in her direction. He walked into the hall and examined himself in the mirror, reaching up to pull out a strand of gray hair. "I'll be home late tonight," he called out, picking up his briefcase.

Jane did not respond. She slammed dishes into the sink and ran the water.

On the way to school Lauren decided to open up a conversation. "Daddy, can we talk?" she began, determined to get through to him.

"Not today, Lauren," he said, his eyes fixed on the road ahead. "I'm not in the mood."

"When *will* you be in the mood?"

"Stop bothering me."

Her life was breaking into little pieces and all her father could say was "Stop bothering me." Once she'd felt she could go to him with any problem, now there was a cold war between them. Didn't he care that he was driving her away?

When he dropped her off she didn't even bother saying goodbye.

Dawn Kovak lingered near the lockers. She and Dawn were not exactly close friends, but Dawn greeted her as if they were. "Did you hear what Nick did to Stock?" Dawn asked.

Lauren was immediately alert. "What?"

Dawn was determined to draw it out. "You mean you haven't heard?"

"No. Are you going to tell me or not?"

Dawn smoothed down her tight skirt. "No need to get edgy."

"I'm not edgy. If you have something to tell me, go ahead."

"Well, from what I hear, Nick knocked Stock on his ass." Dawn couldn't help giggling.

Lauren waited to hear more. "Are you sure?"

"It happened outside the drugstore. Stock was on his way in with a couple of guys, and Nick was on his way out. They got into some kinda beef and Nick creamed him. Funny, huh?"

Even though she was dying to hear all the details Lauren attempted to stay cool. "Is . . . is Nick all right?"

"To tell you the truth," Dawn replied matter-of-factly, "me and Nick—we don't see each other anymore."

Lauren nodded. "Oh."

"Look," Dawn said, suddenly sympathetic, "I got the message about how he feels about you. I wouldn't interfere with that."

Lauren felt tears sting her eyelids. Nobody had spoken to her about Nick before, there wasn't anyone she could confide in. "My parents won't allow me to see him," she said miserably. "I don't know what to do."

Dawn looked suitably concerned. "Yeah, Joey told me. Listen," she added jauntily, "parents are a pain—maybe they'll change their minds."

Lauren shook her head. "Not my parents." She paused for a moment. "I feel so bad about everything. It's my fault Nick got kicked out of school. I mean, if it wasn't for me . . ."

"Don't sweat it. He's happy working down at the gas station, beats school any day. And it's *not* your fault. Stock's the one that had his parents do the dirty."

"I know you're right, but sometimes I wake up in the morning and all I want to do is run away."

Dawn nodded understandingly. "We all get that feeling."

"Really?"

"Sure. It's natural."

A couple of girls rushed past on their way to class. "C'mon, Lauren, you'll be late," one of them called out.

She hesitated for a moment. "What are you doing for lunch today?"

Dawn was surprised. "Who? Me?"

"I don't see anybody else standing here."

"What I normally do. Hang out. Why? You wanna eat with me?"

"I'd like it if we could talk some more," Lauren said.

Dawn seemed pleased. "So would I."

After dropping Lauren off, Phil drove straight to his office. Before going upstairs he stopped in at the hardware store and picked up the new kitchen scissors Jane had ordered.

Kitchen scissors, he thought grimly. She's probably going to stab me to death.

He collected them in the morning because he knew by the time he was ready to go home the last thing he'd be thinking about was running an errand for his wife.

Upstairs he unlocked his office door and entered. Eloise, his secretary, had not yet arrived. The place smelled stuffy and humid. He threw open the windows and settled behind his desk, thinking that perhaps he should have allowed Lauren to talk to him in the car. It wasn't right, this distance between them. If things were different at home maybe it would be easier for him to communicate with his daughter, but there was so much tension between him and Jane that he didn't seem to have the time to deal with anything else.

He considered calling Benjamin Browning. They'd been almost ready to conclude a business deal when Lauren had broken her engagement; after that, he'd been unable to reach him.

The hell with it! Picking up the phone he dialed Benjamin's office before he changed his mind.

A secretary answered, cool and efficient. "Who may I say is calling?"

"Phil Roberts."

"Just one moment, Mr. Roberts, I'll see if he's available." A count of ten. "I'm sorry, Mr. Roberts, Mr. Browning is tied up in a meeting. May I take a message?"

"Yes, I've called several times. I need to speak to him as soon as possible. Can he return my call."

"I'll see Mr. Browning receives the message. I'm sure he'll get back to you."

Yes, I'm sure he will, Phil thought sourly.

Harlan told Aretha Mae he had a sore throat.

"Is it bad?" she asked.

"It feels real bad," Harlan lied.

"Where's your sister?" Her see-all eyes searched the empty trailer.

"She ain't back yet," Harlan said.

Aretha Mae fixed him with a steely stare, daring him to tell a fib. "Is she comin' back?"

He refused to meet her stare. "I dunno."

Aretha Mae screwed up her face, knowing perfectly well Cyndra wasn't coming back. She'd known it on Friday when the girl had come to her with some story about going away for the weekend.

She started to poke around the trailer—all of Cyndra's favorite things were gone, and Nick's too. So he'd run off as well. She wondered if she should tell Primo. No. She'd wait and see if he noticed his only son was missing—it would probably take him weeks—that's how much he cared.

In a way she didn't mind now that she knew Nick was with Cyndra. At least he'd keep a watchful eye on her, and maybe the two of them together could forge a better life for themselves.

"It's okay," she told Harlan. "You can stay home."

He was delighted, he hadn't thought he'd get away with it. Harlan never told anybody about how bad school was, the names they called him—"nigger" and "dirt poor" and "stinking bastard." He'd gotten used to it—he'd even gotten used to defending himself when they beat him up.

As soon as Aretha Mae left for work he sneaked into her trailer to see if he could scrounge some food. Primo was in his usual position, fast asleep with the television blaring. Harlan noticed his mouth was wide open and he couldn't help wondering if anything ever crawled in. Stifling a chuckle he crept over to the refrigerator and peered inside. He spotted a chicken leg and without considering the consequences grabbed it and hurriedly slipped out of the trailer before he was discovered.

Primo heard the door bang shut and woke up. He sat up, scratching his stomach. Even though it was early it was goddamn hot—he could feel the sticky sweat trickling down his body.

He got up, went to the door and stepped outside. A skinny mutt growled at him. He picked up a beer can and hurled it at the mangy animal.

Lately Primo found himself getting restless. He'd never liked staying in one place for long. Aretha Mae might be a good woman, but he was bored. After a while, being with one woman always bored him. Maybe the time had come to move on—after all, there was a whole country out there, and plenty of other women who'd be only too happy to take him in. He was still a fine-looking man. Yeah, fine-looking *and* a stud. What more could any woman ask?

Continuing to scratch his belly he headed for the outhouse and relieved himself.

When he emerged he caught Harlan sitting on the steps of his trailer chewing on a chicken leg. "Whaddaya starin' at, boy?"

Harlan lowered his eyes. "Nothin'."

"Don't give me that nothin' crap. How come ya ain't in school?"

Harlan didn't look up. "I ain't feelin' good," he muttered.

Aretha Mae and her chickenshit kids—they were always getting sick. Except Cyndra. His daughter. Now, she was a real nice-looking girl. If she wasn't his own flesh and blood he would certainly consider bedding her down. She needed an experienced older man who could teach her a thing or two.

"Wanna take a ride?" he asked Harlan.

The boy's eyes widened. Primo had never spoken to him before, let alone offered him a ride. "Where to?" he asked suspiciously.

"Into town, unless you got a better idea."

"Nope."

"Okay. Hop in."

Primo wondered why he was being so generous allowing the kid to tag along.

Because there was nothing to do in Bosewell, that's why. It was a one-horse hicksville town. No decent bar, no dancing girls, no nothing.

A new thought began nagging inside his head. If he decided to leave Bosewell, would he have to take Nick with him?

Nah, why should he? The boy was old enough and ugly enough to manage on his own. Besides, Aretha Mae seemed to have taken a shine to him—let *her* have the responsibility for a while.

Not that he was taking off today. Right now he was riding into town only to stock up on beer and pretzels. He'd leave the following weekend—right after Aretha Mae came home with her paycheck. There was nothing to stop him from borrowing it.

He'd leave in the middle of the night, that way he'd be a couple of hundred miles away before they realized he was gone.

Primo Angelo deserved a life too, and the sweet thing was, if there was nothing out there for him he could always come back. Aretha Mae would always be waiting.

Eloise Hanson arrived at Phil Roberts' office at twelve noon exactly. She worked for him three afternoons a week, typing and filing. Not that there was much to file lately—business was grim.

Eloise was a small plump woman in her mid-thirties, with pink cheeks, a scrubbed complexion and gentle brown eyes. Widowed a year previously—her husband was killed in a freak accident at the canning plant—she'd needed extra money to support herself and her elderly mother.

At first the relationship between herself and Phil Roberts had been strictly businesslike, but as the months passed they'd formed a close bond that eventually turned into a love affair.

Both of them felt guilty.

Both of them hated the duplicity involved.

Both of them could not keep their hands off each other.

As soon as Eloise walked into the office, fanning herself and mur-

muring about the heat, Phil realized that work was over for the day. He took her hand and led her into his private office. "No work today," he said, squeezing her moist palm.

She blushed a little, knowing full well what he had in mind. "But there's letters to get out."

"Too bad."

She accepted his desire without question and slowly began unbuttoning her blouse.

Phil went to the outer door and locked it, then pulled the shade down and hung the CLOSED sign.

He knew Jane suspected the affair was still going on, even though he'd assured her it was absolutely over. But he couldn't stop. Eloise was such a caring woman, so giving and kind. Most of all she was a tiger in bed—a woman without inhibitions. She made Phil feel like a real man in her arms.

Not that sex with his wife hadn't always been good; over the years they'd enjoyed a satisfactory relationship—satisfactory bordering on dull. Eloise was different—she brought out a passion in him he'd thought was extinguished. Eloise allowed him to relive the excitement of his youth. After all, he was not even fifty, surely he was allowed this final fling?

Recently Jane had given him an ultimatum. "Fire her," she'd said, her tone allowing no argument.

"Why should I?" he'd replied, struggling to maintain control of his marriage. "She's an excellent secretary. And you know there's nothing between us anymore."

"I couldn't care less," Jane had replied. "I do not want that bitch anywhere near you."

Jane never swore. To hear her say "bitch" was quite shocking.

Phil knew that firing Eloise was inevitable, but he kept on delaying the moment. Eloise was his escape, and without her—what exactly did he have?

Lauren and Dawn sat on the grass together sharing a tuna fish sandwich.

"I know you went out with Nick," Lauren said, not anxious for the details, but unable to stop herself from finding out how serious it had been.

"It was before he started seeing you," Dawn explained. "As soon as you came into the picture it was over." She shrugged. "Look, I understand. I've met plenty of boys like Nick. I'm like a stopgap, you know? I'm there when they need me and then they move on. He loves you—he never loved me."

"Can I tell you something?" Lauren said hesitantly.

"Go ahead," Dawn replied, biting into the sandwich.

"It's . . . it's embarrassing."

"Ha!" said Dawn. "Trust me. I've heard it all. *Nothin'* embarrasses me."

Lauren sighed—a long weary sigh. "It's just that my parents are very strict, and I haven't been allowed to see Nick in nearly two months and . . . I don't know what to do."

"What is it?" Dawn asked. "You can tell me."

The words were difficult to say, but Lauren managed to get them out. "I . . . I think I'm pregnant."

Until she actually said it out loud she hadn't been prepared to believe it. Now that she'd voiced her suspicions she felt a great wave of relief.

"Damnit!" Dawn said. "How late are you?"

Lauren studied the grass. "Almost six weeks," she mumbled. "I don't dare tell my parents. I . . . I have to see Nick. I have to tell him."

"Sounds like a good idea to me."

"How can I?"

"How *can't* you is more like it. If I were you I'd head straight over to the gas station and tell him. You shouldn't have to handle this alone."

"What if they find out?"

"You can't be any worse off than you are now, can you?"

Dawn had a point. "I'll do it," she decided.

"Maybe the two of you can run off and get married," Dawn said, getting carried away. "*Very* romantic."

"That'll *really* thrill my parents."

"Stop worrying about them. Talk it over with Nick. The way I see it, you've got two choices—marry him and have the baby, or get an abortion."

The word "abortion" petrified her. If there was a baby growing inside her she would never consider doing it any harm.

"Has this ever happened to you?" she asked.

"To tell you the truth, no. But I always take precautions. Didn't Nick wear a rubber?"

Lauren couldn't believe she was discussing anything as intimate as this with Dawn. "No . . . he told me he . . . uh . . . pulled out."

"Oh, Jesus!" Dawn looked disgusted. "*Never* let 'em tell you that, it's the oldest line in the world. That and 'Let me just lay down next to you, I swear I won't put it in.' " She stood up and held out her hand. "Come on, get up, we gotta make plans. If you skip out of school now an' make it over to the gas station you can hear what he's got to say an' decide what you'll do. If you're lucky you'll be back before your mother gets here."

"You're right," Lauren said, drawing a deep breath. "It's the only answer, isn't it?"

"Sure—it's just as much *his* responsibility as yours. He's the asshole supposed to take precautions. An' don't worry, whatever you decide —I'm your friend, an' I'll help you if I can."

Lauren nodded gratefully, and felt sorry for all the bitchy things she and Meg had said about Dawn in the past. "Thanks," she said, squeezing her hand. "You've been great. I owe you one."

28

Early Monday morning they made it into Chicago. Dirty, tired and hungry but totally elated.

"This is my kinda town, Chicago is," Joey sang happily.

"Enough with the singin'. Where we goin'?" Nick asked.

"Yeah, where?" Cyndra joined in. "I'm beat."

"Hey," Joey said, "I got it all under control."

"I wish you'd get my stomach under control," Cyndra complained. "Traveling on that stinkin' freight train all night has made me starvin'."

"Okay, okay, I get the message. Let's go in here."

They entered a dingy-looking café. Cyndra pulled a face while Joey ordered bacon and eggs, coffee and orange juice.

"Can we afford it?" she whispered. "Maybe we shouldn't be blowing our money like this."

"It's okay," Nick said. "We deserve a decent breakfast."

"This is the plan," Joey said, taking charge. "After we eat I'll make a few calls. Don't worry, we'll be sleeping in beds tonight."

"I hope so," Cyndra said wearily. " 'Cause I can't take another night sleeping rough." She went off to the restroom to wash up.

A rag-clad old tramp approached their table. "Gotta dime?" he wheezed.

"Buzz off!" Joey said sharply.

Nick reached in his pocket and fumbled for loose change, handing the old man a quarter.

"What in hell're you doing? We might need that," Joey said indignantly.

"It's like a superstition," Nick replied. "Never turn a beggar down."

"Oh. Some superstition. They'll be following you like the freakin' Pied Piper!"

Cyndra returned from the ladies' room, having brushed her long dark hair and washed her face. "I feel better now," she said, ravenously attacking the runny eggs and greasy bacon.

"This'll have to last us until dinner," Joey warned, grabbing a piece of toast and mopping up his eggs. "Think I'll go make those calls now."

Fifteen minutes later he was back. "Friends," he said sourly. "You can shove 'em."

"What happened?" Nick asked.

"Well, like, y'know, I had this best friend at school. He told me there's no way we can go to his house on account of he's havin' trouble with his dad—so strike him off."

Cyndra leaned forward. "Who else did you call?"

"This girl I used to go with. But when I told her there were three of us she begged off. So then I called my cousin."

"I thought we were forgetting about relatives."

"Don't sweat it. He changed his number—and the new one's unlisted."

"Is that it?" Nick asked. "These are the friends and relatives that were gonna put us up?"

"Hey, things change," Joey said. "We've got enough money for a hotel."

"Not for long," Nick said. "We've only got enough money for three or four days, then we're on the street."

"We'll get jobs," Joey said.

"What jobs?" Cyndra asked.

"I'm gonna try out at a few comedy clubs," Joey said cheerfully. "Face it—I'm young, I'm hot, I'm theirs!"

"I suppose I could do some waitressing," she said thoughtfully.

"And you can get a gig at a gas station, Nick," Joey said.

"If I wanted a job at a gas station I'd have stayed in Bosewell," Nick retorted sharply.

"Stop bitchin'," Joey said. "We're here. We're outta Bosewell. Something good'll come along."

After an hour of traipsing the streets they checked into a fleabag hotel with flashing neon signs, vibrating beds and in-house porno movies. While Joey and Cyndra were registering as Mr. and Mrs. Pearson, Nick slipped around to the back alley. As soon as they reached their room they let him in through the fire escape.

"Some dump!" Cyndra complained, trying out the lumpy bed.

"You were expecting the Plaza?" Joey countered.

"Quit it," Nick said. "I'm not listenin' to you two fight all night long."

They began studying the newspaper, circling job opportunities. Joey found what he was looking for and got ready for action. He combed his hair, slicked it down with oil, put on his best jacket and said, "I'm visiting the Comedy Club. How old do I look?"

Cyndra leaned back narrowing her eyes. " 'Bout seventeen."

"You're full of it." He turned to Nick. "Whaddaya think?"

"You could pass for twenty."

"I'm growin' a beard, that'll do it."

Cyndra wrinkled her nose. "Ugh . . . I hate beards."

"You hate everything," Joey said.

"No, I don't," she argued.

Nick was getting edgy. "C'mon, you two," he said.

"Listen to this." Cyndra pounced triumphantly, reading aloud from the paper. " 'Beautiful young girls wanted for modeling jobs. Ability to travel abroad essential.' Sounds great." She jumped off the bed and paraded around the room. "I could be a model, couldn't I?"

"Sounds great," Joey mimicked. "They'll have you on a slow boat to China with a needle in your arm."

"Huh?"

"That's what they do to girls once they get hold of 'em. Ship 'em off to whorehouses in Bangkok."

"You and your imagination."

"I'm not kiddin'."

"I'm gonna take a walk," Nick said. "See you two later."

"Yeah, yeah," Joey said. "I'm doin' the same. Cyndra, you're on your own, so don't go signing with no modeling agency unless you check it with me first."

"Sure, Mr. Bigshot," she said sarcastically.

Joey grinned. He liked her sassiness. "You'd better believe it. We'll meet back here in a coupla hours."

Trudging around the streets of Chicago, Nick felt his adrenaline begin to pump. Walking the streets was a kick—people-watching, getting the feel of the city. He passed a couple of help-wanted signs and went inside, only to find both positions filled. Who wanted to work in a hamburger joint or a barbershop anyway?

After a while he passed a restaurant/bar with a sign in the window. What the hell—he'd make a pretty good bartender. He ventured inside the dim interior and checked it out. The place was dingy, with low lights and a tired stripper gyrating to a gloomy-sounding Glen Campbell on the jukebox. There were few customers.

He headed toward the bar, where a gnarled old man with a crew cut and bloodshot eyes stood guard. "Yeah?" the man rasped. "What kin I getcha?"

"I'm interested in the job," he said.

The man snorted and turned away. "Round the back."

"What job is it?"

"Washin' dishes."

"That's not exactly what I had in mind."

"What *didja* have in mind?" the man said, picking up a glass and giving it a cursory polish with a grubby cloth.

"Your job."

"Ha-ha, the kid's a comedian. Get your skinny ass around the back."

Nick decided he was better off repairing cars than washing dishes, but since he was here anyway, he made his way into the alley, coming face to face with a large rat balanced on top of an overflowing garbage can. He dodged past it and entered through the back door into a filthy kitchen.

A very thin man in what once might have been a white apron sat on a stool, his legs propped on a countertop. He was smoking a cigarette, blowing lazy smoke rings toward the ceiling. On the stove a huge pan of fries sizzled in a sea of greasy black oil.

"Yeah?" the man said, looking down his long thin nose.

"I was wondering 'bout the job," Nick said.

"You wanna do some washin', jump right in," the man said, gesturing toward a chipped sink piled high with dirty dishes.

"How much?"

"Two fifty an hour—cash."

"That ain't enough."

"Who d'ya think I am—Rockefeller? You want the job or not?"

"How many hours a day?"

"A coupla hours lunchtime, two or three in the evenings."

Thirteen bucks a day if he was lucky, and he'd still have mornings and afternoons free to go on auditions. "Make it a straight three bucks an hour an' I'm yours."

"Don't go bargaining with me, kid. I can get a Mexi t'do it for half the price."

"Why don't you?"

The man blew smoke in his face. "Oh, you got a smart mouth too, huh? Fuckin' Mexis break everything."

"Two seventy-five," Nick said.

"Jesus!" The man slapped his forehead. "Start now and you got the job—or shift your ass outta here. Take it or leave it."

He took it. It sure beat walking the streets.

29

By the time Lauren reached the gas station she was hot and tired. The front area was deserted, so she made her way to the office and tapped on the door.

George sat behind his desk, going over some outstanding accounts. "Yes?" he called out.

"Excuse me," she said, putting her head around the door. "I'm looking for Nick Angelo."

"Nick don't work here no more," George said gruffly.

"He doesn't?"

"Nah—he quit."

She was stunned. How could he quit his job just like that? She was about to ask more questions but the phone rang and George settled himself into a conversation.

She left the gas station, trying to decide what to do.

You've gone this far, Roberts. May as well go all the way. Take a bus over to the trailer park and find out what's going on.

She was more nervous about telling Nick than facing up to her parents, but it had to be done. What would he say when she told him she was pregnant? Oh, God! Would he hate her? She couldn't stand it.

She hurried to the bus stop and waited ten minutes before the bus arrived. It was stiflingly hot and close, and she was beginning to feel nauseous.

"Bad weather up ahead," the driver said, taking her fare.

What was he talking about? It was a beautiful day, much too hot, but it certainly didn't look like rain.

"Thunderstorms," the driver said, nodding his head knowingly. "I can hear 'em miles away."

Settling into a window seat she looked outside—there wasn't a cloud in the sky.

As soon as the bus began to move she started thinking about her father. Phil Roberts had always taught her to be honest and true, so why couldn't she be honest with him? Because that's what she really wanted to do.

On impulse she jumped off at Main Street, deciding to visit him at work and make one last attempt to communicate.

By the time she reached the stairs leading to his office she'd made up her mind exactly what she would say. She'd tell him her life was over if she wasn't allowed to see Nick Angelo. And then she'd tell him about the baby.

The shade was down on his office door, and the CLOSED sign displayed. Disappointed, she went downstairs to the hardware store and spoke to one of the Blakely brothers.

"When will my father be back?"

"He's upstairs, Lauren."

"He's not, the office is closed."

"I'm almost sure he's up there. Here—take the spare key, you can wait for him."

She took the key and went back upstairs. Her father was probably out having lunch. This break was good, it would give her time to compose herself. When he came back she'd be ready with a perfectly reasonable speech that he couldn't fail to understand and respond to.

She put the key in the lock and let herself into the small reception area. As soon as she stepped inside she knew she wasn't alone—there were strange muffled sounds coming from the inner office.

He's being robbed, was her immediate thought. Without thinking she opened the door and stood on the threshold.

212

Eloise, her father's secretary, was spread-eagled naked across the couch. Crouched above her, also naked, was her father.

Lauren's hand flew to her mouth and she gasped. Eloise let out a little screech of horror, and Phil Roberts turned his head around to meet his daughter's shocked stare.

"Lauren!" he said, rolling off Eloise and frantically grabbing for his pants. "Oh, my God! This is not what you think. Lauren, what are you *doing* here?"

She turned around and ran from the room, stumbling down the stairs, trying not to cry. *This* was her father? *This* was upstanding Phil Roberts—the man she'd looked up to all her life?

He was a phony. He was a nothing. And she'd never ever forgive him.

Primo Angelo lumbered into the liquor store and bought four six-packs of beer. Harlan trailed behind him.

When he was finished in the store and the van was loaded he said, "I'm starvin'. Wanna grab a bite?"

Harlan could hardly believe his luck. "Yes, *sir*," he said quickly. "I'se always hungry."

"Where can we find us a good burger?" Primo asked.

Harlan pointed down Main Street. "The drugstore."

Primo set off with Harlan loping behind.

Louise greeted them with a smile, a menu and a crisp "Hi there, folks" as they sat down at the counter.

Primo nodded. Nice-looking piece of ass. Good tits too. "Coupla burgers," he said. "Make 'em plump an' juicy an' fast." He winked suggestively. "Just like you, honey."

The smile vanished from her face. "Cheeseburger, chiliburger, or plain?" she asked curtly.

"Make it two cheeseburgers—well done," Primo said, undressing her with his eyes. He could see little beads of sweat between her breasts and it began to excite him. He'd had it with Aretha Mae, she was old and dried up, he needed somebody younger, juicier—somebody like this hot-looking waitress with the big tits and sassy ass.

Louise stopped by the kitchen, gave the order to Dave and went in the back room grumbling to herself. Some men had no manners. All they thought about was sex.

She removed her purse from the shelf and took out her lipstick and hairbrush. Then she fluffed out her hair, teased her bangs and applied more lipstick. She always liked to look her best, especially when dealing with sexist jerks. Just as she was putting everything away she noticed the letter Nick had left for her to give to Lauren lying on the bottom shelf.

Can't give it to her if she ain't been in, she thought.

Nick had marked it PRIVATE and URGENT. If Lauren didn't show up soon maybe she'd hand it to her friend Meg to pass on.

Louise propped the letter up so she wouldn't forget, and returned to the kitchen.

The school secretary phoned Jane Roberts at one o'clock. "Mrs. Roberts, I'm sorry to have to tell you this, but it seems Lauren is missing again. She was here this morning and now she appears to have left."

Jane's lips tightened. "You mean she's not in school?"

"I'm sorry, Mrs. Roberts, but I must warn you that if this behavior continues . . . Well, I don't have to tell you the consequences."

"Thank you." Jane put down the phone and immediately dialed her husband's number. Nobody answered.

Why did Lauren have to put her through this? Wasn't it enough that Phil had been sleeping with his secretary? Wasn't it enough that she'd been humiliated by the Brownings' rejection?

Jane's perfect life was falling to pieces around her and she couldn't stand it.

She snatched up her car keys and rushed from the house.

Lauren ran down Main Street until she was away from her father's office and the whole sordid scene. She didn't stop running until she reached the bus stop.

Pictures of her father, bare-assed, pumping away on top of Eloise kept playing before her eyes.

Now it all became clear why her parents were always fighting. Her father was having an affair, and her mother probably suspected.

Oh, God! Was this the man who'd told her how to live her life? The man she'd respected and looked up to?

She wanted to cry, but tears wouldn't come. Poor Mommy, she thought miserably. Poor me.

There were so many thoughts crowding her head she thought it might crack wide open.

The bus trundled up and she leapt on. There was no doubt about where she was going now. She had to see Nick, he was the only person she could talk to. The only person in the world she could trust.

Two women got on the bus and sat across from her.

"I just spoke to my sister," said the first woman, a straggly blonde. "She told me they're having a big thunderstorm over in Ripley."

"Yes?" The other woman did not seem particularly interested. She was several months pregnant and looked exhausted.

"Heard a rumor we might be expecting a twister around these parts," said the blonde.

The pregnant woman shook her head. "Not a chance. It's beautiful here today—we're lucky."

Lauren tuned out. Her life was destroyed and these women were discussing the weather.

What was she going to do, that was the big question. *What was she going to do?*

Primo took a five-dollar bill from his pocket, rolled it into a tight cone and attempted to poke it down Louise's cleavage.

She slapped his hand away, glaring at him. "What the hell you think you're doing?"

"Giving you one helluva tip."

"Hey, mister—you can take your tip and stick it up your—" She caught Harlan watching them. "Ah, forget it."

Primo got up and lumbered to the door. Harlan grabbed a few stray french fries from the basket on the counter and followed him out to the van.

"You saw that bitch in there," Primo said sourly. "Women—mark what I say—they're all whores. You don't want nothin' t'do with any of 'em. Remember that." He sprung open a can of beer and took a couple of hearty swigs, then passed the can to the boy. "Try it," he commanded.

"Don't wanna," Harlan replied, kicking the asphalt.

"Try it!" Primo repeated. "Be a goddamn man."

Gingerly Harlan took the can and managed a few sips, almost choking.

Primo laughed, grabbing the can back.

He felt like action.

He felt like doing something.

He felt like getting laid.

"It's not your fault, Eloise," Phil Roberts kept on assuring her.

Eloise, dressed and pink-cheeked, sat on the office couch sobbing into a dainty lace handkerchief. "She'll tell your wife, I know she will."

"Not if I get to her first," Phil said, attempting to calm her. "I can explain what happened. Lauren's a good girl—she'll understand."

"What is there to understand?" Eloise raised her voice. "What we had together was special and now it's . . . it's dirty."

"It's not dirty," Phil objected.

"Yes, it is," Eloise insisted, continuing to sob. "Everything's ruined."

He didn't know how to cope with her. "Go home," he urged. "Let me take care of this. By tomorrow it'll all be forgotten."

Eloise shook her head. "Your wife will destroy my reputation."

Prudently, Phil had not told her that Jane already knew about their affair. "Go home, Eloise," he repeated firmly. "I have to find Lauren."

I have to find her before she gets to Jane and opens up her mouth.

By the time the bus reached the stop nearest the trailer site it had started to rain—huge wet droplets. And yet the sun was still shining and the air remained muggy.

Lauren had visited Nick's trailer only once, but she was certain she could find her way from the bus stop. She walked quickly down the country lane, trying not to think about her father anymore. Nick would solve all her problems. Nick would make everything all right.

It was a strange day, what with the heat and the rain—there seemed to be a stillness in the air, everything was so quiet. A van roared past her. She kept her head down and continued walking.

Eventually she spotted the trailer site up ahead and quickened her pace. A pack of dogs foraged by the overflowing piles of garbage. How could Nick live here? How could he put up with such a slum?

She recognized his trailer and hurried toward it. A big man was getting out of the van parked outside, a small black boy by his side.

The man glanced up. "Lookin' for someone?"

"Yes . . . Nick Angelo. Do you know if he's home?"

"Nick's my boy."

"I beg your pardon?"

"My boy, my son. Who're you?"

"Are you Mr. Angelo?"

"Yeah—that's me, all right. I'm the good-lookin' one in the family." He roared at his own humor, and patted her on the arm.

So this was Nick's father, this big untidy lout with a can of beer clutched in his right hand and a smarmy gap-toothed smile. Perhaps this wasn't the right time to be visiting.

"I . . . I don't want to disturb anyone," she said unsurely. "Maybe I should come back another time."

"Disturb? What's to disturb? Come on in," Primo said, flinging open the door of the trailer.

Harlan attempted to attract her attention. "If you're lookin' for Nick—"

Primo pushed him roughly aside. "Come in," he insisted. "Nick'll be here soon. You can wait, I'll enjoy the company."

Reluctantly she entered the cramped trailer and almost gagged—the stench of stale beer and sweat was overwhelming.

Harlan tried to follow them, but Primo shoved him out, kicking the door shut. He gestured expansively. "Take a seat, anywhere'll do. Want a beer?"

"No . . . no, thank you. Is Nick here?"

"The kid'll find him."

Primo checked her out. She was a pretty girl, a very pretty girl.

More than likely Nick had been slipping her a slice of the old Angelo magic. Like father, like son. Yeah, the Angelo men—real studs.

Lauren felt extremely uncomfortable as she hovered nervously near the door wishing Nick would appear.

"Will ya sit down," Primo insisted. "He'll be here soon. So . . ." He leered at her. "You two are old friends, is that it?"

"We go to school together. That is, we did—until Nick . . . uh . . . left."

Primo snapped to attention. "Whaddaya mean, left?"

She hesitated; evidently Nick hadn't told his father about getting expelled. She corrected herself quickly. "Oh . . . I mean *when* he leaves . . . to go to his job, you know?"

"Yeah, yeah—his weekend job down at the gas station." Primo ran his tongue across his teeth. "Didja try there?"

"They told me he'd quit." She knew as soon as she said it that she shouldn't have.

He squinted at her. "Whaddaya mean, quit?"

"Uh, for the day. He quit for the day."

"Oh." Primo sprang open another can of beer. "Wanna swig?"

"I really have to be going, Mr. Angelo, my parents are expecting me."

He moved over to her, so close she could smell his foul breath. "Pretty girl like you, bet there's always someone waitin'."

Now she felt more than uneasy. His huge physical presence was threatening. Very carefully she began to edge toward the door.

With one fast move he blocked her. "Where ya goin'?"

"I . . . I told you, I must get home."

His voice turned to a lewd whisper. "You an' Nick doin' it? You an' my boy gettin' it on?"

Her stomach turned, and she tried to move. He lunged forward, grabbing her breast.

"Don't touch me! Don't you dare touch me!" she yelled, shrinking away from him.

Primo chuckled. "Hey—feisty little chickie, huh? If Nick's doin' it to ya, why can't I?"

Her eyes flashed angrily. "You'd better let me out of here or I'll scream," she said, trying not to panic.

AMERICAN STAR

"Who's gonna hear ya, girlie? Ya think anyone around here cares?"

Out of the corner of her eye she noticed a kitchen knife lying on the side of the sink. Slowly she backed toward it.

Primo was enjoying himself. "C'mon, chickie, loosen up. Ya fucked the boy, don'tcha wanna fuck the man?" he said, leering lecherously as he moved closer.

Her back was up against the sink. Carefully she maneuvered one hand behind her, groping for the knife. "I said let me out of here," she repeated in a low angry voice, managing to get a firm grip on the knife.

"When I'm ready," Primo replied, fiddling with his belt buckle. "When I'm *good* an' ready."

Outside the sky suddenly darkened and lightning flashed across the window, followed by heavy peals of thunder.

She clutched the knife tightly. "You'd better let me go or—"

He guffawed. "Or *what*, princess?"

The lightning flashed again, once more followed by huge rumbles of thunder. Outside the sky turned even darker, and the light rain swelled to a heavy downpour.

Primo took no notice, so intent was he on getting what he wanted.

She decided that if this man touched her one more time she would stab him.

Outside Harlan started hammering on the door. "Lemme in!" he shouted. "Lemme *in!*"

"Get lost!" Primo shouted back, unzipping his fly. "Get the fuck outta here!"

Harlan continued to yell and hammer on the door. He sounded desperate.

A strong wind howled eerily outside the trailer and the rain turned into pelting hailstones.

"C'mere, girlie," Primo said, pulling at her as she tried once again to dodge past him.

"Don't!" she warned.

He was in no mood to listen to her objections. He grabbed her—forcing his fleshy lips down on hers.

At school she'd learned self-defense and she put it to good use—bringing her knee up hard and sharp, catching him in the groin.

219

He let out a grunt of pain, but managed to hold on to her—bending her backward until she could feel his disgusting hardness pressing up against her, and she knew she had to do something drastic. Gripping the knife behind her back she readied herself for action.

Primo pulled at her skirt, pushing it up and tearing at her panties. "C'mon, y'hot little bitch, you're gonna love this," he muttered, dropping his pants.

She lunged with the knife, blindly striking out as the trailer began to rock in the wind and there was a frighteningly loud roaring sound.

Tornado—the thought flashed through her mind. *Oh, God, it's a tornado!*

Jane Roberts was driving toward Main Street when the sky suddenly turned ominously black and from out of nowhere giant hailstones began pounding the windshield.

She pulled over to the side of the street, petrified, and waited for the ferocious rain to stop, prayed for it to subside—for she had lived in the Midwest all her life and knew what this kind of weather could bring.

Louise peered out the wide front window of the drugstore and yelled to Dave, "Honey, you'd better come on out here right now an' get a load of this weather. It's raining hailstones bigger than golf balls."

Dave had hardly taken one step forward when in the distance they heard a thunderous roar, getting louder by the second.

"Shit!" Dave said, running to the window.

"What?" Louise asked, catching his note of alarm.

"Sounds like a twister to me. Jesus! Can you see it out there?"

Indeed she could. A writhing gray funnel of death and destruction. And it was heading in their direction.

. . .

Eloise was at the door of Phil's office, ready to leave, when the sudden loud howling wind forced her to stand still. She turned to Phil. "What's that?" she asked, her voice quavering with fear.

He looked concerned. "I . . . I don't know. Put on the radio."

Eloise ran to the portable radio on her desk and switched it on. A country-and-western singer twanged about her man doing her wrong.

The howling wind was getting louder by the second, and outside the sun vanished and the sky turned black.

"Find the news," Phil snapped.

"I'm trying," Eloise said, frantically searching for the right station.

"Try harder. I think we're in trouble."

Stock and Mack were in the middle of football practice on an open field, while Meg was nearby rehearsing a new routine with the cheerleading squad, when the coach spotted the tornado in the distance and began yelling, "Everybody inside! Everybody into the gym! Hurry! Go now! Hurry!"

Stock and Mack looked at each other. The sky was darkening, but they hadn't thought a little bit of rain would interfere with football practice.

Stock started to say, "What's his problem—" when Mack spotted the powerful cone bearing down on them.

"Holy shit!" he said hoarsely. "We'd better move."

Mr. Lucas ran out of the main building. "Inside!" he yelled. "Everyone get under cover. Run!"

Mack dashed over and grabbed Meg by the hand. She wished it was Stock. "What's the matter?" she asked. "What's all the panic?"

"We gotta get inside," Mack said. "Can't you see? There's a tornado on the way."

Aretha Mae hurried to the side exit of the factory, looked outside and shuddered. There, only miles away and moving fast, was an enormous, howling, writhing funnel of gray dust bearing down in their direction, destroying everything it passed.

Aretha Mae had never been a religious woman, but now she crossed herself and fell to her knees. "Save Harlan, God," she whispered. "Please, God—save my little boy."

31

"Mop the floor."

"I wasn't hired to mop the floor."

"Fuckin' *do* it. I got health inspectors up my ass."

Q.J. was the boss. Rat-faced, with long greasy hair, an aquiline nose and slit eyes. He wore a grubby white suit, cheap black shirt and bright green tie. He wasn't very tall and he walked with a limp and smoked thin cheroots. He hadn't reached forty yet, but was well on the way if he didn't get knocked off first. Q.J. had plenty of enemies.

Nick grabbed a mop and went to work. He'd only been there a few hours and was already thinking of quitting.

"Where'd ya find *this* bozo?" Q.J. demanded of Len, the so-called chef.

Len looked down his long thin nose. "He walked in off the street. I hired him on a temporary basis."

"Tell him I don't expect no lip."

"Yeah, yeah, I'll tell him."

They spoke about him as if he didn't exist. Surely they realized they were fortunate to get anyone to work in such a crummy place?

The tired-looking stripper he'd caught a glimpse of earlier strolled into the kitchen wearing nothing but a short kimono and a bright yellow hairband.

"Hiya, Q.J."

"Hiya, doll."

"Lousy business."

"It's that time of year."

She opened the big industrial refrigerator, reached for the milk, drank from the carton and put it back.

"That's a filthy habit, Erna," Q.J. grumbled. "Some poor schnook's gonna get your spit in his coffee."

"They should be so lucky." Erna yawned, reaching inside her kimono for a vigorous scratch. "Who's the kid, Len?"

"We're tryin' him out," Len replied. "If he can break less than zero he's got himself a job."

"He's cute," Erna remarked, with a little wink in Nick's direction. "Put him out front—make him a busboy."

"Excuse *me*," Q.J. interjected. "*I'm* runnin' this place."

"Just a suggestion," Erna said, throwing Nick another wink. "Maybe the ladies wanna look at somethin' for a change."

"Shit," Q.J. said, shaking his head at Len. "Now I gotta listen to hirin' crap from your wife."

Len ignored him, he was busy pulling the innards from a chicken.

Nick wondered how Joey and Cyndra were doing. Before the night shift began he wanted to get back to the hotel and check in. He took a quick peek at his watch—it was almost six, which meant he'd been cleaning up for three hours.

"What time you want me back?" he said, addressing himself to Len.

"Whaddaya mean—back?" demanded Q.J., stepping over a box of wilted lettuce stashed on the floor. "We're comin' up to busy. You'll stick around till we close."

"He told me a coupla hours lunchtime, an' two or three in the evenings," Nick said, nodding at Len.

Q.J. shrugged. "What can I tell ya? He lied."

"Do I still get paid by the hour?"

"Yeah, yeah," Q.J. said impatiently, shooting his cuffs, revealing oversized pearl and gold cufflinks.

Nick wondered if they were real. "When's payday?" he asked.

225

"Friday. Jesus! That's all I need—a fuckin' dishwasher with a mouth!"

"Leave him alone, Q.J. He's workin' hard." So spoke Erna—his new guardian angel. "This place looks almost clean, for once."

By the time he got out of there it was past one in the morning. If his figures held up he'd made himself over twenty bucks. But, jeez, he was tired—ready to drop, and now he couldn't remember where the dumb hotel was.

He walked the streets for an hour before giving up, diving into the subway and curling up on a bench outside the men's room. He'd find the hotel in the morning, right now all he could think about was sleep.

Just before oblivion hit he thought about Lauren, and he fell asleep with a smile on his face.

Hands awoke him. Frantic hands, insistent hands. He opened his eyes to find a well-dressed elderly man bending over him, struggling with the zipper on his jeans.

"What the hell!" He shoved the man's hands away.

"I'll pay you," the man said, a feverish gleam in his eyes. "I'll pay you good. Ten dollars to blow you—or if you'd sooner the other way around I'll—"

Nick leaped up, startling the man, who fell back and cowered against the wall.

"I . . . I can go to fifteen," the man offered, licking his lips. "Even twenty . . ."

"Fuck you!" Nick snarled, running down the platform toward the stairs. "*Fuck you, pervert!*"

"No need to get—"

Nick made it up to the street and fresh air. He took a deep gulp. Shit! If this was the big city he'd better learn to watch out.

He glanced at his watch; it was past seven and the streets were already busy. Now that it was light it didn't take him long to find the hotel, sneak past the front desk and make his way upstairs to their room.

Cyndra and Joey were asleep. Nice. Like they'd really been worried about him. He gave Joey a hefty shove.

"Wassup?" Joey mumbled, opening one eye.

"I'm back, that's what's up."

Joey struggled to sit up. "Where were you, man?"

"Workin'. Where were *you?*"

Joey was impressed. "You got a job?"

"No big deal. Washin' dishes. I'll do it till I score somethin' else."

"Washin' dishes," Cyndra said, surfacing from under the covers. "I didn't leave home to do that."

"Yeah, well, *you're* not doin' it, are you? *I* am," Nick replied. "An' it's only till we connect."

"That'll be soon," Joey said confidently, leaping out of bed. "Real soon."

Unfortunately, Nick discovered, he was the only one who'd found work. Neither Cyndra nor Joey had been so lucky. Secretly he was proud of himself. He'd proved he could manage on his own, and that was a big achievement—maybe he should have run from his father a long time ago.

Later, when he reported for work, he felt more at home. The foraging rat by the garbage cans seemed like an old friend, and Len in his soiled apron even threw him a friendly wave, cigarette ash scattering everywhere.

Nick Angelo, dishwasher. Some beginning.

But it was better than nothing.

Cyndra might be only seventeen but she knew the look—it was in most men's eyes as soon as they saw her.

This man was no different. This skinny little jerk with a bald spot, glasses and a nervous tic.

"How old are ya?" he asked, picking his nose.

She was interviewing for a job as an usher in a movie theater. How old did you have to be to direct people to their seats? She took a wild shot. "Twenty."

"Got references?"

"Nope."

He stopped digging for treasure and peered at her through his thick glasses. "No references, huh?"

Big deal. Try a smile. "This would be my first job," she said politely.

The man stared at her breasts. "I'd hire ya—but the management needs references."

"How can I have references if I've never had a job?" she said reasonably, wishing she'd worn a heavier sweater.

The man pushed at his glasses. "Can't risk it."

This was her fifth interview of the day—probably her fiftieth for the week. She'd been out looking every day, and so had Joey. How come Nick walked in off the street and scored an immediate job? It wasn't fair.

She wondered if she wrote to the canning plant back in Bosewell if they'd mail her a reference.

To whom it may concern: Cyndra Angelo worked her black ass off for several months making sure an extra peach didn't fall into the wrong can. She stood on an assembly line for ten hours a day and we paid her minimum wage. Oh yes, and every man in the place tried to fuck her.

No way. She'd left without giving notice. Gallagher, the foreman of her section, was probably still pissed off.

She left the movie theater and hit the streets again. It was hot and her feet hurt. She sat down on a bench by the bus stop and tried to figure out her next move.

Use your looks, a little voice whispered in her head. *Make 'em work for you.*

She remembered an interview a couple of days back. DANCING GIRLS NEEDED, the ad had stated. She'd gone to a loft in the city and lined up with about twenty other girls while a shirtless man with a video camera had filmed the line. When he was finished he'd said, "Okay. Now the nude shots. Anyone who don't wanna strip get out now."

She and three other girls had beat a hasty retreat. The rest had started to disrobe.

What would have happened if she'd stayed?

She shuddered, not wanting to know. No way was she parading around naked, it wasn't her style. And she did have style. Whatever happened to her, whatever the future held, she always had to believe in herself—otherwise she was finished.

"I gotta coupla friends—they both need jobs," Nick blurted out.

Tonight Q.J. was in a maroon velvet smoking jacket well worn at the elbows. As far as he was concerned Cary Grant better watch out. "Whatcha think this is? A fuckin' charity setup?" Q.J. said, pulling a face at Len as if to say *Who is this schmuck? And why is he workin' for me?*

Len pounded on a slab of rabbit shortly to be served up as Chicken Surprise. "Ya don't want conversation, don't come in the kitchen. This kid never stops. He thinks he's an actor."

"An actor?" Q.J. managed to look amazed. "Only *I* would hire a fuckin' dishwasher who thinks he's a fuckin' actor."

As usual they were talking about him as if he didn't exist. That was okay. He was used to it by now. Two weeks working at Q.J.'s and he was used to anything. The place was a dump—but it had turned out to be a popular dump. It hadn't taken Nick long to find out that Q.J. was a reformed house burglar who'd spent so much time in jail that a couple of years previously he'd decided to give up his life of crime and open a restaurant/bar with his brother-in-law Len—a former waiter at one of Chicago's more fashionable hotels. Erna, Q.J.'s sister, had declared herself in as head stripper. Every time she wasn't around Q.J. complained. "Ya gotta retire her, Len. When she takes it off, half my customers get up an' leave!"

"*You* tell her" was Len's standard reply. "*I* have to sleep with her."

Q.J.'s clientele consisted of the more colorful elements of Chicago's criminal population. Strictly small-time, but they all had money to spend, and Q.J. made sure everyone had a good time—in spite of Erna and her dance of the seven veils.

Q.J. was a genial host who did a bit of fencing on the side, and under all the tough talk he was a real easy touch. Which is why Nick decided to repeat his words. "I gotta coupla friends—they both need jobs."

"Do I look like an employment agency?" Q.J. demanded, throwing his arms wide. "I gotta pay nine people a week—ten if ya wanna include the cleaner who don't clean shit. I am not"—he raised his voice for effect—"a fuckin' refuge for fuckin' teenage schmucks from the East."

"West," Nick corrected.

Q.J. threw him a filthy look. "Now I gotta stay outta my own kitchen on account of your mouth. What'd I do to deserve this?"

Len reached for his cigarette smoldering on the countertop. He took a puff, causing thick ash to drop on the pounded rabbit flesh. Neither Q.J. nor Len seemed bothered.

"Can I bring 'em in?" Nick asked, expertly stacking clean glasses ready to return to the bar.

"No," said Q.J.

"No," said Len.

"You'll like 'em both," said Nick.

Two nights later he arrived at six with Cyndra and Joey lurking behind him.

Q.J. took one look at Cyndra and rolled his eyes. "Too pretty," he said. "The broads'll hate her. Can't have a stripper better lookin' than the customers—they don't like it."

"I'm not a stripper," Cyndra said hotly, glaring at Nick.

Q.J. squinted in her direction. "What are ya, doll? A brain surgeon with tits?"

"A singer."

"A what?"

"You heard me."

Q.J. adjusted the collar of his striped shirt and loosened his cerise tie. The girl was a beauty—a little dark for his taste and dangerously young, but she had class. Maybe his customers would go for her if he had Erna dress her up in a tight red dress with plenty of cleavage. Yeah—maybe he'd be Mr. Nice Guy and give her a chance.

"I gotta be crazy," he said, shaking his head. "One night. Ten bucks. If they don't like you you're out."

"What about me?" Joey asked. "I'm a—"

"Save it, sonny. I did my good deed for the day."

Joey knew when to shut up.

Cyndra's singing debut was inauspicious. Dressed up by Erna in a tight revealing gown she hated, with teased hair and too much makeup, she stood in front of a boozy crowd and warbled her version of Aretha Franklin's "Respect." A mistake. The only singing Cyndra had ever done was in private, and although her voice was pleasantly husky she had no idea how to use it.

After a few minutes the crowd became restless. "Take it off, sweetie!" yelled one man, and others soon took up the chant.

Standing at the back of the room, Q.J. chewed on a toothpick and scowled. He'd thought he might have made a discovery—but as usual he was wrong. The girl had faked him out, convincing him she could do something she wasn't capable of.

"You fuckin' her or what?" asked Petey the Frog, one of his regulars —his bug-eyes bulging.

"Nah, just givin' her a chance," Q.J. replied, smoothing down his velvet smoking jacket.

"C'mon, ya *gotta* be fuckin' her," Petey the Frog said, slurping his drink.

"Too young," Q.J. said shortly, walking away.

Cyndra finished to desultory applause and a few more raucous cries of "Take it off!" She ran from the stage.

"I quit," she told an amazed Q.J.

"*You* quit?" he managed. "*You* fuckin' quit? I'm firin' ya, doll."

She glared at him. "You can't fire someone who already quit."

"And I ain't payin' ya, either," Q.J. added, red in the face.

"Oh, yes, you are," she said fiercely. "I performed. You'll pay. It's not my fault your customers are a bunch of stupid apes."

Q.J. had never come across a girl like Cyndra before. She was young, but she had guts and he couldn't help admiring her. It was a shame she had no talent.

His first wife had been like that—Sassy Sarah, everyone had called her. She'd run off with their electrician while he'd been languishing in jail. His second wife had chosen the plumber. He'd been single now for eight years, and that's the way he planned to stay.

He paid Cyndra her ten bucks. She didn't seem particularly grateful. "I don't have to do this," he informed her.

"Yes, you do," she replied, walking out into the night.

Q.J. did not appreciate her attitude, a little ass-kissing would have been nice.

"Don't bring in no more of your friends," he warned Nick.

"You shoulda let her practice or somethin'," Nick said.

Q.J. shook his head at Len. "What the fuck's goin' on here? I got a dishwasher lippin' off, an' a broad that can't sing shit givin' me a hard time. Do I deserve this?"

"That's life," Len said, dipping his finger into a bowl of cream.

"Shit!" said Q.J. "*Shit!*"

"Listen—" Nick began.

"One more word outta you an' you're fired," Q.J. said gruffly.

Erna entered the kitchen beaming. "Big hit, huh?"

"With all due respect," Q.J. said to his sister, "you wouldn't know a big hit if it landed on your ass an' bit you!"

By the time Nick finished work and got back to the hotel Cyndra and Joey were waiting outside with their bags packed. It was two in the morning.

"What's up?" he asked, dreading the answer.

"We got thrown out," Joey said, stamping his feet against the cold night air.

"How come?"

" 'Cause we owe 'em."

"But I gave you the money to pay."

Joey looked sheepish. "I kinda lost it in a street hustle."

"Jerk!" muttered Cyndra.

"Hey—this place cost too much anyway," Joey said quickly. "Tomorrow we'll get us a one-room apartment—it'll be cheaper."

Nick was angry. He was still the only one working—and now Joey was taking his hard-earned money and blowing it on street con games for dumb tourists. Maybe it was time to split up.

"I'm cold," Cyndra said, sounding like a little girl. "Where'll we sleep?"

She was his sister, he couldn't desert her. "C'mon," he said. "We'll find you a nice comfortable park bench, cover you with newspapers an' you'll sleep like a baby."

She recovered her edge. "Gee, I can't wait."

Joey snapped his fingers. "Whaddaya want? The penthouse at the Ritz Carlton?"

She looked at him as if he were a lowly worm. "Yes," she said. "And one of these days that's exactly what I'll get."

"Sure," Nick agreed. "But tonight it's the park, so let's hit it."

They picked up their belongings and set off.

As they trudged toward the park he began thinking about Lauren and how much he missed her. By this time she'd have read his letter, and maybe if he got a post office box and wrote again, care of Louise, she'd reply.

The first thing they had to do was find somewhere to live. Joey was right—the hotel, cheap as it was, had been too expensive. They should have moved weeks ago.

An icy wind blasted them as they turned the corner. Joey stopped to gather a stack of old newspapers sticking out of a garbage can— disturbing a mangy cat. It ran off down the street screeching. Two drunken old tramps staggered by. A couple of junkies huddled in a doorway, busy shooting up.

Cyndra clung to Nick's arm, shivering. "I'm frightened," she whispered.

"Don't worry," he said, trying to reassure her. "We'll be all right."

She clung tighter. "Promise?"

"Hey, listen, kiddo. As long as you hang out with me I'll never let you down. Okay?"

"Yes, Nick."

He may have sounded full of confidence, but it was a cold hard world out there and sometimes he was frightened too.

32

It all seemed to happen at once—one moment Lauren was fighting off Primo, and then everything became a horrifying deadly blur. First the howling wind, followed by a thunderous roar as the tornado bore down on them, catching the trailer in its path, scooping it into the air and carrying it along for several hundred yards as if it were made of papier-mâché.

Lauren could hardly remember anything, as she'd been hurled from the door to the ground outside and knocked unconscious. When she came to, the tornado was off in the distance, sweeping a path of destruction, ripping up everything as it headed for the center of town.

Lying on the ground, she groaned, lifted her hand and felt blood on her cheek. She tried to sit up, overcome with an overwhelming sense of despair as she attempted to remember exactly what had happened.

Primo . . . grabbing her . . . tearing at her clothes . . . the knife.

Oh, God, the knife! Had she killed him?

Panic-stricken, she staggered to her feet and forced herself to think clearly. All she could remember was the power of the tornado descending, and being propelled from the door as if by some magic hand as the trailer was lifted up and swept away.

Somehow she'd been saved. Why?

She looked around the trailer site—it was more or less obliterated, everything gone. Even the trees had been plucked from their roots.

Living in the Midwest, she'd heard about tornadoes all her life but had never experienced one. Now the reality was upon her and she saw for herself the devastation it could cause.

In the distance she could still see the gray funnel twisting on its way, its awesome destructive power demolishing everything it encountered.

There was no more rain, just an eerie stillness, a deathly silence.

She tried to force herself to move, but her legs felt weak and could hardly hold her weight. Somewhere a dog barked mournfully.

I've got to get home. They'll be so worried about me.

She began to walk. Back toward town. Back to the house she hoped was still standing.

The tornado swept down Main Street like a lethal weapon, cutting its deadly path with incredible strength. Everything in its way was sucked up into its white-gray funnel. Trees, people, animals, cars—it was not selective.

Picking up strength as it traveled on its way it hit Main Street at its peak, propelled by winds of up to two hundred and fifty miles an hour.

The plate-glass windows of the drugstore caved in, sending great shards of glass smashing to the ground.

Louise held tightly onto Dave, fervently praying.

He dragged her out into the street as the ceiling collapsed and falling debris crashed around them. Protecting her as best he could, he threw her to the ground and lay on top of her—both of them trembling with fear. A sheet of glass sliced through his leg, cutting it off below the knee.

Louise let out a long anguished scream as the blood from Dave's injury pumped all over her.

The tornado continued on its way, demolishing the Blakely Brothers hardware store, above which Phil Roberts and Eloise clung together in his office. They hardly knew what hit them. The very last words

Phil Roberts heard was Eloise screaming, "I never meant to do it, God. Forgive me for my sins. Please forgive me!"

And then there was nothing.

Jane Roberts' car with her inside was swept up into the wind funnel and carried along for almost a mile. She died of shock.

The car, containing her body, was recovered twenty-four hours later. Miraculously, it was still perfectly intact.

Bosewell High School suffered a direct hit. As the students raced into the gym, the tornado sucked the roof off the building, pelting everyone with flying glass and jagged chunks of concrete. Crashing debris hit a gas main, causing a major fire.

Meg managed to grab hold of Stock as he hung on to the climbing rails, the only part of the gym that remained. She held on for dear life, trying to ignore his hysterical sobs and keep a clear head.

Mack had vanished—sucked away in the awesome cone of dust.

"Help me!" Stock sobbed hysterically. "Somebody help me!"

"I'm here," Meg cried soothingly. "Don't worry, I'll look after you. I'm here."

Aretha Mae watched the factory vanish before her very eyes. She stood in the middle of the destruction completely unharmed and continued to pray.

By the time the tornado left Bosewell fourteen people were dead, over a hundred and fifty injured. More than sixty buildings were damaged or destroyed, and the town declared a disaster area.

In the big story nobody bothered to mention Bosewell—for the killer tornado cut a path of death and destruction throughout the Midwest, making the small town of Bosewell only a minor victim.

By the time the story hit the major news services, Bosewell was hardly mentioned.

BOOK
TWO

33

CHICAGO, 1979

Nick lay back in bed, his eyes following the naked redhead prowling around his tiny one-room apartment. Her name was DeVille and she was a natural redhead.

He liked watching her in his home, it sure beat observing her gyrate onstage while dozens of horny old men got off ogling her considerable charms. She was, at twenty-six, an older woman, but only by four years, which fazed neither of them.

DeVille had a sweep of long hair, pale aquamarine eyes, pouty lips, voluptuous breasts and a sunny disposition. She'd been living with him for almost six months.

"Can I fetch you anything, sweet thing?" she asked, prancing around his apartment, all curves.

"Yeah." He leaned back in bed, putting one arm behind his head. "Get over here."

DeVille did not argue, she never argued. Sometimes he wished she would. He'd heard of easy, but she was ridiculous.

She approached the bed and stood beside him. He reached up and touched one perfect size 36 tit—no silicone—DeVille was all natural. The only phony thing about her was her name.

Rolling her extended nipple between his fingers he made a suggestion she was not about to turn down.

DeVille was pleased. Her last lover had been twenty years older than her and a grouch. Nick was a real treat.

"My, oh my!" she exclaimed, pulling the sheet off him and widening her eyes. "What big . . . *thighs* you have."

"All the better to grab your ass!" He pulled her on top of him and they both laughed as she straddled him with her long white legs. DeVille liked being on top. He didn't mind, he knew it was her one power play.

They started to make frantic love—DeVille was a screamer—their neighbors did nothing but complain.

When they were finished he rolled out of bed and strolled into the cramped bathroom.

"How about I make pancakes?" DeVille called out.

"I ain't hungry," he said quickly. The one thing she couldn't do was cook.

He noticed a spider crawling along the side of the tub. Picking it up by one of its legs he carefully placed it on the windowsill and watched it dart to safety across the fire escape.

"I'll make coffee then," she sang out.

At least she could do that. He stepped into the rusty tub and turned on the shower—as usual getting nothing but a trickle of lukewarm water.

He had a hangover. The night before had been a long one, plenty of action, and he hadn't gotten home until three in the morning.

Who'd have thought Q.J.'s would become *the* place? And who'd have thought he'd become the manager?

Yeah, some success story. From dishwasher to manager. And all it had taken was five years. Wow!

"What shall we do today?" DeVille asked, popping her head around the bathroom door.

"I'm easy."

"Maybe we could catch a movie—there's a new Paul Newman."

Yeah—Paul Newman. That meant he'd definitely get laid again. "Sure," he said easily.

By the time he emerged from the bathroom, DeVille was dressed. On Sundays she liked to play at being ordinary. She'd put on jeans and a sweater and braided her long red hair. Looking at her today nobody would guess she performed one of the horniest acts in town.

"Oh, I forgot to tell you. This letter came for you yesterday," she said, handing him an envelope.

He studied the writing on the front—it was from Cyndra. "How many times I gotta tell you? When I get mail I want it right away," he said, irritated.

"I told you—I forgot."

The envelope looked in bad shape. "What did y'do, steam it open?"

"As if I would!"

"As if you wouldn't."

DeVille had a jealous streak he didn't appreciate.

"Is it from your sister?" she said, peering over his shoulder.

"You *did* open it," he accused.

"No, I did not. Her name's on the back."

It was a stupid thought, but one of these days he still hoped he might receive a letter from Lauren. Yeah—a real stupid thought. Lauren was his past, long gone. He'd written her many times and never gotten a reply. After a while he'd given up. It was obvious she didn't care about him.

But that didn't mean he couldn't think about her once in a while, did it? He imagined her still in Bosewell, married with kids, happy, never giving him a second thought—she probably didn't even remember his name.

He opened Cyndra's letter. She'd left Chicago with Joey over four years ago. The two of them had taken off when the winter got too cold and neither of them could keep a job. They'd tried to persuade him to go with them, but by that time he was settled at Q.J.'s doing everything from taking over the bar to running errands for Q.J.

Cyndra had stayed in New York with Joey for a couple of years, until eventually she'd met some sharpshooter called Reece Webster, who'd lured her out to California with a few phony promises. She was still with him. From what Nick could gather the guy was married, but on the brink of leaving his wife. He'd been on the brink for the last two years.

He scanned her letter.

Dear Nick:

Well, things are good in Los Angeles, you'd really love it here. It's hot all the time and there's these great palm trees everywhere —but I guess I've told you that enough times—right?

Why don't you come visit me? I've got plenty of room if you don't mind sleeping on a sofa bed. Reece is never here on weekends so we could have fun and you know how much I miss you.

As far as my career . . . well, I'm taking singing lessons—ha-ha! Aren't you glad? I'm also meeting lots of people Reece says can help me.

I haven't heard from Joey in a while. I think he's driving a cab. You know Joey, always waiting for the big break. Aren't we all— ha-ha!

I'm serious, Nick—please think about coming out here even if it's only for a long weekend.

I love you and I miss you lots.

As always,
Your sister,
Cyndra

She wasn't the world's greatest letter writer, but at least she bothered to write.

"You ever been to California?" he asked DeVille, folding the letter and putting it in his pocket.

"Once," she replied. "When I was eighteen. There was this rich guy with his own private plane. He flew me and three other girls to a party in Vegas. We put on a show *they* didn't forget in a hurry!"

"What kind of show?"

"Stripping, parading the goods, what else?"

"Did you ever do any hooking?"

Her mouth tightened. "Why are you asking me that?"

"I'm throwing it into the conversation."

"Throw it out again, Nick," she said, glaring at him. "I take my clothes off, and that's *all* I do."

"Yeah, yeah, I'm sorry. I don't know why I said that."

"Nor do I." She marched into the bathroom, slamming the door behind her.

She'd sulk for five minutes and then come out. DeVille never stayed angry for long.

Q.J. had this theory about women. He considered them all hookers under the skin. Sometimes he'd give Nick the benefit of his wisdom. "You gotta look at it like this—when they marry a guy, what the hell ya think they're doin'? They're havin' sex for money, right? So the husband screws her one night an' buys her a dress the next day. The poor schmuck pays for everything. Why don't he leave a hundred buckerooneys on the bedside table an' call it quits?"

Q.J. was a true cynic. Maybe that was the way to be. Nick had no intention of ever getting married. Every time DeVille so much as hinted he'd laughed, not taking her seriously.

Once again his thoughts drifted back to Lauren. He couldn't help thinking about her—she hovered at the back of his mind, a distant memory he couldn't forget. He'd hoped over the years that Joey or Cyndra would go back to Bosewell for a visit—but neither of them seemed inclined. As far as he knew, Joey had never contacted his mother, and Cyndra had no urge to get in touch with Aretha Mae, although she occasionally mentioned Harlan. They both felt guilty about leaving the kid. "When I make it I'll go get him," Cyndra said.

Yeah. Sure.

Once in a while he thought of calling Louise at the drugstore—just to find out what was going on in town. But something always stopped him. The truth was he really didn't want to know.

Over the years he'd worked hard, helping to make Q.J.'s the successful place it was today. Five years ago it was a hangout for petty con artists and their one-night stands, offering nothing but bad food and a couple of tired strippers. When disco got really big he'd started badgering Q.J. about dumping the strippers and bringing in a disc jockey.

"Are you outta your fuckin' skull?" Q.J. had said. "My customers get off on the girls. Anyhow, we ain't got no space for dancin'."

"Make it," he'd urged. "You gotta get into this disco thing before it's over."

"I hire a fuckin' dishwasher an' all of a sudden he's tellin' me what to do."

"I ain't a dishwasher no more."

"What are you then?"

"Your assistant."

"If you say so."

Q.J. was too cheap to hire a disc jockey, and too nervous to risk losing customers by firing the strippers, so he'd compromised by making Nick the disc jockey and persuading Erna to stop stripping—putting her in charge of two new girls he hired. Business had picked up immediately.

Nick was triumphant. "I told ya," he'd said.

"Yeah, yeah, you told me," Q.J. had replied. "Like I didn't already know."

Nick really got into the music. It was a kick hanging out at the record stores listening to all the new sounds and picking out the latest hits.

The sound system Q.J. elected to put in was shit, but he quickly learned how to work the room, mixing the old with the new—a little bit of Elvis, followed by Al Green, throw in some Bobby Womack, then calm them down with Dionne Warwick and Smokey Robinson.

When he wasn't working the turntables he was behind the bar.

The regular bartender didn't like it. "Get that ratty kid away from me," he'd complained, "or I'm outta here."

There was nothing Q.J. liked better than a threat. Plus he could get away with paying Nick half the money he was paying the old man. "So quit," he'd said.

The bartender did, and Nick had found himself in charge of the bar too. "We gotta hire somebody else," he'd complained. "I can't play records *and* run the bar."

"Jesus Christ, you're gonna break me," Q.J. complained.

"No," he'd corrected. "I'm gonna make you."

Erna was his biggest supporter. Even Len got into the spirit of things by hiring an assistant chef who could actually cook. Q.J.'s really took off.

Not that anybody had ever thanked him. He didn't need thanks—a steady job was enough.

He considered the situation. He'd walked in off the street five years ago with exactly nothing, and now he was the son Q.J. never had. Not bad. Not good. He'd come to Chicago hoping to be an actor and done nothing about it. He was twenty-two years old—if he didn't start soon he never would. While he stayed at Q.J.'s there was no time for anything else, not even acting class. He'd managed to save a couple of thousand dollars over the years, and now California beckoned. The letter from Cyndra was a sign. If he didn't make a move he'd be stuck at Q.J.'s forever, wearing cerise shirts and shooting his cufflinks just like Q.J. himself. A frightening thought!

DeVille bounced out of the bathroom. She was pretty, sexy and amiable.

It was over. Six months was his limit. Besides, he couldn't take her with him, excess baggage was never a good idea.

"Are we going to the movie?" she asked.

"Sure."

God, she had a great mouth.

It would be tough kissing it goodbye.

34

PHILADELPHIA, 1979

"Excuse me, Miss Roberts."

"Yes, Mr. Larden?"

"I notice that it's raining outside, and I wondered if I might offer you a lift home."

"That's very nice of you, Mr. Larden, but my cousin is meeting me."

"Oh." Mr. Larden stared at her. He was a man of medium height in his thirties with thinning hair and a drooping mouth. He was also a married man with two children, one dog and several hamsters. He was her boss.

"Are you sure, Miss Roberts?" he asked hopefully.

"Yes, I'm sure, Mr. Larden."

They played this game all the time. He pretended to be the concerned boss always looking out for his secretary's welfare. She pretended that he really did want to give her a lift out of the kindness of his heart because it was raining outside. They both knew this was a lie. He wanted to get her into bed any way he could.

Lauren had worked for him as his personal secretary for two years now, and she knew she had to leave or go completely crazy.

"Well," he said, collecting his briefcase, "I'll see you tomorrow then."

"Yes, Mr. Larden."

She waited until he'd left before picking up the phone. "Brad," she said in a low voice, "I can't see you tonight."

"What do you mean you can't see me?" he spluttered.

"It's difficult to explain now. Let's talk tomorrow." She put the phone down quickly before he could argue.

Bradford Deene, her cousin. Good old Brad. Without him she probably couldn't have gotten through the last five years. But their relationship was sick, it had to stop, and she was the one who was going to end it.

Five years ago she'd arrived in Philadelphia a shivering wreck. Her mother's brother, Will, along with his wife, Margo, had met her at the airport.

"We're so sorry, dear, so very very sorry," Margo had said, but she hadn't shed a tear.

Will seemed more sincere. "Your mother was a wonderful woman —always a good sister to me. We shall miss her."

The Deenes had taken her to their house on Roosevelt Boulevard. It was a nice house, but it certainly wasn't home. Brad, her nineteen-year-old cousin, was away at college and they allowed her to stay in his room. At night she overheard them whispering, Margo saying, "What are we going to do with her? We can't keep her here."

And Will answering, "Lauren is my sister's daughter, Margo. She has no other relatives. We *have* to take her in. After all, she's only sixteen."

"I know, I know. But for how long?"

Jane and Phil Roberts had both perished in the deadly tornado that had practically totaled Bosewell. Lauren remembered very little of the nightmare. She'd arrived in Philadelphia still numb with shock. And shortly after arriving she'd had to tell Margo she was pregnant.

Her aunt had gone completely crazy. "How did this happen? Were you raped?" she'd demanded.

"It just . . . happened . . ."

"Was it that boy you were engaged to? Stock? Because if it was we can force him to marry you."

"No, it wasn't Stock."

"Who was it then?"

"It doesn't matter."

"Your poor parents. They'd be so . . . so disappointed in you."

"I want to have the baby," Lauren had said quietly.

Margo had shaken her head. "Absolutely out of the question. It's enough that *you're* here—we cannot look after a baby too."

"There *is* no choice in this matter," her uncle had said. "You'll have to have an abortion."

She remembered the termination as if it were yesterday. Margo had taken her to the gynecologist, a bald man with sleepy eyes and rubber-gloved hands. "What have you been up to, young lady?" he'd said with a jovial wink as she lay on the cold hard examining table, feeling naked and vulnerable beneath the paper garment the nurse instructed her to wear.

"Come along, put your legs in the stirrups, dear."

He'd probed and poked until she could stand it no more.

"I don't want to lose my baby," she'd whispered.

"It's nothing," he'd said. "Don't worry about it. Next time you open your legs be a little more careful, that's all."

Then they'd given her an injection, and she remembered nothing much at all except the harsh feel of cold steel between her legs.

After that there was no more baby, no more Nick.

At the time she'd thought about him every second of the day, but now she'd forced herself to stop. Nick Angelo had left her, run out of town without so much as a goodbye, and she'd never heard from him again—not even after the tragedy.

In a way she hated him. He'd used her for his own selfish reasons and then dumped her—leaving her pregnant and alone. She was shocked that he'd left. No note, no word, no nothing. She hardened her heart against him, but for some inexplicable reason she still didn't want to lose his baby.

Margo and Will insisted she go back to school. She did so reluctantly because she had no choice.

One night Margo and Will had called her into their living room and given her the bad news. "Your father's estate left nothing. Death taxes took what little there was. He was heavily in debt."

"I'm sorry, Lauren," Margo said. "There's no money to send you to college. You must understand that we can't afford it. We've worked hard all our lives to allow Bradford all the advantages he's had, and now we're entitled to enjoy what's left."

"I don't want to go to college," she said. "As soon as I graduate from high school I'll find a job."

"You could always try for a scholarship," Will ventured, feeling guilty. "After all, you're a smart girl."

They didn't understand that she meant it when she said she had no wish to attend college.

For several years she'd had nightmares about the tornado. In her mind she could see it sweeping down on the trailer—and sometimes in her dreams the tornado would turn into Primo. He would be part of it—leering at her . . . touching her . . . saying lewd things—until he forced her to raise the knife and strike.

She'd killed Primo.

Or had she?

The uncertainty drove her crazy.

As soon as she graduated from high school she'd taken a job at the local bank and started saving money. The moment she had enough she planned to move out of the Deene household.

Since coming home from college Brad was always around. He was good-looking with curly brown hair and a ready smile. He was taller than Nick, more muscular. She still compared every man she met to Nick, it was a habit she couldn't break.

By the time she was nineteen she'd saved enough money to move out. She had good secretarial skills and immediately found a better job at Larden and Scopers, a law firm. Mr. Larden himself had interviewed her and informed her she was perfect—exactly what he was looking for.

Her life was simple until Brad complicated it. He'd dropped by her apartment one night, stayed too long and drunk too much. Then he'd confessed he thought he loved her, and somehow or other they'd ended up in bed even though they both knew it was wrong. She'd tried to make it one time only, but he wouldn't let her. He'd talked her into it, and once in she couldn't get out. Besides, it felt good to be with someone who cared.

Their affair had been going on for several months and she was suffocated with guilt. She wanted out. All she had to do was tell him.

She left the office and took the bus to her apartment, running the last few hundred yards to her building, getting soaked.

Brad was inside, sitting on *her* couch, his feet up on *her* table watching *her* television.

"I told you I couldn't see you," she said, removing her raincoat.

"You didn't mean it," he replied.

"I want my key back," she said, clicking off the TV.

He frowned. "What's with you lately?"

"Brad, you know this isn't right. It has to end."

"No way, baby." He settled back, totally at ease.

The way he said "baby" made her stomach turn. She knew for sure she wasn't the only girl he was sleeping with.

"Please," she said. "I want it to be over."

He held out his arms. "Come over here."

"No, Brad."

"Are we playing hard to get?" He wouldn't leave and she couldn't make him.

"What if I told your parents," she threatened.

"You wouldn't do that."

"I might."

"They'd blame you."

"Do you think I care? They never wanted me to come and live with them anyway."

He considered her threat. He wouldn't put it past her. "What is it, the wrong time of the month?" he asked, clicking the television back on.

She had a plan. If he wouldn't go, she would.

A week later at the office Christmas party, a drunken Mr. Larden grabbed her in his office, trapping her up against his desk.

She knew exactly how to deal with men who tried to force her to do something she didn't want to do. She grabbed a letter opener and stabbed him in the arm.

Mr. Larden yelled out his surprise and pain. "Are you *insane?*" he shouted.

"Try taking no for an answer," she said, making it to the door.

"You're fired," he said.

"Good."

By the time Christmas arrived she had every detail of her departure planned. On Christmas day she went to Margo and Will's for lunch —they'd been a lot nicer to her since she'd moved out and they weren't obliged to support her. Brad was there with a girl named Jennie. The two of them spent the entire day giggling and necking.

"I think they might get engaged," Margo confided in the kitchen.

"That's nice," Lauren said. If he'd brought his girlfriend to make her jealous it wasn't working.

Sitting at the dining table she noticed Brad's hand creep under the table and up Jennie's thigh.

"You know," Margo said, turning to Lauren, obviously unaware of her son's furtive adventure, "you're perfectly welcome to bring a date here. Are you seeing anyone?"

Lauren shook her head. "No."

"A pretty girl like you," Will said cheerfully. "You should have dozens of boyfriends."

"She's probably hiding them from us," Brad said, laughing confidently as his fingers played with the elastic on the panties guarding his girlfriend's moist crotch.

Lauren sighed. He was good in bed and he knew it. He played her like an expert, touching everything in just the right way.

Later that night when he'd gotten rid of Jennie, he arrived unannounced at her apartment. She allowed him to make love to her for the last time, only he didn't know it was the last time, he was under the misguided impression she was going to be available for him whenever he felt like it.

As soon as he left she hurried to the shower, washing him away forever. Then she packed, and early the next morning she took a cab to the bus station and boarded a Greyhound bound for New York.

She left no forwarding address. As far as she was concerned she'd been in mourning long enough.

Lauren Roberts was about to start a new life.

35

Several things convinced Nick it was time to move on, not the least being the Carmello Rose incident. Carmello was a short grizzly man in his fifties with a beak nose, dark skin and a raspy menacing voice. He was a rumored Chicago hit man who visited Q.J.'s from time to time, always with several nubile young girls in tow, always with an eye to picking up more.

This particular night he arrived with only one woman—a tall redhead in her late thirties with large breasts and a sour expression.

"Fuck!" Q.J. said agitatedly. "That broad's his wife."

"So," Nick asked, "what's the big deal?"

"You'd better make sure nobody says nothin' 'bout none of the other skirts he's been hangin' out with—'cause if his wife finds out she'll blow his shriveled ass to Cuba an' back. She's a wild woman."

"You worry too much," Nick said calmly. "I'll take care of Mr. Rose myself."

And why not? Carmello Rose was known for leaving hundred-dollar tips.

When he got near the table and took a closer look he had a feeling he'd seen this woman somewhere before. She was wearing a dangerously low-cut black cocktail dress, and he couldn't keep his eyes from straying down her generous cleavage.

252

Carmello caught him catching a peek and fixed him with a frog-eyed stare that said all right to look, but no touching.

"What can I get you, Mr. Rose?" Nick asked.

Carmello ordered a bottle of champagne.

"I just found out it's his wife's birthday," Q.J. said agitatedly, stalking Nick behind the bar. "Get Len to arrange a cake."

"What does his wife do?" Nick asked.

"What does she *do*? What the fuck you *think* she does—looks after him."

"Then how come he's always hangin' out with other women?"

Q.J. looked testy. "We don't know nothin' 'bout that, do we? Take him a bottle of the best—my compliments."

"How come *you're* not going over?"

" 'Cause Carmello frightens the crap outta me. Is that a good enough reason? Ya just gotta look sideways at his old lady an' he has a freakin' fit."

"Y'know, I got a feeling I've seen her somewhere before."

"Jesus, Nick, ain'tcha got enough broads of your own? This one's too old for you anyway."

"Who's interested? I just wanna recall where I seen her."

Q.J. shook his head. "Forget it."

He took the champagne to the table, informing them it was from Q.J. "On account of it bein' Mrs. Rose's birthday an' all," he said with a smile.

Carmello grunted.

"Thanks, sweetie," Mrs. Rose said.

Was it his imagination or did she throw him a wink? He took another peek at her impressive breasts and it suddenly came to him. She was the woman whose car he'd gassed up in Bosewell a few years ago. The one in the sweater with the attitude. Who could ever forget those tits!

"How's your sister?" he asked, pouring her a glass of champagne.

She ran her tongue across her front teeth and darted a nervous glance at Carmello. "Huh?" she said blankly.

Carmello snapped to attention. "Whadda *you* know about her sister?"

"She lives in Bosewell, right? I used to live there too."

Obviously he'd made no impression on her. She had no idea what he was talking about.

"Hey—I gassed your car a coupla times. You were visiting your sister, remember?"

Carmello threw her a suspicious look. "You know this guy?"

"No, I certainly don't," she snapped, three large diamond rings flashing on her fingers.

"He sure seems to remember you."

"Everyone remembers me," she said defiantly.

"Hey, listen, no big deal," Nick said quickly, sensing trouble. "I musta made a mistake," he added, pouring more champagne into Carmello's glass before walking away.

Five minutes later he was in the stockroom when Carmello entered, kicking the door shut behind him. Before he could say a word Carmello took out a gun and shoved it in his stomach.

He lost his legs, it was like they weren't even there. "*Jesus!* What the hell you *doin'?*" he mumbled, panic-stricken as his life rushed before his eyes.

"Ya wanna know what *I'm* doin'," Carmello snarled, jabbing him with the gun. "What the fuck was *you* doin' with my wife?"

His throat was so dry he could barely speak. "I gassed her car, nothin' else."

"You gassed her car, huh? That it?"

He was breaking out in a cold sweat. "That's all. I was only a kid— I swear to you." Jesus! He needed to pee in the worst way.

Carmello shoved the gun into his stomach even harder. "Swear a little louder, ya dumb punk. Get down on your knees and fuckin' swear."

"It's the truth—God help me, it's the truth."

"Turn around an' get down on your knees, fuckhead."

Maybe Carmello was going to shoot him, maybe he wasn't. He'd never know, because at that moment Q.J. opened the door and walked in on them. "Everything all right?" he asked calmly, like he didn't know anything was going on, although of course he did.

Reluctantly Carmello put his gun away. "Sure, sure. The kid an' me—we was talkin'."

And that was that. Crisis over. But Nick knew the time had come to get out.

254

Two days later he visited Q.J. in his office.

"I quit," he said.

"You *what?*"

"You heard me."

"Sure I heard you, but I don't believe what I'm hearin'."

"I've been in Chicago long enough."

Q.J. glared at him. "Yeah. Long enough to learn everythin' I know, is that the deal? You're gonna open your own place. I shoulda known it." He got up, marching angrily around the room. "I took you in, treated you good, now you're gonna stab me in the heart."

"That's not it," Nick said. "I'm plannin' on takin' a trip to California."

Q.J. rubbed together nicotine-stained fingers. "What for?"

"For a chance."

"I gave you a chance. Ain't that enough?"

"I always had this thing 'bout gettin' into acting. If I don't try it now I never will."

Q.J. snorted his disgust. "Act, shmact. You're in the bar business, that's where you belong."

"When I get settled I'll call, let you know how I'm doin'."

"Who gives a shit? All I care about is you stayin' here. You're my manager, you take care of things. How about showin' some appreciation?"

"When I came to work here I never said it was a lifetime thing," he explained, hoping Q.J. would understand.

"Jesus!" Q.J. rolled his eyes. "You can't trust nobody no more."

"I'll stay till you find a replacement."

Q.J. was steaming. "I don't need nobody else. Don't worry 'bout a thing—you ungrateful little prick. Shift your ass outta here, see if I give a shit."

He knew Q.J. didn't mean it. "How about I stay around for two weeks?" he suggested.

"Do what you want," snapped Q.J.

Later Erna grabbed hold of him. "There's a rumor you're going to Hollywood," she said, thrilled at the thought.

"Yeah, I'm gonna give it a shot."

She nudged him slyly. "Like me to come with you?"

"Uh—I don't think Len would appreciate it."

She giggled. "Perhaps you're right," she said, tugging at an escaping bra strap. "I had a chance to go there once. I coulda been a famous starlet." She winked knowingly. " 'Course, it meant sleeping with a fat old producer, so I stayed here, married Len, and now look at me."

"You're happy, aren't you?"

"I'm married to Len, that doesn't make me ecstatic."

"He seems like a nice guy."

"He's no Q.J."

Erna had confirmed his suspicions—she definitely had a crush on her brother.

When DeVille heard the news of his imminent departure she flew into a fury because he hadn't told her himself. Usually she left the club before him, but this particular night she stayed, joining a customer's table—something she never did.

Nick realized this meant trouble. If he was smart he'd have taken off without telling anybody.

At closing time, DeVille dumped the customer and left with him, hanging on to his arm. She was drunk and angry—not a happy combination.

"Y'know something, Nicky," she slurred in his ear, well aware that he hated being called Nicky.

"What?" he said, steering her unsteady body into a cab.

"You're a son of a bitch, that's what you are." She nodded, confirming the assessment. "Yeah, a son of a bitch."

"Hey, listen, I *was* gonna tell you," he said. "But I had to tell Q.J. first, I owed him that."

"You owed him that," she mimicked. "And what do you owe me?"

He raised an eyebrow. "You think I owe you somethin'?"

"Bastard," she spat out.

The cab driver—a weary veteran—glanced warily in his rearview mirror.

"Goddamn bastard," DeVille said, hauling back in an attempt to slap him. "We live together—doesn't that mean *anything* to you?"

The cab swerved over to the side of the street and the driver turned around. "I don't want no trouble," he said. "Out. Both of you."

"It's all right, man," Nick said, gripping DeVille firmly by the wrist. "There ain't gonna be no trouble. Keep driving."

"The last couple had a fight in my cab wrecked it," the driver muttered sourly.

"I said keep driving," Nick repeated. "I'll take care of you good."

Still muttering under his breath the driver set off.

DeVille began to cry. Her anger he could take, but crying always got to him. "Hey," he said, trying to comfort her. "I'm only going for a month or two."

"You're lying," she cried, leaning all over him, getting mascara on his one and only jacket.

"Maybe I'll send for you."

"Now you're *really* lying," she sobbed.

DeVille was no fool, she knew it was over.

As soon as they reached his apartment she began to pack, hurling her things into a suitcase, well recovered from her crying jag. "I thought you were different," she yelled. "But no way. You're just like every other guy—selfish, self-centered, all you care about is your precious dick."

She looked good when she was angry and somehow or other they ended up in bed. DeVille thought if she was the best she'd ever been he might take her with him. It was quite an experience. At four o'clock in the morning their neighbors couldn't take the moaning and groaning any longer and called the police. They ended up hysterical with laughter.

In the morning they parted company. DeVille was sober and tense and in a funny sort of way dignified.

When she left he almost missed her—only almost.

"You're a scumbag, you know that? No loyalty." Q.J. was on a kick and he didn't intend to stop.

"Leave the kid alone," Erna said, coming to Nick's defense.

Q.J. glared angrily at his sister. "Did I ask for your input?"

"No, but—"

"I treat him like a son," Q.J. interrupted. "Groomin' him, y'know what I mean?"

"Grooming him for what?" Erna asked sharply. "To be in the bar business all his life like us? Who wants that?"

They were at it again, talking about him as if he wasn't there.

Len entered into the conversation. "He'll be back," he said, nodding wisely. "It's too hot in California."

Q.J. didn't seem so sure. "Ya think?" he said.

"No," said Erna spitefully. "He won't be back. Why would he?"

On his last night Q.J. relented and threw him a big farewell party after the bar closed. For the first time he wondered if he was making the right move. Everybody was so warm and friendly. The waitresses, strippers, Erna, Len—even Q.J. In a way this was his family now— the family he'd never had.

DeVille put on a show—and what a show it was! Enough bumping and grinding to turn on a priest! Maybe she wanted him to know exactly what he was leaving behind. He knew all right, but he still couldn't help himself.

Q.J. clapped him around the shoulders. "Ya know somethin', Nick, if y'ever wanna come back, y'got your job waitin'. I ain't never said that to nobody who worked for me before. Consider yourself honored."

"I consider myself honored," he said, grinning.

"In the meantime," Q.J. continued, "when ya get to L.A. I want ya t'look up my ex-partner."

"Who's your ex-partner?"

"Some guy used to be known as Manny the Menace, now he's strictly legit. Call him Mr. Manfred and don't go mentioning his nickname—it drives him beserko."

"What does he do?"

"Runs a car service. Respectable. Just like me."

Nick burst out laughing. "Whoever said you were respectable?"

"Very funny." Q.J. smoothed an imaginary crease in his pinstripe pants which did not go with his bright red jacket and green polka-dot tie.

"You're sure this guy is straight?" Nick asked, thinking that tonight Q.J. looked like a waiter in a whorehouse.

"Would I lie to you?"

"Yes."

"Go see him, Nick. He'll give you a job. All ya gotta say is I'm callin' in the favor he owes me. Q.J.'s collectin'—that's what ya tell him. He'll know what you mean."

"Shouldn't you contact him first?"

"We don't speak."

"So why would he want to—"

"Trust me." Q.J. scribbled on a piece of paper and handed it over. "Here's his number. Do like I say and phone him soon as y'get there."

"Thanks," he said, shoving the paper in his pocket. It was certainly better than arriving in L.A. cold.

Erna hugged him, covering him in her cloying scent. "Don't forget about us now, you hear me?"

"How," he said, grinning, "could I ever forget *you?*"

She giggled coyly. "Not much chance of that."

Len was his usual stoic self. They shook hands. "You'll be back," Len said knowingly.

"Maybe—one of these days."

Now he was really beginning to regret his decision to leave. He had no idea what Los Angeles was like. He had no friends there, no job, just Cyndra, and he hadn't even warned her he was coming, figuring a surprise would be good.

In the morning Q.J. was on the missing list. "He don't like good-byes," Erna explained, as she and Len drove him to the airport. "Gotta see you off in style," she added with a saucy wink.

They couldn't park, so they dropped him off curbside. He grabbed his carry-on bag from the trunk and stood on the sidewalk waving to them as they drove away in Len's two-toned gold Chevrolet with the dented front fender.

As soon as they were gone he felt alone, but only for a moment. Then he picked up his bag, turned and strode purposefully toward the airline desk.

The Greyhound bus delivered Lauren into New York at noon. She waved goodbye to the driver, collected her suitcase and stood alone in the middle of the busy bus station.

Before she could take two steps a scruffy-looking man stinking of cheap aftershave approached her. His long greasy hair hung in strands around her face, and a cigarette dangled from the corner of his chapped lips. "Hiya, lovely. Lookin' for a place t'stay?"

She was no naïve little country bumpkin getting off the bus in New York ready to be picked off by some lurking pimp.

"I have somewhere, thank you," she said, giving him a withering look.

"Just askin'. Can't do more than that, pretty chick like you."

She hurried away, only to be accosted a few yards later by a dark-skinned man in a filthy white suit who sidled up behind her. "Wanna be a model?" he said, speaking out of the corner of his mouth.

She kept walking.

"Wanna be a model an' make a lotta bucks?" he said, keeping pace with her.

She ignored him.

"Wanna fuck me?"

She stopped, turned to look at him and said in a very loud voice, "Leave me alone or I'll call a cop. Got it, pervert?"

He slunk off.

Outside the bus station she found a cab and gave the driver the address of the Barbizon Hotel for Women.

"How many times you get hit on in there?" the driver asked, shoving his foot on the gas and zooming away from the curb, missing another cab by mere inches.

"Enough," she replied, gazing out the window at the dirty sidewalks, scurrying crowds and snarled traffic.

It was like a dream. Here she was, finally in New York, and she was free, she had nobody to answer to except herself.

She'd booked a room at the Barbizon before leaving Philadelphia. She'd also been buying the New York papers and circling job opportunities, setting up several appointments by phone.

After she'd unpacked and settled in, she took a walk over to Fifth Avenue. Oh, yes, it was just like *Breakfast at Tiffany's*. The same wide street, the same expensive stores. She found herself outside Tiffany's staring into the windows like a tourist. She stifled a giggle—all she needed now was a cat and she was all set!

The next day she awoke early. It was autumn and the weather was brisk. She dressed carefully in a simple dark blue dress, low-heeled shoes and her mother's pearls. On top she belted a navy trench coat. She'd pulled her thick chestnut hair back, securing it with a barrette, and wore very little makeup. The plainer the better, she thought. But there was no disguising the fact that at twenty-one Lauren was a natural beauty with her perfect oval face, unusual tortoiseshell-color eyes and dazzling smile.

Before doing anything else she opened a bank account and deposited her four-thousand-dollar savings. Then she set off on the first of three interviews.

The first one was with a law firm housed in a tall chrome and glass building on Park Avenue. There she was interrogated by an attractive black woman, who asked her a series of probing questions and made her fill out a personality analysis form. After that she had to sit in a room and produce a sample of her typing.

The woman timed her. "Excellent!" she exclaimed. "Where can we reach you?"

Her next interview was with a firm of accountants on Lexington Avenue. The building was not so nice, although it was near Bloomingdale's and she'd certainly heard plenty about Bloomingdale's. The man who interviewed her was a junior partner. He was friendly and didn't seem on the make. He read through her references twice and asked if she could start the following week. She told him she'd have to let him know.

Her third interview was with a modeling agency on Madison Avenue called Samm's. They'd advertised for a booker. Lauren had no idea what a booker did—but working at a modeling agency might be fun, and she could certainly do with a little fun in her life.

A harassed girl in a purple jumpsuit told her that she'd made a mistake and better come back the next day because there was nobody to see her.

"I can't come back tomorrow," she said. "My appointment was for today. I have two other jobs under consideration and I have to make a decision."

The girl looked at her like she was nuts. "So don't come back," she said. "Take one of the other jobs."

"I'd like to make a choice," Lauren said. "Why can't somebody see me today?"

"They're all over at the big photo shoot for Flash Cosmetics. Is that a good enough reason for you?"

She went downstairs, found a phone booth and looked up Flash Cosmetics. Then she called their office. "Can you tell me where the ad photo session is taking place?" she asked. "This is Lauren from Samm's."

"Sure, just a moment," said the voice on the other end of the phone. Two minutes later she had the information—a photographer's studio on East 64th Street.

She walked to the studio. It only took her fifteen minutes and when she arrived she informed the receptionist that she had something to deliver from Samm's. The girl told her to go to the studio in back.

She made her way down a narrow corridor which led into a large, brightly lit studio jammed with people.

The first person she noticed was a short, flamboyant man hovering behind a camera, while several other people stood around watching. In front of the camera languished the most startling-looking girl Lauren had ever seen. She was an exceptionally tall blonde with masses of curly hair, huge blue eyes and pouty lips, encased in a low-cut, slinky, silver sequined gown. Lauren recognized her as Nature, the current darling of the fashion magazines.

"Get yer finger out, Antonio," Nature screamed. She had a voice like a fishwife and a cockney accent that could sharpen knives. "I'm freezing me balls off."

"Close your legs, darling, maybe that will help," murmured a thin fortyish redhead standing to one side.

Lauren hovered on the periphery.

Nature struck a pose.

Antonio started shooting. *"Bellisima,* darling, *bellisima!* You are the most fantastic woman in the world!"

The more he flattered her the more Nature loved it. She postured and preened, making intimate contact with the camera, her glossy lips quivering with emotion, her big blue eyes mesmerizing.

Antonio shot several rolls of film before calling for a break.

Everybody clapped. Nature threw her head back and laughed, sounding like a demented parrot. "Me bleedin' feet are killin' me," she roared, collapsing into a chair while a makeup artist and hairdresser rushed forward to attend to her every need.

"Excuse me." Lauren tapped one of the camera assistants on the arm. "Can you tell me who the executives from Samm's are?"

"Over there." He jerked his thumb in the direction of the redheaded woman.

Tentatively Lauren approached her. The woman was in the process of lighting up a long thin cigarillo.

"Uh . . . excuse me," she said. "My name's Lauren Roberts. I had an appointment today with someone at Samm's, but the girl told me everyone was here."

The woman dragged on her cigarette and stared at her. "Too short, too heavy, too eager."

Lauren frowned. At five feet seven she'd never been called short—and as for heavy . . . no way. This woman was definitely peculiar. "I beg your pardon?" she said hotly.

"You'll never make it, darling. You don't have the attitude."

"I'll never make what?"

"A model. Isn't that what you want to be? Isn't that what they all want to be? Although, I must say, it's *très* original, following me to the studio."

She stood her ground. "I didn't follow you anywhere. And nobody's ever called me heavy before."

"For a real person you're not the least bit heavy. For a would-be model you're grossly overweight."

"We had an appointment," Lauren said. "Someone was supposed to interview me about the booker's job. I went to your office and the girl said there was nobody to see me."

"So you decided to come here?"

She couldn't stop herself from staring at the woman's blood-red inch-long nails—talons, her mother would've called them. "Yes."

"In that case you get high marks for using your head. Can you type?"

"I sent in my résumé."

"Can you type?" the woman repeated impatiently.

Don't get aggravated, Roberts. Stay cool. "Yes, I can type."

"Can you answer phones?"

She couldn't keep the sarcasm out of her voice. "It sounds like a really challenging job."

The woman was unfazed. "Oh, don't worry, dear, it's challenging all right. I'll try you out. Be at the office at nine o'clock tomorrow."

"*If* I decide to take the job, I can start Monday."

The woman looked at her like she wasn't quite sure she'd heard correctly. "If you *decide* to take the job? My God, little Miss Independent, aren't we?"

"I have two other job offers I'm looking into."

"And what would you do if I said this offer was only open now, this very moment, and if you turn it down don't bother coming back?"

There was a brief silence, broken by Nature screaming, "Get yer bleedin' arses in gear—I'm ready ter shoot."

Lauren took a moment to consider the possibilities. She could accept the job with the law firm, but she already knew what that would be like—boring, boring, boring. Or she could say yes to the accounting firm—another laugh a minute. Her third alternative was to take the job with this bossy, redheaded woman. It could prove to be interesting.

"Well?" the woman said abruptly. "Are you joining us or not?"

"What's the salary?"

"Not enough," the woman replied brusquely.

"I need to make a decent salary. I have to get an apartment and afford to eat."

"You can share an apartment and starve. Builds character. Let me know when you make up your mind. You have exactly five minutes to think about it. After that, my dear girl, this job opportunity is over."

37

Reece Webster had her exactly where he wanted her—pinned beneath him, waiting for the big moment, almost begging. He knew he gave her good loving, the best she'd ever had, so he could afford to keep her hanging.

He paused in mid-thrust. "What's your name, little lady?" he demanded.

"Cyndra," she gasped.

He prolonged the moment. "Cyndra what?"

"Don't torture me, Reece."

"Cyndra *what?*"

"Cyndra Webster."

He laughed, and let her feel him move inside her. "Who owns you now?"

She moaned, almost there. "You do."

"An' who's gonna love you till you drop?"

"You are."

Now he heated up the action. "And who am I?"

"You're . . . my . . . husband."

"Damn right, baby. Damn right!" He let rip and she came on cue. What a stud! Nobody did it like he did.

Cyndra shuddered and rolled away from him, curling her beautiful body into a tight ball. Some guys might be offended by her immediate withdrawal, but not Reece Webster—he was a man, a real man, and he could take it. In fact, it was a relief—women who wanted to cuddle and talk after sex gave him that *Let's get outta here* feeling.

The good news was he'd finally had the smarts to shed his first wife, a going-nowhere blonde, and two days later he'd turned around and married his little darkie songbird. Now *this* was a girl destined to go places, and *he*, Reece Webster, was going right along with her. Cyndra Angelo was an investment. He'd married her to protect himself.

Reece Webster was five feet ten inches tall, with sandy hair, a thin blond moustache, slit eyes and a penchant for wearing flashy cowboy clothes, even though he'd been born in Brooklyn. At thirty-eight he was sixteen years older than Cyndra, but as far as he was concerned this was a good thing. It meant she didn't know as much as he did. He could mold her any way he wanted, and that's exactly what he was doing.

They'd met in New York at a club where her boyfriend was working as a bouncer. Joey hadn't stood a chance once Reece Webster moved in.

After introducing himself as a personal manager he'd asked her what she did.

"I'm plannin' to be a professional singer," she'd said, very full of herself.

"Then you just met the man who's gonna make you a star," he'd replied, equally confident.

Corniest line in the world, but it worked every time.

At first his interest had been purely sexual. A quick lay and on to the next. But she wasn't interested in accompanying him to his apartment. She had no desire for a quickie—not even when he'd told her he produced records and had something to do with the rise of John Travolta's career. Both lies, of course—but who was listening?

Usually he didn't like them so young—but there was something special about Cyndra, so he'd continued the pursuit, reeling her in carefully. He'd hired a studio for a couple of hours and paid for her to cut a demo. She'd had no idea what she was doing—but there was a voice there somewhere, and he'd decided that if he could bring it out they'd be rolling in dollar bills.

"I'm goin' back to Hollywood," he'd told her casually one day. "Yeah . . . Hollywood's the place a girl like you could really score."

"Well . . ." She'd hesitated. "One of these days Joey and I—"

"Forget about Joey. He's a loser. Hang out with him an' you'll end up like him. On the other hand—come with me an' I'll do somethin' 'bout that singin' career of yours."

And so it came to pass that she finally dumped Joey, and drove with Reece cross country in his shocking pink 1969 Cadillac, consummating their relationship in a Holiday Inn somewhere near Albuquerque.

Once they'd settled in L.A. Reece had arranged singing lessons for her. He wasn't disappointed, she was a natural.

Now, two years later, all his hard work and well-invested money was hopefully beginning to pay dividends. He'd managed to interest a couple of record companies in her—and they were both considering meeting with her and maybe cutting a demo.

In the meantime he'd married her. Reece knew a life-time meal ticket when it stared him in the face.

Curled up in a ball, knees hugging her chest, Cyndra couldn't figure out why she didn't feel any different. She was married, for God's sake. Married! And yet she still felt the same.

Well, she'd only been married one day, she reasoned. Maybe she'd feel different tomorrow.

She thought about Aretha Mae and wondered what she'd have to say about this. For the first time since leaving Bosewell, she almost considered going home. Just for a visit, of course—a very short visit. She'd ride up in Reece's big old Cadillac and Harlan would come running to greet them. God, he must be a big boy now—sixteen. Aretha Mae would cook up some of her special fried chicken and greasy fries. What a treat!

The only problem was she'd never told Reece about her poor beginnings. He thought she came from a nice middle-class family. As far as he knew, her mother was a housewife and her father made his living as a car salesman. She didn't have the nerve to tell him the truth. The fact was she was ashamed of where she came from.

Reece Webster had entered her life at exactly the right time—just when she and Joey were beginning to fight nonstop. New York was tough, she'd had seven different jobs and it was getting her down. If she'd had to serve one more plate of beans and hash she knew she'd go nuts.

When Reece Webster first came on to her she'd thought he was just another on-the-make hustler. "You haven't even heard me sing," she'd said scornfully, when he announced he'd make her a star.

"I don't have to," he'd replied. "With your looks all you gotta do is open your mouth an' every guy in the place will do the fandango. Get it?"

Yes, she got it. He didn't have to tell her about men and their reaction to her.

Joey had been furious when she informed him she was leaving. "What do you know about this guy?" he'd said.

"Enough," she'd replied.

"You're making a big mistake."

Maybe she was and maybe she wasn't, but she had to take the chance. It was time to leave, so she'd packed up and taken off in spite of Joey's objections.

In Los Angeles Reece had set her up in what she considered total luxury. A nice apartment on Fountain Avenue, no roaches or rats, and a palm tree outside her window. A palm tree! She thought she was in heaven.

Reece vacillated between staying with her and spending time with his wife, who lived in Tarzana. For two years he'd promised to get a divorce, now he'd done it, and they'd jumped in his Cadillac, driven to Vegas and gotten married.

"Just you wait," Reece had said. "When you're rich an' famous we'll do it again. An' this time the world will come. You'll see, honey. You'll see."

The first thing that hit Nick when he stepped off the plane in Los Angeles was the sunshine—dazzling, blinding sunshine. And his next impression was one of a laid-back casual friendliness, the like of which was not evident on the streets of Chicago.

Out on the sidewalk with the sun beating down he hailed a cab and gave the driver Cyndra's address.

On the ride in he took in the scenery. Wide streets, tall dusty palm trees and a proliferation of gas stations, fast-food chains and used-car lots. Pedestrians were sparse on the street, but cars were everywhere.

As they got closer to town the greenery overwhelmed him. Every garden seemed to be filled with exotic plants and every street lined with trees.

He couldn't help feeling excited. After all, this was the real thing, he was in Los Angeles for crissake. Hollywood. Land of the movies. Jeez! If he was lucky he might even bump into Dustin Hoffman or Al Pacino walking down the fucking street!

The cab pulled up in front of Cyndra's apartment house—a three-story pink stucco building. He jumped out and checked the row of buzzers by the main door. Sure enough, one of them was marked with her name. He pressed it and waited.

Five minutes later when she still hadn't replied he realized he should have called.

A well-preserved woman in tennis whites and running shoes walked up to the door, balancing two bags of groceries. "Hi," he said.

"Hi," she replied, groping for her key.

He went to help her with the grocery bags. "Can I give you a hand?"

She flashed a row of perfect white teeth. "Why not?"

Hmm . . . in Chicago she'd have told him to get lost. People were obviously more trusting in L.A.

He balanced her grocery bags in one arm, picked up his bag with the other and followed her in as she opened the gate.

The first thing he saw was a swimming pool. Holy shit! Cyndra must be rolling in it.

Around the swimming pool there were several apartments.

"You wouldn't happen to know where Cyndra Angelo lives?" he asked.

"Are you a friend of hers?"

"I'm her brother."

"Apartment three, across the other side."

He handed her groceries over. "Thanks."

She smiled again. "You're welcome. Have a nice day."

"I plan to, but thanks anyway."

He went over to Cyndra's apartment, knocking just to make sure, and when nobody answered, placed his bag against the door and tried to decide what to do. Since this was his first day in L.A. and there was nobody out by the pool he decided to take a swim. Stripping down to his shorts he leaped in, splashing around like a fish. Goddamn it! This was luxury!

He spent the afternoon on a lounger catching some rays and waiting for his sister. By six o'clock it was obvious she was going to be late. Other people were arriving home from work and entering their apartments. A couple of them gave him strange looks.

He knew he'd better make a move before someone became suspicious. With a few deft strokes he used his credit card to spring her lock. Nobody was around to notice as he slipped inside. Mental note —make sure Cyndra got herself a decent lock.

He looked around. Little sis was living pretty good. He opened the refrigerator and uncovered a dish of cold spaghetti. It looked inviting, so he ate it, then he drank from a carton of milk and began roaming around the small apartment. He didn't mean to be nosy, but he couldn't help checking out the bathroom cabinets and opening up the closet. There was definitely a man in residence—some asshole who favored cowboy boots and ten-gallon hats.

On top of the Sony stereo in the living room was a framed picture of Cyndra with an older guy. He picked it up and studied it.

So this was the notorious Reece Webster. The man looked old enough to be her father—skinny and blondish with a thin mouth, droopy moustache and shifty eyes. Cyndra looked sensational in a sexy tank top and shorts. Little Cyndra was all grown up.

He lit a cigarette and settled in front of the television. After a few minutes he dozed off.

When he awoke it was way past midnight and the cigarette had burned a hole in the arm of the couch. There was still no sign of Cyndra, so he grabbed a blanket from the bedroom, curled up on the couch and went back to sleep.

Cyndra didn't want to go home. She'd fallen in love with Las Vegas.

"This place is the best," she told a dumbfounded Reece.

"This place is a pisshole, honey," he replied, amazed that anyone could actually like Vegas.

"Then why did you bring me here?"

"Because this damn pisshole is gonna make us a whole lotta money."

"How?"

"You're gonna be a star here, baby. I can feel it."

She wanted to believe him. She basked in his enthusiasm. "I am?"

"Sure you are. I set up appointments tomorrow for you to meet the talent scouts from a couple of the big hotels. You're gonna impress the custom-made pants off 'em."

"How'll I do that?"

"By lookin' sexy an' singin' for 'em, sugar."

"Why? When we've got those record companies waiting to cut demos with me back in L.A.?"

"Good business," Reece said, very sure of himself. "Never put it all in one place. When we go in an' see these guys you listen—don't talk."

That night he took her around all the best hotels. The Sands. The Desert Inn. The Tropicana. Cyndra was thrilled, she'd never seen anything like the lavish hotels with their multi-colored fountains, oversize sculptures and enormous colorful casinos filled with middle America losing their hard-earned money.

"Consider this little tour an educational trip," Reece said as he swaggered from hotel to hotel masquerading as a Texas millionaire in his cowboy boots and ten-gallon hat. He jerked his thumb at a singer in the lounge at The Golden Nugget. "You see her? She can't sing for shit, but she sure puts in a pretty appearance."

"Why are you telling *me*?" Cyndra asked.

" 'Cause, Mrs. Webster, not only do you look good, but you can sing too. An' we're gonna use everything we got to make you bigger and better than anyone else."

Reece made her feel she could achieve anything. "Can we stay a couple of extra days?" she begged, "Can we? *Please*. After all, it *is* our honeymoon."

He tilted his hat. "What'll you give me if I say yes?"

She smiled. "I'll make it simple. Anything you want, Reece. Anything at all."

· · ·

Nick awoke in the morning uncomfortable and hot. There was no Cyndra around, she must have taken off somewhere. He should've called to let her know he was coming. Shit! Too late now.

He helped himself to a banana, made a cup of instant coffee and then sauntered outside to the pool.

An athletic-looking girl in a one-piece swimsuit swam laps, her brown arms and legs flashing through the inviting blue water.

"Hey," he called out. "Any chance you know where Cyndra Angelo is?"

The girl took no notice of him as she pounded the water, hardly coming up for breath. He squatted down beside the pool waiting for her to surface.

After a few minutes she swam to the shallow end and climbed out, shaking herself like a shaggy dog. The girl wasn't pretty in a conventional way, more interesting-looking—with a pert face, snub nose and bright blue eyes. She was five feet three with a sensational compact body and very short red hair.

"Excuse me," he said. "I'm trying to find Cyndra Angelo."

"Who're you?"

"Her brother."

"*You're* her brother?" she said disbelievingly, grabbing a towel and drying herself. "Cyndra never mentioned she had a brother."

"I flew in from Chicago—figured I'd surprise her. I guess it wasn't such a good idea."

"What did you do, break into her apartment?" she said knowingly, toweling a bronzed thigh.

"Technically, yeah, but I know she'd want me to make myself at home."

"Tell *that* to the super."

"Is he around?"

"I wouldn't dig him up if I were you, he'll throw you out."

"So you can't help me?"

"Come to think of it, I did see Cyndra walking out of here carrying a bag on . . . let's see . . . maybe it was Thursday. She's probably away for a long weekend."

"Today's Tuesday. I'll wait."

The girl threw him a suspicious look. "Are you sure her boyfriend's going to like that?"

"Who is this boyfriend?"

She laughed. "He's okay—if you like drugstore cowboys." She finished drying herself and walked toward her apartment on the other side of the pool. "See ya," she called over her shoulder.

She certainly had a body. "Yeah—see ya. Uh . . . what's your name?"

She turned around at her apartment door. "Annie Broderick. Oh, and by the way, if you rip her off, I *can* identify you to the police. And I will."

He stared at her quizzically. "Do I look like I'd do a thing like that?"

"No. You look like an actor. Worst kind." She entered her apartment, slamming the door behind her.

She couldn't have said anything nicer if she'd tried. An actor, huh? Some compliment. He hadn't performed in so long he wondered if he still remembered how.

By noon he was bored, sitting around waiting was not his style. Out of curiosity he picked up the phone and called the number Q.J. had given him.

"Manfred Glamour Limousines," a woman's voice said.

Glamour Limousines—was she kidding? "Let me speak to Mr. Manfred," he said quickly, before he changed his mind.

"Who's calling?"

"Tell him . . . Uh, tell him it's a friend of Q.J.'s."

Her voice rose. "Q.J.'s?"

"Yeah—he'll know who you mean."

There was a long wait. A very long wait. So long that he almost hung up. Then a gruff voice snapped, "Who's this?"

"You don't know me," he explained, speaking fast. "But your ex-partner said I should give you a call when I got to L.A. Q.J. mentioned you might have a job for me."

"Who the fuck are you?"

"Nick Angelo. I ran Q.J.'s bar in Chicago."

"And what ya got in mind t'do for me?"

"Anything you want if it's legit."

"I don't fuckin' believe this," Manny grumbled. "Ya pick up a phone, mention that putz to whom I don't speak no more, and ya really think I'll give ya a job?"

"Hey, listen, if it's a problem, forget it. Q.J. insisted I call. He told me to say Q.J.'s collecting—for that favor you owe him. But if it means nothing to you . . ."

A weary sigh. "Come in and see me."

"When?"

"Be here in an hour."

"Where's here?"

"Sunset past La Brea. You can't miss it." Manny hung up without so much as a goodbye.

Nick decided to go for it. After all, he had nothing to lose.

38

"Don't you ever date?" Nature asked, studying her face in a large magnifying mirror she'd extracted from her enormous purse.

"Not if I can help it," Lauren replied.

"Not if you can 'elp it," Nature shrieked in her sharp cockney tones. "Cor blimey—that's a funny one. Me, I can't get through the day if I don't 'ave a fella waitin' for me at the end of it."

"You're you and I'm me," Lauren said sensibly.

"Bleedin' right," Nature agreed, searching for imagined blemishes on her perfect peaches-and-cream skin.

Lauren had been working at Samm's for three months. It was certainly different. Definitely not boring. In fact she was so busy she never had time to think about anything except work. A booker, she'd soon found out, did everything for the band of models who trudged in and out of the place like a constant parade of dazzling beauty. They were all gorgeous, but every one, it seemed, had a screwed-up personal life.

Nature, Samm's most famous client, was the most screwed-up of all. She'd taken to dropping by and sitting on Lauren's desk so they could chat. Nature had confided she was fed up with people who brown-nosed her to death.

"You're like a real person," she'd told Lauren. "I can talk to you, you're so sort of normal."

That's nice. But I have work to do.

The phone at Samm's never stopped. Along with Nature, the agency handled three of the other top models in New York—Selina, Gypsy and Bett Smith. At the agency they were known as the Big Four. Selina was a willowy blonde with cat eyes. Gypsy was Eurasian, exotically beautiful. And Bett Smith was an all-American blonde with a cute snub nose and just enough freckles.

Samm herself had turned out to be the woman Lauren had encountered at the photo session she'd crashed. Samm Mason, former top model, now a very successful agent.

In the late fifties Samm had been one of the top models in the country. When she retired she'd opened her own agency, and over the years built it into a formidable rival to Eileen Ford and the Casablanca Agency. Samm was tough, but it worked for her. She ran a tight operation, protected her girls and expected everybody in her employ to do the same. "I know how easy it is to get treated like a piece of shit in this business," she'd often tell her employees. "That's not going to happen to any of my girls. Not while they work for me."

Lauren palled up with an American-born Chinese girl named Pia who'd worked at the agency for several years as Samm's personal assistant. Without Pia to help her through the early days she might have given up. It was certainly nothing like working in a law office—the modeling world was chaos. People on the phone day and night screaming for this girl or that girl. The models yelling that they didn't want to go to Alaska, they would prefer to do the shoot in the Bahamas. Boyfriends calling up, men trying to track them down, clients complaining. Lauren's job was to see that everybody arrived in the right place at the right time. She was also expected to keep everyone happy. She soon became adept.

After a few weeks Pia had said, "You're doing okay, Samm's really pleased. Are you having fun?"

Fun was not exactly the best way to describe her first couple of months in New York. She'd hardly had time to think, let alone have fun. Early on Samm had asked if she minded working weekends. Like an idiot she'd said she didn't mind. But still, she had nothing else to occupy her time, and it meant making extra money. She'd moved from the hotel to a one-room apartment in the Village. It wasn't the perfect location. Upstairs an angry woman practiced the piano at all hours. And downstairs a young boy who claimed he was a performance artist turned tricks.

The good thing about being in New York was there was never time to feel lonely, she was always busy doing something.

"So," Nature said, leaning across her desk. "Last night I met this tall geezer, sort of a Eurotrash type. He was 'anging out at one of the discos. Bleedin' hell, he came on so strong even *I* couldn't fight him off—an' that's sayin' something!" Nature snorted with laughter. "Bloody Italians—they've got their hands all over you before you so much as find out their name. Good job I know 'ow to fight back. Kick 'em in the cobblers an' run. Me mum taught me that."

"Did you go out with him?" Lauren asked, thinking that a kick in the balls from Nature was enough to kill any normal man. Nature was over six feet tall and extremely well built—not skinny like her main rival, Selina.

"Out with 'im? *In* with 'im is more likely," Nature chortled. "He dragged me back to 'is hotel and we 'ad a party."

"What kind of party?"

"What kind of party do you think? Some grass, plenty of rock 'n roll —although 'e wanted to play Julio Iglesias. I put a stop to that *dead* quick, I can tell you."

Lauren finished typing a sheet of paper and handed it over. "Here's your instructions for the Acapulco shoot. You leave on Thursday. I've arranged a car and driver to pick you up at your apartment and you'll be back the following Tuesday in time to be in the studio Wednesday morning for the *Cosmopolitan* cover session."

Nature grabbed the piece of paper barely glancing at it. "Acapulco," she snorted. "It's so bleedin' hot."

"Have you been there before?"

"About ten times."

Lauren sighed—sometimes she envied the models and the exotic trips they all seemed to take for granted. "It must be absolutely marvelous," she said wistfully.

Nature made a face. "If you like sunshine and a bunch of dark geezers runnin' about all over the place. Personally, if I 'ad me choice, I'd be back in London with me mum 'aving a nice cuppa tea."

"How long is it since you've been home?"

"Must be a year now. Samm promised I can take a few weeks off at Christmas."

"Do you need her permission?"

Nature chortled. "Don't knock it when it's all happenin'. Samm got me where I am today. I listen to what she 'as to say, she's a smart old bird. Which reminds me, I gotta see 'er. Is she by 'erself?"

"Let me buzz her."

"Thanks, darlin'. You're such a sweetie."

Samm was available. Nature marched into her office, leaving Lauren with the ever-ringing phones. There were two other bookers, but neither of them paid as much attention as she did. She hadn't intended to make herself indispensable, but deep down she knew everyone depended on her. It was a big responsibility—but at least she felt needed.

The rest of the day passed quickly—everything happening at the usual breakneck speed. By the time she was ready to leave she was wiped out.

Pia caught her by the door. "It's Samm's birthday next week, the girls want to throw her a surprise party. She'd hate it. What'll I do?"

"If she'd hate it, tell them no."

Pia tapped long red fingernails on her fake Chanel purse. "Have you ever tried telling those spoiled bitches no?"

"You can do it."

"It's Samm's big one," Pia worried. "I suppose we *should* have a party. Can you make arrangements for food and music, flowers and whatever else you think we need? Selina's offered the use of her boyfriend's apartment."

"Which boyfriend?"

"Haven't you heard? She's in love again."

It was a well-known fact that the models changed boyfriends as often as they changed their panties. Men were one of the perks of the business.

"Who's she in love with now?" Lauren asked.

"That English rock star, Emerson Burn." Pia giggled. "When Nature finds out she'll kill her—she thinks anything British is automatically hers."

Lauren tried to remain cool. In a way it was all too much. One minute she was sitting in Philadelphia slogging away at a job she hated with a boss who was always chasing her—not to mention her affair with Brad—and now here she was in New York mixing with models and rock stars. Emerson Burn was famous. And she was going to meet him. Emerson Burn! It wasn't so long ago that she'd had his poster on her wall hanging next to John Lennon.

Calm down, Roberts, he's only a person. And from the sound of his publicity not a very nice one.

"Can I depend on you to handle it?" Pia asked, already on her way out. "I'd do it myself but you're so good at everything—so organized."

I'm not so organized, she wanted to scream. *I'm twenty-one years old and I'd like to have a life too.*

"Sure," she said. "Leave the numbers on my desk and I'll get started tomorrow."

"Gee!" Pia peered at her watch. "It's past seven, my guy's gonna kill me. We're seeing *Manhattan*. I'm crazy about Woody Allen. Can you check all the lights are off and lock up?"

Thanks a lot, Pia. Why don't I collect your paycheck too?

She took the subway home, ignoring an elderly flasher in the requisite grubby raincoat.

Two giggly girls sitting opposite her screamed with laughter when the flasher turned his attention on them. "Get it blown up an' frame it!" one of them yelled, making a rude gesture.

The flasher slunk off down the train, searching for more docile victims.

Lauren stopped at the corner market near her apartment and bought a can of beans and a loaf of bread. Another gourmet dinner coming up, she thought wryly.

Since arriving in New York she hadn't been out once. Her routine was work and home—it didn't deviate. A couple of guys had asked her for a date—one a photographer who'd dropped by the office to see Samm, and the other an assistant to Samm's accountant. She'd declined both offers. Who needed the hassle of a man? She certainly didn't.

Nick Angelo.

Every so often his name popped into her head for no reason at all, and she found herself wondering where he was and what he was doing, and most of all—was he happy?

Who cared? Nick Angelo was her past. She told herself she didn't give a damn if she never saw him again.

39

Manny Manfred was without doubt the fattest man Nick had ever seen. Manny wasn't just fat, he was gargantuan—with beady eyes, layers of jowls and chins and dyed yellow hair sporting inch-long black roots. He sat in a specially made Naugahyde chair behind a cluttered desk, sucking 7-Up through a straw and tossing handfuls of cashew nuts into his greedy little mouth. He was not what Nick had expected. Q.J. and Manny together must have been the sight of the century!

"I'm Nick."

"So what?"

"You told me to come by."

"Oh, yeah, Q.J. sent ya."

"That's right."

"Whaddaya want?"

"A job. Part time. I need to be free to go on auditions if they come up."

"What auditions?"

"I'm an actor."

"Says who?"

"Says me."

Manny shifted his enormous bulk and sighed. "Can ya drive?"

"Yes."

"Can ya drive good?"

"Yes."

"Ya got a clean license?"

"You bet."

"See Luigi. Tell him I said t'put you on the airport run."

"Is that it?"

"Whaddaya want—a kiss an' a cuddle? Scram."

He scrammed. Saw Luigi—a bullet-headed man with a broken front tooth and a sour expression—got a short lecture on the do's and don'ts of driving a limo and was told to report back at eight p.m. It was as easy as that.

It wasn't so easy getting back into Cyndra's apartment. The super pounced on him just as he was using his credit card on her door. The super was a ferocious-looking man with shoulder-length dreadlocks, two gold teeth and a take-no-prisoners attitude. He clamped his burly hand on Nick's shoulder. "What you up to, mon?"

He attempted to explain.

The super was having none of it. He threw him out.

Nick realized he was lucky to get away without the Dreadlock King calling the police.

He hung around outside the building until Annie Broderick emerged. She looked different in clothes. A track suit covered her curvy body, and a baseball cap hid her short red hair.

"Remember me?" he said.

"No," she said.

"Sure you do," he said, laying on the irresistible green-eyed stare.

"What do you want?" she asked, unimpressed.

"Your help."

She walked over to an old brown Packard and opened the door. "Why?"

He spread the charm, waiting for the usual reaction. " 'Cause you know me. We're friends."

She seemed surprised. "We are?"

"Sure we are," he said persuasively.

Annie had wasted enough time. "Now, listen," she said sharply. "Cyndra's brother—or whoever you are—stop bugging me. I may look like an easy touch, but trust me—no way."

"I'm not after your money," he said, quite affronted.

"That's good, 'cause I don't have any."

"All I want to do is leave a note for Cyndra. Tell her where she can reach me."

"Who's stopping you?"

"The super's on my case—I can't even get my bag outta her apartment. I need to explain."

"Explain to me. I'll pass it on," she said, waiting expectantly.

He didn't say a word.

"Well?" She was getting impatient. "Where shall I say you'll be?"

"I don't have a place."

Now this is where she was supposed to feel sorry for him and offer the use of her couch.

"You don't have a place," she repeated blankly. "Too bad."

So much for the old Angelo charm. This female had a cold heart.

"No—but I got a job," he said quickly, as if that might change her mind.

"Good for you." She glanced meaningfully at her watch. "I'm late for class."

Maybe she was a dyke—anything was possible. "Just tell her I was here and I'll be calling her. Okay?"

Annie nodded and took off.

He spent the rest of the day wandering around Hollywood—checking out the stars' names embedded in the sidewalk, mooching through a small shop filled with still photos from movies and finally ending up at Farmers' Market on Fairfax, where he ordered corned beef and cabbage from one of the many open-air counters offering all different kinds of traditional fare.

He thought about what he was going to do next. Money was no problem, he'd left Chicago with twelve hundred bucks in his pocket —not bad considering he usually spent it as fast as he earned it. If he wanted he could rent an apartment and get himself settled—although it made more sense to wait for Cyndra to get back and camp out on her couch for a few weeks until he got the feel of the city and decided whether he wanted to stay or not.

Renting a car was definitely a priority. He'd soon realized that in L.A. the buses ran infrequently and did not cover the city. There was no subway, so a car was a necessity. He looked up rentals in the yellow pages and arranged a month-long deal on an old Buick.

Behind the wheel of the car he felt a lot more secure. At least he had a place he belonged—somewhere to call home.

"Ya ain't plannin' on wearin' what ya got on?" Luigi demanded, squinting at Nick with a disgusted expression.

"What's wrong with what I got on?"

"Ya gotta be fuckin' kiddin'." Luigi ran his hand over his bullet-head. "Ya look like a bum."

They glared at each other. This was not an auspicious start.

"I don't have anything else," Nick said. "I lost my bag."

"There's a closet in there." Luigi indicated the back room. "Find somethin' that fits you. And for crissakes, move it—you're on the airport run."

"Who am I meeting?"

"Mr. Evans. He's a businessman. Ya hold up the card with his name on it, ya escort him out to the limo, ya shut the privacy glass, an' you drive him anywhere he wants to go. Oh, an' remember t'drive nice an' smooth. Mr. Evans don't like no sudden stops."

"Sure."

"An' another thing—no talkin' unless he speaks first. Them's the rules of the game. These people pay good money for a limo, they don't want no conversation."

Ha! Like he was looking for meaningful communication with a total stranger. What kind of schmuck did Luigi take him for?

He searched through the closet in the back room and found a pair of black pants, a dark jacket and a none-too-clean white shirt. The clothes didn't fit properly but what the hell—he'd be sitting behind the wheel of a car anyway.

There were a couple of other drivers back there, smoking and playing cards. Neither of them took any notice of him.

Luigi thrust a form at him. "Fill it out," he ordered.

He put down Cyndra's address and lied about his driving experience, writing that he'd driven for a limo company in Chicago. That information took the edge off Luigi's scowl.

Idly, he wondered what favor Manny owed Q.J. One of these days he intended to find out.

Luigi gave him a silver limousine to drive. It was shined and pol-

ished pretty good, but once he got in he realized the limo had seen
better days. The back, where the passengers sat, was all spruced up
with a single rose in a glass vase, a bowl of fresh fruit and side compartments stocked with booze. But in front the leather covering the
seat was cracked, and there were plastic strips peeling off the windows. So much for Glamour Limousines. The car reminded him of a
gorgeous girl with the clap.

"Ya know the way to the airport?" Luigi asked.

He had no idea how to get there but he nodded anyway. As soon as
he left the garage he parked the limo on a side street and studied a
map he'd found in the glove compartment. No big deal. L.A. was all
straight roads going in different directions like one big board game.
He clicked the radio on and zoomed out to the airport listening to
Jimi Hendrix at full volume.

He reached LAX twenty minutes early and had no idea where to
park. Traffic cops were everywhere—yelling and shouting, making
sure all the vehicles kept moving.

Rolling down his window, he waved ten bucks at a porter and asked
where he could put the car.

The porter grabbed the money and obligingly told him where to
leave it so he wouldn't get a ticket.

His passenger arrived on a flight from Switzerland. Mr. Evans was
a swarthy man with patent-leather hair and wrap-around black
shades. Kind of strange at ten o'clock at night, but Nick was getting
used to the foibles of people who lived in Los Angeles.

Mr. Evans had no luggage except a snakeskin briefcase that he
clutched firmly to his side, snarling ungratefully when Nick attempted
to take it.

"Only trying to help," Nick said with a shrug, leading the man to
the limo.

Mr. Evans lived in a high rise on Wilshire. Nick dropped him off
and waited for a tip, a word of thanks, anything.

Mr. Evans was not into pleasantries. He walked into his building
without a backward glance.

"Screw you too, buddy," Nick muttered, deciding that maybe the
life of a limo driver was not for him.

Back at Glamour Limousines, Luigi sat in his office picking his nose while speaking on the phone. "I'm gonna hump your juicy ass off, sweetie. I'm gonna—" He stopped abruptly when Nick entered. "What the fuck *you* want?" he asked, covering the mouthpiece.

"I brought the car back. Thought you'd like to know I delivered your passenger safely."

"Whaddaya want, a medal?" Luigi was like a lesser version of Manny—they'd obviously both graduated from the same charm school.

"Same time tomorrow?" Nick asked, wondering what kind of woman Luigi had panting on the other end of the phone.

"Yeah," Luigi snapped, anxious to get back to his sweetie.

"I'll be here."

Maybe.

If nothing better comes along.

He got in his rented Buick and cruised down Hollywood Boulevard, finally stopping at a motel and booking a room for the night.

"Wanna hooker?" the desk clerk asked, reluctantly shifting his attention from a well-thumbed porno magazine.

"Not tonight."

The clerk regarded him suspiciously. "Why don'tcha?"

He didn't bother replying.

Lying on a lumpy bed watching Johnny Carson do his monologue he wondered if he'd made the right move leaving Chicago. He'd left a good job at Q.J.'s, a great-looking woman—and for what? A fleabag motel and a shit job servicing other people.

He'd give it a couple of weeks and if things didn't improve he was on a plane out of there.

Emerson Burn had a mane of hair better than any girl's. Lauren couldn't help staring. She'd been a fan for so many years, loved his music, and now she was in his presence. It didn't seem possible. His thick, shaggy, honey-colored hair fell way below his shoulders. His eyes were a dreamy gray shadowed by long curling lashes. His nose was aquiline and his lips surprisingly full for a man.

You're staring, Roberts.

I can't help it!

Lauren wasn't alone with him. Also present were his manager, his publicist, his personal assistant and Selina, who—clad in a leopard-skin cat suit—prowled his apartment as if she owned it. Selina was incredibly thin and almost as tall as Nature. She had straight white-blond hair that hung to her waist and incredible cat eyes set in a classically beautiful face. She kept fixing her eyes on Emerson as if to say *This is mine and I don't want anybody touching it.*

"So," said Emerson, standing up and stretching, "I guess that's it."

Even though he was in his late thirties he was still in great shape. He wore skintight black leather pants on his long skinny legs, scuffed boots and a white shirt with some kind of ridiculous frill down the front. Ridiculous or not, on him it worked.

Lauren, busy making notes, realized he hadn't looked at her once. And why should he? She was only the hired help.

Selina floated over to Emerson and kissed him full on the mouth, making sure everyone noticed the little bit of tongue play she indulged in. "You're such a sport, letting us use your apartment," she sighed. "Samm's going to be absolutely amazed."

"S'long as we 'ave fun, darlin'," he replied, putting his arm around her, pressing her in the small of her back and guiding her in for another kiss.

They kissed as if nobody else was in the room—in fact their smooching session went on for so long that Lauren thought they were going to leave the meeting and rush off into the bedroom. Nobody else seemed to take any notice. She imagined they'd seen it all before.

When the kiss was finished so was Emerson. "Bye, everyone," he called, striding to the door.

His entourage leaped to their feet and followed him.

"Later, strong man," Selina whispered, blowing him more kisses.

As soon as he was gone Selina stopped being the ethereal little flower and turned into the tough ball-breaker she really was. "Are we all organized, Laura? I don't expect any fuck-ups."

"Yes, Serina," Lauren replied sarcastically. "Everything's under control."

"It better be," Selina said threateningly, as if Lauren was her personal slave. "And"—she spun around—"if Samm finds out about the party before it happens I'm holding you personally responsible."

Lauren decided that of all the girls Selina was the worst bitch.

Back at the office Samm gave her a blast. "And exactly where have you been all morning?"

"I had to go to the dentist," she lied.

"Not good enough," Samm said curtly. "Make dental appointments on your own time, not when you're supposed to be working."

"I don't have any personal time," Lauren explained. "You've got me working weekends and I'm here late every night. I had a toothache —what was I supposed to do?"

"Hmm . . . I suppose you had no choice," Samm said, giving in. She frowned. "I hate to say it, but this place is chaos without you."

"You managed very well before I came along," Lauren pointed out.

"Yes, well, that was then and this is now. Let's get back to work." Samm tapped her painted nails on her desktop. The polish looked like the high-gloss finish on a new car.

Lauren sat down and prepared to take notes.

"First I want you to send a bottle of champagne to Antonio," Samm said. "He had a vile time on the Selina shoot. I'm really going to have to talk to that girl before she trips over her own ego. Oh, and then call Flash Cosmetics, they need Nature in the studio on the same day she has that big *Vogue* shoot. Tell Nature she'll have to start earlier. Ignore her screaming. After that talk to *Swimwear* magazine, they need all the girls on the tenth. I've told them it's impossible to get anybody out to the Virgin Islands before the twelfth—but they're insisting. You deal with it, Lauren, you're so good with people."

"Consider it all taken care of," she said, getting up.

As soon as she reached her desk Pia was beside her whispering, "Everything okay?"

"All systems go."

Pia looked relieved. "You're so good at this!"

Yes, Pia. I should be doing your job and making your salary.

At lunchtime several of the girls stopped by the office with a cake.

"God, I hate birthdays," Samm said, reluctantly blowing out the candles. "Who told you all?"

Nobody owned up.

"At least she thinks it's over and done with now," Pia murmured. "Boy, will she be surprised!"

"How are you getting her up to Emerson's apartment?" Lauren asked. It was the one detail she hadn't been in charge of.

"Selina's taking her. She's told Samm that she and Emerson have a surprise, and they want to tell her personally."

"Did Samm fall for it?"

"Absolutely. She thinks they're planning marriage, and she's all set to talk them out of it."

Later, Nature managed to corner her at her desk. She was all blond hair, blue eyes and glowing Acapulco tan. "I can't believe Selina 'as bagged Emerson Burn," she complained. "She's not 'is type, too

290

bloody skinny. He likes a bird with a bit of meat on 'er bones—me, fer instance!"

"Do you know him?"

Nature licked her lips. "No, but I intend to."

Lauren sensed trouble ahead.

As soon as she could she left the office and raced over to Emerson Burn's apartment to check on all the arrangements. She was wearing a pleated skirt and a plain blue sweater, her hair pulled back in a thick braid. There was obviously not going to be time for her to get back to her apartment and change into something more festive. So what? Nobody cared how she looked, as long as she stayed in the background and did her job.

Selina was already there, floating around the apartment issuing orders. Emerson's four servants hovered with surly expressions. They did not appreciate every single one of his girlfriends coming in and trying to take over.

"Thank God you're here," exclaimed Selina. "Go and talk to the caterers. Check that they know what they're doing. Oh, and Laura, you did make sure everyone was told to be here promptly at eight o'clock?"

"All taken care of. And by the way, my name is Lauren, not Laura."

"Whatever." Selina waved a beautifully manicured hand in the air.

Bitch! Lauren thought as she hurried into the kitchen to confer with the caterers.

Various members of Emerson's entourage skulked around unhappy because he'd thrown open his apartment for Samm's surprise party.

After she was done with the caterers she viewed the flower arrangements, checked out the guest list with a burly guard at the door and finally found a moment to spend alone.

Locking herself in the guest bathroom she gazed at her reflection in the mirror. Was this how she planned to spend her life? Arranging parties for other people to have a good time? She'd wanted to become a famous New York stage actress. Now she was this unimportant little gofer doing things for other people. Lauren Roberts—invisible.

Somebody tried the door of the bathroom. She ignored them, they could wait.

Now there was hammering on the door.

Angrily she flung it open and came face to face with Emerson Burn.

"Who're you?" he demanded.

"Lauren," she replied, curbing a strong desire to reach out and touch his shaggy mane of honey-colored curls. "From Samm's Agency. I'm organizing the party—remember? We did meet."

He shook his golden hair and took her arm. "Follow me, I want you to 'ear something."

"Pardon?"

"Don't argue," he said, grabbing her arm and leading her down a plushly carpeted corridor into the back of the apartment where he'd built a state-of-the-art recording studio. "Sit down and 'ave a listen to this."

Exactly who did he think he was bossing around?

"Mr. Burn," she said, "I have no time to listen. I'm trying to organize a party for you—I have to see that everything runs the way it's supposed to."

"This is *my* bloody apartment. *I'm* paying for the bleedin' party, so sit down and shut up."

He sounded like Nature. Maybe the two of them *did* belong together—after all, they shared the same accent.

She sat stiffly on a chair while he marched over to a control panel and pressed a couple of buttons. Suddenly the room was flooded with sound.

She recognized his voice immediately—that sexy, cocksure rasp. She'd been thirteen when he'd burst onto the scene and taken America by storm with his most famous single, "Dog Days and Wild Women."

The song playing was a love song, not the romantic kind—but a driving, hard song called "Viper Woman."

"Listen to this and tell me what you think," Emerson said, pacing up and down his studio.

She studied his leather-clad legs. "Does it matter what *I* think?"

"Yeah, you're the public," he said, speaking quite slowly as if she was an idiot. "You're the girl in the street. You won't kiss my ass—you'll tell me the truth." He turned up the volume, almost blasting her out of the room.

The lyrics hammered her senses.

She loves me for my money
She loves me for my power
She even goddamn loves me for my big fat car
She's a Viper Woman
Loves to rock 'n roll
She's a Viper Woman
She only got one goal
Oh yeah!
Money money
Sex and honey
She got her eye on it all
Money money
Sex and honey
This bitch is pretty damn cool!

The record certainly wasn't vintage Emerson Burn.

He turned the volume down and stared at her. "Well?"

"It's . . . it's okay," she said, standing up and smoothing her skirt.

"Okay." He repeated "okay" as though it was a dirty word. "What are you—deaf?" Then he raised his voice. "It's my new single, for crissake. It's a fuckin' *hit!*"

Obviously he didn't care to hear the truth. Maybe she should lie and say it was the best thing she'd ever heard.

Oh, the hell with it, why should she?

"I don't like it," she said. "I don't appreciate you calling women bitches. If it's a love song, why isn't it more loving?"

"Who the *fuck* do you think you are?" he exploded. " 'Viper Woman' is one of the best things I've ever recorded."

"Who the hell do you think *you* are?" she blazed back. "I'm not some burned-out groupie who's going to tell you it's wonderful if I don't think so. You asked for my opinion and you got it."

"Get the fuck outta my sight," he snarled. "You don't know shit."

She was furious, but there was nothing she could do. A party was about to take place and she had to make sure everything ran smoothly.

With as much dignity as she could muster she left the room.

. . .

293

"I knew this was going to be a good day."

Lauren turned around and faced Jimmy Cassady, the photographer who'd asked her out a few weeks earlier.

"Hi," she said, glad to encounter a friendly face.

"Hi," he replied with a smile.

She groped for conversation. "Do you think Samm was surprised?"

"Surprised?" he laughed. "More like pissed."

"I guess it's not much fun being forty."

"Forty?" He laughed even louder. "You think Samm's forty? The woman is fifty."

"What?" Lauren was amazed. "She doesn't look it."

"She doesn't even look forty," Jimmy said. "Samm's a phenomenon. Have you seen pictures of her when she was modeling?"

"No."

"Dynamite!"

Lauren's eyes darted around the crowded party. Most of the guests had arrived on time and when Samm put in an appearance with Selina on one side and Emerson on the other they'd all screamed "SURPRISE!" right on cue. And now everything was going so well she thought she might sneak out.

"What's *your* story?" Jimmy asked, lighting a cigarette.

She turned to look at him. He was in his early thirties, short and wiry with a pointed face and hair that was thinning on top and long in the back. He wore it in a ponytail. He also wore John Lennon eyeglasses and tight blue jeans. The jeans immediately reminded her of Nick.

Sternly she put Nick Angelo out of her head.

"I don't have a story," she said, deciding she could exit through the kitchen without anyone noticing.

"Everyone has a story," he replied confidently. "And I'm interested in finding out yours."

She shrugged. "Small-town girl, came to New York, got a job. That's it."

"There's a lot more to you than that. I could tell the moment I asked you out."

"Not used to getting turned down, huh?"

He drew on his cigarette and regarded her with a contemplative expression. "You're not married, are you?" He looked pointedly at her left hand, bereft of rings.

"No, I'm not married," she said defensively.

"Going steady? I don't notice a guy with you."

"I'm not seeing anyone."

"Then why can't we go out?"

Good question, but she owed him no explanation. "Has it occurred to you that I might not want to?" she said, hoping to put an end to the conversation.

He refused to be put off. "Is it just me or does everyone get the big no?"

"I'm leaving," she said, and then added, "Everything's going nicely, they don't need me anymore."

"You organized this event?"

"Right." She began slowly edging toward the kitchen.

He followed her. "You did a pretty fine job, but you'd better not leave."

"Why?"

He gestured over to the far corner. "Because Selina is just about to kill Nature. Take a look."

Lauren looked. Nature was all over Emerson Burn, who lounged on a couch, his leather-clad legs stretched out before him. Her shrieking laugh could be heard all the way across the room.

Selina hovered behind him clad in a floating chiffon dress, her cat eyes signaling immediate danger.

"It's not my problem," Lauren said.

"How come?" Jimmy asked. "You're known around the office as the solver of all problems."

"I am?"

He grinned. "Yeah. Have you any idea what they call you behind your back?"

She wished he'd leave her alone. "I'm sure you can't wait to tell me."

He seemed amused. "Miss E."

Now she was really irritated. "Miss E.? What's that supposed to mean?"

He laughed. "Miss Efficiency."

"Oh, thanks a lot," she said, not exactly thrilled with the title.

He pressed on. "It's true, isn't it? You do everything for everybody. You've made yourself indispensable. How long have you been there

—three months? The other bookers must love you. I bet even Pia's getting nervous about her job."

How come he knew so much about her? "What are you talking about?"

He stubbed his cigarette in a nearby ashtray. "I'm talking about you. You're the ideal personal assistant—and don't think it's escaped Samm's notice, because nothing escapes Madam."

"I'm not after anyone's job," Lauren said. "I'm perfectly happy doing what I'm doing."

He stared at her from behind his John Lennon specs. "Yes?"

"Yes," she replied defiantly, preparing to take off.

"Oh, shit!" he exclaimed.

"What?"

"Take a look at them now."

She glanced over at Selina, Nature and Emerson in time to observe Selina slowly and deliberately pour a full glass of champagne over Emerson's head.

"Leave 'em to it," Jimmy said, putting a restraining hand on her arm just in case she was about to take care of that problem too. "They'll work it out between 'em."

Emerson Burn was now on his feet, stoned and swaying, champagne dripping down his face. "Yer stupid bleedin' cow," he shouted. "You've ruined me bleedin' 'air."

"Yeah," Nature joined in. "Look what you've done."

"Stay out of it, bimbo," yelled Selina.

"What'd you call me?" Nature yelled back.

And before anyone could stop them they were at each other like a couple of wildcats, tearing at hair, clothing, earrings—anything they could get their hands on.

Emerson prevented anyone from getting near them. "Let 'em at it," he shouted happily. "This is the best part of the bleedin' party."

"Come on," said Jimmy, taking Lauren's arm. "I'm escorting you out of here."

Before she could argue he steered her to the door and they slipped away into the night.

Cyndra stormed around her apartment raging in disbelief. "Someone's been in here. I don't believe it! Look, Reece, *look*, there's cigarette butts in the ashtrays and a burn hole on the arm of the couch."

"Even better," Reece shouted from the bedroom, where he was investigating further. "Instead of taking *our* stuff they've left a bag here."

"What?" she said, marching into the bedroom to see what he was talking about. Sure enough, there was somebody's bag full of clothes. She began searching through it.

"I don't understand," Reece said, scratching his chin.

"*I* do," Cyndra said, pulling out a pair of worn jeans. "This is Nick's stuff."

"Who's Nick?"

"I told you about him—he's my brother."

Screw it! Reece thought. *Relatives! That's all I need.* "How'd he get in? An' where is he?" Reece demanded.

"Knowing Nick, he broke in. Is there a note or something?"

"That's a helluva thing, breakin' into a person's apartment," Reece grumbled.

"Oh, like *you* wouldn't."

He chewed on his lip. "How long is it since you've seen this brother of yours?"

"Going on four years."

Reece's imagination began running wild. Cyndra, his little darkie beauty, probably had a brother who was over six feet tall and black as his patent-leather shoes. What's more, it was likely that he'd want to beat the shit out of him. "You gotta be careful of relatives," he cautioned.

She turned on him angrily. "Nick's my brother. I love him."

"Well," Reece said, hoping the brother would not put in a return appearance, "there's nothing we can do about it. I'll store his bag in the closet and we'll see if he contacts you. One thing, honey. If he does—I've had experience—don't get too cozy with relatives, 'cause they come to stay and then you can never get rid of 'em."

"Thanks, I'll take your advice," she said sarcastically. "I'll throw my own brother out on the street and hope he doesn't bug me again."

If they'd been married longer Reece might have smacked her, he didn't appreciate sassy women. But he knew that the moment you hit a woman you had to have her in a position where she couldn't leave, and since they'd only just gotten married, she might take off on him, and then where would he be, what with the money he'd laid out on singing lessons, clothes and all the rest.

"I'm going to a meeting," he said, adjusting the tilt of his Stetson.

She didn't reply. She was too busy thinking about where Nick might be.

The second night of working for Glamour Limousines Nick landed the airport run again. This time his passenger was an anorexic woman producer with cropped hair and a bad temper. Julia something or other. She sat in the back of his limo snorting coke and talking nonstop on a portable phone.

When they reached Bel Air he got lost in the winding hills and she screamed at him, calling him a dumb fuck and a stupid prick. He almost stopped the car and threw her out, but wisdom prevailed.

When they reached her house she changed moods and invited him in.

"What for?" he asked.

She had desperate eyes and bad breath. "A fuck."

"Sorry—got another job."

Sweet revenge. Not that he'd have fucked her even with somebody else's dick.

So far he was not having a wonderful time in L.A.

That night he stayed at the motel again, and in the morning he called Cyndra.

"Nick!" she exclaimed excitedly. "I've been waiting for your call, I *knew* you were here. I went through your bag and unpacked it. Naturally I had to wash all your clothes, you filthy hog. Nothing's changed, huh?"

"Where've you been?" he demanded. "I came all this way and you weren't even home."

"Where are you?"

"In some crappy motel on Hollywood Boulevard."

"Get over here fast! You'll stay with me and Reece. Hurry up, I'll make you breakfast."

"Since when do you cook?"

"This is California. I take it from the freezer, put it in the toaster and call it waffles. You'll *love* my cooking!"

He made it over to her apartment as fast as possible, parking his car on the street.

She greeted him at the door, almost jumping up and down with excitement. Throwing her arms around him she hugged him tightly and dragged him inside.

"It *was* you, wasn't it? You broke into my apartment."

He grinned. "What else could I do? You weren't around, so I spent the night here, an' when I came back the next day the super wouldn't let me in."

Cyndra giggled. "Don't mess with Rasta. He's a wild man."

They went into the tiny kitchen, where she poured him coffee and toasted her famous frozen waffles.

"So where were you?" he asked again.

"Guess," she said, grinning happily.

He hated playing games. "I can't guess."

She took a deep breath. "I got married."

Oh, great. "You did?"

"Yes—me and Reece got married in Las Vegas." She looked at him with a half-guilty, half-delighted expression—seeking his approval. "Oh, Nick, I hope you like him. He's helping me with my career—he really cares about me."

"Good. 'Cause if he didn't I'd have to kill him," Nick said, making it sound like a joke.

"He does. You'll see. I mean, when you first meet him you might think he's a tiny bit older than me and, y'know, like maybe his cowboy clothes are kinda silly, but he's gonna help me make it big."

"If you say so."

Her marriage had taken him by surprise. He'd imagined them sharing an apartment and hanging out together just like Chicago. Now she had a husband and there was no way he could stay.

He tried to find out more. "What does this character do?"

"Personal manager," she said proudly.

"Who does he manage?"

"Who do you think? *Me*, of course!"

Of course. "So how does he make money?"

She waved her hands vaguely in the air. "I don't know, he has an office he goes to. We don't discuss money. He always has enough."

Sometimes his sister was extremely naïve—how could she not know what her husband did?

"You'll stay here," she said. "The couch turns into a bed—you'll be very comfortable."

It was different now. He was certainly glad to see her, but he didn't plan on moving in. "No, it won't work out—not with you bein' newly married an' all."

She couldn't hide her disappointment. "You've *got* to stay here, Nick."

How could he resist her big brown eyes? "Maybe just for tonight, but then I'll find my own place."

"You can listen to my tapes," she said proudly. "They're professional. I'm a real singer now."

"Yeah?" He remembered her singing debut at Q.J.'s—a total disaster.

"I've been taking lessons," she said. "Reece has a record company interested in cutting a demo with me. And when we were in Vegas I met a couple of the talent bookers at the big hotels, and they might hire me to sing in one of the lounges."

"Sounds great."

"And it's all because of Reece."

"I'm glad you're happy."

"So what made you come to L.A.? I thought everything was going so well in Chicago."

Yeah. Going so well—all the way to nowhere.

"I finally decided I hadda give acting a shot. You know it's what I've always wanted to do."

"This is the right place. Maybe Reece can be your manager too."

Sure. Bring him in on a family package.

When Reece arrived home he and Nick sized each other up, circling warily.

Nick thought Reece looked like a dumb asshole with his fringed suede jacket, stupid cowboy hat and droopy moustache. Not good enough for Cyndra by a long way. And too old.

Reece was relieved to discover that Nick was white. All day long his imagination had been running riot—Cyndra's brother had been getting bigger and blacker as the day progressed. Now here was this skinny white kid, and he didn't feel threatened at all.

"What do you do, Nick?" he asked, going for the friendly brother-in-law approach.

"I was running a bar in Chicago, but I came out here to get into acting."

Reece couldn't help himself. "Yeah—you and every other schmuck in town."

"Excuse me?" Nick said, holding his temper in check because he didn't want to upset his sister.

"Oh . . . no offense. I mean kids come to Hollywood all the time tryin' to make it. Everyone wants to be a star."

"Oh, I'll make it," Nick said confidently.

"That's nice," Reece replied. "Y'see, with me behind her, your sister's gonna be a big star."

"Is that why you married her?" he asked, hitting pay dirt.

Reece glared at him. "I married her 'cause I love her."

"That's nice," Nick replied, giving him a long hard stare. "Because if anyone ever hurts my sister, they're dead."

Reece couldn't wait to corner Cyndra in the kitchen. "How long is he gonna stay?" he asked agitatedly.

"Only for the night," she said, not catching his concern. "I'm trying to persuade him to hang around longer. Why don't *you* talk to him?"

"Sure," he said, although he had no intention of doing so. The sooner the brother was out of their way the better.

The next morning Nick sat at the kitchen table studying the newspaper, circling apartment possibilities. "I'd like to get a place at the beach," he said.

"That's easy," Cyndra replied. "I've heard the rent is lower in Venice. We could look around later today."

"Good idea," he said, folding the newspaper.

Later, when they were driving along Santa Monica he asked her if she ever heard from Joey.

She brushed back her long black hair. "I wish I did. I wrote him several times, he never bothered to reply. The last time I called, someone said he'd moved and left no forwarding address."

"Sounds like Joey."

She nodded wistfully. "Sometimes I miss him. We shared so much together."

Nick felt the same way. "Yeah, we did, didn't we?" he said, thinking of the good old days when the three of them had faced the world alone—hitching rides, sleeping on park benches, sharing a motel room.

The first apartment they looked at was a rathole with broken windows, stained carpets and barely hidden roach motels. As soon as they got outside, Cyndra said, "Ugh, if that's the kind of places available I still say you should stay with us. Reece wouldn't mind. He likes you."

Sure, Nick thought. Like a rat loves a cobra.

"Will you think about it? Please?"

He promised he would, but of course he wouldn't. One night with Reece Webster was one night too many.

The second apartment they saw was better. Unfortunately the rent was too high, so they moved on. The next three were hopeless. On their sixth try they found a pleasant if somewhat rundown house on the beach in Venice divided into one-room apartments.

The landlady—a slovenly woman in a grubby orange robe and fluffy bedroom slippers—showed them a front-room apartment overlooking the beach. It was a large, sunny room with a small kitchenette.

"No bathroom?" Nick asked.

"You share with the other apartment in front," the landlady said, a cigarette dangling from the corner of her mouth.

"I dunno—"

"The tenant is never there—she travels all the time, so you more or less got it all to yourself."

He looked at Cyndra. "What d'you think?"

"It certainly beats anything else we've seen."

"You superstitious?" the landlady asked, picking tobacco from her teeth.

Nick noticed a hole in one of her slippers. "Why?" he asked, trying not to stare.

" 'Cause a guy died in here last week. Hung himself." She hoisted an escaping bra strap. "I'm up-front about it—don't wanna fool you. If you're into that karma thing, you may not wanna live here."

He shook his head. "Karma thing? Shit, the rent is right an' it's on the beach—I'll take it."

Cyndra squeezed his hand. "Reece and I will help you fix it up. If we all come here next weekend with a bucketful of paint we can make it look terrific."

"You got yourself a job. And you," he said, turning to the landlady, "got yourself a tenant."

After leaving a deposit he drove Cyndra back to Hollywood. She talked all the way about old times and the future and her career. Finally she just threw it into the conversation. "Did you ever hear from Lauren? Remember—that girl you liked in high school?"

As if he was going to forget. Was she crazy? He would *never* forget Lauren.

"Nope. I guess she dumped me," he replied, making it sound casual. "I wrote her a lot—she never replied."

"She probably married that big jerk she was engaged to," Cyndra said, rolling down the window. "Strick—wasn't that his name?"

"Stock."

"Oh, yeah, Stock." She giggled. "Dumb oaf! Hey, remember that New Year's Eve when he broke your nose?"

"What a prick!"

"And then a few weeks later you beat *him* up."

"Those were the good times," he said dryly.

"Would you ever go back?"

"Would you?" he countered.

She hesitated. "Only if I was a star. A real big star. I'd be driven into town for a visit in a fancy limo and I'd show 'em *all* who I was— every damn one of them." Now she was warming to her subject. "I'd be wearin' one of those big fox fur coats like Diana Ross, an' some kinda slinky sequined dress. And I'd have a carload of presents for Aretha Mae and Harlan."

"Do you miss him?" Nick asked, pulling up at a stoplight.

Her expression was wistful. "Sometimes I feel bad about leavin' him behind—kinda guilty."

"Yeah, I know what you mean. But we couldn't have taken him."

"I know."

"Hey—maybe we'll *both* make it big an' we can go back together. How's that?"

She nodded enthusiastically. "Yeah! We'll show that damn town a thing or two."

As he was dropping her off at her apartment they bumped into Annie Broderick getting into her car.

"I see you two found each other," Annie said. "Is he really your brother?"

Cyndra nodded happily, clinging to his arm. "Absolutely. Didn't you believe him?"

"You aren't exactly the same color," Annie said bluntly.

"We share the same father, but not the same mother," Cyndra explained matter-of-factly.

"I was only looking out for your interests," Annie said, pushing her hand through her short red hair. "Didn't want some stranger breaking into your apartment."

"You looked after her interests, all right," Nick said. "I almost had to sleep in my car."

"At least you've got a car. Think yourself lucky."

"Thanks, Annie," Cyndra said quickly—defusing the situation.

"What's *her* problem?" Nick asked, as soon as she left.

"It's tough being a single girl alone in L.A."

"No boyfriend?"

"She's into her career."

"What does she do anyway? She said something about going to class the other night."

Cyndra looked amused. "What do you *think* she does? What do you think *everyone* does in L.A.? She's an actress of course."

"So—how do you get into this class of hers? Do you have to pay?"

"Dunno—never been. Talk to Annie about it."

"Maybe I will."

A few weeks later Nick had settled into the L.A. routine. He had his job at Glamour Limousines. He had his apartment at the beach. He'd even started to work out a little and eat healthier foods, and he spoke to Cyndra on the phone every couple of days.

All she could talk about was the deals Reece was about to make on her behalf. He didn't trust Reece. The guy had "con artist" written all over him—he'd seen enough cheap hustlers in O.J.'s to recognize that combination of smarmy charm and bullshit a mile away. Still . . . it wasn't his business, Cyndra seemed happy enough.

One day he asked her for Annie Broderick's number.

"Why? Are you plannin' on taking her out?" Cyndra asked.

He hadn't considered it, but it wasn't such a bad idea if he wanted to find out more about her acting class. Plus he was feeling horny. Oh, was he horny! Of course, Annie Broderick was not his usual type, too gamin-looking and short, but he had to admit she did have a sensational body—and it had been too long between pit stops. He was even starting to miss DeVille.

Cyndra gave him Annie's number. He waited a day and called. "I'd like to buy you lunch," he said, expecting an immediate yes.

"Why?" she asked suspiciously.

Oh, shit, he was going to have to work for it. " 'Cause I kinda think we got off on a downer, an' I don't have many friends here."

She was silent.

He was prepared to work—but not that hard. "Hey—big deal. You wanna have lunch or not?"

She was not exactly filled with enthusiasm. "Maybe."

Didn't she realize this was Nick Angelo calling? "Maybe. What's that supposed to mean?"

"Well . . . can you come to where I work?"

"Tell me where."

"The Body Beautiful on Santa Monica."

"Are you kidding me? What's the Body Beautiful?"

"It's a health club."

Glamour Limousines. The Body Beautiful. They sure loved to foster illusions in L.A. "Okay," he said.

"I get a break at noon."

"I'll be there."

Body Beautiful was in a big white building on Santa Monica. The place was alive with people hurrying in and out, all wearing shorts, tank tops, cut-outs, tights, every kind of variation on workout gear.

"Can I help you?" asked a California blonde perched behind the reception desk, her perky breasts covered by a white Body Beautiful T-shirt.

"I'm looking for Annie Broderick," he said, checking out her attributes.

She caught him looking, fluttered long fake lashes and smiled. "Oh . . . you must be Nick."

He was surprised Annie had mentioned him—maybe she liked him better than she'd let on.

"Is she around?"

"She's getting changed. She'll be with you in a minute." The girl's smile brightened. "I understand you're new in town."

"Sort of."

"How did you meet Annie?"

"She lives in the same building as my sister," he said, noticing that she wasn't wearing a bra.

"Hmm . . ." She eyed him hungrily. "I wish *I* did."

He knew a come-on when it hit him in the face. "What's *your* name?" he asked, going along for the ride.

Annie cut him off at the pass by appearing at the reception desk. "Let's go," she said briskly, taking his arm and leading him out of the building.

"Where are we going?" he asked, thinking she looked healthy and glowing and really quite attractive—even if she wasn't his type.

"There's a health food place across the street. Have you ever tried a turkey burger?"

"Is that like a hamburger without the taste?"

She smiled. "Come on—you'll love it."

"I will?"

"Yes, you will," she said firmly.

They crossed the street, entered the restaurant and sat at a window table. Annie immediately ordered two health burgers. "Turkey, soya and seasonings. It's the most delicious thing you've ever tasted," she assured him.

"I'm drooling!"

"You're funny."

They exchanged smiles.

"So," he said, "you work at a health club, eat healthy foods and exercise in the pool. What are you in training for—the Olympics?"

She tapped her fingers on the table. "I don't know if I told you or not, but I'm really an actress. That's why I have to stay in great shape."

"Isn't being a good actress enough?"

"Producers expect you to have a Raquel Welch body."

"In case you have to do a nude scene, huh?"

"Maybe."

"Would you?"

"If it was an integral part of the story."

He burst out laughing. "Come *on*—that's like me saying I read *Playboy* for the articles."

She couldn't help laughing too. The waitress delivered their turkey burgers. Nick looked at his suspiciously.

"Go ahead, taste it," Annie encouraged.

"Can I have ketchup?"

"You can have anything you like."

"Anything?" he teased.

"Within reason," she replied, beckoning the waitress. "Susie, bring us a couple of glasses of the big A and a bottle of ketchup."

"You come here all the time, huh?"

"It's convenient." She paused for a moment. "Uh, Nick, I'm sorry if I seemed a little tense with you when we first met, but I had no idea who you were. And it seemed kind of strange—you know, Cyndra being, well . . ." She hesitated, then blurted it out. "Black."

"Yeah—I see your point."

The waitress brought the ketchup and two large glasses of deep brown liquid.

He picked up his glass. "What's this?"

"Pure apple juice," she explained. "No preservatives. Drink up—you'll enjoy it."

"Jeez! I've *really* gotta get used to you."

"Maybe you'll have a chance," she said casually.

Was he finally getting through? "Cyndra told me you go to acting class," he said, smothering his burger in ketchup.

"That's right."

He took a bite—it wasn't half bad. "Howdja get into that?"

She sipped her apple juice. "If you're not working you have to study, it's important to keep on learning."

"What kind of class is it?"

Her eyes shone with enthusiasm. "It's an actors workshop. We do all kinds of interesting things. Scenes from plays and movies. Improvisation. A lot of working actors go there."

"Yeah?" he said, taking a gulp of apple juice. "Sounds interesting."

"It is."

He studied her pertly pretty face. "Have you ever had a professional job? Like in a movie or on television?"

She looked pleased that he'd asked. "As a matter of fact I've been in three commercials."

He was impressed. "I guess you've got an agent then?"

"How come all these questions, Nick?"

He decided to confide in her. "Why do you think? Listen, I had a great job in Chicago running a bar—I was the king of my own little kingdom. But ever since high school I've had a thing about acting."

"You can't just do it. You have to be good."

"Oh, I'm good," he boasted.

"Glad to hear it, because one thing you need is plenty of confidence." She sighed. "It helps when you get rejected twenty times a day."

He had no intention of getting rejected. Once he got through the door—whoever's door it was—he was going to make such an impression they'd never let him go.

"I'd like to come to class with you. I could sit in back and watch."

"I don't see why not. You're allowed to observe two sessions, after that you have to pay—that's if Miss Byron accepts you."

"Who's Miss Byron?"

"Joy Byron—the best acting coach in town."

If she was the best, he wanted her. "When can I come?"

"How about tonight?"

"No, nights are out. I got this gig driving for a limo company."

"I had a friend who sold a script to a producer while he was driving him to Santa Barbara."

"Really?"

"It can happen. You have to find out exactly who you've got in the car and go for the pitch. That's what my friend says. It certainly worked for him. His point is if they can afford to hire a limousine they must be someone."

He remembered Luigi and his ferocious scowl. "I got strict orders not to talk to the paying customers."

"You don't look like a man who follows orders."

She was right, it was about time he found out who he was driving and did something about it.

"I'll let you in on a little secret about this town," Annie confided, her bright eyes meeting his. "I've been here three years, and if there's any way you can make a connection, go for it. Don't let anything stand in your way."

He leaned across the table and took her hand, which was surprisingly small and soft. "Thanks, I like good advice."

They finished lunch, and as they were parting company she suggested he might want to come to class with her on the following Saturday.

"Sounds good," he said. "I'll pick you up."

"Okay. I'll see you at four."

That night, when Luigi assigned him Mr. Evans again, he was not exactly thrilled. This Evans guy was a deadbeat, no connections to be had there.

It turned out to be the same routine as before. The same bad-tempered face, the same briefcase clutched to his side, the same nontip. Nick had a good mind to tell Luigi he didn't want to drive him again. He'd talked to the other drivers and found out that most customers handed out cash tips on top of the percentage added to the bill. No chance with this tightwad.

"That Evans guy is a real cheapo," he complained to Luigi when he dropped the limo back. "Do me a favor an' stop assigning me to him."

"Am I hearin' right?" Luigi demanded, eyes bulging. "Mr. Manfred gives ya a job outta the kindness of his fuckin' heart—an' now you're mouthin' off an' tellin' me who ya will an' who ya won't drive."

"I'm entitled to an opinion," he said stubbornly.

"You're entitled t'suck my nuts if I tell ya to."

"I guess I'll pass on that tempting offer."

Luigi made a rude gesture. "In your eyes, punk."

The next night when he reported for work Luigi greeted him with a knowing sneer. "Mr. Manfred wants t'see ya."

"What about?"

"Do I strike ya as a fuckin' information center?"

Manny Manfred greeted him looking fatter than ever. It didn't seem possible, but could he have gained another twenty pounds?

"How's it goin', Nick?"

Surprise. The fat man remembered his name.

"Okay," he said carefully.

"An' the actin' thing? Any auditions yet?"

"I'm lookin' into it."

"That's the way t'do it," Manny said, reaching into a bowl of jelly beans, grabbing a handful and stuffing them into his surprisingly small pink mouth.

Nick noticed he was wearing a Rolex—the heavy gold watch gleamed as it caught the light.

"I talked to Q.J.," Manny said, munching away.

"You did?"

"He likes ya."

"I know."

"He trusts ya."

"I should hope so. I worked for him nearly four years."

Manny spat out a red jelly bean. It landed with a disgusting blob of spit on his huge knee. He brushed it to the floor.

"Loyalty an' trust—them's the things ya can't buy."

"Right." Nick waited for the pitch he knew was on its way.

"So . . ." Manny said, not disappointing him. "I got a proposition."

"Yeah?"

"Ya look like a smart kid."

Jeez! Compliments! From the fat man himself.

Big fucking deal.

"I can handle myself," he said carefully.

"That's what I like t'hear," Manny said, beaming. "Soon as Luigi told me ya was complainin' I knew ya wasn't satisfied sittin' behind the wheel of a car—drivin' some rich motherfucker ya knows you're better than."

"It's a job."

"An' so's what I got in mind for ya."

"Is it legal?"

"Are you bothered?"

"Why don't you tell me about it?"

Lauren had been out with Jimmy Cassady several times—four dates exactly—the last two ending with a chaste kiss on her front doorstep. Now they were on their fifth date and she knew that tonight he expected more. Not that he actually came out and said so—he wasn't that obvious—but she'd picked up little signs here and there, and after a quiet dinner in a romantic Italian restaurant he hailed a cab, and instead of giving the driver her address he gave him his.

"I want you to hear the new Joni Mitchell album," he said, putting his arm around her.

"I'd love to," she replied.

Well, Roberts, what are you going to do?

I don't know.

You'd better decide.

I can't.

Why?

Good question. Why couldn't she decide?

The answer came out of nowhere.

Because I still love Nick Angelo.

"You're quiet tonight," Jimmy said, taking her hand in his. "Something I said?"

She shivered, trying to block the memory of Nick from her mind. "No, I'm tired. I had a tough day."

"Too tired to listen to Joni Mitchell?"

He was asking one question with his mouth and another with his eyes.

"I can't think of anything I'd rather do," she replied, while voices continued to scream inside her head.

All he wants is a quick lay—that's what they all want.

You sound like your mother.

I'll sound like her if I want!

"We're here," he said, paying the driver and helping her from the cab.

She followed him into the elevator—filled with trepidation. Jimmy Cassady seemed like a genuinely nice guy.

Sure, they all do until they get what they want, and then they dump you, run out on you, leave you alone and pregnant. Leave you . . . leave you . . . leave you . . .

"What are you thinking?" he asked, squeezing her hand.

"Nothing," she said, banishing Nick from her thoughts and concentrating on Jimmy. What did she know about him? Not that much. He'd told her he'd come to New York from Missouri seven years ago and started out as a photographer's assistant—moving out on his own four years later. For the past three years he'd been building his reputation as one of the most innovative photographers around with his stark black-and-white images.

In the course of talking to some of the girls she'd discovered nothing about his personal life. Usually the models gave chapter and verse on every photographer they'd worked with—including graphic details of size, sexual preferences and how many times they liked to do it a night. There were no reports on Jimmy—except from Nature, who'd worked with him once and then announced, wide-eyed with surprise, "Well, 'e's gotter be gay, 'ein't 'e? 'Cause 'e din't even hit on me once!"

After their fourth date, when he'd dropped her outside her apartment with only a kiss, she'd thought that maybe Nature was right. But tonight she knew it wasn't so, he had that look in his eyes and she was well aware he was all set to make the big move.

His apartment wasn't an apartment at all—it was loft space, divided into compartments by six-foot stucco walls that stopped far short of the soaring ceilings. His furniture was minimal modern—everything either black, white or stainless steel. Stark, like his photographs.

"This place is amazing," she exclaimed, wandering around, taking in every detail. "Did you design it yourself?"

He laughed. "No professional decorator could come up with this. Besides, I happen to like it."

"So do I," she said, exploring further. "But you have to admit—it *is* different."

"That's *why* I like it," he said, following her into the compact stainless-steel kitchen. He moved closer. "That's why I like you," he added, unexpectedly pinning her up against the cold steel of the refrigerator door and kissing her on the mouth. No stalling. No "Would you like a drink?" or "Can I give you a tour?" He didn't even bother putting on the Joni Mitchell album he'd been talking about all night.

Just the kiss.

Hard and sensual. Not like his usual goodnight peck. This was definitely the real thing.

She gasped for breath, but he didn' t stop.

For a moment she resisted, her body rigid—not allowing him to get too close.

He persevered, and slowly she felt herself begin to respond—a warmth sweeping up her body, a tidal wave of desire so long repressed that it took her by surprise—rendering her helpless to resist.

After a few minutes his hands moved down to her breasts, touching, feeling, stroking.

She began a halfhearted objection. "Jimmy . . . I don't know . . ."

"I do," he said, hands creeping down the neckline of her dress, moving around to the back and unhooking her bra.

And all the while his lips remained on hers, his insistent tongue exploring her mouth, his warm breath all over her.

She threw her head back and surrendered as he exposed her breasts and his lips traveled slowly down to the tips of her nipples.

Gently he pushed both her breasts together, tonguing her nipples simultaneously. Then his hands moved slowly to her back, working the zipper on her dress and it fell to the floor.

She closed her eyes, trying not to think of Nick, trying to forget him once and for all. This was all happening so fast, and yet she felt powerless to stop him.

"You smell so good," he whispered.

It didn't matter anymore, nothing mattered. She'd reached the point of no return, he could do whatever he liked.

He picked her up and carried her to the bedroom, placing her gently in the middle of his large waterbed.

She lay back and opened up her soul to him. There was no choice anymore, she'd been lonely too long.

And Nick Angelo was never coming back.

"I'm getting married," Lauren said, nervously clenching her fists.

Samm glanced up from a contract she was studying and raised her oversized horn-rimmed glasses. "What did you say?"

"Married," she replied, as if this wasn't a major announcement.

Now she had Samm's full attention. "I don't believe it!" the older woman said, placing her glasses on the desk.

"It's true," she managed, sounding a lot calmer than she felt.

Samm reached for one of her long thin cigarillos, her blood-red nails lethal weapons. "And may I ask to whom?"

"Jimmy Cassady."

"*My* Jimmy Cassady?" Samm was very possessive of all the photographers who worked with her girls—she felt every one of them belonged to her.

Lauren nodded. "I guess so."

Samm was silent for a moment while she digested this unexpected information. Then she said, "Isn't this rather sudden?"

Lauren felt like a schoolkid standing in front of the principal. Why was she putting herself through this? She didn't owe Samm an explanation. "We've been seeing each other for six weeks," she said. *And sleeping together for three*, she wanted to add, but didn't. Her sex life was her business.

Samm picked up a thin gold pen and tapped it on her lacquered desktop. "Six weeks is not a long time to get to know someone."

"Long enough for me," she replied, thinking that she certainly didn't need a lecture from Samm.

"Don't you think—" Samm began.

"Congratulations would be nice," Lauren snapped, shattering her "good little Lauren" image once and for all. "Oh, and I'm giving you two weeks' notice—Jimmy wants me to work with him."

Samm was too wise to say another word. Lauren was obviously under Jimmy Cassady's influence and nothing she said would make any difference. Men! They'd caused her more problems over the years than she cared to think about. Usually it was the models who got hooked by a glamorous playboy or some fast-talking would-be manager. She certainly hadn't expected Lauren to get swept away.

Samm might be skeptical, but the girls in the office thought it was sensational news. Pia seemed especially pleased for her. And when Nature heard, she made a special trip to the office, shrieking, "This is bleedin' smashing! So, 'e's not a fag after all!"

Trust Nature to come right out with it.

From the moment they'd slept together Jimmy had started talking about marriage. He wanted to do it immediately. "What's the point of waiting?" he'd demanded.

The point of waiting is to decide whether we're making a mistake.

Samm was right—six weeks was not a lot of time to get to know somebody. But the more she got to know Jimmy, the more special she decided he was, and certainly different from the other men she'd come across in New York.

Even so, at first she'd said no.

"Why not?" Jimmy persisted.

She could think of no good reason.

He'd pressed until she finally changed her mind. Jimmy was attractive, serious about his work, a good lover, and he genuinely seemed to care for her. Besides, she was swept up in the excitement of his desire. And the thought of belonging to someone and being safe was too tempting to resist.

She didn't love him—whatever love was. But maybe that would come in time.

Once she'd said yes, they both agreed they should do it as soon as possible. For one rash moment she'd considered calling her aunt and uncle in Philadelphia, but then she'd changed her mind. Who needed Brad knowing? Besides, both she and Jimmy wanted the ceremony to be as simple as possible.

"What about your family?" she'd asked.

"We lost touch," he'd said vaguely.

"How come?"

He'd raised an eyebrow. "Am *I* questioning *you?*"

Soul mates.

Pia announced she wanted to throw her a wedding shower, but she was soon overruled by Nature, who decided a proper bachelor-girl bash was more in order. "You deserve it," Nature announced cheerfully. "You work ever so hard lookin' after us all, now it's our turn to do something for you."

In a way Lauren wished she hadn't told anybody. Maybe it would have been better if they'd just done it quietly with no fuss.

Too late now, Nature had plans.

Lauren protested, but Nature—as usual—refused to listen. "Be at me apartment next Saturday at six o'clock. And don't expect to get home until three in the morning—that's if you're lucky!"

There was no point in fighting Nature, she was like a great big Mack truck. The safest thing to do was climb aboard and enjoy the ride.

As the days passed Lauren realized leaving Samm's was going to be a wrench—she'd made so many good friends there. But Jimmy assured her it would be fun for her to help him out at his studio, and it didn't seem like such a bad idea.

Meanwhile there was so much to do. They had to take blood tests, get a marriage license—and finally she went shopping with Pia, searching for the perfect outfit, which Samm insisted on paying for.

By the night of the wedding shower she was a wreck. Nature was in top form, screaming and yelling all over the place. She'd ordered a convoy of limos for the night, and following behind the limos she surprised everyone with six leather-jacketed bikers sitting astride their Harleys.

"Ein't it nice 'aving an escort," Nature joked, winking conspiratorially at the convoy of guys. "Muscles an' black leather—me favorite combination!"

First they went to an Italian restaurant, where everyone presented Lauren with their gifts. She managed to put a good face on it, opening the presents one by one and dutifully exclaiming that each gift was exactly what she wanted.

Nature presented her with a huge black vibrator, which elicited much mirth around the table.

When she was finished with her gifts, one of the better-looking bikers swaggered into the restaurant, hit a button on a tape machine and proceeded to do a raunchy strip to the Stones' "Satisfaction." He was merely the appetizer, because from there they all piled back into the limos and headed for a male strip club.

Lauren watched in fascinated amazement as the guys at the club proudly presented their assets—thrusting them into the eager audience's faces.

"Too many dicks," Pia said solemnly.

"Don't you mean assholes?" Lauren murmured, longing to get out of there.

Nature was in her element—hooting and hollering at the guys to take it off, sticking ten-dollar bills down their G-strings, loving every minute.

At last it was over, and they dropped her back at her apartment. She fell thankfully into bed. As far as she was concerned the evening had been a nightmare—like some dreadful hazing ceremony. Still . . . they'd meant well, and she was lucky to have people who cared about her.

The next day she gave up her apartment and moved all her things over to Jimmy's place. That night they ate dinner by candlelight and made love. For the first time since leaving Bosewell Lauren felt she finally belonged somewhere, and she knew that her decision to marry Jimmy was the right one. She fell asleep in his arms, happy and content.

The day before the wedding Pia picked her up and took her over to her place. "You can't stay with your future husband the night before the wedding," she scolded. "It's big bad luck."

In the morning Nature arrived, breezing through Pia's apartment, bossily taking over. " 'Ere," she said, removing a large sapphire ring from her finger. "You'll wear this. It covers borrowed, blue *and* new. Now all we've got to worry about is getting you something old."

Pia produced a pair of exquisite filigree earrings. "These were my great-grandmother's," she said, handing them over. "I'd be honored if you wore them."

Lauren put on the oyster satin suit Samm had bought her, Pia's earrings and the sapphire ring.

Nature peered at her critically. "I wish you'd let *me* fix your 'air."

"I like it just the way it is."

"Yeah, all neat and understated," Nature replied. "Unlike me," she added, fluffing out her blond curls.

"You look beautiful, Lauren," Pia whispered.

They set off in a white stretch limousine—Nature's choice. "Shut your eyes and pretend you're a rock star," she giggled.

By the time they arrived at City Hall Lauren's stomach was doing somersaults. The driver helped her out of the car and she entered the building, flanked by her friends.

They bumped into Samm by the elevator. "How are you feeling?" Samm asked, chic as ever in a scarlet Chanel suit.

"Nervous," she replied.

"It doesn't show. You look lovely."

"Thanks." Her throat felt dry as she clutched her corsage of white orchids and wished that everything was over and done with.

Pia and Nature ushered her into a side room to await the arrival of the bridegroom. Jimmy was coming alone. When she'd asked him who his best man was, he'd replied he didn't want one. "I travel solo," he'd said.

Fine with her. Maybe that's why they got along so well.

She couldn't sit still. She got up, pacing nervously up and down the small room, her mind racing this way and that. A few minutes seemed like an eternity.

Nature kept checking her watch. " 'E's bleedin' late, ein't 'e," she finally said in an exasperated voice.

"Maybe it's the traffic," Pia said, giving her a warning look.

"Yeah, well, bleedin' traffic or not, 'e's late. S'not nice to be late for your own wedding."

After fifteen minutes, Pia slipped out of the room, found a pay phone and called Jimmy's apartment. There was no answer.

Nature cornered her in the corridor. "What the 'ell's going on? Where *is* the scummy bastard?"

Pia shook her head. "I have no idea."

"You wait downstairs," Nature said, "while I keep 'er busy here."

Another twenty minutes passed and Jimmy still hadn't shown up. Pia called Samm out of the room and Nature joined them in the corridor for a conference.

"Looks like 'e's dumped her," Nature said. "What a lowlife!"

"Has somebody called his apartment?" Samm asked.

"Yes. I did," Pia said. "There's no answer."

Samm shook her head, she'd had a feeling about Jimmy Cassady.

"What shall we do?" Pia asked.

"Fuck 'im!" Nature said. "Men! They're all no bleedin' good."

By the time an hour had elapsed it was obvious Jimmy wasn't coming. Lauren took the news stoically, although she was breaking up inside.

Pia, Nature and Samm accompanied her back to his apartment. There was a note pinned to the refrigerator door.

Sorry! Gone on assignment to Africa. Be back in a few months. You can stay at the apartment until you find a place.

Lauren read the note twice before handing it to the others.

"Bastard!" exclaimed Nature, scanning it quickly.

"Oh, dear," said Pia.

Samm was more eloquent. "That lousy son of a bitch! I never trusted him."

Lauren felt totally blank. Another rejection. It didn't matter. Nothing mattered. One thing she knew. She would never trust any man again. Never. Of that she was sure.

The proposition was this—Manny wanted him to take the limo across the border into Tijuana, pick up a passenger at the Tijuana Sunset Hotel and then drive back into the U.S. It sounded simple enough.

"That's it?" Nick asked warily.

"Easy, huh?" Manny leaned back in his oversized chair, double chins wobbling.

"Sure," he replied. "Depending on what the passenger's carrying."

"Let's make it none of your business," Manny said, rubbing his chin. "That way you don't know from nothin'."

Nick decided he wouldn't trust Manny with a nun, but he sensed an opportunity to make money, and since his stash from Chicago was fast running out he investigated further. "How much?"

Manny shot him a knowing wink. "More than you're making now."

"Listen," he said, "I don't know what I'm bringing in, but I ain't crossin' the border for less than two grand."

'That's a lotta money."

"The way I'm hearin', it's a lotta risk."

"Okay, okay," Manny said grudgingly.

The fat man had agreed too readily. Nick immediately wished he'd asked for more. "When's this supposed to take place?" he asked.

"Sometime next week. Things are bein' set up now."

"Who's the passenger?"

"A schoolkid."

"A schoolkid?"

"Yeah. Wanna make something outta it?"

Nick knew he was stepping onto dangerous territory. There was no way Manny's activities were legal. Did he really want to get involved?

Yeah—for two grand he *really* wanted to get involved.

"I got somebody for ya t'meet," Manny said.

"Who?"

"A special broad, so keep her outta your dirty mind."

Oh? Like he was going to hit on a girl that had anything to do with Manny. Fat chance.

Manny hit a buzzer and the door opened.

"Say hello to Suga," Manny said, presenting her as if she was the Queen of England. "Suga an' me—we been together five years. Married for two," he added proudly. "Happy as a coupla sandbugs."

Suga was twenty-three, looked sixteen and acted as if she was twelve. Her dress of choice was black rubber, barely making it to the top of her chubby thighs, worn with lace-up white boots and as much fake gold jewelry as she could manage without falling down. She was top-heavy, short, her flesh was rosy and her hair shoulder-length spikes of dyed blond with inch-long black roots. She smoked nonstop, chewed gum and bit her nails.

Stationing herself next to her husband she stared balefully at Nick. She had small beady eyes surrounded by too much makeup and mean little lips curved in a perpetual sneer.

"Suga's a classy broad," Manny said, talking about her as if she wasn't present. "Helps me with a lotta things."

Yeah, Nick thought, I bet she does.

"I figured you two should meet," Manny continued, touching his wife on the thigh, "on accounta it's Suga you'll be collectin' in Tijuana."

Jesus Christ, what was he getting into? "You said it was a schoolkid."

"Don't worry—she'll be dressed like one."

"You're putting me on."

Suga spoke up, her voice a shrill squeak. "Screw you," she said, chewing gum like an angry cow.

This was going to be some trip.

Joy Byron's acting class was held in an empty warehouse on the wrong side of Wilshire. Joy Byron herself was an elderly Englishwoman with a voice like a hacksaw. She wore a long flowered dress on her bony body and carried a parasol, giving her a somewhat eccentric Madwoman of Chaillot look.

Nick would never admit it to anyone, but he was dead nervous. "So . . . uh, like, what do I do?" he asked, trying to sound cool.

"Nothing," Annie said. "You're merely an observer. Will you relax."

"Okay, okay," he said, wondering why he was putting himself through this.

She grabbed his hand. "Come on, I'll take you over to meet her."

Reluctantly he allowed himself to be led across the room.

"Miss Byron," Annie said, "this is a friend of mine. Is it okay for him to sit in?"

Joy Byron turned around and studied him. "And what is your name, young man?" she asked in imperious tones.

"Nick," he mumbled.

"Do we have a surname?"

'Nick Angelo."

"Lose the 'o.' " She gestured theatrically. "Nick Angel—I can see it on marquees now."

"Yeah?"

"But of course." She turned to speak to another student and Annie pulled him away. "She likes you."

"How do you know?"

"I can tell."

He grinned. "Yeah, well, I'm not just anybody."

"That's what I like about you, Nick—no ego. Come on, we'll grab a seat over here."

His eyes darted around the large musty room. There was a bunch of guys in T-shirts and jeans doing their best Brando imitations, and lots of pretty girls who seemed to take themselves much too seriously. Actors. Just like him.

When everybody was settled Joy Byron stood at the front and addressed the class. "Today we shall speak about motivation," she said. Long dramatic pause. "When I worked with Olivier, Gielgud, in fact *all* the English greats, one of their first thoughts before going onstage was motivation, motivation, what exactly *is* my motivation."

Nick could see this was going to be different from drama classes with Betty Harris way back in Bosewell. And he was right. Joy Byron reveled in lecturing her students on what she thought they should know, talking a great deal about her fabulously successful career in England.

"Was she some kind of big star over there?" he whispered to Annie.

Annie nodded, eyes shining. "She's a great teacher."

"How come she gave it up?"

"I don't know."

Halfway through the class Joy summoned two of her students to the front and instructed them to improvise a scene expressing anger. Nick watched carefully as the two young actors went to work.

They were good.

He was better.

After they were finished Joy stood up again, gave a long harsh critique and then invited the class to comment. Some of the students couldn't wait to pick the two actors to pieces, while a few of them were quite flattering.

"You have to take the good with the bad," Annie murmured. "Everybody has their say. Believe me—it can be brutal up there."

He couldn't make up his mind whether to get involved in this shit. Acting in Bosewell was one thing, but this was Hollywood and who needed criticism?

On his way out Joy Byron stopped him, laying a dainty blue-veined hand on his arm. "You've got the look, dear boy," she said in her gravelly English voice.

"I have?" he replied carefully.

"Oh, yes. I always recognize it," Joy said. "You've got the look."

He took a deep breath, inhaling her scent of musty roses mixed with mothballs. "Yeah, well, uh . . . glad to hear it."

She fixed him with watery eyes. "On your next visit you'll perform something for me."

"I haven't joined the class yet."

"Ah, yes, but sometimes I accept students without fees. We'll see. Next time come prepared."

"What did she say?" Annie wanted to know as soon as they were outside. When he told her she got really excited. "My God, you never even did anything and you made an impression on her."

"Maybe she's horny," he joked.

Annie was unamused. "That's not funny," she said sternly. "Joy Byron is a true professional."

He took her arm. "Hey, there's something I've been meaning to ask —do you have a permanent guy in your life?"

"Why?" she asked suspiciously.

"I thought you'd help me out. Like if you don't have a boyfriend you'd come by my place on Saturday night."

There was a long pause before she answered. "Nick," she said hesitantly, "I'm not looking to get involved with anybody."

"Hey, who's asking? All I want you to do is read with me. I have to prepare something, don't I?"

"Oh." She was embarrassed at having gotten the wrong impression. "I'd be happy to."

Saturday night his landlady was having her usual weekend party. He ignored the hangers-on lingering outside and steered Annie straight through to his apartment. The smell of marijuana was overwhelming. "Don't breathe too deeply," he joked. "One lungful and you're stoned for the rest of the week!"

She walked over to the large windows overlooking the beach. "How did you find this place?"

"Cyndra helped me."

"Nice view."

"Yeah, I was lucky."

The landlady's stereo blasting reggae almost blew them out of the room.

"This is the downside," he explained. "She throws a party every Saturday. You gotta be in the mood." He opened his refrigerator and inspected the contents. "How about a drink? I got root beer or Coke. Take your choice."

"Both bad for you," Annie said. "I'll have plain water."

"Don't you do *anything* that's bad for you?" he teased, reaching for a glass.

"Not if I can help it," she said primly.

He found his precious signed copy of *Streetcar* and flipped it open to a scene he particularly liked, handing it to Annie. "How about I read Joy a scene from this?"

"Hmm." She flicked through the pages. "You want to do it with me?" she asked, settling on the couch.

"Do I want to do *what* with you?" he replied, still teasing.

Her cheeks were flushed. "Nick, get serious."

He moved in on her, knowing he shouldn't. "I *am* serious," he said, sliding his arm around her shoulders and pulling her close.

She was vulnerable and jumpy as he began to kiss her. Feebly she tried to push him away.

"Relax," he coaxed, well aware he had her nailed. "You gotta have *some* fun in life," he added, pressing his lips down on hers.

Just as he was getting somewhere they were interrupted by a loud knock on the door. Annie seized the moment to wriggle out of his grasp and jump guiltily to her feet.

"Ignore it," he said. "It's probably someone looking for the john."

"You'd better see who it is," she said, glad of the distraction.

"Jeez, just when we were gettin' comfortable, huh?" he said, walking over to the door and flinging it open.

Standing there was DeVille carrying a suitcase.

"Hi, honey," she said. "I'm here."

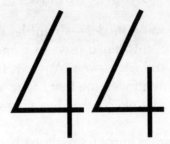

Pia wanted Lauren to stay with her, but Nature insisted she'd be more comfortable at her place. Lauren couldn't care less where she went—Jimmy's betrayal had left her without any feelings. It didn't matter, nothing mattered. She packed up her things and moved into Nature's huge white apartment without an argument.

Nature was delighted. She led Lauren into the guest bedroom, announcing proudly, "This is where me Mum stays. You'll like it. It's ever so cozy."

Lauren decided it was a good place to hide. Maybe she'd stay forever—who needed the real world?

Nature yelled at her assistant to cancel all her appointments for the rest of the week.

"You can't do that," Lauren protested. "You have the *Vogue* shoot, and the Antonio session for *Harper's*. You're booked solid."

"I can bleedin' do what I want," Nature replied tartly. "I'm not a bloody work machine. I understand what you're goin' through—the truth is it 'appened to me once."

"What happened to you?"

" 'Course it was when I was young an' innocent—ha-ha!" Nature threw herself down on the bed, ready to talk. "There was this geezer

327

I was seeing before I was a model—a right layabout. I worked in an 'airdressing salon, and this bloke used to come in all the time. 'E seemed ever so nice. And sexy—wow! Anyway, the truth is 'e dumped me—just like that. Ran off with me best friend an' married her. I bet 'e's sorry now—she's a fat old cow an' I'm a big star . . . well, sort of. I never forgave 'im."

"I had no idea," Lauren murmured sympathetically.

"I'm not gonna bloody advertise it, am I? After that I got meself discovered an' flown to New York. Never looked back. 'Course, me Mum's not thrilled—but I am. It's great gettin' away from the family. Where's your family anyway?"

"I don't have anybody," Lauren said, admitting it for the first time. "My mother and father are both dead."

"Oh, sorry, luv."

"That's all right."

Nature jumped up. "Well, listen, you're welcome to stay as long as you want."

And that's exactly what she did. For two weeks she hid away in the guest room, huddled under blankets watching television day and night, until Pia visited one day, marched into the room and said, "Okay, enough. Time to get back to work. Samm says your job is waiting."

She shook her head. "No. Too many bad memories."

"You can't force her," Nature said, entering the room.

"Staying here doing nothing certainly won't help her," Pia said sharply, not appreciating Nature's interference.

Lauren spoke up; after all, it was her they were discussing. "Pia's right. It's time I found an apartment and another job."

"Jobs aren't so easy to find," Pia warned. "If you're smart you'll come back to Samm's."

"I've got it!" Nature shrieked, joining in as usual. "I've bleedin' got it!"

"What?" Lauren asked.

"You'll work for *me*! You can be my new assistant. It'll be a lot more fun than sitting in an office picking up the bleedin' phone all day."

"I don't know," she said unsurely.

Nature was on a roll. "So now you don't 'ave to move out. It'll be nice 'aving you 'ere permanently—someone to talk to when I get 'ome."

"Yes, very nice," Pia interjected. "Don't do it, Lauren. You'll be on call twenty-four hours a day."

"Well?" Nature said, flashing her big blue eyes.

Lauren shrugged, she had nothing else in mind. "Why not?"

Pia sighed. "You'll regret it."

"No, she bleedin' won't," snapped Nature.

And that was that.

Sometimes Lauren thought it was the best decision she'd ever made and sometimes she thought it was the worst. Working for Nature filled her days, and living in the same apartment filled her nights. If she'd thought she had no life working at Samm's, she certainly had none at all working for Nature, although it was never boring.

Nature did not lead a dull life. As her personal assistant she was expected to do everything from collecting the dry cleaning to watering the plants. She soon delegated to the maid the duties she had no wish to do, and concentrated on getting Nature's life as organized as possible—which was not easy, because Nature was a true gypsy and had thrived on chaos for years.

"You're fantastic!" Nature said one day. " 'Ow did I ever manage without you?"

"Beats me," she replied dryly, thinking was this her lot in life—to be the girl nobody could manage without?

Nature had aspirations to an acting career. "Can't be a model forever," she confided. "I gotta grab all the opportunities I can."

"You're twenty-two," Lauren pointed out. "What's your hurry?"

"I won't look like this for long. Once the lines start 'appening an' I get a bit of sag here and there, it'll be over."

"You're crazy," Lauren said. "You've got another twenty years of looking great."

Nature shook her head. "Twenty years? You must be jokin'! All those little sixteen-year-olds sneakin' up behind, sniffin' at me heels, wantin' what I got. This modeling lark ein't easy."

Lauren realized it was true—modeling was not easy, and the most successful girls worked hard to keep themselves at the top. Nature never allowed herself to gain an extra pound. Every day—no matter how early she had to get up—she worked out for a solid hour, pushing her strength to the limit.

Emerson Burn arrived back in town from a world tour. Nature read about it in the *New York Post* and immediately hatched a plot. She had Lauren call his apartment.

"Tell 'im I wanna 'ave a dinner party for 'im."

"When?"

"Any night 'e likes. Now that 'e's dumped that stupid Selina cow I'm in with a chance."

Lauren called and spoke to his personal assistant, who rudely informed her Mr. Burn's social calendar was full.

She waited a day and phoned again, saying it was Candice Bergen. This time she was put right through.

Emerson Burn sounded like a male version of Nature. " 'Allo?"

"Emerson Burn?" Lauren asked, just to make sure.

"Candy Bergen?"

"No, this is Lauren Roberts—Nature's assistant. She'd like to invite you to dinner next week."

He sounded disappointed. "I thought you was Candy Bergen."

"Your secretary must have gotten your calls mixed up."

"Okay . . . dinner with Nature. She's on."

"What night?"

"Tuesday—eight o'clock. But only if she'll cook."

Lauren choked back laughter. Nature in the kitchen—that was a good one. "Do you have any special requests?"

"Yeah. Tell 'er I want roast beef, Yorkshire pud and roast potatoes."

When Lauren informed Nature of his request she panicked. "Oh, Gawd! I can't bleedin' cook. Can you?"

"Don't worry, we'll hire a caterer."

"I don't *want* a bleedin' caterer," Nature wailed. "This has gotta taste like a 'ome-cooked meal. Look—find a cooking school and learn. Then I'll pretend I made it. 'Ow's that?"

Lauren laughed. "It's different."

And that's how she found herself attending a cooking class learning how to make roast beef and Yorkshire pudding. She learned fast.

The night of Nature's date with Emerson she prepared the meal, gave strict instructions how to serve it, then retreated to her bedroom in the back of the apartment.

At three a.m. she awoke, walked quietly out of her room to turn the lights off in the living room, and discovered Nature and Emerson asleep on the white bearskin rug, naked and wrapped in each other's arms.

For a moment she stood quite still, staring at them. Then she felt too much like an intruder and hurried back to her room, closed the door and attempted to sleep.

It was impossible.

She knew the time had come to move on. No more hiding behind Nature. She had to resume living.

45

On the morning of the Tijuana run Nick awoke at seven. He wasn't into getting up early, but today he was on edge and found it impossible to sleep.

DeVille lay quietly beside him. DeVille with her pale red hair and glorious white body. He hadn't sent for her, but she'd arrived anyway, and since she was standing on his doorstep he'd taken her in. He'd tried to explain to Annie, who pretended it didn't matter, grabbed her purse and ran out of his apartment like she had a rocket up her ass.

He wasn't sure whether she was angry with him or not. Probably she was. Women were like that—overly sensitive.

For a couple of days he'd lost himself in sex. It was so good it should be illegal—especially with DeVille, who knew everything he liked and made sure he was the happiest man on the block.

"I can get my own apartment if you want," she'd offered, not really meaning it.

"That's a good idea," he'd replied, not really meaning it either, and they'd fallen back into bed.

Now she'd been at his place for five days and he knew it was time for her to go—only he hadn't gotten around to mentioning it.

Tomorrow I'll do it, he thought. Give her fifty bucks and ease her out gently by telling her that living together was not a good idea on account of his career.

What career?

The career he was going to have after Joy Byron saw him perform and found him an agent—who in turn would secure him his first professional acting job.

Confidence, you had to have confidence—and he was brimming with it.

By eight o'clock he'd taken a run on the beach, eaten a healthy breakfast of bran and bananas and got himself mentally ready for his first phone call of the day. He called Annie.

"Hey, listen," he said. "Remember I was supposed to work on some kinda scene for Joy Byron?"

"Yes?" she said in her *Who gives a damn* voice.

"You promised to help me out. I haven't had a lot of time this week—"

"I can imagine," she interrupted.

"I've found the scene I want to do. I thought I'd drop by tomorrow and read through it with you."

"I'm working tomorrow," she said coolly.

"I'd really like to rehearse before I do it for Joy," he said, hoping to persuade her.

"Miss Byron," she corrected. "Nobody calls her Joy."

"You *will* read with me, won't you, Annie?"

"Did I say I would?"

Time to turn on the charm, not so easy over the phone—he did better in person. "Are you pissed at me?"

"Should I be?"

"I dunno." A short pause. "Hey—about DeVille arriving on my doorstep—she's an old girlfriend from Chicago who blew into town with nowhere to stay. She'll be moving on soon." He glanced over at DeVille—still asleep on his bed. DeVille wasn't moving anywhere.

There was a long awkward silence, finally broken by Annie. "I bumped into Cyndra yesterday," she said. "She'd like to hear from you."

"I've been meaning to call her."

"What are you waiting for? She *is* your sister."

"I'll call her tomorrow. I'm driving to Mexico today."

"Mexico?"

"Yeah, I'm picking up a passenger. Somebody's kid is getting out of boarding school."

"Boarding school—in *Mexico?*"

"You think I'm making it up?"

"I'm never sure what you make up and what's the truth."

He got off the subject. "So . . . can I see you tomorrow?"

There was another long pause before she finally said, "Okay, I guess so. Come by at five, we'll go to class together."

"I'll be there," he said, hanging up.

After scoring the two grand he was going to tell Manny goodbye. One trip was enough. Soon he'd have an acting job and wouldn't need this crap.

Manny had told him to go out and buy a chauffeur's uniform. He'd done so reluctantly. Jeez! There was nothing worse than dressing up in a uniform, feeling like somebody's lackey.

The uniform hung in his closet. He took it out, looked at it, put it away and went back to bed.

DeVille groaned in her sleep as he snuggled up behind her, letting her know he was awake. Tomorrow he really would tell her to leave. May as well make the best of this last opportunity.

"I finally heard from your brother," Annie remarked, rubbing suntan oil on her legs.

"What's he up to?" Cyndra asked, turning on her lounger beside the pool. "I call him all the time—he's never home."

"That's because his girlfriend came in from Chicago."

Cyndra sat up. "*What* girlfriend?"

"Some tall showgirl type with long red hair."

"Jealous?"

"Who, *me?*"

"Come *on*, Annie. I *know* you like him."

"Well . . . I must admit I thought there might be something between us, but that was before I found out he was the Don Juan of the out-of-work actors."

Cyndra nodded knowingly. "Nick's always been like that. Back in high school he could have any girl he wanted."

"You should have warned me."

"I didn't think you were planning on getting involved."

"*You're* the one who gave him my phone number."

"I had a feeling you two might be good together."

"Listen, the *last* thing I need in my life is a guy who can't keep it in his pants."

Cyndra laughed. "Okay, okay, I get the message." She glanced up as Reece emerged from their apartment wearing a pair of flashy madras shorts with several heavy gold chains swinging around his neck.

Annie greeted him with a desultory wave. "Hi, Reece. Another hard day's work?"

"Don't look like *you're* exactly bustin' your ass," he said, throwing her a dirty look before settling down on the lounger next to Cyndra.

"Reece likes to work on his tan," Cyndra said quickly.

"You don't have to explain nothin' to her," Reece snapped.

"I wasn't explaining."

Annie jumped up before they got into another fight. Lately she'd heard a lot of yelling coming from their apartment. "What's happening with that demo record you were supposed to do?" she asked, to change the subject.

"These things take time," Cyndra said.

Annie stood up and stretched. "I guess they do. See you guys later."

Luigi managed to ignore Nick when he arrived to collect the car. Nick ignored him back as he made his way through to Manny's office.

"The uniform suits ya," Manny wheezed, looking him up and down. "Now, make sure ya got this right. Ya drive across the border, pick up Suga from the hotel an' drive straight back to L.A. If they stop ya at the border ya don't know from nothing. Ya was hired to pick up a schoolkid." He sucked on his cigar. "Who was ya hired by?"

"Prince Limos," Nick said, reciting his part.

"Yeah—no mention of Glamour. Ya got the address I gave ya?"

"All set."

"Did Luigi put new plates on the car?"

"They're on."

"Okay, you're ready."

Yeah. As long as I don't get busted.

What was he bringing back? He hoped it wasn't drugs.

Who was he kidding? Sure, it was drugs. What else could it be?

On the drive to San Diego he played Rolling Stones tapes nonstop, making the trip in record time. He was ahead of schedule, so he parked the car in an underground garage and sat in a Burt Reynolds movie killing time. After that it was all the way to Tijuana.

Once there he parked outside the hotel and searched the lobby looking for Suga.

He couldn't see her. Shit! Manny had said she'd be standing right in front.

Just as he was about to approach the desk an apparition sneaked up behind him and tapped him on the arm. It was Suga, looking twelve. Scrubbed of makeup, her hair in braids, a school cap on her head and in full uniform, she resembled a truculent tomboy.

"Are you blind?" she hissed from the corner of her sulky mouth. "I been standin' here forever."

He did a double take—the transformation was remarkable.

"Pick up my goddamn suitcase," she commanded, marching outside.

He followed her, carrying the case, which weighed a ton. Maybe he should spring it open before they crossed the border and check out the contents. For all he knew he could be carrying a goddamn body, it was heavy enough.

Suga stood next to the limo, stamping her feet impatiently.

He sprung the trunk open, loaded the suitcase, then got into the driver's seat.

"Bust your ass outta here," Suga squeaked, jumping in the back. "I hate these runs—they make me wet my pants."

"How many times you made this trip?" he asked, sliding the car away from the curb.

"Too many," she replied, popping bubble gum.

They drove in silence for a while, until he couldn't contain himself any longer. "What's in the suitcase?"

"Did Manny say you could ask questions?" she snapped. "Whyn't ya just drive. You're making your money—what do you care?"

He eased the limousine along the crowded streets. Now he was getting nervous. Two grand was one thing, but it wasn't worth getting busted.

Yeah, well, two thousand was a lot of bucks, he reasoned. It would take months of real work at Glamour Limousines to score that kind of money—especially with clients like cheapskate Evans. Although right now, as he headed toward the border, Mr. Evans seemed like a dream passenger.

Suga didn't care for his Rolling Stones tapes. "Turn that crap off," she whined. "I hate Mick Jagger."

He saw no reason to take her lip. "Anybody ever told you to shut up?"

"Oh?" she said sarcastically. "*You're* gonna tell me? Big fat chance."

"How much older than you is Manny?"

"Mind your fuckin' business."

"Why'd you marry him?"

"Get fucked."

So much for conversation with little Miss Charm.

There was a long line of cars at the border. It was getting dark and he was more nervous by the minute.

Suga sat in the back, chewing gum, perfectly calm.

By this time he imagined the suitcase was filled with cocaine. They'd throw him in jail for fifty years if he was caught. Never again. This was *it*.

By the time they reached the guard, he was sweating through his clothes.

The guard leaned down and looked through the window. "Do you have any fruits, vegetables or plants?" he asked, peering into the back of the car.

"No, just one juvenile delinquent I'm delivering to her parents," Nick said pleasantly. Jeez, he actually sounded cool!

"Okay," the guard said, walking away.

Okay? Did that mean they could go?

Apparently it did. He put his window up and drove the car out of there.

"Faster!" Suga urged from the back.

"I gotta stop an' take a piss."

"No!" she yelled. "Get away from the fuckin' border."

By the time they reached San Diego he was on a high. It was so easy, like nothing. Christ, he could make this trip twice a day if he had to. He checked out the rearview mirror. Suga was busy wriggling out of her schoolgirl clothes and struggling into a short skirt and tight sweater.

"Hey," he said. "Now you can tell me. What's in the case?"

"Two hundred and fifty thousand buckerooneys," she said casually. "Wanna take it an' run off together, Nick?"

"Are you shittin' me?"

She hitched her skirt down. "Would I do that?"

"No drugs?"

"You think I'd have anything to do with drugs?" she sniffed indignantly. "What *I* need is to find me a guy with enough balls to split. Manny would track us, but we'd have the money, wouldn't we? We could vanish good."

Two hundred and fifty thousand dollars! Holy shit! What if he dumped *her* and took off by himself?

For a moment he thought about it. But only for a moment. He had no desire to spend the rest of his life running from Manny Manfred.

"Well?" Suga challenged. "You got the balls or not?"

The little bitch was testing him so she could report back to Manny. "Whyn't you shut up," he said.

"Dumb prick," she muttered. "I meant it, you know."

He never found out if she was putting him on or not, because as soon as they got back to the garage she jumped out of the car and vanished.

Luigi opened the trunk, removed the suitcase and brought it to Manny's office.

"When do I get paid?" Nick asked, following him.

"Don't sweat it. Nobody's leaving town," Luigi said.

I made a mistake. I should have gotten the money up front. Now they're gonna screw me.

"I did the run, I took the risk. I want my money."

"Later," Luigi threw over his shoulder.

He followed him all the way into Manny's office, where Luigi put the suitcase down. "I want my money," he repeated.

"Yeah, Nick, sure," Manny said, producing a thick bankroll and peeling off hundred-dollar bills. "Here ya go, ya did a nice job."

He didn't trust the fat man. Standing in front of his desk he counted the bills. "There's only a thousand here," he said.

"That's right," Manny answered, reaching for a handful of cashews. "A thousand for the first run, two grand for the second."

"No. We had a deal—two grand for this run."

"Tell ya what I'll do," Manny said magnanimously, crunching on the nuts. "I'll split the difference. Ya get fifteen hundred for this run, an' two an' a half for the next. How's that?"

Nick was angry. "Who the fuck d'you think you're dealing with?"

Manny's voice hardened. "Some punk kid who's lucky to have a job."

"I want my two thousand, Manny, or you'll regret it."

Manny's beady little eyes froze. "*I'll* regret it? You're *threatening* me?"

"I know what's in the suitcase."

"Howdja know that?"

Suga might be a pain in the ass but he wasn't about to put her away. "Do I get my two grand?"

Manny wheezed with laughter. "You're okay, kid. O.J. said ya was." He peeled off ten more bills and handed them over. "Ya can work for me any time."

Yeah, like he wanted to. Snatching the money, he walked out.

"See ya tomorrow," Luigi called after him. "Mr. Evans is comin' back t'town. Nine p.m. LAX. Don't be late."

Fuck Mr. Evans.

Fuck Glamour Limousines.

He had his two grand—this was the last they'd see of him.

"You can't leave," Nature shrieked.

"I have to," Lauren said.

"But why?" Nature demanded petulantly. She was so used to getting her own way that she didn't understand the word no.

Nature was involved in a full-fledged affair with Emerson Burn. It was not peaceful—another reason why Lauren had decided to move on. Their screaming fights were legendary. Even worse, their passionate reconciliations.

Valiantly she tried to explain. "I feel like I'm living in your shadow. It's time I got my life back on track."

Nature pouted. "We're having fun, ein't we?"

"Yes, but it's not enough for me."

Reluctantly Nature accepted defeat. "What will you do? Work for Samm again?"

She shook her head. "I was thinking of starting my own business—kind of a . . . you know, like a Girl Friday."

"Girl Friday? What's that?" Nature asked, hooting with laughter.

"Someone who does everything. I'll put myself out for hire and people will pay me by the hour. I can even work for you occasionally."

"That's nice."

"Actually, I've been speaking to Pia and she's going to be leaving Samm's."

Nature raised a skeptical eyebrow. "Pia's quitting? Samm'll have a freaking fit."

Lauren hadn't planned on confiding in Nature, but now she couldn't stop herself. "We've already talked about going into business together. We'd call ourselves Help Unlimited."

Nature nodded. "Sounds good to me—but only if I can get you back any time."

Lauren grinned. "Pay my hourly rate and I'm all yours!"

Help Unlimited was an instant hit. Word traveled fast, and before they knew it Lauren and Pia were inundated with clients. In fact so many that after the first three months they had to hire two helpers. It was a hectic existence. One day Lauren found herself watering houseplants in a Park Avenue duplex and the next organizing a fantastic midnight dinner for thirty on top of the Empire State Building!

Pia had met a man she was crazy about. His name was Howard Liberty, and he was an executive with Liberty and Charles—one of the most prestigious advertising agencies in New York. Howard was short and sandy-haired with a pleasing personality. Lauren liked him immediately.

"Good, because we're talking marriage," Pia admitted excitedly.

Nature's affair with Emerson Burn continued on its erratic course. Once in a while he would call on the services of Help Unlimited, but Lauren always made sure Pia dealt with him. Somehow she never felt comfortable in his presence.

Every so often someone tried to fix her up, even though they knew she wasn't open to a new relationship. She'd erected a wall around her emotional life and it was there to stay. All her energy was directed toward creating a successful business.

"What are you gonna do—stay celibate?" Nature asked.

"I don't have to jump in and out of bed to be happy," she replied calmly. "I'm building a business."

"You're *really* strange," Nature said, shaking her head. "No way *I* could go without sex."

Big surprise!

Pia and Howard fixed a wedding date. "I hope this doesn't mean you'll be leaving the business," Lauren said.

"No way!" Pia replied adamantly. "I certainly don't plan on sitting home having babies."

"Good!" Lauren said, relieved.

One Monday morning Nature called at six a.m. Lauren groped for the phone in her sleep.

"It's me!" Nature screeched. "I'm in Vegas. I bleedin' got hitched, didn't I?"

"Hitched?"

"Married, of course! Me an' Emerson finally did it."

"Oh, no," Lauren mumbled.

"What do you mean, *Oh, no?* 'Ang out the flags. I'm bleedin' Mrs. Emerson Burn, ein't I!"

Lauren couldn't think of a worse combination. The two of them together were much too volatile, they'd kill each other. She struggled to sit up. "Why did you do it?"

"Oh, this is nice," Nature said. "You're the first person I call, an' all I get is negative shit. We're in *love*, Lauren. In love!"

"Does the press know?"

"Not yet."

"When they find out you'll be inundated."

"Emerson's calling 'is manager. I expect they'll arrange a press conference. Can you fly out here to be with me? I'll pay."

"You don't have to pay. If you want me, I'm there."

"We're flying back to L.A. this afternoon. Emerson's a bleedin' maniac at the tables—there's no controlling 'im. Gotta get 'im outta 'ere quick. Tell you what, why don't you meet us at 'is L.A. house tomorrow? Oh, an' do me a big favor."

"Name it."

"Call Samm an' tell her. If I call 'er, she'll only scream at me."

Samm took the news stoically. It wasn't the first time one of her girls had run off and married a rock star, and it wouldn't be the last.

Pia wasn't thrilled when Lauren informed her she was flying to L.A. "You know I'm getting married next week. I need you here," she said.

"I'll be back," Lauren assured her. "All the arrangements are in place—everything will go smoothly. And I promise you I'll be here."

"*Why* do you have to go?" Pia complained.

"Because Nature is my friend," Lauren said.

"Ha!" Pia exclaimed. "Nature likes you because you do things for her."

Trust Pia to be cynical. "Thanks a lot."

Pia sighed. "What will you do? Sit by the pool watching them fight while I run the business all by myself?"

"Come on, Pia," she said persuasively. "I've never been to L.A. I'll only stay a few days."

By the time she'd organized her departure, Nature and Emerson's marriage had hit the airwaves in a big way. Even though Nature had said there were no press present, photographs of them began appearing everywhere. Nature in a short white minidress lovingly feeding Emerson wedding cake. Emerson in black leather, his mane of shaggy hair falling way below his shoulders. Nature grinning. Emerson scowling.

They looked happy.

They looked stoned.

Lauren sat on the American Airlines flight studying the *New York Post*. A picture of Nature and Emerson dominated the front page.

"Rock stars," sniffed a blue-haired woman in the next seat. "They're all degenerates, you know."

Lauren ignored the woman and closed her eyes. She was en route to L.A. It was a long way from Bosewell.

Embarking from the plane she felt like a movie star. A uniformed black driver greeted her at the gate and accompanied her to the luggage carousel, where she pointed out her one small suitcase.

He looked surprised. "That it?"

"That's it," she replied, sure it must be a disappointment for him having to meet a nobody like her. But he seemed quite cheerful as she followed him outside to the limo.

Everything in Los Angeles seemed bigger and better. The sky was bluer, the trees greener, and the limousine she climbed into was longer and more luxurious than any limo she'd ever seen. It was white with black windows, and inside there were tiny lights dotted all around the sides.

"Ever been to L.A. before?" the driver asked as they cruised along the freeway.

"Never," she replied, settling back into the luxurious leather upholstery.

"It's a trip," he said, peering at her through the rearview mirror. "I've been out here ten years now. Came from Chicago. Name's Tucker."

"And you like it better here?" she asked politely.

"L.A. life is easy."

"How long have you worked for Emerson Burn?"

"Six months. He's a good guy. Sometimes I get to travel with him."

"I guess his marriage surprised you."

Tucker laughed. "When it comes to rock 'n rollers, *nothing* surprises me."

Emerson lived in a mansion high in the hills of Bel Air. A guard waved Tucker through, and the huge gates closed behind them as the limo snaked its way up a long winding driveway. At the top of the hill was the largest house Lauren had ever seen.

As soon as the limousine drew up to the front door Nature came running out, wearing a red polka-dot bikini. "You're here!" she screamed happily. "About bleedin' time." They hugged warmly. "Come on in," Nature said, pulling her through the massive front door. "Welcome to me ever so 'umble home."

The house was a palace. High vaulted ceilings, old masters on the wall and heavy overstuffed furniture. " 'Course, it's not exactly my taste, but I'll soon get 'im to change everything," Nature said matter-of-factly, dragging Lauren through a domed-ceiling hallway toward the pool in the back.

"It doesn't look like his taste either," Lauren remarked, taking in everything.

"Some queen decorator did it," Nature said off handedly. "Probably wanted to give 'im one." She laughed at the thought. "C'mon outside an' congratulate the bridegroom."

Emerson Burn rested on a lounger beside an enormous blue pool wearing nothing but a black Speedo bikini.

Lauren's eyes traveled to the bulge. Either he used padding or everything you saw up on stage was the real thing.

His shaggy mane was bunched into a ponytail emerging from a black baseball cap. Ominous black shades covered his eyes. On either side of him was a small table. One held a phone, a tall jug of apple juice, two bottles of Stolichnaya vodka and several glasses. The other table was piled high with scripts.

Nature bounced over. "You remember Lauren, don't you, darling?"

Emerson removed his shades and stared at her with his dreamy gray eyes.

Lauren stared back, wondering if he used mascara on his long curling lashes. "Uh . . . congratulations," she mumbled.

"Thanks," he said, putting his shades back on and lifting his chin to catch more sun.

"Come back inside," Nature giggled. "I'll give you the grand tour."

By the time Nature had dragged her all around the huge mansion, Lauren was exhausted. "Can I take a shower?" she asked hopefully.

"Yeah, 'ave a sleep, too, 'cause tonight we're gonna party!"

"I didn't come here to party," she objected. "I came to help you out."

"Don't need any help, luv—Emerson's got sixty thousand people working for 'im. I'm entitled to 'ave a friend visit, ein't I? I just got married, for God's sake." She paused by a mirror in the hallway, attracted by her own reflection. "Hmm . . . I'm gettin' fat," she remarked, pinching her slim waistline.

"No, you're not," Lauren said firmly. "How can you say that?"

"It creeps up on you, luv," Nature replied, frowning as she turned this way and that, inspecting her body. "Oh, by the way, what did Samm say?"

"She wasn't exactly ecstatic."

"I *bet* the old bag wasn't. Did you tell 'er to cancel all me bookings for the next month?"

"No, I thought we'd discuss it first."

"There's nothing to discuss."

"Just because you're married doesn't mean you should give up your career."

"Who's givin' it up? But I ein't workin' me bleedin' arse off when I can stick with Em." She lowered her voice to a confidential whisper.

" 'E can't be trusted, y'know. 'Ave you any idea what happens on these tours? Rock stars got dumb little groupies crawlin' all over 'em like bleedin' fungus. I'm gonna travel with 'im, protect me interests."

"You won't be very popular if you cancel your bookings."

"This ein't a popularity contest," Nature retorted, flinging open a door and leading Lauren into a large sunny room overlooking the pool. " 'Ere's your room."

"Oh, my God! It's bigger than my apartment!"

"Everything's bigger and better in California," Nature announced. "You'll soon get used to it. How long can you stay?"

"Three days."

"You 'ave t'stay at least a week."

"I can't run out on Pia."

"She'll manage."

"Three days, Nature."

"Four days."

"Okay. Deal."

Nature smiled knowingly. "By that time you'll be beggin' to stay longer. 'Ave a lie-down—someone will wake you at six."

Lauren took a shower in the marble bathroom and then lay in the middle of the king-size bed. Within minutes she was asleep.

When she awoke it was late in the afternoon. She wandered over to the window and observed Emerson Burn in the pool. He was swimming laps as if his life depended on it. Anything to keep in shape.

Her first Hollywood party and everyone was dressed to over-kill. The mansion, owned by a record tycoon, was bigger and better than Emerson Burn's. Servants abounded.

" 'Ave a gander over there," Nature said, nudging Lauren sharply in the ribs. "It's Jack bleedin' Nicholson, ein't it? Wanna meet him?"

"No," Lauren said, horrified at the thought.

Nature giggled. "When you're out with me you can meet anyone you want. Who do you fancy?"

"I fancy sitting in a corner by myself."

"You're 'aving fun, ain'tcha?"

"You know my idea of fun. I prefer to watch."

346

"Very kinky!"

"Do me a favor—go off with your husband and enjoy yourself. I'm perfectly happy."

Nature didn't need much encouragement. "Okeydoke. I'll check you later."

Looking around, Lauren couldn't get over the fact that there were more waiters than guests. She requested a club soda from one with a blond crew cut and found a corner for herself, trying to remember everything she saw so she could tell Pia.

Not only was Jack Nicholson present, but she recognized a whole slew of other famous faces. A smiling Burt Reynolds, a gorgeous Angie Dickinson, a strutting Rod Stewart, a dignified-looking Gregory Peck.

The little girl in her said, *Why didn't I bring my autograph book?* The big girl said, *I don't want to be here. Let me out!*

Everybody kissed each other, only their lips never touched. Conversation seemed transient. The women wore jewels the like of which she'd never seen.

Nature reveled in it. Lauren watched her as she fluttered from person to person. Emerson didn't follow her around, he sat at the bar and everybody came over to pay homage. He was a rock star. It was his due.

Lauren found it easy to blend into the background. Although at one time she'd been the prettiest girl in Bosewell, she certainly didn't impress anybody in Hollywood. Not that she was trying. In fact, as usual she'd played down her looks—her hair was neatly drawn back, she wore no makeup and her simple outfit blended into the background. Nature often screamed at her about the way she dressed, and Pia was into giving lectures claiming she didn't make the most of herself. "I'm perfectly happy the way I am," she'd told them both.

By midnight she was ready to leave, but Nature was still going strong and Emerson showed no signs of moving. The house had its own discothèque—a mirrored room with flashing strobe lights, black granite floors and a wasted-looking disc jockey.

Lauren managed to grab hold of Nature as she fluttered by on her way to dance. "I'm falling asleep," she whispered. "Do you mind if I go?"

"Don't worry," Nature screeched. "We'll be out of 'ere soon."

"Maybe I can take the car and send it back for you?"

"Do what you want," Nature replied vaguely, continuing on her way.

Tucker was outside talking to a group of drivers. "They're not ready," Lauren said, "but I am."

Tucker nodded. "I'll bring the car around."

Sitting in the back of the luxurious limo she closed her eyes all the way back to Emerson's mansion. When she arrived she couldn't wait to fall into bed.

Sometime before dawn she was awakened by a screaming fight between Nature and Emerson.

What else was new?

The next few months passed quickly. Nick had his apartment, a stash of money from the Tijuana job and Joy Byron's class to keep him busy. Joy Byron had turned out to be the teacher of his dreams. She didn't criticize, she nurtured—carefully watching every move he made. The other students in the class couldn't wait to pick everyone's performance to pieces. Fuck 'em. As long as Joy thought he was good, that's all that mattered.

"I've decided to give you extra coaching," Joy announced one day, her watery eyes darting around the room.

"Can I afford it?" he asked, half jokingly.

"Probably not," she replied crisply. "But you'll pay me back . . . one day."

He began visiting her rundown house way up in the Hollywood Hills on a regular basis, and in her dusty living room he got to do anything he wanted. Joy Byron had bookshelves piled high with every play ever written, it was better than a trip to the library. She allowed him to indulge himself—reading with him, giving him pertinent advice on diction, posture, timing, makeup, the best lighting and camera angles.

"This information is invaluable," she said. "You, my dear boy, are going to be big."

He wasn't intimidated by her. "Hey—*I* know that," he replied cockily.

"Good," she said, unfazed by his arrogance. "Confidence is everything."

When she came on to him he was taken aback, the woman had to be at least sixty-five. He quickly made up a fiancée, a true love, waiting patiently for him in his hometown.

Joy did not believe him, but she backed off anyway, remarking that she had plenty of lovers and certainly didn't need the likes of him.

He wondered if it would make any difference in their student/teacher relationship. It didn't.

Annie was not pleased. The only time he ever saw her was in class and she'd taken to ignoring him.

"What's the matter?" he asked one day. "You're treatin' me like I got a bad case of B.O."

"You used me," she said, turning on him full of pent-up anger. "All you wanted was an introduction to Joy, and now that you're her pet project nobody hears from you. I don't appreciate being used, Nick."

"Hey—what's wrong with me gettin' everything I can out of this?"

Annie refused to be placated. "You're kissing her ass."

It didn't take long to realize most of the other students felt the same way. Well, fuck 'em. If they didn't like it that was their problem. He fully intended to learn everything he needed to know.

Joy announced she was putting on a student production of *On the Waterfront*. Naturally she gave Nick the coveted Marlon Brando role. This did not go down well with the rest of the class, who resented him even more.

So far Joy had advised him not to seek out an agent or manager. "Many important people come to my shows," she informed him. "I'll find you the right agent. Follow my guidance, dear boy, and we can't fail."

That was okay with him, he had no desire to traipse around agents' offices getting a series of turndowns.

DeVille was still living in his apartment, somehow she'd never gotten around to moving out. He didn't mind, it meant he didn't have to go looking for sex—she was always ready and available. Occasionally he asked her to read with him. She wasn't half bad and soon started dropping hints about maybe accompanying him to class.

That, he didn't need. He was having trouble enough—he could just imagine what would happen if he showed up with DeVille on his arm.

As for Manny Manfred and Glamour Limousines, he'd never gone back. As long as he had enough money, who needed to work for a living?

Cyndra had called to complain she never saw him. "I'm going to be playing Vegas," she said, full of enthusiasm. "Reece has me booked to sing at one of the best hotels. Will you fly out?"

He'd assured her he would, but he still hadn't gotten around to it. He was too busy putting all his energy into preparing for his upcoming role.

In between rehearsals he continued to spend most of his time at Joy's house. The night before the big event she came on to him stronger than ever. "I bring people luck, Nick," she announced grandly, her bony hand hovering dangerously near his thigh.

"Yeah?" he said warily, backing off as usual.

Her watery eyes bored into his. "If I told you about some of the men I've slept with, famous men . . . powerful men. They all claim I bring something . . . *special* into their lives."

By this time her hands were all over him.

He knew there was no way he could get it up, and yet he couldn't risk alienating her. "Joy, you're a very attractive woman," he said, speaking fast while desperately removing her hand from his leg. "But like I said—I got this fiancée, an' we promised we'd never cheat on each other."

Joy muttered something lethal under her breath and threw him out.

He drove back to his apartment hoping he hadn't made a mistake. *Hell, no—gotta have some principles.*

When he arrived home DeVille was sitting in a chair facing the door. Next to her were two packed suitcases.

"Going somewhere?" he asked, throwing off his jacket.

She smiled a trifle sheepishly. "I'm finally moving out. Remember, we discussed it a couple of months ago?"

He threw open the fridge and surveyed the meager contents. DeVille was a lousy housekeeper. "I didn't ask you to go," he said, reaching for a can of beer.

She pushed back her pale red hair. "I know, Nick, but I've stayed long enough."

"Where's your next stop?"

She lowered her eyes, almost afraid to tell him. "I met this guy."

Funny, but he wasn't at all jealous. "Yeah? What guy?"

"A producer."

He snapped the can open. "A *real* producer? Or some Hollywood phony?"

"He's asked me to live with him."

"How come you never mentioned him before?"

"It didn't seem necessary."

Nick wasn't used to being walked out on, but so what—there was no way he was begging her to stay. If she wanted to get conned by some would-be producer it was her problem.

That night he slept restlessly. He had a hunch that starting tomorrow everything was going to be different.

"Come over here, darlin'," Reece said, patting the empty seat beside him.

Cyndra hesitated, she had no intention of sitting with Reece at the small round table in the cocktail lounge of the busy downtown casino. The night before, she'd joined him and two of his so-called "friends." As soon as she'd sat down he got up and vanished for over an hour. The men had started making suggestive remarks and trying to grope her. She soon put them straight. When Reece returned he was furious. "Those were important guys," he told her. "*Real* important. What's the matter? You dumber than you look?"

His words had stung like a slap. How dare he talk to her in such a way—he never had before. But since they'd been in Vegas he'd changed, and it wasn't for the better. First of all there was the matter of the hotel where she was to perform. Reece had assured her it was going to be one of the big ones. "Which one?" she'd asked, imagining her debut was to be at the Sands or the Desert Inn.

"It's a surprise," he'd said mysteriously, not looking her in the eye.

Some surprise. A downtown dump full of hookers and hustlers with only a piano player to back her—a surly Puerto Rican who could barely speak English and was usually half drunk.

"What happened?" she'd asked furiously.

"We gotta get you more experience before we hit the big time," Reece explained. "This is a fine start, honey."

Reece talked a good game. First the demo recordings which failed to take place. Now Vegas and this crummy place.

Cyndra told herself she shouldn't blame him—at least he was trying. But he'd made such big promises and look where they'd got her.

When they returned to their motel room she'd refused to speak to him. Now he was sitting in the audience like nothing had happened, expecting her to join him.

Well, screw him, he could think again.

She narrowed her eyes and checked out the table. At least he was alone.

Hmm . . . he probably wanted to apologize.

Hmm . . . maybe she'd give him a second chance.

He got a real buzz performing before an audience—a sensation he'd never felt before. Better than sex—almost orgasmic in a way. Jeez! This was it. Give him a steady diet of applause and he'd be a happy man.

Joy hovered at the side of the stage, encouraging, criticizing, whispering in his ear every time he came off. Do this. Do that. More gestures. Use your voice.

Fuck you, lady, I'm flying! I don't need your help.

And the audience loved him. They fucking loved him! Marlon, move over—Nick Angelo is here to stay!

By the end of the show he was on fire, adrenaline pumping through his veins like pure heroin.

Joy was pleased. She had a big smirk on her face, especially when half the audience came piling backstage to congratulate her.

He wished he knew who was important and who wasn't, it wouldn't do to waste his charm on the wrong person. He looked to Joy for guidance. She was deluged by people.

"Not bad," Annie said grudgingly, passing by with a group. "We're going to the Hamlet on Sunset. Want to join us?"

Hamburger Hamlet was not exactly what he had in mind to celebrate his triumph. Plus Annie was really beginning to piss him off. Why couldn't she tell him he was fantastic, what was with this "not bad" shit? She was such a downer.

"Maybe," he mumbled. *If nothing better comes along.*

Joy beckoned him. "Nick, come over here—I want you to meet someone."

The someone turned out to be Ardmore Castle—a small time agent well known for his penchant for good-looking young actors.

"Hello, Nick." Ardmore had anxious eyes, plump jowls and a hungry expression. He was chasing fifty.

Joy moved away. Nick nodded, scanning the room. Ardmore Castle's reputation preceded him. Maybe Joy figured if *she* couldn't have him, then Ardmore was in with a chance.

The agent fixed him with a lecherous stare. "I enjoyed your performance."

"Uh . . . thanks."

"Very macho."

"Yeah, well, it's written that way."

"You brought something special to it."

Major eye contact. Jeez! Where was Joy when he needed her?

Ardmore cleared his throat. "Perhaps you'd care to join me at my house later. I'm having a few friends drop by."

"Gee . . . sounds great, but I got a date."

"Bring him," Ardmore said boldly.

"It's a her," he responded quickly.

Ardmore realized he was getting the brush. He pursed his lips. "Suit yourself."

"I intend to."

"*Very* bold. For an unknown."

Joy descended on him, accompanied by a hatchet-faced middle-aged woman in a man's pinstripe jacket and black pants. The woman brushed past Ardmore as if he didn't exist.

"Hello, Frances dear," Ardmore said, determined to be acknowledged.

She blew cigarette smoke in his face, barely nodding in his direction.

Joy grabbed Nick's arm in a proprietary way. "Nick dear, meet

Frances Cavendish, the casting director." She said "casting director" in meaningful tones. He got the message.

Frances didn't bother with pleasantries. She was a strong-jawed woman with an *I take no prisoners* demeanor. She was also fast-talking and to the point. "My office. Tomorrow. Noon," she said, flicking a business card at him. "Might have something for you."

Deftly Joy plucked the card from his hand. "We'll be there, Frances dear," she said, smiling sweetly.

"Don't need you, Joy. I'm sure Nick can walk and talk on his own."

What was this little scene? He felt uncomfortably like a piece of meat lying on a slab while the dogs sniffed around deciding who'd get lucky.

Ardmore expressed his disapproval. "You need an agent," he said. "Someone who'll protect your interests."

"Yes," Frances said dryly. "Someone who'll allow you to keep your pants on."

Nick took a deep breath, snatched Frances Cavendish's card back from Joy and mumbled, "I'm outta here."

"Where are you going?" Joy asked, hands fluttering.

"Gotta get some fresh air. See ya."

And he was gone before any of them could object.

48

Nature took on the role of tour guide, deciding that Lauren had to see everything there was to see in Los Angeles.

"Can we take a break?" Lauren begged, after they'd been to Disneyland, Universal City and Magic Mountain all in one day.

Nature looked surprised. "What for? You're only here a few days—we gotta do everything we can. Besides, I've never been to any of these places myself. It's a kick!"

While they were out exploring, Emerson lay out by the pool working on his suntan and reading scripts.

"He's looking for a movie for us to do together," Nature confided.

Sure, Lauren thought.

Every day around noon the rock star's entourage arrived at the house and stayed until he threw them out—usually not until two or three in the morning. They laughed at his jokes, assured him he was the best thing since Elvis and freebied all over the house.

The pack was led by his manager, Sidney Fishbourne—a lanky man in his forties with shoulder-length frizzy black hair.

Sidney was usually accompanied by April—a thirty-year-old married redhead he referred to as his executive assistant, although everyone knew she was his mistress.

The rest of the entourage consisted of Emerson's clothes designer, his makeup artist, his hair-stylist and his personal publicist.

The group spent most of their time discussing Emerson's image for his upcoming world tour.

"You gotta get wilder," Sidney insisted. "Break a few guitars, throw stuff around the stage, get the girls screaming."

"No fuckin' way," Emerson said adamantly. "I'm not doin' all that sixties shit again."

"He should be involved in a cause," his publicist said, twirling her worry beads. "Perhaps something to do with nuclear power or the environment."

"It's all in the clothes," his designer insisted. "No more black leather. I think suits."

"Suits are old," Sidney snapped. "We gotta start appealing to a younger audience."

His designer persevered. "Sophistication is very in."

"Who gives a shit," Emerson said flatly, and that was the end of the suit discussion.

Nature complained to Lauren that she felt left out. "All we ever talk about is 'im. What about *me*? I'm famous too."

"You married a rock star," Lauren pointed out. "His first interest is obviously going to be himself, especially with a world tour coming up."

"It's not that I'm jealous or anything," Nature continued. "But I'm hardly the bleedin' girl next door. I *should* get more attention, don't you think?"

"It depends," Lauren said carefully. "Do you really *want* attention from that bunch of ass-kissers?"

Nature giggled. "You're right, as usual. Who cares about them?"

"What you *should* do is get back to work. You're not the type to sit at Emerson's feet. Show him you're independent—that's why he married you, isn't it?"

"Hmm . . ." Nature wasn't entirely convinced. "I dunno."

"Well, *I do*," Lauren said forcefully. "*Never* give everything up for a man."

It didn't take long before Nature and Emerson were embroiled in another of their famous fights. This one was triggered by April, who innocently remarked she'd seen Selina, Nature's archrival, on television discussing her first movie role.

"Ha!" Nature said spitefully. "What's *she* playing—dumb cunt of the year?"

They were all sitting in the breakfast room picking at an array of salads and fruit plates. Emerson was into losing a few pounds, which meant no real food allowed.

"C'mon, luv," Emerson said mildly. "Selina's never done anything to you."

That was all Nature had to hear. She exploded in a jealous rage, lashing out at everyone.

"Got the rag on, 'ave we?" sneered Emerson, furious with her display of temper in front of everyone.

"Fuck you!" Nature screamed, picking up her plate of Caesar salad and flinging it in his face. "Go back to Selina if that's who you really want!" And with that she stormed out of the room.

Lauren was embarrassed for both of them—Emerson with small pieces of oil-covered lettuce stuck to his face and hair, and Nature, who'd made a jealous fool of herself in front of everyone.

Emerson glared at his entourage. "Get the fuck out," he commanded. "Show's over for today."

Obediently they all filed out. Lauren started to follow. "You don't 'ave t'go," Emerson called after her.

She pretended not to hear and hurried upstairs to her room, where she called the airline and booked a flight back to New York the following morning. She'd kept her promise and stayed four days. It was more than enough.

Later that afternoon she ventured down to the pool. She'd seen Emerson leave in the limo, and Nature had not returned from her lunchtime exit.

Lying out in the sun with nobody around was wonderfully peaceful. No rock music blaring. No Nature shrieking. No entourage making inane conversation.

She closed her eyes and allowed her mind to drift—thinking about Bosewell and her parents, Meg, Stock, all the old crowd. And finally Nick.

Oh, God, she didn't want to think about Nick. She tried to keep him out of her thoughts as much as possible—it wasn't worth reliving memories so bittersweet and painful.

Nick Angelo with his black hair, green eyes and killer smile.

Nick—whom she'd given herself to totally.

Nick—who'd taken off without so much as a goodbye, leaving her pregnant and alone.

She opened her eyes, forcing him from her thoughts. Standing over her, straddling the end of her lounger, was Emerson.

"What are you doing?" she asked, startled.

"Watching you," he replied, and she smelled the liquor on his breath.

She attempted to move her legs so she could get into a sitting position, but moving meant touching his crotch—and oh no, she could see his hard-on, the brief bikini he wore did nothing to hide it.

Stay calm, she warned herself. *Stay in control and nothing will happen.*

"Is Nature back?" she asked, trying to sound casual as she quickly pulled up the top of her swimsuit.

"I want you t'suck my cock," Emerson announced, swaying drunkenly.

Voices screamed inside her head. *Don't react! Don't panic! Stay cool!*

There was a long moment of silence. Neither of them moved. She noticed the small, spiky black hairs on the inside of his thighs and the tiny spot of moisture staining his bikini.

"Emerson, don't do anything you'll regret later," she said, trying to keep her voice even.

"Who says I'll regret it?" he slurred.

Where were the servants? Or Tucker? If she screamed would they hear? Would they care?

Damn Nature for putting her in this position.

She remembered Bosewell and Primo and that fateful day five years ago.

I think I killed a man.

No. The tornado killed him.

She'd never know the truth.

Her mind began to race, formulating a plan of action. If she raised one knee sharply and unexpectedly she'd catch him right on target, probably giving her enough time to run. But where would she run to? Surely if there was no one in the house she'd be putting herself in an even more vulnerable position?

Emerson stuck his fingers in the top of his bikini and began pulling it down.

Perfect! As soon as it was down far enough he'd immobilize himself and she'd make her move.

She made one more attempt to warn him off. "Don't do this, Emerson. Please don't. You're drunk. You're not thinking straight."

He looked surprised. "C'mon, Lauren, you know you've been dyin' t'suck my dick ever since you got here."

They moved together like clumsy ballet partners. He pulled his bikini down. She brought her knee up. He fell to one side, cursing. She struggled to her feet and started running toward the house. A count of three and he was behind her, kicking his bikini away from his ankles, running naked.

She sprinted across the marble terrace, hardly daring to glance behind her because she knew he was close.

He caught her by the steps to the house, slammed her from behind, and they both fell to the ground.

"Gotcha!" he yelled triumphantly, as if they were in the middle of a fun game. Then he pinioned her arms behind her head and rolled on top of her. "Now I'm gonna fuck you like you never been fucked before," he rasped, gripping both her arms with one hand while attempting to roll the top of her swimsuit down with the other.

"Don't you have enough girls," she gasped, turning her head. "Girls who *want* to be with you. Understand me, Emerson—*I* don't."

"Better believe it, baby. You'll want me so much you'll be beggin' for it," he said, ripping at her swimsuit, rolling it down around her waist and grabbing her breasts. "You hear me? *Beggin'* for it."

He tore at the crotch of her swimsuit, pushing it to one side, doing his best to enter her.

"You son of a bitch!" she screamed, suddenly losing all control. "LEAVE ME THE FUCK ALONE!" If she'd had a knife she would have stabbed him, just like she'd stabbed Primo.

Now he was really enjoying himself. He had her where he wanted and there was no way she could escape. "Temper! Temper!" he mocked. "Mustn't use dirty words. Mummy wouldn't like it."

She felt the tip of his penis about to force an entry and she was filled with despair.

Suddenly a new voice filled the air. "You dirty low life, scumbag *rat!*" It was Nature's unmistakable shriek. "You lying, cheating, mother-fuckin' *pig!*"

Emerson's hard-on deflated.

Lauren seized the moment and rolled out from under him, pulling up her swimsuit, fighting back angry tears.

"And as for you—" Nature turned on her, blue eyes blazing. "I thought you was me bleedin' friend. But you're just like all the rest of the slags—couldn't wait t'get your hands on me old man."

"Now wait a minute—"

"Get outta me house," Nature shouted, her cheeks red with anger. "I *never* want to speak to you again."

Emerson began to rock with laughter. He had no intention of coming to her defense.

What a couple, Lauren thought. The truth was they deserved each other.

She ran into the house without looking back.

49

"Are you straight?" Frances Cavendish asked, as if it was the most normal question in the world.

"Want me to pull down my pants an' prove it?" Nick replied, damned if she was going to embarrass him.

Frances leaned back behind her desk and adjusted the diamanté-studded glasses covering her flinty eyes. "Go ahead," she drawled, challenging him.

"Don't try me, lady," he warned, still trying to figure her out.

Frances laughed—a big bawdy laugh. "The kid's got attitude. I like it."

He didn't appreciate her talking down to him. "The *kid* is a hell of an actor. What I need from you is a job."

Coolly Frances appraised him, dragging on her cigarette. "What's your professional experience?"

"I done a lot of stuff," he mumbled.

Frances' expression said she didn't believe him. "Do you have a résumé? A tape? Photographs?"

"Uh . . ." He trailed off. She wasn't going to do anything for him. He'd made the trip to her fancy office for nothing. Frances Cavendish, casting agent. She must have known he had no experience. The old broad probably got off on humiliating people.

362

Frances continued to drag on her cigarette and squinted at him. "Are you fucking Joy Byron?"

"Now wait a minute—"

"No. *You* wait a minute," she said sharply. "You slouch in here in your tight jeans with your bad-ass scowl expecting exactly what?"

"You asked me to come," he fired back.

"Did I?" She took off her glasses and studied him further.

He felt her gaze penetrating beneath his clothes. She wanted a fuck. That's what they all wanted. And if he wasn't giving it to Joy—who at least treated him like a human being—he certainly wasn't giving it to this one. He turned, making his way toward the door. There was no point in hanging around.

Frances stopped him at the threshold, her voice strong and commanding. "I'm sending you on an audition."

He threw her a look. "Yeah?"

"It's a small role—but juicy."

"I got all the juice you want."

"I'm sure you have," she said coolly, putting her glasses back on. "Conditions."

"What?" he asked suspiciously.

"Take my advice and get rid of Joy—she'll hang around your neck like a cement block. Oh, yes, and stay away from agents like Ardmore Castle. If you get the part I'll recommend a legitimate agent to take care of you."

He felt obliged to defend Joy—after all, she'd been good to him. "Joy's a great teacher," he said.

Frances was having none of it. "Joy's an old hack living in the past. Drop her now, Nick, before it's too late."

"You're a hard lady."

"I'm honest—an almost impossible attribute to come by in this town."

He wondered what she wanted. Then decided he had nothing to lose by asking. "So . . . uh . . . what am I gonna owe you?"

"Occasional escort services. When I need you. Get yourself a tuxedo—you already have the attitude." She paused, inhaling deeply, heavy smoke drifting from her nostrils. "Escort duties end at the door. Which is more than you can say for Joy or Ardmore. Do we have a deal?"

This was some straight-talking old broad. "What's the part?"

"Small-time hood with a heart of mush. It's a minor role—but showy. I'm sending you over to meet the director and producers. If they ask about experience, lie. Tell them you've done stock, Off-Off-Broadway and commercials. If they ask for photos refer them back to me. I'll make an appointment for you to have photographs taken later this week. You'll pay me back when you get your first check."

He couldn't figure her out. "Why are you doin' all this?"

"Because when you make it you'll owe me. I like that. Write down your number. I'll call you tomorrow and give you their reaction."

He was apprehensive. "You mean I'm goin' on an audition *now*?"

She stubbed her cigarette out in a full ashtray, immediately reaching for a fresh pack. "Unless you'd prefer to wait a day or two."

He didn't hesitate. "Lady—I'm ready."

"That's *exactly* what I thought."

"You'll do things my way, or you're gonna find yourself doing nothin' at all." So spoke Reece.

Cyndra felt a shiver of fear. This was not the man she'd married— the laid-back cowboy with the big promises. This was someone else— a stranger. "You'd better stop getting on my case or I'm likely to walk," she said sharply, challenging him.

He caught her with a slap to the face, taking her by surprise. "Get it into your head—you're my wife," he said harshly. "*My wife*, do you understand me? I fucking married you—that means you belong to me, and you'll do anything I tell you to do."

Her hand flew to her face, stinging from his slap. "I don't belong to *anybody!*" she yelled.

"That's where you're wrong," he yelled back. "And if you don't believe me, maybe you'll believe this."

To her horror he pulled a gun from his belt and waved it in her direction.

She backed into a corner of their motel room, her eyes wide with fear. "Reece . . . Reece, what are you doing?"

"What the hell you think?" he replied.

"Where did you get a gun?"

He strutted around the room. "I always had it. Never know when it might come in useful. Man's gotta protect himself."

She took a deep breath and tried to stay in control. "Put it away . . . put it away *now*."

"I got your attention, huh?" He smiled slyly, pleased with himself. "So maybe you'd care to give some of that attention to my friends 'stead of making me look like a jerk."

Her mouth was dry, she couldn't believe what was happening. Within the last few minutes her life had crumbled around her. Wasn't it enough that she'd had to escape from Bosewell? Did she have to escape from this man, too?

"Listen to me *good*, bitch," Reece said. "I found you bumming around New York—now you're singin' in Vegas, so don't ever forget it's *me* got you here. An' if I expect you to be nice to my friends, then you'll do it. Understand?" As he spoke he waved his gun in the air.

"Yes, Reece," she whispered.

"Say it louder," he commanded.

"*Yes*."

"*That's* what I like to hear." He stuck the gun back in his belt. "Tomorrow night mebbe I'll have a coupla guys join us after the show, an' you'll be nice to 'em, honey. You'll do whatever I tell you t'do."

She nodded blankly.

Later, when he was asleep, she thought about creeping from the room and running. But where could she run to? If she took off she knew Reece would come after her.

With a feeling of deep despair she realized there was no escape. Once more she was trapped.

Nick did exactly what Frances had told him to do. He lied. When they asked him about his experience, he made up a traveling stock company he'd performed in, then mentioned a few commercials and several original Off-Broadway plays. In fact, he lied pretty good.

There were two producers in the room—a tall nervous man who sat in the background staring, and a middle-aged woman with great legs that she kept on crossing and uncrossing. The director was Italian-American, short, with swarthy features and a shock of greasy brown hair.

Nick checked them out. Three assholes all in a row. Fuck it. He wasn't nervous—although the casting assistant was really pissing him off. When they read together she didn't know acting from shit. But still, the three assholes seemed to like him—in fact they made him read through the scene twice.

When he'd arrived the receptionist had handed him several pages of dialogue. He'd had half an hour to study them. He'd also had half an hour to study the other actors waiting to go in. Talk about a cattle call—you could feel and smell the competition.

He remembered Frances' words—"small-time hood with a heart of mush"—and that's who he became. Not Nick Angelo, an actor chasing a role, but a small-time hood with a heart of mush. Some fucking description!

He finished reading the second time and waited for their reaction.

"Good seeing ya, Nick," said the director, dismissing him as though they were old friends.

"Thank you," said the woman producer, crossing her legs again while eyeing him contemplatively.

The tall man said nothing.

Before he could think about it he was out of there.

He stopped at the reception desk and spoke to the girl. "How long before I get to hear?" he asked.

She looked amused. "New at this?"

"Nah . . . Well, yeah, I guess. I'm new in town. I was, uh . . . workin' in Chicago an' New York."

"Oh, you're a New York actor," she said, a little bit impressed. "Don't worry, you'll soon get to know the routine. Sometimes these auditions go on for months. They see you, like you, then they see fifty other guys. After that maybe they'll call you back. You never know."

"So it's like a long wait?"

She shrugged. "Face it. This town is a crapshoot."

She was using his dialogue! He wondered if she ever got to listen in on the producers' conversation after the actors left the room.

"Hey, what's your name?" he asked, going for the friendly approach. "And when do you wanna have dinner?"

"Marilyn," she replied, still smiling. "*Married* Marilyn," she added, holding up her hand to display a wedding ring. "But thanks for asking anyway."

Outside in the parking lot he contemplated driving back to Frances' office and giving her a rcport.

Nah. Instinct told him he should wait until he heard from her. But now he was high from the audition and there was no way he could sit around waiting for the phone to ring. He decided to pay Annie a visit.

She was vacuuming when he arrived and didn't look thrilled to see him. "Oh, the big star is here," she said, continuing to vacuum.

He pulled the plug from the outlet. "What *is* this crap with you?"

She sighed. "How many times have we had this conversation? Like last night—why didn't you join us at Hamburger Hamlet? What *did* you do, take off with Ardmore Castle?"

"You calling me a fag, Annie?" he said, feigning indignation.

"I'm not calling you anything, but you . . ." She shook her head. "Oh, I don't know, Nick. You confuse me."

"I went home—alone."

"That's nice."

"I met this casting director—Frances Cavendish. I dropped by and saw her today and she sent me on an audition."

"What audition?"

"Small part in a movie."

"Did you get it?"

"Dunno."

"Did you read?"

He grinned. "I was great!"

"Mr. Modest."

"Listen, if *I* don't sing 'em, who will?"

She pushed the vacuum over to a corner closet and stored it. "Are you coming to Joy's class tomorrow night?"

He wandered around her small apartment. "I kinda figured I might drive to Vegas, see Cyndra. Beats sitting around waiting for the call to tell me I didn't get the part. This is like difficult shit."

"Nobody ever said it was easy."

"Whaddaya think? Should I go to Vegas?"

"Cyndra would love to see you."

"How long's the drive?"

"Five, six hours, I'm not sure."

"Wanna come?"

She shook her head but he could tell she was tempted. "C'mon, live dangerously. Throw a few things in a bag. It'll be fun," he said encouragingly.

Annie began to relate a list of excuses.

Nick shot them all down.

An hour later they were on their way.

Back in New York Lauren refused to talk about her L.A. trip.

"What happened?" Pia was anxious to know.

"Nothing," she replied quickly. "Exactly nothing."

"Why aren't you telling me anything?" Pia complained. "And how come if Nature calls you don't want to speak to her? *Something* must have gone on."

Lauren's only desire was to forget about L.A., and with that in mind she threw herself back to work. In her spare time—of which there was little—she began attending a self-defense class, studying French and also taking a gourmet cooking class. These activities left her no time for a social life, and if anyone tried to fix her up they got a blank "No thanks."

Shortly after getting back she attended Pia and Howard's wedding in the garden of his uncle Oliver's house in the Hamptons. Oliver Liberty was one of the founders of Liberty and Charles. He was a distinguished-looking man in his late fifties, with a dry sense of humor —the complete opposite of his wife, Opal, a vacuous blonde he'd married on the rebound after an expensive divorce from his first wife of thirty-one years.

It was a beautiful wedding. Lauren sat back and daydreamed about how it might have been if things had been different with Jimmy. She even allowed her mind to drift back to Nick. So many years ago . . . but when she thought about him it still hurt and she shut off the thoughts abruptly.

After dinner Oliver Liberty strolled over and sat down beside her. "I hear you and Pia are building quite a business," he said, one eye on his flashy wife, who was cavorting on the dance floor in a too tight red dress.

"We're doing okay," she replied, adding with a smile, "I'm sure you can't wait to steer all your clients in our direction."

He nodded. "Always thinking ahead. That's what I like—a smart woman."

If that's what he liked, how come he'd married the blonde—who, according to Pia, had an IQ of zero?

"So . . . will we be getting your clients?"

He smiled. "I'm sure, Lauren, you always get exactly what you want."

Shortly after Pia moved out the calls started. The first one came at two o'clock in the morning. Lauren groped for the phone in her sleep, mumbling a groggy "Hello."

"I wanna talk to you," a familiar voice said.

She knew immediately it was Emerson Burn. For a moment she held her breath before quietly replacing the receiver.

He called back within seconds. "Don't 'ang up on me," he complained. "That's not nice."

"What do you want?" she asked, amazed at his nerve.

"It's about time we got together," he said confidently.

"Are you crazy?" she said, struggling to sit up.

"Seems like a normal request to me."

"Have you forgotten what happened in L.A.?"

"Nothin' happened."

"That was because Nature came back."

"What are you gettin' so uptight about? So I came on to you. Big deal. Most girls would give their left tit to 'ave me come on t'them."

"I don't *believe* this. You tried to rape me, and the only reason you didn't get away with it was because your wife came home. Your *wife* —remember her? She used to be my best friend—now she no longer talks to me, thanks to you. You're an asshole, you know that?" She slammed the phone down.

It rang again immediately.

She took the receiver off the hook and buried it under her pillow.

The next day three dozen red roses arrived at the apartment with a note. The note read, *Sorry! E.* She dropped the flowers off at a nearby hospital.

A few days later while lunching with Samm she casually inquired about Nature.

"Did you two fall out?" Samm asked, raising an elegant eyebrow as she picked at her tomato and lettuce salad.

"You know what Nature's like better than anyone," she replied cagily, sipping a glass of water.

"That's true," Samm replied with a weary sigh. "The girl can be absolutely impossible. I don't know what she sees in that mangy rock star, he looks like he's in desperate need of a shower—several in fact. Those leather pants stick to his body like tacky tape—and I *do* mean tacky."

"So they're still very much together?"

"About as close as two enormous egos *can* be," Samm said dryly. "You *do* know she's been bad-mouthing you all over town?"

Lauren sighed—this was all she needed to hear. "She has?"

"I wouldn't worry—nobody takes her seriously."

Emerson called again the following week. "Changed your mind?" he asked casually, like they chatted every day.

"About what?"

"Gettin' together."

The man was in ego overdrive. "I have a news flash," she replied sharply. "You've finally met the one person who doesn't want to go out with you."

He was not to be put off. "If you're worried about Nature, she's in L.A."

"I thought she came with you on every trip to hold your hand."

"Nah, can't 'ave her trailin' me, can I? S'not good for the image. Come on, we'll hit a few clubs, 'ave us a time."

"You know what, Emerson?"

"*What*, babe?"

"Stop calling me."

It seemed inconceivable that Emerson Burn had decided to pursue her. Did he honestly think that a near rape was prelude to a romantic relationship?

Three months after getting married Pia announced she was pregnant. "Howard and I talked it over, and we want you to be godmother."

"I'd be honored," Lauren replied, thinking how lucky Pia was to be married to the man she loved *and* pregnant.

Help Unlimited was doing so well that they'd finally rented proper office space. Pia decided to keep working until a month before the baby was due. "I'm not the sitting-at-home type," she explained. They now employed six people, which gave Lauren the luxury of choosing the jobs she wished to do. Since she'd taken the cooking course, small dinner parties were her forte. She enjoyed organizing incredible meals, and it also kept her busy most nights—which suited her fine.

Sometimes, late at night, when she was lying in bed, a wave of unbearable loneliness swept over her. But she'd decided it was better to be lonely than to suffer another broken heart.

Now that Pia had moved out of the apartment they'd shared, she decided to redecorate. It wasn't the most luxurious place in the world, but it was comfortable and cozy and she was happy there. Weekends she liked nothing better than strolling along Eighth Avenue exploring the antiques shops and picking out special things.

One Saturday afternoon she was walking across from Park to Madison Avenue, when she noticed a long white limousine crawling along the curb behind her.

She quickened her step, but the limousine kept pace, and when she stopped at a street corner the door of the car was flung open and Emerson Burn leaped out. He grabbed her arm and spun her around to face him. "You been avoiding me," he said accusingly.

Was he so dumb he really thought she was ever going to talk to him again?

"What now?" she said, attempting to shake his arm off.

His grip tightened. "Get in the car an' I'll tell you."

"Forget it."

"I ain't forgettin' it, darlin'," he said loudly. "*That's* the friggin' point."

Two girls spotted him and froze as if they'd just seen Jesus.

Emerson's bodyguard jumped out of the car. "Time ta split, Em," he said, watchful eyes raking the street.

Emerson ignored him.

The girls clutched each other, bracing themselves for the rush.

"You ain't bein' fair t'me," Emerson complained, holding tight. "I wanna explain. I was drunk. I had a problem."

"Now look—" she began.

The girls sprang into action—sprinting toward him with purposeful looks in their eyes. The bodyguard saw them coming. So did Emerson. "Oh, shit!" he exclaimed. "Here comes trouble."

Lauren felt a thump in the small of her back and was rudely shoved aside as one of the girls moved in on him.

"I'm insane about everything you do!" the girl yelled hysterically, pulling at his jacket. "I love you! I *really really* love you!"

Before Lauren could think about what to do the bodyguard bundled Emerson into the limo—somehow pushing her in behind him. The car immediately took off.

"Well," Emerson said, "that settles it. You're trapped, darlin', an' there ain't nothin' you can do about it."

51

"I've never done anything like this before," Annie said, throwing Nick a sideways glance.

He laughed. "Anybody would think we were planning on robbing a freakin' bank!"

"You know what I mean. Taking off like this, it's . . ." She looked at him questioningly. "I guess it's fun."

"*Now* you're beginning to learn."

They'd been driving for several hours. The freeway ride was long and boring, but the thought of seeing Las Vegas for the first time excited both of them. "Hey, how much money you got on you?" he asked, realizing he hadn't come prepared.

"About fifty dollars. Why?"

" 'Cause we're gonna blow it, that's why."

"Oh, no, not with my money," she said indignantly.

Grinning, he steered the old Chevrolet onto an off ramp. "C'*mon*, Annie, you gotta take *some* chances in life."

"It's my rent money," she objected.

"So we'll double it. How's that?"

She glanced over at him. "You know, Nick, you're really strange."

"Oh, so now I'm strange. What's *this* leading up to?"

"Can I be honest with you?" she asked earnestly.

"You can be whatever you like," he replied, pulling into a Chevron station.

"It's just that sometimes it seems you're coming on to me, and then other times you act as if you're my brother."

Oh, shit—the last thing he needed was Annie developing a crush on him. But then again, why not? DeVille was long gone and he was bored with the endless stream of one-night stands he could have any time he wanted.

"Are you interested in me or not?" she asked, putting it firmly on the line.

He stalled for time. "Is this a proposition?" he said lightly, winding down his window.

"I . . . I need to know."

"Hey, I'm here with you, we're driving to Vegas."

"Is that your idea of a commitment?"

Commitment! The very word gave him nightmares. What was it with women and commitments? Why couldn't they take it day by day?

The gas station attendant leaned into his window—saving him a reply. "What'll it be?" the old man asked, scratching his grizzled beard.

"Fill her up," Nick said. "An' check the oil an' water while you're at it."

"Well?" Annie demanded, not letting him off the hook.

He took his time before replying. "We're goin' on a trip," he said carefully. "Whyn't we take it nice an' easy and maybe we'll find out."

Reece Webster sat back in the smoky atmosphere of the small casino bar and watched Cyndra sing. She was good. She was *really* good. So how come she wasn't getting anywhere? The record labels hadn't liked the deal he'd proposed, and the bigger hotels had said she needed experience. Experience, goddamn it! He was giving her experience, and what kind of thanks was he getting? Exactly nothing. Cyndra had no appreciation of the things he did for her.

Well, what did he expect? Women were all takers and Cyndra was no exception.

He hoped he hadn't wasted his time marrying her. He'd been so sure she was going to be his ride to the big time—now all he did was pay the bills. The money she made at the casino didn't even cover his expenses. Some dud investment. He'd put two years into singing lessons and grooming and it simply wasn't paying off.

His narrow eyes raked the room. Several men were watching Cyndra with that look on their faces. Reece knew the look well. It was the *I wanna fuck your brains out* look.

He studied her dress. Not sexy enough. She needed more cleavage and maybe a deep slit in the skirt. She had great tits and long legs. He'd have to deal with that. He'd have to pay for it too.

Cyndra was beginning to remind him of his first wife. That bitch had dragged him down like a lead weight, all she'd been capable of was grabbing everything he had. Now Cyndra was falling into the same category, and it was about time he did something about collecting on his investment.

The other night he'd overheard a couple of guys talking while Cyndra was on stage. "I wouldn't mind a piece of that," one of them had said.

"Yeah, with gravy all over it!" the other one replied.

Reece had sidled over. "Wanna meet the little lady?" he'd offered. " 'Cause if you do, I'm the man can arrange it."

Both men had nodded eagerly, so Reece had negotiated a deal. The problem was he'd forgotten to tell Cyndra, and when he'd sat her down with the two guys and they came on to her she insulted them both. The men were real riled up—and who could blame them? Much to his chagrin he'd had to return their money.

So what the hell was wrong with a little light hooking on the side? Convincing Cyndra was a bitch. Except that today he'd asserted himself—put the fear of God into her. *That's* what women expected—a little fear in their lives. They had to know who the boss was.

Sipping his malt whiskey he scoped out likely prospects, focusing on a stocky man sitting alone at a corner table watching Cyndra like he'd just discovered candy for the first time. The man was middle-aged with a florid complexion. A brightly colored Hawaiian shirt and open sandals on his feet announced tourist.

Casually Reece wandered over. "Howdy," he said, tipping his cowboy hat.

The man looked up. "Do I know you?"

"No," Reece said, "but I got a strong suspicion you'd like to."

"Get your homo ass away from me," the man said, his florid face reddening even more.

"You got it wrong," Reece replied, scowling. "I ain't that way. I came over here t'do you a favor."

"What favor?" the man asked suspiciously.

Reece gestured toward Cyndra. "Y'see that little lady standing up there? She's what I got in mind for you, but if insults is what I get— then we got no more conversation." He turned to go.

"Wait a minute," the man said.

Reece stopped. "You interested or not?"

The man glanced around furtively. "I'm interested," he said, lowering his voice. "How much will it cost me?"

"Did you win or did you lose? 'Cause if you lost you can't afford this baby."

"I won at craps."

"Then you're a lucky son of a gun, 'cause she's gonna cost you two hundred and fifty."

The man licked his lips and thought quickly. His flabby wife was upstairs sleeping off the effects of winning at the slots. His snotty teenage son was out chasing girls. This was the opportunity of a lifetime and he didn't want to blow it. But two hundred and fifty bucks was an awful lot of money, he could buy a second television for that much money. "I . . . I don't know," he said hesitantly.

"You don't know," Reece repeated, as if he couldn't believe what he was hearing. "You got a chance for a piece o' that and *you don't know?*"

Sweat beaded the man's thick neck. "Is she good?" he asked hoarsely. "Is she worth it?"

Reece tilted his cowboy hat even further back on his head. "Are you shittin' me? Does Kentucky give fried chicken? Does Cadillac give the smoothest ride goin'? Man, this little lady is the best *you* ever had."

They came upon Las Vegas like a shimmering jewel sitting in the middle of the desert. It was dark and they'd been driving for hours without any light at all. Now in the distance they saw the city spread out before them and it was a startling sight.

"It's incredible!" Annie gasped.

Nick grinned. "I told you—you gotta get out an' do things. No good sittin' on your ass all day expecting . . . I dunno—" He looked at her quizzically. "What *do* you expect, Annie?"

She shrugged. "I work hard, go to class . . . one of these days I'll get a break."

"Yeah, I guess that's what we all think." He pulled the car over to the side of the road, sliding his arm around her shoulders. "I'm glad you came."

"So am I."

They were silent for a while, staring at the mirage ahead—at least that's what it looked like in the middle of the barren desert. Finally he broke the silence. "I never asked you before—where's your family?"

"They're in Florida, where I grew up. I left three years ago and took the bus out to L.A." She snuggled closer. "What about you? Cyndra's never talked about your family. Where are your parents? Do you have any other brothers or sisters?"

He drew away from her on the pretext of reaching for a cigarette. "No sad stories," he said, shaking loose a Camel. "Cyndra and me— we got a father in common, a real charmer. Neither of us has seen him in years."

"You don't speak to him?"

"Nope."

"That's a shame. Family is all we really have."

"Yeah, well, you ain't met mine," he said flippantly.

"What about your mother?"

He struck a match and lit up. "She died when I was sixteen. Left me."

"She didn't leave you, Nick," Annie said softly. "Dying is not exactly making a choice."

He didn't need to dredge up any more memories, it was painful enough without having to talk about it.

"Hey, can we quit this conversation? Let's appreciate what we got in front of us. Take a look at that view!"

"It's beautiful," she murmured.

"Yeah," he said, starting the car. "Let's go get us a piece of it."

"This is my friend," Reece said.

Cyndra nodded, not looking anywhere near the man in the Hawaiian shirt.

"My *good* friend," Reece added, in case she hadn't quite gotten the message.

"Uh-huh," she said dully.

The man nudged Reece. "When we gettin' out of here?" he asked, perspiration beading his forehead. "It's not good for me to be seen with you people. Where we going anyway?"

"Close by," Reece replied reassuringly.

"You're not like those con people I seen on TV?" the man said anxiously. "They lure you to a room with a girl, take your money and beat up on you."

Reece tipped his cowboy hat. "Do I look like a con man?" he said, his lip curling. "Does she look like a con woman? Don't worry, partner. You are about to have the dream trip of your life."

Cyndra caught snatches of the conversation. She knew what Reece expected, he'd made that very clear, but she still couldn't believe it.

"Okay, hon," Reece said, all nice and friendly. "Let's go so you an' this fine gentleman can get to know each other better."

"I'm warning you," she hissed under her breath, just loud enough for him to hear. "I'm not doing this."

His hand strayed toward his belt. "Cooperate, hon. I told you this mornin'—I been carryin' you too long, it's about time you gave something back."

The three of them walked out of the casino into the parking lot, where the humid night air enveloped them like a heavy cloud. She wondered what Reece would do when she refused to go through with this. He'd probably blow her head off—he was crazy enough. But still, he wouldn't be in the room watching them, and once he left she'd tell the guy the position she was in—appeal to his better nature. He looked like a family man, although he sure didn't smell like one. He stunk of beer. She shuddered—his smell reminded her of Primo.

They drove to the motel in Reece's shocking pink Cadillac. By the time they got there the man was sweating even more profusely.

"Take my license number," Reece suggested, sensing that this dude could back off at any moment. "It'll make you feel more secure."

"No, no, I trust you," the man said, although he didn't. "How'm I gonna get back?"

"I'll stay around," Reece said. "Whistle when you're done an' I'll drive you."

Cyndra got out of the car and stood stiffly beside it.

"Get your cute little butt to the room, honey," Reece said coaxingly. "An' don't forget t'leave the door open for our friend." He waited until she was out of sight and then snapped his fingers, it was time for business. "Gotta have cash," he said. "No cash, no pussy."

The word "pussy" turned the man on. Feverishly he counted out several large bills.

Reece checked it through twice. When he was satisfied he said, "Room eight, near the pool." Then he winked. "Do the double loop for me, partner, compliments of the house."

When Cyndra reached their room she thought about locking the door. But she knew it wouldn't work—if she didn't let the man in Reece would only kick the door down.

She was pretty, she was young, she had talent—why hadn't her career taken off? If it had, everything would be all right. Reece was doing this to punish her. *How about divorcing him?* a little voice whispered in her ear. *How about getting out while I still can?* But she knew it was hopeless, he'd never let her go unless she paid back every cent he'd spent on her.

There was a knock on the door. Swallowing hard, she smoothed down her dress, walked over and threw it open.

The man barged past her into the room, his Hawaiian shirt sticking to his chest. "Let's do this quick," he blurted. "I'm about ready—so hurry it up."

"I'll fix you a drink," she said, stalling for time. "There's a Coke machine down the hall and we got Scotch or vodka. What'll it be?"

"Nothing," he said, already fumbling with the buttons on his fly.

She noticed the gleam of a wedding ring on his finger. "Does your wife know you're doing this?" she asked sharply.

He stopped short. "What's my wife got to do with anything?"

"I . . . I just wondered, that's all."

His eyes darted around the room, settling on the bed. "I do it the conventional way," he announced. "Whyn't you lie back and take your clothes off?"

"I'm not a conventional girl," she replied quickly, continuing to stall.

"I don't got all night," he said, glancing at his watch.

"If you'd sooner forget it . . ." she ventured.

He jumped to attention at that. "I paid good money for you."

"How much?"

"What's it to you?"

His words infuriated her. "It's *me* you're supposed to fuck, isn't it?"

He reached over, pinching her left nipple through her dress. "I'm not used to women talkin' dirty."

She shrunk away. She was no hooker and she wasn't about to act like one. If Reece wanted to blow her head off, then so be it. "There's been a mistake," she said, her voice a dull monotone.

His eyes began to bug. "What mistake?"

In the same flat voice she said, "I don't do this sort of thing."

"But I was told—"

"I don't care *what* you were told. Zip up your pants and get out of here. Go home to your wife."

Without any warning he burst into tears. "I knew I shouldn'ta come here," he sobbed. "I knew it was a bad thing to do."

Cyndra was taken aback, she'd expected a violent reaction, not this. "Look," she said, showing some compassion. "I'll get Reece to drive you back to the casino. He doesn't have to know nothing happened."

The man continued to sob.

"We'll tell him it was the greatest. That way we'll both come out of this okay—you'll look like a real stud and I won't get my head bashed in." Gently she began steering him to the door. "It'll work out, you'll see. We'll—"

With a sudden spurt of anger he threw her arm off and choked out a frustrated "What about my money?"

"I can't help you with that."

"I paid good money for you. I want it back."

"You'll have to ask Reece, and if you ask him he's gonna know."

The man seemed to have recovered from his crying jag. Now he was red-faced and angry. "I want my money," he said stubbornly.

"I told you—I don't have it."

"Then you'd better get it, you cheap little hooker."

"He's got a gun," she said in a flat voice. "He could blow both our heads off. Whyn't you do us both a favor an' go quietly?"

"This was a setup all along," the man said bitterly. "I seen you people on television, you had no intention of putting out."

"Listen, mister, you're the one started to whine like a baby."

"You black bitch—if I'm not getting my money, I'll sure get my money's worth." Unexpectedly he grabbed her, his wet lips slobbering all over her neck.

She shoved him off, but he came at her again.

Suddenly she was back in the Browning house in Bosewell and he was Mr. Browning—grabbing her, forcing her to do things. Every bad memory flooded over her.

"I . . . won't . . . do . . . this," she screamed, kicking out.

"You'll do it unless I get my money back," he said, roughly squeezing her breasts.

Was money all anybody cared about? Mr. Browning's words hung in the air—*black cunt . . . black bitch . . .* She could hear his voice, his insults. It was like it had all happened yesterday.

They fell back on the bed and her screams became louder. Somebody knocked on the dividing wall yelling, "Shut up!"

The door flew open and Reece marched in. "What in hellfire's goin' on here?" he demanded, narrow eyes pinning Cyndra accusingly.

"He . . . he . . . tried to attack me," she gasped.

"Damn whore," the man muttered. "The bitch wouldn't give me nothin'."

"I left you two to have a good time," Reece said patiently, tapping one of his pointy-toed cowboy boots on the frayed carpet. "An' all you're doin' is fighting. *'Course* she's gonna give you any sweet thing you want." He threw her a warning look. "Get it together, hon, or you *know* what'll happen."

"Screw you, Reece," she spat. "You can't treat me like this."

His hand hovered near his belt. "Oh, I can't, huh?"

The man decided the time had come to get back to his hotel room and his flabby wife. "I want my money," he said, making one last attempt to claim what was his.

"No refunds," Reece snapped.

"You had no right to pull this on me," Cyndra said, tears stinging her eyes. "I'll divorce you, that's what I'll do."

Reece stood dangerously still. "Honey, you'll do what *I say* you'll do."

"Why don't I take my money and leave," the man suggested, not liking the way this was going.

"Shut your mouth an' stay out of this," Reece said, not even looking in his direction. This was between him and Cyndra, and she had to learn a lesson.

"Maybe what I *should* do is call the cops," the man threatened. "You stole from me."

Reece jumped to attention, pulling back his jacket and revealing the gun stuck in his belt. "You ain't going nowhere, partner."

"Aw, Jesus!" the man groaned, the color draining from his face. "Aw, sweet Jesus!"

Reece turned his attention back to Cyndra. "Get your clothes off. I hear one more scream outta this room an' you *know* what'll happen."

The man began slowly edging toward the door.

Cyndra stared at Reece, a deep rage burning inside her. "You know what, Reece—you're nothing but a dumb pimp," she said, the words spilling out. "In fact, that's all you're capable of—pimping. How does it feel to be pimp of the year? Pimp of the fucking century?" Her voice rose. "How does it feel to know you CAN'T DO ANYTHING ELSE?"

The person next door hammered on the wall again.

"You callin' *me* a pimp?" Reece yelled. "Well, what does that make you? A whore, honey. A drippin' blood-suckin' whore."

"Oh, I ain't no whore, mister. Don't you get it? *I ain't no whore!*" She leaped off the bed, furious.

Removing the gun from his belt Reece waved it in her face.

"Don't threaten me," she yelled hysterically. "You can't control my life. You can't control *me*." She lunged at him, grabbing for the gun.

The man reached the door, sweat coursing down his face. These two were crazy. And he was equally crazy to have come here.

His hand clutched the doorknob as Cyndra and Reece struggled for possession of the gun. His hand was so slick with sweat he couldn't get it open.

And then a shot rang out. One lone shot.

The bullet ricocheted off the wall and hit the man in the back of his head. He fell to the floor without a sound. There was a long moment of frozen silence.

"Oh, *shit*," Reece said, panic-stricken. "Look what you done, you crazy bitch—you shot the dumb motherfucker. You killed him, you stupid cunt. You gone and goddamn killed him!"

52

"I'm not as bad as you think," Emerson said.

"How do you know *what* I think?" Lauren replied, sliding along the leather seat as far away from him as she could get.

"It's not exactly difficult figuring you out."

"Figure this out, Emerson. I'd like to get out of this car, and I'd like to get out now."

He shrugged. "Okay, I'll admit it. I was bombed outta my skull and I gave you a hard time. So I'm sorry. I'll make it up to you."

She shook her head. "What does it take to get you to understand that I don't want anything to do with you?"

He began to laugh. "That's what I like about you. You're different from the rest of 'em. You can even string two words together."

"So can Nature," she snapped.

"*You* try living with Nature," he said gloomily. "It's a bloody nightmare. Anyway, we split—didn't she tell you?"

Lauren leaned forward and tapped on the smoky black glass separating them from the driver.

"Whattaya doin'," he asked, lounging back and stretching out his long leather-clad legs.

"Telling your driver to stop the car."

He looked amused. "I thought I told you—you're my prisoner."

"This is kidnapping."

He shrugged. "So arrest me."

She sat back, trying to decide what to do. In spite of everything there was no denying that he was a very charismatic figure, and if she really wanted to face up to it she *was* attracted to him in spite of what had happened. Besides, what did she have to lose? Exactly nothing. Nature wasn't talking to her anyway.

"Okay," she said, with a weary sigh.

"Okay what?"

"I'll have lunch with you. Impress me. Dazzle me with your charm. Show me that you're really just like the boy next door."

He chortled with laughter. "Babe, I 'aven't been like the boy next door in twenty years."

"Make an effort."

"For you—anything."

He took her to a small Italian restaurant on Third Street. The jovial owner ushered them to a table in the back, treating Emerson like a king. His bodyguard stayed at the front of the restaurant, scanning the sidewalk for trouble.

"Champagne, caviar, what'll it be?" Emerson asked, tossing back his mane of hair.

She glanced at her watch. "It's three o'clock in the afternoon."

"So?"

"So I'll have a small green salad and some pasta. Then I have to go. Besides, this place doesn't have champagne and caviar."

"Wanna bet? I can get anything I want any time I want," he boasted.

"And if you don't get it you take it. Story of your life, right, Mr. Burn?"

"What's with this Mr. Burn crap?"

"I'm giving you a little respect, you should try it some time."

He leaned across the table, staring directly into her eyes. "You're beautiful, y'know that? You got somethin' I really get off on."

She hit him with a little light sarcasm. "Gee, you certainly have a way with words."

He didn't seem to mind. "It's me upbringin'," he said cheerfully.

"Where was that?"

"Elephant an' Castle—or Asshole, as we liked to call it back in the good old days. Sorta Brooklyn with a cockney accent."

"You and Nature have a lot in common—including a country."

He laughed derisively. "Me and Nature 'ave exactly nothing in common."

"You married her."

"Big friggin' deal. I 'ad a hangover at the time."

"Is that your excuse for everything?"

"Oh, now you're gonna give me the *You drink too much* speech."

"I really don't care what you do."

"You're wrong."

"About what?"

"About not caring. From the first time I saw you I knew we had something goin'. You were like this little mouse runnin' around organizing that party for Samm up at my apartment—remember? I noticed you immediately 'cause you seemed different—that's what I like about you."

"I'll tell you what you like about me," she said crisply. "You like the fact you can't have me, because you're so used to having every girl that breathes, and now finally somebody says no. *That's* the only thing you like about me."

"Wrong."

"I don't think so."

"Whyn't we put it to the test?"

"How?"

"Sleep with me an' see if I'm still around tomorrow."

"Very funny."

"Glad I got you laughin'."

After lunch he decided he had to buy some books, so they stopped at Doubleday's on Fifth Avenue. Two minutes after leaving the limo, word was on the street and he was mobbed. He grabbed her hand and ran her back to the limo. As soon as they were inside, the car took off.

"Home. Mine," she said breathlessly.

"Deal," he replied. "I'll pick you up at ten."

"I'm asleep at ten."

"Tonight's different. Be dressed and ready to hit the town."

"I didn't say I'd go out with you."

"You didn't say you wouldn't. Just remember, I could have kept you prisoner for the rest of the day, but I'm letting you go. Now you owe me."

"Exactly nothing."

"Do you always 'ave to 'ave the last word?"

"Yes."

Upstairs in her apartment she found herself unable to settle down. This was crazy. Emerson Burn was a dilettante rock star. She wanted nothing to do with him. Or did she?

How come you had lunch with him, Roberts?

Why shouldn't I?

Do you find him attractive?

Yes, as a matter of fact I do.

The phone rang and she grabbed it, ready to tell Emerson she was definitely not going out with him that night, or any other night for that matter.

"Hi," Pia said brightly. "What are you doing?"

"I just walked in. Why?"

"Howard and I want to take you to dinner."

"I don't like the sound of your voice."

"What's wrong with my voice?"

"Whenever you use that tone there's always some single guy you think is perfect for me."

"I resent that," Pia said indignantly. "As a matter of fact, we're dining with Howard's uncle, and we thought it would be nice if you made up the foursome."

"Where's his wife?"

"At their house in the Hamptons."

"Hmm . . ."

"Lauren, we're talking about Howard's *old married* uncle—he's hardly likely to jump all over you."

"He's a man, isn't he?"

"Oh, *please!*"

"Okay, I'll come."

Pia was so used to getting a no that this was a surprise. "We'll pick you up at eight," she said quickly, before Lauren changed her mind.

Hmm . . . dinner with Howard's uncle. At least it got her out of the house, and when Emerson arrived and found nobody home maybe he'd take the hint and leave her alone.

Or then again, maybe not.

53

She didn't know how long she'd been sitting there, she only knew that Reece had gone and left her. Left her with a dead man lying on the floor.

She crouched on the bed, hugging her knees to her chest, her eyes wide with fear, while the man's body lay in a huddle behind the door.

"*I* didn't shoot him, *you* did it," she'd screamed at Reece when it happened—breaking away from him, her body trembling.

"Oh, no no *no, baby*, I don't take the rap on this one," Reece had said, frantically stuffing his clothes in a suitcase and running for the door.

"You . . . can't . . . leave . . . me," she'd said, the words sticking in her throat.

"Just watch me, honey," he'd said, throwing the gun at her.

And then he was gone.

At first she'd thought about calling the police. In fact, she wouldn't have been surprised if they'd turned up, because the people next door must have heard the gunshot. But nothing happened. Absolutely nothing. So she stayed on the bed too frightened to move, knowing she should have followed Reece and taken off. But how could she? He had the car and all their money—she was left with nothing.

So she sat in the middle of the bed, tears rolling down her cheeks, clutching the gun—her only protection.

Her life was over and there was nothing she could do about it.

"This is just like I've seen it on television!" Annie exclaimed. "Look at all these lights!"

"Yeah, this is really something," Nick agreed, pulling into the parking lot of a downtown hotel.

"Where are we going?" she asked. "Shouldn't we find Cyndra?"

"First we're gonna gamble. That's what you're supposed t'do in Vegas."

"Nick . . ."

"Try an' enjoy yourself, Annie," he said teasingly. "Today's your day for takin' chances. Bring it t'the edge—you never know, you might enjoy it." He got out of the car, grabbed her by the hand and they ran across the parking lot into the hotel lobby.

"Holy shit!" Nick exclaimed, taking in the banks of slot machines all in constant use. A grin spread over his face. "Y'know, I always wanted to do this." He groped in his pocket for change, coming up with several quarters. "C'mon, pick a machine—we're gonna win big time!"

"We are?" she asked unsurely.

"You bet your ass we are!"

They played the slots for two hours straight, ending up ten dollars ahead. By this time Nick had the fever—he was all set to carry on, but Annie was ready to quit. "We'd better go find Cyndra," she said. "It's one o'clock. What will they say when we turn up in the middle of the night?"

"They won't care. Tomorrow night we'll hear Cyndra sing, then we'll drive back to L.A."

"I can't take off work again tomorrow," Annie objected.

"You'll call in sick. Big deal."

She sighed. "You're making me as bad as you are."

"Hey—that can only be an improvement, right?"

"Thanks a lot!"

Armed with directions they drove to the motel where Cyndra and Reece were staying. It was not the most glamorous place in the world —just a few rooms located around a small pool.

"I bet they're asleep," Annie said accusingly. "I told you we should have come earlier."

"I bet they're not," he retorted confidently. "Nobody sleeps in Vegas."

They parked the car, found the room and knocked a few times, getting no answer.

"I gotta stop making a habit of this," he grumbled. "I'll spring the lock—no problem."

"You can't do that," Annie said, alarmed.

"Yeah, *right*," he said, working his magic on the lock and pushing the door open.

The first thing they saw was Cyndra sitting in the middle of the bed holding a gun. The second was the body slumped on the floor behind the door.

"Oh, my God!" Annie gasped.

Cyndra stared at them blankly while Nick edged his way toward her. "Take it easy," he said, speaking fast. "Take it real easy." Gently he removed the gun from her hand. "What happened?"

She covered her face with her hands and began to sob. "Oh, Nick . . . Nick . . ."

He put his arms around her, cradling her to him. "C'mon, baby, you can tell me."

Slowly she began to choke out her story. "Reece wanted me to . . . to sleep with this man. He brought him to our room . . . and then . . . then the guy wanted his money back because I wouldn't do it, and . . . and . . . Reece took out his gun . . . we were fighting . . . and . . . it went off. It was an accident, Nick, it really was."

"Where's Reece?"

"He ran."

"And left you like this?"

"What's going to happen, Nick? Nobody's gonna believe me. The cops won't understand."

Cyndra was right, she wouldn't stand a chance.

He went over to the man, staring down at his immobile body, hoping this was all a big mistake and that the guy would breathe, move, *something*.

No such luck.

"I'll phone the police," Annie said, pale and shaken.

"No," he said quickly. "This don't look so good." He turned back to his sister. "You're *sure* you didn't know him?"

She shook her head. "Reece picked him up in the casino. I never saw him before."

"So there's no connection between the two of you?"

"Not unless we were seen leaving together."

He bent down, gingerly groping inside the man's jacket for his wallet. It was imitation leather and contained five hundred dollars, a couple of credit cards and a driver's license in the name of George Baer.

"We gotta get him out of here, an' fast," he muttered, thinking aloud. "Yeah, that's what we gotta do."

Annie asserted herself. "No. What we must do is call the police."

"Will you shut up about the cops," he said, glaring at her. "Cyndra's in trouble, we gotta help her."

"I can't be an accessory," Annie said stiffly.

"I'm asking you a favor."

"It's too big a favor."

He pinned her with his green eyes. "I'm worth it, aren't I?"

She hesitated. "I . . . I don't know."

"Do it for me, Annie," he said persuasively. "Nobody has to know what happened here tonight."

"*I'll* know," she said vehemently. "And I can't live with it."

She was getting on his nerves. Fuck her if she didn't want to cooperate. "If that's the way you feel you'd better take a walk."

"Don't you understand," she said, her eyes filling with tears. "This is wrong."

"Cyndra's my sister—she needs me, so get off my fuckin' case."

"I'm not leaving," Annie said stubbornly.

"If you're staying you're helping, an' that makes you part of it."

"What are you going to do?"

"I'll deal with it, okay?" he replied, tired of her questions.

He coaxed Cyndra off the bed and told her to pack her things. Then he stripped the blanket from the bed and began rolling the man's body in it. No easy job. There was blood everywhere and Annie's accusing eyes nailed him every move he made. Sweat enveloped him. His mouth was dry and his heart pounding. Shit! He didn't even know if he was doing the right thing, but if he was to get Cyndra out of this mess there seemed to be no other alternative.

Finally he had the body wrapped in the blanket. The next move was to get it out of the stinking motel room and into the trunk of the car.

"Nick, I'm really frightened," Cyndra said, clinging to his arm.

"Don't be," he said, sounding more confident than he felt. "It's almost taken care of. I'm gonna drive the body out to the desert and bury it. You two'll stay here until I get back."

"No," she said sharply. "I can't let you do this alone. I'm coming with you."

"If you're going, so am I," Annie said, quickly joining in.

The two of them were beginning to drive him crazy, but it was probably safer to take them with him. "Okay, okay," he said reluctantly. He went outside and took a look around. When he was sure it was all clear, he backed his car up as close as he could get. Then, still keeping a wary eye out, he dragged the body out of the room and somehow or other bundled it into the trunk.

By the time they set off everyone was on edge.

"We're taking this nice and easy," he said, trying to keep them both calm. "If we get pulled over for anything—anything at all—stay cool, right?"

He drove carefully out of town through the gaudy neon-lit streets until they reached the quieter outskirts, and eventually the desert. Then he drove another half hour before pulling over to the side of the road, lugging the man's body from the trunk, dragging it across the sand for what seemed like an eternity—and then digging a shallow grave with his hands.

When he was finished he rolled up the blood-soaked blanket and carried it back to the car. "We'll bury this somewhere else," he said, throwing it in the trunk. "Don't want any connection between the body and the hotel room."

"What about the gun?" Cyndra asked anxiously.

"I'll get rid of it on the way back to L.A."

"This is a nightmare," Annie said, shaking her head. "I wish I'd never met either of you."

"Well, sweetheart, you did, an' now you're part of it, so shut up," he said roughly, not in the mood to listen to any more of her complaints.

Within minutes they were on their way back to L.A.

54

"I made a mistake," Oliver Liberty said.

"Excuse me?" Lauren replied.

They were sitting in an exclusive New York club, sipping brandies while Pia and Howard clung together on the small dance floor. The sound of Frank Sinatra singing "In the Wee Small Hours of the Morning" flooded the darkly paneled room.

Oliver puffed on a long thin cigar—it somehow suited his aquiline features. "I said I made a mistake," he repeated.

"About what?" she asked politely.

"When my wife left me I was very angry. We'd been together for over thirty years until one day she decided she'd had enough. She became an overnight feminist, and suddenly I was the enemy."

"That's not good."

"An understatement, my dear."

"So you met Opal—"

"And foolishly married her."

Lauren wasn't sure she wanted to hear this. Sitting in a nightclub listening to Howard's uncle tell her all about his failing marriage was not her idea of heaven. But then again, she'd had a nice enough time. They'd been to an expensive French restaurant, talked about everything from politics to the latest fashions, and although he might not be the youngest man in the world, he certainly had an abundance of charm.

"Are you sure you should be telling me this?" she asked.

"I can talk to you," he said, nodding as if to reassure himself. "You have a certain quality."

"What quality is that?" she asked lightly.

"Something in your eyes. An understanding. And let us not forget, you're also a very beautiful woman."

This certainly seemed to be her week for compliments. "I'm flattered," she said, "but I'm no psychiatrist."

"I didn't say you were," he replied, nodding toward the dance floor. "Shall we?"

"Okay," she said, getting up.

He stubbed out his cigar, took her hand and led her onto the crowded floor. For a moment he held her at a discreet distance, and then without warning pulled her into his embrace. "I've already spoken to my lawyers," he said.

"About what?" she asked, inhaling his expensive aftershave.

"A divorce."

"Why are you telling me?"

"Because you're easy to talk to, and I want to see you again. That's if you don't mind being in the company of an older man." He smiled when he said it, taking the curse off his words.

She thought about saying *I have no intention of getting involved*, but it seemed presumptuous to assume anything at this early stage, so instead she murmured, "I'd like that."

"So would I," he replied. "How about tomorrow night?"

Outside the club Oliver's Japanese chauffeur and sleek black Rolls waited patiently.

"Not bad, huh?" Pia whispered, climbing in the back while Oliver and Howard discussed business on the sidewalk. "Do you like him?"

"He's married," Lauren whispered back. "Stop trying to fix me up."

"Ah, but he's getting a divorce."

"Pia, he's old enough to be my father, maybe even my grandfather."

"So what?"

"Do me a favor—quit trying to matchmake."

They dropped Howard and Pia off first, and then the Rolls proceeded to Lauren's apartment. On the street she spotted Emerson's limousine parked outside her building. The last thing she was in the mood for was another confrontation. Turning to Oliver she said, "Do you have a guest room?"

He looked at her quizzically. "A guest room?"

"There's somebody I want to avoid and, uh . . . it seems to me if I went home with you it would save me a problem."

"Certainly," he said, only too happy to oblige.

Located in a stately old building overlooking Central Park, Oliver's apartment was sumptuous by anybody's standards. The ceilings were high, the rooms large and the view incredible. He led her into the living room and offered her a drink.

She shook her head. "I have to work tomorrow. Would you mind if I went straight to my room?"

"Not at all," he said, leading her down a spacious corridor into a guest bedroom. "Can I get you something to sleep in?"

"Maybe an old shirt?"

"I'll be right back."

She explored the tastefully decorated room, obviously designed by a woman—certainly not his current wife—perhaps a decorator?

Picking up a silver frame she studied the photograph of a younger Oliver and a woman who was obviously his previous wife. They made a handsome couple.

Oliver returned and handed her a plastic-wrapped toothbrush, a tube of toothpaste, a silk shirt and a hairbrush. "All settled?" he asked, smiling.

She smiled back. "Thank you, I've got everything I need—you must have done this before."

"No, Lauren," he replied seriously. "I can assure you I haven't." He hesitated at the door. "Tell me, my dear, exactly *who* are you avoiding?"

She shook her head. "Nobody important."

The next morning she was dressed and ready to leave by eight-thirty. A housekeeper greeted her in the hallway. "Mr. Liberty has already left. He asked me to tell you that his driver is downstairs waiting to take you wherever you wish to go."

She felt a tinge of disappointment—she'd hoped to see him, but apparently he was an earlier riser than she.

She had the driver drop her at her apartment, where she quickly changed clothes. No messages from Emerson. She felt relieved—or did she? Too confusing, she couldn't make up her mind.

At the office Pia bombarded her with questions. "What do you think of him? I told you he's getting a divorce, didn't I? Hmm, he *is* attractive, isn't he?"

Lauren shook her head. "*Stop* fixing me up."

"I'm not fixing you up, I'm trying to marry you off! One day you'll be old and shriveled—what then?"

"I'm sure I'll be very happy, thank you."

Pia pulled a face. "You know what, Lauren—you're a hopeless case. Oh, and by the way, Emerson Burn called you three times this morning. What does *he* want?

"If I knew I'd tell you."

"*Sure* you would."

"I would."

"Oh, yes, and pigs will wear tutus and fly down Fifth Avenue!"

"Very funny."

"You don't need a rock star, Lauren. You need Oliver. He's stable, rich and crazy about you."

"I'll tell his wife."

"Ex-wife."

"Not yet."

"Sooner than you think."

"Yeah?"

"Yeah."

55

Back in L.A. Nick found two messages from Frances Cavendish. Good sign? Bad sign? He didn't know. He'd brought Cyndra and Annie back to his place because he figured it wasn't safe for either of them to go to their own apartments, but now they were getting on his nerves. Cyndra wandered around in a daze, and Annie complained hotly because he hadn't dropped her home.

"We gotta get our stories straight before anybody goes anywhere," he said. "I'll call Frances Cavendish back—then we'll talk."

Annie glared at him. He ignored her.

"Where have you been?" Frances said testily.

"Out of town."

"In the future leave a number where I can reach you."

Who the fuck did she think she was talking to? "Yes, *ma'am*," he said, biting back a sharper retort.

"They like you, sonny," she drawled, calming down. "They like you a lot."

"What does that mean?" he asked suspiciously.

"They want to see you again. In fact they might even test you."

"Is that good or bad?"

She made an exasperated sound. "How long have you been in this business, Nick? A test costs them money—if they're paying, of course it's good."

He wound the phone cord around his wrist, snapping it back and forth. "When do I get to do this?"

"Today. Be at my office at ten." She hung up before he could reply.

Well, why not? She knew he'd be there. He was an actor after all, and when a casting agent says jump it's all systems go.

Annie had stationed herself by the door. "I want to go home," she said, daring him to say no. "I want to go home now."

"Okay, okay. But Cyndra stays here. And listen carefully. If Reece shows up, you know nothin'. You never went to Vegas, you've been with a girlfriend for the last twenty-four hours. Got it?"

She continued to glare at him. "Yes."

"And don't go making any phone calls you might regret. Whatever happened in Vegas—it's history."

"If you say so," she said tightly.

"What's that mean?"

"I've never had to bury a body before."

"I said forget about it, Annie. It never happened."

"Maybe *you* can pretend it never happened. I can't."

"Okay. I'll take you home." He glanced over at his sister. She sat by the window, staring out. "Cyndra, you stay here. Don't answer the door or the phone. I'll get back soon as I can."

She nodded dully.

Annie gave him the silent treatment on the drive to her apartment. Her attitude was shit, but there was nothing he could do about it. "Call you later," he promised, dropping her off on the street.

She didn't say a word as she marched inside. He had a strong suspicion she was going to cause trouble. Regrettably there was nothing he could do about it.

The woman producer had eyes for him. No mistaking that hungry look.

The tall man hated him. Probably a closet queen with a yen he didn't want to let loose.

The director was into pleasing everyone.

"I don't think we need to test him," the woman said. "Do you, Joel?"

The tall man shrugged. "Whatever."

"I'm happy," the director said.

Nick sat in the room listening to them talk about him as if he wasn't there.

"Shall we have him read again?" asked one of the casting people.

"Not necessary," said the woman, tapping her foot impatiently.

"The camera'll love him," said the director, running a hand through his greasy brown hair. "He's got the eyes."

"I'd like to see his body," the woman said, crossing her legs, silk stockings crackling.

He wasn't sure but he thought he caught a glimpse of a sexy garter belt.

"Would you mind removing your shirt?" said one of the casting people.

Where was Frances when he needed her? Nobody had warned him he'd have to strip off.

"There's a scene in the movie where you're in bed with the hero's girlfriend," the director explained. "Can't have you looking better than the star."

They all laughed.

He stood up and awkwardly removed his shirt.

"Fine," said the woman.

"No competition," said the director.

"We'll get back to you," said the tall man.

Getting out of there was a pleasure.

Outside, he sat in his car trying to relive the events of the last twenty-four hours. He'd buried a body, for crissakes. He'd buried a fucking body in the Nevada desert, and that made him an accessory to murder. Jesus. Maybe Annie was right. Maybe they should have called the police and let Cyndra explain.

No way. She wouldn't have stood a chance.

The woman producer strode out of the building and got into a cream-colored sports Mercedes. She wore large mirrored sunglasses and a knowing smile.

401

Nick wondered who she was fucking. The tall man for sure. The director—maybe.

He hadn't liked removing his shirt in there, it was demeaning. He was an actor, not a stripper.

The woman drove off and he followed her for a while. Her Mercedes sped down Sunset. He drew alongside her at a stoplight and said, "Hi." She looked at him as if she'd never seen him before in her life.

"Nick Angel," he said, dropping the "o," just as Joy had advised.

"Do I know you?" she said, adjusting her huge mirrored shades.

Bitch!

He gunned the light and drove straight home. Cyndra was gone. This wasn't his day.

His landlady was sunning herself outside. "You're two days late on the rent," she reminded as he rushed past.

"You'll get it."

"I'd better or you're out."

Money was a problem. He'd almost blown the Tijuana stash and there was nothing coming in. If he paid his rent there'd be hardly anything left.

"Did you see my sister leave?"

"Your sister," his landlady sneered. "No, I didn't see your *sister*."

He jumped back in his car and headed for Annie's.

"We're going to the police," Annie said. She was dressed and ready for action, a silent Cyndra by her side.

He'd arrived just in time, they were almost out the door.

"You can't do that," he said.

"Oh, yes, we can."

He appealed to Cyndra. "I helped you out—you go to the cops now an' it'll be me who gets it. Don't kid yourself—we'll all be in deep shit. Is that what you want?"

"I don't know . . ." she said unsurely. "Annie says it's the right thing to do, otherwise this'll always be hanging over us."

"Fuck!" he muttered angrily, turning on Annie.

She backed away.

"Don't you understand?" he said angrily. "It's *too goddamn late*. We're in this together an' we'd better learn to trust one another, so stop this runnin' to the cops shit. I can't take it every time I leave the house."

"But—" Annie began.

"But nothing—you do this again an' so help me I'll—"

"You'll what?" she asked defiantly.

He'd almost raised his arm to her. He'd wanted to strike out—just like Primo, just like his father. Oh, God! There was no way he'd ever allow himself to become like that fucking loser. He slumped into a chair. "Don't do this to us, Annie. You gotta let it go."

Her eyes filled with tears. "I'm trying."

"Try harder."

She nodded, acquiescing.

They were safe—for now—but who knew how long it would be before she spilled it all? Annie was dangerous. But he had a solution, and the sooner he put it into action the better.

Emerson dropped out of sight and Oliver moved in. Lauren had never been courted before, and it was strangely seductive. Oliver sent her flowers every day, called at noon without fail, always checked out his plans with her, and never so much as attempted a goodnight kiss.

After three weeks of this courtly treatment she was beginning to wonder what was wrong with her.

"He adores you!" Pia confided, perching on the side of her desk. "He told Howard."

"That's nice," Lauren replied, busily organizing a pile of papers.

"Stop being so cool and in control," Pia said, hardly able to hide her exasperation. "What do *you* think of *him?*"

"He's a very charming man."

"You're so noncommittal."

"What do you *want* me to say?"

"Have you slept with him?"

"Pia—if I had, you'd be the last to know."

"Why?"

"Because since you've become a married woman you do nothing but gossip."

Pia's eyes gleamed. "Is he sensational in bed? Older men are supposed to have fantastic technique." She giggled slyly. "I hear they give great head."

"I wouldn't know."

"What are you waiting for?"

Good question. What *was* she waiting for?

Actually she was waiting for Oliver to make a move. The fact that he hadn't intrigued her. Was there something wrong with her? Did she turn him off? It was about time she found out.

Later that week they went to the opening of a Broadway show and the party afterward. Oliver seemed to know everyone—the musical comedy actress who starred in the show, a slew of New York socialites whom he jokingly called night runners, a famous senator and his equally famous model girlfriend. Lauren guessed that he probably even knew Emerson Burn—crazy Emerson who'd flashed into her life and vanished just as quickly. A good thing—because he was definitely trouble. She'd read that he'd left on a world tour.

On the ride home they discussed the evening. Oliver enjoyed filling her in on everyone—he had interesting stories and was not shy about telling them. According to him the musical comedy actress liked other women, the senator wore red sequined stockings to bed, and the model only slept with men worth over ten million dollars.

"How do you know all this?" she asked, studying his distinguished profile.

"I'm in advertising. It's my business to know everything."

"Then who's going to be the new Marcella girl? I hear they want Nature but she's holding out for too much money."

Oliver frowned, he hated it when somebody knew something before he was prepared to tell them. "Who told you that?"

"Samm."

"If she was worth it, I'd recommend they pay her."

"You don't think she is?"

"Too many covers in too short a time," he said brusquely. "Her face is overly familiar."

"Is it your account?"

"Between us?"

"No. I'm taking an announcement in *Ad Weekly*."

"Very amusing, Lauren."

"Well?" she pressed. "*Is* it your account?"

"It wasn't, but it will be."

"Really?"

"They're coming in tomorrow to see what we have to offer."

"And what *do* you have to offer?"

"A surprise."

She grinned. "I love surprises."

"Good."

The car drew up outside her building. She'd never asked him in before, but the time seemed right. "Would you like to come up for a drink, Oliver?"

He shook his head. "I didn't want to bother you with this before, but my charming wife has detectives following me. Apparently she feels she'll get even more of my money if she can prove I'm sleeping around."

"I asked you up for a drink, nothing else."

"My dear, *I* know that. But I would never put you in a compromising position."

Thoughtful as well. He was turning out to be the perfect man.

"Tomorrow night—I'll pick you up at eight," he said.

"Not possible, I'm catering a dinner."

"Have someone else do it."

"No."

"Why not?"

She hated it when he tried to tell her what to do. "Because I want to do it myself."

He started to say something, then changed his mind. Lauren had that determined look, he knew better than to argue.

57

Things happened fast. "You've got the part," Frances told him over the phone. "Shooting begins in two weeks. I've made an appointment for you to see an agent friend—she'll handle the deal. And I've booked a photo session with another friend of mine. The session's gratis—all you have to pay for are the prints."

"Hey, Frances—this is great. I—"

Frances was a fast talker. "Saturday night. Escort duties. You're taking me to an industry party—wear a suit."

He started to say something but she cut him off again.

"I'm putting you on to my assistant, she'll give you the details. Oh, and Nick, don't forget who got you started."

"Frances, I—" But she was gone.

He had a role in a fucking movie. He was about to get an agent. He was going to be a star! Things were definitely moving in the right direction.

His new agent was a short middle-aged woman named Meena Caron. She had dark cropped hair and thick no-nonsense glasses. She was with a large important agency, which was reassuring.

"It's two days' work," she said, all business. "You'll be shooting in New York. They'll fly you in the day before—tourist—only above the title gets first."

"What does that mean?"

"Above the title?"

"Yeah."

She looked at him quizzically. "You *are* new to the business, aren't you."

"Gotta learn sometime," he said cheerfully.

Meena tapped a silver Cartier pen on her desktop. "*Stars* get their name above the title. The star of your movie is Charlie Geary. He's young, red-hot and a real-life pain. Stay away from him—he'll do his best to get you fired. And don't try to screw the leading lady—that's Charlie's privilege."

Oh, yeah?

"Who's the girl?"

"Carlysle Mann. Very pretty. Very crazy."

"I never went for crazy."

Meena didn't crack a smile. "As soon as you get your photos bring them in. There's a pilot at NBC you could be right for. You *can* act, can't you?"

"Frances wouldn't've sent me to you if I couldn't."

Meena stood up—she was finished with him. "Frances has her own reasons for doing things. You look good. I'm sure she's taking you on the party circuit."

He didn't answer. It was none of her goddamn business. Maybe he should have opted to go with Ardmore Castle instead of this storm trooper.

The photographer Frances set him up with was a tall gawky woman who worked fast, shrieking directions at her harassed assistant. Didn't Frances ever deal with men?

She circled him like a predatory animal. "Stop trying so hard," she kept telling him. "For God's sake, attempt to look natural. Dump the put-on scowl, it's so phony."

He hated her too. He was used to women falling all over him. The agent and the photographer didn't appear to give a fast fuck.

After the session he figured he should go home—check up on Cyndra. But then again, Joy was probably wondering where he'd vanished to, and he didn't want her mad at him. Christ, this was like walking a tightrope without a net. Surrounded by women and he wasn't even getting laid.

Joy greeted him frostily.

He told her about the movie.

"Bit part," she said, screwing up her nose in disgust. "You should have held out for better."

"At least it's a job. My first professional one."

"Crap movie. Crap director."

Why couldn't she be pleased for him instead of criticizing everything? "Gotta start somewhere," he said easily, refusing to let her get to him.

"Ha!" she sniffed.

He told her about Meena Caron.

"Second rate."

"She's with a big agency," he pointed out.

"You'll get lost. You should have signed with Ardmore."

"I don't like Ardmore."

She narrowed her eyes. "Who said you have to like people. It's what they can do for you that counts."

Maybe. Maybe not. But right now Joy was bringing him down, so he got out of there fast and stopped by to see Annie at the health club. She was suitably cool.

"My movie's shooting in New York," he said. "Maybe Cyndra can stay with you while I'm away."

"*Your* movie," she sneered.

He'd had it with her attitude. "Yeah. *My* fuckin' movie. Two days' work—it's more than you're doin'."

She looked hurt. "Thanks, Nick. Remind me that I can't get a job. Remind me that every time I go on an interview all they want is a six-foot blonde with big tits."

He did his best to soften her up. "Two days, Annie. I can't leave her alone."

"Why not?" she said bitterly. "I'm here to do anything you want. Right?"

Slowly Cyndra recovered and tried to think positively. After all it wasn't her fault, *she* hadn't shot the man, Reece had. It was *his* gun, *his* responsibility.

Damn Reece Webster. He'd gone. Vanished. Good riddance.

"I'm moving back to my apartment," she told Nick.

"You can't do that," he said, trying to reason with her.

Cyndra had a strong stubborn streak. "Why not?" she asked, tilting her chin, preparing for a fight.

" 'Cause you're not ready."

She sighed, brushing a hand through her long dark hair. "Stop worrying about me, Nick. I won't go to the cops, nor will Annie."

"An' what'll you do if Reece comes back?"

"He won't."

"You don't know for sure."

"Look—if he does, I'll tell him the guy got up an' walked away."

Was she stupid or what? "The man was dead, Cyndra, fuckin' *dead*."

"Reece doesn't know that. He ran out of there so fast he doesn't know anything. Go off and do your movie, it's a great break for you. It'd be nice if *one* of us made it."

He couldn't argue with that.

Frances worked a room good. She knew everyone and everyone knew her. Nick trailed behind, feeling out of place and inadequate in his rented suit. He was in a freakin' mansion, for crissake—the like of which he'd never seen. It made the Browning house back in Bosewell look like a shack.

Frances ordered a drink and made him carry it. She didn't bother introducing him to anyone—not that anyone seemed interested in meeting him, they looked right through him as if he didn't exist. As the evening progressed, so did his aggravation. He felt invisible, un-important—it wasn't a feeling he enjoyed.

Dinner was seated, and he was not seated next to Frances. He found himself between a fat woman in a maroon cocktail dress and an older man in an ill-fitting tuxedo. He didn't have to be a genius to figure out it was the worst table in the room.

The fat woman talked to a vivacious blonde on her other side. The older man morosely sipped his drink.

Frances was across the room at a table filled with familiar faces. Everyone at her table was laughing and talking. Shit! How did he get stuck in these situations?

He gave conversation a shot, asking the man what he did.

"Banking" was the cold reply.

"You work in a bank or you own it?" he said, going for the flippant approach.

The man was unamused.

After a while he got up and made his way outside to the bar. Two waiters were sneaking a smoke. "Anybody know who's giving this party?" he asked.

"Some studio exec," said one of the waiters.

"That's his daughter," said the other waiter, gesturing across the well-kept gardens, where a young blonde was entwined around a guy with long hair. They were making their own entertainment.

"At least someone's having a good time," he mumbled.

It took forever before Frances was ready to be escorted home. He got behind the wheel of her old Mercedes and gunned the engine.

"Did you enjoy yourself?" she asked, puffing on a cigarette.

Was she kidding?

He stared unseeingly at the road ahead. "I had a lousy time."

She couldn't have cared less. "Really?"

"Those people don't wanna know you unless you're important."

"That's Hollywood, dear," she said matter-of-factly. "Make the most of it—when you're famous they'll be crawling all over you."

He liked the sound of her words. Glancing at her quizzically he said, "You really think I'm gonna be famous, Frances?"

She blew smoke in his face and regarded him with her flinty gray eyes. "Yes, Nick. As a matter of fact I think you're going to be very famous indeed."

58

"I'm finally divorced," Oliver announced over the phone. "Tonight we're celebrating."

Lauren was at work. Cradling the receiver under her chin she doodled on a yellow legal pad. "How did it happen so fast?" she asked.

"We made a deal. My ex-wife loves deals."

She drew a circle and enclosed it with a square. "Congratulations, Oliver."

"Thank you, my dear."

"Where are we going?"

"We're staying home. My chauffeur will pick you up at seven." A slight pause. "Oh, and Lauren . . . bring a toothbrush."

Was this his way of telling her they were finally going to consummate their relationship? Hardly romantic, but Oliver was nothing if not to the point.

She went home early, washed her hair, took a leisurely bath, rubbed perfumed cream into her skin and thought about the evening ahead. She liked Oliver—he was entertaining. He had panache and style, wore great suits, always got the best table in restaurants. He was a good dancer, charming and witty.

But I don't love him.

So what? Who do you think is going to come rushing into your life? There are no Prince Charmings left.

But I don't love him.

Get real. He's the man for you.

He's old enough to be my grandfather.

It doesn't matter.

She dressed carefully, still thinking about what lay ahead. She'd slept with three men. Nick—who'd gotten her pregnant and dumped her. Brad—her bad-seed cousin. And Jimmy—who'd taken off the day of their supposed wedding. Some trio.

Except Nick was special.

Bullshit. Nick Angelo was nothing but a loser.

I loved him.

No, you didn't.

I still love him.

For God's sake!

Oliver's apartment was filled with white orchids, his favorite jazz pianist—Erroll Garner—played background music on the stereo, the lights were low and Oliver was in a very good mood indeed. He greeted her with compliments and a glass of champagne, while the butler served small wedges of toast loaded with caviar from a silver tray.

"I don't like caviar," she said, wrinkling her nose.

Oliver looked amused. "It's an acquired taste. Acquire it, my dear. You'll soon grow to adore it."

They ate in the dining room with candles lighting the table and Erroll Garner giving way to the smooth sound of Ella Fitzgerald.

Lauren picked at her food and gulped two glasses of wine, wondering if she should encourage him.

A little late, Roberts. You've encouraged him for three months. Why stop now?

After dinner he dismissed the servants and led her into the darkly paneled library, where they sat in front of a wood fire sipping brandies.

"I don't usually drink—" she began.

"I know," he interrupted, removing the glass from her hand and leaning over to kiss her.

This was not the first time they'd kissed, but it was certainly the most intense. She was glad she'd had the champagne and the wine at dinner and now the brandy.

God, she was nervous!

He moved slowly, kissing her for a long time before suggesting they go into the bedroom.

Her affair with Jimmy had taken place over a year ago—she hadn't been with anyone since, and yet she did not feel that incredible rush of excitement. Instead she felt apprehensive, as if she was about to embark on a trip she might regret.

The bedroom was filled with red roses, their seductive scent in the air. Oliver touched her lightly on the cheek. "Do you want to undress in the bathroom? There's a robe in there for you."

She hadn't planned on undressing herself, but that was apparently what he expected.

Shutting the bathroom door she stared at herself in the mirror. Little Lauren Roberts. High school prude. About to embark on a sexual adventure with a man who was older than her father. Oh, God!

For a moment she flashed onto the memory of Phil Roberts that fateful day in Bosewell. Her father and his woman. Her father and that cheap tramp.

And then she saw Primo, leering at her with his wild eyes. She could almost feel his beer gut pushing up against her and hear his filthy laugh ringing in her head.

You killed him, Lauren.

I'm not sure . . .

Oh, yes, Lauren, you killed him all right.

She removed her clothes and put on the silk robe Oliver had so thoughtfully provided. The material was soft and sensuous. She pulled it around her protectively.

He was waiting under the covers with the lights off. A single candle lit the room. The scent of the roses was overwhelming.

Standing next to the bed she slipped the robe from her shoulders, allowing it to fall to the floor.

"You're so beautiful," Oliver murmured, holding the covers open.

She dived for safety.

Slowly he began stroking her naked body—apparently in no hurry, content to touch and caress her, until she felt herself longing for more.

Tentatively she stretched her hand beneath the sheet, reaching for him. To her surprise and disappointment he was not hard.

"Don't worry, it'll happen," he murmured unconcernedly. "Lie back, my darling. Before anything else I plan to make you feel wonderful."

His head began to move down her body, his tongue tracing little patterns on her breasts and stomach as he descended, until finally his head was between her legs and his fingers started prying her apart—all the better for his tongue to gain entry.

She gasped. This was a first and she was unprepared and wary of what to expect.

"Relax, my sweet, relax and enjoy," he said soothingly, his tongue flicking in and out with practiced ease.

"Oh . . . my . . . God," she whispered. This was so intimate, so private, and yet—she had to admit—so breathtakingly enjoyable.

She threw her head and arms back, allowing herself to fall into the beauty of the moment.

He held her open with his thumbs—all the better to penetrate as far as he could.

Was this what Pia had been talking about when she'd said older men gave great head? Was this it—because if it was, Oliver certainly knew what he was doing.

Before long she began to feel little shock waves of pleasure. They started in her toes and traveled up her entire body, causing her to moan softly. Shivering uncontrollably she threw her legs wide.

He devoured her with a passion until she climaxed with a long-drawn-out cry of ecstasy.

Oliver surfaced, a smile on his face. "I can't think of a better time to ask you." He paused for a moment. "My beautiful Lauren, will you do me the honor of becoming my wife?"

"Let me see the ring," Pia said for the hundredth time—at least it seemed to Lauren it was the hundredth time.

She held out her hand while Pia admired the four-carat emerald surrounded with baguette diamonds. "Gorgeous!" Pia sighed.

Lauren patted her friend's ever-growing stomach. "Gorgeous!" she said enviously.

"Seriously, Lauren, I'm so happy for you."

When I'm thirty he'll be almost seventy, Lauren thought. *When I'm fifty he'll be dead.*

"Is he okay about you continuing to work?" Pia asked.

"About as okay as Howard is with you."

"That's encouraging. Howard begs me daily to give it up."

Lauren looked perplexed. "Why is it that men are always so threatened by working women?"

"Because it means we have our own money," Pia said wisely. "And with our own money comes independence. Samm is my shining example."

"Samm is a lonely old spinster."

"But a beautiful one. *And* she doesn't have to wash anyone's socks."

"Pia, you have a maid."

Pia giggled. "I'm only joking. I *love* washing Howard's socks!"

Lauren knew that was something she'd never have to do. It was quite obvious Oliver had no plans to change his lifestyle. He was very comfortable, a man of habit. He had his live-in housekeeper, two daily maids, a butler when he entertained and his trusty Japanese chauffeur. At the office he had a slew of assistants who obviously adored him.

They planned on getting married in the Bahamas, where Oliver kept a bank account and a house. "You'll love it there," he'd assured her. "It's very peaceful and the people are delightful."

Their target date was six weeks, two months after their first bedroom encounter.

Since that night nothing much had changed. Oliver was totally into pleasuring her, and when she tried to reverse the situation he always had the same answer. "Give me the joy of making you happy now—when we're married it'll be different."

She didn't fight it, there was no hurry. After all, she was marrying the man—she had the rest of her life to make him the happiest man alive.

59

Working on a movie was a new experience and Nick immediately knew he was going to love it. He'd arrived in New York to be met at the airport by a car and driver—not a limo, only a sedan, but it sure beat taking the subway. They had him staying at a small hotel near Times Square where most of the crew were, and upon arrival he found a typed call sheet giving him instructions for the next day.

In the meantime, he had to meet with Waldo, the men's costumer. They spent the afternoon shopping in the Village. Actually he could have used his own clothes—because they ended up purchasing tight jeans, a black shirt and a leather jacket.

"Do I get to keep the clothes?" he joked. "They'll blend right into my closet."

"Only if it's in your contract," Waldo replied, fussing with the leather jacket.

"My agent's got the contract."

"Then it's probably too late." Waldo stood back and surveyed him. "Steal 'em," he said archly. "They'll never notice."

Nick laughed. "*Now* you're talkin!"

"I'm surprised you got this role," Waldo remarked, pursing his lips.

"How's that?"

417

"Our macho young *star* is hardly going to be thrilled when he sees you."

"Oh, you mean Charlie?"

"Do you know him?"

"Nah, never met him, but we'll get along."

"Don't be so sure."

"C'mon, Waldo, believe me—I get along with everyone."

How wrong he was. Charlie Geary was the jerk everybody said he was. A former television star, Charlie had hit the movies in a big way with two box office bonanzas. He was shorter than Nick, had a baby face, a shock of reddish hair and a bad cocaine habit. The moment he saw Nick he was on the director's case.

"What the fuck you hire him for? *I'm* supposed to be the star of this movie."

"We gotta have someone who looks halfway decent," the director replied. "In the movie he's in bed with your girlfriend—why else would she hop in the sack with him?"

Charlie's baby face creased into a sour expression. "Do I give a fuck? Do I care? Fire him."

"Too late," the director said.

"Don't fucking tell *me* it's too late," Charlie replied, his eyes popping. "Because I'll tell you it's never too late for me to walk."

The director conferred with his producers. The producers, who'd had enough of Charlie Geary and his enormous ego, said they weren't firing anyone.

Their first scene together took place in a bar. Charlie Geary was at a table with his cronies and Nick had to enter the shot, exchange insults with Charlie and walk off camera.

Although Charlie only had a few lines, he managed to blow them every time. The director kept calling "Cut" and going for another take.

Nick had his lines down pat. He loved the feeling on the set, the family atmosphere, the way everybody fussed around him. Plus it was a real blast being in front of a camera.

Make the most of it. You're only here for two days.

Because of Charlie the scene took all day, continuing into overtime. The director was pissed, the producers more so as they worked into the night.

Waldo took Nick to one side. "You'd better plan on being here an extra day," he said. "They'll never get to your scene with Carlysle by tomorrow."

"Hey—I'm here for as long as they want me," Nick replied. "I could really get used to this."

Back at his hotel he tried calling the number he had for Joey.

"Joey moved outta here a year ago," a female voice said. "I took over the apartment from him."

"You got any idea where he went?"

"Yeah, there's a number somewhere."

"Can you find it?"

She did not sound enthusiastic. "I dunno."

He went into persuasive overdrive. "I'd really appreciate it if you could."

"You visiting or what?"

"I'm shooting a movie here."

Her voice perked up. "Oh, you're an actor?"

"You got it."

"Well, um . . . you here alone?"

"Find me the number an' we'll talk."

Her voice heated up considerably. "Whyn't you come over and I'll give it to you personally."

"Because I need to call him now."

"I like actors."

Oh, shit! Why did he always get saddled with the maniacs? "So I'll send you an autographed picture. Be a sweetheart an' get me the number."

She finally delivered, and he called Joey. A stoned woman answered.

"Joey around?" he asked.

"Who wants him?"

"An old friend."

"He owe you?"

"No, I told you—I'm an old friend."

She snorted derisively. "Sure, same old story. It's always an old friend, an' he always ends up gettin' his brains beat out. I told you, mister, he ain't here."

"Tell him it's Nick—Nick Angelo. Okay?"

"Wait a minute." She kept him hanging on for a while, then she got back on the phone and gave him the address of a club. "You'll find Joey there."

This was like playing hide-and-seek. Find Joey in the big city. Christ!

The club was a dump. Nude photos displayed outside proclaimed SEVEN BEAUTIFUL GIRLS—TOTALLY NAKED. An Indian bouncer slumped wearily on a canvas folding chair picking his nose. It cost ten bucks to get inside, and once there he was immediately pounced upon by a topless waitress with droopy tits who offered him a complimentary glass of champagne and the choice of a hostess to sit with him.

He declined both offers. "I'm lookin' for Joey."

She lost interest in him and jerked a finger toward the bar.

He walked over. It was not difficult finding Joey—he was the only customer. Nick tapped him on the shoulder. "Joey?"

Joey spun around. "What the fu—Jesus! *Nick?*"

"Yeah, it's me."

Joey almost fell off the barstool. They hugged awkwardly and grinned at each other.

"How're you doing, man?" Nick asked, thinking that Joey did not look good at all. He was skinny and pale, with dark circles under his sunken eyes and a nervous facial tic. "Don't even tell me—you look like shit."

Joey managed a weak grin. "Thanks. S'good to see you too." He dragged on his cigarette. "How come you're here? I heard you were livin' in L.A."

"Can you believe it—I'm in a movie."

"A movie, huh? You're finally doin' that acting thing."

"Yeah, well, I stayed in Chicago for a while—then moved to L.A., found myself an agent, went on this audition and got lucky. It's only a small role, but at least I'm workin'."

Joey snapped his fingers at the girl behind the bar. She bounced over wearing nothing but a short sequined miniskirt and long fake eyelashes. "Get my movie star friend a beer—an' don't water it down."

"Anything you want, Joey," she said, squinting at Nick. "Movie star, huh? What you been in?"

"Never mind," Joey said, waving her away.

The girl moved off and Joey gestured around the dingy club. "Classy joint, huh? My place of work. I come on between strippers— the crowd really gets off on me. I'm doing stand-up like I always wanted."

Yeah, and from the looks of you that's not all you're doing.

"That's great, Joey."

"Don't give me polite crap. This gig is about as great as a rattlesnake up your ass. I'm doin' a shit job in a shit place, but it's all I got right now." He stubbed out his cigarette, immediately reaching for another. "So," he said, rubbing his bloodshot eyes. "What's happening with Cyndra? You seen her?"

"She married that Reece Webster guy—who incidentally turned out to be the creep of the century. He's not around anymore."

"What's she doing?"

"She was singing in a Vegas hotel. Small stuff, but she'll do okay."

"We kinda lost touch."

"Looks like you lost touch with everyone."

Joey laughed ruefully. "It's always that way, huh?"

"Did you ever make it back to Bosewell?" Nick asked.

"No. Did you?"

"Nope."

"I guess once we got outta there, that was it."

The topless bar-girl delivered his beer in a cracked glass. "Enjoy," she said, holding out her hand for money.

"Put it on my tab," said Joey, irritated.

"Your tab's overdrawn."

"I said put it on my fuckin' tab," he snarled.

She flounced off.

"You look like you could do with a break," Nick said. "How about flyin' to L.A. an' staying with me for a while?"

"Oh, yeah—an' give up my job?"

"There's plenty of comedy clubs in L.A."

"I can't afford to take the chance."

"Why? You got such a wonderful life here?"

"Nah. I'm living with this girl."

"Somebody special?"

"If I told you, you wouldn't believe me."

"Try me."

"She's a hooker."

"Okay, so I believe you."

They both laughed.

"Seriously. She's the proverbial hooker with a heart of gold. I met her at a party. She likes having me around. I like being around. She pays the rent an' I give her what I can. It works out okay."

"Hey, Joey," shrieked a blowsy blonde. "Get your ass up on stage. *Now.*"

Joey shrugged, stubbed out his cigarette. "My boss. Charming lady. Hang around, Nick, catch the act."

"I'd love to, but I got an early call tomorrow. Whyn't you come by the set? Here, I'll give you the address." He scribbled it on a piece of paper and handed it over. "Drop by tomorrow an' we'll talk about you coming to L.A."

"Yeah, maybe."

When he got back to the hotel he called Cyndra. "Everything okay?"

"Everything's fine."

"No sign of Reece?"

"No."

"Is Annie behaving herself?"

"I told you, Nick, everything's fine. Stop worrying."

He cleared his throat, ready to give her the big news. "Guess who I saw tonight?"

"Who?"

"Joey."

There was a long silence. "How is he?" she finally asked.

"Not in great shape. I'm trying to talk him into flying back to L.A. with me."

"Not on my account. I've had it with men."

"Listen—the three of us went through some hard times together. Be nice to hang out, huh?"

She answered a touch too fast. "I told you, Nick, don't drag him back because of me. I'm not interested."

"I get the message."

She changed moods. "How did the filming go today?"

"It's a trip."

"What's Charlie Geary like?"

"A stoned prick."

"Really?"

"Wouldn't kid you."

"Y'know, Nick, I've been thinking. Tomorrow I'm going to contact the record company Reece was dealing with and see if they're still interested in me."

"Sounds like a good idea."

"You think so?"

"What's to lose?"

"That's how I feel," she said, glad to have his confirmation.

"I'll call you tomorrow," he said. "Take care, little sis."

"Bye, Nick."

Nick ran into Charlie Geary early the next morning in the makeup room. Charlie was not a pleasant sight. The famous actor was wasted, he looked worse than Joey.

"Boy, did I have a night last night!" Charlie boasted. "Even though I say it myself, I got a cock that never quits. I had this little pussy creamin' herself all over me. I mean she was comin' an' comin'."

"Shut up, Charlie," the makeup girl said wearily.

"Don't tell *me* to shut up, sweetheart. You wanna stay on this film you'll suck my dick if I tell you to."

Nick sat down in the second chair. Charlie stretched and burped in his direction. "So—where'd they dig you up from?"

"I been around," Nick said.

"Yeah?" Charlie yawned, throwing his arms back, almost hitting the makeup girl in the face. "Couldn't tell it from your performance. You really fucked up yesterday—I hate working with amateurs."

He was not about to take this little asshole's shit. "You got a short memory—it wasn't me that fucked up, it was you."

"Don't bother with him," the makeup girl murmured, moving past. "He's not worth it."

"What did you say, cunt?" Charlie demanded, almost falling off his chair.

"Why don't you leave the girl alone?" Nick said.

"Why don't you get fucked."

Fortunately an assistant entered, summoning Charlie to the set. He got out of the chair unsteady on his feet and lurched to the door.

"He's stoned," the makeup girl said.

"No kiddin'?" Nick replied.

Later, on the set, Charlie played the same game—screwing up his lines, forgetting cues, generally messing up.

Nick noticed the two producers conferring in a corner. The woman wore a bright scarlet suit, her long legs in matching tights and very high heels. The tall man had assumed a permanently grim expression, while the director ran around looking frantic.

After the lunch break Charlie failed to appear at all. The assistant director said she couldn't get him out of his trailer. Forming a group, the two producers and the director stormed off to personally escort him to the set. They returned with no Charlie.

"Tell you what, Nick," the director said. "We'll shoot your close-ups. Charlie's not feeling good—he may not be able to do the rest of the scene this afternoon."

As little as Nick knew about production, he realized this did not bode well for the shoot. But screw it, he wasn't complaining—close-ups sounded good to him.

Joey did not show, so at the end of the day he called him. This time Joey picked up the phone himself.

"Where were you?" Nick asked.

"Had a meetin'."

"You couldn't've come by after?"

"Hey, man, what's the problem?" Joey said belligerently. "We don't see each other for a few years—you come back inta my life an' I'm supposed t'jump?"

"Forget it. I'll see ya."

"C'mon, Nick, don't go gettin' pissed. I'll be there tomorrow. Right now I got a lot on my mind."

"Anythin' I can help out with?"

"Nah. Just small problems."

"See you tomorrow."

"Bet on it."

Nick settled back to study his script. Tomorrow he had his big scene

with Carlysle Mann and he didn't want to blow it. This filming shit
was seductive.

He fell asleep with the script clutched tightly in his hands.

The next morning he was sitting in makeup at seven a.m. calm as can
be, when the A.D. entered looking flustered.

"They need to see you at once," she said.

"Who needs to see me?" he asked patiently.

"The producers."

"Yeah?"

*Oh, shit. This is it. Charlie Geary's getting his way and I'm about
to be canned.*

"He's nearly through," the makeup girl said, blending dark pancake
on his neck.

Yeah, sweetheart, you can say that again.

"There's a crisis," the A.D. said. "They need him immediately."

"Better let you go," the makeup girl said.

He got out of the chair and followed the A.D., silently rehearsing
his objections.

It didn't matter what he said, he was out and he knew it.

Lauren was frantic, suddenly there seemed so much to do before she left for the Bahamas. Pia was not much help—seven months pregnant, she waddled around with a smile on her face, arriving late and leaving early. Lauren didn't blame her, but still it left most of the responsibilities of the business to her.

"I wish Howard and I were coming with you," Pia said with a wistful sigh, obviously expecting Lauren to say "Why don't you?" But she'd decided it was going to be her and Oliver—nobody else. She'd experienced one wedding where everybody stood around waiting and the bridegroom didn't show up, and she did not plan on doing it again.

"Who'll run the business while I'm away?" she worried.

"*I* will," said Pia.

"You're hardly here anymore."

"Don't obsess. I'll be around all the time while you're away."

Lauren knew that the business only survived because of her personal touch. She'd gained such a good reputation, especially with her dinner parties. Lately, all Pia took care of was the financial side.

She had one more dinner to organize before leaving for the Bahamas. This was at the house of Quentin and Jessie George. Quentin was the managing editor of *Satisfaction*, the avant-garde magazine of the moment, and Jessie was a social whirlwind. She'd catered dinner parties for them before and it was always an enjoyable experience. The Georges put together an eclectic group of guests, mixing politics and fashion, rock 'n roll and movies. Jessie was a delightful character —a woman of indeterminate age, not conventionally pretty, but loaded with style.

The night before the dinner Lauren visited their brownstone to go over the final details. Jessie had heard about her upcoming marriage and couldn't wait to complain. "I suppose we'll be losing you," she lamented. "You won't want to do this anymore."

"I didn't say that," Lauren objected.

"Ah, but Oliver will never let you."

"Oliver's not going to control what I do or don't do."

Jessie nodded knowingly. "Darling, when you're married you'll see."

"Jessie, when I'm married I'll see nothing. I'll carry on exactly the way I please."

"Hmm," Jessie said. "That's what I thought when I married Quentin, and look at me now."

"It seems to me you have a fantastic life."

"Some would say so." Jessie waved her bracelet-adorned arms in the air. "Now, let's get down to business. I have a brilliant idea for hors d'oeuvres—imagine scooped-out melon balls filled with golden caviar. Doesn't it sound divine?"

Oliver was very much involved with the Marcella girl campaign. Marcella was a hugely successful cosmetics company in Italy that was all set to take a large chunk out of the American market. They planned to rival Revlon and Estée Lauder. Now that Oliver's firm had landed the account, the search was on for the perfect girl. So far they'd tested and photographed at least thirty candidates.

Lauren viewed the photos and videotapes with Oliver. He was extremely critical—this one was too glamorous, this one too old, this one too young and so on.

"Your expectations are too high," she said. "I can see at least seven or eight of them who'd be great."

"No," he said, shaking his head. "None of them have it. The Marcella girl has to have a special quality that appeals to the public, something that makes women say, 'I want to look exactly like her—and if I wear Marcella makeup I can.' She has to have a certain ordinariness, combined with that magical something else."

"I've no idea what you're getting at."

"It's a quality. Grace Kelly had it. Marilyn didn't. Ingrid Bergman had it."

"Who's Ingrid Bergman?"

"Never mind." He stared at her closely. "You have it."

"I have what?"

"The quality I'm talking about."

"Is that good or bad?"

"If you were in the running for the Marcella girl it would be good."

She walked over to his desk and helped herself to an apple from a bowl of fruit. "Fortunately, Oliver, I'm not."

He frowned, looking at her intently. "But you could be."

"You *are* joking."

"No," he said, very seriously. "I'm not."

She laughed. "Oliver, I am *not* a model, I do not want to be a model, I am perfectly happy doing what I'm doing, so kindly forget it."

"Will you do something for me before we leave?"

She sighed. "What?"

"Will you let my people organize a photo session with you?"

She crunched her apple. "Now why would I do a thing like that?"

"Because it would be very helpful if I could show them exactly who I'm looking for."

She flopped into an armchair. "You're so funny."

"Then humor me."

"I don't have time."

"Do I ask for much, Lauren? Wouldn't you enjoy having your hair done and your makeup and wearing beautiful clothes? It could be fun."

"It might be your idea of fun, but believe me, I have better things to do."

"Please, Lauren—for me? As a wedding present. Think of the money you'll save."

428

"Oliver—"

"Yes?"

She weakened. "Well, as long as you promise not to take it seriously."

"You have my solemn promise."

Humoring Oliver turned out to be more enjoyable than she'd thought. To go into a studio and be totally made over by professionals was an interesting experience. Pia thought it was a hoot and insisted on accompanying her. They giggled like a couple of schoolgirls as the makeup artist and hairdresser went to work.

"At least you'll have some incredible photographs to show your grandchildren," Pia said, perching behind her on a high stool.

"*What* grandchildren?" Lauren exclaimed. "I haven't even got any children yet—let's not get carried away."

"You *are* going to have some, aren't you?" Pia asked anxiously. "I need a playmate for mine," she added, patting her huge belly.

"I guess so," Lauren agreed. "But give me time to enjoy my marriage first."

"You got fab 'air, darlin'," said the English hairdresser, his cockney accent reminding her of Emerson. "The color needs livening up a bit, an' you're in desperate need of a cut. Apart from that you're perfect!"

"I've always had long hair," she said, alarmed.

"Yeah, but it's just 'angin' there, 'ein't it? Let me work it over—leave it to me."

"Don't take off too much," she said, when he started wielding his scissors.

"Trust me, darlin', you'll be thankin' me."

She shut her eyes and hoped he knew what he was doing. The makeup artist was next. He came at her with a pair of tweezers, plucking at her eyebrows, squinting at the shape of her face.

"I don't like to wear much makeup," she said.

"Nor do I," he said tartly. "What we have to do here is the illusion of no makeup at all while I create *the* most incredible face."

And so they transformed her. Lauren Roberts, small-town beauty, was turned into Lauren, face of the moment. The hairdresser had added ever so subtle light streaks in her chestnut hair, and the cut had given it more body and shape, so that although it still fell below her shoulders, it was fuller and more flattering.

The makeup artist had worked on her face with a palette of natural colors—playing with browns and beiges, bringing out her eyes in a way they had not been emphasized before.

"My God!" Pia said. "You look fantastic!"

"Oh, thanks a lot," Lauren said jokingly. "Was I such a dog before?"

"You know what I mean. You've always been pretty, but my God, now you're absolutely stunning!"

Next it was the photographer's turn. Antonio worked fast, with a minimum of fuss and the maximum of assistants. He knew exactly what he wanted, and even though Lauren had never been in front of a camera before, she fell into the poses easily, having watched Nature so many times. It was a kick. There was great music playing, she was dressed in beautiful designer clothes. When it was all over she confided to Pia that she'd actually enjoyed it.

"Who wouldn't?" Pia said, shaking her head in amazement. "You really *do* look incredible."

"I wish you'd stop saying that. God knows what I must have looked like before."

"I can't wait to see the photos," Pia said.

"And I can't wait to wash this makeup off."

Later, Oliver asked her how she'd enjoyed the session. "It was okay," she said, laughing. "Never again, though. You can only talk me into it once."

The next morning was a different kind of frantic. She left early for the market accompanied by a couple of her college student assistants. They picked out fresh fruit and vegetables, and then stopped to buy flowers. Jessie and Quentin were very particular, and that's exactly the way she liked it.

"Have Oliver come to the dinner," Jessie urged, when she arrived at their house.

"No way," she objected. "I don't want him sitting there while I'm working."

"But I adore Oliver—he's so droll," Jessie said. "At least have him drop by to pick you up."

She called Oliver at his office. "Do you want to come by later and pick me up from the Georges' dinner party?"

"I'd like that," he said.

"Jessie particularly requested you. How well do you know her?"

"We had a hot and steamy affair once."

She almost believed him. "Oliver—*did* you?"

He laughed. "No, my dear. I am not the hot and steamy affair type."

"You could have fooled me."

"Ah," he said. "Wait until our honeymoon."

From four o'clock on she commandeered the Georges' kitchen. It was the kind of kitchen she liked, large and spacious, with all modern conveniences. The menu she'd planned was one of Jessie's favorites. Vichyssoise followed by rib-sticking chicken casserole with creamy mashed potatoes, lightly sautéed carrots and creamed spinach, all accompanied by a healthful chopped salad.

"I love it when you serve those kinds of meals," Jessie told her. "It makes people feel comfortable and relaxed, and when they're in that sort of mood the conversation *really* sparkles. Oh, dear. Lauren, what am I going to do when Oliver takes you away from all this?"

"I'll still keep the business," she said. "I'll cook occasionally."

"Shall we bet on this?" Jessie suggested.

Lauren grinned. "Only if it's cash."

Later Oliver called her at the Georges'. "Remember how you said the other day you loved surprises?"

"Did I say that?"

"Yes. Well, I have a surprise for you."

"What is it?"

"If I told you, it wouldn't be a surprise. When I come by later I'll bring it."

"Does it have four legs?" she asked, remembering her recent request for a puppy.

"Be patient, my dear. I'll show you later."

Carlysle Mann was pretty beyond belief. She had one of those etched faces with alabaster skin, huge blue eyes, a snub nose and a beguiling overbite. She was petite, with baby-fine blond hair curling around her face, and a perfect figure.

For the first time in his life Nick felt intimidated meeting somebody. He'd seen her in a couple of movies, but actually meeting her was something else.

"Hi," he said, almost shyly.

"Congrats," she replied, pretty blue eyes gazing into his. "This is some great break for you."

Yeah, congratulations were definitely in order. He had not been canned. Instead he had gotten the chance of a lifetime. While Charlie Geary was being rushed off to a drug rehab center, he, Nick Angelo—excuse me, Nick Angel—had been presented with the big break. He'd been given the lead in the movie, and it was a career-making role—that of a young hood who reforms, finds true love and ends up as the hero.

"You've got the look," the woman producer had said, crossing and uncrossing her elegant legs.

Yeah, I've got the look, all right. A look you didn't even recognize when I pulled alongside you in my car in L.A.

"We're giving you this chance," the director had said, "in the hope you'll deliver."

"We've spoken to your agent," the male producer had added. "You'll probably want to give her a call."

Want to give her a call? Holy shit! He couldn't believe this was happening. Charlie was dumped and he was in.

"I can do it," he'd blurted. "I've studied the script—I can do this good."

"That's exactly why you're getting this opportunity," the woman had said.

The truth was they didn't have much choice. Charlie Geary was out of action and they couldn't afford to shut down production while they waited to negotiate for another star. They were prepared to take a chance on Nick.

The next few days were crazy time. His main worry was Cyndra and Annie. Could he trust them alone in L.A.? Would they be all right without him? Or would Annie go running to the cops, ruining everything? It was a chance he had to take.

He called them both. Annie sounded sulky as usual. She didn't even rustle up any enthusiasm when he told her about his lucky break.

"Tell you what," he suggested. "Give me a few days, then maybe you can fly to New York for a weekend. I'll spring for your ticket and room. I talked to my agent, I'm making okay money."

"I don't think so," she said coolly.

"C'mon," he persuaded. "You want to see New York, don't you? You've never been here."

"I'll let you know."

Cyndra was genuinely thrilled. "You'll be sensational, Nick," she assured him.

"I'll do my best. Can't do more than that."

His agent had been suitably businesslike. "It's an excellent opportunity for you to show them how good you are. Of course, you're still very inexperienced. It may not work out—don't get your hopes up."

"How come they went with me?" he asked.

She told him the truth. "This is not a big-budget movie. If they wait for a name replacement for Charlie it'll hold them up and cost them money they can't afford. You're there, and as far as they're concerned you seem capable of doing the job. Carlysle's name will carry the film. Oh, and Nick, remember what I told you. Don't screw her—it'll get in the way of your performance."

"You told me not to screw her before because it would get in the way of Charlie Geary. Now he ain't around."

"Nick, you're new to this business—*don't screw her.*"

Frances expressed the same sentiments. "Save everything you've got. Getting laid takes time and energy. Put all that sexual juice into your performance."

Once he met Carlysle he knew exactly where all his sexual juice was going. They'd hit it off immediately. He asked around and found out her story. She'd been a child star since the age of eight, now she was twenty-two, recently divorced from a rock 'n roll drummer and very career-oriented. She had a mother who usually accompanied her on shoots, but so far had not arrived in New York.

"Watch out for the mother," Waldo warned. "The woman is a complete nightmare."

"Why are you telling *me?*" he asked.

"Because we all know what's about to happen between you two," Waldo replied, with an evil chuckle.

Nick laughed. "How about fillin' *me* in?"

Their second day on the set Carlysle invited him out. "I have to go to this dinner party tomorrow night," she said. "My mother was coming with me, but since she's not here . . . will you take me?"

She gazed up at him with her big blue eyes and he wasn't about to say no. "Yeah, sure. Should we go from the set?"

"No, I'll have to go home and change first. Pick me up at my apartment."

"I thought you lived in L.A."

"I do. I've got a house in L.A. and an apartment here."

Wow! This girl really had it all together. "What time?" he asked.

"The dinner starts at seven-thirty, but they probably won't sit down to eat until nine. Get me at eight-thirty and we'll make a late entrance."

"Uh, what do I wear?"

She smiled. "Whatever you like. I'm sure you look fine in anything."

Cyndra was determined the incident in Vegas was not going to drag her down. She'd come so far and she was not allowing it to pull her under. It was unfortunate, but it was her past—just like Mr. Browning, her abortion and all the other bad things she'd gone through.

Annie, on the other hand, kept insisting they had to do something about it. If Nick knew, he'd throw a fit. "You'd better shut up about this," Cyndra warned her. " 'Cause the only thing you can do is get us all into big trouble."

"You agreed with me at first," Annie reminded her.

"I was upset then. I wasn't thinking clearly. Understand, Annie, Nick is right, it's *our* secret, and if none of us blow it we'll keep it that way."

"How can you forget what happened?" Annie demanded. "That poor man—what about his family? Don't you *care?*"

"Stop giving me that poor man crap," Cyndra said angrily. "He was in a motel room with me, wasn't he? He thought I was a hooker. You should have heard the names he called me."

"He didn't deserve to die for it."

"It was an *accident*, Annie. Reece didn't shoot him purposely, it was just one of those things. Like when you get on a plane you don't expect it to crash. When you go for a ride in a car you don't expect it to be totaled. These things happen."

"I still think—"

"Will you shut up!" Cyndra said, finally losing her temper, her dark eyes blazing. "Shut up about it, Annie."

She went through her apartment and packed all of Reece's clothes into two suitcases, stacking them in a closet by the front door. Nick had suggested that as he was going to be in New York for at least six weeks she should give up her apartment and move into his. Since she didn't have any money, it struck her as an excellent idea. He'd also left her his rented car to drive, so at least she was mobile.

Searching through Reece's papers she found the name of the producer he'd been dealing with at Reno Records. Marik Lee. She called him on the phone.

"Where's your manager?" Marik Lee asked, sounding guarded.

"You mean Reece Webster?"

"That's the guy."

"He's no longer my manager."

"Good," he said.

"Good? How come?"

"Drop by and we'll discuss it."

She didn't need a second invitation. Within the hour she was at his office—dressed to make an impression in a tight red dress which showed off her figure and flattered her glowing skin. Her hair, dark and lustrous, fell almost to her waist.

Marik Lee did a double take when she walked in. "*You're* Cyndra?" he said, standing up.

She nodded, checking him out. He was black, a little overweight and kind of homely-looking, but he had nice eyes and a big friendly smile. "Why do you sound so surprised?" she asked, sitting in a chair across from his desk and crossing her legs.

His eyes wandered. "I had no idea you were so . . . so pretty."

"Thank you," she said demurely, accepting the compliment.

"Now tell me," he continued. "That guy you were hitched up with —that, uh, Reece Webster. He definitely out the picture?"

"Yes," she replied. "Very definitely."

"Between you and me, he was a bad case. We don't like to get involved in those situations."

"What situations?"

"You know what I'm saying. He talked about you like you were a slab of meat, like you'd do anything he wanted. We expect our talent to be able to talk for themselves."

She sat up very straight. "Oh, I can talk for myself all right."

He looked at her appreciatively. "Yeah, I can see that."

She thought about Nick in New York about to get his big chance. She wasn't planning on playing the little sister role, dragging along behind. She had every intention of making it just as big as he.

"Mr. Lee—"

"Call me Marik."

"Marik. Tell me the truth—do Reno Records and I have a future together, or am I wasting my time?"

· · ·

Nick was in the wardrobe trailer trying on different clothes.

"They're very happy with the dailies," Waldo confided sotto voce.

"Dailies?" he said, zipping up a pair of tight black jeans.

"Oh, Nick, *please*. Surely you know what I'm talking about? The dailies are the scenes from the previous day. My friend is the projectionist—I get a full report."

He was pleased. "So they like me?"

"Yes, they certainly do. Why do you think they hired you in place of Charlie? They took one look at your closeups and realized they had something with you. According to my friend the camera simply loves you." He reached for a pair of cowboy boots. "Try these, please."

Nick grabbed the boots and sat down. "Yeah, well, I always knew I could do this," he said, pulling on the left boot.

"You can do it, all right. Although, of course, there's no such thing as a sure thing. You might have what it takes and the audience can still hate you."

"No way they'll hate me," he said confidently. "I'm putting everything I've got into this performance. They're gonna respond. You'll see—they're gonna respond big time."

"I'm sure they will," Waldo said, selecting a denim jacket from the rack. "And what are we wearing tonight when we take little Miss Madam out?"

He pulled on the other boot and stood up. "How come my date with Carlysle is public knowledge?"

"This is a film set, Nick. If you fart in the privacy of your dressing room everyone knows about it."

"Great!"

"Just be careful with little Madam. She appears to be angelic, but watch out."

He grinned. "Hey, Waldo, this may come as a big shock to you, but when it comes to women I know my way around the block an' back again."

"Actresses are not women," Waldo murmured. "Oh, dear me, no."

Nick burst out laughing. "You're a character, you know that?"

"You have been warned," Waldo said primly. "Nobody can say you haven't been warned."

"Thanks, but I guess I'll take my chances."

Waldo rolled his eyes.

"Hi," Carlysle said, greeting him at her apartment door wearing nothing but a welcoming smile and a skimpy bath towel wrapped sarong style around her body.

"Uh . . . hi," he said, standing on the threshold.

"Come on in," she said. "As you can see, I'm not quite ready."

Oh, he could see, all right!

She led him into a comfortable living room and waved him in the direction of a small bar. "Fix yourself a drink. I'll be quick—I promise."

"Take your time," he said, checking the place out.

"Ooops!" Her towel slipped and she quickly hitched it up, but not before he caught a glimpse of her large, rosy, disturbingly erect nipples.

She noticed him looking and giggled, her blue eyes widening. "Isn't it stupid the way we all try to hide ourselves? Wouldn't it be better to walk around without anything on? After all, we weren't born fully dressed, were we?"

"Works for me," he said, opening the refrigerator behind the bar and extracting a beer.

"Good," said Carlysle, dropping the towel.

Instant erection. He didn't even have time to think about it.

"Why don't you take your clothes off, too?" she said, with an innocent little smile.

"Hey—"

"You're not shy, are you?" she teased.

No, baby, I'm not shy, but I am used to being the instigator and this is a different trip.

He shrugged off his jacket and began unbuttoning his shirt.

Carlysle was not a patient girl. She ran toward him and went right for his zipper, pulling down his pants and underwear. Before he knew what was happening she had him in her mouth giving him one of the finest blow jobs known to man! He came in record time because it was so unexpected and so good, and the truth was he hadn't gotten laid in a while and he was beyond horny.

"Ah . . . Jesus!" he groaned. "That was . . ."

"Yes?" she asked breathlessly, still on her knees.

"Pretty . . . damn . . . good."

"Good? Surely you mean sensational?"

"That, too. C'mere," he said, reaching for her breasts.

She jumped to her feet, skipping out of his range. "Later," she said in a little-girl voice. "Gotta get dressed. It wouldn't do to be late for the party, would it now?"

The guests had all arrived, the hors d'oeuvres had been served and Lauren began her own private countdown to dinner. Her two assistants, Hilary and Karen, knew her well, anticipating her every request. Actually, the truth was she'd trained them so efficiently they could probably do it without her. Which was good, because when she and Oliver were married she'd have to delegate a lot more. Oliver had already told her he wanted her to travel with him, and why not—she was dying to see Europe. He took six weeks' vacation every year, traveling through Italy, France and England. Help Unlimited would just have to manage without her for a few weeks.

Jessie popped into the kitchen. "Almost ready," she said, beaming in her severe, men's style velvet suit. "The melon and caviar was a riot!"

"We're all set when you are," Lauren said, adjusting the flame under the sautéed carrots.

"Spectacular!" exclaimed Jessie.

One of the things Lauren liked about catering dinners for the Georges was their unbridled enthusiasm. Quentin was exactly like his wife. The two of them enjoyed life, and it was infectious.

"Who's out there tonight?" Lauren asked Hilary, who'd been busy serving the hors d'oeuvres.

Hilary recited a list of celebrities—including a controversial black politician, an avant-garde dress designer, a famous ballplayer and two movie stars. Jessie sure loved to mix people up.

Lauren decided Oliver would be happy when he dropped by. He enjoyed hanging out with celebrities. She didn't. If she was lucky she wouldn't have to emerge from the kitchen all night long.

"Did you like it?" Carlysle giggled, holding tightly onto his arm in the back of her limo. "Was it the best—the very *very* best you've ever had?"

He grinned lazily. "The best."

She squeezed his arm. "Don't lie to me, or I'll have to do it again—right now in the car."

He laughed. "Sure."

Her blue eyes sparkled. "You think I wouldn't?"

"I'm positive you would."

"Want me to?" she asked, stroking his thigh.

He felt himself getting hard again. "What about the driver?" he said.

She pressed a button and the black privacy glass slid up. "Oh, he's not getting any—he's *definitely* not on my list."

Before he could question her about what list that might be, she was on him again—going for his zipper with practiced hands, springing him free, and bending her blond head.

He gave himself up to the moment, pressing the top of her head, forcing himself into her mouth as deep as she could take him.

This time he lasted longer, and when he came it was an explosion. "*Shit!*" he exclaimed, falling back on the leather seat. "Holy *shit!*"

She laughed triumphantly. "I'm good, huh?"

"You're great."

"The greatest?"

What was it with this girl? All she wanted to hear was how great she was. "Yes," he said.

"The greatest you've ever had?"

He reached for her breasts again, but she slapped his hands away. "We're here," she said. "Didn't you notice the car stop?"

"Sweetheart," he sighed, "I didn't notice anything but you."

He'd said the right thing. Carlysle beamed like a cat who'd just devoured a saucer of cream—and in a way she had.

"Later I'm gonna fuck you," he said.

"Later I'm going to let you," she replied.

Grinning, they alighted from the limo and entered the house.

The vichyssoise was served. The guests were happy. In the kitchen Lauren concentrated on the mashed potatoes, making sure they had just the right combination of cream, butter and milk. Cooking was therapeutic. She really enjoyed creating a meal and watching as all the empty plates came back into the kitchen.

"Carlysle Mann just arrived," Hilary said. "She's *sooo* pretty."

"You're pretty too," Lauren said crisply. "You're as pretty as any movie star."

"No way!"

"Yes, you are."

"She's got fantastic skin," Hilary said enviously.

"Talking of skin—did you see the guy she's with?" Karen said.

"Cute," they both said in unison. "Very *very* cute." They burst out giggling.

Oh, to be young again, Lauren thought. Hilary and Karen were so bright-eyed and full of life. She was only six years older than them, but sometimes she felt like a staid old lady. "Come on, girls, concentrate," she said. "Let's get this meal on the road."

Carlysle's hand began creeping up his leg again. Shit! She was actually doing it in front of all these people. And important people, too. He glanced around the table and couldn't believe he was sitting among them.

"Hey—stop that," he whispered.

"Why?" she whispered back.

" 'Cause somebody's gonna see."

"So what?" she replied.

"So what? You're crazy—you know that?"

She leaned very close and nibbled on his earlobe. "If I had my way I'd give you a blow job right under the table now."

This girl was not bluffing. "You would too, wouldn't you?"

"Ooops! I dropped my napkin—excuse me." She started to dive under the table.

He grabbed her arm, stopping her. "Don't you dare!" he warned.

"So, Carlysle sweetie," said Jessie, turning in their direction. "How's your new film going?"

"We only just started," said Carlysle, abandoning her under-the-table plan. "I guess you heard about Charlie? He has a kind of . . . uh, virus."

"I'm so sorry. Is he in the hospital?"

"Not exactly. Well, sort of—yeah, I guess you could say he is."

"I always thought you two made such an adorable couple," Jessie said.

"Uh . . . thanks."

Jessie turned away to talk to the politician on her other side.

Nick nudged Carlysle. "I didn't know you and Charlie were a couple."

"We weren't," she said shortly.

"Then why'd she say that?"

"We went on a few dates—that's not exactly being a couple."

He imagined her on her knees in front of Charlie and he wasn't too thrilled. But still, he hardly knew her, he couldn't start acting possessive at this stage.

Soon she began trying to unzip his jeans again, her hands working feverishly. "Give me a break!" he said, catching a look from the dress designer on his other side, who had orange hair and an attitude.

Carlysle giggled. "Stop acting like a prude."

This girl was a wild one.

Oliver arrived during the dessert stage.

"The dinner was simply divine," Jessie informed him. "You're marrying the best cook in the world."

Oliver was amused. "I'm not marrying Lauren for her cooking, Jessie dear."

"I'm sure you're not."

He put his head around the kitchen door. Lauren was busy organizing desserts. She'd baked two *tartes tatins*, and a batch of double chocolate brownies.

"You're busy," he said.

"Very astute," she said.

"Jessie wants you to come out and join the party."

"I can't do that. Anyway, I'm not dressed."

"You're more beautiful than any of the guests."

"You're such a smooth talker, Oliver."

"Which is *exactly* why I'm where I am today."

She ladled whipped cream into a crystal bowl. "Oliver, please—I'm trying to get this together."

He nodded understandingly. "Very well, I'll go and sit down and wait patiently. When you're ready I'll take you home."

What about her surprise? She'd been looking forward to a puppy all night, but then again, he couldn't bring it to the Georges' house. Maybe he had it waiting at home.

Everybody carried on about the delicious desserts. Jessie had squeezed Oliver in between Quentin and a vivacious book editor with teased black hair. Suddenly she stood up, tapping the side of her champagne glass. "Listen, everyone, I have an announcement," she said, beaming around the table.

Nick felt Carlysle's hand slide inside his zipper. This was wild, but he couldn't help being aroused.

"I know you've all enjoyed the excellent food tonight, and I'm bringing our chef out to allow you to thank her personally. You may also congratulate her, because she and Oliver Liberty are engaged. You all know Oliver, but I don't think you've met his lovely fiancée." Jessie beckoned a waiter. "Have Lauren come out," she said.

In the kitchen Lauren was mortified. "I'm not going out there," she said, backing into a corner. "What does she think this is—a show?"

Karen gave her a little shove. "You have to, she's waiting."

"Oh, no!" Lauren groaned.

"Oh, yes!" Karen and Hilary chorused, enjoying every minute. They loved working for Lauren, and they were delighted to see her get the kind of attention she deserved.

Reluctantly she allowed herself to be propelled to the dining room doorway. If there was one thing she hated it was being the center of attention.

"Ah, Lauren dear, there you are." Jessie raised her champagne glass. "Here's to you."

There was an enthusiastic round of applause from the guests.

She felt like a total fool. Her eyes scanned the dinner table, checking out the guests. She looked once, twice and couldn't believe her eyes. Nick Angelo was there. *Her* Nick was actually at this dinner.

No, it couldn't be.

Yes, it was.

She looked again. He was older, more handsome than ever, skinnier. His eyes were still deep green and intense. His hair that incredible jet black. Oh, God! She wanted to die. The only good thing was the fact that he hadn't seen her. He was all over the girl sitting beside him, who happened to be Carlysle Mann, the movie star.

Desperately Lauren tried to breathe, to recover her composure. *Move slowly. Get out before he spots me. Get the hell out!*

As she turned to bolt from the room he looked up and their eyes met. He was as startled as she was. They gazed at each other in disbelief before she broke the stare and rushed back into the kitchen. She didn't hesitate, grabbing her coat and purse she began running for the back door.

"Where are you going?" Hilary asked, startled.

"I don't feel good. I have to get out of here. Tell Oliver I had to go."

"One of us should come with you," Hilary insisted.

"No—I have to get out now," she said, flinging open the door and racing out of the apartment before anyone could stop her.

"What's the matter?" Carlysle said. "What happened?"

His hard-on had deflated. "Nothing," he said, brushing her hand away as he surreptitiously tried to zip up his pants.

445

"What do you mean, nothing?" she said, her chin tilting belligerently.

He got up from the table. " 'Scuse me, I gotta take a piss."

"I'll come with you. You'd be surprised what we can get up to in the john."

"Hey—Carlysle, I'm not surprised at anything you do. Stay here. I'll be back."

In the hall outside the dining room he grabbed a hovering waiter. "How do I get to the kitchen?"

"Through there, sir. Can I get you something?"

"Nah, it's okay," he said, hurrying into the kitchen.

She wasn't there. He stopped a pretty girl in a striped apron. "Where's Lauren?"

"She left," Hilary said, quite intrigued by this intense-looking guy. "She didn't feel good."

"Where can I contact her?"

"Do you need to have a party catered? We have a very comprehensive service. Here, let me give you one of our cards."

She handed him a card and he stared at it. HELP UNLIMITED was printed in the middle with an address and phone number. In neat script on either side were two names—Lauren Roberts and Pia Liberty.

"You can contact us anytime," Hilary said, wishing he'd flirt with her. "During business hours, of course."

"Oh, I will," Nick said, pocketing the card. "Bet on it."

The couple entwined on the bed made love fast and furiously until they climaxed with a series of grunts and moans.

"Oh, baby, baby, that was freakin' sensational!" said Marik.

Cyndra rolled away from him, flushed and surprised at her own boldness, yet at the same time strangely exhilarated. Marik had only been in her life a week, and she already had him in her power.

"Was it good for you too, baby?" he asked, sitting up and reaching for a cigarette.

"You *know* it was good for me," she replied, coming out with all the right words. "You're an amazing lover, Marik. The best."

They'd been to dinner at a cozy Italian restaurant, following an afternoon in the studio, where she'd finally cut a demo record. Marik had liked what he heard. When they were finished in the studio he'd said, "We're goin' out to celebrate, 'cause when the big boss hears your sound you're gonna be signin' your life away!"

She'd glowed with delight. "Really?"

"Yeah, babe. Really."

Cyndra liked Marik, he seemed nice enough. But more than that, she wanted something from him, and she was beginning to learn that if you wanted something you had to offer a prize in return. Her way of doing this was to get him into bed, where she knew she had the power.

"Do you really like my voice?" she asked again, anxious to hear him repeat the compliment.

"Hey, baby, how many times I gotta tell you? You sound *good!* A little raw in places—nothing I can't fix when we record your first single."

She'd been waiting to hear those words from somebody legitimate all her life. She moved closer to him, brushing her breasts against his chest. "What happens next?"

"Anything you want," he said, puffing on his cigarette with a blissful smile.

"I want a contract."

"Baby, as far as I'm concerned, you got it."

"I want to start making money."

"I'm the man to do it for you."

"And I need somewhere to live. I moved out of my apartment. Right now I'm staying at my brother's."

"Oh, wow, you're in a bad way, huh?"

"I had to get away from Reece. Now I plan to start fresh."

"You will, baby. When the big boss hears your voice and takes a look at you, we're goin' all the way."

"That's exactly what I needed to hear."

He laughed. "Come back here, and I'll show you exactly what *I* need."

Marik was true to his word. Within a week she was installed in a new apartment, she'd signed a contract with Reno Records and finally met the big boss. His name was Gordon D. Hayworth, and he was a powerful-looking black man in his forties.

Gordon D. Hayworth was handsome—he was also married. As soon as Cyndra stepped into his office she'd noticed the family pictures on his desk. A very beautiful wife. And two young children. The perfect American family.

"You've got some voice," he told her. "It's not strong—more soulful and sexy. But I like that."

"You do?" she asked, widening her eyes.

"Yes, I do," he replied. "We'll find the right single for you to record and see what happens."

"Really?"

He looked at her intently. "It's what you want, Cyndra, isn't it?"

"It's what I've always wanted, ever since I was a little girl."

"You must've been a cute little girl," he said, smiling.

She wondered how cute he would've thought she was when Mr. Browning was raping her, when she was having the abortion, and all the other bad things that had happened to her.

"Yes, I was very cute," she said, smiling back.

"We're happy to have you with us, Cyndra," he said, standing up and walking around his desk to pat her on the shoulder in a fatherly fashion.

"I'm happy too," she said.

"We'll be seeing lots of each other."

I hope so, she thought.

He continued to smile as he escorted her to the door.

She walked out of his office and realized for the first time in her life she'd met a man she knew she could fall in love with.

"I'm flying to New York to see Nick," Annie said.

"That's nice," Cyndra replied. "It'll be a break for you."

Annie frowned. "I have to be honest with you. I'm going there to tell him I can't keep quiet any longer."

Cyndra turned on her, her eyes flashing angrily. "No, Annie. How many times must I tell you? It's not just Nick you'll hurt—it's me. And now my career is about to take off, you mustn't do this."

"I have to," Annie said stubbornly. "I can't live with myself and keep this secret."

"Screw you!" Cyndra exploded. "I'll deny it ever happened. Let them go out and search for the body. You'll look like a fool, 'cause I'll deny everything. You're not dragging me down, girl, so don't you try it. I'll tell them you're crazy, I'll tell them you've always been crazy."

"You can say what you like," Annie said, refusing to look her in the eye. "But I'm going to the police when I get back."

As soon as she was alone Cyndra called Nick. "Annie's gonna blow it," she said. "You'd better be prepared to do something about her."

"I know what I have to do," he said.

"Good, 'cause otherwise we've both had it."

449

"What happened?" Oliver said, standing on her doorstep trying to conceal his anger.

"I didn't feel well. I had to get out of there."

He tapped his foot impatiently. "May I come in?"

She wasn't in the mood to deal with him. "I still don't feel good, Oliver."

He walked past her into the living room. "Why didn't you tell me? I could have driven you, my car was downstairs."

She trailed behind him. "I needed some air. I walked halfway home."

He looked at her as if he didn't quite believe what he was hearing. "You left me there and walked home? You left me looking like a fool, Lauren."

"No, I didn't," she said, refusing to admit she might be wrong. "Nobody knew I'd gone."

"I'm sure they did."

"Please, Oliver, I'm not in the mood for a fight. I told you, I don't feel well."

"Do you need a doctor?"

"No, I'll be all right. It was just the pressure of cooking dinner, and

450

their kitchen was so hot, and I just . . ." She sighed. "Oliver, don't you ever feel that you're about to explode?"

"No," he said in an irritated voice. "And if I did I would tell you."

"Thanks," she said listlessly.

"Sometimes, Lauren, I don't understand you."

He could say that again. Perhaps she should enlighten him before it was too late.

"There's a lot about me you don't know. Maybe we should think about this marriage thing."

Now he was really aggravated. "I don't have to think about it, and neither do you."

"If I told you about my past you might change your mind."

"Oh, now you're going to tell me you have a hidden past, is that it?"

"It hasn't all been exactly 'Little House on the Prairie.' "

"Listen, my dear, everyone has secrets. I have no need to hear yours. I love you, that's enough for me."

She was determined to be heard whether he liked it or not. "When my parents were killed I went to live in Philadelphia with my aunt and uncle. I had an affair with my cousin."

"Am I supposed to be upset about that?"

"Then I came to New York, met a photographer called Jimmy and slept with him."

Oliver frowned. He was not enjoying this. "Lauren, how old are you?"

"Twenty-four."

"You're twenty-four years old and you've had affairs with two men. You wouldn't be normal if you hadn't." His tone softened. "You know, darling, I hardly imagined you were a virgin."

"There was somebody else—somebody I knew when I was very young."

"Who was that?" he asked patiently.

"A boy in high school."

"What about him?"

"Oh, nothing . . ." There was no point in telling him about Nick. "Please, Oliver, I really need to be alone. We'll talk tomorrow. Go home."

"I was going to give you your surprise," he said, refusing to budge.

"Give it to me tomorrow."

His mouth hardened into a thin tight line. "Very well," he said, obviously not at all pleased. "Get a good night's rest." He pecked her on the cheek and left.

As soon as he was gone she paced around her apartment a nervous wreck. God! She was so confused. She didn't know what to do or what to think. She'd never imagined running into Nick. As far as she was concerned he was out of her life forever. And yet there he was, sitting at the dinner party with that Carlysle person, and every feeling she'd ever had for him came flooding back over her. She'd loved him so very much, she would have given her life for him.

Seeing him again had unnerved her. Her memories of him were so vivid. And he'd looked so good, so great, so fantastic.

Get real. Nick Angelo is your past.

It doesn't have to be that way.

Yes, it does.

Had he seen her? Had he recognized her? Their eyes had met for an instant and yes—she knew without a doubt he'd recognized her.

If only she could tell somebody, but there was nobody to confide in. Who would understand about her and Nick? They'd say it was a teenage fling, a stupid little affair. But it wasn't. She'd lived for him and he'd crushed her.

Why was she getting in such a state over Nick Angelo? He was a son of a bitch. He'd dumped her like all the others. He'd set the pattern.

Well, she'd show him. She was marrying Oliver Liberty, a man of substance. And when she was Mrs. Liberty he couldn't touch her ever again.

The next morning she woke up and fervently wished it had all been a dream. She showered, brushed her teeth, put on her makeup, dressed and went to the office.

As soon as she walked in, Pia was on her case. "Nick Angelo called," she said. "He sounded anxious to reach you. Who is he?"

Her stomach did a somersault. "Nobody important. Tear the message up."

On her desk there were a dozen red roses from Oliver and a note asking her to meet him for lunch. She knew he must be feeling anxious, they were supposed to leave for the Bahamas in two days and her behavior had obviously unsettled him.

"Uh, Pia . . . do me a favor," she said, staring at the roses.

"Yes?"

"If Nick Angelo calls again, say I've left town. In fact, you can tell him I'm about to be married, and don't give him any other information."

"Who is he?" Pia asked curiously.

"Oh, just somebody I knew a long time ago in high school."

"He's got a great voice," Pia said. "Kind of sexy."

"That's nice," she replied, wishing Pia would get off the subject.

Oliver was waiting when she arrived at the restaurant. "Feeling better today?" he asked, solicitous as ever.

"Much better, thank you," she said, sliding in beside him.

"Good. Because I have your surprise."

"Does it bark and eat plenty of food?"

"No, my dear, it is not a puppy. You know how I feel about puppies. I refuse to have them peeing all over my Persian rugs."

"Then I'm very disappointed, Oliver."

"You won't be," he said, groping for a large envelope on the banquette seat. "Take a look," he said, handing it to her.

"What is it?"

"Open it and you'll see."

She opened the envelope and pulled out a large poster. Staring at her was her own image. Above the photograph in bold lettering were the words THE NEW MARCELLA GIRL! "What's this?" she asked.

"You can see what it is. It's your photograph from the session."

"I know, but why does it say the new Marcella girl?"

"Because, my darling, that's exactly who you're going to be."

Carlysle tried every way she knew how, but she could not get any further action out of Nick that night. Unbeknown to her he was in a state of shock because he couldn't believe he'd run into Lauren after all those years. It was all he could do to escort Carlysle home.

"Aren't you coming up?" she asked as he helped her from the limo.

"Nah, early call," he explained.

"So've I," she pointed out. "We could go into the studio together."

"I got a headache," he said.

"*You've* got a headache?" She laughed hysterically. "Isn't that supposed to be *my* line?"

She went for his zipper again. He slapped her hand away.

"What happened?" she demanded. "I thought we were having a good time."

"We were. It's nothing personal."

"God, you're behaving really strangely."

He was behaving strangely? Had she ever thought about her own behavior?

"Look, I'll see you on the set tomorrow," he said.

She marched into her apartment building without a backward glance. Her driver took him back to his hotel.

He couldn't get over seeing Lauren. What exactly was she doing in New York? And who was the old guy she was engaged to?

How could she be engaged to a man old enough to be her grandfather? And how come she hadn't acknowledged him? She must have busted her ass getting out of there so fast.

He had so many questions and he needed answers. It wasn't that he was going to forgive her for not answering his letters, but it would be nice to find out why.

At the hotel there was a message from Annie. He returned her call.

"I'm coming in," she announced.

"Oh . . . that's great," he said, thinking it wasn't so great. The last thing he needed was Annie.

"I'll be arriving tomorrow at four. Will you meet me?"

"I'm on the set," he said. "But I'll arrange to have someone there."

"We have to talk," she said.

Oh, Christ! Cyndra was right, this didn't sound good.

First thing in the morning he called Help Unlimited. A female voice said, "Pia Liberty. Can I help you?"

"Yeah, let me talk to Lauren."

"She's not in yet."

"I need to get in touch with her, like immediately."

"I'll see she gets the message."

"Maybe you can give me her home number."

"No, I'm sorry."

"We're friends from way back."

"I'm sure you are, but we never divulge personal numbers. Why don't you call again at ten?"

He took off for the studio. Carlysle greeted him with a scowl, she was obviously unused to not getting her own way.

He studied his script, conferred with the director and tried to throw himself into character, but it was difficult holding his concentration. As soon as he got a break he rushed to the phone. "Is Lauren in yet?"

"I'm sorry, you've missed her. She's left town. She's getting married, you know."

"Is this Pia?"

"Good memory."

"Listen, Pia, I *have* to talk to her. It's very important."

"I gave her your message. Maybe she'll call you."

"You don't understand. We really go back a long way."

"She said she'd contact you."

"She did?"

"Yes."

He hung up the phone feeling depressed. What was he chasing her for anyway? She'd dumped him. What more could he have done than written her a hundred times without receiving one single reply.

The truth was—if he wanted to face up to it—Lauren Roberts had never wanted him. It had all been a game for her. Nick Angelo—the jerk from the wrong side of the tracks, and pretty little Lauren Roberts who'd amused herself at his expense.

Well, screw her. Let her go off and marry some rich old man. What did he care?

But deep down he did care. And although he'd never admit it, seeing her again had stirred up every painful memory of the love he'd once had for her.

He wanted Lauren to be his past. Somehow he knew it wasn't possible.

Annie had her own agenda, Nick knew it as soon as she arrived on the set direct from the airport. In New York she looked very Californian with her deep suntan, athletic body and brightly colored clothes.

"Who's she?" Carlysle demanded, the moment Annie hit the set.

"A friend," Nick replied.

Carlysle smiled a secret smile. "I bet she doesn't give head like I do."

Waldo, hovering on the sidelines, raised his eyebrows and tut-tutted.

"She's not my girlfriend," Nick explained to Carlysle.

"You haven't fucked her?" Carlysle questioned.

"No."

"But she wants you to."

"Why do you say that?"

"Take a look at her, Nick. She's mooning after you like a baby who wants to suck mama's tit." Carlysle giggled wickedly. "Only it's not your tit she wants to suck."

"Has anybody ever told you you've got sex on the brain?"

"Something wrong with that?"

One thing about Carlysle, she wasn't a clinger. She didn't give a damn who he was sleeping with—which was just as well because he didn't plan on answering to anyone.

He introduced Annie to the director, which pleased her. Later she sat in his chair and watched while they shot a restaurant scene. When it was done she reluctantly admitted he was good.

"Thanks," he said.

"Joy would be proud of you. Aren't you glad I took you to her class?"

Was this her subtle way of telling him that if she hadn't taken him to Joy Byron's class none of this would have happened?

Filming finished shortly before seven, and they took a cab back to his hotel.

"I booked you a room," he said. "It's one floor up from me. Oh, and they need to know how long you're staying."

"That depends on you," she said in an edgy voice.

Shit! Why did it depend on him?

"What d'you mean?" he asked.

She stared straight at him. "How long do *you* want me to stay?"

Carlysle was right, Annie was waiting for him to make a move, and unfortunately the only way he could stop her from opening up her mouth to the cops was to make her his girlfriend.

They ate Chinese food in a nearby restaurant, talked about the movie and L.A. and Cyndra's record deal. Then they got down to the real reason she'd come to New York.

"I suppose Cyndra warned you," she said, sipping tea. "I'm sorry to do this to you, Nick—but it's too big a burden for me to carry any longer."

"Yeah," he said, thinking about how to handle her. "I understand."

She was surprised. "You do?"

"I know how difficult it must be for you, Annie. You're all alone, you've got nobody to talk to . . . you're trying to get connected and acting jobs aren't easy to come by. Yeah, I understand." He moved right along, talking about Joy and the class and her job at the health club.

She was confused. She'd expected him to try to talk her out of going to the police and she'd had all her arguments ready. But no, he'd gone completely in the opposite direction and she was at a loss.

On the walk back to the hotel he put his arm around her, held her hand and told her how pretty she looked. By the time he got her to his room on the pretext of rehearsing the next day's scene, she was all his. But still he proceeded carefully, and when he started to undress her she was more than ready.

He took it slowly—pacing himself, going at her speed, which was slow. She did have a terrific body, compact and muscled, but not really his type—he liked his women more on the voluptuous side.

When they finally made it he was shocked to discover she was a virgin. "You must be the only virgin left in Hollywood," he joked, trying not to hurt her as he went for the final thrust.

"Don't joke about it, Nick," she gasped. "I believe in waiting."

He broke through and felt her gush. Then he proceeded to make her very happy indeed.

By the time he was finished he knew the cops would be the last place she'd go.

Annie stayed a week. The moment she left he resumed with Carlysle, whose only comment was why hadn't the three of them got it on.

"You're somethin' else," he said, shaking his head.

With Annie safely back in L.A. they proceeded to have sex whenever and wherever they could. It became a standing joke that if either of them was needed on the set they had to be pried apart first. Their on-screen love scenes were sizzling, especially when Carlysle did things to him under the sheets that nobody knew about except the two of them.

He got to see the dailies and knew it was working for him. He and Carlysle had great chemistry.

Most nights they went out. Carlysle was invited everywhere, and there was always a party or an opening. She really got off on public sex—the more dangerous the better. They'd done some form of sexual activity everywhere from the first night of a Broadway show to the toniest restaurant. And he never made a limo trip without Carlysle giving him one of her famous blow jobs.

"Don't you ever get tired?" he asked, only half jokingly.

"I've got the rest of my life to get tired. Live for the moment, Nick —we won't be around forever."

If she carried on at this pace she'd wear out his dick! And then where would he be?

The female producer started paying more attention to him. He figured her to be in her early forties, but extremely well preserved. One day she informed him she had a script she'd like him to read and invited him up to her hotel suite.

"Can I come too?" Carlysle begged.

"No," he said firmly.

"She wants to fuck you," Carlysle said.

"According to you everyone wants to fuck me."

"When this movie comes out they will. You can take odds on it."

Carlysle, as usual, was right. The producer poured him a vodka on the rocks and sat opposite him, crossing and uncrossing her long elegant legs while he attempted to read the script. She'd already informed him it was under wraps and could not leave her hands.

Twenty pages in and she dropped her skirt, revealing a black lace garter belt, stockings and a black bush. She obviously did not believe in panties.

He remembered the stoplight where she'd ignored him, and he fucked her good.

Afterward she asked him what he thought of the script.

"Not bad," he said confidently. "But the fuck was great."

Carlysle wanted details. She savored every juicy one, and it turned her on so much that they made out in an alley behind the latest hot disco where they were attending a party.

Meanwhile he called Annie every other day. She sounded fine. He was relieved, at least he had her under control.

One day he received a distraught call from Joey's hooker girlfriend. "Those bastards beat Joey up good," she said. "He's in the hospital."

As soon as he finished work he rushed over to visit. Joey lay in a public ward with bandaged limbs and a pulped face. His eyes were mere slits and his lips swollen to twice their size.

"This is really nice," Nick said cheerfully. "Can't leave you alone for a minute. How'd it happen?"

"Got in a fight," Joey mumbled.

"What with—a meat truck?"

Joey tried to raise his arm. "Don' make me laugh."

Later he talked to Joey's girlfriend again and found out the true story. Joey owed big money on account of a heroin habit he wasn't about to quit.

"I'll take care of it," Nick promised, and he went to Carlysle and asked to borrow money so he could help Joey out. "I wanna put him into some kind of clinic—get him straight," he explained. "It costs, an' I don't have that kind of bucks. This'll be a loan—I'll even pay interest."

Carlysle was unconcerned. "My mother handles all my money," she said, blithely dismissing his problem. "I can't touch it."

You could if you wanted to, bitch.

He went to his producer. She asked questions. Satisfied with his answers, she agreed to the loan in exchange for an option agreement making him available for her next film.

In Los Angeles Meena Caron objected bitterly. "I'm hearing excellent reports, Nick. It would be suicide to tie you up now."

"Gotta help a friend," he explained, and signed the agreement.

Before the movie was over the word was out. There was a new hot property on the horizon. And his name was Nick Angel.

"Do you, Lauren Roberts, take this man, Oliver Liberty, to be your lawfully wedded husband?"

She hesitated for only a second. "I do," she said breathlessly.

"Do you, Oliver Liberty, take this woman, Lauren Roberts, to be your lawfully wedded wife?"

He turned to look at her, his eyes full of pride. "I do."

They stood on the terrace of his house in the Bahamas overlooking a glorious never-ending white beach and a bluer-than-blue ocean. The setting was idyllic. Lauren wore a simple white dress and flowers in her hair. Their witnesses were Oliver's housekeeper and her husband—a friendly black couple who did nothing but beam happily.

When she said "I do" Lauren felt a shudder of apprehension. She was giving her life to another human being. She was joining with Oliver and things would never be quite the same.

It's what you want, isn't it, Roberts?

No.

Don't think that way.

What I want is Nick Angelo.

Oh, for God's sake.

Oliver bent to kiss her and she quickly shut out the images of her past.

461

Later that night they dined quietly, just the two of them on the terrace overlooking the sea.

"So, my darling," he said, clasping her hand. "How do you feel?"

She wasn't sure how she felt. "Lightheaded, I guess."

"That's good, because I feel I'm the luckiest man in the world," he said, clinking his champagne glass with hers.

She sipped her champagne and listened to the soothing sound of the surf.

I'm Mrs. Oliver Liberty.

He's forty years older than me.

I don't care.

You've married a father figure.

That's not true.

After dinner Oliver retired to his study to make a few phone calls. "It'll give you time to relax," he said.

Why would she require time to relax on her wedding night?

She wandered around the house, finally settling in the master bedroom. It was a light and airy room, decorated in earth tones, with another picturesque view. There was an intricate white lace cover on the bed and piles of luxurious cushions. She wondered who'd decorated it, wife number one or wife number two? She decided it was wife number one—far too tasteful for wife number two.

In the pale beige limestone bathroom she took a shower and slipped into the sheer white nightgown she'd purchased specially for her wedding night. By the time she returned to the bedroom Oliver was lying on the bed in silk pajamas perusing a stack of mail.

"Don't you ever stop?" she asked, standing silhouetted in the doorway.

"I believe in taking advantage of every moment. This is correspondence I didn't have time to deal with before I left."

She moved over to the bed. "Was it absolutely necessary to bring it on our honeymoon?"

He must have noticed her tone of annoyance, because he pushed the mail to one side. "I'm sorry," he said, reaching for her hand. "You, my darling," he continued, looking at her for the first time, "are absolutely ravishing."

Will you ravish me tonight, Oliver?

Will you ravish me until I can't breathe?

"Thank you," she murmured.

"Come over here," he said, pulling her down onto the bed.

This was the first night of their married life and she wanted it to be memorable. So far their sex life had not progressed very far. Oliver kept telling her that when they were married things would be different, and she was ready for the change. She needed a man to take her on a passionate trip. Only Nick had managed to satisfy her every need, and she craved that same satisfaction.

Oliver began to kiss and caress her. She responded with a passion she'd kept hidden from him before. "Oliver, tonight should be memorable . . ." she murmured, voicing her thoughts.

"Isn't our lovemaking always memorable?" he asked smoothly.

No, it's not. We've never made love properly. All you've done is make love to me with your tongue.

She demonstrated with actions what she wanted to do to him. As she began to bend her head, he stopped her abruptly. "What are you doing?"

"I'm going to make you very happy."

"No, Lauren. I don't like you to do that."

"But you do it to me all the time. In fact, that's all you do."

"Because you deserve it."

Deserve it? What kind of comment is that?

"Oliver, let me do this to you. You know you'll love it."

"No, Lauren, I will not love it. I refuse to see you in that position."

"I only want to please you," she said.

"I know, my darling, but that doesn't please me. It's an act I associate with sex for sale. It's demeaning and I don't expect you to do it."

She was shocked by his words. Surely, when two people were married nothing was demeaning if it was something they both desired? But if that was the way he wanted it, so be it.

They kissed and caressed some more. His hands fondled her breasts, stroking her gently. Then his head began traveling down her body, heading for what he considered to be his proper destination.

Some women might be wild with joy at the thought of a man who gave them nonstop oral sex, but she'd had enough. Especially as he wouldn't allow her to do it to him.

463

"No, Oliver," she said, moving. "I want you to make love to me properly."

"But, my darling, you enjoy every second of what I do to you."

"Tonight it should be different," she said, reaching to feel his hardness, and disappointed to discover he was only semi-erect.

"Lauren, my darling," he said, drawing away.

"Yes?"

"I have no desire to disappoint you."

"Why would you disappoint me?"

"Because I'm not twenty-five."

She couldn't help being sarcastic. "Oh, really? And I thought you were."

"Don't be flippant. When I was a young man I made love all night long. When I got to be older I realized there were other pleasures that could give a woman more joy than anything else."

"What are you saying?"

"I'm not sure I can satisfy you in the way you expect."

"Why can't we try?"

"It's simply that . . ." He hesitated. "Well . . . since I had my pacemaker—"

"Pacemaker?" she said, alarmed.

"Surely I mentioned it? About two years ago I had a heart irregularity, nothing serious. My doctors decided a pacemaker would solve the problem."

"You never told me, Oliver."

"I probably didn't think it was that important."

"Of course it's important. We're married. I should know everything about you."

"Why? Would it have made a difference?"

"No . . ." Her mind was racing. A pacemaker. Did that mean he was sick? If they made love could he suddenly die? Oh, God, what had she gotten herself into?

He got up and walked over to the window. "I'm sorry, my dear. You're right, I should have told you."

She tried to make it easier for him. "Well, you didn't and now I know. But we can still make love, can't we?"

"Yes."

464

"Then come back to bed. I'm not demanding. All I want is to be close to you."

They stayed in the Bahamas for ten days, during which time Lauren realized she'd married a man who was not prepared to consummate their marriage in the normal way. The truth was he wanted to make love to her his way or not at all. And although his way was very pleasant, it was hardly the same as being joined together with another person.

Oliver was also obsessed with business. She'd thought that once he was away from the office he'd be able to relax. She'd imagined long walks on the beach, swimming, snorkeling, maybe taking a boat out. She did all of those things by herself, because Oliver spent most of his time on the phone.

Occasionally the subject of the Marcella girl came up. When he'd first suggested the idea she'd said a very resounding no. However, he wasn't prepared to take no for an answer. Every other day he asked if she'd changed her mind.

"I told you, Oliver, I'm not a model, nor do I want to be."

"I understand," he replied. "But this is hardly a modeling assignment. You'll be spokesperson for Marcella. You'll also make a lot of money, become well known and enjoy every minute of it."

She disagreed. The idea of making money was appealing, but she had no wish to become well known.

Pia called from New York. "Well? Are you going to do it or not?"

"Not," she said firmly.

"You're blowing an opportunity if you don't," Pia said. "What have you got to lose? Oh, and by the way, take a look at yesterday's *Daily News*. There's a photo of that Nick Angel guy—the one who called you. You didn't tell me he was an actor. And you certainly didn't tell me he was gorgeous."

When Lauren hung up she immediately searched for yesterday's New York papers. Sure enough, on page five of the *News* there was a picture of Nick with Carlysle Mann. She studied the picture, then read the copy:

Carlysle Mann, out on the town with her new co-star, Nick Angel. Carlysle and Nick are shooting Night City *on location in New York. Word has it that Nick lights up the screen, especially in the sex scenes—of which there are many. Ladies, look out . . . he could be your new Saturday night rave . . .*

Nick was actually in a movie! She could hardly believe it. Nick Angel—whatever happened to Angelo? God! He was a professional actor! He'd done what they'd both talked and dreamed about.

She stared at his picture again, and hated Carlysle—which was stupid, because she didn't even know her. Then she read the copy through three times, folded the paper and put it in a drawer.

Later that day she approached Oliver. As usual, he was on the phone.

"Hang up," she said, standing in front of him.

He covered the mouthpiece. "What's the matter?"

"Hang up. I have to talk to you."

He excused himself and put the phone down. "I hope this is important," he said irritably.

"It is."

"Well?"

"I'm accepting."

"You're accepting what?"

"I'll be the Marcella girl."

He perked up. "Really?"

"Yes, Oliver. And I want Samm to be my agent. She'll negotiate my price."

He laughed. "*She'll* negotiate your price?"

"I'm expensive," Lauren said. "But if you want me you'll pay."

Back in New York Pia waddled around looking like she was going to drop the kid any moment. Lauren realized that if she was going to embark on this Marcella girl campaign, then it was time to think seriously about Help Unlimited.

"What do you want to do?" she asked Pia. "You're having a baby, you've got Howard to look after. Maybe we should dissolve the business."

"I *like* having the business," Pia said. "Although I suppose you're right. I won't have the time to spend there. And if you get the Marcella job, neither will you."

It was sad, but they decided the best thing to do was to close it down.

Lauren met with Samm, who was quite amused by the turn of events. "Do you realize how many of my models will want to scratch your eyes out, darling?" she said. "They'll say you used your influence with the boss."

"No, Samm—he used *his* influence with *me*. But I want a killer deal, otherwise I'm not doing it."

Samm nodded. "I like killer deals. Are you giving me permission to walk in and make the deal of the century?"

Lauren smiled. "That's *exactly* what I'm doing."

"And can I stroll casually away if they don't care to accept it?"

"I wouldn't expect you to do anything else."

"Lauren, you're my kind of girl."

Oliver came home that night with raised eyebrows. "Are you insane? You're asking for more money than a top model."

"Sweetheart, this was your idea, not mine. If Marcella would like me to represent them, then this is what they'll have to pay."

He shook his head. "I didn't realize I'd married a tough businesswoman."

"It wasn't my idea to be the Marcella girl, kindly remember that."

"I've talked with the client," Oliver said. "They have my recommendation. I've also given them several other suggestions. The final decision is theirs."

"Good," Lauren said. "Because I don't care either way."

Although deep down she did. Deep down she knew that she wanted to be somebody. Just like Nick Angel was going to be somebody. She didn't want to be left behind. She wanted to be just as important as he was destined to be.

"You need a publicist," Frances said.

"What for? I'm getting plenty of publicity. Carlysle and I are all over the columns."

"You need somebody to shape an image for you. Give you a profile—a very high profile."

"Forget it. I don't have the money."

"What did you do with the money you got for the option agreement you so foolishly signed against Meena's advice?"

He shrugged. "I had a friend in trouble. That was the deal."

"How sweet," Frances said, dragging deeply on her cigarette. "He has a kind heart."

"I always thought it was cool to help out friends," he said, throwing himself on her couch. "Isn't that the way it's supposed to work?"

"You really are a genuinely nice person," said Frances, sounding surprised.

"So I guess you've got a publicist you want to recommend," he said, reaching for a cigarette, deciding it was his turn to blow smoke in *her* face.

"You have to admit, you *do* like my recommendations," Frances replied. "Your new photographs are excellent, and Meena is doing well for you. Of course, she could do better if you hadn't tied yourself up with that ridiculous option deal."

He shrugged. "What's so ridiculous about signing for another movie? A couple of months ago I couldn't have gotten arrested. Why the big fuss?"

"Learn to understand this business," Frances said sternly. "From all reports, when *Night City* comes out you're going to be hot. When you're hot is the time to act. But since you've tied yourself up for another film, Meena cannot do anything for you."

"Yeah, Frances, but I'm not a total jerk. I don't have to do the film immediately. There's a clause in there that says I can do something else if they're not ready by a certain date. It's cool."

"So now you've decided to be your own lawyer?"

"Hey, I've been meaning to talk to you about that. Can you recommend a good lawyer?"

"There's a cocktail party tomorrow night," Frances said. "You'll take me. There'll be several top lawyers there. You can quietly audition them."

"I don't know if I can make tomorrow night."

She looked at him sharply. "Nick, I don't expect you to forget our deal so early on in our relationship."

"Okay—I'll make it," he said.

He'd only gotten back to Los Angeles the day before after nearly two months shooting in New York, and although he'd spoken to Annie on the phone he hadn't seen her. He'd promised to take her out the next night for a welcome home dinner. Now that Frances required his company he'd just have to switch nights on her.

Frances wrote down the name and phone number of a publicist and handed him the paper. "Go see her," she said.

"Another woman?"

Frances narrowed her flinty eyes. "What's the matter? Don't you like dealing with women? Believe me, dear, they'll look after you much better than men."

Like she was telling him something new.

Marik, Cyndra had decided, was too nice for his own good. He treated her like a princess. Initially she'd lured him into bed—although he didn't take much luring—to get him under her power. Now she had him where she wanted him and more besides, because not only was he producing her single, but he was also her attentive and caring companion. The trouble was she didn't want a companion. She was perfectly happy making it on her own. Being married to Reece had been enough companionship to last her a lifetime.

Marik was a California boy. He wanted her to meet his mother and sisters. She said no until she ran out of excuses, and then she accompanied him one sunny Sunday afternoon. His family lived in the Valley and they were all equally as nice as Marik.

Unfortunately, he was in love with her. She liked him, but she certainly didn't love him.

Gordon Hayworth was another matter. Every time she saw him she experienced exquisite little chills running up and down her spine, and a nervous stomach that drove her crazy. He dropped by the recording studio when she was making the demo and through the glass she spied him talking to Marik. She wanted to stop everything and go over just to be near him.

Casually she asked around. Usually the secretaries had the scam on everyone, but Gordon had no scandal attached. He was married to a beautiful ex-model and never came on to anyone else.

Gordon Hayworth had a presence and dignity she'd never observed in a man before. And she wanted him almost as much as she wanted a big career.

Marik was excited. The song he'd found for her was called "Child Baby," written by a couple of up-and-coming songwriters. He'd put together a backup ensemble that really complemented her voice, and the arrangement was a killer.

"Reno Records is behind you all the way, baby," he told her. "When this little old record hits the airwaves, people gonna find out about you big time!"

The next weekend Marik wanted to take her to Palm Springs. He was so anxious to please, she didn't want to disappoint him, even though she'd sooner not have gone.

They drove down on Friday night in his white Corvette and stayed at a small hotel set against a backdrop of magnificent mountains.

"What was the story with you and that Reece guy?" Marik asked as he unpacked his overnight bag.

"Why?" she said carefully, unfolding her clothes.

" 'Cause I'm interested. He said you were married. True or false?"

"No, we weren't married," she said quickly. "We lived together for a while. I was young and stupid—I didn't know any better."

She didn't care to tell him the truth. If he'd known she was married to Reece it may have affected their business relationship, not to mention their personal one.

Later that night they sat outside in the bubbling Jacuzzi gazing up at the stars.

"This is oh so very very nice," Marik said, stretching his legs.

"Yes, it's really pretty," she replied.

"No, baby—*you're* really pretty."

She threw her head back, her long hair trailing in the bubbling water. "So, tell me, Marik, how long have you been with Reno Records?"

"I've kinda been around Reno for five years."

"Where were you before that?"

"I put in time at a couple of the big companies. Produced some damn good artists. Then Gordon came along and offered me this job. It was a chance to do bigger and better." He laughed. "Gordon kinda stole me away."

"I expect he's good at that," she said.

His hand touched her leg. "Yeah, Gordon's a powerful personality. He's sure heavy on charisma."

"Why don't you tell me about him, he seems like an interesting guy."

"He had a small record company in New York, sold it for mucho bucks and moved out to L.A. about ten years ago. Then he started Reno, and the rest is a big success story."

"Is he married?" she asked, knowing full well that he was.

"Yeah."

"Who's his wife?"

"She was a top model but gave it all up when they married—Gordon didn't want his wife working."

"Are they happy?"

"Very happy." His hand snaked up her leg. "Hey, baby—what's with all the questions?"

"I should know who I'm working for."

"Stick with me, girl, and you don't have to know nothin'!"

He held open his arms and she moved into his bubbly softness. California was so health-conscious, she wondered if Marik had ever thought about attending a gym. He should firm up his pecs, work on those stomach muscles. She didn't want to hurt his feelings by asking.

He was a good kisser, so she leaned back and let him have his way. Marik was taking her all the way to stardom—why fight it?

Bridget Hale, Nick's new publicist, reminded him of a thinner, less cheerful Meena. What did these women have—a club? At least she seemed to know what she was doing, she'd already set him up for two interviews later in the week—one with a news service for a piece that would run throughout the country, and one with a popular entertainment weekly. He'd done a few interviews on the set and found it to be kind of a kick talking about himself.

Bridget trained him in the ways of the world. "We have to make up an interesting background for you," she said. "I don't know where you're from and I don't particularly care. We'll start from zero."

"I'm from the Midwest," he said.

"No, I don't think so. Something foreign will do. Your father was in the CIA—you were raised in China. Let me work on it."

"You gotta be kidding."

"Another point to remember—never tell them your age. Let them guess. And Hollywood loves a loner. The more mysterious you are, the better."

"How come?"

"Because when you're on the cover of *Time* we don't want some nosy journalist visiting your hometown and checking with all your old friends. If we can maintain it, mystery is the best, remember that."

"So what *do* I say when they ask me?"

"That you don't believe in pasts, only futures."

He laughed. "Sounds good to me."

"Frances and Meena are very high on you," she said. "And their praise does not come easily."

"They haven't seen me on film yet."

"Frances and Meena hear everything first. If you're good in this movie, then they're aware of it."

He knew he should visit Joy, but he also knew she'd do nothing but bitterly criticize everything he'd done, and he wasn't in the mood for that. While he was prepared to acknowledge her help in introducing him to Frances, he was not prepared to listen to her negative comments. He wanted to feel good about himself. He was finally on the road and the main thing was to enjoy it.

He'd gotten Joey out of the hospital in New York and now he was safely stashed in a drug rehab clinic somewhere in the middle of the country. As soon as Joey was through with his treatment he'd arranged for him to come straight to L.A.

In the meantime there was Annie to deal with.

They had dinner at a little restaurant near the Santa Monica Pier, and talked about what they'd both been doing. Toward the end of dinner she leaned across the table and fixed him with a penetrating stare. "Nick, am I going to move in with you?" she asked. "Is that what we're planning?"

He hadn't been planning anything of the sort, but it was obviously what she expected. He stalled for time, finally saying, "Uh, you mean you'd give up your apartment?"

She nodded. "If we're going to be together it seems only sensible. Why waste money paying rent on two places?"

The last person he'd lived with had been DeVille. Toward the end he'd felt beyond claustrophobic. "Are you sure it's what you want?" he asked, hoping she'd say no, but knowing she'd say yes.

"Very sure," she said firmly, just as he'd predicted.

He knew if he backed away she was going to start with the *I'm going to the cops* crap again. He couldn't afford to take the risk.

"If that's what you want, you should move in."

"Are you sure, Nick?"

He took her hand and squeezed it. "Yeah, 'course I am."

What a lie. He liked Annie as a friend. He didn't love her, and the last thing he wanted was to live with her.

Trailing Frances around another industry party was the same old story. However, he felt a little more secure. He'd starred in a movie and a couple of people seemed to know who he was even though the movie hadn't come out yet.

He felt even more secure when he bumped into Carlysle. He'd missed the on-the-edge excitement of being with her. This was a different Carlysle from the girl he'd known in New York. She wore a neat little dress with a Peter Pan collar and a sweet angelic smile. "This is my mother," she said, introducing him to an untidy-looking woman who practically ignored him. "Mommy, this is Nick Angel—he starred in *Night City* with me. Remember? I told you about him."

"Oh," Mommy said. "So you're Nick. I hear you've done a good job."

"I'm hoping," he said.

Carlysle did not make a pass at him. Carlysle was a different person when she was with Mommy.

After the cocktail party Frances took him to dinner. "So, you did fuck her," she said, studying the menu.

"Who?"

"Carlysle. It was all over New York."

He grinned. "I had no choice."

"A word of advice," Frances said, sipping a J&B on the rocks. "Never let your cock interfere with your career."

"I'll remember that, Frances," he said, trying to keep a straight face.

A week later Annie moved in. He hated having to share his closet. She hated the fact that the bathroom was down the hall. "I'll look for something better," he promised, although he was fond of his little place by the beach.

Six weeks later he was invited to view a rough cut of the movie. Annie and Cyndra accompanied him. He sat in the theater sweating, wondering what it was going to be like seeing himself on the screen. He'd attended a couple of days' rushes, but that was it. Meena, Frances and Bridget were in the audience. Having them there made him extra nervous. He nodded at his two producers—the woman didn't even crack a smile. Carlysle was there with her mother, looking demure.

Cyndra squeezed his hand. "This is so exciting!" she whispered.

"Yeah, almost as exciting as your record debut. When's it coming out?"

She grinned. "Two weeks. I can hardly stand it!"

"We'll celebrate," he said.

"You *bet* we will."

He wished something would come along for Annie. He knew she must be feeling left out, working at the health club watching their careers take off while she never got a break. It couldn't be much fun.

When the lights dimmed he slid down in his seat, barely able to see the screen. Carlysle got star billing. He got: INTRODUCING NICK ANGEL AS PETE.

Jesus! That was his name up on the screen. He'd actually made it —he was in a fucking movie!

The film was fast-paced, gritty and surprisingly good. At the end of the screening there was a burst of spontaneous applause. Bridget was smiling—unusual for her.

Frances came up to him. "I like the film, I like you in it."

"Lunch tomorrow," Meena said on her way out. "It's about time you met the head of the agency."

Cyndra was more excited than anybody. "Oh, God, this is so great! You're fantastic, Nick, you really are!"

Annie was more controlled. Naturally. It wasn't in her nature to get excited about anything.

The three of them went to a restaurant on the Strip, where they celebrated with double margaritas and huge steaks.

Later, at home alone with Annie, he felt like making love, but not with her, she didn't turn him on. He was only with her because he had to be—it was a sad thought.

But tomorrow was another day and he'd figure out something—maybe.

He lay awake for a long while thinking about the movie, wondering what would happen next.

Eventually he fell asleep with a smile on his face.

Lorenzo Marcella was the quintessential Italian man. Tall, exquisitely dressed in the finest Armani had to offer, proudly handsome in an aristocratic way. His dirty-blond hair was longish and lightly touched with silver at the temples. His jewelry was discreet, and solid gold of course. His car was a black Maserati—not exactly ideal for Manhattan, but he would not dream of letting down the image. He was forty-two years old and the sole heir to the family fortune. While he waited to inherit he'd been sent to America to spearhead the Marcella girl launch.

Lorenzo had no idea Lauren was married to the head of the powerful advertising agency Liberty and Charles—the very agency that was handling the Marcella account. And even if he had, it wouldn't have made any difference. "This is the girl we use," he announced, picking out Lauren's photo from a select group.

"She's expensive," Oliver said, trying to curb his amusement, for he'd known there was no contest.

"How expensive?" Lorenzo demanded.

"Very," Oliver replied, straight-faced.

"Does she represent any other product?"

"No," said Howard, sitting in on the meeting with several other Liberty and Charles executives.

Lorenzo studied Lauren's photographs one more time. "Then we sign her to an exclusive Marcella contract. I don't mind what she costs. She is the girl."

"Good," said Oliver. "I think you've made the perfect choice."

Lorenzo flashed a movie-star smile. "But of course!"

"Well, my dear," Samm said, her cat eyes gleaming. "You *are* the new Marcella girl—it's a done deal."

"You got my price?" Lauren asked.

"Yes, this was a record breaker and I am very happy indeed. Of course, as I mentioned before, most of my models will want to kill me. They'll blame me for not getting *them* the job. You're going to be a star."

Lauren laughed. It didn't seem possible. "I'll be in a lot of magazines, and my face will be around, but that hardly makes me a star, Samm."

"Just you wait," Samm said, nodding wisely. "Hollywood will come chasing after you. Didn't you once tell me you wanted to be an actress?"

"That was a long time ago."

"Well, sweetie, you're hardly ancient. How old are you now?"

"I'll soon be twenty-five."

"An old hag," Samm laughed. "I'd like to see Jimmy Cassady's face when he picks up the first magazine with you on the cover."

"Being the Marcella girl does not mean I'll be on any covers."

"Oh," Samm said acidly, "if they want you at *Vogue* you'll turn them down?"

"Yes, I told you—I'm doing this for the money."

"I'm sure Oliver can look after you very nicely."

"Yes, he can. But I prefer to be independent."

"You *do* know that Nature was up for this job, don't you?"

"How is she?"

"Living in L.A. with a producer."

"What happened to Emerson?" Lauren asked, trying to sound casual.

"According to Nature, he sent her a telegram from Japan announcing he was ending the marriage. By that time she'd moved in with her producer, so she didn't much care. Don't you read the gossip columns?"

"Actually, I don't."

"Smart girl. Who needs to fill one's mind with trivia."

Oliver, who'd been so enthusiastic at the idea of her being the Marcella girl, was now not so pleased. "Perhaps I've created a monster," he said.

"Don't be silly, Oliver."

"I know what's going to happen. I'll never see you."

"Representing Marcella will not take all my time. I've read the contract carefully. Two photo sessions a year, six public appearances and one commercial."

He shook his head. "You have no idea how much of your time they'll require."

"You were the one that got me into this in the first place."

She was confused. She hadn't wanted a career in the public eye, but now it seemed that's exactly what she was about to have. All she'd really wanted was to marry Oliver and live a happy, fulfilled life. Only this was not to be, her husband could never fulfill her. Oliver could not make love the way she expected, and whenever she raised the subject he dismissed it as though it wasn't important.

Did he really think she was going to want nothing but oral sex from him their entire married life? If the truth were known, he'd tricked her into marriage. He should have told her about the pacemaker.

Meeting Lorenzo Marcella was an experience. The only Italian man she'd ever come in contact with before was Antonio the photographer, and he was gay. Lorenzo was the complete opposite. He kissed her hand, gazed into her eyes, inundated her with white orchids and told her she was the most beautiful woman who'd ever breathed.

"You *are* my Marcella girl," he said. "You will make every woman in the world want to be you. And every man want to be with you."

She backed off, his avid attention made her edgy. "I'll do my best," she said.

"Ah, but your best is going to make me a very happy man," Lorenzo crooned, continuing to gaze into her eyes.

They were at a luncheon in her honor—arranged so she could

meet the other executives from Marcella. "Did you tell them we're married?" she whispered to Oliver.

He shook his head. "No. I imagine they'll find out soon enough."

"But he's coming on to me."

"Take no notice, my dear. Italian men come on to every woman. Whether they be six or sixty—it doesn't make any difference to them."

Obviously, Lorenzo's outrageous flirting did not bother Oliver, so she went along with it.

"I will have a wonderful party to present you to the press," Lorenzo told her. "It will not be another boring press conference. It will be a fantasy ball—and you will make a divine entrance in the middle of the party."

"I will?"

"Yes, *bellissima*. You shall introduce Marcella Cosmetics to the world as only you can. Everyone will fall in love with you—just as I have."

"You have?"

Lorenzo flashed his dazzling smile. "But of course!"

The next few months proved challenging and exciting for both Cyndra and Nick. Neither of them could really comprehend what was happening to them.

"It's like a dream come true," Cyndra said. "Can you believe it, Nick—you and me? My record's taking off and your movie's a big hit. It's incredible."

It *was* incredible. If he wasn't stuck with Annie he might have enjoyed it a lot more. He was so tired of faking his emotions, pretending to be someone he wasn't.

Annie was smothering him. Because her own career had failed to go anywhere, she leeched onto his—voicing her opinion on everything. This was exactly what he didn't need. It was enough he had Frances giving him advice, Meena handling his career and Bridget guiding him through the maze of hungry press.

He also had his producer friend anxious for him to start her next movie. He'd read the script. It was not exactly what he wanted to do. Meena said they'd try to get him out of the contract.

"How?" he'd asked.

"With the right lawyer we can do anything," she'd replied confidently.

Night City had launched his career. It was one of those low-budget films the critics loved and the public flocked to. His reviews were excellent and suddenly he was an actor people were talking about. He'd followed Bridget's advice and made up a past for himself, not revealing too much.

"Try not to smile in interviews," she'd told him. "Cultivate that moody look. Women love it."

He did as she asked. Especially with the reporter from *Satisfaction*. They ran a cover story on him that blew his mind. He was on the cover of a fucking magazine and everybody in the world was going to see it!

In the meantime, Cyndra's record was getting plenty of air play. Gordon Hayworth had financed a trip for her and Marik to visit some of the most influential disc jockeys in the country. Marik loved the idea of traveling with her, but she wasn't so thrilled. She would have preferred that it was Gordon accompanying her.

Shortly after she got back Nick took her for a long drive. It had been a while since they'd been alone and had a chance to talk privately. He drove his rented car to Paradise Cove and parked. It was a beautiful September day and they got out and strolled along the beach.

"So," he said, stopping to flip pebbles in the sea. "How you feelin', kid?"

"Sensational! What about you?"

"The agency is trying to get me out of that contract. They have another film for me to do. This time it's a big movie with an important director."

"Is it what you want, Nick?"

"Yeah, I'm doing all the things I always dreamed of."

"So am I," she said. "Thanks to you."

"Why me?"

"Because you're stuck with Annie. You've saved us both."

He shrugged. "Annie's a nice girl."

Cyndra pinned him with her eyes. "But she's not the girl for you, is she?"

"You can talk. Marik's not the guy for you—but sometimes we do stuff to make things work."

"How do you know Marik's not for me?"

"I see it in your eyes."

"Oh, thanks a lot, Nick. Am I that obvious?"

"Hey—I'm your brother. I should be able to read you, huh?"

She stopped walking and flopped down on the sand, hugging her knees to her chest. "Wait until *that* little item hits the press."

He zoomed another pebble and watched it skim across the smooth surf. "What, that I'm your brother?"

"Somebody's bound to find out."

"I've been thinking," he said, squatting on the sand beside her.

"What?"

"Now that we're both getting all this publicity, maybe it's time to go back to Bosewell."

"Really, Nick? Y'know, sometimes I wake up in the middle of the night and I get all these guilty feelings about leaving Harlan."

He nodded. "I know what you mean."

She rushed on. "I always thought I'd send for him, but it was never the right time. It would be nice to go back and let them see how well we're doing—although I'll catch hell from Aretha Mae."

He frowned. "God knows why I'd want to see Primo."

" 'Cause you wouldn't let me go by myself."

"You really think we should do it?"

"Definitely."

"Okay—so this is the plan," he said, jumping up.

"What?"

He reached out his hands and pulled her to her feet. "Now that I'm in a position to buy a car, I'm gonna get me the biggest, reddest Cadillac you've ever seen. And I'll take delivery in Kansas, then we'll drive to Bosewell. How do you like *that* image?"

She began to laugh. "With fifty copies of *Satisfaction* on the back seat so you can hand them out. Right?"

He grinned. "Hey—Bosewell's a small town, maybe they haven't heard."

"But we'll tell 'em, huh?"

"If we're goin' back we gotta do it big time."

"Right on, Nick. When shall we do it?"

"How about next weekend."

"Just the two of us?"

He nodded. "Just the two of us."

They flew to Kansas and took a cab directly to the car showroom. When Nick saw his gleaming red Cadillac it was one of the happiest moments of his life. He'd always dreamed about it, but he'd never actually thought the day would come.

The dealer handed him the keys with a shit-eating grin. "Enjoy. This little baby's gonna give you plenty of pleasure."

Nick tried to stay cool—had to keep up his image. He was getting good at it.

"Uh . . . thanks."

"Finest car on the market."

"I know."

"Liked you in *Night City*."

"Thanks."

He finally got rid of the dealer. Then he sat behind the wheel of the Cadillac with Cyndra beside him and let out a whoop of joy. "Holy shit! I got it! It's all mine! It's all fuckin' mine!"

"It's so fantastic," Cyndra said, bouncing up and down on the seat.

"Hey, get a load of the radio, look at the chrome, feel the leather. I *love* this freakin' car. I goddamn *love* it!"

She leaned across the seat and hugged him. He started the engine and switched on the radio.

"It's my record!" Cyndra screamed. "They're playing my record!"

"Shit!" he said, grinning. "This day belongs to us!"

Their plan was to drive to Bosewell, visit Aretha Mae and Harlan, take a walk around town and then drive back to L.A. Nick had estimated it would take them a couple of days, but they'd both decided they needed the break.

When he and Cyndra had first talked about visiting Bosewell he'd hoped that Joey might come with them. He'd called him up and asked. Joey said no.

He wasn't about to argue, and Cyndra was hardly disappointed. "Joey's a loser," she'd said. "He always was and he always will be."

When Joey got out of the drug rehab clinic he'd run straight back to New York. Nick had decided he'd done all he could.

Later that day they arrived in Ripley. Nick had booked them the biggest suite in the best hotel. They ordered room service and recalled old times. Then they drove around the city, and Nick detoured past the spot where the motel he'd spent his first night with Lauren was situated. The motel had been replaced with a gas station. So much for memories.

Cyndra stared out at the grimy streets. Maybe it wasn't such a good idea coming back. She was starting to remember all the bad things. What if she came face to face with Mr. Browning? Would she talk to him?

Hell, yes! She had nothing to be scared of now.

Early Saturday morning they set off for Bosewell. In the back seat of the car were stacks of Cyndra's single and piles of *Satisfaction* with Nick on the cover.

"We should've found out if *Night City* played there yet," Cyndra said, snapping open a can of 7-Up.

"Don't worry, I already did," he said, laughing. "I had somebody call—it was on a month ago."

"Where's our first stop?" she asked, sipping from the can.

"The trailer park, where else? Then we'll go to the drugstore and drive up and down Main Street."

She giggled. "Handing out records and magazines!"

"Right on!"

Suddenly she felt anxious. "Oh, Nick, I hope we've made the right move. It feels so strange being back, doesn't it?"

He glanced out the window. "It sure does. Small-town people stuck in a one-gas-station town. I bet nothing's changed."

"You're probably right."

He'd gone to the bank before he left and withdrawn a thousand dollars in cash. He planned on making an extravagant gesture and handing it to Primo. Let the asshole see what a big man his son had become.

Here, Dad, thought you might need some money.

Fuck you, Dad. Make the most of it because I'm never coming back.

He drove straight to the trailer park. They were both startled to discover it no longer existed. In its place there was now only wild brush, overgrown grass and huge mountains of garbage.

They looked at each other in surprise. "Probably moved the trailers somewhere," Nick said. "We'd better drive into town—see what we can find out."

She squeezed his arm. "Nervous?"

"Yeah. How about you?"

She nodded.

When they reached Main Street they both realized it did not look the same. The buildings were different. Everything was different. It was almost as if they were visiting an alien place.

"What the hell happened around here?" Nick said. "I don't recognize anything."

"I guess they've made a lot of improvements," Cyndra said. "Look how built up everything is."

He drove slowly down the street. "Christ! Where's the freakin' drugstore?"

"Look over there," she said, pointing. "Isn't that where Blakely's Hardware Store used to be? Now it's like one of those mini shopping malls."

He pulled into a parking space and they got out in front of a bookstore and a fast-food place—both new stores.

"Do you see anybody you know?" he asked.

She shook her head.

"Some triumphant return, huh?"

"How are we going to find anybody?"

"We'll ask."

They walked into the bookstore. "Can I help you?" said a woman with frizzy gray hair.

"Yeah, as a matter of fact you can," Nick said.

Standing on a ladder behind the woman was a girl stacking books on a shelf. She took one look and did a double take. "Oh, my goodness!" she said, almost falling off the ladder. "Aren't you . . . aren't you Nick Angel?"

"Uh . . . yeah."

"I saw *Night City*," she said excitedly. "I saw it three times!"

"I guess you enjoyed it."

She could hardly speak. "Oh, I did! I did!"

The woman was looking at him with a new respect.

"How long's this store been here?" he asked.

"Five years," she said. "Although I've only been working here for two. Can I find you a particular book? We have a very large selection."

"There was a hardware store here before. Uh . . . Blakely's Hardware. Have the Blakely brothers still got a place in town?"

The woman shrugged. "I don't know—never heard of them."

The girl stepped forward, clutching a raggedy piece of paper. Her hand was shaking. "Can I have your autograph?" she asked, staring at him as if he was Clint Eastwood.

He and Cyndra exchanged glances. "Yeah, sure," he said, self-consciously scribbling his name.

She took the scrap of paper and gazed at it in awe.

They walked out of the bookstore and stood on the sidewalk. "This is what I think we should do," he said.

"What?"

"Go see George at the gas station. He'll know everything."

They got back in the Cadillac and drove to the gas station—a familiar sight at last. There didn't seem to be anybody around, so Nick got out of the car and walked into the office. Sitting behind the desk, speaking on the phone, was Dave.

"Hey," Nick said in a loud voice. "I got a red Cadillac outside needs a lot of attention. Anyone around here care?"

Dave didn't look up but waved his hand as if to say *Don't bother me, can't you see I'm on the phone.*

"Where's George?" Nick said, speaking even louder. "Tell the old bastard to haul his lazy butt out here."

Dave covered the mouthpiece of the phone and glanced up. " 'Scuse me?"

Nick burst out laughing. "You fuckin' old fart."

Dave's mouth dropped open. "Holy cow! Nick! It's you, ain't it?"

"You bet your ass it is." He beckoned Cyndra into the office. "You remember my sister, Cyndra. You've probably heard her record on the radio."

"Sure have," Dave said, beaming widely. "Everyone's heard it. You two are famous around here."

"We are?" Nick said, getting off at the thought.

"I saw your movie. Haven't gotten so lucky with Louise in a long time."

Nick walked around the familiar office, remembering old times. "Oh, Jesus, it's good to see your ugly face," he said. "We went to the trailer park—it's gone. We drove down Main Street—everything's different. Where's the drugstore? Where's Blakely's? We come back and nothing's the same."

Dave nodded. "Since the tornado there's been a lot of changes."

"What tornado?" Cyndra asked.

Dave rubbed his chin. "You weren't here when it happened?"

Cyndra looked concerned. "When was that?"

"The big tornado of 1974. The whole town was darn near wiped out."

Cyndra stepped forward. "What are you talking about?"

"Gone. Everything gone. People killed, devastation. You must've read about it."

"Oh, Jesus," Nick said. "We didn't read anything. We didn't know —we were in Chicago."

Dave shook his head. "I'm sorry I had to be the one to tell you."

"What about my mother?" Cyndra asked, clasping her hands tightly together. "Do you know where Aretha Mae is?"

"Plenty of people left town," Dave said. "There weren't any jobs here—not until we started to rebuild."

"How about Louise?" Nick asked. "Is she okay?"

"She's doing good," Dave said. "Fact is we've managed to have us a few kids. They keep her busy."

"Hey, at least there's some good news," Nick said.

"You can say that again," Dave said, reaching for his crutches behind the rickety old desk.

Nick glanced down and saw that half of Dave's leg was missing. "Oh, jeez—what happened?"

"The tornado," Dave said matter-of-factly. "Cut my damn leg in half. One of these days I'm gonna get myself a false limb. Can't afford it now, what with the kids an' all. But I manage—doesn't bother me that much."

"How am I going to find my mother and Harlan?" Cyndra asked. "I have to find them."

Dave propelled himself around the table. "I don't know what to tell you. Maybe Louise knows—she's always in on everybody's business."

"Where is she?" Nick asked.

"Stop by the house. She's at home with the kids. It'll give her a thrill to see you. We watched your movie together. Couldn't darn believe it was you up on the screen."

"Are the Brownings still in town?" Cyndra asked.

"Yep. You know what they say—when the poor get poorer the rich get richer. He built another store, he's got two places now. They're still living in that big house. The tornado never touched them."

"Give Louise a call and tell her we're coming," Nick said.

Dave shrugged. "I would if we had a phone. Things been tough around here these last few years. Ring the doorbell and say hello— she'll be real glad to set eyes on you."

"Where's George? I'd like to say hello before we go."

"George fell victim to the big C. Died last year."

"I'm sorry, Dave. That's too bad."

"Yes, we were all sorry to see him go. He left me this piece of property, makes life a little easier."

"I'm sure it does."

Outside the gas station they sat in the Cadillac and stared at each other.

"Shit!" Nick said. "Nothing but bad news. I don't fucking believe it."

"We have to find Aretha Mae and Harlan," Cyndra said. "They must think we deserted them."

"We didn't desert them. We had no idea what happened."

"I only hope they're all right."

"Primo would've taken care of them."

"Get serious, Nick. Your old man probably ran the moment it happened."

"Yeah, you're right. But don't worry, we won't leave until we find 'em."

Louise was not the same sharp-tongued woman they'd once known. She looked twenty years older and thirty pounds heavier. She stared at Nick with saucer eyes, as if she was a fan. "OhmyGod! OhmyGod!" she kept repeating, wiping her hands on a grubby apron. A couple of whining toddlers crawled on the floor of the untidy living room and a baby cried lustily in its crib. The place was rundown and a mess. So was Louise.

"Let me make you a cup of coffee," she said, after she'd gotten over her initial shock. "I can still do that."

"I'm sorry about Dave," Nick said, shaking his head. "I never knew. We took off for Chicago—and that was the last we heard of Bosewell."

"You're lucky to have missed it. A lot of people lost everything. Fortunately, there weren't too many died, but it was an unbelievable scene, like someone dropped a big fat bomb on us."

"Who got killed?" he asked.

"Remember that girl you liked—Lauren Roberts?"

"Lauren's okay," he said quickly. "I just saw her in New York."

"No—not her, but both her parents. Her mother was carried away in her car—literally swept up into the air. It was terrible. And her father was in his office when the entire block got wiped out. He was killed instantly. So was his secretary."

Nick suddenly realized that Lauren had probably never received any of his letters. "Uh, Louise—do you remember if you handed Lauren that note I gave you the night I left town? I know it's dumb to ask after all that's gone on, but did she ever get it?"

Louise shook her head. "You've got to be joking. The drugstore was completely destroyed—nothing left except rubble. Me an' Dave —we're lucky to be alive."

"It must've been tough for you."

"It was tough for everyone," she said. "Especially Lauren. We all felt so bad for her, she took such a big loss."

"I'm trying to find my mother and brother," Cyndra said. "They lived at the trailer park."

"That was completely destroyed too," Louise said. "But I heard Aretha Mae went back to work for the Brownings." She shrugged. "Look, I wish I could tell you more. It was one big nightmare for everyone."

"What about Betty Harris—is she still in town?" Nick asked.

"You mean that acting teacher?"

"Yeah."

"If I recall, she moved to New York—even though the houses on that side of town weren't touched. People got nervous it could happen again. Trouble is, with three kids I don't get around much anymore. I used to know everything. Now I'm trapped in the house all day."

"Mommy! Mommy!" One of the toddlers tugged at her apron, his chocolate-covered face crinkling into tears. "I'm hungry!"

"I gotta feed 'em," she said apologetically. "It's been a treat to see you both. You here for long?"

"Just long enough to find Aretha Mae and Harlan," Nick said.

"Try the Brownings. I'm sure they can tell you where she is."

"Thanks, Louise." He leaned forward and kissed her warmly on the cheek.

She blushed. "You were always a nice kid, Nick. You deserve every bit of your success."

The Browning mansion looked the same as ever, although after living in L.A. it was not the palace they'd both once thought it was.

"Is it okay to walk up to the front door and ring the bell?" Cyndra asked unsurely.

"What do you wanna do—go around the back and use the service entrance?"

"I don't know, Nick. This is so strange . . ."

"What is it with you and the Browning family? Just because your mother worked for them—"

"It's more than that."

"Wanna tell me about it?"

"Not now. Maybe on the drive back to L.A."

They rang the bell and waited.

The door was opened by a plump blonde in tennis shorts with heavy thighs and a dissatisfied twist to her mouth. She stared at them, they stared at her, and then her mouth fell open and she said, "Nick Angelo," in reverent tones.

He didn't recognize her. "Do I know you?" he said politely.

She laughed gaily. "Do you *know* me? I was your first girlfriend in Bosewell. I'm Meg."

"Meg?"

"Remember *The Poseidon Adventure?* When you made me sneak you in the back without paying?"

He recognized her. It was Lauren's ex-best friend, Meg.

"What are you *doing* here?" she asked, looking flushed.

"What are *you* doing here?" he countered.

She sucked in her cheeks and stood up straighter. "I'm Mrs. Browning. Stock and I got married five years ago."

"No kidding."

She nodded. "Nick, we're all so excited by your success. The whole town's been talking about it ever since your movie played here. And, Cyndra dear, nobody can believe you're doing so well. Oh, I'm so rude leaving you standing on the doorstep. Do come in."

"We're trying to find out what happened to Cyndra's mother," he said, following her inside the house. "We heard she was working for the Brownings again."

Meg looked blank. "Cyndra's mother?"

"Aretha Mae," Cyndra said.

"Oh, yes, of course, she's your mother. Well, as far as I know, Aretha Mae went to live in Ripley, it must have been a year or so ago."

"Do you have an address for her?" Cyndra asked.

"No," Meg said. "I have no idea where she went." She turned to Nick again—far more interested in speaking to him. "You look wonderful," she gushed. "We saw *Night City* twice. Stock loved it. He's such a fan of Carlysle Mann. Is she nice? What's Hollywood like? We're both so *proud* to be your friends—we always knew you'd make it."

He couldn't believe the crap that was coming out of her mouth. Stock had hated his guts. And so had she. What a couple of major phonies.

"Is Benjamin Browning here?" Cyndra asked.

"He's in the breakfast room. Do you wish to see him?"

"Yes, maybe he can help me with the information we need."

"This is so exciting," Meg said, leading them through the hall, tugging at the back of her shorts, failing to hide ripples of cellulite.

"So you married Stock." Nick said, thinking to himself *So you married the asshole. Well, somebody had to get stuck with him—it may as well be you.*

"We have two adorable children," Meg announced proudly. "Miffy and JoJo."

"We only just heard about the tornado," Nick said. "Must've been a tough time here."

"It was terrible. You have no idea—the destruction was tragic."

491

"I heard about Lauren's parents."

"Yes, it was a terrible tragedy. She was devastated. Went to live with her aunt and uncle in Philadelphia. We lost touch a long time ago. I have no idea where she is now."

"You two were such good friends."

"We were children," Meg said. "Babies."

They all trooped into the breakfast room. Benjamin was sitting at the table drinking coffee and reading a newspaper. He looked up, startled. Cyndra was satisfied to see that he was older, grayer and fatter.

"Remember me, Mr. Browning?" she said, standing in front of him, hands on her hips. "Or should I call you Benjamin?"

He stumbled to his feet. She noticed he'd grown a thin Hitler-like mustache.

He stared at her, his mouth twitching. "What are you doing here?" he said.

"Looking for my mother. I thought you might be able to help me."

His shifty eyes darted this way and that, searching for an escape.

"You were always very close to my mother, weren't you?" Cyndra continued, watching him squirm.

He cleared his throat and shot a filthy look at Meg for letting them into his house. "Aretha Mae moved to Ripley," he said.

"Do you have an address for her?"

"I'll get it," he said.

"I recall coming to this house so many times," Cyndra called after him as he left the room. "I have so many fine memories, Mr. Browning . . . Benjamin. Don't you?"

Meg, oblivious to the tension, said, "Stock is playing tennis, but I know he'd adore to see you both. Can you come back later? We could all go out and have a drink—wouldn't that be nice?"

"We gotta get back to L.A.," Nick said. "We only came to see Cyndra's mother and my dad."

"Oh, yes, your father," Meg said.

"What about him?"

She looked embarrassed. "I really don't want to be the one to tell you."

"Tell me what?"

"He's . . . he's dead."

Nick felt absolutely nothing. He knew he should be upset, but the news didn't affect him. "How did it happen?" he asked blankly.

"The tornado," Meg replied. "I'm so sorry."

Mr. Browning returned with Aretha Mae's address written on a piece of paper.

"Why did she leave?" Cyndra wanted to know.

"I have no idea," he replied, his face an impassive mask.

"She wasn't hurt in the tornado?"

"No. Her trailer was destroyed, which is why Mrs. Browning and I took her in out of the kindness of our hearts."

"What a prince you are," Cyndra said sarcastically. "And did you take Harlan, my brother, in too?"

"He came here for a while and then went to Ripley. Your mother followed him."

"Thank you so much . . . Benjamin. C'mon, Nick, let's go."

They sat in the Cadillac and contemplated the latest information.

"Are you upset about Primo?" she asked, squeezing his hand.

"I guess I'm supposed to be . . ."

"It doesn't matter if you're not. You don't have to feel guilty."

She was right. Primo had never given a shit about him—why should he care?

But still, Primo *was* his father, and he couldn't help being affected.

"So many changes here," Cyndra murmured. "And we knew nothing."

"You know what this means," Nick said, starting the car. "Lauren never got my letters. She must've thought I ran out on her."

"It was a long time ago."

"You don't understand. *I* was mad at *her*. I thought *she* didn't care. A few months ago I saw her in New York."

"You never told me."

"I was at a dinner party with Carlysle. Lauren was catering it. She was engaged to this old rich guy—one of the guests. I tried to contact her the next day, but I was told she'd gone off to get married."

"Did you speak?"

"No, we made eye contact, an' you know what? It was like time stood still."

"Really?"

"I always loved her, and I guess I always will."

"Don't go getting romantic on me, Nick. I can't stand it."

"There'll never be another girl like Lauren."

"Listen to you—it's pure soap opera."

"Fuck you, Cyndra. I've got to find Lauren and explain what happened."

"Didn't you tell me she got married?"

"It doesn't matter—I have to see her."

"I wouldn't mention this to Annie if I were you. She might not appreciate it."

"Annie has nothing to do with this."

"I know, but be careful. Annie could rock our future."

"Don't worry. I'm more aware of it than you."

"I'm sorry, Nick."

"About what?"

"Vegas. What happened there."

"It's nothing. Everything's gonna work out just fine. Now let's go find Aretha Mae and Harlan."

Apparently it did not concern Oliver one little bit that Lorenzo Marcella was launching a kamikaze attack on his wife.

"I'm going to tell him we're married," she informed Oliver.

"Do whatever you wish, my dear. But I can assure you, it won't make any difference to the attention he pays you. Italian men are incorrigible."

"Don't you care?"

"Naturally I care. However, I trust you. You know how to handle yourself."

She didn't understand him. He refused to make love to her, and now a much younger, attractive man was all over her and it didn't appear to bother him. As a matter of fact, the more time she spent with Lorenzo the more she enjoyed his company. He was outrageously phony, but his charm was addictive. His latest plan was for her to come to Italy and visit the big Marcella factory.

"Can my husband come too?" she asked.

They were in his office on Park Avenue, only it looked more like a luxurious apartment. Sheepskin rugs on the floor, an enormous white desk, oversized couches and leopard-skin throws.

"You mention this husband all the time," Lorenzo said. "And yet I

495

have never seen him. Who is he? Tell me and I will have him killed."
He smiled.

She smiled back. "You know my husband, Lorenzo."

"I do?"

"I thought somebody would have told you by now."

"Told me what?"

"My husband is Oliver Liberty."

Lorenzo looked at her with a quizzical expression. "You are not serious?"

"Yes."

"I do not believe you."

"Why would I lie?"

"He's too old for you."

"That's rather a presumptuous thing to say."

"You are young, beautiful, vital. Oliver is—how do you say in English? Ah, yes, he is over the mountain."

"You don't have to be young in years to be vital. Oliver has a tremendous amount of energy—probably more than you and me put together."

"Ah, well," Lorenzo said, sighing. "I will simply have to steal you away from him."

She laughed. "You're incorrigible."

"But you like it."

She had to admit that she did. Lorenzo made her smile. He made her feel young and lighthearted. Living with Oliver had turned into all business.

Pia gave birth to a baby girl, a golden child they named Rosemarie. Lauren was appointed godmother. She loved going over to Pia's apartment and cradling the baby in her arms, all her maternal instincts sprung to life. The thought occurred to her—if Oliver never made love to her, how was she going to get pregnant?

As the months passed she found herself drawing away from him. If he didn't want to make love to her properly, she didn't want him to touch her at all. Whenever she tried to discuss it he walked away as if it didn't matter.

You made a mistake, Roberts.

I'm getting good at that.

One Saturday afternoon she went by herself to see *Night City*. She sat in the dark movie theater and watched Nick up on the screen. He was so good. His intensity worked for the camera. When he was in bed with Carlysle Mann she closed her eyes—she couldn't bear to watch.

Their affair was long ago and far away—and yet it seemed like yesterday. Maybe she should have taken his call the day after the Georges' dinner party. Instead of speaking to him she'd run off to the Bahamas and married Oliver. Foolish girl. She should have listened to Nick.

Too late now. Nick Angelo was a movie star, and she was about to be launched upon an unsuspecting public.

"Lorenzo wants us to go to Italy," she told Oliver.

"I can't go anywhere," he replied. "I'm in the middle of landing an important client."

"What client?"

"Riviera Champagne."

"Surely you can get away for a few days?"

"No," he said abruptly. "The owner is coming to town. It's a personal thing. Only I can talk him into switching his account to Liberty and Charles."

"Can't Howard handle it?"

"Howard is *not* me, Lauren. I'm training him, but it will take time and experience before he can pull an account from another agency the way I do."

"Do you mind if I go with Lorenzo?"

"What is this trip for?"

"He wants me to meet the other Marcella executives and visit the factory. He feels that if the campaign works in America they'll want me to spearhead the whole European campaign. I've spoken to Samm, she likes the idea and so do I. Of course, it will mean more money."

"Are you asking me what I think?"

"Yes."

"Then you should go—it's important."

"You wouldn't mind?"

"Of course not."

Screw Oliver. He honestly didn't care. He was sending her to Europe with an eligible, devastatingly attractive Italian lech.

"It's settled then," she said.

The next morning she had coffee with Pia in her apartment.

"You're going to Rome with Lorenzo?" Pia said, almost spilling her coffee.

"Oliver seems to think there's nothing wrong with it."

Pia leaped up. "Ha! Howard wouldn't let me exchange a handshake with Lorenzo Marcella! Those Italian men are lethal—especially when they look like him."

"Why?" Lauren asked casually. "Do you think he's attractive?"

"What a ridiculous question. The guy is devastating—he looks like a movie star."

It wasn't his looks that attracted Lauren, it was his attitude.

"When do your ads start appearing?" Pia asked.

"They'll be in the Christmas issues, which means they'll hit the stands at the end of November."

"Wow, that's exciting."

"Can I see the baby?" Lauren asked.

"She's sleeping."

"Why don't we wake her?"

Pia grinned. "Why not?"

The private jet was the most luxurious form of travel Lauren had ever imagined.

"It's nothing," Lorenzo said, with a sweeping wave of his hand.

His idea of nothing was a state-of-the-art cabin fitted out with stereo equipment, a kitchen, a marble bathroom and a bedroom in the back. The interior of the plane was decorated as lavishly as any penthouse apartment. It was the company plane, but Lorenzo had full use of it whenever he wanted.

"I'm sorry your husband was unable to accompany us," he said, strapping himself into the seat next to hers, not meaning a word he said.

"I'm sure you are."

"No, really, *bellissima*. I would never pay attention to another man's wife."

He could have fooled her. "Have you ever been married?" she asked.

"No, my princess, I have yet to meet the woman of my dreams. Besides, we have but one life to live—why confine oneself to the same meal every day?"

She wrinkled her nose. "You're beginning to sound like a chauvinist."

"What is a chauvinist?" he asked innocently.

"You know what I mean—comparing a woman to a meal. That's hardly very nice."

Watching her closely he said, "You are the most beautiful woman in the universe. I love it when you speak. The way your mouth moves, the way your lips quiver. Everything about you is so . . . so tempting."

"You're full of it, Lorenzo."

It was her first trip to Europe and she couldn't help being excited.

Lorenzo was amused. "I have crossed the Atlantic so many times that I have lost count," he boasted.

"Lucky you," she replied, fastening her seatbelt and tensing for takeoff. Every time she flew it made her nervous.

Lorenzo seemed totally at ease. He took her hand and turned it palm up.

"Ah . . . you, too, will be very lucky," he said, studying her palm. "I see it here."

"What, Lorenzo?"

"Did I not tell you that my grandmother was a gypsy? I read palms, I can foresee the future."

"And what do you see in my future?"

"You will be very famous, and very rich. Ah, you notice this broken line here—it means you will have a divorce."

"Lorenzo," she scolded, pulling her hand away.

"No, no, my princess, I am not joking." He took her hand again. "Maybe lots of bambinos—two, three, ah, yes, four." He frowned. "I see something else," he said, peering closely.

"What?" she asked, alarmed.

"I see they are not American babies—they are half Italian."

She began to laugh. "You're bad, you know that?"

"Ah, yes, I have been told many times. But I am not bad where it matters."

"And where's that?"

"In the bedroom."

He had seductive eyes, a thin nose and sculpted cheekbones. She liked looking at him, and so did the two stewardesses, who paid him avid attention.

After takeoff they sipped champagne, ate a delicious meal, and then Lorenzo watched a movie while she fell asleep.

He woke her gently when they were preparing to land. "Ah, *bellissima*, you were exhausted. Twenty minutes and we will be in my home country."

She struggled awake and went into the bathroom to repair her makeup and brush her hair. What had her life become? Here she was on a plane with a very attractive Italian while her husband had elected to stay behind in America. She knew she was going to be tempted. It was inevitable.

Let's see how you handle this one, Roberts.

I can do what I want.

There was a welcoming committee waiting to greet them. A small child in a long white dress rushed to present her with a bouquet of roses. She accepted it gracefully, although several of the thorns stuck into her flesh. A television crew captured every moment.

Lorenzo introduced her to several people at once. They shook her hand and kissed her on both cheeks. She was overwhelmed by all the attention.

Lorenzo rushed her out of the airport into a limo, which sped through the streets of Rome as if it was competing in a race. She hardly had a chance to view the sights. The limo deposited her at the Villa Marcella, where the guest suite was bigger than the apartment she'd lived in when she was single in New York.

"Tonight you will rest," Lorenzo said. "And tomorrow there will be a big reception gala in your honor." He put both hands on her shoulders and placed a tender kiss on each cheek. "I have things to do now. Anything you want, just ring. Tomorrow, *bellissima*."

The next few days were magical. Rome was the most beautiful city she'd ever seen. Lorenzo arranged a tour for her and she saw everything from the incredible ruins of the Coliseum to the Appian Way and all the fine buildings and monuments in between. She particularly loved the narrow cobblestone streets and colorful sidewalk cafés.

She met Lorenzo's family. His father was an older version of him and his mother was a frighteningly chic blond woman. Everybody treated her like a queen. She visited the factory and met many of the employees. Her picture was everywhere.

"They love you," Lorenzo said. "They have named you the innocent American girl."

"I'm not so innocent," she said.

"You have that special quality Grace Kelly possessed. It's very appealing to Europeans."

She'd expected him to make a pass, but Oliver was obviously right —Italian men flirted a lot, but took it no further.

On their last night in Rome he invited her to dinner at an open-air restaurant located near the bottom of the Spanish Steps. She'd expected it to be the usual group of people, but it turned out to be just the two of them.

"Tonight we enjoy the typical Italian meal," he said. "No champagne, no caviar. We have pasta, a little fish, plenty of vino—we relax."

He amused her with stories about his past and she found herself having a wonderful time. Later he invited her back to his apartment. "You will see the best view in Rome," he boasted. "Or maybe you'd prefer to go to a disco?"

"No, I'd like to see your apartment."

She knew she was treading on dangerous territory. She'd drunk too much wine and the city was so seductive, luring her to misbehave.

He held her captive with his eyes. "Are you sure, Lauren? I don't want to force you to do anything you do not wish."

501

"All I'm doing is coming back to your apartment."

He smiled. "Yes, *bellissima*, that is all." Although they both knew this was not the case.

His apartment did indeed have the best views in Rome and was furnished most luxuriously.

"Now is the time for champagne," he said. "To finish the evening."

He poured them both a glass, put Billie Holiday on the stereo and held open his arms. "Good Morning Heartache" serenaded her and for a moment she thought about Nick. Then she closed her eyes and allowed Lorenzo to sweep her into his arms. They danced slowly, their bodies pressed closely against each other.

I wonder what Oliver is doing now?

Ha! Working. What else.

You never loved him, Roberts. Why did you marry him?

That's my business.

Lorenzo's fingers pressed through the thin material of her dress. When he started to lower her zipper she didn't stop him. He peeled the dress from her shoulders and expertly unhooked her bra.

She knew she was about to be unfaithful to her husband, but somehow she couldn't stop herself.

Aretha Mae stared at Cyndra as if she'd seen a ghost.

"Mama?" Cyndra said softly, shocked at how thin and wasted her mother looked. "Mama, it's me, Cyndra."

Aretha Mae shook her head in disbelief.

"Can we come in?" Cyndra asked, standing at the door.

"Oh, girl, lookit you," Aretha Mae said, speaking in a low shaky voice. "You so pretty."

Cyndra's face lit up. "Yes, Mama, you think so? You really think so?"

"I should be spanking your ass," Aretha Mae said, recovering her composure. She peered at Nick. "And what you have to say for yourself?"

Christ! This was just like being a kid again. "It took us a while to find you," he mumbled.

"I would've left you an address if I'd known where you run off to," she said tartly—the same old Aretha Mae.

They followed her into the small room she called home. The place was cluttered with stacks of newspapers and magazines. On the mantel were two old photos of Luke, surrounded by several burnt-out candle stumps.

"What are you doing now, Mama?" Cyndra asked, running her finger along the mantel and finding thick dust.

"Don't work no more," Aretha Mae said, fiddling with the glasses hanging on a string around her neck. "Don't have to. Got me some money, 'nough to manage on."

"Is Harlan here?" Nick said, anxious to see him and get the hell out.

"What you wanna know 'bout him for?" Aretha Mae said suspiciously.

"Is he okay, Mama?" Cyndra asked. "The tornado happened after we left. We knew nothing about it—we only heard today. Were you all right?"

" 'Bout as all right as a person can be when their home gets destroyed," Aretha Mae snapped.

Cyndra sat down on the worn old couch. "If I'd known I would've come back."

Aretha Mae pursed her lips. "You did right, girl, gettin' out."

"I'm a singer now," Cyndra said proudly. "I got a record, they're playing it on the radio. And Nick's in a movie."

Aretha Mae shook her head from side to side, her expression blank. "Don't get out much," she muttered, her voice weak again.

"Maybe Harlan knows?" Cyndra said hopefully. "Where is he?"

"I don't see your brother no more," Aretha Mae said sharply.

"Isn't that why you moved to Ripley—to be close to him?"

Aretha Mae stared accusingly at them both. "Who told you those lies?" she demanded.

"Mr. Browning," Cyndra said, frightened by her mother's strange behavior.

"You saw that cracker?" Aretha Mae sneered. "Why'd you see him?"

"We had to track you somehow."

"Why'd you go near him?" Aretha Mae asked, narrowing her eyes. "You shouldn't've done that."

" 'Cause I had to find you."

"You found me, girl. Here I am."

"We heard about Primo," Nick said.

Aretha Mae began to cough, the harsh sounds racking her thin body.

Cyndra jumped to her feet. "Are you all right? Mama? You sound terrible."

"I feel fine."

"Have you seen a doctor about your cough?"

"Doctors! Ha!" Aretha Mae shrieked with crazy laughter.

"You should see one. You're too thin."

Aretha Mae frowned. "Don't go tellin' *me* what to do, girl."

Cyndra tried to put her arms around her mother. "I'm sorry I left you. I always meant to write. I know I didn't, but that doesn't mean we can't be close now, does it?"

Aretha Mae darted across the room to escape her daughter's embrace. "You always saw things your way, Cyndra. It always had to be your way or nothin'."

"That's not true," Cyndra objected.

"Oh, yes, it is."

"No, it's not."

"Where're you living?"

"We live in California. Los Angeles."

"That Hollywood place—fulla sex an' drugs an' all those bad things I read 'bout," Aretha Mae said churlishly.

Cyndra laughed. "It's not full of sex and drugs. Maybe you'll visit me one day. I'd like that."

"*I* wouldn't."

"So tell us about Harlan. Is he working?"

"You don' want nothin' t'do with him."

"Why not?"

"He got himself in trouble."

"Maybe we can help," Nick suggested.

"You don' wanna help him, oh dear me, no."

"That's our choice."

Aretha Mae glared at him. "You don' wanna help no pansy boy."

"What?"

"Pansy boy. Sells himself down on Oakley Street. Gets in a car with anybody, he does. He ain't my son no more. Luke's my son—the only one I care about. Him and Jesus."

"Jesus?" Cyndra said, glancing quickly at Nick.

"Yes, girl, Jesus. An' you better learn to repent your ways. Otherwise, Jesus gonna shut you out, an' your fancy black ass gonna burn in hell."

"Mama, I never did anything wrong."

"Oh, yes, you did wrong, girl," Aretha Mae said, her eyes burning feverishly. "Oh, yes, you led Mr. Browning on. You led him into Satan's bedroom."

"I didn't," Cyndra said, her eyes filling with tears. "You know I didn't."

Aretha Mae sat down in an old chair, wrapped her arms across her chest and rocked back and forth. "Deny all you want, but Jesus knows, Jesus sees."

Nick took Cyndra's arm. "We gotta get goin'."

"Don't *say* that, Mama," Cyndra said, pushing his hand off. "Don't say that to me."

Aretha Mae cackled. "An' the guilty shall burn in hell. An' the fire'll take out their eyes. An' a girl like you—a temptress—will be the Devil's playmate. You done things no decent person can forgive."

Cyndra was frantic. "What are you *talking* about? I didn't do anything. Benjamin Browning *raped* me—you know it."

A strange smile snaked around the corners of Aretha Mae's downturned mouth. "You sinned, girl. Mr. Browning—he be your daddy. An' you let him sin with you." Her voice rose. "You gonna burn in hell. Oh, yes, you are."

"He's not my father," Cyndra screamed angrily.

"He be your daddy for sure, girl. When you got rid of that baby you murdered your own brother. You killed Luke, too, didn't you?" She leaped up. "You killed Luke, you little whore!"

Nick grabbed Cyndra's arm again and physically dragged her out of the room. She was sobbing hysterically. He pulled her down the stairs and into the street.

"What's she talking about?" Cyndra yelled. "Nick, help me, tell me what she's saying? What's she trying to do to me?"

"Can't you see she's crazy. God knows what happened here."

"I have to see Harlan."

"Okay, okay—we'll find him."

"When?" she demanded.

"Now," he replied, pushing her into the car.

They drove to Oakley Street, parked the Cadillac and sat in it and waited. After a while Nick left her in the car and went into a nearby bar to find out what the action was.

"You can get anything you want on Oakley Street," the bartender told him. "Only ya gotta watch out—it can look like a girl, it can talk like a girl, but you're likely to find a big old surprise swingin' between its legs."

"Transvestites, sweetie," crooned a fat woman sitting at the bar downing a vodka. "This street is crawling with them. Now, why don't you sit down with me, buy me a drink and I'll tell you everything you ever wanted to know."

"Thanks. Another time," he said, hurrying back to the car. Cyndra had been crying.

"You don't wanna take any notice of Aretha Mae," he said, trying to comfort her.

Her voice was shaky. "She said Benjamin Browning was my father. Do you know what that means?"

"She doesn't know what she's talking about."

"Oh, yes, she does. She's telling the truth. I'm sure of it."

"Hey," he said flippantly. "Look on the bright side—if Benjamin's your father you can claim half his money when he drops."

"Be serious, Nick. You don't seem to understand. When I was sixteen Benjamin raped me, and my mother did nothing. He made me pregnant, and I had to have an abortion. You remember when you came to live at the trailer? I was in Kansas—getting rid of my own father's baby."

Nick decided this trip was a horrible mistake. They'd have been better off leaving Bosewell in their past, where it belonged.

By dusk the transvestites began to hit the street in full drag. Several of them cruised past the car in pairs, bending down to peer in the window.

"We're looking for Harlan," Cyndra said, talking to them in a friendly voice. "Do you know him?"

"What's wrong with me?" lisped a beefy six-footer in a long blond wig and transparent white minidress.

"You're lovely," Nick said. "But we want Harlan."

"If the bitch puts in an appearance I'll send her over," the man said, patting his wig.

"I've got a big feeling we're not gonna like this," Nick said.

"He's still my brother," Cyndra said fiercely. "And if Aretha Mae's telling the truth—you're not."

He was hurt. "Hey, Cyndra, we'll always be brother and sister. It doesn't matter who your father is."

"I know, I know," she nodded, sorry for what she'd said.

They sat in the car for a long while, watching the parade of drag queens.

"How will we recognize him?" she asked. "What if he's all dressed up? We left a little boy behind—now he's a man."

"I hate to point this out," Nick said. "But black faces aren't exactly heavy on the street."

"You're right."

Around nine o'clock Cyndra thought she spotted him.

"Are you sure?" Nick said, peering into the darkness.

"I don't know, but like you said, black faces aren't exactly common."

"Okay, whyn't I go see." He got out of the car and approached what appeared to be a black woman in a scarlet dress, feather boa and long black wig. "Harlan?" he said, edging close so as to get a better look.

"Don't you mean Harletta?" the creature shrieked.

"Harlan, it's me—it's Nick."

The creature put a finger to its chin. "Do I know you? Have I *had* you?"

"Harlan, for Christ's sake, it's Nick. Cyndra's in the car. Come talk to us."

The creature backed further into the shadows. "Harletta never goes anywhere unless she's paid handsomely."

He fumbled in his pocket and produced several bills, which he shoved at the creature. "Get in the goddamn car!"

"Oooh!" Harlan shrieked. "I love it when you talk rough."

And so that's how they found Harlan. A drugged-out street hustler. An embittered young man who'd had no chance to be anything else. They took him back to their hotel and talked to him for hours, but he showed no desire to change his life. He laughed at them.

"Come back to L.A. with us," Cyndra pleaded, practically in tears.

"My friends are here," Harlan replied, roaming restlessly around the hotel suite.

"Your friends are on the street," Nick pointed out. "Hookers and hustlers. What kind of friends are those?"

"At least they're here when I need them," Harlan sniffed, suddenly pulling off his wig and throwing it petulantly across the room. "You two ran off an' left me. You don't know what it was like after you'd gone. There was no money, no place to live. Aretha Mae had to take charity from that Benjamin Browning pig."

"Did he touch you? Did he do anything to you?" Cyndra asked.

"What do you think?" Harlan replied, his grotesquely painted lips twisting contemptuously.

"I'll kill that bastard one of these days," Cyndra said, staring blankly ahead. "I'll blow his fucking head off."

"Calm down," Nick said.

"He deserves it."

"Oh, yes," Harlan agreed. "An' I'll watch. Front-row seats, please," he added archly.

They couldn't persuade Harlan to leave with them. But he did accept some money and reluctantly promised to keep in touch. Not that either of them believed him. "We'll be lucky if we ever see him again," Nick said.

Finally they got in the red Cadillac and made the long drive home to Los Angeles.

The moment he arrived back Nick sold the car.

"I don't understand you," Annie complained. "Why would you do that? You've dreamed about owning a Cadillac all your life."

"There's a lotta things you don't understand about me, Annie," he said.

"Maybe we should try spending more time together," she suggested.

Wasn't it enough they were living together? What did she want from him?

He went out that night by himself and called Carlysle from a phone booth. "Are you with your mother?" he asked.

"She's out of town," Carlysle replied. "Why? Want to party?"

"Yes."

"Come on over."

When he arrived at her house he found she was not alone. There was another girl there, an exotic Indonesian model. The three of them ended up in the Jacuzzi playing games he'd never played in school.

He lost himself in a round of hedonistic pleasures. He needed the release. By the time he left Carlysle's house he felt better.

The next day Meena informed him they'd gotten him out of his contract for the movie with the woman producer and arranged a deal for him to star in *Life*—a big-budget movie about a young killer and his father.

"This is an excellent break, Nick," Meena said briskly. "Top director, first-class production. And here's the best news—I've doubled your money."

He wasn't as elated as he should have been. He had Lauren on his mind and somehow or other he knew he had to see her.

He went home and told Annie that he had to go to New York for two or three days.

"Can I come with you?" she asked hopefully.

"No. It's business." He kissed her on the cheek. "See you in a couple of days."

At the airport he wrote out a check for six thousand dollars and sent it to Dave. It was all the money he had in his account. But he was lucky, there was more coming in.

He made the evening flight. Soon he would get to see Lauren, one way or another. He didn't know what he'd say to her. He only knew that he had to resolve the situation. And the sooner the better.

72

Lauren was filled with guilt because she'd slept with Lorenzo. It had only happened once—the last night she was in Rome—and she had no excuse. The experience was memorable—which made her all the guiltier because she would have preferred to forget it.

Maybe I take after my father, she thought miserably. *Why should I feel guilty—he obviously never did.*

Upon their return to America, Lorenzo behaved like a perfect gentleman. She told him she regretted it had happened, it would never happen again, and would he please never refer to it.

"I respect your wishes," he'd said. "But when you get rid of your husband, I will be waiting."

Oliver suspected nothing. "How was your trip?" he asked.

"I wish you'd been with me," she said.

"Next time," he promised. "In fact, I was thinking that in the summer we might cruise the Riviera on a yacht."

"That would be nice, Oliver. Can you get the time away?"

"I'll make time."

She'd already done the photographs for the Marcella girl campaign, and now it was time to shoot the commercial. Digging down into her past she drew on her acting experience, relaxed and had fun in front of the camera. It was quite an elaborate commercial and took a week to shoot.

Lorenzo visited the set every day, still behaving like a perfect gentleman. He did nothing more than flirt with his eyes—but, oh, those Italian eyes! She remembered their one night together in Rome and her body screamed out for more. It was only her mind that kept her from doing anything about it.

You're a married woman, Lauren.

You don't have to keep reminding me.

She enjoyed making the commercial, being the center of attention. It made her feel special—like she really mattered in the scheme of things.

Now that Oliver possessed her he paid less and less attention to her. Work, as usual, came first.

She decided that if he could put work first, so could she. Over lunch with Samm she told her that if any other good modeling jobs came along she was prepared to do them.

"I thought you weren't interested in modeling," Samm remarked, sipping a glass of white wine.

She picked at a salad. "I've changed my mind."

"You won't be able to represent other products, but you can certainly do photographic work," Samm said thoughtfully. "I'll see what I can get you."

"Get me the cover of *Vogue*," Lauren said with a persuasive smile. "You know you can do anything."

Samm waved to a fashion editor, leaned back and also smiled. "My, my, aren't we getting ambitious."

"Why not? It's about time."

"By the way," Samm said. "Did you hear about Jimmy Cassady?"

"What about him?" Lauren asked coolly. As far as she was concerned he was ancient history—even hearing his name failed to bother her.

"He emerged from the closet."

"Huh?"

"Gay, my sweet. Positively festive in fact!"

So there was the answer to that little mystery.

Most weekends she spent with Pia, Howard and the baby. Sometimes they stayed in town, other times they drove to Oliver's large estate in the Hamptons, where he spent most of his time in his study on the phone—relaxing was not for him.

Sunbathing on the beach one day Pia said, "Do you realize you have three homes now? The apartment in New York, the house in the Bahamas and this house."

"They're Oliver's homes," Lauren said, enjoying the hot sun. "I never chose any of them."

"If you feel that way you should sell them and buy something else. Be nice to start fresh, wouldn't it?"

Lauren reached for the suntan oil. "I'm sure Oliver would let me do exactly what I like. He probably wouldn't even notice."

"Hmm," Pia said. "Do I detect a note of dissatisfaction?"

She rubbed the greasy oil over her legs. "You detect a note of I've married a man who never stops working."

"Ah," Pia said wisely. "That's *why* you have three houses."

"Very quick."

Pia looked thoughtful. "I think Howard's following in Oliver's footsteps," she said pensively. "He didn't come home last night until nine o'clock. Maybe he's got a mistress."

"Howard?" Lauren started to laugh. "I can't imagine Howard with a mistress."

"Why?" Pia said, quite affronted. "Don't you think he's sexy?"

"To you he's sexy—to other women he's your husband."

"Sometimes I wish we'd kept the business," Pia said wistfully. "I love Rosemarie and looking after her, but playing mommy is not my life."

"Get a job," Lauren suggested, lying back.

"I don't want to go that far. Being my own boss is one thing, but working for somebody else—no, that's not for me. Unless you'd like me as your personal assistant—I'd be very efficient."

"I'm not busy enough for an assistant," Lauren murmured, closing her eyes.

"You will be. Wait until the ads start appearing. And Samm tells me you want to start doing other work."

"I wouldn't mind."

"Nature's turned to acting, you know."

"Really?"

"Yes, she's living with this producer guy and he's put her in his movie. She's the new discovery on the block."

"That'll make her happy."

"And I read in one of the columns that Emerson Burn gets back from his world tour this week."

"You're a regular little gossipmonger."

Pia sighed enviously. "You certainly have some interesting ex's. And when you came to work at Samm's we all thought you were so quiet."

"Emerson's not an ex."

"Is Nick Angel?" Pia asked curiously. "You never speak about him. He sure was anxious to talk to *you*, though."

"I went out with Nick in high school," she said casually, like it meant nothing.

"Wow! High school—was he gorgeous then?"

"Yes," she said very quietly. "He was."

As soon as Nick arrived in New York he called Help Unlimited. The operator told him the number was no longer in service.

"Shit!" he said, slamming down the phone. He thought for a moment, then called Carlysle in L.A.

"Oh, boy!" she exclaimed. "That was some good time! I didn't realize you were so adventurous."

"Yeah, well, that makes two of us."

"Can you come over now? My friend's still here."

"I'm in New York."

"Shame."

"I need a favor."

"What?"

"You remember that dinner party you took me to when we were shooting *Night City*?"

"We went to so many places."

"The hostess had on all those crazy bracelets."

"You mean Jessie George."

"That's the one. What's her number?"

Carlysle giggled. "Oooh, Nick, isn't she a little old for you?"

"I need to ask her something."

"Wait a sec, I'll get my book."

She gave him the number and he hung up and dialed.

All he had to say was "Nick Angel," and Jessie knew exactly who he was.

"Nick, how nice to speak to you," she said. "I so enjoyed *Night City*. Memorable performance."

"Thanks."

"What can I do for you?"

"Do you have the number of Help Unlimited?"

"Unfortunately they're not in business anymore."

"They're not?"

"No. But I do have another caterer I can recommend."

"Remember that girl . . . the one who did all the cooking?"

"Do you mean Lauren?"

"Who was that guy she was about to marry?"

"Oliver Liberty. They got married in the Bahamas."

"What does he do?"

"Oliver owns the biggest ad agency in New York—Liberty and Charles."

"Can you give me his home number?"

"Certainly. By the way, I'm having a dinner party tomorrow night. I'd love you to come."

"Well, uh, I don't know . . . I'm only here for a few hours. Gotta get back to L.A."

"What a shame—Oliver and Lauren will be here."

"Maybe I don't have to get back so fast," he said quickly.

"Eight o'clock. Casual. I'm putting you on my list."

So, Lauren had actually gone ahead and married the guy. This wasn't good news. But then again, all he wanted to do was apologize, it wasn't like they were going to fall into each other's arms. A long time had passed. They were both different people now.

Yeah, sure. And what else was new?

Odile Hayworth was the most exquisite woman Cyndra had ever seen and she hated her on sight. Gordon belonged to Odile. Odile belonged to Gordon. It was patently obvious.

Marik had arranged a cozy dinner for four at a French restaurant and Cyndra was loathing every minute of it. Odile was uncommonly pretty, with amber eyes, fashionably short black hair and a wide smile. She was also at least thirty-five.

Old, Cyndra thought. Surely he needs someone younger?

"Marik tells me you used to be a model," Cyndra said politely, not that she cared.

"Yes, I was—until Gordon came along and rescued me," Odile replied, squeezing her husband's hand. He squeezed hers back.

How sweet, Cyndra thought.

"I saw her across the room at a crowded party," Gordon said. "Took one look and knew my life was over."

They all laughed.

"Hmm," Odile said, pretending to sound cross. "Your life was only just beginning, *and* you know it."

He grinned. "She's right. Before Odile I was a womanizer. After I met her I repented."

"Oh, yes, did you repent," said Odile, smiling at her husband. "Before you met me you were a *dog!*"

Marik took Cyndra's hand in his. "I kind of feel the same way myself."

This was news to her. She knew he liked her a lot, but he'd never expressed any serious intentions.

"It looks like you two are pretty cozy already," Odile said. "Do I hear moving-in-together noises?"

Gordon sipped a glass of brandy. "We like to see our artists happy. And I have some news, Cyndra, that should make you very happy indeed."

"Yes?"

"Your record broke the top forty."

She was wild with excitement. "It *did?*"

"True."

"Oh, this is so great!" She turned to Marik. "Did you know about this?"

He grinned sheepishly. "Yeah, I knew, but Gordon's the boss, he wanted to tell you himself."

"I needed some good news in my life."

"Baby, you're gonna get all the good news you can handle," Marik said.

Later they made love. She thought about Gordon at home with his pretty wife and his two little children. He'd never so much as second-glanced her. She was a recording artist—*his* recording artist, and that was all she meant to him. One of these days he'd look at her in a different fashion. One of these days he'd want her as much as she wanted him.

Cyndra knew there was no such thing as an ungettable man.

Later that night Nick dropped by to catch Joey's act. The club had not improved in his absence, nor had the lackluster hostesses.

Joey was funny. He had genuine talent—a talent he was pissing away in this joint.

"You promised you were comin' out to stay with me," Nick said.

"Hey, man, you're like a nursemaid," Joey complained. "Stop checkin' up on me."

"Tell you what—you come to L.A. an' I'll try to get you a role in my new movie."

Joey's lip curled. "Oh, big star now. You can get me a role, huh?"

"Maybe. But not if you're sitting on your ass in New York."

"I ain't sittin' on my ass, man. I'm workin' for a living."

Nick took a good look at Joey. He wasn't an expert, but he could've sworn his friend was back on drugs.

"I'm sending you a ticket," he said.

"I can buy my own ticket."

"Hey, listen—I got more money than you. Take advantage of it while you can."

"Fuck you," said Joey, grinning.

"Likewise," Nick replied.

He called Meena when he got back to the hotel. "I need a favor."

"Just tell me one thing," she said, sounding annoyed.

"What?"

"Who said you could fly to New York without telling me?"

"Am I supposed to check in?"

"No, but you *are* supposed to be in costume fittings tomorrow morning at nine a.m. sharp."

"I'll be back in forty-eight hours."

"In the future, tell me."

"Yes, Mommy."

"Hilarious, Nick," Meena said dryly. "What's the favor?"

"I got this talented friend. I'd like him to have a part in the movie."

She couldn't control her amusement. "Who do you think you are —Burt Reynolds?"

"At least get him in for a reading."

"What part did you have in mind?"

"He'd be good as the jail snitch."

"They've got someone they like."

"Make 'em see him, Meena. He's good."

"Very well, Nick, I'll try to arrange it. By the way, what *are* you doing in New York?"

"My publicist taught me one thing."

"What's that?"

"Always keep 'em guessing!"

In the morning he took a brisk walk through Central Park. A couple of girls recognized him, clutched each other and fell into fits of hysterical giggles.

Back at the hotel he called Jessie and told her he was definitely coming to her dinner.

"I'm delighted," she said. "Will you be bringing a date?"

"No, I'll be alone." He paused for a moment. "Uh, Jessie . . ."

"Yes?"

"Put Lauren next to me."

"You mean Oliver's wife?"

"Yeah. You see, Lauren and I . . . we, uh . . . we knew each other a long time ago."

"I wasn't aware of that."

"We lost touch, so it would be nice to catch up on old times. No big thing—but if you can seat her next to me I'd appreciate it."

"Of course, Nick. I look forward to seeing you."

Jessie put the phone down thoughtfully. Far be it from her to read anything into it, but it did seem rather odd that at first Nick had called to get Oliver's number and now he was requesting that Oliver's wife be seated beside him.

Oh, well, it wasn't for her to question, it was just for her to do. She had an interesting group planned, and Nick Angel would make it even more so.

If her instincts were correct it was going to be quite an evening.

Lauren had been back from her trip to Rome for five weeks when she realized something was wrong. She'd been feeling queasy for a few days, and when she checked her calendar she realized she was late. This was unusual, because she was never late.

One big thought loomed at the center of her mind—was she pregnant?

Once she'd started to think about it she couldn't stop. She went to the gym and vigorously worked out. Then she came home and sat in a hot bath for an hour. She wanted a baby, and yet it wasn't possible because Oliver had never made love to her. So, if she *was* pregnant, how was she going to explain it?

I will not have an abortion. I will not kill another baby.

What are you going to do now, Roberts?

I don't know.

See where your little jaunt in Rome got you?

Shut up! Shut the fuck up!

There was only one answer. She had to get Oliver to make love to her properly.

He arrived home from the office early for a change.

"Can we talk?" she asked, handing him a martini.

He seemed distracted. "If we're going to the Georges' tonight, I have several calls to make before we leave."

"Oliver," she said evenly. "I'm requesting a conversation. Is that too much to ask?"

"Of course not. I am merely pointing out I must make these calls before we go. Can our talk wait until later?"

"You're always tired when we come home."

"I won't be tired," he promised. "I'll make time for you."

Oh, how generous! The truth was he was beginning to get on her nerves.

She wondered if she could cancel the dinner engagement. If they didn't go she'd have Oliver to herself and maybe, just maybe . . .

You have to get it up before you can get it in, Roberts.

I told you—shut the fuck up!

The thought of calling Jessie and canceling out at this late hour was not one she relished. Jessie would throw a fit, especially as they hadn't seen her in a while.

With a sigh she realized they'd have to go.

She put on a simple black dress, brushed her hair and took extra care with her makeup. Then she stood back and surveyed her image. Since she'd been doing the Marcella girl campaign there was a certain glow about her. Oliver called it the glow of success.

She wondered if it was the glow of having great sex with Lorenzo.

Once.

Once was not enough.

She was too guilty to do it twice.

Walking into the Georges' apartment she felt as if she should head straight for the kitchen and start cooking.

Jessie had gathered together her usual interesting mix, it would not be a dull evening.

She lifted a drink from a passing waiter, and spoke briefly to one of Oliver's competitors from a rival agency.

"Congratulations," the man said, standing too close. "I've seen the Marcella ads—they're very sleek. Trust Oliver to find the face of the year and marry it."

"I'm glad you like them," she said, backing away. "You have excellent taste."

He chortled. "So does Oliver."

She had her back to the door, but she sensed somebody important entering. Turning around she was startled to see Emerson Burn. His mane of hair was longer and wilder and he had acquired an even deeper suntan. Pale beige leather pants emphasized his long legs and he wore a stylish fringed jacket. The girl with him looked about twelve.

It didn't take long before he made his way over to her. "How you doin', luv?" he said, as if they were best friends. "I 'ear you got married."

"I hear *you* got divorced," she responded coolly.

He didn't seem too concerned. "It was bound to 'appen. Nature drove me bleedin' bonkers. Crazy bird."

Lauren indicated the young girl hovering by the door. "Is that your daughter you're with—or a date?"

"Ha-ha, still a comedian."

"You always bring out my sense of humor, Emerson."

"That's not exactly what you bring out in me." He pointed at Oliver across the room. "Is that the old geezer?"

"Don't call Oliver an old geezer."

"He ain't exactly in the first flush of youth," he said, scrutinizing her. "You're lookin' pretty good. Marriage must agree with you."

"You should know. How many times have you done it now?"

"Enough to know better."

Lorenzo swept down on them. His suit was impeccable. His accent was charming. He kissed her on both cheeks. "Ah, *bellissima*, every other woman in the room pales beside you."

"Cor blimey," Emerson said. "I've 'eard a load of cobblers in me time, but this takes the cake."

"Emerson, meet Lorenzo Marcella."

"It is my pleasure," Lorenzo said, proffering a manicured hand. "I listen to your music—it brings me much delight."

"What do you do, Lorenzo?" Emerson asked.

"He owns Marcella Cosmetics," Lauren said quickly. "It's an Italian firm whose products are just about to hit the American market."

"Em." Emerson's petite young girlfriend marched determinedly over with a frown on her face and a plaintive whine in her voice. "You left me standing over there by the door. I don't know anybody here. How can you do that to me?"

"Shush, luv, there's grownups present."

"Yes," Lorenzo said, ignoring the interruption. "Lauren is the Marcella girl. Starting next month you will see her face everywhere."

"Well," Emerson said cheerfully, "it's a pretty enough face."

Shortly before dinner she began to feel queasy. She hurried into the bathroom, soaked a towel with cold water and held it to her forehead.

I'm pregnant.

How do you know?

Because I do.

Then it's your own fault.

Oh, God! How was she going to explain it to Oliver?

Sweetheart, I know we've never had proper sex, but something miraculous has happened. We've had an immaculate conception.

It didn't sound too convincing.

When she emerged from the bathroom everyone was seated. She entered the dining room and slid into her seat. Lorenzo was on her left. "Are you feeling all right?" he asked solicitously.

"Fine, thank you."

She turned to see who was seated on her other side and could not believe it.

"Hi, Lauren," said a familiar voice. "It's been a long time."

Nick.

Nick Angelo.

Her past swept over her, rendering her speechless.

Their eyes met and locked together. For a moment she couldn't catch her breath. She felt her heart pounding in her chest and she didn't know what to do. There was no escape.

"Hello, Nick," she said weakly. "This is a surprise."

"I guess we're destined to meet at Jessie's parties, huh?" he said.

"It seems that way," she replied, trying to sound as casual as he.

Oh, God! His eyes were the same piercing green. His hair still jet black and curly. He still had the indentation in the middle of his chin which drove her totally crazy.

"It's good to see you," he said, thinking that she looked more beautiful than ever.

"You too," she murmured.

They talked all the way through dinner. She never turned to her other side and Lorenzo was not pleased.

They started off with superficial talk, gradually getting more personal, until eventually he mentioned his trip back to Bosewell and that he'd heard about her parents and how sorry he was.

She nodded. "It was a frightening time."

"You do know I wrote you," he said, staring at her intently.

"No, I didn't know that."

"Yeah, many times. I guess there was nowhere for the letters to go. I also wrote you a long letter when I left town explaining why I had to leave."

"Where did you send it?"

"I left it with Louise at the drugstore. She said she never had a chance to give it to you, but I didn't know that until I went back." He continued staring into her eyes. "How're you doing?"

"Fine," she said, not knowing how she was managing to talk at all.

"So you got married," he said.

"Yes. That's my husband at the other table," she said, pointing Oliver out.

He took a good look. "I don't wanna be rude or anything, but isn't he too old for you?"

"You *are* being rude," she said, trying to breathe evenly.

He grinned. "Yeah, well, remember me? I was never Mr. Polite."

She couldn't help smiling back. Yes, she remembered him, she remembered him only too well. For a moment she got lost in his green eyes and it was all over. "I thought you didn't care," she murmured.

"I thought the same about you."

She broke the stare and grabbed her glass of wine. Her hand was shaking and she wished it wasn't, but there was nothing she could do about it. "It was a long time ago—we were both very young."

"Yeah," he agreed. "Little kids."

"Not that little."

He leaned closer. "You're so goddamn beautiful."

She gulped more wine. "Nick . . . I . . . ."

"Yes?"

"Oh . . . nothing." Desperately she tried to change the subject. "Who else did you see in Bosewell?" She held her breath, waiting for him to tell her his father was dead.

How did he die, Lauren?

You killed him.

"Saw your old friend Meg. Guess what?"

"What?" she asked breathlessly.

"She married that asshole Stock Browning."

"No! Really?"

"Are you surprised."

"Well . . . I guess they do make a perfect couple."

"Jeez! What a pompous prick he was. And you were engaged to him."

"Only by default," she said quickly.

"Don't use big words on me."

She picked up her wine glass again. "Remember the night he broke your nose?"

"Oh, yeah," he said ruefully. "Like I'm gonna forget that. You took me home with you and your parents were really thrilled."

"And in the morning we drove to Ripley."

He fixed her with another long stare. "Now *that* was memorable."

"Very," she said, returning his look.

He shook his head. "Jesus, Lauren—it seems like such a long time ago."

She turned the stem of the wine glass in her hands. "I thought about you a lot, Nick. Where did you go?"

"Chicago. Got a job in a club, ended up doing everything. Bartender, disc jockey—you name it, I did it. Then I moved to L.A."

"It must have been exciting."

"Hey, anything was exciting after Bosewell." He hesitated for a moment, then added, "Missing you wasn't."

"Did you think about me?" she asked softly.

"Every single day."

"Me too."

"There's something I need to say—"

"Lauren." Lorenzo had had enough. He jabbed her sharply in the ribs. "Introduce me to your friend."

She was shaken back to reality. "Oh, uh, this is Nick . . . Nick Angelo."

He cleared his throat. "It's Angel now."

"Of course. How could I forget." She began to giggle hysterically. "Angel. What kind of name is that?"

He grinned. "Hey—it's my professional name, don't make fun of it."

"Oh, well," she said, still giggling, "in that case—Lorenzo, meet Nick Angel. We used to go to high school together."

"We used to do a lot of things together," Nick said, catching her with his eyes.

They exchanged intimate smiles.

I love you, Nick. Nothing's changed.

Get real, Roberts. You're a married woman carrying another man's baby. You do not need any more complications.

Lorenzo did not appreciate this situation one little bit. He sensed competition and reacted fiercely. The husband was one thing—easy to deal with. But this man was a threat, and Lorenzo did not like threats.

"Recently Lauren and I were in Rome together," he said, snaking a possessive arm across her shoulders. "Ah, such a romantic city! Have you been there . . . Rick?"

"It's Nick," Lauren said quickly, moving so that she dislodged his arm.

"Whatever," Lorenzo said disdainfully.

"No," Nick said. "But I may make a movie there next year." He was lying—but screw this Italian prick who quite obviously had big eyes for Lauren.

"Gina Lollobrigida is a very good friend of mine," Lorenzo said, adjusting a perfect silk cuff.

Nick looked at him blankly. "Gina who?"

"Gina is one of the biggest movie stars in Italy. And a great beauty."

"This'll be a contemporary film," Nick said, winking at Lauren.

She pushed her chair away from the table and stood up. She was feeling queasy again.

"You look pale, *bellissima*," Lorenzo said, leaping to his feet.

"No . . . no, I'm fine. I'll be right back," she said, glancing over at the other table. Oliver was making conversation with Emerson Burn. Good. She had enough to handle with Nick and Lorenzo surrounding her.

The guest bathroom was occupied, so she made her way down the corridor to Jessie's bedroom, where she sat on the edge of the bed and attempted to think straight. It was all too much. Oliver, Emerson, Lorenzo . . . and Nick.

The only person she really cared about was Nick. In fact, she loved him just as much as she always had. He was in her heart and in her soul, but she was trapped in an impossible situation, and there was nothing she could do about it.

Nick walked in, startling her. "What's going on, Lauren?"

"Uh . . . nothing."

"Can I see you?" he asked urgently.

"You are seeing me."

His green eyes captured hers. "You know what I mean."

She knew exactly what he meant.

He walked over and stood very close, pulling her to her feet.

She was melting inside. Falling . . . falling . . . And when he began to kiss her it was like time stood perfectly still and nothing else mattered. They kissed feverishly.

His hands touched her face. "Oh God, Lauren, I missed you so much."

She managed to push him away, fighting for her life, desperately trying to gain control of the situation. "Nick, you're forgetting something. I'm married. *Very* married."

"Get a divorce."

"It's not that easy."

"We'll make it easy."

"No . . . I . . . I can't."

He kissed her again, forcing her to be silent.

She closed her eyes and she was sixteen again, and there was no more pain. She was safe with Nick, she'd always been safe with him.

He held her tightly and she felt his urgent desire pressing against her. She knew she should break their embrace, but she didn't have the strength.

"I love you, Lauren." He whispered the words she was waiting to hear. "I've always loved you."

She wasn't sixteen anymore. She was a grown woman and she could do what she liked.

How do you know he's not lying to you? It's easy for him to say he wrote you. But remember—he left you pregnant, and now you're pregnant again.

"Nick . . . I . . ."

It was too late to protest. She was just as caught up in the passion of the moment as he was.

They fell back on the bed locked in a dangerous embrace.

His hands began exploring her body beneath her clothes and she lost all sense of time and place.

"I love you, Lauren," he kept repeating like a mantra. "I love you . . . love you . . ."

A woman's voice interrupted them. "Excuse *me*."

Guiltily they broke apart.

Jessie hurried over to her dressing table, pretending she hadn't noticed what they were up to. "Lauren, Oliver is looking for you," she said casually, picking up a silver hairbrush. "Oh, and Nick, why don't you stay here for a few moments."

Lauren felt her cheeks burning. She adjusted her dress and fluffed her hair. Real life was back with a vengeance.

"Call me, I'm at the Plaza," Nick said in a low voice. "I'll wait for your call."

She nodded, knowing she wouldn't call.

It was too late to go back.

Nick Angelo was her past. It had to stay that way.

BOOK THREE

1988

74

The crowds went crazy. Totally berserk. Nick could hear them before he left the safety of his limo, screaming his name, yelling hysterically. Annie sat beside him, impassive as usual. He took another swig of Scotch from the leaded glass in his hands, put it on the carpet of the limo and said to his bodyguard, "Okay, let's go."

Igor, an enormous bald black man, said, "Yes, boss," in a feathery little voice that was at odds with his looks.

They had a routine. Igor left the limousine first and met up with his other two bodyguards who followed in a backup car. Then the three of them formed a shield around Nick, and Annie trailed behind as they made a rush for the entrance of the theater.

It was the premiere of Nick's new movie, *Hoodlum*. Press and paparazzi were lined up on either side of the red carpet, thrusting cameras at him, screaming his name. They were almost as bad as the fans.

He'd learned how to handle it. Stare straight ahead, don't look to the left or right—just keep walking, never stop.

Stardom.

It was a pisser.

The crowds tonight were unruly. They began trying to break through the barriers, struggling with the police holding them back.

He quickened his step, holding on to Annie's hand, dragging her along behind him. After all, she was his wife, it wouldn't do to lose her.

The crowd began to chant, "NICK! NICK! WE LOVE YOU! WE LOVE YOU!"

Yeah, it was all very nice, but sometimes he felt like such a phony. Who was this person they'd created? This icon? Was it really him? Was it really Nick Angelo?

They made the lobby of the theater, where he was greeted by his agent, Freddie Leon. Meena Caron no longer handled his career, he was now looked after by Freddie, the head of a rival company to Meena's—I.A.A.—International Artists Agents.

Freddie was a poker-faced man in his early forties, with cordial features and a quick bland smile. His nickname was "the Snake," because he could slither in and out of any deal. Nobody ever called him the Snake to his face.

Since Nick had been with him—which was over four years now—Freddie had guided his career to superstardom status.

Freddie gave Annie a quick peck on the cheek and then ignored her. She was Mrs. Angel. She deserved an acknowledgment, but that was about it. Stars' wives had to know how to stay in the background, look attractive and keep quiet.

Annie was not good at it. Her anger bubbled beneath the surface like a volcano about to erupt.

Freddie put his arm around Nick's shoulders and they walked into the theater together—the superagent and the superstar. The celebrity-filled audience turned to look. These two men were Hollywood royalty.

Mrs. Freddie Leon waved to Annie and they exchanged empty kisses on the cheek.

Everybody was smiling except Nick. Bridget, his original publicist, had taught him well. Moody was best. Moody worked every time.

Bridget was no longer his publicist. He was now represented by Ian Gem, a wiry P.R. dynamo with flat red hair that looked like a wig, although it was all his own.

Nick sat down in his reserved seat with Freddie on one side and

Annie on the other. He wished he'd brought his drink in with him, but that would have caused Ian to throw a fit. It wouldn't do to be seen drinking in public.

Why the hell not? He could do whatever the fuck he liked.

Carlysle Mann walked down the aisle and waved at him. She was with her new husband—a studio head with a tired expression and crinkle-cut hair. Christ! Living with Carlysle was enough to make anybody exhausted.

He and Annie rarely exchanged words anymore. Nearly seven years of a loveless marriage and they were growing more apart every day. The more famous he became, the more hostile Annie was. She would never forgive him for the career she'd never had.

He'd married Annie for two reasons: one—the anonymous body buried somewhere in the Nevada desert; two—the fact that she was pregnant. He had a daughter now—the one light of his life. She was named Lissa.

The audience settled into their seats, twisting and turning, greeting him, waving, blowing air kisses, generally brown-nosing. These were the same people who'd once ignored him. Fuck 'em. He could play the Hollywood game as well as anyone.

He'd seen the movie at least fifty times. One of the enjoyable things about making movies was the editing process. He'd gotten into that on his third movie, and now with every film he made, he liked to sit in with the editors—viewing the film frame by frame, shaping it to make it exactly what he wanted.

He knew he was only allowed to do this because he had the power. Last week he'd told Freddie that he wanted to direct.

"Whatever you want," Freddie had replied, totally unfazed.

Being a superstar meant never having aspirations you couldn't achieve.

The lights began to dim. Nick hunched his shoulders and slid down in his seat. It was all so unreal, this movie stardom shit. He'd done nothing to deserve it, and yet he was now at a height where the atmosphere was so heady he could hardly breathe.

Nick Angel, superstar. How had it all happened?

He tried to think—clear his mind. Every day there was so much going on, so many demands on his time. He never had a moment alone. Sitting in the darkened theater was a pleasure—no one to bother him, no fucking leeches clinging to his every word.

Annie fidgeted beside him. Annie who'd turned into the definitive Hollywood wife. She gave to charity—yes, Annie was extremely generous with *his* money.

This was the first time she'd seen *Hoodlum*. She hadn't gone to any of the screenings or sneak previews that gauged early audience reaction. No. Annie had told him she didn't care to sit through his latest movie more than once. Bitch! If she could find an opportunity to put him down she did.

According to Annie he'd sold out, become a movie star instead of the fine actor he could have been. *Bullshit*. What was wrong with making six million bucks a movie? He noticed she had no trouble spending it.

They'd moved three times in the past seven years. First the modest little house above Sunset with a breathtaking view of the city. Then the larger house in fashionable Pacific Palisades. And finally the Bel Air mansion.

Who needed a fucking mansion? He certainly didn't.

Annie was into decorating. She'd surrounded herself with a bunch of gay interior designers and they all had a high old time spending, spending, spending.

His name appeared on the screen and there was a ripple of applause. He didn't have to turn in a performance, they loved him anyway.

He wasn't quite sure how it had happened—he only knew it had happened fast. From modest success to cult superstardom. Three easy steps. Meena Caron had taken him the first two levels and then Freddie Leon had whisked him into the stratosphere.

The movie started and his image filled the screen. His co-star was a moody blonde with a downturned mouth and smoky eyes. They'd had an affair. It was one of the perks of being a superstar, you got to fuck whoever you wanted—and leading ladies were up for grabs.

Freddie could do the same thing if he wanted, but Freddie never availed himself. He'd once told Nick that the high he got from a great deal was far more satisfying than any transient fuck.

Lucky Freddie. He had his power-base agency, an attractive, intelligent wife who'd been his college sweetheart and a couple of well-behaved teenage kids. He had it all.

Nick did not consider himself so lucky—although some might say he was the luckiest man in the world. How many red-blooded males would love to be in his position? He was a star. He could have any woman he wanted. People laughed at his jokes. He got the best tables in restaurants. He was feted wherever he went. He was adored, worshiped and loved.

But it wasn't enough. He didn't have Lauren.

He often thought about the last time he'd seen her in New York at Jessie George's dinner party. When they were together it was like no time had passed. They'd ended up in the bedroom, about to renew their relationship when Jessie had interrupted them.

Lauren had promised to call. He'd never heard from her again. Five long gut-wrenching days he'd sat in his hotel room waiting, before he was forced to fly back to L.A. to start the new movie. When he got back he'd tried to contact her, but she refused to take his calls.

Soon after their meeting in New York, photographs of her had started appearing in all the magazines. He'd been prepared to forget her, but it wasn't possible. There she was staring out at him—that beautiful, incredible face. The Marcella girl.

Over the years she hadn't gone away. As his star had risen, so had hers. She was probably the most famous model in America now. And he was probably the most famous movie star.

But it wasn't enough. Not by a long way.

When he returned to L.A. after the New York trip Annie had been waiting as usual. He'd been considering having a talk with her, saying it wasn't working out. But he was sure if he did, she'd run straight to the police. She had him where she wanted him—and she knew it.

Annie had greeted him with unexpected news. "We're having a baby."

What did he have to lose? Lauren was married, and obviously didn't want anything to do with him, so he'd married Annie because he didn't like the idea of his baby growing up with no father.

Bridget and Meena had thrown a fit. According to them marriage was a career killer. They'd made him keep it secret for two months, until one day Annie had blurted it out to a reporter—by accident, she said, but nobody believed her.

After that she'd started getting the attention she thought she deserved. Mrs. Nick Angel got a lot more kudos than plain Annie Broderick.

Joey had finally made his way out to the Coast, and Nick kept his promise and got him a part in his movie. Joey had taken to California immediately, and Nick was so pleased that he'd made it a ritual to put Joey in every movie he made. Eventually Joey had overdosed on his minor success. Three years after coming to live in L.A. he was found dead in his girlfriend's apartment with an empty vial of crack beside him.

Nick had not blamed himself. He'd done everything he could for his friend—but drugs won. Joey's death was inevitable.

Sitting in the theater, Nick began getting that old restless feeling. Watching his face on the screen drove him crazy. Sometimes he wished the fame had never happened. Hadn't he been happier in Chicago running the bar for Q.J. and living with DeVille? No pressure then. Now there was so much fucking pressure he sometimes thought he'd explode.

He got up.

"Where are you going?" Annie hissed.

"Gotta take a leak."

He walked outside, grabbed an usher and handed him a hundred-dollar bill. "Do me a favor. Run to the liquor store and buy me a quart of Scotch. Keep the change."

"Yes, *sir*," said the kid, fully impressed.

He paced around the lobby until the usher returned with the bottle, then he went into the john and took a few solid swigs. The strong liquor burned a hole in his stomach. He hadn't eaten all day—had to keep the gaunt look, had to keep the Nick Angel image.

Peering in the mirror he wondered why it had happened to him. Yeah, sure, he looked okay, but he was certainly no Redford or Newman.

Shit! The trouble was he had everything, and yet he knew for a fact it could all vanish tomorrow.

Why wasn't he happy?

Because he was living with a woman he didn't love, and it made him feel empty inside.

He swigged enough Scotch to give him the strength to go back to his seat.

As soon as he sat down Annie smelled the liquor on his breath. "Couldn't you wait?" she said in an angry whisper.

Screw you. Get out of my life. Go to the police if you want. I've paid for burying that body a million times.

And yet at the back of his mind he knew she could ruin everything if she exposed him.

Cyndra was unconcerned, but Cyndra lived in her own world, she thought nobody could touch them.

After the movie there was the obligatory party. He didn't mingle—he didn't have to. He sat at a table with Freddie, while people trooped over to pay their respects.

"Sometimes I feel like the Godfather," Freddie joked, loving every minute of his silent authority.

"You've got the power," Nick said, gulping a glass of Scotch.

"So've you," Freddie replied, sticking to Perrier.

Nick got along with Freddie because Freddie didn't give a damn about anything except the deal. There was something likable about his steely single-mindedness.

Freddie's wife, Diana, engaged Annie in light conversation. They weren't exactly bosom buddies, but Annie was about as friendly with Diana as she was with anybody.

Annie was no social butterfly. Women didn't warm to her, because she was too critical and outspoken. She was also bitter and a bitch. She and Cyndra had stopped speaking long ago. Cyndra knew that Annie had forced him into marriage, even though he tried to deny it. "Listen, I made her pregnant," he'd explained. "I wanted to be a father to my baby." Cyndra wasn't having it.

He had to admit that he loved his little girl, she was quite a character. The only time he was really at peace were the afternoons he spent with Lissa—teaching her to swim in the pool, running around the garden with her, watching her play with her toys.

Annie always managed to spoil their times together. She'd appear at just the wrong moment and summon Lissa in for a piano lesson or a dancing class.

"Leave the kid alone," he'd say.

"I want her to have all the advantages I never had. Don't try to stop her progress."

"Fuck you, Annie."

It had become his lament. *Fuck you, Annie.*

Hoodlum was well received. The critics loved it. Right now he could do no wrong. Each movie he did received more and more praise.

"The brooding intensity of Angel's performance propels this movie to new heights," read one glowing review.

"Angel scores again! A dark performance filled with pain and bitterness as only Angel can portray it," read another.

He'd thought about taking a break, maybe visiting Hawaii with Lissa and the nanny.

Annie soon put a stop to that. "She has to go to summer school," she said. "I want her to learn Spanish."

"She's only six years old," he objected. "Give her a chance to have some fun."

Annie glared at him. "You control your career. At least let me control what happens to our child."

Over the next few months he met with the writer and director of his upcoming movie, *Miami Connection.* It was the kind of role he hadn't tackled before and he liked it a lot. A young cop who gets caught up in a drug scam, is coerced by the villains and eventually turns the tables.

The search was on for a co-star. The director wanted a big name. Freddie, who had very good instincts, suggested they go with somebody new.

"Let's discover somebody," Freddie said enthusiastically. "I'm in the mood to make a new star!"

Carlysle Mann phoned Nick and told him she wanted the part.

"It's not up to me," he said.

"You're full of shit," she said.

Ah, Carlysle . . . still as sweet as ever.

A few days later he was having lunch in the private dining room at the I.A.A. offices when Freddie picked up a magazine and threw it across the table.

"Take a look at this girl," he said. "She's the top model in the country. I've been asked to represent her. What do you think? Should we bring her out for a screen test?"

Before Nick looked at the magazine he knew who it was.

Lauren.

"Yeah," he said. "I'll test with her myself. Fly her out."

75

Lauren sat behind the desk in her Park Avenue office. The room was light and bright, furnished with sleek bird's-eye maple furniture and comfortable beige couches. On the walls were framed covers of all the top fashion and women's magazines featuring her. The Lauren Roberts image dominated. Sexy. Sweet. Thoughtful. Provocative. She could be anything the photographer required—hence her enormous success. A block of *Vogue* covers took pride of place. She'd asked Samm for one cover. She'd got it, and gone on to be their favorite cover girl for the last seven years.

Concluding a meeting, she stood up, walked around her desk and shook hands with the two men and one woman. "I like your ideas," she said. "Put everything in writing and I'll give you my decision."

"As soon as possible, I hope," said one of the men, his bull neck flushed with the thought of success.

"It's your move," Lauren replied, smiling.

"I think we can lay out a deal that'll please you."

"Good. I'll look forward to it." She ushered them from her office and closed the door. "No way," she said, turning to Pia, who sat unobtrusively in the corner.

"How come?"

" 'Cause they're a nickel-and-dime operation. I knew it was a waste of time meeting with them."

"They're offering you a lot of money for one simple exercise video."

"What do you want to bet it's all deferred payments? I'd sooner deal with legitimate people and make less money."

"In that case, why did you agree to see them?"

Lauren grinned. "To test out my gut instinct. Trust me, it's still working."

Her secretary buzzed. "Mr. Liberty on line two."

She picked up the phone. "Oliver, what can I do for you?"

It struck Pia that she talked to her husband as if they were working colleagues rather than man and wife.

"Okay," Lauren said, rather irritably. "I know. I'll be there." She put down the phone and glanced at the art deco Cartier clock on her desk. "Oliver's getting panicky. I promised I'd go to the Raleigh cocktail party. Damn! I'm running late. Do you think I have time to go home and change?"

"You look great," Pia said, and marveled at exactly how great Lauren looked. She was staggeringly beautiful, although it was no longer the innocent, somewhat naïve beauty she'd once possessed. Lauren was sleek, almost feline with her long thick chestnut hair streaked with blond, unusual tortoiseshell eyes and full sensuous lips.

At thirty she was more stunning than she'd ever been. Glossy, slick, but still with that faint vulnerability—Lauren was the face of the decade.

Sometimes Pia thought she envied her. Other times she knew she didn't. Lauren had everything, and yet she had nothing. She had an empty marriage, no children, a business empire and great fame, but she was always chasing more. She wanted to be tops at everything she did. It wasn't enough that she was one of the most sought-after models in the world, that she had lent her name to a very successful clothing line, that she had co-authored a beauty book. Now she was looking into an acting career.

"Why don't you take some time off and enjoy your success?" Pia said to her one day. "You're always in such a hurry to conquer new mountains."

"I love working," Lauren had replied. "Working is my life!"

No wonder she and Oliver got along. Twin personalities.

Her car was waiting outside her office. She had her own limo and driver—preferring not to share Oliver's. Their schedules were never in sync, so they needed separate cars.

She told her driver where to go, then reached for the day's newspapers, stacked neatly on the seat opposite her. She did not believe in wasting time, and car trips allowed her the perfect opportunity to scan the papers.

She went through the *New York Post* in record time, perused the *Wall Street Journal*, glanced at *Newsday* and stopped at a column piece in the *News*. It was a short gossip item about Nick. He'd been spotted out and about with his latest leading lady. Nothing new about that.

Hmm, if Nick Angel had screwed every woman he was linked with he'd be dead.

She put the paper down and frowned. She wished she could stop thinking about him. She wished that he would vanish. But this was not to be. Nick Angel was a superstar. He was everywhere she went.

She thought about the last time she'd seen him, in Jessie George's New York apartment and shivered. Every so often she relived that night in her head. Being in the same room with Emerson, Lorenzo and Oliver was unnerving enough—but when she'd seen Nick everything had changed. At first it had been so good to see him, so wonderful, and she'd gotten carried away with the moment. But it was only for a moment, because reality soon reminded her that she was a married woman. And not only that, she was pregnant—or at least she'd thought so at the time.

A week later she'd gotten her period. It had all been a false alarm.

"Probably the European trip threw you off schedule," her gynecologist had told her. "It often happens."

If there wasn't Oliver to consider she would have been a free person. She'd thought about calling Nick and seeing him again, but she didn't have his number in L.A.—although it would have been easy enough to find if she'd really wanted to. But did she?

She woke up one morning a few months later and realized that yes, she did. Maybe if she divorced Oliver there'd be a chance for her and Nick to be together after all.

She'd decided to use her connections, find out where he was and call him.

Before she had a chance, the papers were full of the news. Nick Angel had gotten secretly married.

With a dull feeling of hopelessness she'd known it was too late for her to do anything.

Lauren arrived at the cocktail party late. Oliver glowered at her. "It was important for me that you be here earlier," he snapped.

"I'm sorry," she replied coolly, not really sorry at all. "I was in a meeting. Surely you understand better than anyone that business comes first?"

She knew why he wanted her there. People were impressed when they found out she was his wife.

After the cocktail party there was a boring dinner with business people Oliver wished to impress. She excused herself and left early, much to his chagrin.

Back at the apartment there were several messages on her private answering machine. Two were from Lorenzo.

Ah, sweet faithful Lorenzo. He'd never given up hope, even though he was now a married man. He'd wed a beautiful eighteen-year-old Italian girl, but he still lusted after Lauren.

She called him first. "What can I do for you, Lorenzo?"

He laughed. "You know what I would like you to do for me, *bellissima*."

"Cut it out, Lorenzo. It's late, I'm tired and I'm not in the mood for your phony Italian bullshit."

"Ah, such a lady. Whatever happened to the sweet innocent girl I used to know?"

"She grew up."

"I was thinking," he said. "Would you entertain the idea of adding a line of cosmetics to your fragrance line?"

Lorenzo sure knew how to make a girl interested.

"It's a great idea—when did you come up with it?"

"Your fragrance has been so successful, the other directors and I thought it might be a good idea if we started a limited line. We would call it the Lauren Roberts Collection. You like that?"

"I like it," she said enthusiastically. "Can you stop by my office, say at noon tomorrow, and we'll discuss it?"

"But of course," he replied, pleased because he had her full attention.

She hung up the phone and smiled. The more she achieved, the better she liked it. Three years ago Marcella had financed her with her own scent collection. It had been an enormous success. To branch into makeup would be an interesting challenge.

Being a model had never been enough. She felt that her beauty was a gift and that taking advantage of it and forging a good professional career was an excellent way to handle that gift. Her business acumen she'd developed. In a way it was much more important to her than merely looking good. She wasn't going to be a model forever. She was thirty now and she had to protect her future.

There were several more messages on her answering machine. The only call she decided to return was the one from Samm. It was past eleven, but Samm was a night person.

"I'm not waking you, am I?" she asked.

"Not at all," Samm replied. "I was hoping you'd get back to me tonight."

"What's up?"

"Can you fly to Los Angeles tomorrow?"

She laughed incredulously. "No, Samm, I cannot fly to Los Angeles tomorrow. What are you talking about?"

"I'm talking about that big chance you've been waiting for."

"I've had plenty of big chances," Lauren replied. "And I'm not waiting for anything."

"Short memory," Samm said crisply. "For the last eighteen months you've been badgering me about a film career."

"And you've told me it's not something I should pursue. You said models do not make good actresses—all they do is make fools of themselves."

"Yes, Lauren, but when you talk I listen. You're very smart."

"Thanks, Samm. Coming from you I guess that's a compliment."

"Without your knowledge I've been speaking to Freddie Leon. Do you know who he is?"

"Oh, come on, I took the straw out of my hair a long time ago."

544

"Anyway, I thought if you were going to have representation in L.A. it should be the best. As you know, Freddie handles only a very few clients, and they're all top stars."

"So?"

"So, he's interested in representing *you*. He wants you to fly to L.A. tomorrow to test for the new Nick Angel movie." There was a long silence. "Lauren—are you there?"

"Yes, I'm here."

"Will you do it?"

She took a deep breath. "Yes, I'll do it."

"How many times must I tell you, Marik? I have no desire to get married."

"But, baby, baby, we're so good together."

"I know," Cyndra relented—but only a little. Marik was the sweetest man she'd ever met and she didn't want to hurt his feelings. "I don't see us married," she said.

Actually she did see them married, but it was impossible. Somewhere out there was a man named Reece Webster, and she had no idea where. All she knew was that she was legally married to him, and there was nothing she could do about it.

Or maybe there was. Lately she'd been considering confiding in Gordon. He was an important and powerful man, and now she was his important and powerful recording star. If she went to him in strict confidence, maybe he could help her.

Of course, she wouldn't tell him anything about the shooting, that was privileged information. She would just tell him she was once married to this guy who'd run out on her, and how could she get a divorce.

Over the years Gordon and she had forged a good friendship. There'd been one little glitch three years ago when she'd come right out and confessed her feelings for him. He'd sat her down and talked to her like a father. "Cyndra," he'd said, "when you find what *I* have, you never want to risk losing it. You're a beautiful and fine woman, and I love you in my own way. But Odile is my life, and nothing will ever change that."

Strangely enough she'd understood exactly what he was saying and accepted it. Since that time they'd been best friends.

Marik and she were still an item. It was better to be with one guy than fight off the lines of men that came sniffing around after she became a star.

Stardom. Nick hated it. She loved it. What a trip! She'd had eight hit singles and three mega-albums, and now she was even contemplating the offer of her own television series.

One night she and Nick had started laughing about it.

"Maybe there was something in the water at Bosewell High," he'd joked. "It's crazy that we've all made it so big. You, me and Lauren."

"What about the rest of them?" she'd asked.

"Yeah, well, you had to drink the water and *then* get out fast," he'd explained, laughing. "That's the way it works."

A year ago she'd persuaded Aretha Mae to come and live with her. The old woman was very sickly and stayed in her room all day muttering to herself.

"Are you out of your mind?" Nick had said. "What do you want her around for?"

"Because she brought me up. Because she busted her ass so I could go to school and have food on the table. And I couldn't live with myself if I didn't take care of her now."

Marik also thought she was nuts. "I hate the way that batty old lady looks at me," he complained.

"What do you mean, looks at you? She never comes out of her room."

"She spies on me from her window."

"Big deal. It shouldn't bother you."

"She's loco—and you know it."

"Yeah, but she's also my mother."

Neither she nor Nick had achieved any success with Harlan. He'd never contacted them. They weren't even sure if they had the right address anymore, but they both regularly sent money.

"One of these days," Cyndra said, "I'm gonna ride into town in a big old limo with an entourage and a couple of strong bodyguards. Then I'm gonna find Harlan, throw him in the back of my car and bring him back here."

Nick had no doubt that one day Cyndra would do it. She was strong-willed enough.

Every couple of weeks she and Nick spoke on the phone.

"Why don't you ever come by the house?" he asked.

"You know why. I try to avoid that wife of yours—she's such a bad-tempered witch."

"Lissa misses you."

"Really?"

"You know she likes seeing you."

"So bring her over to my house. Maybe she'll lure Aretha Mae out of her room."

He changed the subject. "Lauren's coming to town."

"How do you know?"

"Because she's testing for my new movie."

"I'm proud of you, Nick. How did you fix that?"

"Freddie's thinking of representing her. He suggested it."

"Oh, and you didn't exactly fight it?"

He laughed. "Nope. I guess not."

"You'd better not let Annie find out," Cyndra warned. "She'll slice your balls up and lay 'em out for the fans."

"You got a graphic way with words."

"How long is it since you've seen Lauren?"

"I look at her every day. All I have to do is pick up a magazine."

"You're not exactly out of the limelight yourself, Nick. Anyway, she's still married, isn't she?"

"Yeah."

"Then you're both perfectly safe."

"Gee, thanks. That's just what I wanted to hear."

Freddie was totally unaware that Nick and Lauren were already acquainted. He sent one of his minions to meet her at the airport, and then visited her when she was installed in a bungalow at the Beverly Hills Hotel.

He called Nick later. "I'm not usually impressed," he said. "But I have just met the most beautiful woman I've ever seen. And sweet too. And sharp. And intelligent."

"You met Lauren, huh?"

"What's with the Lauren bit?"

"Neither of us advertises the fact, but we went to high school together."

"You're kidding?"

"No, I'm not kidding."

"Then how come you didn't nail her? She's gorgeous. And you know me, Nick. I do not get enthusiastic about anybody."

This was true. Freddie rarely noticed or commented on women. Sexual chemistry was not his thing.

"Uh . . . do me a favor," Nick said. "Keep this information to yourself. I'm not sure Lauren wants people knowing. And I certainly don't think it's a good idea to spread it around."

"Why? What's the big secret about going to high school with someone?"

Nick sighed. "We did more than go to high school."

"You *did* nail her?"

It was so unlike Freddie to talk like one of the guys that he was quite shocked. "Hey, Freddie," he said sharply. "Maybe *she* nailed *me*. What's the difference? I don't answer questions like that."

Freddie didn't seem to notice his aggravation. "She's *really* beautiful, Nick."

"I know."

After he hung up he was unreasonably pissed off. What the fuck was Freddie getting interested for? Before he had a chance to think about it further, Annie buzzed him on the intercom.

"Dinner's ready," she said.

They had a cook, but recently Annie had been attending a gourmet cooking class and now, three nights a week, they were treated to her culinary concoctions.

He went downstairs, sat at the dining room table and toyed with a plateful of pumpkin ravioli.

"Don't you like it?" she asked accusingly.

"It's bitter," he replied, pushing it around the plate.

"God, I can never do anything right, can I?"

"You asked for my opinion."

"You're at home now, Nick," she said angrily. "You're not on show for the fans. You don't have to make a fuss about everything—I'm not waiting on you hand and foot, so don't expect me to."

"Annie, you know what?"

She turned on him, eyes blazing. "What?"

"Aw, shit . . . forget it."

That night he couldn't sleep. He lay in bed imagining Lauren ensconced in the Beverly Hills Hotel. What was she thinking? Was she looking forward to seeing him as much as he was looking forward to seeing her?

Annie came to bed wearing her peach peignoir. It signaled sex.

Christ! Occasionally he did it with his wife. He had to, didn't he? He never would have thought that sex could become a chore, but it was.

The next morning he was up early and out of the house before Annie awoke. Lauren was going to be testing with him. He didn't want to keep her waiting.

The studio limo picked her up at seven. She wore jeans, a sweat shirt, baseball cap, huge shades—and no makeup.

"Morning, Ms. Roberts," the driver greeted her, checking her out in the rearview mirror. He was young and good-looking, standard Hollywood fare. "It's a clear day today. No smog."

"That's nice," she said.

"Unusual," he said.

Damn, he wanted conversation and she wasn't in the mood. Once she would have humored him, been polite, chatted all the way to the studio even though she didn't want to. Now she was a different Lauren, no longer into pleasing everyone. She raised the privacy glass, cutting him off in midsentence.

Pia had wanted to come with her, but she'd said no, this was one trip she had to make by herself. This trip was a test. She was all grown up and she wasn't about to turn to mush when she saw Nick again.

Arriving at the studio she was hustled straight through to makeup. "I have my own ideas," she said to the makeup artist.

"Fine with me," the girl said. "I'll do whatever you want."

"I see this character as tough-looking, yet with a vulnerable streak. Smoky eyes, natural eyebrows, not much lipstick."

"Sounds good," the girl said.

Lauren had studied the script on the plane. As usual, the female role was somewhat passive, but if she got the part she had lots of ideas.

"I heard a rumor that Nick Angel is coming in to test with you himself," the girl said in a reverential tone.

Lauren wasn't surprised. She'd known he'd be around. Well, she was prepared. They were both married now—they were even.

"He's a nice guy," the makeup girl went on. "His wife's a real pain, though. She doesn't visit the set often, but when she does—oh boy, run for the hills. You'd think she was royalty."

"Is she an actress?" Lauren asked.

"From what I hear she tried to be and never made it."

"Oh," Lauren said. She'd seen pictures of Nick with his wife. She wasn't the woman she'd imagined he'd marry.

I am not tingling with anticipation, she told herself sternly. *When I see him I will not fall to pieces like I did last time. I'm a different person now. I've finally grown up. It's been a long time.*

Yes, Roberts?

Yes.

They met on the set, so there was no time to get personal, as they were surrounded by people.

"Hey, congratulations on all your success," Nick said, a polite but friendly stranger. "It's really great to see you again."

"You too, Nick. You're amazing. I can't believe your career."

He smiled. "I know—it's good, huh?"

She smiled back. "Very good."

He peered at her closely. "Now, let me see—there's something different about you."

She grimaced. "Yeah, wrinkles—I'm older."

"You—*never.*"

"Thank you."

The director came over to introduce himself, and ask her if she was comfortable with the scene. She assured him she was. "I've studied the script. I understand this character."

"Good," said the director, moving off to confer with the cameraman.

"Freddie Leon's very high on you," Nick said, impressed with the way she handled herself. "He thinks you could be big."

"I'm glad I have the opportunity to test for this movie. You know I always loved acting."

He nodded, remembering Betty and their acting class in Bosewell. "This sure takes me back. Remember *Cat on a Hot Tin Roof?*"

She smiled. "How could I ever forget it?"

"You were the actress then," he admitted. "I was the amateur."

"And now it's the other way around."

"Hey, don't knock it—you're just as famous as I am."

She nodded. "It's funny, isn't it?"

"Yeah. Cyndra and I were talking about it the other night. We decided there must have been something in the water at Bosewell High."

"In that case—"

"I know what you're gonna say," he interrupted, laughing. "So what happened with Stock an' Meg and all the rest of 'em? The scam is this—you had to drink the water, *then* get out of town."

They were both quiet for a moment before she continued their conversation. "Congratulations, Nick," she said. "I haven't seen you since you got married. I understand you have a child."

"Yeah. Lissa's a little beauty."

For one painful moment Lauren thought about the baby she'd aborted. Nick's baby. She'd never told him. She'd never told him about what happened between her and his father, either. It was better that way.

The director returned and asked if they were ready.

"Let's do it," Nick said. "Let's make it as good as old times." He looked at her. "Right, Lauren?"

She took a deep breath. "Right, Nick."

He made sure the scene went smoothly, filling her in on camera angles, lighting and the best way to play to the camera. "It's different than working in the theater," he explained. "You play it down instead of up. The camera catches everything."

He obviously hadn't seen her commercials. She knew exactly what she was doing.

When they played the scene, he gave it to her—wanting her to get the role. They were finished before lunch. "Okay," he said. "I'm buying."

"No, Freddie Leon is," she replied quickly. "He's sending a car for me."

Nick felt a stab of jealousy. What the fuck was Freddie up to? "Am I invited?" he asked lightly, walking her back to her dressing room.

She shrugged. "I don't know—you'd better ask Freddie."

"Hey—I don't have to ask, he's my agent." He paused for a moment. "You don't *mind* if I come, do you?"

She stopped at the door to her dressing room. "Not at all."

"I'll have someone call Freddie and tell him I'll bring you to the restaurant. Why don't I meet you here in fifteen minutes?"

As soon as he left she rushed to the mirror, staring at her reflection.

Nothing had changed. Absolutely nothing. She was still as hooked as she'd ever been.

Tough luck, Roberts.

Screw you.

Freddie dominated lunch. He was charming, funny and completely unlike himself. They ate at Le Dome on Sunset, sitting at a round table in the back room. Nick settled back and watched Lauren in action. She was different, he decided. More sophisticated, stylish and definitely more worldly. But underneath the gloss he knew there was still the same sweet Lauren he'd fallen in love with.

"You know," Freddie said with his new charming smile. "This lunch was for me to persuade Lauren to become an I.A.A. client. I guess I can't do that with you sitting in on the meeting, Nick."

"You're doing a pretty good job," he replied, determined to stick around.

Lauren sipped a glass of Perrier, well aware of the interaction between the two men. "It's so good to see you again, Nick," she said, as if they were nothing more than polite strangers. "And meeting you, Freddie, is a pleasure."

He wanted to touch her so badly he didn't know how he controlled himself. And he wanted to smash his best friend, Freddie Leon, in the face.

Eventually Freddie left the table to go to the john.

Nick waited until Freddie was out of sight and leaned across the table. "Can we have dinner tonight?"

She kept her voice even. "I'm planning on taking the late flight back to New York."

"You just got here," he pointed out.

"I know, but I have an important meeting tomorrow morning. Marcella has offered me a deal to start my own cosmetics line."

"Oh, like you're not busy enough?"

She was immediately defensive. "How do you know how busy I am?"

"I read the papers. You're always in the New York columns doing this and that."

"I read the papers too, Nick," she replied, staring straight at him. "You're always in the paper, screwing this and that."

He laughed. "Nice talk."

"How's your marriage?" she couldn't help asking.

"How's yours?" he countered.

Their eyes met and there was a long moment of silent intimacy.

Freddie bounced back to the table. "Lauren," he said, "I know you're not making any decisions today, but I'll be in New York next week, so why don't we have dinner and talk about it then?"

Why don't we have dinner and talk about it then? Nick couldn't believe what he was hearing. This was Freddie—faithful Freddie. Freddie Leon with a definite hard-on.

"I'd like that," Lauren said. "Do you get to New York often?"

"Only when it's important," Freddie replied, homing in on her.

"Are you taking Diana?" Nick interjected.

Freddie shot him an annoyed look. "No."

"Who's Diana?" Lauren asked.

"Freddie's wife," Nick replied. "Terrific woman. They've got a couple of great kids. You should meet the family."

Freddie continued to glare at him. Lauren looked from one to the other. She knew exactly what was going on and it amused her.

Freddie signed the check, and they got up to leave. "I'll drop Lauren back at her hotel," he said.

"That's okay," Nick said. "I'll take care of her."

"As a matter of fact," Lauren said, "I'm not going to my hotel. I thought I'd stop by Neiman's and do some shopping—I never get time in New York."

"My offices are right there," Freddie said. "Maybe you'd like to come up and meet some of the other agents."

"Not today. Perhaps next time."

"Yeah, stop hustling her, Freddie," Nick said. "She hasn't signed with you yet."

"She will. Won't you, Lauren?"

She smiled her dazzling smile. "I'll have to see."

Lauren walked around Neiman Marcus in a daze. She hadn't seen Nick in seven years, and yet he had this incredible effect on her. She was still the same stupid wreck.

What kind of hold did he have over her?

What kind of hold did she want him to have?

She sighed. They were both married. It was an impossible situation.

She wandered through the designer collections—tried on a Donna Karan jacket, picked out a couple of Armanis and charged it all to her American Express. Shopping was not her thing, but it was better than going back to her hotel and sitting there until she had to leave for the airport.

"Hey—"

She turned around, startled. It was Nick. "What are you doing here?" she asked, her heart pounding uncontrollably.

"I'm taking my fucking life in my hands," he said.

"What do you mean?"

"I don't travel anywhere without bodyguards. I'll get mobbed in here."

She laughed. "Oh, come on, nobody's taking any notice of you. This is Beverly Hills, they're used to movie stars."

A saleswoman rushed up to him. "Can I have your autograph for my daughter?" she gushed. "She loves you. She sees every movie you're in."

He shot Lauren a triumphant look.

"And you're the Marcella girl, aren't you?" the woman continued, turning to Lauren. "My daughter loves you, too. Oh, this is so thrilling!"

They both signed the piece of paper she proffered, and then Nick took Lauren's shopping bags and said, "Let's go, we're getting out of here. Walk swiftly and don't make eye contact."

She giggled. "You sound like the CIA."

He took her hand and she found herself beginning to melt.

The valet had his car waiting outside. Nick slipped him a twenty.

"Get in, fasten your seatbelt—we're gonna talk whether you like it or not."

"I told you," she protested, knowing it was useless. "I have a plane to catch."

"I'll see that you do."

She got into the passenger seat of his red Ferrari. "I thought a Cadillac was the car of your dreams," she said, remembering how he used to talk about it all the time.

"It was—but the dream turned into a nightmare."

"Oh, not so patriotic anymore?"

"You could say that." He revved the engine and zoomed off down the street.

"Where are we going?" she asked.

"To the beach. I have a house there."

"Of course you do," she said dryly.

They didn't talk in the car. He put on a Van Morrison tape and concentrated on his driving. She stared straight ahead as they sped down Wilshire on their way to the Pacific Coast Highway.

It took twenty minutes before he made a dangerous left turn into a winding driveway, pulling up outside a shuttered house. "This is my retreat," he said. "The only place I get any privacy."

"How do you know your wife's not here?"

" 'Cause she doesn't know about this house. I bought it without her. I needed somewhere that's all mine. A place that's not filled with servants, ringing telephones and people driving me crazy."

"You don't sound too happy," she said, as he helped her from the car.

"Hey—I got a lotta demands in my life, don't you?"

"Yes, but I love every one of them."

"That's because you've turned into a workaholic. Can't pick up a magazine without seeing you."

"Can't go to the movies without seeing you."

They both began to laugh, breaking the tension.

He pulled out a key, opened the massive door and she entered paradise. The house was located on top of a bluff with full-length windows overlooking the ocean. Perched on the edge of the grounds was an infinity swimming pool—creating the optical illusion of disappearing into the sea, even though it was hundreds of feet above it.

"This is absolutely breathtaking," she said, as they strolled outside.

He placed his hands on her shoulders, turning her toward him. "You never called me in New York. I sat in that fucking hotel room for five days waiting."

"I would have, if I'd thought we could be together."

"Why *can't* we be together?" he said urgently. "Let's cut out the shit. You know as well as I do it's what we both want."

"Nick, be serious. I'm still married, and now you're married too."

"Are you happy, Lauren?" he asked, staring at her.

"No," she replied, getting lost in his green eyes. "But what's that got to do with anything?"

"How about this for a plan," he said. "We could both get divorced."

She shook her head. "You make it sound so simple. Life isn't like that."

"Life's what you make it, Lauren. We've both worked hard, why *can't* we be together?"

"Are you suggesting I go home, say, 'Hey, Oliver, I went to L.A., met this old friend of mine and I've decided to divorce you.' You think he'll accept that? And what about you? What'll you say to your wife? 'Hey—Lauren's back. Goodbye.' She's the mother of your child, Nick. You have responsibilities."

He refused to take no for an answer. "If we really wanted to we could work it out."

She shook her head again, trying desperately to stay cool. "I don't know if I want to, Nick. What kind of a life would we have together?

You're this big movie star, and I work all the time. We'd never see each other."

"Why are you making it so difficult?"

"I'm not. We're two different people. This isn't Bosewell, we're not kids."

He kissed her, taking her by surprise.

She didn't fight it. They stood quietly on the terrace entwined in each other's arms, their lips pressed closely together.

"I love you," he said very quietly, drawing back. "I always have and I always will. Nothing's gonna change that."

She felt weak. "Don't say it, Nick."

"I have to, because it's the truth."

They began to kiss again. Feebly she attempted to pull away. "I must get back, my plane . . ."

"I don't give a shit about your plane. You're staying here tonight. We'll have a night together neither of us will ever forget."

Oh, yes, that's what I want. That's what I really want. "Nick . . . you don't understand. I can't . . ."

"Hey, Lauren—this is the way it's gonna be," he said forcefully.

She continued to fight it. "I don't know . . ."

He still wasn't taking no for an answer. "Well, I do."

His lips were on hers again and all was lost.

She'd promised herself that after the pregnancy scare with Lorenzo she'd never cheat on Oliver again. But this was her life and she had to live it. Damn the consequences. Nick was right. They deserved one magical night together.

Nick awoke first. Rolling over he stared at Lauren asleep beside him. Jesus! She was the most perfect, most beautiful woman in the world—everything he remembered and more.

He got out of bed, moving quietly so as not to disturb her. He'd known when he purchased this house it would come in useful one day. The only person who knew about it was Freddie—he'd arranged the deal and paid for it with money Annie was unaware of.

Christ! Annie. He hadn't phoned her—she'd be freaking out. She'd probably called the police by now and reported him missing. He could just imagine the headlines. NICK ANGEL VANISHES. WIFE INHERITS EVERYTHING. Oh, yes, Annie would love that. She'd finally be the center of attention. Maybe it would even kick-start her acting career.

He knew he wasn't being fair, it wasn't Annie's fault she was a pain in the ass. It was just that the guilt of what they'd done in Vegas weighed heavily on all of them.

He padded barefoot and naked into the kitchen. There was nothing in the fridge except champagne and 7-Up. He opened the cabinet and found a can of orange juice. Then he picked up the phone and called home.

Annie answered with a terse "Yes?"

"It's me."

"Where are you?"

"I'm at a friend's."

"Oh?" she said icily. "And what friend is that?"

"Don't question me, Annie," he warned.

"Then don't treat me like a fool. You're with a woman, aren't you?"

"Hey—wherever I am and whoever I'm with, I'm letting you know I'm okay and I'll be home later."

"Maybe you shouldn't bother coming home."

"Is that a threat, Annie?"

"I don't appreciate being treated like nothing."

"We gotta talk," he said.

"Maybe *I* should have talked a few years ago."

He knew exactly what she meant and it was time they got it out in the open, but not now, not on the telephone. "I'll be home later," he said.

She slammed the phone down.

He took a deep breath. There was no way she was going to ruin his day. Swigging orange juice from the can he realized it was the first morning in a long time that he hadn't wanted to add vodka to it.

Back in the bedroom Lauren was still asleep. He sat on the bed and stared at her. She was naked, covered only by a thin silk sheet. Her skin was smooth and white and very soft. He ran his fingers across the tips of her breasts. She sighed and made little groaning noises. Slowly she opened her eyes. "I thought this was all a dream," she murmured, stretching luxuriously.

"We actually got to spend the night together," he said. "First time we did that."

She sat up, hugging the sheet to her chest. "Oh, God! I missed my plane."

"I love you," he said, stroking her arm.

She tried to sound firm. "Nick, this is hopeless."

"What's hopeless? I'll speak to Annie, you'll talk to Oliver. We'll work it out, Lauren. We've waited long enough."

She sighed. "You make it all sound so easy."

"It *can* be easy, if it's what we both want."

"I'm not so sure."

"You're wrong."

"It's more complicated than you think, Nick. We're not two unknown people. The press will be after us, watching our every move.
Everything we do will be public knowledge."

"So what else is new?"

"It's not just you—now you have a child to consider. What about
her?"

"Trust me, Lauren. We'll work it out."

She sighed again, completely hooked—he had some kind of hypnotic power over her. She was too weak to resist, and what's more,
she didn't want to. His love embraced her and she wanted more.

"If you say so," she murmured.

"I say so," he said, cradling her in his arms and kissing her very
very slowly. "I want you to know that last night was the most incredible night of my life. And you are the most incredible woman."

"Last night I should have been on a plane," she said ruefully.

"But you weren't. You were in bed with me where you belong—
and you have to admit it was the greatest."

Why was it that every time she was with him her heart started to
race and her body tingled? Yes, he was right, it was the greatest and
she couldn't deny it. Together they had something very special.

They continued to kiss, slowly at first, but more heatedly as his
hands began to explore her body.

She craved his touch. He electrified her. Sex with Lorenzo had
been pleasurable. Sex with Nick was beyond anything she'd ever
known. He took her to new heights and then back again.

Eventually they made love fast and passionately. He teased her—
taking her almost there and then making her wait until she begged for
more.

"Tell me what I want to hear," he said urgently. "Tell me—I want
to hear you say it."

She couldn't stop herself. "I love you, Nick. I always have."

It was noon before they even thought about getting dressed.

"I've got to go," she said, reaching for her clothes.

"Why?"

"Because I have to get back."

"Do you want to?"

561

She touched his chin. "Silly question."

Before he could convince her not to, she called the airline and booked another flight.

"We'll stop by your hotel, pick up your bags and I'll drive you to the airport," he said. "Maybe I should come with you."

"Oh? You'll sit there while I tell Oliver? That'll be very helpful."

"You're right," he agreed. "I'll take care of things here, and we'll talk tomorrow. It won't be like last time."

"No?"

"We're going to be together."

"Do you think so?"

He bent to kiss her again. "I *know* so."

She flew back to New York filled with confusion. The last forty-eight hours seemed like a dream. She'd come out to California so full of confidence, knowing she could handle any situation, especially Nick Angel.

But no, it was not to be. Once she was with him all her resolve failed, and having spent the night in his arms she knew there was no going back. It was time to tell Oliver their marriage was over. And when she was free, if Nick was able to extricate himself from *his* marriage, they would be together. It was truly their destiny.

Halfway to New York she realized she hadn't called anyone to tell them she was arriving a day late. Knowing Oliver, he'd be too busy to notice, but Lorenzo was probably furious she'd missed their meeting. She'd called her driver from LAX and told him to be at the airport. Her plan was to go straight to the office, reschedule her meeting with Lorenzo and then tell Oliver they had to talk.

It was raining in New York, the skies were black and heavy with thunder.

"Pia Liberty would like you to phone her as soon as you arrive," her driver informed her.

She picked up the car phone. "Hi, Pia. I'm back."

Pia sounded distraught. "Oh, Lauren, thank God! I've been trying to reach you."

"What's the matter?" she asked anxiously.

"It's Oliver. Last night he had a massive heart attack."

"Oh God, no!"

"Go straight to New York Hospital, Lauren. Come quickly."

"As far as I'm concerned," Freddie Leon said, "she's got the part. You want her, don't you?"

"Ask a stupid question . . ." said Nick.

"The studio people ran her test early this morning—they love her. In fact they're ready to make an offer." He paused. "And guess what?"

"What?"

Freddie looked pleased with himself. "I'll negotiate her deal."

Nick reached for a cigarette. "I've never seen you so interested in a woman."

"Me? Interested?" Freddie said casually. "I'm a happily married man."

"Yeah, yeah, just like all the rest of 'em."

"What is it between you and her, Nick?" Freddie asked curiously. "I sense there's more to this."

"I told you," Nick replied, speaking slowly. "We're old friends."

"So if I *was* interested . . ."

"Forget it," he said sharply.

Freddie nodded knowingly. "That's what I thought."

Nick had stopped by to see Freddie on his way home because he wasn't ready to face Annie. He had a feeling he should talk to his lawyer first, fill him in on all the facts. But no, surely Annie wasn't going to come up with the same old threat? And if she did—would they ever find the body in the desert? It must have decomposed by now, nobody would be able to identify the man. And how could they pin it on him anyway?

When he finally got home the housekeeper handed him a note from Annie.

"Mrs. Angel and Lissa have gone away for a few days," she informed him.

"Where to?" he asked, aggravated.

"Mrs. Angel didn't say."

He was pissed. Annie had known he wanted to talk to her, she'd done this purposely. And how dare she take Lissa without telling him where they were going.

Angrily he walked into his study, threw himself into the leather chair behind his desk and ripped open her letter.

Dear Nick,

I refuse to be humiliated in this fashion. It is common knowledge in Hollywood that you sleep with whores. I do not intend to be made a laughing stock. If your behavior continues, I will take Lissa and you will never see your child again.

You should also remember the information I have. Information that has been a burden for me to keep all these years and would be a great relief for me to reveal to the authorities.

I like being Mrs. Angel and I plan to remain Mrs. Angel, so I suggest that if you continue to whore around you be more discreet. Remember what is at stake.

Your loving wife,
Annie

He read the letter twice and couldn't believe it. Bitch! Blackmailing bitch! She wasn't going to quit until they were both dead.

He picked up the phone and called his lawyer. "Kirk, I need to see you. Can you drop by the house this afternoon?"

Kirk Hillson, like Freddie Leon, was one of the Hollywood power elite. As a top lawyer he had plenty of clout and knew all the right people in all the right places. Nick had a feeling Annie was not going to be easy to get rid of, he would need Kirk's full support—which meant there could be no secrets. It was about time he got the Vegas thing off his mind. All he'd done was bury a body—he hadn't murdered anyone, for Christ's sake. The way Annie carried on you'd have thought he'd pulled the fucking trigger.

He didn't mind paying Annie a bundle—after all, he could certainly afford it. But there was no way he was allowing her to give him a hard time when it came to seeing Lissa. His daughter, along with Lauren, was the most precious thing in his life, he'd fight for her all the way.

When Kirk arrived he told him the whole story, omitting only Cyndra's name. It wasn't fair to involve her until he checked it with her first.

Kirk, a sleek, well-preserved man with startling horse teeth, was noncommittal. "It makes you an accessory," he remarked, sipping a glass of unchilled Evian.

"I know," Nick agreed. "Why do you think I've stuck with Annie all these years?"

"On the other hand, maybe she imagined the whole thing," Kirk said, getting up and walking to the window.

"What do you mean?"

"Well—what's she going to prove? Does she know where you buried the body? Do *you* know?"

"I kinda remember," Nick said hesitantly. "I think I know where I drove to—but I can't be sure."

"By this time the evidence will be gone, believe me."

"Yeah, but is it worth taking a risk?"

Kirk glanced at his Rolex—he was late for a golf game. "With no more proof than she has, they won't touch you. You're Nick Angel."

"Then I want out," Nick said firmly.

"Have you met someone else?" Kirk asked.

"There *is* someone else," Nick explained. "She's been in my life a long time—it's just that we've never gotten together before now."

"Is she worth it?"

"She's worth anything it'll cost me."

"It would be better if there wasn't somebody else," Kirk said, admiring his manicure. "You know what they say about a woman scorned?"

"Annie won't be scorned. She doesn't give a shit about me anyway. All she cares about is the money and status. She's pissed my career took off the way it did and she never made it."

"I've heard that story a hundred times," said Kirk. "But whatever you say she'll try to hurt you."

"I want out," Nick repeated. "It's time."

"Does she have a lawyer?" Kirk asked.

"You're her lawyer."

"I can't represent both of you. Perhaps I should recommend someone. By the way, have you told Freddie?"

"Not yet."

"You should bring him in on this."

"You mean tell him about Vegas?"

"Not at this stage. But he should know you're planning to divorce Annie."

"I'll tell him."

"Excellent." Kirk headed for the door. "I don't foresee any problems. If you're prepared to give her ninety-nine percent of your money we'll be fine."

Nick laughed. "Jeez, lawyers' humor—just what I need."

Kirk smiled. "It'll cost you, so I hope your freedom's worth it."

"You know something, Kirk? I'd pay her every dime I had if I could be free tomorrow."

And he meant it. Being with Lauren was the most important thing in his life. He couldn't wait.

78

Aretha Mae had been bedridden for several weeks. Cyndra had nurses there day and night to look after her. The doctor had recently informed her that Aretha Mae was suffering from bronchial pneumonia and should be in the hospital.

"No hospitals," she said firmly. "I want her at home where I can watch her."

"She'd get better care in the hospital," the doctor pointed out.

"No," Cyndra replied, remembering what had happened to Luke. "My mother stays here."

Marik tried to persuade her. "C'mon, baby, let them take her to the hospital."

"No," Cyndra said flatly. "Those places kill people."

"She's dying anyway," Marik said.

"Oh, that's encouraging."

But she knew he spoke the truth. Aretha Mae did not have long to go.

Every evening at six o'clock she went into her mother's room and sat with her. She held her hand, the frail little hand that had once cooked greasy fries and bacon, slapped her kids, brought them up and allowed them to survive.

"How you doin', Mama?" she whispered, leaning in close.

Aretha Mae stared up at her. "I soon be with Luke," she said. "Soon be happy."

"Mama, I have something to ask you," Cyndra said, speaking softly.

"Yes?"

"You have to be very truthful with me. You must promise."

"Tell me, girl. What is it?"

"Who's my real father?"

Aretha Mae looked up at her with sunken eyes and was silent for a long while. "Benjamin Browning—he be your father," she said at last.

Cyndra nodded. She'd known it was true the first time Aretha Mae had told her, but she needed to hear it again. "Is there any proof?" she asked.

Aretha Mae nodded weakly. "There's a letter in the bank in Bosewell. You'll get it when I die."

"You're not gonna die, Mama."

"I don't mind dying, girl. I be with Jesus, an' my sweet baby Luke."

"No, Mama, you are *not* going to die," Cyndra repeated fiercely.

Aretha Mae smiled mysteriously. "I always knew you'd survive, girl. I was always sure."

Later that night Cyndra sat with Marik and talked about her past in a way she never had before. He listened quietly while she told him about Benjamin Browning, the rape, the abortion, and all the other bad things that had happened to her.

"Oh, baby, baby, I had no idea," he said, holding her tight.

"Why should you?" she replied. "It's my pain—I can handle it."

"That Benjamin Browning must be one bad son of a bitch," Marik said. "We could have somebody sent down there who'd fix him good."

"No," she said sharply. "Benjamin will pay for his sins, just like Mama would want him to. But it'll be my way."

The next day she signed a contract to star in her own television show. She took the contract home and proudly waved it in front of Aretha Mae. "You see, Mama? You see? I'm gonna be on television all over the country. Everybody will watch me. Everybody in Bosewell. What do you think of that?"

Aretha Mae smiled a sad little smile and managed to nod her head. "You be a star, girl. You did real good."

And then she shut her eyes and died peacefully.

Cyndra threw herself on her mother's body and started sobbing. The nurse called for Marik. He rushed to the room, took Cyndra in his arms and comforted her.

"I want you to be my wife, baby," he crooned. "It's time you had somebody looking after you."

"We'll see," she said between sobs. "We'll see."

Nick couldn't believe she was doing it to him again. Lauren had been gone for two days, and although he'd left countless messages on her private answering machine she still had not returned his calls. What was it with her? She'd done the same thing to him in New York when he'd sat in his hotel room waiting for five days. This time he wasn't going to stand for it.

He contacted a girl who worked at I.A.A. in New York and told her to go to Lauren's office.

"Make sure she calls me immediately," he said. "And don't leave until you see her. I'll be waiting by the phone."

The girl did as he asked and then called him in Los Angeles. "I'm sorry, Mr. Angel, Ms. Roberts is at the hospital."

"What's wrong?" he asked, panicking.

"Her husband had a heart attack."

"A heart attack?" he repeated blankly.

"Yes. I spoke to her personal assistant and she said she'd get a message to Ms. Roberts that you're trying to reach her."

He put the phone down and shook his head. Had Lauren told her husband and then he'd promptly had a heart attack? Was it Oliver's way of hanging on? Jesus, this was not good.

Freddie called and said, "You're not going to believe this."

"What?"

"Lauren Roberts turned us down. According to Samm, her New York agent, she doesn't want to do the part."

"Why not?"

"Her husband's in the hospital."

"He's going to be all right, isn't he?" Nick asked flatly.

"Nobody knows. Apparently she's at his bedside day and night."

It was bizarre. Fate brought them together every so often, and fate split them apart. If he knew anything about Lauren at all, he was certain she would not leave Oliver while he was sick.

"Any suggestions?" Freddie asked.

"About what?"

"Your leading lady."

"Give it to Carlysle. She wants it."

"I don't think the studio'll go for Carlysle Mann—she's old news."

"She's not even thirty, for crissakes. She's right for the part. Tell 'em I want her, that should do it."

"Are you sure?"

"Very sure."

And he was. Carlysle Mann was exactly what he needed to get him through the next few months. Because Lauren was not going to be around. Of that he was sure.

Oliver smiled weakly. "Somebody should have told me I was over-doing it."

"They did. Constantly," Lauren replied, fussing around his hospital bed.

"They did?" Oliver asked innocently.

"Yes. *I* told you, and Howard, and Pia. We all did. Nonstop work and no play makes Oliver a candidate for a very big heart attack."

"It wasn't that big."

"With a pacemaker anything's big."

A nurse entered the room carrying more flowers. The room already resembled a flower shop.

"I'll slow down. I promise."

Lauren nodded. "If you wish to stay around I suggest you do."

He held out his hand. "Come over here, my beautiful neglected wife."

Inexplicably her eyes filled with tears. She was so relieved he was alive. According to Pia, if their butler hadn't been working late when Oliver collapsed he would not have survived.

While your husband was almost dying, Roberts, you were in L.A. in bed with Nick Angel. Proud of yourself?

I didn't want this to happen.

Well, it did, and you're lucky he's still here.

Every time she cheated on him something bad happened. First the false pregnancy, now this. It was a sign. She and Nick were not meant to be.

He squeezed her hand and gazed helplessly into her eyes. "I'm making plans," he said. "We'll go to Rome and Venice. We'll travel together. I don't know what I'd do without you, my darling. I'd be lost."

He was her husband and she was fond of him, but if she were to tell the truth he was more like a father figure than a husband. He'd never made love to her. In fact, for the last four years they'd had no physical contact at all.

Oliver was almost seventy. She was thirty. Oh, God! She was absolutely and totally trapped.

"Don't worry, Oliver," she said. "I'm here. I always will be."

Later that night she called Nick.

"I heard," he said.

"I don't know what to say."

"You don't have to say anything. I understand."

"I can't tell him now—not while he's sick. Maybe in a few months when he gets better."

"Lauren, you don't have to explain to me."

"But I do. This time I didn't want to leave you hanging."

"I'll always be hanging."

"Don't make me cry, Nick."

"Look, you must do what you have to do. I'm divorcing Annie whatever happens. I don't intend to stay in a meaningless relationship."

"Yes, well, your wife's not lying in a hospital bed."

"Can we at least speak?"

"It's not a good idea."

"You're killing me, Lauren, you really are. You come into my life every so often, screw me up, and vanish. You're fucking killing me."

"Nick, if it means anything at all, I love you. I truly love you, but I can't leave this man, not now."

"When you're free, call me," he said. "I hope I'll still be waiting."

Nick attended Aretha Mae's funeral with Cyndra. She was buried at Forest Lawn, and there was a good turnout of people showing their respect for Cyndra.

"Actually, Nick," she told him, "they're showing their respect for my stardom, but what do I care?"

"Are you sure she wanted to be buried here?" he asked. "Maybe you should send her body back to Bosewell?"

"I thought about it," she said. "But then I remembered she had nothing but bad times there. She'll rest in peace here."

A few weeks later she informed him she was going back to Bosewell.

"What do you want to do that for?"

"Marik's coming with me," she said. "I have people to confront before I can be at peace with myself."

"Are you crazy?" he said. "You're a big star now. Why go back? If the tabloids get hold of your story you'll be sorry."

"I don't care," she said stubbornly. "It's something I have to do."

He realized her intentions. "You're after Browning, aren't you?"

She nodded.

"How does Marik feel about this?"

"He'll go along with me."

"And Gordon? Have you told him?"

"No," she said irritably. "I don't have to tell him. He's not my father confessor."

"Maybe you should listen to his advice."

"I know what his advice will be. He'll tell me not to go, just like you. But some things are unavoidable."

"Well, lotsa luck, Cyndra. You know I mean it."

"Want to come with me, Nick?"

"You've *gotta* be kidding. I wouldn't go back there for all the money in the world."

That afternoon Annie arrived home. Lissa rushed into the house first, raced up to him and threw herself into his arms. "Daddy! Daddy! I missed you *sooo* much!"

"I missed you, too, little kid," he said, hugging her tightly.

"Gotta go pee!" she giggled, wriggling out of his arms and running off.

Annie marched in with a sour face.

"Where the fuck have you been?" he demanded.

"With friends," she said coldly, going to the bar and pouring herself a drink.

He followed her. "What friends?"

"The same friends you were with. How do you like it when *I* vanish?"

"Don't ever take off with my kid," he said sharply. "Don't ever do that to me, Annie, because you'll regret it."

She arched her eyebrows. "*I'll* regret it?"

"I want a divorce," he said.

"No," she replied, sipping straight gin.

"It's too late. I've already talked to my lawyer. I want out of this marriage. Neither of us is happy. It's not good for Lissa—all she ever sees us do is fight."

"Didn't you read my note, Nick? I *like* being Mrs. Angel. There's no way I'm letting you go."

"You have no choice, Annie."

"Oh, but I do. You seem to forget what I know."

"I'm not forgetting anything. Kirk will recommend a lawyer for you. I'll be fair with you, but it's over."

"Oh, yes," she said spitefully. "It'll *really* be over when I tell everything I know."

"You know something, Annie?" he said wearily. "You've held this over me for too many years now—I don't give a shit what you do or who you tell. I'm through—get that into your fucking head. I'm through."

"You'll regret it. I'll take Lissa and you'll never see her again," she said, playing her trump card.

"Oh, no, that's where you're wrong," he said curtly.

"Your career will be over, Nick."

"You can't touch me, Annie."

She smiled contemptuously. "We'll see who's right."

Oliver's recovery was slow, but true to his word he began to take it much easier. This affected Lauren because she was used to getting on with her own career and not worrying about Oliver being lonely or wondering where she was. Now he demanded her full attention.

She informed Lorenzo she did not wish to proceed with the cosmetics line at this particular time.

Lorenzo was upset. "What will you do? Stay at home and look after an old man?"

"I don't think it's any of your business."

"You cannot waste your life like this, Lauren," he said, genuinely concerned. "You are at the peak of your career, you can achieve anything."

"I'm taking some time," she said quietly. "I have to look after Oliver. He needs me."

Samm was equally outraged. "You fly to Hollywood, test for a role in a Nick Angel movie, get the part—and then tell me you can't do it. I don't believe this!"

"Samm, sometimes life comes before fantasy. Making a movie is fantasy, being with my husband is real life. I'm looking after him until he's better."

Samm shook her head, too perplexed to argue.

"And another thing," Lauren added. "No more modeling assignments until I feel Oliver is back on his feet."

"You have your commitment to Marcella," Samm pointed out.

"I'll keep that commitment. Right now put everything else on hold."

As soon as Oliver was out of the hospital she accompanied him to their house in the Hamptons, where they spent several weeks sitting around doing nothing. She bought him piles of magazines and books, classical tapes and videos.

"You know, I rather like doing nothing," Oliver confessed. "Especially with you beside me."

She smiled wanly. "I thought you might."

"We've spent so little time together over the last few years. I'm going to make it up to you, Lauren, you'll see."

She tried not to think about Nick. It was quite obvious their relationship was not to be, and Oliver's heart attack was God's way of warning her. She'd been blessed in so many ways. Having Nick was not part of the deal.

When Oliver was feeling better she booked them on a long cruise and they took off for several months.

She'd thought about phoning Nick before she left, but then decided against it. They both had their lives to lead. They had to do it separately.

"C'mon, stud—fuck me!" Carlysle urged in a feverish voice. "C'mon, Nick, fuck me good."

She was unbelievable. What the hell did she *think* he was doing?

"Hey, we're already rocking the trailer back and forth," he pointed out.

She laughed hysterically. "What do you care? You think the crew don't know what we do in here all the time? You and me, Nick Angel, we're a pair—right?"

"Yeah, right," he said, giving it to her just the way she liked.

She caught her breath. "Mmm . . . that's nice. We should've gotten together a long time ago."

"We did get together a long time ago," he panted.

"No, I mean permanently. Like married."

He started to laugh. Only Carlysle managed to fuck and carry on a conversation at the same time. "You want to get married?"

"I've tried it twice," she gasped. "You could be third time lucky."

Oh, God, he was almost there. "Did you say lucky?"

"Hmm . . ." She let out a deep groan. "Don't forget I knew you when, and I *screwed* you when. All these little girls running after you now—they want you because you're Nick Angel. I had you when you were nothing. Remember?"

"Yeah, I remember," he said, thinking about the apartment in New York and the way she'd greeted him in nothing but a bath towel.

"Think about it, Nick," she said, speaking very fast. "You're getting divorced—we'd be good together. And we wouldn't have to worry about that whole boring faithful thing. I could bring girls home for you whenever you wanted. You know how you love threesomes."

He groped for a nearby bottle of vodka and took a healthy swig.

"Shouldn't drink when you're working," Carlysle admonished. "Especially when you're fucking."

One final thrust and he climaxed.

Carlysle joined him, letting out a blood-curdling scream.

Someone hammered on the trailer door.

"God!" exclaimed Carlysle, struggling into a sitting position. "You'd think they'd be used to us by now." Giggling, she yelled out, "Who is it?"

"You're wanted on the set, Ms. Mann. Is Mr. Angel there?"

"Haven't seen him," she yelled back, pulling on her panties. "Try his trailer."

He got up and zipped up his pants. Carlysle made him feel like a teenager. Dirty sex on the floor. Getting it on anywhere they could. Getting it on anywhere that would make him forget Lauren.

He took another swig of vodka from the bottle. Carlysle wagged a finger at him.

"Don't sweat it," he said. "It works for the part."

"Okay, okay."

He left her trailer and returned to his.

"Your lawyer called," said his personal assistant.

"Anything interesting?" he asked.

"Yes, he left a message for you to call him. Something about Las Vegas."

Las Vegas. So Annie was finally making her play. They'd been separated for a couple of months. He'd become a weekend father, seeing Lissa on Saturdays and Sundays, taking her on jaunts to Universal, Disneyland and the movies—always accompanied by his bodyguards. He didn't like it.

At least Annie hadn't gone through with her threat to keep Lissa from him. But still . . . being a weekend father did not cut it.

Grabbing the portable phone, he waved his assistant out of the trailer and called Kirk. "What's going on?" he asked.

"I don't want to discuss it on the phone," Kirk replied. "How about a drink later?"

"Come by the set. I don't know what time we'll be through tonight. Could be shooting late."

Kirk sighed. "I don't do sets, Nick."

"For me you'll do it," he said persuasively.

"All right, have your secretary call my secretary with the address. And I hope the location is in Beverly Hills, because my Rolls doesn't leave the vicinity."

"C'mon, Kirk, you're such an old pussy. We're shooting downtown—risk it."

"No, Nick. Call me when you get back to your house. I don't do downtown."

"I'll be tired when I get home."

"Do you want to hear what Annie is planning or don't you?"

"Okay, okay, I'll call you."

He didn't need to hear what she had planned. He already knew. She was going to screw him, and she was going to screw him good.

Cyndra arrived in Bosewell in a blaze of glory. She did it the way she'd always wanted to—in a huge limo, followed by two backup limos containing her entourage. She wore a red fox coat, wild extensions in her long dark hair and a glamorous gown. The town of Bosewell wished to present her with the keys to the city at a special luncheon ceremony. The prodigal daughter was returning a huge star.

A TV crew followed her, recording her visit to be made into a television special. Small-town girl makes good. Now a big, big star. What could be better?

Returning with Nick seven years earlier had been a small happening. Now she was coming back as a megastar.

Marik was by her side—along with two publicity people from the record company, a producer from her new television show, her personal makeup artist, her hairdresser and her clothes coordinator.

They all stayed in the big Hilton in Ripley and made the cavalcade limousine journey to Bosewell on Saturday morning.

They were escorted into town by the Bosewell police and taken straight to Town Hall for a reception in her honor.

The town turned out in force. Cyndra looked around as she was led inside and recognized many of the faces. Nobody had given two cents about her welfare when she'd lived in Bosewell. Now they were fawning all over her—touching and grabbing, telling her how wonderful she was and how they were so proud of her and how they'd always known she could do it. Well, fuck 'em. Let 'em weep.

A dark woman wearing too much eye makeup and a tight orange dress grabbed her arm. "Hi, Cyndra. Remember me?"

"Dawn," she said, remembering immediately.

Dawn Kovak beamed. "What a memory! We were at school together."

"We sure were," Cyndra said, recalling that Dawn had been one of the few people who'd talked to her. "Still here, huh? I thought you'd have gotten out long ago."

Dawn waved her hand, flashing a sizable diamond ring. "I stayed," she said. "And last year I married Benjamin Browning." She beamed triumphantly. "His wife died a few years ago, so now *I'm* Mrs. Browning. Ain't that a kick? Now everyone has to kiss my ass!"

"*You're* Mrs. Browning?" Cyndra said, barely concealing her surprise. "*You* married Benjamin?"

Dawn nodded happily. "Yeah. And you can imagine the scandal. Not much goes on here, but when I bagged him, boy, was there an uproar! Stock went nuts—couldn't accept it. Ben and me, we hadda throw him an' his wife outta the house. She's such a pain anyway."

The crowds were pushing and shoving. Marik attempted to hustle her along.

"I'm sorry, Dawn, I can't talk now," she said.

"I'll see you later," Dawn said, moving off into the crowd.

There were so many people and they all wanted a piece of her. One by one they came up to her saying things like "You remember me?" "What fun we had in school." "It's so good to see you again!"

Some phony group. If she wasn't Cyndra, big singing star, they wouldn't even remember her name.

So Dawn Kovak, the school tramp, had bagged the richest man in town. In fact, Dawn had bagged her daddy. Well, they were all in for a big shock.

She saw Stock fighting his way through the crowd to get near her. Stock, once the handsome football hero, was now thirty pounds overweight with heavy jowls and a puffy red face. An overweight Meg clung to his side.

The TV crew captured every moment as they finally fought their way over to her.

"I always knew you'd be a star," Meg said breathlessly. "When you visited a few years back I said to Stock, 'She's going to be such a big star.' I love your records. You know, we were planning on coming out to Los Angeles with the children for a vacation. What do you think? We'd adore to see your house."

Stock eyeballed her with lecherous eyes. He'd been one of the worst offenders at school, calling her dark meat and other offensive names. She wondered how he was going to take the fact that she was his half sister.

"Is your daddy around?" she asked him.

"You heard the news?" Stock said, scowling. "He married Dawn. He's damn senile."

"It's shocking," Meg added in a hoarse whisper. "She only married him for his money. But we're seeing a lawyer. We're not going to let him change his will. Stock's entitled to everything."

Cyndra smiled. *That's what you think.*

"How long we gotta stay here, baby?" Marik asked. "I'm getting depressed."

"Just long enough for me to attend the lunch," she assured him. "Then they'll hand me the keys to the city an' we're on our way."

"I still don't understand why you wanted to do this," he grumbled. "This town treated you badly. Why *did* you want to come back?"

"You'll see," she said, smiling sweetly.

She had not revealed her plans to Marik, but they were all in place. She knew exactly what she was going to do.

They were finally seated. The lunch was long and boring. People got up and made little speeches about what an excellent student she'd been, how they'd all known she would do so well. Even the school principal spoke glowingly of her.

Eventually it was time for the presentation. The chief of police stood up, made a short speech and handed her the keys to Bosewell. A round of applause rippled through the room.

She smiled and got to her feet.

"A long time ago this town was my home," she said, speaking clearly. "I lived in the trailer park. Nobody took much notice of any of us then, but we were just barely surviving. My mother worked as a maid. In fact she worked for the illustrious Browning family, who I'm sure you all know." She shot a vindictive glance at Benjamin, sitting with his new wife. "Oh, the Browning family was very good to my mother. They used to give her their cast-off clothes and leftover food."

A buzz echoed around the room.

"And when I was a little girl," Cyndra continued, "my mother took me with her to their house. It was always fun at their house. Well, let me put it this way—I was too little to understand what fun was all about, but I think Mr. Browning had a good time. He used to come into that back room when I was a little girl and pat me on my cute ass, and run his hand up my panties, and sometimes he even lifted my dress so he could *really* get a good feel."

A murmur of consternation from the crowd.

Cyndra checked to see that the TV cameras were recording everything. They were.

"Yes," she continued. "That filthy bastard abused me good when I was a child. And then when I was a young girl, he raped me." She paused for effect. "I was sixteen and a virgin. His wife was out shopping at the time, and his spoiled bigoted son was at school, screwing all the girls. Mr. Browning raped me, and called me every foul name he could think of. I had to go to Kansas to get an abortion. Before my mother died she told me the truth. When she first went to work for the Brownings she was a young, innocent girl. Benjamin Browning raped her too. And you want to hear the twist to this lovely American folk story? I'm his daughter. *I'm* Benjamin Browning's daughter. And I have a letter to prove it."

The room erupted.

"Oh, baby, baby, when you do it, you really do it," muttered Marik. "Let's get the hell outta here, and fast."

Cyndra refused to be stopped. "I've come back to town," she said in a loud clear voice, "because I know there's nothing you all love better than a good old American success story. And I thought you'd enjoy hearing the truth."

Cyndra's story made every TV news program in America, and she was thrilled. "I *had* to bring it out in the open," she explained to Marik. "I needed to. It was my life and he tried to ruin it. Now I've ruined his. I'm a survivor, but there's lots of kids out there who'll never survive—because their fathers or uncles or somebody else is abusing them every day. This is something we shouldn't hide. I refuse to be ashamed anymore."

"Right on, baby," Marik said. "I'm with you all the way."

Marik had supported her royally. On the way back to L.A. she'd made him stop in Ripley, and with her two security guards they'd searched for Harlan and kidnapped him just as she'd sworn to do. They'd found him in a bar dressed in tattered clothes and drugged out of his mind. He hadn't recognized her at first, but when he had he'd broken down in tears and allowed himself to be taken without a fight. He was such a pathetic sight. She'd vowed there and then that she'd look after him and help him make a decent life for himself. He was her brother and she loved him.

Back in L.A. she'd put him into a private clinic to break him of his habit, visiting him every few days.

Three weeks after getting back she and Marik were married in a lavish ceremony in Beverly Hills.

She'd long forgotten about Reece Webster. As far as she was concerned he was dead.

"She wants five million dollars in a bank in Switzerland. This demand is separate from the divorce settlement."

"Shit!" Nick exclaimed.

"I know," Kirk agreed. "Apparently it's the price of her silence." He paused. "Is it worth it or do you wish to take a risk?"

"I don't know," Nick said, pacing up and down. "You tell me."

"You're a big star. You'll make a lot more movies. In the long run five million dollars won't mean that much to you. My advice is to pay it."

"Jesus! She's getting half my money as it is, and she wants another five million bucks on top of it. How greedy can you get?"

"I've seen worse," Kirk said. "In Hollywood it's often this way. When the husband is famous and the wife isn't, there's always resentment. Usually the wife came to Hollywood to be an actress. Instead she marries a famous man, and has the compensation of being a wife with clout. When that clout is taken away she wants revenge—usually the revenge is financial."

"And what about Lissa?" Nick said. "Can I spend as much time as I like with her? I don't want to have to ask permission to see her. I refuse to be a weekend father. Oh, yeah—and when I'm not working I'd like her to be able to come and live with me."

"If you're agreeable to the financial terms I'm sure we can work it out."

"Do I have the money?"

"I've spoken to your business manager. Right now it's tied up in bonds, but he can make arrangements. Yes, you have it, Nick. You're doing pretty damn good."

"Okay," he said. "If this is what it takes to get my freedom."

"Good," Kirk said. "I'll have the papers drawn up."

"Fast, Kirk, fast."

As soon as Kirk left he called Carlysle. "I'm lonely," he said.

"Naughty boy, I just left you. We did it three times today in the trailer—what more do you want?"

"Come over. Bring a friend."

She pretended to be insulted. "I'm not a hooker, you know."

"What's the matter, Carlysle? You getting old?"

These were the dreaded words for any actress. "I'll be there," she said. "Who do you fancy?"

"Remember that Indonesian friend of yours? Is she still around?"

"No, she's in New York. But there's this girl I met on the set the other day—she's an extra. Great bod. I'll see if I can contact her."

She turned up an hour later with Honey, a seventeen-year-old nymphet. Honey had huge eyes, a delectable mouth, an unbelievable body, and she was a fan.

"I can't believe I'm here with Nick Angel," she sighed, gazing around his house in awe.

"You won't be unless you shut up," Carlysle said sharply. "Don't talk, enjoy. That's the way he likes it."

He got through half a bottle of Scotch and still managed to make love to them both. Honey was one of the most obliging girls he'd ever come across. Anything he wanted she did.

In the end Carlysle got jealous. She could see he was really getting off on Honey and she didn't like it.

"Don't forget your promise," she whispered as they left.

"What promise?" he slurred, squinting at her.

"After your divorce—you and me, we'll be together."

He might be drunk, but he wasn't that far gone. "I never said that."

"Oh, yes, you did."

"Oh, no, I didn't."

When they finally left he staggered up to bed and got two hours sleep before his early call.

He got through the week, and on Friday night he stayed sober, preparing for his Saturday visit with Lissa.

He picked her up early in the morning.

"Where are we going today, Daddy?" she asked.

"Wherever you want, sweetheart."

He took her to the toy store and out to lunch. But even with his ever-watchful bodyguards it was impossible. Everywhere he went people stopped him, requesting autographs, wanting to take his photograph, telling him how much they loved him. There was no privacy.

Lissa was upset. "I don't like it, Daddy," she said, beginning to cry. "Why can't people leave you alone?"

"Hey, kid—my sentiments exactly."

Eventually they went back to his house and Lissa settled in front of the television, watching a video of *The Sound of Music* for the hundredth time. "I like this movie, Daddy," she said, cheering up. "It's nice."

He didn't take Lissa home when he was supposed to.

A furious Annie called up. "Where is she?"

"She wants to stay here tonight," he said.

"She can't," Annie replied.

"What are you going to do about it?"

"I'll get a court order."

"You won't get a court order until Monday."

"You'd better send her home, Nick. I'm warning you."

"Stop threatening me, Annie. It's over."

He went into the kitchen and told the cook to make Lissa a hamburger and a milkshake. Then he sat beside her and watched the film.

An hour later Annie was at his door. She barged into the house. "Lissa, come with me," she said, her tone brooking no argument.

"No, my daddy says I can stay here tonight," Lissa said defiantly, curling up on the couch.

"You see," Nick said. "She *wants* to stay here. There's nothing you can do."

Annie turned on him. "You son of a bitch."

He stood up. "Don't use language like that in front of Lissa. And let's not fight in front of her either."

Annie's lip curled. "I can't imagine why I ever married you. You're nothing but a piece of shit."

"Oh, and I suppose you're Mother Teresa."

Annie went up to Lissa and grabbed her by the arm, yanking her off the couch. "You're coming home with me."

Lissa's eyes filled with tears. "Daddy! Daddy! You said I could stay."

Annie was in a rage. "You're coming with me, you little bitch!"

Nick tried to stop her. "Don't talk to her like that, Annie."

"I'll do what the fuck I want. I don't have to listen to you, I *hate* you." She pulled the reluctant child toward the door.

Lissa began screaming.

"Don't do this, Annie," he said, going after them. "Can't you see she doesn't want to go."

"I'll do what I damn well please."

He wanted to slap her, but he couldn't do it in front of his daughter —this scene was traumatic enough for Lissa to deal with.

He followed them outside. Christ! Money, fame, none of it mattered when it came to Lissa.

Annie shoved the child into her car. "Don't you ever pull this stunt again, Nick, or you won't see her at all."

"Quit threatening me, Annie, 'cause I'm through taking your crap. I'm talking to Kirk about this."

She jumped into the car. "Your high-priced Beverly Hills lawyers can't help you get Lissa," she sneered. "I'm her mother, she'll always stay with me." She started the car and roared off down the driveway.

"Don't bet on it," he yelled after her, filled with an impotent fury.

It was the last he saw of either of them. Their car was in a head-on collision. Neither Lissa nor Annie survived.

BOOK FOUR

DECEMBER 1992

81

Two overripe teenagers in short black knit dresses with black hose and "fuck me" shoes boogied the night away beneath the midnight tent, where lights sparkled like ministars and an assortment of predators circled the dance floor on the lookout for a score of some kind or the other.

Honey Virginia, bleached blond hair pulled demurely back, finely tuned body clad in strapless lace, sat on Nick's knee, purring sweet sexual promises into his ear.

Diana Leon, sitting across the table next to her husband, watched from the corner of a jaundiced eye. Nick Angel never failed to amaze her. His capacity for everything was overwhelming. Honey entered his life on and off, and in between Nick covered the waterfront.

Diana often urged Freddie to talk to him. "Does he practice safe sex? Does he understand about AIDS?"

Freddie always placated her. "I'm his agent, not his sex therapist."

"But he's so . . . irresponsible. You *should* talk to him. You're his friend."

Freddie knew better than to discuss women with Nick Angel. Nick was a legend, having steadily laid every fuckable woman in Hollywood since he'd first arrived in town. It was surprising he could still get it up. But then again, little Honey could raise the dead if the mood took her, and Nick was by no means dead—just a touch jaded. And at age thirty-four showing definite signs of wear and tear. Freddie decided that maybe he *would* have a talk with him. Nick was getting out of control, it was becoming increasingly obvious. It had been a steady slide since Lissa's death in the car crash with Annie. At first Nick had been inconsolable. He'd gone off to a retreat and stayed there for several months. When he returned it was like nothing had ever happened. He refused to discuss the accident. But Freddie knew he was breaking up inside. Nick had always been a drinker, and as the months turned into years his habit escalated.

"You should get into one of those twelve-step programs," Freddie had suggested one day. "I think you've got a problem."

Nick had turned on him, green eyes full of a deep hidden anger. "You think it's time I started looking for a new agent, Freddie?" he'd asked.

Freddie knew when to back off. It was one of his strengths.

"Can we go?" Diana whispered in his ear. She hated parties and had only attended this one because the woman for whom the party was being given was Freddie's latest client—a blond video superstar called Venus Maria.

"Five minutes and we're out of here," Freddie promised.

Honey removed herself from Nick's knee, stood up and stretched. Every man at the party craned his neck to get a better look at her spectacular body.

Nick had been with her for four years on and off. In between he screwed all his leading ladies and anybody else he fancied. He was playing a dangerous game—AIDS was not selective.

Diana was getting restless. She rose from the table. "Good night, Nick. Good night, Honey dear," she said politely.

Nick leaned back. "Are you two going?"

"Past my bedtime," Diana said with a stretched smile.

"See ya," Nick said. He'd always considered Diana Leon a tight-assed broad. The older she got, the more tight-assed she became.

Honey decided to join the two overripe teenagers on the dance floor. She put them to shame with moves even strippers hadn't thought of.

Nick watched her. The next morning they were leaving for New York. He had a birthday coming up and he didn't care to celebrate it in Los Angeles. Not that there was any cause for celebration—getting older was a pisser.

Two years ago he'd purchased a New York apartment. He liked having a place in the same city as Lauren, although they hadn't seen each other in four years. She'd called him when the news of the accident hit the headlines.

"Is there anything I can do?" she'd asked, full of concern.

Yes, be here with me, he'd wanted to say. But he knew she wasn't going to leave Oliver.

He decided it was time to get the hell out. Honey was still busy on the dance floor. He walked over and pulled her by the arm. "C'mon, we're going."

"I don't wanna . . ."

"I *said* we're going."

She followed him dutifully. Twenty-one years old and an idiot, but with the best body in town. That was all right—he wasn't interested in conversation. Meaningless sex. His life.

"Why did we have to leave so early?" Honey complained in the car on the way home.

" 'Cause I might feel like flying the plane tomorrow. If I do I want to be able to see where I'm going."

He'd been taking flying lessons for a couple of years, it was the one thing he did where he tried to remain sober.

Back at the mansion Honey did a slow striptease for his benefit.

She was undeniably luscious.

He watched her for a few minutes, then passed out.

She might be luscious, but he'd seen it all before.

"You look tired, *bellissima*," Lorenzo said, full of concern.

"Thank you," Lauren replied crisply. "That's just what I want to hear when I'm about to go before the camera."

"The camera loves you. You will always look beautiful. Me—I know you too well, and you do look tired."

"I *am* tired," she confessed. "I had so much more energy when I was working all the time. Every morning was a challenge—I'd get up and there was always something new to do. Now that Oliver's retired I do nothing but sit around at home."

"Why?"

"Because he likes me there. It makes him feel secure."

"You don't have to do this, Lauren."

"Yes, I do," she said defensively. "I'm his wife."

"You don't love him."

"What's love got to do with it?"

"When I married my wife I loved her. When I fell out of love we got a divorce."

"Well, Lorenzo, you do things in a much more simple fashion than I do. I believe in loyalty and sticking with somebody through bad times."

"Oliver is perfectly healthy now."

"I know, but he got used to not working. He liked it so much he decided to retire."

"That doesn't mean *you* have to waste your life."

"I'm doing the new Marcella campaign," she said. "What more do you want?"

"Yes, but that's all you're doing. Before, you were so vital—everything excited you."

"I guess I'm not excited anymore, Lorenzo. This is the last year I'll do the Marcella campaign. As you know, we're moving to the south of France."

"Lauren, you're making a mistake—shutting yourself away from the world."

"It's not a world I particularly want to be in anymore. Anyway, the south of France is beautiful. And Oliver's found this wonderful old farmhouse way up in the hills—miles from anywhere."

Lorenzo shook his head. He simply didn't understand her.

It was Sunday afternoon and Cyndra was entertaining. She paused at the top of the stone steps leading to her patio. She paused just long enough for people to notice she was making an entrance.

Smiling at her guests she watched Marik leap to his feet. He was always so attentive and concerned about her welfare. He was also a consistently good lover. It was a shame he wasn't more attractive.

Don't think that way, she scolded herself. *Marik is the best thing that ever happened to me. He's kind and caring, and he genuinely loves me. Apart from that he's a talented producer, and he made me a star.*

Behind her, Patsy, their plump English nanny, carried their little girl, Topaz. Topaz was the pride of her life. Three years old and adorable. Cyndra would do anything for her child. So would Marik, he worshipped their daughter.

Cyndra greeted her guests graciously, going from table to table, smiling and chatting warmly.

Marik crept up behind her, hugging her tightly. "You look fantastic, woman," he said, nibbling her ear. "Every year you get better-looking."

"Thank you, dear."

Out of the corner of her eye she noticed Gordon and Odile arriving. Gordon was still her best friend. She confided in him, went to him for advice, discussed most things with him, including the incident in Vegas—which he'd told her to forget about.

She went over to greet them. "Hi, Gordon."

"Hi, beautiful," Gordon said, kissing her on both cheeks.

"Hello, Odile," she said with a smile.

"You're looking hot, Cyndra."

"Thank you. From you that's a compliment."

Over the years she'd actually gotten to like Odile. Yes, she was beautiful and, yes, she was Gordon's wife. But she was also an extremely nice woman.

Gordon and Odile were Topaz's godparents, along with Nick, who was godfather number one. She was upset Nick hadn't been able to come. He'd flown off to New York complaining he was depressed.

"Why don't you stay here for your birthday?" she'd asked.

"I don't feel like it," he'd said.

She wished he'd dump Honey. That girl made dumb look intelligent. But Nick was on some sort of self-destruct course, he didn't seem to care about the company he kept. Ever since the accident he hadn't been the same man. Unfortunately he blamed himself.

"It wasn't your fault," Cyndra repeatedly assured him.

"If I hadn't been fighting with Annie, it would never have happened."

"No, Nick, you mustn't think that way."

But he did, and she knew there was nothing she could do about it.

Maybe Nick would have a good time in New York. At least he'd be away from the pressures of Hollywood, and there was always Harlan to keep him company.

Ah, Harlan . . . what a character he'd turned out to be. After kidnapping him and getting him off drugs, she'd moved him in with her. He'd quite taken to Hollywood, and met an older man whom he decided to go work for as his valet. When the man died of AIDS two years later Harlan had not wanted to stay around. Cyndra had arranged for him to work for Nick in New York. He loved it.

Marik took her arm and led her over to sit down. She was surrounded by friends and loving family. Little Topaz created a furor wherever she went, running from table to table, giggling and cute.

Cyndra surveyed her guests, her family and her beautiful home.

I'm so lucky. I have everything.

Only sometimes, late at night, the thought occurred to her that maybe she was too lucky. Then she shuddered and hugged herself and prayed to God that her good luck would last. For family meant everything to her and she didn't want to lose it.

82

Reece Webster had not had a good time in prison. For once in his life his looks had not worked in his favor. In jail they were particularly fond of snake-hipped white guys with blond hair and nice looks, and he'd had two choices—give it up or get the crap beaten out of him.

Reece soon learned which way to turn. Not that he was gay. No way. But taking it up the butt from one big black brother, as opposed to watching his ass every move he made, seemed to be the better deal.

Eleven years. Eleven fucking years of his life and now he was out.

He lingered outside the jail in North Carolina, trying to decide what to do first. He wanted a woman bad, but he also wanted a fat juicy steak. An inmate had given him the name of a whorehouse that served up the best women, and food too. What more could he ask for?

He tilted his beat-up Stetson and took the bus into town. He didn't have much money. Fuck! He didn't have much of anything. But he sure as hell knew how he was going to get plenty. He'd studied up on that. In eleven years a man could do a lot of studying.

The whorehouse served him a dried-up steak and a dried-up hooker who'd seen better days. It was not a first-class operation. But any woman was better than none at all.

He wore a condom supplied by the house. He didn't argue because he'd heard it was pretty dangerous out on the streets now. Sex was not the carefree pastime it once was.

He fucked the whore three times.

"You been in jail, dear?" she asked, not particularly impressed by his stellar performance.

"Howdja know?"

"I can tell. You convicts are always the horniest."

Yeah. He'd been in jail, all right. Sixteen years was the sentence he'd been handed, and he was out in eleven for good behavior. Eleven lousy years for something he'd never done.

When he'd split Vegas he'd traveled all the way to Florida, where he'd met a nightclub hostess who took a shine to him and let him move in with her. He hadn't been living with the bitch two weeks when Max, her old boyfriend, returned. She'd omitted to tell him that Max was a convicted felon who specialized in robbing banks. Since Max was with his latest girlfriend—a ditsy redhead—there seemed no need for him to move on, so the four of them had palled up.

"People who work legitimate make me sick," Max told him one day. "Me—I kin take any bank I fancy. I jest walk in, show 'em my gun, scoop out the money an' I'm on easy street."

"What if you get caught?" Reece asked, thinking it sounded simple enough, but there was always a downside.

Max chortled. "You realize how many people git busted? Outta a hundred hits mebbe five people git themselves caught. I been doin' this goin' on twenny years."

"But you were in jail once."

"Only a short time—it weren't nothin'."

They went on a car trip through several states, and Max showed Reece exactly how easy it was. On their ninth job Max blew away the security guard.

They were caught, arrested and charged with armed robbery and murder.

Screw it. He hadn't pulled the trigger, but nobody took that into account—he was sentenced along with the rest of them.

Now he was out and he was bitter as hell. If Cyndra hadn't gotten him into that mess in Vegas, he'd never have met the nightclub hostess in Florida, and he'd never have spent eleven years of his precious life in jail.

Fuck little Cyndra. While he was away she'd become a big star and so had Nick Angel. He'd watched their rise carefully—oh, yeah, he was no fool.

Now he was out and he knew exactly where to go and what to do. Little Cyndra must be worth millions, and he was going to get himself some of that great big score.

Yes. Reece Webster had a plan.

California, here I come . . .

83

The new Marcella photos were done and Lauren had nothing left to keep her in New York. Oliver was anxious to leave. For some time he'd been severing his ties in America, selling the East Hampton house, putting the New York apartment on the market and preparing for their move to France. It was a radical move, but on the other hand, what was the point in sitting around New York when Oliver wasn't working? In France he would have his garden, the view, the tranquil surroundings.

Christ! You're beginning to sound like an old lady, Roberts.

It's my life—I have to accept it.

Pia came by with Rosemarie, a particularly bright little girl, and watched her pack. "Are you sure you're making the right move?" Pia asked, wandering around the room.

"Yes, I'm sure," Lauren said, with more conviction than she felt.

"It's just that everything's so different for you now," Pia remarked. "I mean, you went through a period where you really loved your life, it showed on your face. Now you're kind of like . . ."

"Are you calling me a zombie, Pia?" Lauren asked, gathering together a pile of sweaters.

"You said it, not me."

Lauren placed the sweaters in a suitcase. "I'll do things in the south of France. Maybe even start an interior design business."

"Oh, that sounds very challenging. Decorate houses for senile old millionaires who've moved there to retire."

"Can I come visit, Auntie Lauren?" Rosemarie asked, a polite little girl with a sweet smile.

"Of course you can, darling. Any time you want."

She packed several pairs of Charles Jourdan shoes, and then wondered why she was taking them. Where was she going to wear them? Even in New York they never went out anymore.

"How's Howard?" she asked.

"Howard has turned into Oliver," Pia said. "He works day and night, never gets back from the office before nine, then goes straight to his study, where he spends the rest of the evening on the phone. I told him the other day if this goes on I'm not standing for it."

Lauren laughed. "You know you love it."

"Love what?"

"Being Mrs. Howard Liberty. It's a lot of fun when your husband's the head of a big important company."

"I'm not so sure I do," Pia said thoughtfully. "It was all right for you when you had your high-powered career—but I don't enjoy being the little wife. At half of the parties we go to I'm ignored. He's the big gorilla."

"Pia, I'm sure you're never ignored."

"You'd be surprised."

Lauren shut the suitcase. "Why don't you and Rosemarie stay for dinner tonight?"

"We'd like that. I'll call Howard and tell him if he gets through early enough he can join us."

At dinner Oliver was particularly animated. He was looking forward to the move and it showed.

In the middle of dinner Lauren had a phone call from Lorenzo.

"I have unfortunate news," he said, sounding upset.

"What is it, Lorenzo?" she asked.

"There was an accident in the lab—the negatives of the new photographs are ruined."

"You're kidding me?"

"No, this is a freak thing. It's never happened before. You must stay so we can shoot them again."

"I can't do that. You know we're leaving tomorrow."

"Oliver will have to leave without you. You'll join him a few days later. I'll organize everything as quickly as possible."

"Lorenzo," she said crossly, "this is most inconvenient."

He was more than apologetic. "I know, my darling. For me too."

"What's the matter?" Pia asked, when she hung up.

Lauren sighed. "The Marcella photographs are ruined. Lorenzo wants me to do the shoot again."

"But you're leaving tomorrow."

"That's exactly what I told him."

"Don't worry, my dear," Oliver said, perfectly calm. "I'll go ahead without you."

"You can't fly all that way by yourself."

"I'm not an invalid, Lauren," he said, rather snappily. "Our travel agent has perfectly good people on both ends to meet me and take care of the luggage. I'll settle in and you'll get there when you can. No problem."

"Are you sure?"

"Yes, I'm very sure."

She went into the bedroom and called Lorenzo back. "This better not be one of your crazy scams."

"Lauren, I can assure you."

"Okay, I'll stay. Tell me tomorrow what time we're going to do the photos."

"My darling," he said happily, "you are a princess."

"And you are a prince—the prince of bullshit."

"I'm so glad our relationship gets closer every year."

The next morning she was up early, helping Oliver with last-minute packing.

"How about if you postpone the trip?" she said. "Then I can come with you."

"It's all arranged, my dear. You worry too much."

"I'm coming to the airport," she said.

"You don't have to—the traffic . . ."

"I'm coming to the airport."

She sat next to him in the limo and saw him safely on the plane. Then she rode back to New York, alone and thoughtful. Soon she would be leaving the city and her life would change. She'd come a long way from Bosewell and the little girl she once was.

Nick . . . Every so often he lingered in her thoughts. She wondered how he was, how he was doing. She missed him. She always missed him.

"What do you want for your birthday?" Honey demanded.

Peace. "No celebrations," he said sternly.

"Why not? I get off on birthdays," she said, toying with a strand of her long hair.

He hoped she wasn't planning anything—at twenty-one it was easy to love birthdays, but he was not in the mood.

"I'm telling you, I don't want anything. No surprises," he repeated, hoping she'd get the message.

She pouted. "I'll think of something."

"Don't," he said.

Had he made a mistake bringing Honey with him? He wasn't sure. Sometimes it was nice to have a warm body lying next to him in the middle of the night when he woke up and thought about Lauren. And he thought about her often. Over the years he'd grown to accept the fact that she was an obsession. Only the drinking made her go away.

In the New York apartment there was a stack of scripts waiting for him to read. Word was out that he wanted to make his next movie in New York, and every producer in town seemed to know it. There was a pile of faxes, a ton of mail and a list of phone calls waiting for him.

"Teresa, you deal with this shit," he said, calling upon his assistant.

Teresa had worked with him for a year now. She was the best assistant he'd ever had. He figured she was gay because she'd never come on to him, and that suited him just fine. Before her he'd had a series of assistants who'd looked at him with mournful eyes day and night and eventually confessed undying love. Who needed that?

Teresa was all business. A black-belt karate champion who could also type. The perfect combination.

"I'm taking the week off," he told her. "Don't bother me with anything. You deal with whatever comes up, okay?"

Teresa nodded. She looked like a man. He wondered if she had a girlfriend, he hadn't noticed any lurking about.

Tomorrow he was going to be thirty-five. It was a milestone. Ever since he'd started acting it had always been young Nick Angel. He'd always played the rebel, the kid without a cause. Now he was moving into a different age group. He was going to have to start playing responsible roles, and he wasn't sure if he was ready for it. He still felt like a kid at heart, sometimes a very weary kid, but always young.

He shut himself in his den and put his favorite Van Morrison on the CD player. Honey tried to come in and annoy him, but he waved her away.

Closing his eyes he let the music sweep over him.

He wasn't happy, but he hadn't quite figured out what he could do about it.

84

It wasn't difficult finding out where Cyndra lived. Reece purchased a map to the stars' homes from a street vendor and thumbed through it. Sure enough, there was Cyndra's address printed clearly for all to see.

He chuckled to himself. Sweet little Cyndra. Sweet little bigamist.

Who did she think she was fooling? He reached for the latest copy of *People* magazine. There was a big story on her and he read it for the sixth time. Sitting in his rented car he studied the pictures. Cyndra in her fancy bathroom. Cyndra by her fancy pool. And Cyndra with her cute little girl, Topaz, sitting on her daddy's lap.

Cyndra had gone and married one of her own kind. A producer, they called him. Marik Lee—he was no Billy Dee Williams. But the two of them together seemed like they had it all their own way—and nobody was worried about Reece Webster.

He'd spent eleven years in jail and they didn't give a damn. Motherfuckers! They'd soon find out he was back.

He pulled the car up to a hot dog stand and bought himself a greasy dog with plenty of relish and onions. Life's small pleasures, how he'd missed them in jail.

Later he drove down Melrose, stopped at a store and bought himself a new Stetson and some sharp-looking leather boots. He handed the sales clerk a check that would bounce, but he'd be long gone by the time they discovered it was no good.

He admired himself in a full-length mirror. Still looked good. Still had that lean body and handsome face. Nobody would guess where he'd been for the last eleven years. He could do with a suntan. Didn't have time to wait to get one. Shame.

By three o'clock in the afternoon he was ready to start the action. He knew exactly where Cyndra's house was. He drove up into the hills, through the winding streets, until he reached her security gates. Then he leaned out his car window and pressed the entry buzzer.

A man's voice said, "Yes?"

"Cyndra?"

"No, she's not here. Who is this?"

"I'm here to see Cyndra," he said.

"I just told you, mister, she's not home."

"Then I'll wait."

"Who are you?"

Should he spoil the surprise? Tell this moron that he was her husband?

No, it was better to confront her face to face.

"I'm a relative," he said. "What time will she be back?"

"I can't reveal that information. Leave a note in the mailbox and I'll see she gets it."

What kind of garbage was this? He wasn't leaving any note. He drove the car half a block away, turned it around and sat in it waiting and watching.

After a while a fancy white limousine drove down the street and turned into the gates.

Reece started his car, and as soon as the gates opened he followed the limo in, thinking to himself how stupid these people in Hollywood were if they actually thought a pair of fancy gates were enough to keep anybody out.

He followed the limousine up a long driveway until they reached the grand entrance to an imposing mansion.

A driver got out of the limo, noticed Reece's car behind him and rushed over.

"Can I help you?" the driver said.

The back door to the limo opened and a man that Reece recognized as Cyndra's supposed husband got out. "Hey, Clyde, what's going on?" the man called.

"I'm looking into it," Clyde replied, embarrassed because he was at fault for not noticing the car before.

Reece got out of his car. "I'm here to see Cyndra," he said.

"I'm sure you are," Clyde replied, very hostile. "A lot of people would like to see her. If it's an autograph you want, leave your address and we'll see you get one."

"You don't understand," Reece said. "I'm a relative."

Marik walked over. "What's going on here?" he said.

"I want to see Cyndra," Reece said.

"You shouldn't follow people onto private property. We're going to have to call the police."

"I don't think you'll want to do that," Reece said.

"Look, man," Marik said patiently. "I know you're a fan and you love her. A lot of people love Cyndra—but you cannot follow her into her private home. Get it? Now I suggest you get back in your car and leave immediately, and we'll forget about this."

"You don't recognize me, do you?" Reece said.

"No," Marik said. "I don't."

"Think back," Reece said. "And fuckin' weep. I'm Cyndra's husband."

Cyndra had been crying on and off for hours. In the back of her mind she'd known the good life could not last. One moment she had everything she'd ever wanted, and the next Reece Webster came back like a ghost from the past to ruin it all.

At first she'd tried to deny she knew him. She'd gotten out of the limo, stared him in the face and said, "I don't know this man. I've never seen him before."

"Hey, bitch," Reece had taunted. "Would you sooner I went to the newspapers with this? I'm giving you the courtesy of coming here first."

They went into the house and the story began to unfold. How she'd married him. How he'd used her. And then Vegas. "She shot a guy," Reece said. "Shot him stone cold dead."

"I didn't do it—you did it," she said accusingly.

Marik looked from one to the other and shook his head. Then he stared at Cyndra with hurt eyes. "Why didn't you tell me, baby?"

Her world was crumbling. " 'Cause I never thought Reece would come back."

"Here I am," said Reece. "Would've been here sooner—'cept I got put in jail on a false charge, that's where I've been."

"What do you want?" Marik asked.

"Why, I would imagine that's pretty obvious," Reece said, taking in the luxurious surroundings. "I want my wife back."

"Let's talk straight here," Marik said grimly. "What do you *really* want?"

"Well," Reece said, tilting his Stetson at a rakish angle. "If I can't have the little lady, then I guess I'll have to be compensated for my loss."

"Yes," Marik said. "I understand you want money. And Cyndra wants her freedom. We'll pay. And the money will buy a quiet divorce."

One thing about this Marik guy—he certainly wasn't stupid. "How much you got in mind?" Reece said.

Marik glanced at Cyndra. She was too upset to look at him. "We have to discuss it," he said. "In private. I'll talk to my lawyer and we'll come back to you with an offer."

"It better be a big offer," Reece said. "Oh, and by the way, I thought I might pay me a visit to Nick Angel."

"What's Nick got to do with this?" Cyndra snapped.

"He helped you out, didn't he, sweetheart?" Reece said slyly. "I saw what happened that night. You thought I left, but I didn't—I stuck around, followed you. So, y'see, I know exactly what went on. You took that good old boy out into the desert and buried him. You're all as guilty as hell. I think Nick Angel will want to contribute to my future well-being, don't you?"

"Leave him out of this, Reece. We'll make a deal, but leave Nick out."

"Now, now, don't go getting upset."

Cyndra's mouth twitched dangerously. If she had a gun she'd blow his head off. All her life she'd been a victim, and now, just when she'd thought she was through with being victimized, this creep had to come back to haunt her with his threats.

"Calm down, Cyndra. We'll settle this," Marik said, taking charge.

"We're not talking pennies here," Reece said warningly.

"I understand," Marik replied.

"When will I hear from you people?" Reece asked.

"Tomorrow," Marik said. "Where are you staying?"

"Give me a thousand bucks cash for now, an' I'll contact you to-morrow."

"I don't have that much cash."

"What *do* you have?"

"Five hundred."

"It'll do."

As Marik was escorting Reece to the front door, Topaz came running out of her room. "Mommy! Mommy! Look at my new dress. Isn't it pretty?"

Reece stopped. "Yeah, sugar, that's *real* pretty. You're the image of your mama."

Cyndra turned on him, her dark eyes stormy. "Stay away from her. Get out of my house and stay away from my family."

He shrugged. "Trouble with you, Cyndra, is you got no appreciation. Who gave you singing lessons, taught you how to dress an' fix your hair? You were nothing when I found you hanging out in New York. Now you're a big star. I expect plenty of compensation for all I did."

"You'll get it. I told you that," said Marik.

Cyndra rushed over to Topaz and picked her up. "Come here, sweetie."

"Bye, little girl," said Reece, waving. "See you around."

She ran upstairs with Topaz and tried to call Nick in New York. He was out. She left a message with Harlan for him to call her back. Then she went to her closet and searched behind her clothes for the secret compartment where she kept her most valuable possessions. There, alongside her diamond necklace and earrings, was a small pearl-handled gun. One of her security guards had given it to her as a gift. He'd told her how to use it, too.

"Never hurts for a lady to have a gun," he'd said. "Especially a famous lady like yourself."

She'd never told anybody about the present, otherwise the guard would have gotten fired. But she'd always appreciated it.

She had a feeling she soon might be forced to use it.

85

Lauren called Oliver in the south of France to make sure he'd arrived safely and was settled in.

"I'm perfectly fine," he said. "In fact last night Peggy invited me over for dinner."

Lauren vaguely remembered Peggy—a titled English widow who'd sold Oliver the farmhouse.

"That's nice," she said. "I'll be there as soon as I can."

"You don't have to rush," he said. "It's beautiful here, so peaceful and quiet. I'm very content."

Oh, God! Should she bring her knitting?

Oliver seemed perfectly satisfied with the tranquil life, but she wasn't so sure it was for her. Maybe she was making a mistake after all. She wished she had the courage to tell him. No. It was impossible. This was her life.

Lorenzo called bright and early to inform her that the photo session was on for the next day.

"No more fuck-ups, Lorenzo," she said sternly. "I have to get out of here."

He was hurt. "Please, Lauren, do not insult me."

She got dressed and wandered around the apartment she'd grown to love. It was on the market and every day people came to see it. She hated showing them around and tried to stay out of the way, leaving the tour in the hands of the real estate agent. It had been her home for almost twelve years and she was certainly going to miss it.

She sipped her morning coffee sitting at a table on the terrace overlooking Manhattan. It was a chilly December day, but clear. She loved looking out at the bustling city laid out below her.

The maid brought her the newspapers. She glanced through them quickly, stopping at an item in *USA Today*. She scanned it once, then read it more slowly a second time.

> *Today millions of fans across the world celebrate the thirty-fifth birthday of cult superstar Nick Angel and the opening of his latest movie,* Killer Blue. *A statement issued by Panther Studios disclosed that Nick will not be present at the Los Angeles premiere of* Killer Blue *as expected.*
>
> *A personal spokesman for Angel reported that the actor will spend his birthday in New York.*

Nick was in New York and it was his birthday . . . Was she ever going to forget him?

I can call him if it's his birthday.

No, you can't.

Why not?

Because he'll want to see you and you're leaving for a new life with Oliver in France.

She shut her eyes for a moment, saw his face and wanted to be with him more than anything else in the world.

So why are you punishing yourself, Roberts?

I'm not punishing myself.

Yes, you are. If you want to be with him you should.

I murdered his father.

Maybe. Maybe not.

I murdered his baby.

You had no choice.

She reached for the phone. Her hand hovered over the receiver for a few seconds. Then she shook her head. No, it wasn't right. She'd be tempting fate again—just forget it.

Honey took the second phone call from Cyndra. "He left here early," she said. "I think he's taken his plane up."

"But I need to speak to him," Cyndra said.

"He'll be back later. I'm having a surprise party for him."

"Nick doesn't like surprises."

Honey giggled. "He'll like this one."

"Let me talk to Harlan," Cyndra said.

Harlan got on the phone sounding swishier than usual. Since his move to New York he'd become extremely caustic. "Sister, dearest— and *what* can I do for you?"

"I need to talk to Nick. Is there any way I can reach him?"

"He's *not* in the best of moods," Harlan said. "Raced outta here like he had a ferret playing tag up his ass."

"Tell him to call me as soon as he gets back."

"Will do."

He'd got out of his apartment, left them all standing there, and now he was completely alone.

At the controls of his small plane Nick felt a glorious freedom. There was something about being alone, totally out of reach by anyone—a rarity for him. Oh, sure, he had his retreats, but one by one they got discovered. The *National Enquirer* had the number of his beach house. Every fan in town knew where he lived. Most of his business acquaintances had somehow or other gotten hold of his private phone number.

Now he was cut off from everything and everyone, and it was a wonderful feeling.

Flying was something he'd never imagined himself doing. He'd taken it up because of some macho bet with an old actor who'd appeared in one of his movies. Now he enjoyed it better than anything.

Color me dead.

It was a tempting thought. He could fly this little mother right into the fucking ocean and vanish forever. The ultimate thrill. No more hassles. No more fame. Because the fame was suffocating the life out of him. And there was nothing that made him happy anymore . . . Except Lauren . . .

And what had he done about that situation?

He'd let her get away again. Hadn't even bothered to pursue her.

"Call me when you're free," he'd said. And four years had passed.

She was never going to leave Oliver. She'd stay with him until he dropped.

Well, shit, he couldn't take it anymore.

On a sudden impulse he turned the plane around and headed back to the airstrip.

Reece thought about Cyndra, he thought about her a lot. Damn, she looked hot—a real juicy piece. He'd been right about her all along. Cyndra was a star—and only because he'd had the foresight to pay for her singing lessons and all the rest. The truth was that he'd discovered her before anyone. He was the one who deserved all the credit. Goddamn it! He'd even introduced her to Reno Records. They owed him plenty, too. They should all be sucking his dick.

He was bored in his hotel room, there was no way he was going to sit there waiting to hear from Marik. He had five hundred dollars. The idea was to go out and spend it.

He got in his car and drove down Sunset, cutting up La Brea to Hollywood Boulevard. A sign caught his eye. NAKED LIVE BEAUTIES. TOPLESS, BOTTOMLESS, BIG BARE BABES.

He parked his car, went inside and got himself a seat at the bar, where he watched a long-legged dyed blonde bump and grind as she removed strips of black leather from her sinewy person.

He beckoned her over with a twenty-dollar bill. "Come here, doll. Get that sexy ass over here." He folded the bill into a thin strip.

She edged closer to the side of the bar—which doubled as the stage —and squatted down. He inserted the money into her G-string, grabbing a quick feel at the same time.

"Later," she hissed. "It'll cost you more than twenty."

He was insulted. He'd only ever paid for it once, and that was the day he got out of jail. But still, paying for it wasn't such a bad thing. At least you knew where you were.

He winked at her. She winked back. As far as he was concerned they had an agreement.

After coffee on the terrace Lauren went inside and finished packing. Lorenzo had wanted to come around but she'd put him off. "What are you doing tonight?" he'd asked.

"Staying home."

He'd sighed. "Lauren, Lauren—one more night on the town before you fade into retirement. Please, I beg you."

"Well . . . maybe."

Going to dinner with Lorenzo was a temptation she didn't need. She'd accustomed herself to the life she had now. No sex.

What are you, a nun, Roberts?

No, but I have the strength of character not to play around on my husband.

Oh, get off your soapbox.

At two o'clock her phone rang again. If it was Lorenzo she decided to tell him that she wouldn't have dinner with him after all. Why tempt fate?

"Hey, Lauren."

She held her breath for a moment. "Who's this?" she asked, although of course she knew immediately who it was.

"Nick."

"Nick," she repeated dumbly.

"It's been a long time. How are you?"

"I'm leaving in a couple of days," she said quickly. "Oliver and I are moving to France."

"I want to see you."

"It's not possible."

"Lauren, it's my birthday. Remember old times? You always looked after me on my birthday."

"You know what happens every time we see each other, Nick," she said weakly.

"Five minutes of your time, that's all I need."

"For what?"

"You can't spare me five minutes on my birthday?"

"Oh, Nick, come on, this is ridiculous."

"Be downstairs in half an hour. I'm on my way."

Before she could say anything he hung up.

She paced around the apartment, undecided about what to do. Then she realized that since there was obviously no stopping him she'd better see him.

You don't have to.

Oh, yes, I do!

She felt totally wired as she ran into her bedroom, stripping off the boring silk shirt and skirt she had on and reaching for her favorite faded jeans and a familiar sweatshirt—it wouldn't do to look like she'd tried. Then she brushed her hair, added soft shadow around her eyes and a blusher to her cheeks. She stared quickly at her reflection. Talk about glowing. She looked alive for the first time in a long while.

Here we go again.

She put on tennis shoes, grabbed her Oliver Peoples shades and ran downstairs.

"Do you need a cab, Mrs. Liberty?" the doorman asked.

"No, no, that's okay," she said.

"It's cold out," he said.

"It's not that cold. The sun's shining."

"If you're going for a walk you'll need a coat."

"I'm not walking, Pete. Somebody's picking me up. I'll only be out for five minutes."

What was she explaining herself to the doorman for?

"Oh, by the way, Mrs. Liberty," he said, handing her an envelope. "I was supposed to give you this letter today. Mr. Liberty left it for you. I was about to bring it up to your apartment when you came down. Saved me a trip."

She glanced at the envelope and recognized Oliver's handwriting. Quickly she opened the letter and read it.

My dear Lauren,
I have known for some time now that you are not completely

happy. The truth is, neither am I. I feel that both of us are compromising our true feelings, and that we would be better off apart. I have never wished to be treated as a burden, and whether you know it or not that's what our relationship has become. Over the last few months I have become quite close to Peggy during the course of our negotiations for the farmhouse. She is a wonderful woman—nearer to me in age, and quite ready for a settled life. You, my dear, are not. So I arranged with Lorenzo to keep you in New York. It's where you belong.

I am releasing you, Lauren, because I love you, and we will have better lives apart.

Of course, I quite understand . . .

The letter continued on in the same vein, and she read it filled with mixed emotions. Oliver wanted out! *He* was releasing *her!*

Oh, God! Free at last!

Free to do whatever she wanted!

The timing was unbelievable. And the best thing was she didn't have to feel guilty, because he'd found someone else. Pocketing the letter she peered through the glass doors, impatiently waiting, pacing up and down until eventually she saw the Ferrari approaching—red, of course.

She rushed outside. It had been four years since she'd seen him, and her heart was in overdrive. He looked a little ragged, but it was still her Nick.

He leaped out of the car. "Hey—"

"You're crazy, you know that?" she said, speaking too fast.

He took her hand. "Get in the car."

"Five minutes," she said, her heart beating wildly.

"Yeah, yeah."

Pete was standing at the entrance staring. He'd suddenly realized it was Nick Angel she was with. Before he could recover she jumped in the car and Nick took off.

"Happy birthday," she said.

"You're my present," he said.

"I am, huh?"

"I need to tell you something."

"What?"

"I've waited for you ever since I left Bosewell, and I'm not waiting any longer."

She sighed. "Nick, don't do this to us again."

"Why?"

"Because . . ."

"Listen, Lauren—I love you and you love me. You can't fight it any longer."

For a moment she thought how simple it would be to agree with him, because that's what she really wanted to do. But there was too much he didn't know about her. He didn't know she'd killed his father. He didn't know she'd killed his baby. And if he knew those things he wouldn't want to be with her anyway.

She glanced at her watch. "Your five minutes are up."

"What five minutes?" he said, steering the Ferrari onto the highway.

"You agreed to five minutes."

"I lied."

"Oh God, Nick, don't start."

"I'm taking you for a ride in my plane."

"I'm not going in your plane."

"Oh, yes, you are."

"No way."

"Will you shut up? Just shut up for once."

Why did I let him talk me into this?

Because you wanted him to.

So do like he says—shut up and enjoy it.

She leaned back in her seat and didn't say another word.

Forty-five minutes later they were at the private airstrip. "Come on," he said. "Out."

"I told you, I'm not going in a plane with you."

"Maybe I should knock you out and carry you over my shoulder. What do you think?"

"You're crazy, Nick Angel."

He grinned, so happy to see her. "Yeah, yeah, you told me that before. Shouldn't come as a shock to you."

She knew she should back out, but she was already drawn into the game. She got out of the car and walked with him to the plane.

"Another five minutes," she said sternly.

"Sure," he said.

She shook her head. "This is the last time I'm going anywhere with you, Nick."

"Hey—never say never."

"Why not?"

" 'Cause you could live to regret it."

He took her hand and helped her aboard.

"Five minutes," she repeated.

"Hey—whatever you say."

"How much do you think he wants?" Cyndra asked.

"It's not the money," Marik said. "It's what he can do to us."

"What do you mean?" she said fearfully.

"Think about it," Marik said, sounding calmer than he felt. "Over the last few years you've had massive national publicity. You've been on all the shows talking about pride and strength and women not allowing themselves to be abused. How do you think it'll look if Reece spills his guts?"

"Where's he staying?" she said, thinking about how she could put a stop to Reece Webster once and for all.

"Our driver followed him. He's at the Hyatt on Sunset." Marik peered at her suspiciously. "Why do you want to know?"

"Why not?" she said flatly.

"You're not to try and talk to him," Marik said warningly. "You're to leave this to me and Gordon."

"What's Gordon got to do with it?"

"We'll need his help," Marik said. "I've already called him. He's coming right over."

"Damn!" she said.

"What?"

"I don't want him involved."

"Cyndra, baby," Marik said patiently. "This is big-time stuff. We've got to work it out carefully. A payoff has got to mean just that. A one-time score—no coming back for more. We need Gordon's brain in on this."

"All right," she said reluctantly. "But I don't want to see him—it's too humiliating. I'm going to bed."

He came over and kissed her. "Don't worry, baby. It'll all be taken care of."

You bet it will, she thought. *By tomorrow morning Reece Webster will be history.*

The sinewy blonde took him back to her apartment, fucked him, then demanded three hundred dollars.

He laughed in her face.

"Pay up, bastard," she said, "or I'll set my boyfriend on you."

"I'm Reece Webster," he said disdainfully. "That's who I am. Not some dumb john off the street."

"I don't give a cocksucking crap *who* you are," the blonde replied. "You're payin' an' ain't that the truth."

Reece zipped up his pants, pulled on his boots and reached for his Stetson. He'd been threatened by bigger and better than this dumb cooze. "You ain't worth three bucks, let alone three hundred," he sneered.

"I hate cheap cocksuckers," she said.

"And I hate cheap whores," he said, walking through her front door.

She picked up a heavy glass ashtray and hurled it after him. The jagged edge of the ashtray hit him on the side of the head, making a deep gash in his temple and knocking his hat to the floor.

"Bitch!" He reached up and felt sticky blood pumping from the cut.

She ran over and slammed the door shut, leaving him out in the hallway.

At least he hadn't paid the whore.

He stooped to pick up his hat and felt dizzy. For a moment he slumped against the wall, his hand holding the wound. Soon his hand was covered with slippery blood.

Better get out before her boyfriend arrives, he thought, feeling quite unsteady on his feet. The goddamn bitch had hurt him. She'd pay for this.

He staggered downstairs, blood dripping onto his jacket and soaking through the fabric.

Out on the street a woman walking past took one look at him and quickly shrank back.

Christ! What was going on? He hardly had the strength to walk.

He blinked once, twice, tried to clear his head and remember where he'd parked his car.

The streetlight cast an eerie glow. He sat down on the curb, putting his head in his blood-soaked hands. Nausea overcame him and he threw up.

Goddamn it, better get to his car and get out of here.

Cyndra crept into Topaz's room and watched her baby sleeping. The little girl was so cute. She had a snub nose, wide eyes and Marik's tight curly hair.

Carefully Cyndra extracted her thumb from her mouth. "No buck teeth, Topaz," she whispered softly. "Gotta think beautiful."

Back in her own bedroom she went to her closet and changed into a black track suit. Then she pulled her hair severely back, covering it with a squashy Garbo-type hat. Large sunglasses completed her disguise. Unrecognizable, she thought. As Cyndra, her public image was cascades of long dark hair, shimmering gowns and provocative makeup.

Reece Webster was threatening her future. Marik thought money would solve the problem. Cyndra knew it wouldn't.

She reached for her purse, checked that the small pearl-handled revolver was loaded, and slipped quietly down the back stairway into the garage.

Reece slumped behind the wheel of his car. He was lucky to have made it. He had a headache from hell, and blood was still pumping from his wound. Ripping off his jacket he held it to his head and started the engine.

One hand on the wheel and one hand holding his head, he set off toward his hotel.

Cyndra took the nanny's station wagon—best not to call attention to herself with her Rolls or Marik's Jaguar. She locked the doors—second nature for a woman driving alone in L.A.—and drove down the hill.

The car was weaving. Reece felt it swaying this way and that—he couldn't seem to control it. All he had to do was get back to the hotel, put a dressing on his head and lie down. He'd be fine after a rest.

It occurred to him that maybe he needed to go to an emergency room. But those places were always filled with the lowest of the low— gunshot wounds, stabbings, heroin overdoses. Who needed it? Besides, he should be at the hotel in case Marik phoned. Didn't want to miss the deal of the century.

Three million bucks. That's what he'd decided to ask for. And cheap at the price.

The sound of a blaring horn almost made him swerve off the road. Bastards! Why didn't people concentrate on their driving instead of hassling him?

He saw the hotel in the distance and slowed down.

More blaring horns.

Goddamn it, people didn't know how to behave anymore.

Cyndra found a space on the street and got out of the station wagon, locking the doors with a remote control.

Bump! Big bump!

Fuck, someone hit him. What did he care, it wasn't his car, only a rental.

Christ, his head was getting ready to explode. Was he at the hotel yet? Must be. He could hear noise, confusion. Leaning on the steering wheel he closed his eyes while blood dripped steadily onto his new cowboy boots.

There was something going on outside the hotel. Cyndra hurried along the street, glancing over as she approached the entrance. A car had crossed over to the wrong lane and smashed into two other cars. The hotel doorman was running over to investigate.

A figure was slumped over the driving wheel, his weight on the horn, which let out an incessant noise.

She covered her ears and was just about to detour by when she realized the yellow car, a Chevrolet, looked awfully familiar. In fact it looked like the same car Reece Webster was driving when he'd followed her limo up her driveway.

She stopped, watching, while the doorman, assisted by two other people, opened the door and extracted the driver.

"He's dead," she heard one of them say. "Looks like he bled to death."

She edged closer for a better look as they laid the figure on the ground. No mistaking those cowboy boots. Reece Webster was certainly dead.

"Thank you, God," she whispered, and quietly made her way back to her car.

87

"I didn't know you could fly a plane."

He put it on autopilot and raised his arms. "Look, Ma, no hands!"

"Very funny," she said sternly.

"Hey—" He caught her with a green-eyed stare. "Have I told you lately that I love you?"

"Nick . . ."

"Yeah?"

"Please stop," she begged.

"What? Stop loving you? I'm sorry, but I can't seem to do that."

"I think you can."

"How's that?"

She lowered her eyes. "There's things I've never told you."

"What things?" he asked.

She turned away from him, staring out the window at the clear blue sky, determined to be truthful so there could finally be an end to this.

"Nick," she said hesitantly, "when you left Bosewell, I was . . . I was pregnant with our baby."

"Oh Jesus, Lauren, I had no idea—"

"I know you didn't. I went to the trailer park to tell you—I guess it was the day after you left. Your father was there . . ."

"Yes?" He had a feeling he wasn't going to like what he was about to hear.

"He . . . he tried to attack me," she continued. "And I . . . I stabbed him. Then the tornado came and I don't remember anything else. When I woke up I was on the grass and the trailer was gone. The town was in chaos—my parents were both victims. I was sent to live in Philadelphia with relatives. Shortly after I arrived they made me have an abortion." Her eyes filled with tears. "Nick—they made me kill our child."

It was the first time she'd spoken of any of this and the relief was overwhelming. Suddenly it wasn't her secret anymore—the burden was not hers alone.

"I didn't know," he said. "If I'd known I'd never have left. We would have worked it out somehow. Jesus, Lauren, I don't know what to say except that I love you. I always have and I always will. I'm sorry for what happened. I'm sorry I wasn't there with you, and for everything you had to go through without me."

All these years she'd expected him to be angry, to blame her for what had happened. Now he was the one that was sorry.

"I murdered our baby, Nick," she cried out, in case he hadn't understood.

"Come here, sweetheart," he said, taking her in his arms. "You had no choice. You were a kid—we both were. You did what you had to do—so stop blaming yourself."

It felt so good in his arms. She was at peace. It was as if she belonged there.

"As for Primo," he said, holding her tight, "you didn't kill him—he died of head injuries. It's public record."

"It is?"

"Yup. I had it checked out."

"All these years I thought I'd killed him."

"Why didn't you tell me this before?"

"Because . . ."

"Because what?"

"I don't know."

"You're crazy. And I love you."

"Nick," she said hesitantly, feeling like a kid again.

"Yes?"

"I love you, too."

He grinned. "So what are we going to do about it?"

"We're going to be together."

"We are?"

"Yes," she said, filled with a sudden strength and determination. "Forever."

"Fasten your seatbelt," he said, relinquishing his hold and concentrating on piloting the plane. "We're preparing to land."

"Where are we?" she asked.

"Canada."

"*Canada?*"

"I figured I had to take you somewhere remote, where nobody can bother us—not unless we want them to. There's this little log cabin—"

"How did you arrange it? And how did you know I'd come with you?"

"Hey—it's my birthday."

"Happy birthday, Nick," she said softly.

"Thank you, Lauren."

They stared into each other's eyes and smiled.

The dream was finally coming true.

They were together and they both knew without a doubt that this time nothing would ever split them apart again.